ARIANRHOD'S WAR

The Pirates' Web – Book Two

SANDI CAYLESS

www.sunskerrypress.com

ARIANRHOD'S WAR
The Pirates' Web – Book Two

ISBN 978-1-9993259-4-7

Sunskerry Press
Scotland
www.sunskerrypress.com

www.sunskerrypress.com

CONTENTS

1: NEWS FROM THE WEB

The usual topers holding up the bar in the *Half Moon in a Puddle* were still laughing but hastily ceased when Captain Cinnabar Ahxenta and Commander Tallica Apnis of the *PSS Arianrhod* stepped in. The *Half Moon's* regulars had heard of the message lately sent out from Merkat Three's Port Authority to the great private starship that a matter had arisen relating to her. Those in command of security at Merkat's vast space docks were probably quaking in their collective boots, was the general opinion. The Web at Merkat, that home away from hell that served as a huge port and harbour facility and was open to all comers, or at least those that could cough up the docking fees, was a tightly secured place, or at least that was what its publicity office would like its clients to believe. But PA security had slipped up badly and landed in some serious guano.

"Should we head for a back seat, Jurry lad?" one semi-inebriated barfly asked of his mate. "The last time the *Arianrhod* was in, a month or so ago, we had a few on the deck that couldn't get back up once they'd felt the kiss of Ahxenta's left hook."

"Nobody's here from the Port Authority Malty, and neither are any of the usual troublemakers, so I guess it's safe enough. Just don't stretch your face into a grin if either of them looks this way is all."

Captain Ahxenta's piercing gaze swept the place as she made her way to the bar, where two mugs of a fizzing brew were placed on the counter before she had opened her mouth. Ally, the proprietor and barman of the *Half Moon*, welcomed her and her first mate back into his premises with a nod and the information that his prices had gone up but that she and her first mate would be charged at the old rates this time. And her tab was open, as always. The captain nodded, accepted one of the pots and raised it in token acknowledgement. Commander Apnis did likewise.

"Seen any Guild or Merkat security reps yet, ma'am, or any of the great and the good from the Authority?" was Ally's opening gambit.

Ahxenta fixed him with icy eyes. "My business, not yours."

"Or anybody else's," Tallica Apnis added loudly, looking around.

"Changed my mind, Malty. There's a booth over there with a view of the bar and the door," Jurry whispered to his buddy. "Let's get it before any more awkward customers come in."

As the two scuttled off, Ally dug below the bar and hauled up two small packs of nibbles. "Have these on the house," he urged. "New flavour; you can tell me what you think."

"So what's the story going round?" the captain demanded sharply, ignoring the offer as she looked him in the eye.

Ally shrugged evasively, but realised that she would not be fobbed off by any pretence of ignorance. Settling his elbows on his counter, he leaned forward confidentially.

"They say that despite the tightest security this side of the mapped galaxy, somebody breached the inner belt six repair sheds and made off with your shuttle, the one you'd left for repair – the *Gadfly* was it? And they've scoured the Web from planetside on Merkat Three to the last beacon of the outmost belt and found nothing. They reckon the thief's long gone, but a shuttle wouldn't get far without a ship, so there's maybe a ship out there with your shuttle on board," he ended. "How did you find out, Captain, if you don't mind me asking?"

Ahxenta grinned at him. "You tell me," she invited.

"I heard you got a link from a PA security liaison to look out for a ship stolen from the Web. When you asked why they'd tell you, they *then* said it was your shuttle. Rumour has it you were a tad upset, as you hadn't been informed immediately they discovered the loss but a long time after. The poor sap that took your response hasn't got over it. They say he's on compassionate leave on mental health grounds."

"Very funny," Apnis reproved. "So apart from the badges you and your people are wearing, what else is new this side of zone Alpha?"

"The usual skulduggery, but nothing else matching the theft of your shuttle," said Ally. "That's why the Authority's in a fizz. They expected a spate of copycat crimes apparently, but so far zip, as far as I know. Mind you, the Guild upped its security round the inner repair docks, but apart from the regular petty pilfering, nothing."

"What's with the badge? Trying to pretend you're someone you're not?" *Arianrhod's* first mate persisted, raising an eyebrow.

"Place needed a facelift," Ally told her. "Now you can address my friendly and efficient staff by name instead of "hey you, I'm waiting" or the various other tags that are bandied around by many of my less polite customers most nights. You'll also note we have new menu-vids and better links to Web local external channels."

"So you can keep an even closer weather eye on the traffic in and out you mean," the captain cut in.

"Exactly, Captain. Eating here tonight? The menu's changed too."

"We are: we'll order at the table menu pad."

Ahxenta and her first mate chose a table with a view of the door and set the privacy shield to mute their talk to other ears and reduce external noise. Both were aware that they were the target of many eyes, as Ally's place was unusually busy for the early evening hour by Merkat time. They returned stare for stare and most of those eyeing them soon looked the other way.

"Watching for our reactions," Apnis said, taking a draught of ale. "But Ally's right: even had the perp or perps been able to grab an extra energy cell or three, they wouldn't have got far from Merkat in the *Gadfly*. She's a good little ship but she's not designed for long haul, even if she made the beacon and the bypass."

"Which she could have done," the captain argued as she called up the specials on the menu pad. "But she would have needed fitting up and clearance to leave the Web. The PA has got explaining to do."

"We left the Dockers' Guild an entry key but we left no weapons or anything like that aboard her," Apnis muttered. "Cottontail's team stripped her bare, even of most of her energy cells – you know how light-fingered some of the repair crews are. Without additional cells, just how far do you reckon she would have got?"

"Kelpin or Linza Base are the nearest, but she would still have had to make for the bypass and the hyperspace currents would have been wild for a ship her size. So another ship waiting out there would seem the obvious answer, but it doesn't track," Ahxenta frowned. "Why go to the trouble to steal a shuttle when you could hire one and make off with it, or hitch a lift if you were so desperate to leave? It would take a fair pilot to move the *Gadfly* out of the repair sheds under the noses of Guild and Merkat security when *Arianrhod's* not in port."

"Her repairs were near done they told us. And as we always insist on the best, she'd have been in very good trim – after our firefight with those moon-based bandits out of Lonagan Four, she *was* a tad the worse for wear. But every ship in the sector knows the *Arianrhod's* call-sign and the *Gadfly's* as space pink as most of our other shuttles *and* our insignia's on her hull. She's hardly invisible. Someone sending us a message?" the first mate hazarded.

"Maybe. Azular's theory is that she's not left Merkat, she's hidden here and so are the perps. If that's so she must be cloaked in more stealth ware than the latest ISP battlecruiser, otherwise we'd be able to read her anywhere in or near the Web – and we've tried."

"And *our* snoopware is the best that credit can buy or Azular,

Greffy and Crizz Cottontail between them can come up with," Apnis smiled. "So we take the Port Authority apart, after we've sorted the senior reps from the Dockers' Guild. I'll check with my buddy Kit Biernop. As a member of the Guild security oversight committee and a liaison with Merkat's security, he keeps his nose to the ground: anything related to *Arianrhod* and he's sure to hear about it."

As their meals appeared from the serving hatch, the two unpacked their cutlery and set to. Both had had a busy time since *Arianrhod* had docked and were hungry.

"Watching every mouthful," Apnis remarked, cocking her brow at two uniformed men with blatantly displayed phase rifles at a nearby table, who had an excessive amount of drinkware between them.

A pointed stare from Ahxenta caused the two to shuffle and look away. Having recognised either the duo or their insignia they seemed reluctant to annoy them, despite their own large physiques.

"Friskianx, by the look of the uniforms and the guns, and the cast of features," Ahxenta noted. "There was a Friskie League loader near our berth when we came in. Wonder how long she'd been there?"

"It's a free port, Cap," Apnis shrugged. "They dock where they're told and can eat and drink where they like."

"They usually like the *Green Diamond*. They know our people use the *Half Moon*. But we're all part of one big unhappy family now since the ISP, the Coalition, the NTA and the other half-bit unions formed their big Alliance over that shooting war caused by those malcontent cyber-sods intent on ripping the known galaxy apart. And the war didn't end at the showdown at Skyrtek: there are still pockets of them in hidey-holes all over the place and active, by all accounts."

"And our ever-resourceful raiders are getting back on their feet, better armed and worse-tempered than before, again by all accounts. We've been lucky not to meet with any of them as yet," the first mate replied. "I suppose they're still trying to get back what they lost when the cyber-hostiles took over most of their ops *and* many of them and put them out of business. At least, that's what we figured at the battle for Skyrtek. But if those energy-based lifeforms we met on Kelfennig that blamed themselves for sending out the original cyber-enhanced beings as super-colonists eons ago keep their word to make amends by expediting the take-down of the last hostile bases, it might be a while before any ex-raiders are strong enough to take on *Arianrhod*."

"I'm not so sure, Tallica; those energy-like beings said they'd use subtle influence as a tool on the gang of ex-victims we met crewing those ragtag ships at Skyrtek, but it strikes me that *that* lot would reconstruct, not deconstruct, *and* subvert any hostile base for their own use, especially if they were once raider bases before the hostiles took them and a lot of their residents over."

"Good point Cap, and there must be a lot of leftover tech floating out there in the space lanes. But look who've just come in – Captain Murmur Fleetskup and his best buddy Tommy Buntle. I'd heard the *Tallulah* was in and looking for personnel. He's seen us. But he *has* been hard-pushed to replace the crew he lost to us when we launched the *Emerald* under our flag, so maybe he'll leave us alone."

"Don't count on it. He'll be here to crow over us at the loss of the *Gadfly*," Ahxenta grimaced as the tiresome captain of the *PSS Tallulah* made his ponderous way over, his exec at his heels.

"It does seem that the whole damn Web knows about it," agreed Apnis as she nodded to the pair.

Captain Fleetskup had indeed been made aware of the loss of the *Gadfly*, but he was more inclined to blame lack of care on the part of the Dockers' Guild than to give way to misplaced levity. He had good cause: he knew the captain of the *Arianrhod* only too well and could gauge what her reaction might be. He also had an enduring soft spot for Tallica Apnis, not realising that he was doomed to failure on that front. Tommy Buntle could not help his lips curving in a derisive leer as he sat down at the invitation to join the two at their table but he remained silent. He had felt Ahxenta's left hook once before and was apprehensive of a repeat performance.

"But it's not only you," Fleetskup disclosed in a low tone. "I heard that the *Nyx Warrior* lost a cargo pod the last time she was in, stolen under the eyes of Guild security as it was heading back to the ship after unloading. And it was a new one, but at least it was empty."

Apnis frowned. "How did you pick that up? We met her first mate at Kanelian Juxta a couple of days ago and he said nothing. Though I expect his captain wouldn't want *that* spread about, as Nat Holdspan fancies his ship as the best in the PSS fleet."

"The shiniest, maybe," Ahxenta put in. "She *is* one of the latest in the PSS register. But how did you come by the news?"

"I had a meeting with Port Authority reps about their upping the fees. They used it and the theft of your shuttle as the excuse and told me that Nat's pod had been swiped from the very grapple drones that had been ferrying it back from cargo drop-off. It was a small pod, but they're not easy things to hide," Fleetskup opined heavily.

"I'd say they are, Captain," Buntle disputed. "Most ships use cargo pods and they all look much the same. But they should be secure-tagged and have their ship's call-sign and insignia incorporated into their hulls. Though the *Nyx Warrior* has only been rigged as a PSS for a few months so maybe it didn't."

"Ally's petty pilfering," Apnis huffed. "Some pilfering. But Solmar Treskitt said their last stop-off here had been standard and I can't imagine that Nat Holdspan would have anything but the newest and best tech for his ship, including cargo pods, as she's *Vanguard II* class. The *Warrior* was in Kanelian to pick up an arms shipment for ferrying to Kelpin and then she was heading here for their next pick-up for Selliden, so Sol Treskitt said, so we'll see them soon enough."

"You're here for a while, then, Captain, given the loss of your shuttle?" Buntle asked Ahxenta, an edge to his tone.

"Not your concern, Mr Buntle," she retorted, lifting an eyebrow. "Any more news on other local crime?" she added to Fleetskup as she pushed the remains of her meal into the disposal hatch.

"That's the latest I have," he declared. "Apart from a minor dust-up the *Green Comet* had out in the Belts, but I expect you heard about it as it was sent out over the Ultraviolet III. Order us more beers, Tommy," he added to his exec. "Put it on my tab. Can I buy you a drink, Captain, Commander?"

The two from the *Arianrhod*, exchanging quick glances, thanked him and accepted. It was obvious to both that he had other things on his mind and they were curious to find out what they were. As the privacy shield shifted at the exit of Buntle towards the bar, Tallica Apnis turned a disarming smile on Fleetskup.

"Everything all right with the *Tallulah*, Murmur?"

"Absolutely fine," he responded a shade too quickly. "The *Emerald* still out in the space lanes and earning her keep?"

"Yes. Why?" Ahxenta's ice-water eyes pierced his defences and he shuffled uncomfortably.

He looked away for a fraction before answering. "Dr Greenwing is holding his own as chief medic?"

"Yes. Why?" she repeated, aware of the reason for the question.

"My own CMO is retiring soon and I'll need another. I would up the ante if Greenwing would come back as chief medic. The *Tallulah's* bigger than the *Emerald*, so he would have more responsibilities and hence more pay. And he knows the ship and her crew."

"What's that to do with me? Why don't you ask him directly? He's contracted to the *Emerald* but it's not set in stone and he can move if he wants. I don't hold swords over the heads of my crew to keep them aboard and neither does Captain Goodsocks."

"He was contracted to the *Tallulah* when I lent him to you as a favour!" Fleetskup burst out. "And then you poach him, as well as Goodsocks and Toadflax, my two most senior officers, when you took on the *Emerald*! Three of my best! Not to mention Yellowfork as science officer, though he's wet behind the ears. I still haven't got a suitable first mate and I'm making do with Jesse Inks."

"Here's Mr Buntle," interrupted Apnis. "And, Murmur, we hardly poached Dr Greenwing or your other officers: posts were available aboard the *Emerald* at the time and open to applicants. Four of your crew clearly wanted promotion and a new berth. Melly Goodsocks was up for a command of her own for one and as she's more than capable, she was an obvious choice. You'd evidently trained her well, and the same could be said for Commander Toadflax."

The flattery went a little way to soothe Fleetskup's ruffled pride but in the face of Ahxenta's ill-concealed amusement he continued to mutter crossly until one of Ally's new staff turned up with a tray of frothing mugs. As the woman slapped down four beakers, she was interrupted by one of the two uniforms from the nearby table.

"Hey you! Where's our order? We've been waiting a while."

"On its way," she responded as she slipped her empty tray under her arm and turned to them.

"Yes and so's Merkat's Winter Carnival," the officer growled as he shifted his rifle over to the table edge. "You're slow."

"And you're ugly; but it's a tough galaxy, so deal with it. Where's your credit?"

"Put it on a tab."

"No. Credit slip, please, and *then* I'll bring your order across," the woman replied, swiftly rounding up a few used mugs from their table and looping them over her fingers as she dredged up her card-reader.

Several eyes had swivelled over at the sharp voices, four of which belonged to the two inebriates in their side booth.

"Think we should head for the hills, Malty, or wait for fisticuffs?" Jurry demanded of his mate.

"We're safe enough here," hiccupped Malty. "Last time she went wild there was gunplay and we didn't cop a blast, but we got a couple of pots out of the story later, so there may be profit in it."

"I bow to your authority," Jurry nodded. "Just sit well back," he advised as the Friskianx rose slowly, a hand straying towards his rifle.

"I don't like your attitude," the man snarled, swaying slightly – he had evidently sampled rather a lot of Ally's strong ale.

"And I don't like your face, but you're entitled to your opinion," she shot back. "You can pay at the bar and pick up your stuff there."

She dropped her reader and turned on her heel but halted at the click of a safety catch being released. "You aiming to use that?" she demanded, turning back into the sudden silence. "You *do* know there are weapons restrictions in place here? Means you'll get into trouble," she explicated calmly, looking up at him.

"Is that so?" he sneered as he raised the weapon.

He had no opportunity to bring it to aim, for before anyone could move, the waitress let go of both mugs and tray and relieved him of the rifle by grabbing it, dropping down and twisting. She spun away and was back on her feet in seconds. As he moved to make for her, she tilted it upwards and into his face.

"I wouldn't, if I were you," she advised him as she kneed him in the groin and followed up with a cuff to his ear with the rifle butt as he went down.

"You neither," Ahxenta told the second Friskianx, who had half-risen and grabbed for his own weapon when he saw his mate hit the deck, only to find the *Arianrhod's* captain at his elbow.

He looked sideways to find the business end of the captain's phase rifle in his line of sight. She smiled grimly down at him as he sank back into his chair, eyeing her but not releasing the hold on his gun.

Ahxenta was ready and brought her right hand down forcefully on his arm the second his grip tightened on his weapon, jabbing him so viciously in the ear with her own rifle that he let out a squeal. He rose in fury to face her, his reddened eyes blazing as he swept mugs off the table. He was tall, but so was Ahxenta. She had dropped her rifle and he missed the movement of her fist as it connected with his jaw. His head snapped backwards and he collapsed down into his chair.

It was at that point that the *Half Moon's* security detail, having realised there was a dispute, pushed between the tables to intervene, the loud voice in the van calling everyone to break it up.

"Better late than never," Jurry whispered to his mate. "I wonder sometimes why Ally keeps them on."

"They're ex-law enforcement officers and other assorted types that help out behind the bar, mostly for free beer and whatever they can lift off the troublemakers they work over," Malty explained equally quietly. "Keeps them off the highways and byways and gives them some sort of credentials in case they're hauled up before the judiciary for minor infringements. But I see Ahxenta's left hook is still as fast and accurate as ever. He never saw it coming. Looks like Kerrix can pack a good knee as well – the other one's looking green."

The four security personnel were shortly blearily cognisant of the situation and soon had the duo on their feet with their arms pinned behind their backs. The two were fluent in their own defence and had begun to threaten retribution, but excess of ale and the punishment that they had already received had removed most of their capacity for a fight. They were locked in hand restraints, their ineffectual struggles sending the beer slopping at nearby tables. Their fate would be a couple of hours cooling off in the local cell block of Merkat security and the confiscation of their weapons, the lead guard told them. And then they might be charged with causing affray, he warned, before ordering his fellows to take them away. The secure cams of the *Half Moon* had captured all the relevant data.

"I'll remember *your* face!" the more aggressive of the two hissed at the waitress in passing.

"I doubt it. I'll certainly be trying to forget yours," she responded.

"I'll take that phase rifle, Kerrix," the lead guard told the assistant. "It's evidence."

"Of what? His usual outfit for a night of drinking and dissipation? I'll leave it behind the bar once I've disarmed it. He'll no doubt try to claim it back after his head clears, *if* he remembers where he left it. You can argue with Ally over it, I have work to do."

With that she slung the rifle over her shoulder, thanked Ahxenta for her timely assistance and bent to retrieve the scattered mugs and her dropped tray. The whispering of those closest to the scene grew but most of the patrons were content to turn back to their drinks, giving sly glances over at the deserted table where Kerrix had stacked the rescued crockery and was loading her tray with detritus, and at the backs of the security squad and their detainees.

"Nothing ever changes in the *Half Moon*," Apnis remarked to her captain as the quartet of PSS officers looked at one another. "Your fist okay, Cinnabar? He looked to have a hard jaw and you didn't have time to get your hand shield in place."

"It'll do. Wonder where Ally picked *her* up? She's not the usual run of young and strapped-for-cash apprentices that he usually hires for bar work. And she was eyeing *us* up pretty closely."

"You can ask him later. Here's Captain Nat Hotshot and his first mate just stepped in the door."

2: OLD ACQUAINTANCES

The veils of the holo-door of the *Half Moon* had parted to admit a tall individual wearing the dark uniform that indicated his affiliation to a private starship. The man was sleek and exuded self-confidence as he looked around the crowded space as if expecting to be sized up. His black and bronze badge identified his ship as the *PSS Nyx Warrior* and the pips at his collar suggested that he held high rank, despite his relative youth. He strode to the bar, his companion a step behind.

Ally greeted him equably and asked if he would like to set up a tab. Captain Nathan Holdspan nodded and thanked him, ordering two beers before turning to scan the place for familiar faces. It was a moment before his eyes lighted on Captain Ahxenta, who had been watching him with a sardonic smile on her face. She had released the shield at her table, aware that its privacy would soon be invaded.

"Never fails," Apnis grinned, tilting her head in acknowledgement as Holdspan saluted the four with a sharp nod, a smile and a slight straightening of his form, as if he were standing to attention.

The captain picked up his mug, said something to his mate and set off between the tables. With an appraising glance, he claimed the place recently vacated by the loud-mouthed Friskianx and sat, telling his first mate to do likewise. He greeted the other four by name and asked civilly after their welfare.

The *Warrior* had not long berthed and with most businesses being closed for the day, the captain could not corner the relevant reps in marketing to arrange his next cargo pick-up. He had been told of the theft of the *Gadfly* and brought the subject up, regretting the increase in docking fees that he had also had to face. This led, as it often did when Captain Holdspan was holding forth, to the subject of his ship and her merits out in the space lanes.

"Found out any more about your lost cargo pod, Nat?" Murmur Fleetskup put in. "I assume it was secure-tagged and had your ship's call-sign and insignia embedded?"

"Nothing," Holdspan said shortly, his face darkening. "And it *was* the highest spec available so it was secure; and it was tagged. It seems you can't trust the Dockers' Guild to keep tabs on their own grapple drones in their own space and when on their own business."

"And you'll have had no luck getting compensation out of them, I bet," Buntle conjectured. "*We've* had trouble of that kind before," he nodded at his captain. "They take everything and give nothing."

"I'm on it," the young captain said curtly. "One way or another, I'll get to the bottom of it. On another note, I heard of an attack by raiders on a PSS out by the Crimson Drapes Nebula."

"Where in hell did you hear that?" demanded Ahxenta sharply.

"Who was it?" Apnis queried almost in the same breath.

"I picked it up in the harbour office. There was a small-time trader just in from that sector of the galaxy who said a ship he'd been told was a PSS had been attacked off the beacon at Sevolb," Holdspan replied. "But he couldn't say which one."

"Sevolb?" Fleetskup repeated. "Zone Alpha, then."

"A small-time trader and you believed him?" Ahxenta asked. "Did you ask the source of the news and how he knew it was raiders?"

"He got it in a bar in Lonagan Four, where he claims he's based, from repair-shed dock-rats who told him that a PSS had shipped in for a quick repair job as they'd taken a couple of hits from a skirmish with a raider pack and needed to get their comms gear back on line. If their comms *had* been hit, they'd not have reported it to the Trades Alliance or through the usual relays to the PSS fleet."

"Lonagan Four? Almost next door to the Friskianx and not a place I'd choose for repair, even if I was in a tight spot," remarked Apnis. "Nothing good has ever come out of that neck of the galaxy, but it's close enough to the bypass for a quick turnaround. But why would raiders take out comms? They'd be out for fast hits to disable weapons and then to release the payload. Doesn't stack."

"New tactics maybe," Murmur Fleetskup pronounced. "But why a PSS? We're big ships mainly, and a match for any raider pack, even with a mothership nearby. And after that trouble with hostiles posing as raiders and rumours that they'd taken over raider bases for their own ops, surely the usual scum haven't salvaged enough of what was left to start up big time again?"

"I'd not be too sure of that," warned Ahxenta. "That rat-pack of rebels including ex-raiders we met flying into Skyrtek was well-armed and well-set up and the losses they took were nowhere near enough to put them out of whatever business they had decided they were in."

"Revenge, if I recall," her first mate reminded her. "But that was months ago and I bet they're far better armed and booted now."

"What I didn't get was how the trader managed to miss out on the

ID of the PSS, if it *was* a PSS," Solmar Treskitt interjected. "The PSS fleet's not exactly unknown. I reckon he'd clocked our uniforms and was out to tell more than he knew, just to stir it."

"You could be right, Sol," Holdspan agreed. "He looked too well set up for the owner of a one-man trading rig. And he was interested in what we were carrying and where we were headed, *too* interested I thought. Though he backed off when I asked him why."

Ahxenta and Apnis exchanged glances, the same thought shifting in the backs of their minds.

"This trader wasn't a short, sharp-nosed runt by the name of Bick Micklemouse was he, with a one-man trading rig based on an old Comet Six?" the first mate of the *Arianrhod* asked curiously.

"He called himself Froyd Melson, but the description fits. And he told the rep dealing with his claim that his ship was a Comet Six with innovative engine and cargo-carrying capacity but not a model that rated higher fees for a short stopover. Why?" Holdspan asked.

"We should've left his damn boat parked on Kelfennig and left *him* to be a burden on society," Tallica Apnis snorted. "Looks like he's reinventing himself again and he still has the credit to do it."

"I take it you've heard of this character," grinned Nat Holdspan.

"Probably," Ahxenta replied bleakly. "If ever you meet him again, take everything he says as suspect and tell him nothing about you."

She was interrupted by a buzz on her wrist communit. She tabbed the device to call up the holo. "It's Azular," she said to her first mate. "I need to take a comm in private, so perhaps I'll see you all around tomorrow," she added to the others. "Tallica, you're with me."

The two rose and made for the bar to bid their host goodbye and settle their tab. They had no intention of discussing ship's business within earshot of any of the clientèle of the *Half Moon*.

"Azular's got something on the *Gadfly*, Cap?" Apnis asked softly as the two trod along green level two of inner belt two, making for the transport tubes that would take them to the outer reaches of the belt and then to the lower level docking bays that catered for smaller craft, where they had left their ride.

"Looks like, but he's not saying. He may have picked up a sniff in whatever bars he's been visiting. He'll meet us at the shuttle. I expect he wants to get back aboard and out of mufti. A lone drinker asking leading questions in the places he tends to stop into is likely to raise hackles and encourage the attentions of scallywags."

Dr Azular, the Berzic senior science officer of the *Arianrhod*, spied the two from the entry to their shuttle bay. He detached himself from the wall where he had been leaning and stepped out. Both noticed that his phase rifle was loose and his scanner was in his hands.

"Been tracking our advance," Apnis guessed. "Trouble maybe?"

She was right, for as they hailed him he held up a hand and continued his sweep. Both women released their rifles and backed up against the wall that sealed off their docking station.

"Three, armed and moving this way," was all Azular said.

His analysis was accurate for seconds later three tall figures turned the corner, to pause at the sight of *Arianrhod's* officers. The two males and one female wore uniforms, the sheen of which implied they were armoured. All were bareheaded and sported short-cropped dark hair.

"Indefinite physical characteristics," Azular reported in a low tone as the trio began to move forward again, weapons slightly raised. "All have cyber implants and the one in the lead reads partially Friskianx. He has traces of serocepcin in his system, though no zukivianite that I can read. Capturing data."

Ahxenta ran her eyes over the three as they came to a halt. She did not directly recognise the uniforms or the faces but she had a vague sense of familiarity as she studied the leader. A patch of scarcely visible metalloid attachments at his temples supplied the clue.

"We've met before," she said levelly. "You were in command of a bunch of ex-victims, ex-raiders and other aggrieved persons in one of the ships of that fleet heading from sector sixteen of Beta to Skyrtek months ago. Taking back your own using ships and hardware you'd lifted over the years to build a force that you figured could take out your former masters and give you the upper hand, wasn't it? Except it didn't work. They got rather out of hand and it took the combined forces of most of the galactic allied groups to stop them. And now that the hostiles have been put mostly out of business, you're out to carry on where you and your raider buddies left off?"

"We have no quarrel with you at this time, Captain Ahxenta."

"At this time?" Ahxenta repeated. "So you won't shoot me today, but you might if you meet me tomorrow, is that it?"

The man's eyes narrowed and he hissed in exasperation. "We have no quarrel with you, Captain."

"So why are you following me?"

"We're *not* following you! We're heading for our shuttle, a couple of bays along. We did *not* know you were ahead of us."

The flickering eyes of one of his cronies towards him gave the lie to that and the captain shook her head in disbelief. "You knew damn well. But you'd better move on, if your shuttle's down that way."

There was a fractional pause before he nodded, and keeping his eyes on her, he led his small team past the three from the *Arianrhod* and along the corridor. Azular kept his scanner on them until they had disappeared into one of the entries further along.

"It's shielded and I can't get clear readings, but all three could have done us some damage: those implants give them quite a kick."

"*That* was the commander of that rear renegade ship at Skyrtek?" Apnis asked. "He's looking a bit more human than last we saw him."

"He still has the implants at his hairline but they're smaller and the scars have gone. And he's had a face job, but he's the one. The others I don't recall but they may have been aboard that ship. We have its spec in our databanks, so we could scan for it if we get the go-ahead. Your Guild pal Kit Biernop may be able to help, Tallica," Ahxenta said. "You were going to check with him about the *Gadfly*?"

"I was and I will. But what in blazes were those three up to? They damn well knew it was us and they must have had something in mind if they *were* on our tail. Although how we didn't pick up on them I don't know. Either we're slacking or they're experts. We'd best check our berth very carefully before we even get close to our shuttle."

"Ahead of you there," the captain told her. "Azular, we leave your debriefing until after we're aboard *Arianrhod*. For now I want you to check every atom of the space around and behind that door."

"On it," he responded briefly as he turned his scanner to the entry and began a systematic analysis of the access space.

"This is one of the best docking bays, so the security should damn well be tight," Apnis grumbled. "No-one but those with the relevant clearances should be able to gain access, which means us. And the shuttle should be on *Arianrhod's* screens at tactical and on the Web's auto-surveillance systems, so any breaches would be evident."

"Something went wrong with the Guild's systems for the *Gadfly*," the captain retorted. "And *she* was in the repair docks in inner six, which has supposedly more security than hell's gates. I still need you and Greffy check over the actual records they say they've got, Azular. The Guild reps I *did* get hold of said there had been no alarm called and the cam footage showed status quo – until somebody went down for a look-see and found the bay empty, the *Gadfly* nowhere to be found and the cams all compromised."

"This entry reads clear, Captain. No evidence of tampering and our keys should operate normally. And there are no devices or other irregularities beyond the door space, including personnel."

"So here goes. Keep your phase rifle handy, Tallica, just in case."

Ahxenta pushed her key into the relevant slot and the access panel slid silently into the bulkhead. The light in the bay cut in instantly and the three could see that their shuttle was as they had left her. Azular ran his scanner in continuous sweeps as he moved onward and found nothing amiss, but the captain was wary.

"There might be something behind the shuttle and there are deck hatches and overheads all over. Keep your weapons hot, people."

The three made it aboard without incident and tied themselves in for the short trip to the outer belts and the network of vast lacunae that catered for the largest starships that used the huge facility. The captain took the pilot's seat and had begun to lock down her systems and power up when a light and an alarm on the control panel alerted her to something awry. It was seconded by an expletive from her science officer, who had been carrying out his own checks and had linked to the local schematics grid for their small area of operations.

"Do *not* operate the depressurisation sequence, Captain and don't open the hatch to space!" the Berzic officer spat out. "There's some sort of cloaked device on the outer side of the airlock doors and I don't think it's a part of the station's exterior in this area."

Ahxenta let loose an oath and leant across to check his readings. "Explosive?" she asked.

"Readings are unclear but it's big and I bet the trigger is our exit."

Grimly, the captain called in the situation to the duty officer on board *Arianrhod* and bid her own tactical and weapons stations send out probes to monitor the relevant area. Merkat security she knew would be alert to any incursion into its space and so sent in a priority call using an emergency call-sign. It was answered immediately — when the captain of the *Arianrhod* demanded attention, she got it.

Ahxenta was terse, sending across her officer's readings with a demand to know what had been planted outside the bay holding her shuttle. In the vast expanse of the Web, with nigh on four thousand individual high-security bays, the probability of the event being a random act of sabotage was next to impossible. The inevitable conclusion was that *Arianrhod's* shuttle had been targeted.

Merkat security was quick on the uptake and as speedy in sending out security bots to verify. A rapid response team was on the way, the captain was told, and she and her crew were advised to vacate their craft, as the area would be sealed off both internally and externally.

"Lock up and leave," the first mate grimaced. "So that any further mischief planned for inside this bay can be carried out? Should we set the self-destruct sequence?"

"Very funny," Ahxenta sniffed. "But we leave. I won't risk that something else will go bang under our noses, even if our scans read clear on the way in. Grab your valuables and let's move. You got that, Earbleat?" she added into the open link. "Have science and tactical stations maintain surveillance on this bay and everything near it."

"Roger that, Cap!" the loud voice of *Arianrhod's* second mate and weapons officer came clearly. "I'll warn the rest of our crew Web-side of the problem and that they should watch their backs."

"Do it," was the short reply. "Let's get out of here."

Retracing their steps with care, the three made their way out of the shuttle bay. There they found a detail of panting individuals that were the first wing of the security squad sent in to survey the area and set up a blockade to prevent entry to nearby bays, lest they had been targeted. They also found a clutch of hangers-on that had scented a drama and were there to watch it unfold. Soon after, a second posse of law enforcers dressed in riot gear appeared.

"What are they expecting, Armageddon?" Apnis enquired shortly. "There's nothing to see here but us and the local rumour-mongers."

"And the three that accosted us earlier," Azular noted, indicating the group in the background, who were standing quietly by a far wall.

"And I wonder how long they've been there?" Ahxenta enquired.

"If there's relevant cam footage of this area of deck, we could find out from security?" the senior science officer suggested.

"I suspect we'd come up empty on that," the captain rejoined. "But we're not leaving the area until I get a few answers."

"That could be a while," her first mate told her. "Why don't we get a couple of our own crew on furlough to hang on here and go see what we can dredge up in the Guild or Authority offices? If they're open, that is: we *are* out of usual business hours and then some."

Ahxenta shook her head. "I want to see what else if anything these guys find at first hand. And as our crew Web-side are on leave, they won't thank me for interfering in *that*, whatever they're up to."

An hour later and most of the hangers-on had been moved on or had drifted off of their own accord. Apnis heard a voice at her elbow and found Kit Biernop. As a senior member of the Dockers' Guild and a liaison with Merkat security, he had helped them before in matters best kept private and he was discreet. He was disturbed at the latest outrage and told them that there had been an increase in the numbers of petty crimes in the inner belts recently. He had put that down to the aftermath of the big shooting war that had involved much of the mapped galaxy but serious offences were also rising. He had little on the theft of the *Gadfly*, he had to admit, and was no wiser than others of his Guild as to why and how she had been spirited away. But he would keep his eyes and ears open, he assured Captain Ahxenta.

She had other things on her mind and looked up when a senior Merkat security officer whom she knew strode into view.

"Well?" she demanded, before he could utter a word.

"You were right, Captain: a highly explosive device attached to the outer hatch of the docking bay and triggered to go off at your exit – a magnetic mine. It would have damaged your shuttle badly and taken a chunk out of the superstructure of the hull of that section. And it was cloaked. We got it off with fine beam cutters and remote grabbers. We're manoeuvring it well away from the habited sections to see if we can work out what it is and disarm it."

"And if you can't?" she demanded harshly.

"Then we blow it apart at a safe distance from all Web structures. We have an army of secure bots out scouring the rest of the lower sections of extern inner two. Now that we have the spec of the beast we can speed up the search. But I advise that you don't make for your ship in that shuttle in case there are more surprises in store."

"Advice noted, but I need to get back to my ship, and that's where I'm headed. You can link any more details to me there."

The huge *Arianrhod* hung almost immobile within the delicate red-lit docking struts of her berth in one of the outermost holding areas of the Web, a flickering of light and dark showing that numerous repair and surveillance bots were in action across her pink hull. Her glowing form blotted out the blackness of space as the shuttle drew closer, to fill the view from the forr'ad window of the craft. Ahxenta requested permission to come aboard as she piloted her vessel towards the dark hollow of an outer docking bay. A dozen monitors tracked her on approach and at the corner of her vision the captain could see that the local targeting eyes of her ship's weapons batteries were active.

Docking achieved and the bay pressurised, the crew slipped their harnesses and slid out, collecting their gear en route. The three found an armed detail on the far side: second mate Lieutenant Commander Whisper Earbleat was covering all bases.

The trip from inner belt two had been uneventful, apart from the unusually large number of security craft and shifting tackle operating close to the outer structure of the facility. In the passing, Azular had garnered what data he could from the explosive device that had been captured and was at that point being gingerly manipulated away from the scene. It was large and would have done more than damage to their shuttle had they caught the full blast, was his estimate.

"So it looks like we're still not the flavour of the month in many circles," Tallica Apnis had remarked ironically as they hauled in.

The captain made straight for the bridge with her team. Late as it was, she wanted more answers. With a number of her crew harbour-side, she was very aware that they might be targeted if the *Arianrhod* was the object of local malice. She was not surprised to find that Captain Nathan Holdspan had left a link of enquiry – it seemed that news spread fast where the *Arianrhod* was concerned.

"Nat Hotshot can wait," Ahxenta said acerbically. "Azular, get what you can on the current situation. We'll defer a briefing on your other findings for the time being. Tallica, see if you can get hold of Kit Biernop on the QT and see if he has any more, and get security permission for a sweep for anything resembling that ship we met out near Skyrtek. We have its size, so Biernop should be able to give us the location of likely berths. If any of the locals in port scream, put it down to the security breach. And I still want a word or ten with the senior reps from the Port Authority, over this as well as over the *Gadfly*; and it wouldn't hurt to have the Dockers' Guild, the Trades Alliance and Merkat's Central Advisory Council in as well."

"You'll be lucky," snorted the first mate as she made her way to the comms station to brief the officer and make her links.

"Mr Bellfish, link me into the Ultraviolet III channel and patch it through to my office," Ahxenta ordered her senior comms officer. "I want to give the rest of the PSS fleet the heads up on the state of affairs here, in case any of them are headed into Merkat."

"It's going to be a long night," Lieutenant Box at the navi-helm console mourned dismally to his mate. "I thought the dark o'clock watch would be a breeze, with nothing to do but look at the view."

"You'll be sitting on your own for most of it if you don't shut up," helmswoman Romanna Dox retorted. "And as I've programmed in a series of diagnostics and battle sims, you'll have plenty to do."

The captain was still in the command chair three hours later and deep in thought as she digested the latest. The explosive device that Merkat security experts had distance-scanned before they blew it up was based on technology that was hardly a whisker from the weapons borne by the highly advanced pseudo-raider warships that had caused such destruction during the recent all-out conflict into which the

Arianrhod and her sister ships had been drawn several months before. A number of systems and bases within the mapped galaxy were still on the edge of survival and many would never fully recover.

Ahxenta had sought and gained consent from Merkat security to bring in splinters of the device and her science officers had analysed them. Its skin was based on a meta-jurillium alloy with a molecular signature pointing to an origin of Beta Zegonia 68c, a place known for the quality and cost of its goods, and it was recent in date. The inference was that someone had sourced high-class costly plating, and an outfit out there was using it to produce well-armoured destructive technology for small scale attacks. The operative key, the cloaking system and the type or types of explosive used in the bomb were unknown and were causing head-scratching in the experts dragged away from their rest to carry out urgent tests.

Exhaustive but covert scanning of likely bays for a vessel similar to that of the hostile-based and heavily-armed ship that the *Arianrhod* had met during the conflict at Skyrtek, and which had been one of a small fleet heading into the battle zone, was unproductive. Nothing close to its spec had been found, and as far as Kit Biernop was aware, the Dockers' Guild had not been called upon to repair such a vessel. However, further analyses that Azular and his second Greffy had carried out of the data picked up from the three strangers in the inner two bay levels had indicated that all three were similar to known victims of the late hostiles, all bore extensive cyber implants and all had recently undergone genetic alteration.

"Possibly to aid removal of the last of the technology implanted to ensure their compliance," Azular inferred. "Or to assist in adaptation to additional cyber hardware for other purposes – there were traces of meta-jurillium absorption products in all of them."

Azular now had the bio-records of the three locked into his pet scanner and into the *Arianrhod's* vast data facilities. The leader was part-Friskianx, but the origins of the others were unclear, although their genetics hinted at somewhere near the edges of zone Gamma.

The captain sighed in frustration, flexed her shoulders to ease the tension and was about to release command to the duty officer when a hiss from Bellfish, still at comms, alerted her to new troubles.

"Incoming from Merkat security, Captain! There's been another explosive device found, and this one's gone off!"

3: FISTICUFFS

Ahxenta let loose an oath, calling for details. The message was an alert to all ships in the Web with craft in the smaller docking facilities. There had been a detonation in outer belt five's level nine short-stay shuttle berths. One bay had been badly damaged as a service shuttle had been making its exit. It had recently been repaired and was under auto-pilot for the return trip to its mother vessel. There had been no fatalities, but one dock worker making a final check of the shuttle had just left the bay and had been injured when the inside pressure doors automatically sealed and the external lock covers blew off.

"Damn!" the captain exclaimed. "So we're not the only targets! But was it down to the same perps or a very early copycat crime?"

"Or nothing to do with the bang that nearly took us out," Apnis remarked from her seat alongside. "And I was just about to hit the sack. Had Merkat security not got that far out with its search?"

"The Web's a mighty big place and there's probably only a limited number of search drones available," Ahxenta posited. "They'd have concentrated on the expensive places first as that's where they feel they can charge the highest fees. Outer five *is* out on a limb and one of the furthest out that caters for short-stay traffic. The bays beyond that are usually packed with longer-stay shuttles, the gadabouts of the locals and the wrecks that can't find a cheaper berth elsewhere."

"So they should look for what they found when they analysed the scrap from the bomb that was set to blow out part of *our* bay. There must be enough in the type of explosive and plating they've got that they can do quick passing scans and home in on suspect signals."

"I'll leave you to tell them how to run their ops," Ahxenta told her first mate. "Meanwhile we operate continuous sweeps locally and we tell our crew on furlough to check out everyone and everything and check in with us if they're planning to ship up. We'll carry out our own surveys before our dockside shuttles leave their berths."

"Aye, Cap. We have two out apart from the *Gadfly*. They're both in inner two, close to their pet hang-outs for most of our people."

"The *Half Moon* and the lower level nightclubs, you mean."

"That's what I mean," Apnis grinned as she rose and headed over to comms to start the notifications to the crew off-ship.

An hour later, a call from medbay alerted the two senior officers that they had been on call well over time and should take time out or Dr Ma'Lappis would relieve them of duty on medical grounds. It had been quiet and as the Web kept Merkat planetary time and business was carried out during set hours, most residents were likely unaware of the situation and the Authorities would want it kept that way until they could draft in more personnel to deal with the inevitable outcry.

The second blast was similar to the first, the explosive device's plating had contained meta-jurillium alloy and the major volatile components used in both incidents were high grade but available in small amounts over half the mapped galaxy. Security was searching likely bolt-holes for stores of the stuff and all ships and businesses in the massive port had been updated and asked to assist.

Ahxenta was not impressed: very few of the operations that used Merkat would jump at such bidding, given the high fees they were obliged to pay for the services that were available, was her opinion as she conned over the crew rota.

"We're doing our bit," Apnis said as she cast her eyes over the list. "Pollux Gliss is next for duty officer. I'll swop weapons and tactical as they've both pulled long shifts. Azular, you get off as well. That's that, Cap. We'd best to our sacks if we're to be chewing the ears off the reps from the Port Authority, Merkat security *and* the Dockers' Guild first thing. They sure as hell should be expecting us, as they've been dodging a face-to-face ever since we got in. And Lindell has a couple of sessions in marketing over our next cargo pick-ups."

Early next day the captain and first mate were deep in discussion with senior delegates from Merkat and Guild internal security over the loss of the *Gadfly*. Little had been gained apart from the return of the shuttle's entry key. As far as the Guild reps could work out, the inner and outer airlock doors to the secure bay of the repair sheds in which the *Gadfly* had been docked had been opened only once during her stay. As the action had been classed as a routine exit, it had likely been allowed by the auto systems on release of the proper codes by the pilot of the shuttle, who had to be someone who had access to the key or a clone of it, knew the right codes and was able to operate the ship. Guild security was working on the idea that that was when it had been stolen: it was a normal part of ops that once repairs to a craft had been completed it would be moved to a holding bay, as the repair bay would be wanted for some other vessel. Although final repairs to the shuttle *had* been signed off, the bay had not been assigned to another repair job at that point.

Ahxenta was not satisfied. As *Arianrhod* had not been in port, an exit by her shuttle should have been noted by auto security systems if no relocation order was in place. And very few people would have had access to the repair bay. As the shuttle's entry key had apparently never left the possession of the Dockers' Guild, it had either been returned after the fact or a clone had been made and used. The latter was the most likely explanation. As for the proper codes, those would have been programmed into the key and thus into the shuttle's systems as she was powered up. But authority would have had to be granted for any transfer from whoever had been on duty in the local ops office at the time and secure cams would have had to be running to monitor the move. As docks and ancillary facilities had inevitably to run at all hours, the place should have been manned.

There was a certain amount of shuffling by the agents at the table that did not go unnoticed by Ahxenta and Apnis. The leading Guild security rep at that point was forced to admit that a full investigation into the processes that should have been in place at the time had led to the conclusion that the positional cam systems had been tampered with and bay entry ops overridden, by persons unknown.

"You mean your own people," the captain stated bluntly.

Apnis raised a mocking eyebrow: she and the captain had been briefed first thing by Azular on what he had found the day before in his visits to seedy ports of call around inner belt six. It was common knowledge that there were a number of light-fingered felons among the army of dockers that formed the labour force of the Web. There were also those who made a career of disposing of goods liberated by the larcenous. A lesser known secret was that there were a few clever criminals expert in bypassing security systems who were paid highly for their talents by those who used them. Of the latter, one or two were quite capable of cloning or forging various pieces of hardware, including credit slips, security entry keys, IDs and workforce permits.

Azular had acquired a couple of names of lesser links in the chain of corruption who, rumour had it, had tried their talents near or close to the inner belt six repair sheds at or around the time of the *Gadfly's* loss, but had come a cropper. Just what exactly had been the fate of the two Azular had not been able to determine, but it had raised a little hilarity in those in the know. Azular had also found out that the duo had a mate in the local ops office of internal Guild security whose job was process monitoring and secure cam surveillance. His collusion had been implied, but no-one dared give a name. The science officer had found out thus much and was even then prowling the usual haunts of off-duty Guild personnel in hopes of digging up more from off-duty dock-rats with big mouths and big thirsts.

The Merkat security pair had little to say, being wary of stepping on Guild members' toes, but their enquiries had pointed to big Guild complicity. The repair bay access had been dented but there had been no overt sign of forced entry into the space or any trace of illicit entry into nearby Guild facilities. A few workers had complained that their changing room lockers had been broken into and articles stolen but they blamed their fellows. A thorough search of the vast and complex Web for traces of the missing craft would be fruitless: if security did get wind of the whereabouts of a stolen transport, others would and it would be moved. The shuttle may have been taken from the Web, was so well hidden it would never be found, or it had been disguised or stripped bare and its pieces scattered.

None of these scenarios rang true for Ahxenta and she called for more details, particularly on the ships in port close to the time of the *Gadfly's* disappearance. That cause ruffled feathers, as the privacy accorded to those that used the Web was one of its major advantages, from which *Arianrhod* herself benefited. Apart from which, disclosure of that data was a matter for the Port Authority.

"It damn well isn't when *your* lack of care's resulted in the loss of a very costly shuttle!" Ahxenta snarled in response. "I want permission to have my own people go over that bay. I assume that you haven't allowed its use for any other business, in view of what happened?"

The silence and exchanged glances that greeted that assumption told the captain all she needed to know. "You have, haven't you?"

"You must understand, Captain…" the senior Guild rep began.

"Enough! You haven't heard the last of this, and if I didn't have a meet with reps from the Port Authority, you'd be hearing a helluva lot more right now!" the captain stormed. "Despite the latest attacks that are taking up security's time, this matter will not slip to the bottom of the pile. Do you understand me?"

"Yes, ma'am."

"Good. If you'll excuse me, I *will* see you later."

The silence lasted until the two had cleared the Guild offices and were in a transport tube heading inwards to Port Authority HQ.

"You scared the socks off them, Cinnabar, but it does look like they've hit a brick wall."

"They know damn well it was an inside job, or it had inside help *and* I bet they have an inkle as to who might have had a hand in it. I hope Azular picks up more on his latest jaunt. It's costing me to line his pockets so that he can grease the throats of the dock-rats that'll let slip what their seedy pals get up to behind locked bulkheads."

Azular had picked up more than he had bargained for, Ahxenta and Apnis found out some hours later. After a futile question and evasive answer round with executives from the Port Authority, the two spent a short session with *Arianrhod's* supercargo, Lindell, who had been talking contracts with reps in the main marketing suite. They had chosen the *Sunlight Subspace Diner* for their get-together as it was close to marketing and was well-equipped with privacy shielding for the convenience of customers. Lindell had secured two deals and needed the captain's go-ahead to finalise them. That and lunch being over, the three were about to leave when the captain's wrist communit chirped and a holo-note appeared asking for an immediate response.

"What's to do?" Apnis asked, brows raised in enquiry.

"Soon find out," Ahxenta replied. "It's Flintlock. She's giving zip away and says use the earpiece," she went on, extracting the device from her communit and slipping it into her ear. "Go ahead, Doc."

"Is he okay?" was her next question.

The answer she had from the *Arianrhod's* chief medic gave rise to a quick rejoinder. "He's going nowhere. Keep him there. Tallica and I will head back in one of our other Web-side shuttles. Put me through to Earbleat – she'd best alert the crew on leave that they're a shuttle down and some must be due back up soon. I'll be with you shortly."

"What's happened, Cinnabar?" the first mate asked after the captain's talk with duty officer Lieutenant Commander Earbleat.

"Azular got himself into a tight spot. Lindell, you hang here and complete the deals: I'll update you later. And settle our tab. Tallica, you're with me. Our nearest ride is green eleven, so let's get to it."

The two made quickly to the docking area, the captain maintaining a grim silence on the way which Apnis forbore to intrude upon. Their shuttle sat in a pool of light within the dim interior of its allotted bay. It was one of the larger of *Arianrhod's* surface craft and normally would have been used to ferry several crewmen.

"So what gives, Cinnabar?" Apnis urged as the access panel closed behind them and they took their seats. "I take it Azular made it home on the shuttle we came down in this morning?"

"Yes, he made it. Not one of his better landings; he's creased the bay floor and Crizz is a tad put out. But at least he's more or less in one piece. We'll find out more when we see him," the captain told her as she set the initiation sequence for departure.

The first mate had to be content with that, for Ahxenta said no more than required for shuttle operation and the return to *Arianrhod.*

"You seem overly worried, Cap," Apnis noted as the two headed out of the bay to the transport tube that would take them to medbay. "Something bad has happened to Azular that's got you rattled?"

"He was attacked some time after he left the *Green Diamond* on outer nine. He was making for inner two on a lead and had almost got there. Flintlock says he doesn't know if he was tracked all the way from the *Diamond,* or his trail was picked up along the way."

"It's a mighty long way from outer nine blue seven to inner two," Apnis interposed. "But Azular's not only canny, Cap, he has strong telepathic abilities. He'd have picked up any tail unless it was a damn clever one. And he was in work fatigues: who would target a guy in work gear for robbery with violence?"

"That's what's bothering me. He should have spotted a tail and he wouldn't look as if he was worth the energy for mugging unless it was someone or some people really desperate. And he's tall enough that he wouldn't be picked on as fair game for a bit of passing sport."

"So either he raised suspicion around the place, presumably in the *Diamond,* or he was recognised as one of ours."

"Or as a guy asking awkward questions. A remote cam could have tracked him – he'd be less likely to spot that, though he'd have had his scanner online. Or word had been sent ahead and others were on the lookout. We'll find out more when we speak to him. Flintlock said he'd had a mauling, including a fractured rib, but there's a story."

The medbay of the *Arianrhod* was a well-appointed space close to the central area of the great vessel and it took some time for the two to reach it. Chief MO Axellina Flintlock was there to greet them.

"He's holding up," she told the captain. "He wanted to get up and back to work, but I told him no way. I *have* managed to extract DNA from his fists and fingernails that's not his own and I've got Greffy going over his gear to see if he can get any more on his attackers."

"How many?" Ahxenta queried.

"There were four, apparently. But I don't have enough to give you any definite ID on who or what; early signs indicate the origin of one as near the outer regions of zone Beta near Mellifly, but it's difficult to pin down anyone's planet of origin. And it may not have been one of the bad guys, but you'd best hear his story."

"Four!" Apnis repeated incredulously. "He held off four?"

"I'll let him tell you the tale – I suspect I only got the outline. But go easy on him, Cinnabar: he *has* had quite a pounding and it's taken a lot out of him, though he won't admit it. He's like many of the rest of us – getting a bit long in the tooth for that sort of shenanigans on a regular basis. I'm still amazed he got the shuttle back without more damage to him and it. I've already rattled his cage over it."

The senior science officer was settled comfortably in a side bay off the main medbay. His face bore witness to a couple of well-aimed punches and one of his hands was strapped up but his medical scrubs and his coverings hid the remainder of the damage.

"Captain, Commander," he said equably as the two strolled in.

"You've had some morning," the captain greeted him, hauling over a chair. "Want to tell me about it?"

"I can leave, Azular, if you want a private chat," Apnis offered.

"Sit down, Commander. I expect Dr Flintlock has briefed you."

The first mate grinned wryly as she nodded and pulled up a seat. "So what's the story? You had four on you and you got away in one piece? That was some going and I'm mightily curious."

"I had help," was the dry response.

As the two knew, the science officer had made for outer belt nine and the *Green Diamond*, a seedy eating and drinking den on level blue seven. The place was known as a haunt of dock workers and others that worked and lived in the outer belts, and for various crews whose ships stopped over now and then. Azular wanted more on the two names he had picked up earlier and whose adventures around the inner belt six repair sheds some time before had caused such glee in their fellows. He was also keen to find the friend of the pair who worked in the local ops office and was marked as a corrupt member of Guild internal security. He knew that in the *Green Diamond* he was likely to find one of the dock-rats who had incautiously revealed the rumours doing the rounds of the local workforce during his first visit.

It was as he was talking to this contact, a type who worked aboard the rigs used for hull patch-up of the larger ships in for repair, that he noted others listening in. He had had to feed the man sufficient drink to encourage disclosure, but that had had the side-effect of making him loud as well as voluble, and it had drawn notice. Azular had, however, found out that the two implicated in the affair near where the *Gadfly* had vanished were known for their habit of acquiring cloned keys to craft in for repair and trying their luck in the removal of valuables left behind by the owners. As dock workers they could get into a number of repair bays in various areas of the Web. Such entry was strictly controlled but the men were allegedly sly enough to be able to bypass the restrictions and had been known to use the small hours of low activity to carry out their sorties.

On the night in question and despite the help of their chum in the ops office, the pair had failed dismally. Rumour had it that they were found later by two mates in the local Guild changing rooms stripped to their underwear and minus some prized assets, including hardware and credit slips. Not that they *definitely* had a cloned key, the drunk assured Azular, sufficiently aware to realise his own quandary if word of his indiscretion got into the wrong ears, but they had certainly been up to no good and had paid a price that they were frantically trying to hide from others, especially their bosses.

Azular had not been able to persuade his associate to divulge the name of the corrupt security operator and was unwilling to press him in view of the interest being taken by others, but the man had let slip that the one in question was a regular at the *Port in a Storm* on green level six of inner two. Affecting excess alcohol himself and a pressing matter elsewhere, the science officer took his leave. He was certain at that point that he had not been followed as he was habitually keenly observant and when involved in a clandestine operation, he was extra cautious. His scanner, an integral part of his typical mission kit, had shown nothing to arouse suspicion. There were people in the general area, it being into set business hours, but he had been ignored as just another workman coming on or going off shift.

Inner two was quite a way from outer nine and it had taken Azular some time and transport tube changes to reach the main stop-off area on blue five. He had not been unduly aware of overt curiosity from fellow travellers in transit but as the blue five terminal was busy he had taken a couple of quieter routes down to green ten to avoid the crowds, aiming to head back up to the *Port in a Storm* on green six. Four others had stepped into the final tube, two of whom were in nondescript dark fatigues and appeared to be having an argument. The other two were openly armed and gave green eleven as their stop. He was sure he had not seen any of them before.

It was as Azular disembarked at green ten that he realised he was in trouble. The arguers had hopped out first and turned to him. The science officer had sensed immediate danger and was alert enough to try to run for it when one of the pair behind made a grab for him and clouted him across the side of the head before he was off the mark.

"I made a lot of noise – to attract attention," he admitted.

"Or scare it away," Ahxenta remarked. "You had your handgun?"

"Yes, but I'd no way to get to it; to carry it openly would have given rise to undue interest. All four were trying to pin me down and I got the impression that they wanted me away to a place where they could work me over more easily."

"Interrogation – to find out what you were up to?"

"Yes, ma'am, that's what I figured later as they'd not drawn their guns. At the time, I was more intent on avoiding the fists and boots. And then I heard someone racing up. Whoever it was sounded as if they had a squad on their heels. They smacked into my attackers, one hit the deck and the rest of us were shunted backwards. That was enough of a diversion that I could grab my gun. It was kicked out of my hand but I got hold of it again, as two of them had turned to take on whoever it was that had jumped in."

Azular closed his eyes and took a juddering breath. "I got in one shot, heavy stun, but I took a kick in the ribs that badly winded me. By that time another one was on the deck and there was space enough that I could take a second shot. I don't know if it hit a target, but I felt the gun being taken from my hand and heard another bolt. By the time I'd got something like my breath back, it had gone quiet – I imagine anyone in the immediate area would have run for cover when they realised what was going on."

"You got all four of them?" Apnis asked.

He shook his head. "No: one made off. There were three on the deck when my head had cleared enough to take in my surroundings. I'm afraid I was in no fit state to scan for who or what they were, but my rescuer was searching their pockets. I thought at first she was an off-duty security officer, as she deactivated their rifles and removed the charge caps very efficiently, but I was mistaken."

"How so?" the captain asked.

"She pocketed a couple of things she had taken from my assailants *and* wiped her traces off the guns. And she gave one of them a kick and a very rude word in the passing. She came over to check on me when she realised that I was too stunned to move. I half expected her to search my pockets but she didn't. She checked my pulse and my injuries, asked after my health and gave me back my handgun; and then she said she'd call for assistance from Merkat medbay. I resisted that, as given my mission, I did *not* want Merkat security involved – as they would have been. Did you know there's a small part-time free emergency medical station on green twelve run by volunteer off-duty medbay personnel? They treat those who can't afford or don't want to use medbay: lowly paid workers, the unwaged or those who would rather their hurts were not reported. She took me there, despite my protests. I'd hoped to make for our shuttle on green eleven and call for help from there, but I could not of course, with a stranger in tow. We must have been quite a sight," he said, wincing at the memory. "She had stopped a few blows."

"So who was she?" Apnis asked curiously.

Again Azular shook his head. "I asked when we got to the line of seats outside the med station, but she said she'd only say if I gave her *my* name. I gave a false name and she knew it. But she *did* say that one of my attackers, the one she kicked, was a dock worker. She knew him from somewhere, though she wouldn't say where, and she said he was a bad lot. I didn't press the issue."

"So how come you made it to the shuttle and then thought you'd pilot her back to the *Arianrhod?*" the captain enquired.

He looked away for a moment, discomfited. His friend, clearly in pain, had complained of dizziness and then slid to the deck in a dead faint. Another patient in the line outside the clinic had yelled out that one was down and the investigating medic had called for a gurney to take her away for treatment. Someone else came out to ask if anyone knew her. Azular claimed that he had met her on the way in and knew no more than that she had stopped to help him.

At Apnis' scandalised glance, he qualified his statement. He had recognised the medic who had responded to the initial call as a senior doctor from Merkat's medbay and was worried that his own identity might be revealed once he reached the treatment room. He had thus waited until the disturbance had died down and then shuffled off to make for their docked shuttle on green eleven. There, he had used the onboard emergency medical kit to treat as many of his hurts as he could and for reasons that he himself could not clearly explain, he had not called for help nor set the distress on his communit, but had decided to head back to the ship as quickly as possible.

"I *will* be reporting the attack on you to Merkat security, Azular," the captain informed him. "I want to know who those bozos were and why they picked on you. They're probably long gone by now, but the gunfire may have registered on local sensors or roving secure cams. And if one *was* a dock-rat, it may have been a response to your sneaky enquiries – someone didn't want you digging. But how they tracked you… you weren't bugged, I take it?"

"No ma'am, and I *did* check."

"Dr Flintlock can try her contacts in medbay for more about the woman. There must be records for that emergency station. Give her as many details as you remember. And next time you get beaten up, call for back-up, don't turn one of my shuttles into a guided missile and aim it at the docking bay floor."

"Aye, Captain."

"Meanwhile, no getting back to work: Greffy's quite capable of looking after things while we're in port. Which we won't be for much longer, if Lindell has got those contracts in place. We're heading up to the bridge to see what Earbleat's been doing in our absence."

The two senior officers made off through the bay exit to have a quick word with the chief medic, who was waiting for them.

Ahxenta was serious as they left Flintlock's office. "That was quite a pounding. He won't be fit for more than light duties for weeks. I'd like to know who the bastards were that did it and why *and* how they got to him. If we could find the owner of the spare fists, we might get more clues. We're not much further forward with what happened to the *Gadfly* or where she is now either, and I sure as hell would like to know *that* before we ship out."

The captain checked in with her personnel, made a link to Merkat security about the attack on her officer and then set off Web-side with Flintlock. The latter was headed for the central medbay to meet a friend. Ahxenta was bound for main marketing on inner belt two's green four. Lindell had completed the details of the deals he had been working on, but the reps involved in one of them wanted to talk to the captain, as the clients on Delta Iridium Colony were being sticky.

Arianrhod's supercargo was waiting in one of the open areas of the marketing suite. "Everything's signed and sealed, Captain, this is just nit-picking. They're refusing to disclose the complete manifest until they have your assurances that we're capable of the commission."

"Every damn rep in the sector and out of it knows the *Arianrhod* and her capabilities. *We* know Delta Iridium Colony like the backs of our hands, the clients have dealt with us before and it's not highly sensitive cargo. There's just a lot of it and expensive if we go down."

"That's the problem – I even had to get assurances from the TA office that our insurance is up to date. They're antsy over the increase in crime here and the upping of raider activity out there. I'll need a drink at the *Half Moon* once we're done," he added.

"I'll come with you, but you can pay," was the short response.

4: KERRIX

Two hours and a great deal of wrangling later the captain and Lindell, drinks in hand, were propping up the bar in the *Half Moon in a Puddle*. They were sharing the counter with a stranger in a business suit that would have been smart if it was clean. He looked as if he had been there for a while. His mug had reached rock bottom and he was looking around for assistance, but Ally was busy with orders.

"What do you have to do to get service in here?" he demanded of Lindell, who was closest to him.

"You ask nicely and then you wait," the supercargo replied civilly.

"I'll be over once I've done these," Ally called out. "Merry, take these to booth eight, they've prepaid," he ordered. "And tell Lotty to clear table twelve, they've not put the empties in the auto-hatch."

"Aye, aye sir!" was the bright response as his young aide Merry floated off, the appraising eyes of the businessman following her.

The man turned back to find Ally's help, Kerrix, on the far side of the bar, slapping mugs from a tray to a shelf under the counter. He slowly read the name on her badge, leaning in to make it out.

"Ker-rix," he intoned. "What's a nice girl like you doing in a dive as downmarket as this?"

He was treated to a withering look and a raised eyebrow. "Dealing with idiots, it seems. Get your elbows off the bar."

"I want another drink."

"I'd say you've had plenty," she retorted, snatching away his mug. "Don't you have a home to go to, or a hole to crawl back into?"

"Here's my credit slip: I want another drink."

"Here's my answer: no. I don't intend to clean up the mess when you puke all over the floor. You have had enough, mister."

"You're not so good-looking, now I see you up close," he slurred.

"You want good-looking, try Azure Belle's on green twelve. For now, just shut up and ship out. I've had one hell of a day already, it's not even half over and I'm not adding to it by shovelling you through the door when you can't stand on your own two feet."

"Cool it, Xanna," Ally, who had just come over, cautioned. "I'll get Jox to shift him, that's what he's paid for; wherever the hell he is," he added, tabbing the security button under the counter.

"You'd be as well asking the pink pixie to get rid of him," was the short rejoinder as Kerrix snatched up her tray and made off.

"What's eating her?" Ally muttered to the ever-cheerful Merry, who had sailed up with a tray of used glassware from the far reaches of the *Half Moon's* dim interior. "She's not long come in for her shift and she's taking the heads off the customers."

"Maybe with reason," the girl replied, cocking an eye at the drunk, who, head pillowed on arms, was snoring gently. "I think she's had a bad night. I noticed she was limping when she got in and she's got a couple of nasty bruises under her makeup. Jox jigged her arm earlier and she nearly went through the roof. I'll find out when I get a tick."

The two from the *Arianrhod* had been watching the exchanges in some amusement.

"Where did you find your friend Kerrix?" Ahxenta asked of Ally, who had begun to replenish their mugs. "She's not your usual type of friendly and efficient waiting staff."

"Xanna Kerrix, allegedly, and it's an odd story," he said with an expressive shrug. He propped his elbows on the bar, ready for a chat, one eye on the insensible one further along the counter. "I'll tell you as long as you don't pass it on, Captain – I don't think she'd like it."

"Now I'm *really* curious," Ahxenta told him. "I won't say a word."

"It wasn't long after you were last here, ma'am. We had a gang of bad guys in, real thugs, a crew that had been fixing the main Kanelian Juxta orbital station. They were here on stopover to spend their pay before heading to their next job, and where credit's splashed there's always trouble. Well, one half-drunk rowdy figures he's been short-changed, so he starts on Merry; she's less than polite, he gets nasty, I call my security and step in. The bozo hauls out a gun and fires: it took out half my goods on the wall behind the bar, so it wasn't set on stun. Then he turns it on me. I tell you, his finger was squeezing that trigger… Next thing, I'm on my butt on the floor, a chunk's out of the front of my counter and the guy's on the floor along of me, his head being kicked in. But he was tough: straight back up, drunk and livid, and this fighting fury I'd never seen before at his throat. *She* had him almost out for the count before my security showed."

"Doesn't look like much from here," Lindell noted, with a look over to where the subject of the exchange was collecting used mugs.

"My security guys are clearing the crowd, Merry's tidying up, I'm still stunned and sat on the floor and I see *her* going through the guy's pockets, taking stuff. I haul myself up and start to assess the damage.

Merkat security shows, my people give them the story and they start searching the guy on the deck. Merry's cleaning *her* up by this time. She's sat on a stool as she's taken a few knocks. Naturally I step over to say thanks and ask if there's anything I can do for her in return."

Ally leaned forward conspiratorially. "Guess what she says?"

"Give me a job?" Ahxenta guessed.

He shook his head. "Don't tell the security guards it was me did that, is what she says. I'm just a victim that got caught up in it and I'm fine. Only she wasn't, I could see that, so I got Merry to take her off to the staff room in the back."

"And then you gave her the job?" Ahxenta interrupted.

"It gets better," Ally muttered, casting a wary eye on Kerrix, who had dumped her load and was off for more. "Security frisks the guy on the floor. He still has the gun that did the damage and an ID but nothing else: no credit slips, no other weapons, no loose credit bits. But he'd *paid* for his drinks… I say nothing, they haul him off. I go to see how she is and I find out that the gun didn't miss its target: she caught the edge of the beam down her leg and had hell knows how many cuts and bruises; *and* a broken finger. Obviously, I made to call in a medic but she point blank refuses to see one."

"So what was she hiding, Ally?" demanded the captain. "It can't have been too bad, as she's now one of your paid underlings. You *are* paying her, I take it?"

"Of course I am! What do you take me for? She said she couldn't afford the medical fee and as she wasn't local and didn't have a valid ID, there would be questions. I couldn't help saying what about the goods she'd lifted from that thug, there must be credits there. She laughed and admitted it, but as he wasn't in a position to claim it back and she'd more need of it than he had, she reckoned she was entitled. And as he'd shot her, he'd get off paying that price. I didn't dispute that, but I offered to pay for the medic as it was my place and she *had* saved my butt. I called in one I knew that wouldn't ask questions over the phase-burn and she was in no fit state to argue by that time anyhow. As she'd lifted a couple of loaded anonymous credit slips from the guy, she ended up paying the medic herself anyway."

"That still doesn't explain why she's working in the *Half Moon*, Ally," Lindell pointed out.

"Well, she'd no place to go – we found that out when Merry was set to help her home. So I asked how I could help. *That* was when she said, find me a billet and give me a job."

"Even though she'd no valid ID, had robbed a guy and evidently could throw a punch?" the captain asked.

"She was honest about it and few are. I *did* ask about her, but she said she'd good reasons for not telling who she was and where she'd come from and they weren't illegal or immoral and were none of my business," Ally shrugged. "So I didn't push. I figured I'd find out or she'd move on. Merry offered to find a billet and she got one through a friend of a friend. And so far she's done okay, though I'd bet good credit that this kind of work isn't her usual trade. And I can look in the mirror and see that I'm still here, and that counts for a lot."

"That's quite a story," Ahxenta agreed. "So what do you reckon *is* her usual trade?"

"Undercover agent that took a wrong turn? I don't know. Merry gets on with her okay despite the age gap and says she can be trusted. But I told my partner the story and *she* suggested I scan her for an implanted ID. She got me the loan of a security hand-held reader from one of her mates in the sheds – you'll recall she works in the repair bays of the middle belts."

"And?" the captain probed, nodding.

"She's got three implanted pieces that the scanner couldn't read and registered as invalid: in her shoulder, in her upper arm and in her hand. We guessed that one was an ID and one was a credit reserve, but we couldn't figure the third; maybe another ID or permit but we don't know for sure. She was pissed when she realised I'd scanned her, but didn't raise too much dust as she was grateful for the help."

The two officers were expressing their surprise when a concerned Merry slid over and up to Ally, apologising for her interruption. She had come from the staff room behind the bar.

"It's Xanna," she said. "I know we're going to be busy when the evening crowd gets in but she's in no fit state to be heaving trays about and manhandling drunks, even she admits that. Evrett's always looking for extra shifts so maybe you could pull him in?"

"She looked a bit wild when she came in for her shift. What's up?"

"Had a bit of a dust-up with some slimy heavies this morning, she said; met them on her regular workout run through the lower green levels. They were beating the crap out of some guy and she realised one of them was that dock-rat that battered her friend Vetta from next door two weeks back and got away with it. So she dived in. She said she'd been patched up at that charity med clinic on green twelve, but all you get there's a free bandage and a pain shot, if you're lucky – they haven't the facilities for much else."

"What happened to the guy that got beat up and the thugs doing the beating up?" Ally enquired.

Merry raised her hands in perplexity. "I don't know. She's not very talkative. Said it was okay, she and he got the better of them and got out is all. But she looks like hell."

Ahxenta, brows furrowed, had been listening intently. "You said the med clinic on green twelve? What time this morning?"

"No idea, Captain. Why?"

Ally scented a story and tilted his head sideways, eyes gleaming. "You know something, Captain?"

"I'd like a word with this Kerrix of yours. Lindell, you contact Dr Flintlock: she's probably still in medbay. Get her over on the QT and tell her to bring a full medical kit. And check in with Merkat security to see if they have more on our other matters, but not in here. Come back here once you're done. Do you have somewhere private I can talk to Ms Kerrix without half the galaxy listening in, Ally?"

"There's my office; it's inside the staff room, but they won't listen at the door. Merry, you keep an eye on things and see if Evrett's free for a shift, starting now. Check that Chef and his team are set for the dinner rush, and make sure the rest are on their toes – it's always bad when we're short-staffed. And you'd better get Jox to lever that barfly off my counter or he'll be giving the place a bad name."

"I take it you want mayo with that," was the sharp retort as Merry turned to the bar's comm station to begin the first of her tasks.

"Just do it," Ally snapped. "This way, Captain. You realise half my regulars are watching and wondering what in hell's going on?"

"Let them wonder," Ahxenta said, looking around balefully.

Several pairs of curious eyes viewed the captain of the *Arianrhod* as she followed Ally through the door at the far end.

Kerrix was curled up in the corner of a hard sofa against the back wall, eyes shut tight. Merry had been right, Ahxenta thought: she did look like hell. The woman's head sheared round at the noise of the door and her eyes opened. They widened as they took in the tall commanding officer of the *Arianrhod* at Ally's back.

The proprietor of the *Half Moon* indicated a side door. "My office is that way, Captain. There are chairs, a table and a comm station. Captain Ahxenta wants a word with you, Xanna, in private."

"Why?"

"I'm sure she'll tell you."

Kerrix' eyes flitted to Ahxenta. "Why?" she repeated.

"You'll find out shortly. In Ally's office, *if* you please, Ms Kerrix."

"You're not the boss of me," Kerrix said in a hoarse whisper, her eyes challenging the captain's cool stare.

"No, I'm the boss of you," Ally told her flatly. "And I'm telling you to be civil to the captain and to answer her questions."

Kerrix gave a grim smile and a short, husky chuckle as her gaze flicked over to him and she made to stand. "So you are... Dammit!"

"I've got her. Open the door, Ally," Ahxenta instructed as she caught and braced Kerrix, whose leg had given way as she rose.

The woman had no option but to accept the captain's support to walk into the office. A glance had shown Ahxenta a comfortably padded chair and she made for that, kicking it away from the desk.

"Sit down. My chief medic's on the way; she'll have a look at you."

"Why?"

"Don't be a fool. And stop asking why, it's damned annoying," Ahxenta growled as she pulled over a chair and sat alongside. "Ally, get her a shot of something strong, she looks as if she needs it."

"Aye, aye, Captain."

The two sat eyeing one another in silence until he reappeared with two small glasses of spirit. Ahxenta accepted the goods with a nod and placed them on the desk.

"Shut the door on your way out, Ally," she said. Once the door had closed she picked up a glass and held it out. "Drink."

"So I see."

"You're *really* beginning to bug me, Ms Kerrix. Get that damn well down you."

The spark of the sharp eyes and the set mouth told Kerrix that here was someone it would be better not to gainsay. She inclined her head in accord and took the glass, knocking the contents back in one mouthful. She then began to cough painfully, a rough, rasping sound.

"Bloody hell, what was that, jetfuel?" she finally gasped.

"Close enough," was the dry reply as Ahxenta retrieved the glass and sat back, watching until the spasm had ceased. "You had an adventure this morning on green ten. Tell me about it – and do *not* ask why or I'll get Merkat security in and you'll be telling them."

"Merry told you," she guessed. "And I doubt you'll call security, it's hardly your style, from what I've heard. But I owe you for your help yesterday, I expect. Yes I did." Her gaze slid to an indeterminate spot over the captain's shoulder to avoid the hard stare.

"I usually go for an exercise run along the lower green levels when I'm not in early. I was on green ten and I heard a racket. I stopped to take a look round the corner and saw a gang beating a guy up. He was on the deck, kicking like crazy. I don't like uneven odds at the best of times," she winced. "But then I caught sight of one thug with bright yellow hair – I'd seen *him* at that trade before so I joined in to put a stop to it. *Now* can I ask why you want to know, Captain?"

Ahxenta considered. "Who exactly are you, Ms Kerrix? Your usual trade isn't bar work, not by a long way."

"That's none of your damn business, Captain. And you haven't answered my question. I *have* answered yours."

They were interrupted by a discreet buzz at the door that heralded the entry of Axellina Flintlock.

"Captain?"

"Your patient, Doctor. She's had a bad day. As for your question, Ms Kerrix: that man you saw being beaten up is one of my officers."

That caused an intake of breath and a startled look at the captain. The woman's eyes stayed fixed on her face until Flintlock, scanning complete, extracted a hypo and pressed it to her upper arm.

"What's that?"

"Pain relief. I need to get to your shoulder to replace the strapping and get you better support round your middle. And I'll have to treat your facial bruising before it gets worse. Then I'll fix the right leg – you've got tendon damage and what looks like a fractured toe. And there's swelling around the implanted hardware of your lower limbs."

"Implanted hardware?" Ahxenta questioned suddenly.

"Standard, Cap; bone-strengthening repair, I figure. You've been using your fists as well. And that embedded chip in the pad of your left hand's an ID, I take it, as it's giving out a localised signal?"

At the brief but weary nod, Flintlock continued her ministrations.

The captain ruminated, watching carefully. "What's the purpose of the device implanted in your shoulder?" she asked abruptly.

Kerrix gave her another startled glance, her head skewing round. Her right hand slid up to finger a place at the top of her left shoulder, close to her neck. The location of the device, Ahxenta guessed.

"It's a language analyser-translator," she replied. "It links to aural, neural and vocal networks and assists the learning of new languages. And allows communication until the new linguistics are assimilated."

"That's hardly a standard piece of kit," the captain remarked. "I've never heard the like of it before. Where in blazes did you get it?"

"I've heard of such devices," Flintlock cut in. "Experimental, rare, and you couldn't afford one even if you could source one."

There was no answer, merely a shake of the head.

"None of my business, huh?" surmised Ahxenta. "What about the chip in your arm? Implanted credit reserve?"

"Ally," she said resignedly. "He scanned me covertly just after I started working here. Why is everyone so damn interested?"

"You tell me. You're not what you appear to be on the surface."

"Neither are you. What was your officer doing dressed in fatigues down in green ten, being kicked about by a bunch of ruffians?" was the snappy retort. "How is he anyway?" she added more civilly.

"He'll live. Who was the guy with the yellow hair you mentioned?"

A stubborn look replaced her former expression but her eyelids drooped as another hypo shot by Flintlock took effect.

"I'll need her out for this; it'll hurt, despite the analgesic," said the doctor. "And you'll have to give me a hand to hold her upright until I get this strapping on. She's damn lucky there's little internal damage. A kick in the wrong place could have ruptured an organ."

"What did you pick up in medbay?" the captain asked practically, rising to assist her medic.

"They keep files of what goes on in the free med station on green twelve. They get some rum types in as it's near the livelier nightclubs, but my contact gave me one or two details. I had to tell him about Azular, but he'll keep it close. A female matching her *did* show up early this morning saying she'd got caught up in a fight, but wouldn't say where. The med records show more or less what I've found. They patched her up and advised she head to the main medbay. It was recorded that she said she'd had someone come in with her, but there was nothing else. But her physiology's interesting: the nearest they could get, and my readings confirm, is an origin at the Kirtish edge of zone Mu. It's not conclusive as they've few medical records to go on and there are differences to the records they *do* have."

"Zone Mu? It's the smallest zone of the mapped galaxy but has a large border lapping onto uncharted space," Ahxenta mused. "And it's not under the direct control of any big alliance. As far as we know they're all independents. Part of it is close to the Enigma Nebula, so near one of the original hostile bases that were part of that frigging war we're just out of. I've heard of more trade routes coming online in the area as there's a new double bypass route the independents are building. It cuts from Cassary on the Mu-Kappa-Iota border clear through Mu to Kollaskin Ambit and then back across into Kappa at Wild. And Cassary and Kollaskin both border uncharted edges. It'll bolster their own trade and extend the local star charts. You done?"

"Yes, you can let her go now. Just ease her back into the chair. Stupid ass, she should have gone to medbay," Flintlock grumbled.

"There's allegedly been contact with populated systems beyond

Mu's borders and exploration of unmapped space is going on all the time, as it's part of ISP's mandate. But we *do* know that of the latest civilisations reached and brought into the galactic zone system, most are pretty much humanoid and probably what's grown out of the seeding that went on in the early expansionist phase."

"Too esoteric for me," the doctor told her. "I'll do the leg. The toe's okay so I won't disturb that, though she'd still be better with regular checks in medbay. But if she does originate out that way or close to it, how in hell did she get this far? I've rarely met a zone Mu independent in Merkat and never a medic. They tend to keep very much to their own sectors as far as I know, and you only get the odd rep or two when something big's in the offing."

"She's the least of my concerns. I still want to know who attacked Azular and why *and* how they managed to track him. We're no closer. I'll leave you to finish up and keep an eye on her for a while. I'd better see what else Lindell has found out, if anything. I'll be back."

Lindell had returned to the *Half Moon*, which was now filling up with the clientèle that stopped by later in the day. Ahxenta could tell by his face that little new had surfaced. The two made for a private booth with a good view of the door, watched by many curious eyes.

"What do you reckon went on back there in the staff ready room, Malty?" Jurry enquired of his friend.

"No idea. But we'd best stay close and find out. Ahxenta goes in with Ally, he comes out, gets drinks, goes back in and then comes out again; and then the *Arianrhod's* chief medic heaves to and *she* heads in. And now here's Ahxenta back out and in confab with her supercargo, but no medic. There's a doozy of a story here," was the sage reply.

"So there is," agreed Jurry. "And it may reap us benefits in free ale if we can find out what it is. We'd best make these drinks last."

The drinks had to last, for half an hour went by with no further incident. Ahxenta and Lindell had continued in close discussion and even to the bleary eyes of the topers, the captain did not look happy. The place began to fill as the close of regular business hours passed.

It was a hubbub behind the bar that drew inquisitive looks. One of the *Half Moon's* security guards had come racing out of his burrow to relate some tale to Ally. The latter, mouthing orders, jerked his thumb towards the staff room and then sprinted across to Ahxenta, flinging an instruction to Merry in passing to keep an eye on things.

"Captain, you'd best get back here; there's trouble," he panted.

Ahxenta was on her feet in a second. "Lindell, you're with me. What in hell's happened?"

"This way, ma'am," was all he said as he led the charge across the diner and back behind the counter.

The staff ready room was disordered, with one of the *Half Moon's* young staff moving furniture away from the centre of the floor to the wall and another digging in a closet from which half the contents had already spilled. Ally made straight past them for his office. The door was ajar and the noises of a skirmish could clearly be heard.

Ahxenta's eyes took in the upended fittings and smashed comm station. Two of Ally's guards had a struggling man on the deck and were clapping restraints on him. A dazed Flintlock was inching her way over the floor to a heap in a corner that looked like Kerrix. The captain made for her chief medic and dropped down to her knees.

"Axellina! What happened?" she demanded, stopping the doctor's uneven progress and attempting to slip an arm across her back.

"I'll be fine. Just let me see if she's okay..."

Ahxenta looked up. "Lindell, check her. And call the ship, see if any of our own medics are on shore leave and get them here. Ally, I want an emergency response team from Merkat medbay in here *now*."

"Yes ma'am."

Flintlock was winded and had a bloody nose, and as she moved Ahxenta could tell that she had sustained body blows, for she was wincing and guarding her side.

"We're taking care of it," the captain soothed as one of Ally's staff appeared with an emergency med kit he had just unearthed.

The young man tore the kit open and dug out a medi-wipe pack, which he handed to the captain, his eyes wide and frightened.

"I'll take that Jez; you get back out front and help Merry," Ally said firmly as he snatched the pack and knelt down. "Tell everybody to keep out but have somebody at the door to direct the emergency medics in here as soon as they arrive," he added in a loud voice.

The boy nodded and ran and the barman quickly undid the pack and removed a wipe, running it with practiced fingers over Flintlock's face as Ahxenta held her steady.

"Help's on the way," Ally told her. "My desk-comm's been shot to bits, so there's been gunfire. We deal with the injured and then we find out what's happened, but it looks like just the one guy. My boys have got him pinned and they won't be gentle. Looks like he got in by the back door to the staff room — it leads out to my stores and then by a secure door to the main passage. He must have breached the secure door to get in, but I'll have my people check that later. I called Merkat security as well. They can take charge of *that* bozo."

"I'll be fine, Cap," Flintlock groaned. "I think Kerrix took a shot but I'm not sure, it was all so fast."

Ahxenta looked over to the far wall where Lindell was on the deck beside the woman. He was supporting her and talking to her, but the captain could make out little else. A noise at the entry distracted her: it was the emergency response team from Merkat's main medbay.

"Over there," she directed, pointing, as another body appeared around the door. "Oak!" she called. "This way."

The new arrival sped across and crouched down beside them. His uniform and badge marked him as one of *Arianrhod's* officers and like most of the crew he was prepared. He hauled out a medi-scanner.

"Dr Flintlock's med-kit's over there," Ahxenta indicated the spot. "Fetch it for the doctor, will you Ally?"

Dr Zaiklyn Oak examined his superior quickly, requesting details. All Flintlock could say was that someone had burst through the door waving a weapon and before she could do more than look up she had been pushed to the floor and Kerrix was out of her chair and on him. Their scuffle had given the doctor time to snatch a hypo and try to stick him, but a glancing blow had caught her across the face and a kick in the ribs had left her gasping. Kerrix had been thrown to the side. A shot wrecked the comm and as Flintlock ducked behind Ally's desk, she heard a second shot and the sounds of struggle. She risked a look and saw the man, Kerrix wrapped around one of his legs, turn in her direction with his rifle raised. She spun out of the way just as the *Half Moon's* security team burst in. They forced him down and got the rifle from him. She made it close enough to deliver the hypo that inactivated him to the extent that the guards could deal with him.

"He's cyber-enhanced, I'm sure of it," Flintlock grated. "Ally's back-up boys are big but they struggled. And he tossed Kerrix like a rag doll. But he was aiming to use that rifle on *me*, Cinnabar, I could see it in his eyes. I think he recognised my uniform."

Ally had returned with the med-kit and was listening. A call at the door interrupted him. "Merkat security. I'll deal with them," he said.

"Oak, you look after Dr Flintlock. I want to know what went down and how that bastard knew that she and Kerrix were in here. This was no way an opportunist crime; there's something behind it."

The captain stood up and made her way over to the emergency team, who were in process of strapping Kerrix into a gurney. She *had* taken a shot to her upper arm but it would heal cleanly, the senior reported. Ahxenta could check on her progress with medbay. The woman was conscious and trying to speak, but was given a shot of something and a mask was slipped over her face. The team raised the trolley upwards, locked their patient in place and set off, Ally's voice echoing in their ears that they should use the route to the left through the store and not through the main bar.

"Did you get anything out of her, Lindell?" the captain asked.

He sighed. "I don't know what to make of it. She said that the guy burst in and wasn't surprised to see them, as if he expected them to be there. And she said she was sure that his target was Dr Flintlock. She said he was trying to kick *her* off to get to the doc. She was out of it, so I'm not sure if she was mistaken but she *was* intense about it."

That shook Ahxenta. "Azular this morning, and now Flintlock. It seems that somebody's targeting my people. Ally and I were seen to go round the back, Ally comes and goes and Axellina shows. I come out on my own, so whatever's going on, a medic's needed and she's still in here. So we were watched. I want to see that bastard before security takes him off. You update Commander Apnis and get all our people down here back to the ship. Tell them to watch their backs. And have a shuttle stand by to take us up – we're not hanging around here any longer than we have to."

Ally's two guards, ably assisted by Merkat's team, had got the man under and had searched him, removing two handguns, a set of deadly throwing vanes and a scanner, all of which they had placed out of reach. There was an odd familiarity about him, especially about his mouth, but Ahxenta was sure he was not one of the three that had accosted her, Apnis and Azular the previous day. *Their* leader had been part of a renegade fleet the *Arianrhod* had met some time before and she was highly suspicious that the man at her feet was of that mould. As she scanned his face for signs of implanted hardware she reflected on the dialogue she had had with the commander of the rear ship that day and on events surrounding the encounter – and another rather more painful encounter that she herself had had some months before that on the dusty world of Xerophyte IV.

"Dammit!" she exploded as she bent down for a closer look.

The man's eyes unclosed and flickered as he focussed them on her face, his initial stunned expression melting as it gave way to a defiant stare. That was quickly followed by an icy glance of recognition and then a sneer of utter hatred as he lifted his twisted upper lip.

"Ahxenta," he said.

The four security guards were nonplussed and stared at the captain as her jaw tensed. She had not been mistaken, Ahxenta realised bitterly, as she closely inspected the unattractive face at her feet and then cast her glance over the array of bits and pieces that the guards had taken from him. There was a formidable collection of weaponry.

"Have you scanned him?" she demanded of the senior guard.

"Yes ma'am. He's no ID that we can find, implanted or otherwise, but he *has* complex embedded technology of some sort. Our scanners can't make it out but there's a lot of metalwork in there. I wouldn't like to be on the end of a right hook or a kick from him."

"What's his origin?"

The guard looked down. "I can't tell you, ma'am, not without an ID. We'll have our medics go over him once we've got him in lock-up. He'll be kept in a secure holding cell. How's your officer?"

"She'll live; as for his other victim, that I can't say. *I* want to scan him before you take him away, so stay here."

Ahxenta was clearly incensed. She strode over to her own people to claim Dr Oak's scanner, meanwhile tabbing her wrist communit.

"Tallica? Is Greffy there? If not, get him in. I'll be taking readings of the bastard that hit Flintlock and Kerrix using Oak's medi-scanner and I'll link the data up. I want him to check it against bio-readings in our databases of a bag of scum we once had caged in our brig."

"Greffy's here. Which bag of scum?" the first mate questioned.

"Len Lokterix."

"You what!"

"You heard. The face has changed but the eyes and the attitude are the same. And he knew me," the captain told her. "Stand by."

She returned to her quarry, now alert and sat on a chair, his wrists in heavy restraints behind and curb-cords attaching him to one of his minders. She ran the scanner, which she had linked her communit, over him. Greffy was feeding the data into his bridge station and the results were being relayed by holo-note to the captain, who had inserted her ear-piece to listen to a verbal report.

"You should have records on him in your files," Ahxenta told the

Merkat security pair as the report ended. "He went by the name of Len Lokterix and he'd been working in the repair sheds, so there'll be Guild records. He's Friskianx and is packing serious cyber-hardware. I suggest you go over his quarters. I'd like to be updated on what you find. I also suggest you check out his associates – he may have had help or at least some corrupt friends to do his bidding."

A chirp at her wrist alerted her to a further note from Greffy. She scanned it, her eyebrows rising in surprise. Additional analyses by the science officer showed that Lokterix had gone through recent surgery but there had been no genetic element to it, or traces of substances that would suggest new cyber implantation. A scan of the man's skin, however, had picked up signs of various substances, two of which were integral ingredients in the explosive used in the incidents that had caused the recent security alert.

Ahxenta smiled grimly and briefly related her officer's findings. "Your people are hunting out hidey-holes for stores of the stuff. You might like to include every place that *he* has or might have had access to," she added to the duo from Merkat security.

"Clever, clever, Ahxenta," Lokterix sneered.

"Get him the hell out of here. And tell your chief I'll be in touch."

The captain turned on her heel and marched off.

Ally had by this time collared his own guards and was being given the gist of what had been discovered. He intended to bring charges as his property and one of his staff had been injured. He sent his guards to assess the damage outside and to maintain a watching brief on the *Half Moon*: with the proprietor away, he was well aware that his usual customers could get out of hand.

Ally was also curious as to Ahxenta's former link to Lokterix. She gave him the outline: the man was one of a trio who had attacked her on Xerophyte IV several months back. He had escaped justice there but had later turned up in the Web, where he had got work as a repair operative on a team that had been assigned to the *Arianrhod* after her near-fatal encounter with several hostile warships out at Kifferbuck.

"Whoa! I remember! We were amazed you got her back at all with the hits you'd taken. It took *four* of your sister ships to bring you in. If they hadn't shown when they did, you'd have been nothing but flak."

"Tell me about it," Ahxenta growled. "He was up to no good on *Arianrhod* then but we thwarted him. And after that he turned up on a renegade ship pretending to be a good guy at Skyrtek. I didn't believe it then and I don't believe it now. But no word of this to anyone, Ally, or I *will* have your hide and you'll be sharing a cell with him."

"Understood; and I'd best get the evidence of *this* for my insurers, and get my outer secure door fixed. If *he* got in, others could."

"I'd be grateful if you'd let me know how he did get through your door. But I'll have to get my chief medic back to the ship and into her own medbay, so I'll be using that back door – I don't want more of your regulars' beady eyes on my business. And the least said about what has gone down here the better. We don't want a spate of other incidents on the back of this one. I'll see you before we ship out."

"Aye, Captain. I'll keep my eye on Xanna Kerrix as well. Seems like she's never out of your hair."

"That hadn't escaped me. There's one helluva lot more to your Ms Kerrix than meets the eye. I'll be paying her a visit in medbay, but I've a cargo to load and a ship to ready for our next trip out."

She nodded farewell and made her way over to Flintlock, who had been helped to a chair and was looking fairly composed. Oak was at her elbow and taking readings with the CMO's medi-scanner.

"Badly bruised ribs but no fractures, a couple of strained tendons but no serious internal damage," he reported. "You have a bruised butt as well," he added to his boss. "And I bet it hurts."

"Your diagnosis isn't wrong," was the retort. "Nice to know your time at med-school was well spent. When do we go home, Cinnabar? I want to see the inside of my own medbay."

"As soon as I can arrange it. I want to see my own bridge, believe me. Lindell, what's your status?"

The supercargo had been in constant contact with *Arianrhod* over coordination of the uplift of the last of ship's personnel on leave and reported that the final run was already underway. There was a shuttle standing by for the captain's party in a secure docking bay on green eleven of inner two and the pilot was aboard and waiting their arrival.

"Guild didn't charge us for the space," Lindell said wryly. "Guilty consciences over what they've put us through already. Security's cleared as many of the local highways and byways as possible, so we should have a clear run. The doctor's fit to travel, I take it?"

"She's fit," Ahxenta said dryly. "Let's get what's ours and get the hell out. We'll take medbay's kit. I'll return it when I come back and we take the back door, we do *not* go through the main bar."

"Wise," Lindell remarked as he began to collect their goods.

It was not obvious exactly where Ally's secure back door had been breached as there was very little damage apart from what appeared to be normal dents and scrapes. One of the *Half Moon's* crew was fitting a replacement lock mechanism but the original seemed undamaged.

"New design, ma'am," he replied to the captain's query, eyeing her team curiously and storing up what he saw to pass on to his mates later. "This'll maybe stop another break-in, but it looks like the guy was able to pick the code or bypass the security system."

He stood back to let them pass, watching until they were out of view. Lindell had been right and the trip to green eleven was quiet, with little other foot traffic. They gained their bay and found their pilot waiting. The shuttle was prepped and ready to leave.

The trip to *Arianrhod* took a short while but an inner landing bay had been made ready. The team found an inordinately relieved Tallica Apnis waiting beyond the airlock.

"Been quite a day, Cinnabar," she greeted the captain. "You doing okay, Axellina?" she added to the chief medic. "There's a warm bed waiting for you in medbay."

"Like hell, I've had enough cosseting for one day," was the sour response. "All I want is a very strong coffee and a soft seat."

"Dr Oak, escort Dr Flintlock to medbay and make sure she stays there until both you and the duty medic say otherwise. Lindell, you're with me; you too, Tallica. We'll debrief in my office. I want Earbleat, Greffy and Crizz as well, as we'll need our engines up to speed for a quick exit; *and* I want a lowdown on the state of our defences. What's the situation on the cargo loading, Tallica?"

"Getting there. The manifest's in your office, Lindell. I had the reps liaise with Perla Jute and our loading teams are on standby. Once PA clearances are in place we'll be ready to go. I estimate midday tomorrow, unless you've more business in the Web, Cap?"

"We'll discuss it in my office. Hell, I need a drink, and coffee's not going to hit the spot. Anything else?"

"I've had Nat Holdspan and Murmur Fleetskup bending my ears on what's been going down. Told them to mind their own business, but it seems the news is spreading that *Arianrhod* and her people are attracting the wrong sort of attention. And we had a link from Grey Bluejohn: *Obsidian's* due in three days and he wanted a word over the news you sent out. I updated him privately on the latest and asked him to let the rest of the fleet in on the basics over the Ultraviolet III. Didn't want to spread too much bad news but Grey's had word that the *Hexameter* was involved in a clash out by Stinward and that's off the beaten bypass, though it *is* firmly in ISP territory."

"Interstellar Systems Protectorate not keeping an eye on its own backyard then," Ahxenta surmised. "But given the beating it took at Skyrtek, I'm not surprised. Stinward? Isn't ISP's new shipbuilding dock being built there? As its Central Logistics facility and a key ISP local office are there, and plenty of useful ores in the asteroid belt in the Stinward system, it seems a logical place."

"That may have been one reason for the stand-off with the *Hexameter*: there's a lot of cargo will need to be hauled in that general direction, much of it will be big stuff and the ISP won't be able to do it without commercial assist. So that might mean more trade for us in the long term as many of the PSS ships are the biggest carriers this side of mapped space. Bee Lyvy Coxen saw the outlaws off with no trouble apparently and *Hexameter's* not even had to haul in for repairs, but Grey didn't know what she was carrying or to where; or for whom, for that matter. If it *was* ISP, it would be on the quiet."

The following morning found Ahxenta and Apnis in the *Half Moon* for an early breakfast. Merry was on duty and the captain took the opportunity to ask after Kerrix, assuming that she would be aware of the previous day's happenings and their aftermath.

"I visited her late last night, Captain, but they only let me peep in the iso-bay window. She was awake and waved, but they wouldn't tell me anything or let me speak to her, though I said I was a friend. She looked all out but they said her condition was *satisfactory*, whatever that means," Merry said irately. "A guard was posted outside the bay as she'd witnessed a crime. I said I knew as I was there, but it cut no ice. Ally tried this morning and was told to call back later."

"Same as you got when you linked through, Cap," Apnis noted. "But they've posted a guard? Expecting trouble?"

"Probably. We'll eat and then I'll call in personally. I can call up one or two of Flintlock's contacts if I have to."

"And you're the captain of the *Arianrhod*," the first mate added with a snicker. "They'll let you in."

Apnis was right. After breakfast the two made for medbay, stated their business at reception and asked for the manager. The captain gave him short shrift, refusing a visit to his office and a coffee. She wanted a word with Kerrix and refused to budge. He gave in.

Kerrix was awake and propped up when the two reached the small iso-bay. The captain introduced her first mate, hauled two chairs over to the bed and sat, Apnis carrying out a full scan before they began. Kerrix replied equably to enquiries after her health, lying about her condition – the captain was well able to read the medbay monitors.

"Security guard still there, Captain?" Kerrix asked of her visitor.

"Yes; maybe they think you need watching," was the reply.

"Afraid I'll skip off without paying the bill more like," she sniffed. "What can I do for you? I don't expect this is a social call."

The first mate grinned wryly at the far from deferential tone as the captain called for details of the events of the previous evening from Kerrix' viewpoint. She was keen to hear the woman's ideas on why she and Flintlock had been targeted.

"Targeted?" Kerrix repeated. "You're saying you don't think it was a simple robbery with violence that went wrong?"

"*I'm* asking the questions," Ahxenta advised her. "And no, I don't think it was a bungled robbery and neither do you. You *did* tell my officer that the gunman wasn't surprised you were there. In fact you got the impression he expected to see you, or at least someone. And you were quite adamant that his target was Dr Flintlock. Why?"

She sighed, tilting her head slightly, acknowledging the strike. "He tried to loose himself of me to get a better aim, I'm sure of it. It was as if I was in his way. And he said something like 'get the hell off me' before he kicked me and swiped me with his gun, but I may have misheard: his voice was low and harsh. He fired a shot to keep me down but I don't think he took careful aim. He struck me as a nasty piece of work that would stop at little to get his own way."

Ahxenta nodded: that tracked. "So why did you try to stop him? You shoved my medic out of his way and jumped him. Why?"

"It was instinct on my part, I guess," she shrugged slightly, eyeing Ahxenta. "After all, the doctor *was* trying to help me. And that villain had a murderous look in his eye that I didn't like," she added.

That smacked of evasion and the captain shook her head. "You don't like uneven odds at the best of times, you told me earlier. But your attitude and your actions don't stack. You were not pleased that I'd got my chief medic to fix you up and you were curious as to why my officer that had been attacked on green ten was not in uniform. In other words, you're doubtful of me and mine, yet still you stick your neck out for one of mine. Why?"

Her response came after a short pause in which she studied her questioner closely. "Where are my things?"

Apnis turned a curious glance on the captain, mouthing, "What?"

"Your things?" Ahxenta asked levelly.

"The things I had on me and the gear I was wearing when I was brought in here," she clarified wearily.

"Answer my questions. Why are my people being targeted? Why did you risk yourself for my chief medic? It hasn't benefited you."

Kerrix closed her eyes for a moment, sighing. "I don't know why your people are being targeted: you'll know more than me, I'm sure. And as for… I *am* trying to tell you. Where's my gear?"

"Locker," Apnis said briefly, pointing. "I guess that's where they put it when they took it off her."

An inclination of Ahxenta's head sent her first mate to the cabinet to check the contents. The captain's face was grim and her annoyance rising. She had plenty to do and if this was some sort of game she was in no mood to play it, she informed the woman brusquely.

"Do you usually carry a handgun to work?" Apnis enquired as she held the small piece aloft.

"I work in the *Half Moon*," she shot back. "Are my boots there?"

The first mate exchanged another baffled glance with the captain before resuming her search. "Yes."

"Left boot," Kerrix said tersely.

"One left boot. Looks like a left boot," said Apnis, looking closely at its owner, who motioned her over and held out her hand.

Kerrix took it with curt thanks, upended it, flicked a button on the inner edge and twisted the heel out to expose a hollow. A small metal block filled the space. As the two watched, she removed it, reclosing the cavity before discarding the boot. She held the thing out on the palm of her hand. It was a small, smooth-contoured flat box.

"This charade had better have a purpose," the captain warned her. "I suggest you get to the point."

Kerrix paused for a second, judging Ahxenta narrowly. "In answer to one of your questions: I figure I owe you."

She took the box in both hands, examined it carefully and flipped a catch on the side. It popped open and she abstracted the content – a flat, finely-crafted and incised rectangular key on a slender chain.

"Yours I believe, Captain," she said, holding it out. "It's not the original, I think, but a very good counterfeit."

Apnis whipped out a probe and quickly scanned the item before the captain touched it. Both officers had recognised at once what it appeared to be. The first mate nodded, eyes widening.

"You have one hell of a lot of explaining to do!" Ahxenta rapped angrily at Kerrix, snatching the item from her hand. "I want to hear it now, and quickly: I don't have all day. And you'd better leave nothing out or I'll have your butt in a cell before you can turn round, whether you helped one of mine or not."

"I didn't make that and I don't know who did," Kerrix said tiredly as she eased down into her pillow and looked upwards with a sigh. "I *did* remove it from the person who had it."

Her eyes slid back to the two. "I was in what I found out later was inner belt six, the lower outer levels, near the secure repair docks for small craft. I was in trouble, looking for a safe place, never mind why. It was near empty, a few people but not close. I figured if I could get hold of fatigues or common workwear I could blend in…"

"Cut to the point," Ahxenta ordered harshly.

"I was scanning and read two, armed and closing on my position, so I ducked behind a grille fronting active power boards. I heard and saw them as they went by. They had on dock workers' gear; one had a backpack. The other was listening to a link, confirming something, as he told his mate that Lecky or some such had frozen the screens and cut the auto alerts and local secure cams, so they were good to go; *and* he only hoped the cloned entry key would work. So I figured they were up to no good and trailed them."

"If you were in such trouble, why did you try to find more?"

Kerrix sagged, sighing deeply. "I'd nowhere to run. But to cut to the point: they made for a repair bay with a shuttle in it. *Your* shuttle, I found later. They had a key that got them into the bay, though they had trouble with the entry, so they wedged it open – their mistake. I gave them a minute or two and slid in at the back of them. They were too busy eyeing your shuttle to notice, so I guess they'd not worked on her. The one on the link called to his pal that they'd made the bay and were set to go and then cut the link. I let them get close enough to the shuttle to use the key to make sure it worked and then I took them down with the heaviest stun my handgun could deal."

"So these dock workers were the ones that planned to steal my shuttle, but you got there first?" the captain broke in derisively.

Kerrix shook her head. "They weren't aiming to steal your shuttle, Captain; if they had, they'd hardly have wedged the bay door would they? I'd scanned the pair of them, remember, and I knew that the backpack guy was toting artillery that was part-shielded. I later found out it was a micro-detonator attached to just enough plas-explosive to make a very big bang. Not a normal load for an average docker. I suspect they'd planned to integrate it into your engine compartment in such a way that the first time you fired up her main engine, you'd have been blown to bits. Of course, that's conjecture on my part. But had the repair crews moved your shuttle to a holding bay they'd have used manoeuvring auxiliaries, not her main engine."

Ahxenta was shocked, only half-believing what she had heard, but she was angry enough to demand in what way the tampering would have missed the eyes and scanners of later operatives.

"Her repairs were complete, Captain, or so it seemed. And these guys were dockers, or at least they carried Guild ID. I checked," she added to forestall the next question, "When I removed most of their kit, including their IDs, credit slips and weapons…"

"And clothes, except for their underwear," added Apnis.

Kerrix started at that. "How did…"

"You still haven't told me how my shuttle vanished or where she is now," the captain snapped. "Or how you managed to get two full-grown males out of the bay without being seen or heard or how they didn't spot you. They'll have scanned every step of their route."

"My scanner's powerful and was superior to theirs *and* it emits a masking signal. And I was behind operational power boards. Your shuttle carries emergency medical gear aboard, including a gurney. Got it out, rolled them on, moved one at a time to the nearest Guild washroom along from the bay – the washroom was empty and one of their IDs got me in. And neither of them were big, in fact they were a pair of scrawny weasels, which is how I figured their fatigues might fit me. *And* it was the middle of local rotational night – most places around the Web follow a standard work hour system. And this Lecky guy mentioned had cut the local secure cam and alert systems."

"You've got an answer for everything."

"You seem to have a question for everything," was the wry retort. "Your shuttle's in outer belt nine, lower outside level blue fifteen, bay six eight alpha two. She's camouflaged and tightly docked alongside my small transport, what's left of it."

"How did she get there?"

"I piloted her, obviously. I *am* capable and the cloned key made it possible. The bay's identity coding shows it's a local semi-permanent transport holding station for the use of people here. As I'd lifted the IDs of both the felons who'd tried to get into your shuttle, I had little problem getting in and out after that. *They* weren't going to raise a complaint that they'd been robbed, so their IDs remained valid."

Ahxenta shook her head, wishing that her Berzic science officer had been fit to travel: his telepathic abilities would have helped her. "That doesn't add up," she told Kerrix. "Why move her? Why not leave her where she was, get Merkat security in anonymously?"

"I had no information on Merkat security, but it was clear that the Dockers' Guild was sheltering corrupt personnel. But that wasn't the reason I took her out," she said with a faintly embarrassed grimace. "I had nothing. I needed a base and I needed transport…"

The captain could see where this was going and was livid. "You thought you could commandeer my shuttle?"

"To be honest Captain, I had no idea what I thought I could do. All I could see was a sizeable shuttle in very good trim that had been a target of crime for reasons I couldn't work out. That made it a safe bet that there would be a cover-up that would buy me time. My own shuttle was shot to hell but I had managed to hide her in an outlying place that could take another two small transports. And it was in a seedy part of the Web, though I didn't know *that* then. I needed a base and time to figure my next move, so I used the Guild temporary permission codes locked into the key to get the shuttle out of the repair bay. I'd sealed the bay door on the passage side when I got rid of the no-goods; it was stiff, so the two must have damaged it earlier. And once I *had* got her safely berthed, I used your shuttle as my billet for over two weeks. *That's* why I reckon I owe you. But I'm not normally a thief, Captain. I was in desperate straits, believe me."

"Quite frankly, I'm finding what you say *very* difficult to believe. It seems highly unlikely to me that you were there just when an attempt was made on my shuttle, though hell knows crime is endemic day and night in the Web. And I've heard about your antics in the *Half Moon* before you asked Ally for a job and a berth. But we scanned for my shuttle the minute we docked, we've been scanning ever since and even in lockdown mode, we should have been able to track her."

"I fitted a cloaking system I had aboard my ship. It was one of the few things left that was operative, it isn't standard here and it worked. It also operates as a vis-camouflage system at most wavelengths."

"I'll be checking out your story, Ms Kerrix, even though it's likely to hold me up here. And if I find you're pulling a fast one, you *will* have nowhere to hide, believe me. It'll be the most secure cell in *Arianrhod's* brig that you'll be calling home. Do you get me?"

"Yes ma'am. That key will get you into the bay as well, I adjusted the coding. You recall the location?"

"I've been recording our chat from start to finish, Ms Kerrix, as I'm sure you know. I have the information and the evidence, should I need to call on them later. I trust you also understand that?"

"I do, Captain."

"I *will* be back."

"I bet you will. I doubt *I'm* going anywhere. And Captain?"

"Yes?"

"I'd be obliged if you'd leave my shuttle where she is. There's not much to her, but she's all I've got left."

"Of what?"

"Of everything I ever had."

Ahxenta gave a curt nod. "I'll see you later."

Once clear of medbay and well away from eavesdroppers, Apnis turned to the captain. "That's one helluva story, Cinnabar."

"Part of a story, Tallica, and if only half of it's true, I don't like the implications. But we have a name – Lecky – and a description of the two that she says tried to plant a bomb on the *Gadfly*, as well as the time of the thing. But I need Greffy down here with all the deep-scan gear he's got before we go near outer belt nine *and* I want our own security as back up. This is going to make scheduling tight when we get underway, but I'm not leaving it hanging. Word will have got out about Lokterix and what went on at the *Half Moon* and hushing it up and calling it a bungled robbery won't help. Too many people know."

"You realise that if she *is* telling the truth – and why would she tell such a tale otherwise – and we find the *Gadfly*, there will be eyes that have spied us going in to see *her* just before…"

"Which will make her a target or at least raise suspicions in one or two of those involved, especially if I go back; yes I had figured that. But I'm beginning to think that this Ms Kerrix, whoever the hell she is, is well able to take care of herself – ordinarily."

The captain found a private booth in marketing to make the links to *Arianrhod* and to bring her second mate up to date. Arrangements were made to have Greffy and two security guards shipped over to meet Ahxenta and Apnis close to the bay on outer nine, blue fifteen.

It took them fifteen minutes to reach their target. The captain had used her own shuttle to save time, although the advent of two of the *Arianrhod's* craft in such a sleazy area was liable to attract notice. The two met their team and then made for bay six eight alpha two.

Lieutenant Greffy found naught amiss after cautious scanning of the bay entry, but he could not read the nature of the craft inside. It was a multiple-use space typically holding shuttles owned by private persons or trade interests who shared to save costs. The captain drew out the entry key and slipped it into the reader. The door slid aside to reveal a dim interior in which nothing could be clearly distinguished.

"Lights!" Ahxenta called out as she advanced, rifle in hand.

Her guards and Apnis had also readied their weapons. They were greeted by silence as the light grew. A characterless, grubby space tinted grey extended around them and into an indeterminate murk. The high external airlock doors were limned in red to show that they were secure and in front of them a dark-hulled shuttle sat dim against the dusk beyond. Next to it was a smaller wedge-shaped hulk, its hide pitted and scored. It sat askew, one side lower than the other.

"That bigger boat doesn't look like the *Gadfly*," Apnis remarked.

"Greffy, check out that shuttle but don't go too close," the captain ordered. "Goldwash, get back and shut the bay door and stay there. Hanx, you're with us," she added to her security personnel.

The young science officer was already closing in on the ship, his scanner glowing pinkly as it captured the details and analysed them. "I can't get details, she's shielded. Just a moment…" he murmured as he manipulated his instrument. "It's some sort of cloaking buffer and it's being externally generated – from over there."

He pointed as he headed to the side wall, his scanner held before him. "There's a device here secured to the bulkhead, some kind of chameleon material. I should be able to disarm it."

Quickly fishing out a torch, Greffy warily studied the mechanism. "Commander, if you would hold the light?"

Apnis took it and fixed the beam on a block that resembled a power casing. The young officer carefully unhooked the outer shell to reveal a set of switches. He scanned and then released what seemed to be the main toggle.

Ahxenta was watching the two vessels and her intake of breath warned the others that something had occurred. All five stood staring at what now took up centre stage in the bay.

"Now that *does* look like the *Gadfly*," Apnis observed in a low voice. "So far the story stacks."

"So far," was the caustic reply as the captain made her wary way over to the larger shuttle. "What are you getting now, Lieutenant?"

"She's reading as the *Gadfly* now, Captain. That cloak must be able to shield her from normal sensors as well as disguise her appearance, although any regular scanners might have had trouble picking up her readings – but I brought one of Dr Azular's high-spec probes and we of course have her security ident codes. She's locked, though I don't detect any anti-access ware on the inside."

"That key, or key-clone, should be able to unlock her, according to Kerrix," Apnis stated.

"Only one way to find out," the captain replied heavily as she made her way towards the side of the craft.

<h1 style="text-align:center">6: STORIES</h1>

The metallic pink plating of the *Gadfly* felt cold as Ahxenta passed her hand across the hull of her favourite shuttle. Slowly she slid the entry key into the slot at the side of the panel and stood back. With Apnis' cautionary hand on her arm, she waited for the shuttle to recognise the authority, release the locks and allow descent of the boarding ramp. With barely a whisper the seals broke, the access panel slid into the body of the craft and the internal pressure door released.

"It looks dark in there," the first mate observed into the silence as she peered up the ramp. "She should recognise us: her internal secure systems should be scanning for IDs – unless they're disabled."

In answer, the inner light grew and the two could see the familiar interior. Greffy at their heels requested permission to scan ahead, lest anything had been planted. Ensign Hanx, his phase rifle primed, was inspecting their surroundings with keen eyes.

"Active scan ongoing, Captain," confirmed the science officer. "It reads normal. I don't read any booby traps, although I *am* picking up a trace of hostile tech similar to the hulls and weapons systems of the alien ships we faced in the war – we have that data in every scanner we have, including hand-helds. It's over by the aft section, ma'am."

Ahxenta stepped up the shallow ramp cautiously. The command and second positions on the flight deck area of the ship looked as they always did apart from a strange key plugged into one control board. A set of aft seating had been reconfigured to form a couch, an option if injured crew formed part of the payload. The captain made for the rear of the shuttle and to the point indicated by Greffy.

"This is it, I take it?" she asked the young officer.

"Aye ma'am: the signals are coming from the inside of that pack."

"A backpack she said was full of plas-explosive and a detonator," Apnis rasped. "She brought it in here? That was damned stupid."

"It's inactive, Commander. I would imagine it would need a lot of tuning to set and prime an explosive device if it had had to be carried in personal luggage," Greffy posited.

"Good point," the first mate conceded.

"Go over every atom of this ship and make sure we have no more surprises, Lieutenant," Ahxenta ordered the science officer. "I want to check her current status and fuel supplies. She won't have much, but we should be able to get her back home."

"You plan to fly her out of here and back to *Arianrhod?*" asked Apnis, frowning. "You think that's wise, Cap? Three of our shuttles setting off from the same place in the outer reaches where we never usually show our faces will be noticed. It's probably already been logged that we haven't left Merkat and we *have* loaded all our cargo."

"Our schedules are our business, so nobody had better be wiser; and we request port clearance when we're ready. But you're right, our timetable's slipping and I bet our trip out here will have been picked up. And our people have been targeted so we *are* being watched."

"That brings us back to Kerrix," Apnis pointed out as the captain slid into the pilot's chair and began to check her boards.

"Not necessarily, but I won't risk another visit. I'll send Flintlock if she's fit but it'll have to be tomorrow. She can dig up more on the scum that tried to bomb my shuttle and tell *her* what we've done."

"So you're beginning to put some credence on her story?"

"Thus far: she may be trying to persuade us to trust her and this is an elaborate set-up."

"You don't believe that, Cinnabar."

"No I don't but it would have been a lot more helpful if Azular had been well enough to be in on the talk we had," Ahxenta sighed.

"If Kerrix hadn't dived in there when she did, he might have been a lot worse off," the first mate said as she took the co-pilot's seat.

"Granted. And I bet there's more to *that* tale. Anything, Greffy?"

"I read no incursions anywhere, Captain, and apart from that bag with the device in it, I get nothing else hazardous that should not be here, nor anything missing that should be," was the reply. "Though there *are* a handful of bits and pieces I'm sure don't belong to any of ours. This is one of them," he added as he held up a fine but broken metallic chain with a tiny jewelled locket attached.

"Tidies up after herself," Apnis said ironically. "*Gadfly* seems to be tip-top from where I'm sitting. She okay your end, Cap?"

"It seems her repairs *were* completed. She has one fuel cell with enough in it to get us home and her systems read secure and ready to go. But I want all our flights scanned from *Arianrhod* from start to finish. I'm taking the *Gadfly* home. You'll pilot our shuttle. Gunn's still aboard the shuttle she brought the other three over in and she'll fly that. Hanx will hitch a ride with you in case of trouble. But before we go, I'd like a complete scan of that small boat Kerrix says is her ship. It doesn't look like much from here, but from what we've seen of *her* so far, I'll bet it packs a punch or two."

"Or once did," the first mate said. "Looks like it's seen action. If we wanted it, we'd have to scrape it up and get it out with grapples."

"It's well-shielded, for all its surface damage," Ahxenta reported as she used the *Gadfly's* sensors to scan the craft alongside. "I can make out that it was well-armed but its arsenal must be near dry. But I can't make sense of some of the readings I'm getting."

"I'd like to take scans from outside if you don't mind, ma'am," Greffy, who had been watching events keenly, cut in. "I'm sure Dr Azular would be very interested in what we can pick up."

"I'll bet," Apnis agreed as the captain gave the go-ahead. "This sort of thing is always on his map. But you promised we'd leave it intact, so we can't commandeer it in reparation for the *Gadfly*."

"I don't recall I said intact," Ahxenta disagreed. "If you can get hull or any other samples, Lieutenant, take them."

"Aye ma'am!" the young officer replied with alacrity as he set off.

"You know, once Merkat security and the Dockers' Guild realise we've got the *Gadfly* back they are going to want details big time," the first mate said with a grin.

"They'll get what I give them, Tallica. They can find and plug the gaping holes in their own ops. I'm not their damn minder nor am I their back-up when things go belly-up."

"The Web will be laughing its collective socks off when word gets out – and it won't be long. They've been looking for weeks for the *Gadfly*; we've been back a couple of days and we've got her home."

"Almost got her home you mean; once she's safely berthed aboard the ship we'll see the fur start to fly. Let's check that all's secure out there and with Elsey Gunn and then we move."

It took time to set up the systems that would track all three of the *Arianrhod's* shuttles out of their berths and back aboard. The lower levels of outer belt nine were closer to the lacunae that housed the huge trading vessels that used Merkat Three port than most docking areas and were fairly free of other traffic, but navigation was tricky.

It was with relief that Ahxenta made the *Gadfly's* regular bay and set her down. The captain had ordered her chief engineer and a team on standby to go over every micron of the craft once she was aboard. She and Apnis made for the bridge to be briefed by the second mate on the latest on the attacks on her crew, the attempts by security to trace the *Gadfly* and the second explosion in the Web. The results were scanty: little new had emerged except that Lokterix was using the alias Mak Trebint, his billet was clear and one of his most recent contacts had been traced and grilled. Nothing could be pinned on the latter and he had been let loose, albeit under covert watch. Earbleat had been unable to prise the name of Trebint's crony out of Merkat security as he was held to be law-abiding, although in her opinion, security was worried that *Arianrhod's* crew would carry out their own interview of the man if they knew his name.

Ahxenta also privately contacted the *Half Moon* to check up on the latest. Ally was scathing: his place was crawling with guards who had found nothing; he could not use his own office; his comms system was out; and, his insurers were being awkward over coughing up for repairs. On a cheerier note, his takings were up as many more than usual had come in hoping for a piece of whatever action was going.

By the time she had finished most of her links and was conning over the manifest sent up by Lindell for their current payload, the supercargo, efficient as ever, had managed to source a small contract to carry some light engineering parts to Iris Three, one of the outpost worlds of the much larger Delta Iridium Colony and very close to their next stop-off. The deal could be sealed and the cargo loaded over the next several hours if the captain gave the go-ahead. Ahxenta agreed quickly: not only did it mean a more profitable trip, but it gave her an excuse for the delay to *Arianrhod's* departure from Merkat.

The captain's first link the next morning was to the Port Authority to insist upon an immediate briefing with the senior PA reps and their colleagues from the Dockers' Guild and Merkat security. Complaints of the short notice given were ignored, Ahxenta stressing the urgency of the case in view of the matters to be discussed and the evidence that she intended to present. She copied her message to the Guild and security for good measure, telling the horrified PA rep that she and her officers would be with them as fast as their shuttle could get there. She expected that a secure venue for the conference would be available and she would be bringing her own security back-up.

"You've certainly put the wind up *him*, Cap," Apnis, who had been in the captain's office for the comm, noted with a snort of laughter.

"It's more than wind up him he'll have when he hears the rest of what I have to tell him. But I need to see Flintlock ASAP – if she's not well enough to come, I'll take Flish Ma'Lappis. It'll have to be a medic for the trip to medbay to see Kerrix. With all this going down, I'd best not be seen anywhere near her."

"You think we'll still be under surveillance, Cinnabar?"

"I do. That's one reason I don't want reps from Merkat's Central Advisory Council or the Trades Alliance at the meeting – too many in the know will increase the risks to us. As for our security, Hanx is sharp for all he's young so we'll take him, and as Ensign Marks is big enough to cause heads to turn, he'll be the second."

"Aye, aye, Cap. Standard weapons?"

"Outwardly, yes. I don't want to give the impression we've been intimidated by any of these shenanigans."

"Understood. I'll see to it," the first mate chuckled as she left.

Flintlock had released herself from medbay and was at work in her office: as chief medic she had the final say over medical matters, she reminded the captain. She was keen to renew contact with the odd Ms Kerrix, having heard of the talk in Merkat's medbay and having been privy to a chat that Greffy had had with Azular over events in outer nine. The senior science officer was not fit for social or duty calls off ship, the doctor told Ahxenta, but he had begun to study the material that his second had brought in and was eager to get back to his lab to delve more deeply into the issues raised.

"He thinks there's novel tech we could use, judging by Greffy's scans and samples," she explained. "And if there's novel weaponry involved, you can bet Whisper Earbleat will want her paws on it."

"Figures. But we're going now, Axellina, so grab the necessary if you're sure. And I'll be assigning Ji Lerro as your guard. She looks harmless and is anything but."

In as short a time as it took to marshal her crew and her gear, the captain took the helm of the shuttle and made for inner belt two and the docking facility nearest main marketing.

There were seven waiting when Ahxenta, Apnis and their two security guards arrived. Flintlock and Ji had made for green three and the main medical facility and were long gone. The lead Port Authority rep told them that he had arranged the most secure negotiating room in the marketing suite. The captain immediately enquired how many from the PA, security and the Guild knew of the meeting. The reply was *several*. The captain thus calmly told the reps that given what she was about to say, she had no intention of risking that the assigned room had been tampered with and insisted that they be taken to another, well away from the appointed place.

That was met by a snicker from Biernop of the Dockers' Guild: he knew Ahxenta of old. He agreed at once, to the fuming of the PA reps and dark undertones from the two from Merkat security.

"I'll inform our allocation supervisor of the change," the senior

PA rep advised the captain.

"You will not," was the sharp retort. "I have very little time and I suspect that also applies to all of you. Let's move it."

The party was led to a quiet side room off the main suite. Ahxenta posted both her guards outside, stepped in and hauled out two small devices, which she set up on the central table. The first was a jammer to thwart covert recording and the other was a sweep scanner, she told the group. As Apnis stepped over to the facilities at the wall to fetch hot drinks, the captain began a thorough probe of the room and its occupants, including herself and her first mate.

"I take it there have been major developments, Captain," Biernop remarked as he and his colleagues were swept head to foot.

"Get a drink if you want one and sit down, Mr Biernop," he was cordially ordered.

"Is all this necessary, Captain?" asked senior PA rep Gentrum.

"Yes," he was told shortly as Ahxenta sat a recorder on the table and selected a chair facing the door. "My team and I are fitted with implanted locating pins and we are being monitored from my ship," she added. "Please sit, all of you."

The captain placed a holo-projector on the table and started it off. A holo of the *Gadfly* materialised above the unit. "My shuttle, the one that disappeared from Merkat's inner belt six repair sheds…"

"We're no further ahead, with that, Captain," one Merkat security rep interposed. "As we reported…"

"My people have located the *Gadfly*, Mr Links; she's back aboard *Arianrhod*. Our scanners are clearly superior to yours and we have the means to trace our own that aren't your concern," she said coolly, to the incredulity of most of those around the table. "More to the point, I've found out that the original plan of the culprits was not theft but sabotage, using an explosive device that I also now have. *And* I have the IDs of the two members of the Dockers' Guild who attempted to plant the device, and a name that may or may not be the accomplice, or one of the accomplices, of the two."

As she spoke, the captain called up the IDs of the men identified by Kerrix as the two who had the cloned key and who had tried to break into the *Gadfly*: two of the items found by Greffy in his search of the shuttle had been their IDs, lifted by Kerrix when she searched them. Their names had matched those picked up by Azular during his covert surveys of local drinking dens. Ahxenta sketched out the events of the night in question, advising that Guild security check who was on duty in the local ops office at the time. She then dropped in the name Lecky. It was familiar to all three Guild reps.

"Almot Leckford!" whistled Kit Biernop. "I've often wondered about him. I figured he was light-fingered and had some shady mates but I'd never have guessed he was into that kind of corruption. As for these two, I don't know either of them but they'll be on file. You heard of them?" he demanded of his colleagues, both of whom were full members of the Guild's security force.

One nodded. "Mol Kister and Pullen Selt: ops from the belt repair sheds. Don't know more than their names and their reputations as twisters, takers of bribes and so on, but there's never been anything pinned on them as far as I know. They've got friends in high places, maybe. But you'll need proof of their compliance, Captain."

"You will, you mean," Ahxenta retorted harshly. "I suggest you check them, their billets and their contacts as soon as possible, before they get wind of this talk. That applies to this Leckford guy as well. As Merkat security's aware, two of my crew were assaulted by local thugs, and the one in custody was bent on more than minor affray, given the gear he carried. And there was that explosive device outside the bay in which one of my other shuttles was berthed. I want to know the latest on all of those matters, particularly on the man who was known as Len Lokterix. You should have *him* on file."

The silence was broken by Links, whose latest news on Lokterix was that he had arrived a month before aboard a small passenger ship out of Lonagan Four under the alias Trebint. That he was Friskianx and that his cyber implants packed a punch they knew. The contact that had been linked to him, through credit slips used by him and the associate to buy drinks and meals at the same table and at the same time in the *Green Diamond*, was a recent arrival in the Web and so far had done nothing illegal that was known about.

"His name?" the captain requested icily.

"That I can't…" Links began.

"His name?" she repeated.

"He's a small-time trader called Froyd Melson, also from Lonagan so he could have known this Trebint or Lokterix, but as he's…"

"What?" Ahxenta hissed, her eyes blazing in fury as her first mate let out an oath. "A trader calling himself Froyd Melson? In that case the PA certainly has current records on him. He made a credit claim the other day for overcharging for his berth, as his ship's allegedly an old Comet Six with advanced features. You didn't mention *that*," she rounded on the PA reps.

"*I* hadn't heard," Links replied. "You know this man, Captain?"

"The last time he was in Merkat, a long time back as far as I know, he claimed to be a trader called Bick Micklemouse. He and a gang of cronies from the Coalition Central Council had swung their way into a high-level secure meeting of the TA, the Merkat Central Advisory Council and the Dockers' Guild *and* the senior officers from several Privates, including me and Commander Apnis. They were there with a jumped-up excuse so they could find out what we knew about the increase in raider attacks in the mapped galactic sectors. And we've had dealings with the little runt since."

"The Coalition Central Council?" repeated Kit Biernop. "He runs in big circles for a small-time trader."

"If Merkat security has a covert watch on him they'll know where he is now and *I* want to know. I want words with Mr Melson. Have you anything else to update me with that I should know about?" the captain continued dangerously.

"*I* have nothing else, Captain," Biernop said quietly. "But I *will* see what else I can dig up on this Micklemouse person and on Lokterix. I remember the trouble you had with him last time: he was posing as a Guild repair op so that he could get aboard the *Arianrhod*, for reasons we couldn't fathom at the time, although the *Arianrhod* is what she is and you had just come in after a fight you shouldn't have been able to survive, by all accounts."

"By most accounts," Apnis corrected him. "And it *did* have to do with the damn war we all got dragged into after that. So the war's not over yet by the look of it, or there are factions out there that want to continue the disruption for their own ends. But why us?"

"Lokterix personally had no cause to like us," the captain recalled. "And he's the type to bear grudges. But what's going on here is much bigger than one disaffected agitator. I have a lot to do in a short time so I'll leave you to get on with your work, *once* you tell me where I can find Froyd Melson. You *will* keep me updated on what you find out about your own rogues when you dig them out of whatever holes they're hiding in – which I trust will be soon. And this meeting is of course not to be discussed with anyone."

A quick link to their headquarters allowed Merkat security to pin down the elusive trader and Ahxenta and Apnis collected their gear and made their way out, leaving the reps to their own devices.

"Bick Micklemouse!" the captain stormed in a low voice as they set out for the nearest transport, their two security guards in tow. "I figured it was him from what Holdspan told us in the *Half Moon*, but given the coward he is and what he owes us I wouldn't have thought he'd involve himself in attempts to blow us out of the sky."

"I would bet he didn't know what was going down, whatever his dealings with Lokterix," was the first mate's opinion. "*We* know he's a lying toad that likes his comfort and his own skin, but no matter his motive it would have involved profit, not a love of intrigue."

"You're probably right but I want a word with the little rat. Stupid of him to pick the *Port in a Storm* for whatever he's up to. It's only two levels down from here and he knows our people use the *Half Moon* when we're in port. And he sure as hell knows we're in port."

"The *Port* may not have been his choice, Cap. But he's not as dim as he'd like people to think; we found *that* out on Kelfennig. Maybe he knows he's being watched and he's being smart. We disabled many of his more obscure talents but whatever he is now, he's still an info-sent and I bet he's worked out how to subvert his abilities to his advantage. He can maybe even download what he picks up. Security talked to him about his links to Lokterix after the attack on Axellina, so he knows something bad went down and he'll have worked out it concerned us, though he wouldn't have been given all the details. But I suggest we don't head to the *Port* with Hanx and Marks in tow — our uniforms will cause a stir as it is."

"I agree. You two find a quiet place to hang out but keep within firing range," the captain ordered her guards. "Bellfish will have the record of what we discussed in the meeting and Gliss is keeping tabs on our signals. We've not heard from Flintlock, so I guess she's either in medbay still or has headed out. I'll get Bellfish to update her. But here's green six and the *Port in a Storm* is just a few sections over."

"Pity we don't have Azular with us. He was the only one of us that Micklemouse ever trusted, and his talents are more than useful in a tight spot," Apnis remarked as the captain completed her links.

The *Port in a Storm* was a small bar frequented largely by various members of off-duty Dockers' Guild repair crews and at this time in the morning it was quiet. The advent of two uniforms caused heads to turn and one of them the officers identified at once. A drinker in a classy suit and sporting a large jewelled chrono was not an everyday sight in the *Port* and the small man was conspicuous. He sat alone at a table at the back. His eyes widened and he stiffened as he took in the two. He recognised them and the fact that they were headed in his direction rather than that of the main bar led him to the certain conclusion that he was their object. He half-rose.

"Not so fast, Mr Melson," Ahxenta said, her hand on his shoulder forcing him back into his chair. "The commander and I would like a few words with you. Get us a couple of jars, Tallica, and something for Mr Melson here."

The captain sat down, her eyes not leaving the trader, who shrunk into his expensive suit in trepidation. She continued to stare him out in silence until Apnis returned with three small mugs, setting them on the table as she sat. A deliberate skimming of the room with cold eyes caused the few that were still looking in their direction to turn away and Ahxenta looked back at her quarry.

"I've been hearing bad things about you, Mr Melson," she said as she flicked the table's privacy shield on. "Care to tell me what you're doing here, what you *have* done and to whom you've been speaking?"

The answer was clearly no but the man knew that such a response would cut no ice with the captain of the *Arianrhod*. He took in the scanner that Apnis had extracted and was running over him, licked his lips and began a recital of the trade that had brought him to the Web, aware that Ahxenta was liable to treat every word as a lie.

He had been carrying a batch of coded data shards for a Merkat-based industrial group, but would give no details of his clients, those being private. He had been hired at his last port of Lonagan by a man he had recently met. The change of name he admitted, as too many knew him as Micklemouse and several shady local deals were likely to cause him trouble: his criminal record in relation to contraband cargo was on the files of the Lonagan law authorities. His delivery contact in the Web was a Mak Trebint, whom he had never seen before, but the man was to contact him on arrival. Trebint had called him when he came in, three days before. They had met in the *Green Diamond*.

The captain sat back. "You're still a lousy liar, Micklemouse."

"It's true!"

"You're aware of the recent happenings around the Web as far as the *Arianrhod* is concerned," she stated calmly. "And you *have* been interviewed by Merkat security over one of them."

The man licked his lips and confirmed that it was the case. He had heard of the missing *Gadfly*, the shuttle bay explosion and the assaults on her people. He quickly jumped in to deny his involvement in any of it, and asked after Dr Azular and Dr Flintlock with a degree of sincerity that was so patently feigned that Ahxenta found it hard to control her temper.

"Strange," she hissed. "Dr Azular made it back to *Arianrhod* with no help from Merkat medical facilities; he was not in uniform, nor was the attack on him openly reported. Dr Flintlock was taken back to the ship and not treated here. Their identities were not disclosed and the squad from Merkat security at the incident that involved Dr Flintlock were not given her name. So how come you know that two of my crew were attacked and who they were?"

Micklemouse's jaw dropped visibly, realising too late that he had made a grave error. "Captain, I…"

"We should have fried the little creep when we had the chance, Cap," Apnis drawled as she looked at the small man, whose rapidly blinking eyes gave the clue that he was desperately trying to work out how to lie his way out of the situation.

"I want to know exactly what happened from the moment you met your new contact on Lonagan Four. Drink your drink and let's hear it. I don't have all day and neither do you."

"Captain, I gave you the information out on Kelfennig that helped save your hide!" he began desperately.

"If I recall, it was your alien allies using you as a mouthpiece that gave us the information. It may also have escaped your memory that *Arianrhod* would not have been in the area, nor found you, had it not been for the emergency beacon you set off using stolen hardware, after you'd crashed a few weeks before."

"And while we were fighting a frigging war that was nothing to do with us, you were cosily hid below the surface at Kelfennig," Apnis cut in angrily. "You sat the war out in total safety and we came back once it was over to scrape you and your devious pal Doosbak off the planet. We should have left the pair of you there to rot!"

"We're not here to discuss our previous association, Micklemouse; talk to me now, or we'll be having this conversation in the brig of my ship," the captain told the trader, aware that the name of his erstwhile companion had caused a sharp quiver in the man.

He had met his new associate, Chel Fogrun, in a bar on Lonagan Four at his last stop, the man told them, but his refusal to maintain eye contact and his reflex table-tapping gave the lie to his story and Ahxenta's annoyance was rising. She had been through this type of grilling with him before and was suspicious that his info-sent abilities were not as inactive as they had been left at their last encounter. He was possibly still able to use his senses and his inserted hardware to pick up and store details of the activity around him, including that which would escape normal perception. If he could download data into storage facilities for use by others, his talents would be worth much to many, including friends that knew him well, particularly if they were more devious than him and had links to strategic concerns such as the inner circle of the Central Council of the Coalition.

"So what's your employer Chel Fogrun's real name?" the captain asked shrewdly. "Spendle Doosbak of the Co-Scutter Council?"

"This is as pointless as it's always been where he's involved, Cap," Apnis said coolly as the man's eyes stretched in an unease tinged with fear. "I vote we hand him over to security and they can persuade him to spill the beans. And they won't be as nice as we are."

"Captain, Spendle still has a place in the Coalition Central Council so he has to keep his business life separate. His operations need…"

"Don't make excuses for that weasel and give me the details now. I have two injured crew as a result of your activities and if you don't want accomplice to attempted murder added to your list of crimes, you'd better get on with it," Ahxenta snapped.

Micklemouse was shaking, to the marked interest of some of the other patrons in the *Port in a Storm*. Apnis handed him his drink and told him to take a long swig to calm his shattered nerves.

Once the alcohol was down, the trader began his tale, acutely aware of the recorder set on the table. His buddy Doosbak was using the name Chel Fogrun to run the part of his business that dealt with the dealing in and transfer of sensitive data. Of his other trade links Micklemouse knew nothing, but Fogrun paid him well for carrying out covert missions such as data transfer. A minor trader in a low-key Comet Six one-man ride would not normally be the target of raiders or the crime syndicates that operated throughout the mapped galaxy.

Doosbak, as Fogrun, had approached his old friend on Lonagan in a high-class restaurant and given him his latest job: the delivery of a small case of highly encrypted data shards to be handed to an agent in the Web. The case was passed to the trader just before departure and he was threatened with all sorts of trouble should it fail to reach its endpoint. He had been told that it was destined for a classified commercial interest in the Web, the content was highly confidential and the agent would contact him to collect. He was given a link to the agent, Trebint, who had the key to the case. Once the contents were verified, Trebint would hand over the residue of the fee. The meet went as planned and the exchange was made.

"So far so good," Ahxenta grated. "So how come you knew about the attacks on my people and the explosion outside the bay where my shuttle was berthed?"

"Word gets round, Captain, and there were a lot of people about when the explosion went off. I heard it from one or two sources."

"Who?"

"Just talk in bars; the *Green Diamond* and here," he replied uneasily.

"People talk in bars, you can pick things up. I don't tend to use the bigger restaurants when I'm in the Web on my own."

"And my people?"

"Look, Trebint and I were drinking when we met for the transfer, in the *Green Diamond*, like I told you. We'd done our business, he paid for a few, I paid for a few, you know how it is. And he mentioned the *Arianrhod* and asked if I'd heard of it. I said I had – everybody has. I think he was a bit drunk and he had a few offensive things to say about you and your ship. I didn't say anything," he added hurriedly.

"I bet you agreed with every word," Apnis remarked tartly.

"And he said that you and yours would get what was coming to you one of these days. A lot of people were put out over what you did at Mellifly: a big operation you took out that cost a lot of people a lot of credit."

Ahxenta and Apnis exchanged startled glances but said nothing.

"Go on," the captain ordered harshly. "What else?"

"He'd heard about your stolen shuttle, the one that you'd left for repair. Asked if I knew anything about it, but as I'd only just got in I hadn't heard the story, so he told me. He seemed bothered about it, but that's all. He didn't tell me anything more, I swear."

Ahxenta folded her arms, her lips compressed in anger. "You're beating about the bush, Micklemouse. How did you know that both Dr Azular and Dr Flintlock had been attacked?"

"I saw Trebint again the morning after our meeting," the trader admitted. "I'd stopped into the *Diamond* for a bite and he was there, with a guy that looked like he'd been in a fight. They were talking in a quiet corner at the back. I overheard the guy saying that they'd almost got the nosy type they'd been trailing and were set to get him away to find out more about who he was and what he knew, but somebody else had turned up and there had been gunplay. He had got away, but his mates had been taken down and that was all he knew."

"You overheard? Just walked up and listened in on a private chat, did you? And nobody batted an eye?" the captain asked scathingly.

Micklemouse squirmed. "Well not *exactly*."

"You have exactly two minutes to tell me *exactly* or you're coming with us to Merkat security, who will not only haul *you* into custody, they'll commandeer your ship as well. And for your information, your friend Trebint is already in their hands. But you must know that, as you know what went down at the *Half Moon*, don't you?"

Micklemouse did: he had slipped a phial of short-lived nano-bugs into Trebint's drink at their first meeting on the off-chance that he could pick up profitable information on the cargo he had handed on. The bugs would only tell him where the man was, if he was close enough for the trader's dedicated scanner to work, and would only last in the man's system for a few days, but if he got close enough, Micklemouse had spyware that would allow him to pick up talk. His gear had led him incognito to the *Green Diamond*, where, having spied Trebint and his friend, he had slipped unseen into a nearby booth. Using his listening device the trader heard about the outcome of an attack on a snooper who had been tracked from the *Diamond* to green ten in inner two. Trebint had dismissed his tattered contact and had made a private link to another unknown. That was when he had stated Azular's name as having got away. He then told the unknown to try and track what had happened from his end, as Trebint wanted the unfinished business completed. That had left Micklemouse to assume that the contact must have been a person in a position to obtain the relevant details. That was worrying as far as the trader was concerned as such a person would have to be connected to Merkat security or a similar official body. Trebint then stated that he would make his own arrangements before heading to the *Half Moon* later in the day, as the crew of the *Arianrhod* were known to hang out there.

The trader by this time realised that he may just have stepped into muck that it would be better to step out of and that Trebint was not a man to get on the wrong side of, but being curious as to the mention of the *Half Moon*, he had made that his stop-off for a late-night drink. He had slipped into a table at the back to order at the menu pad and it was at that point that he had been accosted by a couple of the *Half Moon's* regulars, who told him he had missed the excitement of earlier in the evening. Once he had coughed up enough ale to oil their jaws, he heard the whole story, including that one of the reputed victims was the chief medic of the *Arianrhod*. He was by then more than sure that whatever he had picked up had better stay secret, and he had no plans to pass on any of it.

"Believe that if you like," Tallica Apnis snorted.

Ahxenta shook her head. If there were any grains of truth in the story, then it looked like Merkat security itself had been infiltrated, which boded ill for Micklemouse as well as them and their people, as Merkat security was keeping watch on him and they had lately come out of a meeting where it was known that they planned to talk to him. The captain though it wise to inform the man of the situation and advise him to make tracks out of the Web as fast as his Comet Six could fly, lest the repercussions were more than he could handle.

The expression on his face as she told him was sufficient to convince her that he was scared: he had obviously no idea that he was being tailed by security. That and the seriousness of the attacks on the crew of the *Arianrhod* left him in little doubt of his fate if the perpetrators caught wind of the tête-a-tête he had just had with that ship's two most senior officers. He made his excuses and fled.

"We're not being bugged, Cap," Apnis stated as she scanned the surroundings and pointed to the captain's recorder still on the table. "But there are a few heads turning and eyes on us and as he's being tracked by Merkat security you can bet they know we're still in here. And a few round here will have noticed that he talked to us a while and that we probably now know a lot of what he knows."

"That's worrying me. We'll hook up with Hanx and Marks and find out where Flintlock is and what she's found. But it looks like Lokterix and his chums are still in the dark over the *Gadfly*."

"If our meet *has* got into the wrong ears, they'll know we have the *Gadfly* back and some sharp fly might just puzzle out we had help and who it might be, given the help Azular had, our chat with Kerrix yesterday and Flintlock's visit today."

"That had occurred. Let's make tracks — but slowly, as if we'd all the time in the galaxy."

"Aye, aye Cap," Apnis replied as she pocketed her own scanner.

The two had no sooner quit the *Port in a Storm* than their guards made towards them from the corner where they had been waiting.

"What is it?" Ahxenta demanded of Hanx.

"Lieutenant Commander Earbleat requests that you contact the *Arianrhod* immediately, Captain. There's been a problem."

7: A BLUE DOOR

The captain and first mate traded glances as they led their two guards away from the *Port in a Storm*. Ahxenta made for a nearby transport tube, figuring that Merkat medbay on level three was as secure a place as any to call the ship and to seek her chief medic. The tube was occupied by two ensigns in dark uniforms that bore the insignia of the *PSS Nyx Warrior*. The captain nodded briefly, aware that her advent had interrupted their chat and that she was the subject of their keen but furtive stares. The badge of the *Arianrhod* still commanded awe then, she thought wryly, even given their troubles.

Level three was busy as the quartet stepped out but they were not waylaid, possibly because Apnis was scanning ahead and the guards had primed rifles. Medbay reception was hectic but the captain found a comm booth to link to her ship. Her first mate meanwhile set off to enquire after Dr Flintlock at the info-point in the centre of the space.

The captain's face dark with anger as she emerged from the booth told Apnis that all was not well and she hastened over.

"What's to do, Cap?"

"Where's Flintlock?" was the immediate response.

"She's with Kerrix in the senior surgical officer's HQ. The human I spoke to wouldn't say why but did say that the doc had demanded a meet and threatened an official protest if she couldn't see the SSO at once. *And* she insisted on taking Kerrix in, I've no idea why. But what's up with you? The news from Earbleat's not good, then?"

Ahxenta looked around quickly and turned back. "Lokterix was sprung from Merkat's highest security cell an hour ago. As of now they've no idea where the hell he is, though if he's any sense he's well away. Earbleat got Greffy to use our data on the creep to scan our berth, and she's got targeting eyes ready for anything that gets close. I told her to tell Merkat security nothing: if they've been compromised, and now it looks likely, I want them kept in the dark as to how much we know about Lokterix and his like. But I've ordered her to let the Port Authority know that we will treat any craft or piece of kit getting anywhere near *Arianrhod's* berth as hostile and will take them out."

"That'll go down well. Won't the PA think it's a tad drastic, Cap?"

"I don't give a damn; I'm not having my ship under threat. But where's this senior surgeon's HQ then? We'd better find out what's happened that's got Flintlock in a fury. Earbleat didn't mention it."

"It's in section seven-ten, suite twenty six. I'd to get the info at the auto-rep and it didn't ask why I wanted to know, which is just as well. I've alerted the doc that we're on the way but they may not let us in."

"They'd better. Hanx and Marks, you're with us."

The senior surgical officer's HQ was located a way off the main medbay area but was easy to find. The small but dynamic Ji Lerro was stationed outside, eyes taking in all that she could see. She stood to attention when she spotted the captain and her team.

"Lieutenant Ji, what's the problem that Dr Flintlock and Ms Kerrix are locked in verbal combat with the chief surgeon?"

The young officer gave a wry grin as she saluted. "Ms Kerrix was attacked last night, despite the guard outside her bay. *He* was stunned, the assailant tried to knock her out with a hypo, probably to remove one of her implants with a med-extractor, and she lashed out. The racket alerted the on-duty staff and they stormed in. Nobody knows a thing and the perp got away with a bloody nose. Dr Flintlock walked into the furore this morning as Ms Kerrix was trying to discharge herself. The doc took a hand and they've been in there for over two hours. She's expecting you, ma'am."

Flintlock was relieved to hear that Ahxenta and Apnis had arrived and insisted on their admittance. The advent of gun-toting personnel in a secure part of Merkat medbay did not go down well with the staff in the outer office but the captain refused to be parted from her weaponry. In view of what she had heard she not only insisted on retaining it but on having her first mate scan their surroundings and the office into which they were headed. They were clean of all but surveillance cams. Hanx, Marks and Ji she left outside on watch.

Kerrix, Ahxenta noted as she sat, seemed to be fit despite the attempt on her person, but there was a suppressed anger in her that was noticeable as she returned the captain's greeting. Flintlock was spitting quarks over the lack of care and follow-up and told her two colleagues that the woman had taken an injury to her left shoulder, the object of the attack thus being the device implanted there.

Ahxenta's eyes narrowed as she recalled her exchange with Kerrix in Ally's office: the attacker had obviously gone for the language analyser-translator that linked into her bio-system networks.

"I assume that it would have caused very serious damage if it *had* been removed using a standard med-extractor?"

"With the internal links that must be in place, *very* serious damage doesn't begin to cover it, Cap," snapped Flintlock, her eyes flicking to Herta, the senior surgical officer. "It may have been fatal."

"What *is* that device and what does it do?" the senior SO asked. "Our medical probes haven't been able to completely analyse it, and we've tried. It must have internal shielding."

"Not your concern," Kerrix interjected. "It doesn't pose a danger to you or yours and it's essential to me and my survival, *here* at least."

Ahxenta exchanged a look with Flintlock. Whoever had made the attempt either knew what the device was and where it was implanted, or had been guided by someone who did. It could be that Lokterix had sensed a difference between Kerrix and the others in Ally's office and had used his influence from his cell, but the captain doubted it. It *would* take someone highly cybernetic like him to discern the almost-indefinable nuances that such alteration caused in others, and there was a set of beings that Ahxenta knew could do just that – and at least three had been in Merkat recently. She kept her suspicions to herself and asked Herta how the intruder had got access to Kerrix.

The senior surgeon expressed surprise that *Arianrhod's* captain was taking such interest in a worker from the *Half Moon*, but repeated the gist of what she told Flintlock: she had no idea but extra security had been put in place. She was strongly against discharging Kerrix, given her unhealed injuries, but realised that she could do little to stop her; and from an ethical viewpoint she was on very shaky ground. That Flintlock was heartily sick of the argument was so apparent that the captain called a halt, held herself and her chief medic responsible for the health of the ex-patient and told Herta that they were going.

"I have my gear," Kerrix said, holding up a bag. "I wasn't going to leave anything here for any light-fingered criminals to remove."

Once back in reception, Apnis looked around at the large number of people about, many of whom were openly staring at the party.

"Lots of eyes looking and noses twitching, Cap. Where to now?"

"I don't know about you, Captain, but I'm for my billet," Kerrix announced. "I've had enough of this place and I want some peace."

"You're headed nowhere without me. I've guaranteed your health and I now have that responsibility," said Ahxenta, looking down at her. "And I want more than a few words with you."

"I figured you might. My place or yours?"

The captain's eyes flashed at that effrontery. "If you think you're getting a ride to my ship you can think again. Where's your place?"

Kerrix pointed down. "Not too far that way: green twelve, section one, one, four, apartment thirty one. It's around the corner from Azure Belle's Nightclub in fact. You may have heard of that place?"

"Everybody has," Apnis chuckled. "One of your haunts?"

"Not ordinarily," was the short response. "Are you bringing your back-up?" she added to Ahxenta in a tone that lacked the respect that was generally accorded to the captain of the *Arianrhod*.

"Let's move," was the curt response. "Ji, you're with Dr Flintlock and me. Commander Apnis, you take Hanx and Marks and see what you can get in security about *their* problem of an hour ago."

"Aye, ma'am," the officers responded as one, all knowing without being told that the affair in medbay would not be mentioned.

Ahxenta preserved a solid silence on the way down. She knew the area as there were several shuttle berths in its outer sections she used. As the tube panel slid aside at their stop she was not surprised to find the passage outside empty. She scanned all the same, but apart from a secure cam set high in the wall opposite, there was nothing to see.

"Lead on," she ordered Kerrix, to a warning glance from her chief medic and the mouthed word "easy".

Section one, one, four was a dimly-lit passage along which blank doors set either side smacked of very inferior quarters. Number thirty one was partway along and looked the same except for a blue rather than grey door. A scan by the captain confirmed the place empty. She ordered Ji to remain outside. Kerrix dug out a key and unlocked the entry, calling out "lights" as she stalked in and slung her bag on a decrepit sofa that flanked a low table and an armchair.

"Coffee?" she offered. "I don't have anything stronger."

Ahxenta nodded with a word of thanks and looked around. There was a kitchen space with two chairs set under a counter, a hygiene closet, thermo-clean unit, comm station and a bed. It lacked comfort, she thought, noting that the doctor had reached the same conclusion.

Kerrix placed three mugs on the table and invited the other two to sit. She took the armchair, sinking into its squishy depths with a sigh, but was sufficiently aware to notice the captain setting up a recorder.

"So what do you want to know?" she began without preamble.

"Exactly who and what you are; where you hail from; what you're doing here and why; why your ship's no more than a wreck; and why someone or ones badly want your implanted hardware."

An ironic grin greeted the list as she lifted her mug. "My name *is* Kerrix. I was part of the crew of a survey ship out of a world called Norvalla Three; we were on an exploratory into poorly-charted space. As to how I came here... it's a long story. I was in a science shuttle investigating an anomaly and something went badly wrong. What, I don't know. I ended up in unmapped space, no reference points that my nav-gear recognised. The far end of the anomaly, I guessed."

"You're not making sense," Ahxenta interrupted, again wishing that she had her Berzic science officer with her. "How did you get to this anomaly and then end up at a point you didn't recognise?"

"As I said, we were on an exploratory, and we picked up what we thought was a distress. It was not familiar, so we made for the system that seemed to be the source. It *had* been charted but not named, it had a red-orange star and it was listed as having no habitable planets. The signal led us towards the fourth planet. And there it was – a massive structure, a huge piece of defunct technology that read as inert. It was like nothing we'd ever seen but we figured it might once have been a bypass node. But as we got closer, the distress cut and we read an intense wash of energy *within* the structure. We took it for a small periodic wormhole. So I took out my sci-shuttle to check it: a mistake. I got too close, the thing woke up and I was sucked inside an energy vortex without power to haul back. The gravitational forces were huge and I passed out. My shuttle must have switched to auto. I woke up in a place I didn't recognise, but close to what looked like a set-up similar to the one I'd left, with its own planetary system. Only *this* bypass thing seemed dead. I didn't have a lot of power apart from weapons and my shuttle had taken a beating, but I set for it, assuming that *if* it worked I'd end up back where I started. Nothing happened."

"You *did* get as far as Merkat. And I've never heard of Norvalla Three – where is it?"

"I wish I knew, Captain; I've made enquires and *nobody* knows. As for Merkat… the planet close to my exit point as far as I could tell was dead but it was in what may have been the star's liveable zone in the past. I got readings of derelict structures spread across its surface but that was it. The system was close to a nebula that I later found out was called the Enigma – ah, you've heard of it."

"We've heard of it – go on."

"I was in the area for a day and a half, by my reckoning. It was bad, as you can imagine from the size of my ship. I didn't dare land as I wasn't sure I'd be able to take off again and there wasn't enough oxygen in the atmosphere to be worth extracting, even if I could get close in. I *had* activated my distress, though I was aware that it might attract no attention or the wrong attention. In my case it was the latter, so it was as well that I had my cloak operational."

The account of the ship that had come in, its design and the few lifesigns that Kerrix alleged she had detected, led Ahxenta to believe that *Arianrhod* had met similar and she pressed for details. The ship, Kerrix said, seemed to have been in a fight as it was badly damaged, but it was capable of fast flight and it still had weapons. And it was not alone: a short time later, another ship arrived. By this time Kerrix had shut off her beacon and moved towards the planet in hopes of using it or one of its moons as a shield if the need arose.

"Another of the same?" the captain demanded.

"Yes and no," was the reply. "It was of a similar spec but a good bit smaller, it had sustained very little damage and was better manned. But my systems detected bio-variations in its crew: a different species was the best my external sensors could come up with but my cloak limits their active range and sensitivity."

"You have records of those ships? You evidently escaped them."

The response to that was a wry grin and a shake of the head. "Not exactly. But yes, the records are still aboard my shuttle."

That the two vessels had been involved in a deadly cat and mouse game was clear, as the smaller was intent on the destruction of the other. But as the flak that was all that was left of the larger ship flew past her as it was taken down, Kerrix realised that the later arrival had picked up her distress and she had suddenly become the prey.

"They got me. I don't know what kind of high-tech they had but they caught my signal and used tractors to get my ship close enough to scan. They'd made no attempt at contact so I guessed they didn't know what I was and were not going to ask nicely. I'd jettisoned my escape pod to make them think I was making for the planet and would burn up or be hit by bits of flak, but they were smart. They tracked it and pulled it in, no doubt figuring it was empty and that I was still in my shuttle, though they didn't get my lifesigns through her cloak and were hard pushed to make out her shape. I didn't raise my battle-shields nor did I use my weapons, which were shielded in any case. I played dead in other words."

"And they fell for it?" That was Flintlock.

She shook her head again wearily. "No, they were not sure. I don't think they realised what they had; they were very cautious once they'd got my ship and my pod aboard their own. My external scanners had shown me that they'd set weaponry and armed guards around the perimeter before going over my shuttle a scrap at a time with a heap of tech. They'd pressurised the space and their techs weren't masked so I could make out from their faces that they were humanoid. They were talking, which gave my ship and my inbuilt translator enough to start on the language. I learnt later it was called Inter-Lan. As soon as they'd got me aboard I'd bored an aperture through a lower hatch to take in air and equalise my pressure to theirs – it was similar."

Kerrix leant back and gazed at the grimy ceiling, stretching to ease the tension. "They couldn't breach my ship without causing her and them serious damage and my cloak had sufficiently foxed them that they couldn't read specifics. I think they wanted her intact anyhow and were making for a place where they could get to work. There was talk going on with what I assumed was a command unit or base and comings and goings of various people, possibly senior staff – and *they* wanted answers as there were raised voices. But all I could make out visually was the interior of the bay. It was large and there were a few small ships there that looked like one-man fighters."

"You made it to Merkat," Ahxenta cut in. "Care to tell me how?"

"They finally got through my defences. It had been over a day, I was beat and they got a scanner in through a micro-breach. They got my spec; and my inserted ID emits a signal. My ops systems sensed the scanner and I scrambled its uptake and sealed the breach, but too late. I'd got enough of their language to know that they were headed to a base close to the bypass node. They called the node Starfall Exit, or that was the translation I got, so I guessed that they used it. They'd only lately taken over their base – there was a lot they were unfamiliar with – which worked to my advantage once we'd got to it. I realised we'd docked when they all left, shut the internal bay doors and started to depressurise. After a while they opened to space and began to move grapples in to get my shuttle out. So I woke her up."

She grinned at the memory. "I blew my own pod to pieces along with two of their fighters and their grapples. I shot out of that bay like a cork from a bottle. I had to use visuals as I'd no idea where I was, but it was a huge orbital station that seemed to stretch around half the planet it was anchored to. I took out what I thought were comms and sensor arrays close to the bay area of their ship. There were other ships close by, some badly shot up. I moved in amongst them, snugged down under a massive weapons array on the hull of one and shut down everything but my cloak."

"That sounds beyond far-fetched," the captain noted levelly. "And doesn't explain how you made Merkat."

"You're welcome to check my shuttle's records," Kerrix spat back.

"Enough, Cap," warned Flintlock. "You can get the rest later."

"What the hell… they didn't track me right away but I couldn't stay put: there was a lot of rebuilding going on and most of the hulks were crawling with repair bots. So I made for the guts of the wreck I was on until I got my bearings. It *was* shot to hell but had some gear including derelict fighters. I still had enough of my tech that I could capture their outline specs in my portable cloaking projector – that device I used on your shuttle – and generate a visual cloak. I had to find food, energy; my emergency supplies were out and I had to get more. A bad time. I got about using their gear. And learned to steal."

"How long were you there?" the doctor asked.

"Not sure, about thirty Norvallan days. They hadn't given up on me, tenacious bastards. I tried to repair my ship but the tech was too unlike. I did infuse enough of their hull call-sign indicators into my cloak to let me slip aboard a ship that seemed to be a massive cargo, but she was not like any other there. She was whole, looked new and there was a lot of activity round her. I assumed from the goings-on that she was headed for parts fitter to live in, so I stashed as much as I could lift, got my shuttle into her and stuck her like a bug under a ledge in an outer cargo bay. The ship made *this* place in ten days. I broke out as she was docking. There was a lot going on, as I don't think the authorities here were familiar with her lines."

"Do you have scans of this huge cargo ship?" Ahxenta demanded suddenly and suspiciously.

Kerrix looked at her. "You still don't believe me. And yes I do."

"So you just hopped off at Merkat and made yourself at home?"

"Don't be a fool," she snapped irritably. "An anomaly must have shown on their boards and they sent a shot after me that cut through my shields and took out a chunk of plating. But Merkat's a big place, I know a few moves and I was cloaked. I eventually got her into an outlying free berth close to a few old repair runarounds, but what I didn't count on was that they had got enough of an ID signal on *me* that they could track me, and they did. There must have been one or two damn smart scouts on that ship with very clever tech. I spotted a small flyer buzzing about and realised that they'd get me sooner or later. So I set my cloak to chameleon and moved again, but I couldn't get far as that hit had crippled her. So I ditched her, got out and started running. And *that* was why I was on the run at Merkat."

Ahxenta raised a sceptical eyebrow. "Really? And they didn't catch you? You must have had some turn of speed for a runaway who'd been stuck inside a damaged shuttle for days on end and living for thirty days before that as a fugitive in an alien place you didn't know and where you couldn't speak the language."

Kerrix eyed her angrily. "You can believe what you like. I was able to part-blanket my ID to prevent long-distance scans and buy time. And as I told you, my analyser-translator had picked up enough basic Inter-Lan to translate what I needed and it's been doing so since. You note I speak directly *to* you and not through a voice projection interface. And why the hell am I justifying myself to you?"

"*You* stole my shuttle Ms Kerrix," the captain reminded her. "And there's a helluva lot you've not told me, including how some crook knows about your language translator device and is not above cutting you up to get it. I don't have time to find out more but I *will* take you up on your offer to check your shuttle's records, particularly the data on the base you spoke of, the people you were dealing with and the transport on which you say you stowed away to get here."

"If you give me your link details, Captain, I'll send you the files."

"Like hell. We visit your shuttle now and get them. You can download them to a data shard."

At the mute fury in the woman's eyes, the captain added that she had a shuttle in a docking bay on green four near marketing, and they would use that to reach outer belt nine. She carefully avoided her chief medic's eyes as she did so, having noted Flintlock's manifest irritation. They collected Ji at the door and made off.

Apnis, Hanx and Marks were waiting in the marketing reception area. They were surprised to see Kerrix, but hiding their curiosity, they followed the captain towards their ride, Apnis muttering that she would brief Ahxenta later over the state of play in Merkat security.

It took a little time to reach outer belt nine but by the time the *Arianrhod's* shuttle had docked in a bay close to six eight alpha two on blue fifteen the captain had alerted her bridge crew to her status and warned them that she and her team intended to return shortly. As all their cargo had been loaded and final port clearances were in order, the ship would leave as soon as they were back on board. Taking Apnis and Hanx as escort, Ahxenta motioned their guide out of the *Arianrhod's* shuttle and into the passage beyond.

Kerrix called out "lights" as she unlocked the bay door. The space grew brighter and the captain, with Apnis and Hanx behind, followed her in. The cloak projector was still fixed to the side wall, Ahxenta noted, and the ship was as she had last seen her, listing to starboard, her hull scarred by numerous assaults. Closer inspection revealed the depth of scoring and the spot where a section of hull plate had been sheared off. In spite of the shabby façade it took some manipulation for the entry panel to open and the ramp to descend and Ahxenta realised that any intruder would have a tough time trying to break in.

Leaving her first mate and the guard outside, the captain trailed Kerrix up the short ramp, which was set almost amidships but closer to the narrow nose of the shuttle. As she had expected, the pilot's position was at the front and looked tight. A lesser station was set behind and the aft part of the vessel had been rigged as a couch with storage bays above and below. Several bulges indicated more storage, instrumentation and an engine area. Indicator lights were blinking on the control boards but that was all.

Kerrix called for more light as she sat forr'ad and ran her fingers over her console. She invited Ahxenta to sit behind as the ops area lit and systems came on line. The captain's eyes roved the small space. It would be uncomfortable for a lengthy stay but it offered shelter. A stale smell permeating the craft caused her nose to wrinkle but she said nothing as she watched the vis-data records being searched.

"I've overhauled and reconfigured my systems a couple of times since I've been here," Kerrix told her. "They *will* accept a standard data shard. Do you want one of mine or do you have your own?"

"I always have my own," was the laconic response as the captain dug out the requisite article from a side pocket.

As download progressed, Ahxenta scanned the space with a hand-held probe. Many areas were shielded but a flight jacket hung above the couch at the rear caught her eye. She took a visual of the item and its insignia, none of which she could pin to any recognisable system or authority. Finding Kerrix' keen eyes on her, she raised an eyebrow.

"You were a science officer aboard your ship?"

"Science was my background, yes," was the cool response. "I've added records I picked up from around the Web, including visuals of two attempted intrusions into this space. Your data shard, Captain."

Ahxenta accepted it calmly. "By the way, that thug that attacked my chief medic and let loose a shot at you has escaped. He's probably fled the Web, but he had at least one friend and a few associates so I suggest you watch your back – although I suspect you always do."

Kerrix' eyes widened. She had not heard, evidently, but she said nothing, accepting the warning with a quick, affirmative nod.

"On another note, Dr Flintlock and the medics in medbay made a thorough scan of your biosigns and their opinion is that your people may originate in a region close to outer zone Mu, although the data's not clear-cut. If you're searching for your own, that might be a place to start. I'd imagine your systems in here can be configured to search the databases available in every info-point in the Web."

"Dr Flintlock *did* mention it, Captain," Kerrix replied. "Although I don't think detailed navigational charts are available free of charge and I'm sure questions would be asked of those who probe too deeply about acquiring them. Is there anything else you require?"

"I'll go over the data on this shard and let you know, Ms Kerrix."

She stood, having to bend her head to make her way out of the small shuttle, and set off down the ramp. She turned at the bottom to watch as the other made her own way down and sealed the door.

"One thing, Ms Kerrix: what was your rank aboard your ship?"

"Mind your feet, Captain; the deck plates are a little misaligned."

"I asked you a question, Ms Kerrix."

The woman smiled inflexibly up at her. "I've answered sufficient questions for one day, Captain."

"I find you annoyingly irritating, Ms Kerrix."

"And you scare the hell out of me, Captain Ahxenta. You know where to find me, should you need to ask me more questions. I wish you and your crew a safe onward voyage."

The latter was said a little bitterly as she held up the key to the bay entry. Ahxenta took the hint and turned to leave. Apnis, an amused listener to the exchange, shouldered her phase rifle and raised her brows questioningly as she prepared to move off likewise.

"Would you like to be returned to inner two?" the captain asked as the group regained the passage and Kerrix secured the bay door.

"I can see myself home, thank you Captain," was the curt retort as she acknowledged Apnis and Hanx, turned her back and walked casually off down the corridor, the eyes of the other three following.

"She's still limping," the first mate noted. "And you can bet your bottom credit somebody noticed that she was in our company. You reckon there will be comeback on her, if we're out of the picture?"

"I strongly suspect Ms Kerrix can look after herself. But I sure as hell want to see what's on this data shard. If it's a heap of hogwash, I'll kick her butt to oblivion when we make it back here. But we've cargoes to ship and we're already behind time. You can brief me on the bridge as we haul out and we'll have a full update over lunch."

"Roger that. Marks is going over our shuttle and her bay with a fine-toothed comb. And Gliss is monitoring us and every micron of space from here to the *Arianrhod* from tactical, just in case."

"Good call. But don't expect a bonus, you won't get it."

The *Arianrhod* sat apparently peacefully in her assigned dock but the subtle chasing of light and dark over her glistening pink metallic hull signalled to her captain as she brought the shuttle in that an army of monitoring and repair bots was ceaselessly inspecting every micron of her exterior. There had been no signs of incursion into her space but the crew remained at full alert. Ahxenta had scheduled a briefing with her senior officers to review her and her first mate's missions once the ship was on the bypass and on the way to Delta Iridium.

The two command officers made for the bridge as soon as their shuttle was secure. Ahxenta took her chair, stretching to ease tense muscles as she pulled her ops board across to flick over the contents.

"Lieutenant Box, plot us a course via Silshoon and straight down. There's been no raider or other hostile activity reported in zone Delta so we'll take the direct road. Steady as she goes, Lieutenant Dox, no need to overcook the chief's engines."

"Aye, Captain," came the dual response from the navigator and helmswoman from their ops station below the command position.

"Lindell and Perla Jute have sent up the delivery and scheduling specs, Cap. We'll make it with time to spare as long as we don't meet trouble on the road," Apnis told her as she took in her own board.

"We hope. I'm usually grateful to be out in space after a stopover in the Web, but this time I'm more than happy to see the back of it. It's bad enough that out here we seem to be the target of every ill-tempered hostile with a grudge against the galaxy, but in the Web we can usually expect no more than the odd bust-up down at Ally's."

"That's for sure. And now it may be that one of our favourite ill-tempered hostiles is out here and may be gunning for us."

"Lokterix?" the captain asked quietly.

The first mate nodded. "The security reps I spoke to said he had a tracker injected at his med check when they hauled him in and they'd been able to follow its signal to one of the low level docking bays of inner four, but no further. There were two small transports there that headed out soon after, making for ships berthed further out and due for departure. Both ships got away, as the Port Authority wouldn't hold them up on such little evidence."

"Didn't want to get into hot water with their clients, you mean, and lose the business," Ahxenta said shortly.

"More than likely. So the assumption is that he's now well away."

"That's some assumption: Lokterix is savvy enough to know that he'd had a tag inserted. He'd have deactivated it or even cut it out, he's the type. Did you get an ID on the two ships?"

"I persuaded the reps to provide them. One was a medium-sized cargo runner of the Crimson Ensign Line out of Sevolb and heading home. The other was a cargo cum passenger registered at Mellifly but as it was privately owned there was no note of her heading."

"Mellifly! That's a name to conjure with."

"That's what I thought, Cap, and if he *has* skipped port, it would be a probable route. But those ships seem too much of a coincidence, unless he'd planned to head out anyway, after he'd done what he was here for, which included taking out as many of ours that he could."

"He and how many more? He can't be acting alone. Remember what Micklemouse let out in the *Port in a Storm*? Trebint told him that a lot of people were miffed that we took out that hostile shipbuilding base over Mellifly's northern polar region."

"It was more than a big set-up, it would have taken down half the sector if those ships had got out. But Trebint, or Lokterix, said it cost a lot of people a lot of credit? That suggests that the *lot of people* are still around and intent on revenge. I don't like the sound of that."

"Me neither, Tallica. But not long after we took that base apart, the tricksy Colonel Myrtleberry of the ISP told us that *Arianrhod* was identified as the attacking ship, despite the utter destruction of the place. We figured at the time that something or someone had got out. And then she mentioned groups of nameless ships leaving Mellifly in haste? It looks like this war isn't as dead as some think and there are surplus bad guys out there that may not have been actual hostiles but were deeply into making credit out of them and their activities."

"And who've got some handle on where and when we're around to settle the score. We'd best watch our backs," Apnis warned.

"That's what I told Kerrix. Talking of whom, once we're well on the bypass I want to check out this shard she so kindly gave me *and* the readings I got of her shuttle's interior. And I need my rations."

"You and me both. If Azular's feeling better, he'll want to be in on it. I'll check in with Flintlock. She headed straight to medbay as soon as we got in and she was in a temper. Did you have a spat?"

"She reckoned I was over-hard on our strange friend Ms Kerrix."

"From what I've seen of *her* she's able to give as good as she gets. We seem to dig up odd contacts wherever we go," the first mate said with a shrug. "Must be our innate charisma or something."

Once *Arianrhod* was well on her way to her first port, the captain called her senior officers into the briefing. As she waited the arrival of the last of them, she linked her personal scanner to a projector port and began to scrutinise the visual record of what she had picked up from the scruffy shuttle belonging to Kerrix.

"Something, Cap?" Tallica Apnis asked as Ahxenta leant forward to examine one part of the record very closely.

"This jacket looks like a piece of flight kit. I couldn't get the whole thing but check out the insignia: seen anything like those before?"

The first mate took a close look. "New to me," she said through a forkful of food. "But here come Azular and the doc; and Crizz has been around a bit. Maybe one of them has seen something like?"

"Help yourselves to rations and sit," the captain invited. "Feeling better, Azular? Sorry I couldn't stop by earlier, I had my hands full."

"Understood, Captain and I'm much better, thank you."

That was not what the update from her chief medic had shown, but Ahxenta let it pass: she knew Azular well enough to know that he would have been extremely peeved if he had had to miss the briefing.

Meanwhile the chief engineer was studying a holo of the complete shuttle that the captain had set up to one side. "Not seen one like that before, Cap," she said. "Where did she say she hailed from?"

"A system called Norvalla."

"Never heard of it. I don't recognise that uniform or the badges on it either. Anything in our databanks?"

"Nothing I could find, Crizz, but there *are* systems out there that don't belong to any alliance. And there must be hundreds of worlds we know nothing about – the mapped galaxy's a big place. But that's not the only thing I get from this particular piece of kit."

"A lot of trimming around the sleeves and three pips each side of the collar," said Apnis. "Maybe her kind goes in for fancy dress, but I did notice that she was less than polite to you now and then, as if she wasn't used to being contradicted. So what is she or was she?"

"Science was my background, yes," intoned Ahxenta. "That was her answer when I asked if she was a science officer. And she called her boat a science shuttle. That exterior image is Greffy's," she told them, indicating the holo. "*This* is the spec of the interior of the ship, as far as I could get it. I'm not familiar with the design. Anyone else?"

None of the officers present had seen a vessel like it. Second mate

Whisper Earbleat was puzzling out the weapons capability. Azular was more interested in the finer details of the interior and had called up the minutiae that the scanner had been able to record.

"There's a lot of shielding *within* the ship," he noted. "Perhaps it's security for the pilot from unwanted scanning of sensitive systems."

"One of the reasons I suspect she didn't stop me scanning," the captain said. "We'll return to it after we've dealt with what else Tallica and I found. And I also have this."

She held up the data shard containing the information that Kerrix had loaded and gave an outline of what it represented. She also took the step of having her senior science officer examine the shard lest it had been tampered with without her knowledge.

Two hours later the captain leant back in her chair and looked round the table. "I want you to go through that with a fine-toothed comb, Azular, and make sure it hasn't been fabricated in some way – though how the hell you'd fabricate something like that I've no idea."

"It opens one huge can of worms, Cinnabar," was the first mate's opinion, "And suggests that Ms Kerrix wasn't talking hogwash."

"It suggests much more than that, ma'am," Azular said ominously.

His keen eyes had raked the background of a part of the scratchy visual and his quick fingers had pulled up and refined the image that had struck him. "Recognise him, Captain, Commander?" he asked.

Ahxenta looked at the image. "That part-Friskianx commander of that rear ex-hostile ship of the pack out of sector sixteen of Beta! In fact the one we came across not long ago. He said he'd no current quarrel with me, so who is his quarrel with? They're taking back their own all right if they *are* rebuilding those hostile ships damaged, left behind or hauled into that ex-hostile base off the Enigma. I guess that's what the star patterns are showing?" she asked Azular.

"Aye, Captain; the Enigma Nebula *is* in uncharted space, but I can extrapolate. I've captured Ms Kerrix' shuttle's data from the moment she dropped out of what she assumed was the exit node that took her into that area beyond our mapped space. I've no record of the planetary systems in local space but from what I *can* read, the base she mentions may be the one we believe to be sited between the Enigma and the furthest edges of Mu. As the being on Kelfennig told us, their ancestors sent out groups of their own people whom they'd physically altered as colonisers to find habitable worlds beyond their local system, as Kelfennig had been almost destroyed. That may have been one of the outpost worlds and the base was built to orbit it."

"Too many maybes," Apnis interrupted.

"You're right," Ahxenta agreed. "But there is evidence that there was a hostile base in the area and *this* record, unclear as it is, shows that the first ship she recorded *had* a clear hostile configuration, with limited lifesigns aboard – and that brings up its own problem."

"It suggests that there are still pockets of hostiles out there in their big bad ships," Earbleat put in. "But the ex-raider renegades and their hangers-on we met at Skyrtek are out to get them and take over their bases and anything in them they can use. And if *this* can be believed, they seem to be succeeding."

"Exactly," Azular concurred. "You said that the second ship was of a similar design but smaller and with an animate crew that seemed different to the first, though still hostile to her, Captain."

"She took them to be a different species," Ahxenta stated. "She said they got her shuttle and escape pod and brought them aboard, and that's about what this record shows. And she reckons science techs were sent in first to analyse her ship and then command staff. *They* seemed to disagree over what to do with her – which brings us to this guy. Command staff! And we find him in the Web. She also figured she'd come off a local bypass node. Her translator picked up the name Starfall Exit, which I've never heard of. It may be part of a covert system used by what she said she came into Merkat aboard: a massive transport. From what I saw of its spec from the few visuals of the interior and exterior she got, it was nothing like the hostile or ex-hostile specs that we were looking for when we scanned what we could of the Web to work out where those three that waylaid us came from. If they came in on *that*, it's no wonder we didn't find it."

"That poses another problem or two, Captain," said Azular.

"Don't I know it: if these crews of victims and ex-raiders are now the new raiders, it implies that they're not only into upgrading what's left of their own and their ex-captors' ships, but they've started in the boat-building trade themselves. And if they've managed a takeover of most of the hostile bases we think are out there…"

"But we know more or less where the bases are, which gives us an edge. And they must know that we know," Earbleat chipped in.

"And who the hell are this us?" the gruff voice of Crizz Cottontail demanded. "We're traders, not the guardians of galactic peace. The Interstellar Systems Protectorate, with its Coalition, Non-Treaty and Independents allies are the ones that are supposed to keep the space lanes clear. They and the Trades Alliance charge us enough on every load we haul to do it. They have the data on these bases, haven't they? We passed it to Admiral Zillah at Freskat during the damn war that the ISP, with the connivance of the TA, dragged us into."

"They don't have *this* information, Chief," Azular calmly pointed out. "And I expect Ms Kerrix may want it kept that way, at least until she can find her way back to where she belongs. If those who suspect what she is realise she has *this* and that she's in Merkat, she may be in very serious trouble. And as we now have it, so might we."

"Crizz has a point," Flintlock noted curtly. "But *our* people were targeted, even though there was an explosion in another part of the Web. Is it *only* because a lot of people bear a grudge because we took out that hostile shipbuilding base near Mellifly? And where does Lokterix fit in? And Micklemouse for that matter."

"More questions than answers," said Ahxenta. "But the explosives suggested hostile technology that may have come in on this transport that brought Kerrix in a while ago. And it could still be in the Web."

"Not necessarily," Azular disagreed. "Explosives of alien origin must be available and the three we met before the event were ex-victims of the hostiles. Perhaps one at least hails from that ship but he was adamant that he had no quarrel with you, Captain."

"At this time; but we'll have to keep our eyes and ears open for more trouble in the Web. If it's contained and there's no more than usual, then we know we're the target of some body or other. And it has to be a group, as Lokterix alone couldn't have set it all up."

"We're not the only ones," Apnis mused. "The *Hexameter* had that clash at Stinward and the *Nyx Warrior* lost a pod to theft. And Nat Holdspan said he'd heard that an unidentified PSS had a raider pack on her tail out by the Crimson Drapes and had taken a couple of shots, although Micklemouse was the one that told him."

"But we now have reason to believe that at least one of the hostile bases that launched attacks during the war has been taken over by an ex-raider cum ex-victim group and they're setting up on their own account. They seem to have built one bloody great ship that's not in their usual mould and that might only be the start," Ahxenta said firmly. "I can warn the rest of the PSS fleet on the QT over the Ultraviolet III, but we may not be the only potential targets if the raiders get back to what used to be their usual trade of harassing shipping and taking out all that they could. So the ISP and their allies at least need to know, as well as the commercial shipping lines."

"They'll want to know how we know, particularly the military, and they may press the TA to penalise us if we don't cooperate," argued Apnis. "It wouldn't be the first time they tried to revoke our flag."

"Why don't you pass it on to Admiral Zillah?" the chief engineer suggested. "She's ISP, you've dealt with her before, she trusts you and she knows how to get things done. But I wouldn't go in over the usual comms channels and relays."

"Good point, Crizz. Zillah's no fool and she won't push if I can't say where I got the info. She's too savvy not to use it and what's more, she'll believe me: many in ISP certainly wouldn't. So we have a lot ahead of us on the way to Delta. You go over these records more fully Azular, and get Greffy to help. But you're for medbay and you'll stay there until the doc says otherwise. But it would be useful if you could pull out enough to pass to Zillah without bringing in Kerrix – remove any links to her gear and her tech if you can."

"Yes, ma'am."

"Apnis and Earbleat, we're for the bridge. Chief, you'd better make tracks for main engineering. Everyone else, dismissed."

Over several standard days and route changes via the bypass nodes that allowed ships to enter and leave the hyperspace transport system efficiently, the captain had time to contemplate the problems facing her crew. She was mildly surprised that they had met with no trouble and little traffic on the way to Delta Iridium, centrally located in zone Delta and well within ISP-controlled boundaries.

Ahxenta had called as many of her fellow PSS captains as she was able to pass on the news. She had been wary, although she gave her closer friends part of the relevant data with the request that they keep it under wraps. It looked as if the recently-born super-Alliance that had been forged from smaller cooperatives of systems bound to each other by trade, non-aggression and joint assistance treaties was about to be hit with another test of cohesiveness. A unified front would have to be held against emerging threats to zone and sector stability and part of that threat yet again seemed to be coming from outside the limits of currently mapped space.

"Well, the ISP *is* making a lot out of its expansion into unexplored areas," Tallica Apnis remarked as she and the captain talked over the issue. "Probably in an attempt to flush out the last of the hostiles and their hardware, or commandeer it. All the bases we knew of bar one were outside current treaty borders and in uncharted space anyway."

"But *that* one was a doozie," Box stated loudly over his shoulder.

"Shut up and pay attention to your boards," he was told shortly by helmswoman Romanna Dox, his colleague at the navi-helm console. "And stop listening in on other people's conversations, it's rude."

"*You* were listening to the Cap and Commander Apnis and so was everybody else," he accused in a sharp undertone.

"But I don't tell the whole bridge about it," she retorted.

Apnis grinned and continued, "From what Kerrix told you of her ship and mission, *her* people are exploring, so you can bet sentients from systems close by *our* mapped zone edges are doing the same."

"Now and then you hear of another world out there that might be worth the picking, and usually there's nobody about that can tell you to back off and find your own bit of space," was the cynical reply.

"So it's marked as ripe for scavengers to head in and see what they can dig up that's worth a credit or ten on the open market," the first mate said sardonically. "But that shouldn't impact on our problem of why *we* seem to have been marked out for this campaign of revenge. Maybe our actions off Mellifly *have* put a few noses out of joint."

"I gave Grey the gist when I spoke to him, so he'll scout around when he hauls into Merkat. *Obsidian's* still en route as he had a delay at his last cargo pick-up. He'll be Web-side a few days for repairs as his loading gear was damaged at Cygilla Prime. I warned Goodsocks about it as *Emerald's* headed that way with paying guests she took off a stranded cruiser at Marridan. And Pinkhorn's been able to source a cargo for pick-up from Cygilla to Polstarn."

"Handy the *Emerald* being set up for passengers," Apnis remarked. "It's handier still that we appointed Pinkhorn supercargo. If Lindell teaches Perla Jute as well as he did Helly and news gets out, we can hire him out as a supercargo tutor if we hit hard times."

"I'd hope it wouldn't come to that. But the space lanes are quiet, or ships are running silent. We've had nary a hello from anyone."

"Still picking up the pieces from the aftermath of the war – they always say the consequences last longer than the duration, which in a way bodes well for us as we tend to take on commissions that many of the regular mercantile steer clear of."

"Which is why we land in hot water so often," the righteous voice of Box floated up from the well of the bridge.

"Button it, Mr Box," the captain ordered. "But Zillah will maybe enlighten us. I didn't tell her the whole story over the distance comm relays as I bet there are a few unfriendly listening posts out there still active. She knows we're heading in after we drop our cargo at Iris. The thin diamond wafers for crystal comm linkages we can pick up at Freskat will find a market: they're rare at any price as Brown Amber's gem mining ops are nowhere near full production. Lindell's on it but for now I'm heading to medbay to see what Azular's dug out."

"*If* he's still there," Apnis smiled. "Your buddy on Freskat Six has got a supply of the wafers in hand?" she added in a low voice.

"Yes. He had a back stock of quality gems and trade's been slack, so he's been cutting and array-setting to keep his hand in. There's always a market at Coronis on Delta but we can try local comms ops on Freskat and I'll cut him in on the profits. The Freskat Navy must have orders in for comms systems repairs to their surviving ships and for the new ships they're building. They lost a lot in the war."

"They and everybody else; half the damn galaxy needs rebuilt."

"You have the conn, just keep us on track," was the only reply.

Medbay was quiet when Ahxenta arrived. She found her science officer still there: Flintlock had threatened him with physical restraint if he refused to stay put and the warning seemed to have worked.

Azular had linked his medbay info-station to the complex science station in his office and was studying part of the data that he had transferred and enhanced from the shard that Kerrix had loaded. He had also thoroughly examined the shard itself.

"A data shard set into a system has to interact with it and it adapts to a system alien to itself by integrating linkage and other data from the host source. In this case, the ops console of Ms Kerrix' shuttle."

"So in other words you're trying to get more information on her ship and her technology?" the captain commented wryly.

"Quite so, and from what I've been able to work out, some of her tech is way more advanced than ours," he smiled.

"Her cloak and camouflage damn well are, otherwise we should've been able to detect the *Gadfly*," was Ahxenta's rueful observation.

"Yes, that I had noted, as have others," Azular said with a grin.

"Who?"

"Lieutenant Commander Earbleat: she sees such tech as a useful adjunct to what she and her team have already developed for her new version of *Loki*. As you recall, she lost *Loki V* at Skyrtek."

The captain sighed. "And she's never stopped bending my ears over it. I might have known she'd be in for first dibs. One of these days I'll dock her pay for spending too much time and too much of my credit on her favourite toys. Cargo pods are for cargo, not for turning into guided missiles, however useful they are. Who else?"

"I've also had words with Chief Cottontail: if we could duplicate or build on some of Ms Kerrix' tech it would be useful to upgrade our decoy – *that* has saved our hides on a number of occasions."

"And that would be a valuable use of time. But we'd have to get hold of her tech, as we surely won't be able to do it from scratch."

"That *is* the downside, but if Ms Kerrix is still in Merkat when we next stop off, we may be able to carry out some sort of trade?"

"Doing what? Fixing up her shuttle?"

"That, or helping her find a way home, if we do head anywhere near the outermost edges of zones Mu, Kappa or Zeta – they *are* the nearest to this anomalous bypass node she reported."

The captain's terse response of "no way in hell will I have her on my ship!" to the latter proposal resulted in a fleeting frown from Azular, but he shrugged diplomatically.

"There will be ways of getting more data on the anomaly. It must have been reported before, even though it's outside mapped space. I'll run through all I can get on the Enigma and the area round it, as nebulae are often held to be sources of strange phenomena. The Ginseng is a case in point," he added slyly.

The answer to that was a warning glance, but Ahxenta was keen to hear what else the science officer had found. He had not been able to link any other faces in the visual record to the two who were with the part-Friskianx commander at their late meeting, despite his tweaks to the data. But the part-ships and hulks captured by Kerrix' shuttle's sensors were clearly wholly or partly based on hostile tech. One sign of alien origin *and* use was trace zukivianite in many of the wrecks, a large number of which were being overhauled, as shown by the hosts of service bots skittering across their hides. So many that they almost looked to have a bad case of fleas, Azular observed dryly. As for the records themselves, Kerrix had spent time scanning the area beyond the station and had possibly compromised her own safety, as one or two visuals must have required her exit on sorties.

"Her scanners are superb," he noted. "However, few ships seem to be operative, which suggests that these ex-raiders or whoever they are have only recently taken over this base. But they appear to be expedient in turning it into a highly efficient and functional station, and *that* suggests that they have ready supplies of what they need."

"Leading to the conclusion that once up to spec, they'll be more than capable of getting back to work full-time," the captain grimaced. "In other words we'll have the usual raider rat-packs that we've faced over the years but the new breed is tougher, more bad-tempered and very much better equipped than our old adversaries ever were."

"Which in turn means that we'll have to be able to cope: perhaps you should encourage Ms Earbleat to continue with *Loki VI*?"

"Don't push it," she warned. "But that ex-commander we met out at Skyrtek and recently in the Web wasn't up for a scrap with us. And if Kerrix is to be believed and he *had* come in on what looked like a huge merchant ship, what else are these people up to?"

"The being from Kelfennig told us that those used and abused by the hostiles for their own purposes and who had escaped them would be *influenced* to take revenge in the form of recovery of what it called violated spaces – presumably the places of power held by the hostiles and built up clandestinely over the ages until they felt they could take on the existing powers in the mapped galaxy and take them over."

"As in wipe them out," the captain said. "But we took the entity's influencing bit with a pinch of salt as it also said they couldn't control the results. It just didn't want the victims eyeing up Kelfennig. And we figured the hostile bases as former raider dens, raiders being ripe for misuse, but as the hostiles had been on the go for eons before they struck, *they* maybe were behind the raiders all along. But we're back to at least four ex-hostile bases that may be reverting to unfriendly use, with more gear than most planetary systems and run by people that bear grudges against anyone they believe ever did them a bad turn."

"Which may very well include us, at some point," Azular frowned. "You'll pass this on to Admiral Zillah as well, Captain?"

"I feel I have to. The four bases we have reason to believe may be active are all outside charted zones. Lartzeg Trine we can discount: it was blasted to dust and it's well-known now. But Freskat's firmly in ISP territory and the ISP may get more than it's bargained for if it pushes its exploration into areas near those bases. However, we…"

She was interrupted by the distinctive wail of the red alert and a loud request that the captain head to the bridge. She jumped up with an oath. "I thought it was too good to be true! Ahxenta here, on my way. You're staying here, Azular! Greffy can handle it." Calling for details, she shot out of medbay and ran for the closest transport tube.

The bridge was at full alert, with every station manned. The reason for the alarm was a distress call that had been picked up from a ship in normal space just off the beacon. Ahxenta ordered an update on the source as she tied herself into her command chair.

"Difficult to make out, but it's on a PSS channel and they're under attack," Lieutenant Bellfish reported from the comms station.

"Dammit! Battlestations! Cloak up, Dox, and prepare to jump off the bypass! Gunnery crews stand by. Chief, hot up our engines, we'll need them; and make sure every shield is in place. Tactical, set the grid to full. Do we know who it is yet and what they're up against?"

"Three vessels, Captain!" Pollux Gliss at tactical replied loudly as he transferred his display to the bridge holo. "Our cloak's making it tough, but we have one large ship reading as a PSS, two others, much smaller but reading like the hostiles we came up against in the war."

"Greffy, scan those hostiles!"

"On it," he said tersely. "Similar to hostiles we've faced before, subtle differences but no zukivianite traces, repeat *no* zukivianite."

"They've a lot of firepower and they're using it!" Gliss called.

"Got it!" crowed Bellfish. "It's the *Tallulah*, Captain!"

"Might have damn well known," Apnis growled as Ahxenta gave the order to drop the cloak, set attack vector and ready their decoy.

"Shields at maximum and power up those phase cannons! Dox, ready her to go in at high speed. Earbleat, get those hostiles targeted the second they're in your sights and take them down. Hold back on the decoy for now, Greffy. All positions at ready… go!"

"*Tallulah's* altering her position to protect her forr'ad shielding – hostiles are closing and trying to deploy slicer beams!" cried Gliss. "They've seen us! One's changing course to take us on!"

"Launch deflecting drones!" Ahxenta bellowed. "Earbleat, target her comms! Tallica, take auxiliary weapons and get those beams out."

As the ship shuddered to the strikes of phase cannon on her hull, the helmswoman's skilled hands wove an intricate path to outfly her opponent. The smaller ship was highly manoeuvrable and speedy at close range for she wove her own patterns around *Arianrhod's* hull.

"Gunnery crews, fire all weapons! Take her down!"

"Got her!" screeched Earbleat. "She's backing off, heading for the bypass! She won't make it. Why doesn't she launch escape pods?"

As the exploding ball of flak expanded, Ahxenta ordered her ship out of the debris zone and into a position to defend the *Tallulah*. That tactic was enough for the second attacker, for she veered off towards the bypass. She was too late, for a massive burst of torpedo fire from the *Tallulah* caught her stern and she burst apart in a ball of flame.

"Hit her while she's running for cover, why don't you?" muttered Apnis, releasing the restraints tying her to the weapons station.

The captain cancelled the red alert, called for all stations to report in and ordered comms to contact the *PSS Tallulah*.

"Damage to forr'ad shields but they're holding," said Cottontail. "Our hull plates have taken a few bumps but otherwise we're sound."

"We'll need to replace energy cells and torpedoes, Cap," Earbleat stated. "And our smaller charges and deflecting drones. But we're still well-armed enough to take them on again."

"Let's hope we don't have to," Apnis chuckled, scanning her

boards. "We've four casualties, all minor. What's keeping Fleetskup? He should be showing his gratitude for his rescue by now."

As if in answer, Bellfish announced him on the comm and called up the visual. As Fleetskup's moon face materialised in the holo-grid, they could see the chaos of *Tallulah's* bridge. Medics were attending to injured crew, stations were flashing warning beacons and his first mate's position was empty.

"Captain Ahxenta," he pronounced. "Good to see you and thank you for your timely assistance. As you're no doubt aware, we've lost much of our forr'ad shielding, our long-range scanners are down and we've taken casualties. If you could escort us to Delta Iridium I'd be grateful. We could also use a few energy cells if you can spare them."

"I can't spare you energy cells as we've also taken damage."

"Thanks for asking," Tallica Apnis put in *sotto voce*.

"As I'm headed for Delta Iridium, I can provide escort, but you're on your own after that. Care to tell me what happened?"

"They were on the far side of Elf One and out of our scan range when we came off the bypass," Fleetskup told her. "I'd ordered us off for air top-up, our reserves were low."

"Hell, history repeats itself! Given what happened last time you did that, I'd have thought you'd have given it a miss this time!" Apnis interrupted acerbically.

"The war's over, Commander Apnis. It should have been safe. It's a place we've often used as the atmosphere is oxygen-rich…"

"And nobody's there to argue its abstraction," Ahxenta finished. "All very well, but didn't you come in with your guard up?"

"The war's over," Fleetskup repeated. "And naturally we had our shields up. But they must have been on the wait for something and we showed instead. They came at us like bats out of hell."

"Captain!" Greffy warned. "Energy surge from Elf One, a big one. Recommend we get out of here fast!"

"Show me!"

The science officer's readings had just reached the holo-grid when the voice of Gliss cut across the bridge. "It's from a surface station! We're just coming into its range… it's launched a missile spread and it's locked on to us – and the *Tallulah*!"

"All hands battlestations! Break and attack!" Ahxenta called out. "Fleetskup, protect your own and get the hell out of here!"

9: A CASE OF RETRIBUTION

Several searing beams of light cut the sky over Elf One as a spread of missiles lanced through the atmosphere and out into space, to split into two groups above the upper layers. The fast reactions of Dox at the helm had *Arianrhod* spearing up and beyond the deadly shower, but the missiles' guidance system had lock-on and five broke off to follow. *Arianrhod's* crew was however well-versed in battle situations and her meta-jurillium plated hull was packed with a mighty range of artillery, proximity and long-range sensory scanners and a shield grid of short-range deflectors. Her weapons arrays running hot, the ship held a tight course to allow tactical and weapons teams to lock onto and take out the projectiles headed her way. After a heart-stopping ten minutes, the voice of Whisper Earbleat cut the bridge.

"Last one out, Cap! That was close!"

"Getting more power build-up from the surface," Gliss reported. "That station's not out of firepower yet!"

"Then we take it out," the captain snarled. "Greffy, get all you can on that base and anything like it in the vicinity. Dox take us in close. Earbleat, get a bead on it and loose torpedoes, tight spread."

"On it... Forr'ad arrays set! Bring us in close, helm!"

"Down their throats, aye!" Dox called out.

"Take that, you frigging bastards!" the weapons officer bawled as she loosed a tight spread. "On target... on target... bullseye!"

"She didn't miss, then," Tallica Apnis noted, cocking an eye at the captain. "But are there any more hidden defensive posts down there? And where in hell's the *Tallulah*?"

"I don't read any other structures down there, Captain," Greffy affirmed. "But we haven't completed sufficient orbits to rule out the possibility that there may be more buried or shielded. No other large energy sources detected, however."

"And we don't have time to look. That's something else to report to Zillah and to the authorities on Delta Iridium: Elf One's on their doorstep. Gliss, have we any sign of the *Tallulah*?"

"He probably did as ordered and ran for it," Apnis remarked. "Do we know how many of those damn missiles he had on his tail?"

"We're reading her, Captain," Gliss responded. "She's coming into range. She was making for the bypass at speed I think, judging by her ion trail, but she's turned back. She's taken a bit of a beating, though. Looks like at least one missile got through."

"Get Fleetskup on the comm," Ahxenta ordered.

"Linking through now, Captain," Lieutenant Bellfish confirmed. "I have Lieutenant Jesse Inks for you."

"No Fleetskup?" the first mate asked in surprise.

The acting first mate wore a medical patch over one eyebrow and had one arm in a sling, but was seated coolly in the command chair.

"What's your status, Mr Inks?" the captain asked.

"Our hull stopped a missile but one of our empty cargo bays took most of it, ma'am. My gunnery crews took out the other two. We've lost more plating and three forr'ad shields are out, so on top of our previous damage we're in poor shape, but we'll be able to limp along to Delta Iridium. Our cargo's still intact, so that's one mercy."

"Your captain?" asked Ahxenta.

"Is in medbay; he took a fall and was knocked cold. We've several casualties, some serious. No fatalities, but our medbay's stretched," Inks frowned. "You've offered to escort us to Delta Iridium, Captain. Appreciate it, we'll not be able to navigate the bypass easily on our own. What was down on Elf One that caused all that?"

Ahxenta briefed him on their findings. Inks had been in medbay after the first assault but had discharged himself when the alert over the missile attack sounded. He had taken command when the captain went down and was now planning to make for their original stop to drop his cargo and attend to the hurts of his ship and her crew.

The captain reiterated her offer of help and the two ships made ready to leave. It had been decided to take the quickest route to Delta via the bypass, which would take several hours. With little option but to lend the *Tallulah* energy cells, Ahxenta sent a doctor and a nurse-tech over in the shuttle to assist in her medbay until she made port.

Delta Iridium Colony occupied the sixth planet out from its star. The orbital docking and repair station was a well-known and respected facility and the *Tallulah* quickly settled into one of the largest berths. Ahxenta had ordered *Arianrhod* into orbit, registered her presence with the planetary authority and sent a short report on the events at Elf One. The readings taken by Greffy after the missile attack had confirmed that they had originated from a well-armed base station that should not have existed on a world with no sentient presence and little of anything else. The technology certainly bore a similarity to the type of hostile weaponry responsible for the damage during the recent war that had disrupted every galactic zone.

The captain and her first mate had been invited to a briefing with reps of the planetary authority's defence division. She deemed it wise to go, leaving Earbleat, with Lindell as back-up, to supervise payload drop and the return of her crew from the *Tallulah*. Ahxenta's temper was a little ruffled to find that Captain Fleetskup had also been asked to the discussion. That his exec, the ubiquitous Tommy Buntle, was at his side was an added annoyance.

"No Lieutenant Inks?" she greeted her fellow captain with a touch of irony. "As he was the one that got you out of the missile attack with *Tallulah* still in one piece, I'd have thought he'd be here."

"He's busy. We have cargo drop-off as well as a host of repairs to both my ship and many of my crew."

"We noticed that he was injured," Tallica Apnis interposed. "Not serious, I hope, Murmur? You don't want to be left short-handed."

"He'll cope, Commander. So how come the Delta Iridium home fleet didn't spot the building of a base on Elf One and report it to the authorities?" he demanded of the two from the *Arianrhod*.

"It may have been in place for a long time, even before your incident out that way last time we met in this neck of the galaxy. You recall: when you sent out a distress after you met a couple of ships you believed to be hostile," Ahxenta reminded him icily.

"They were!" Buntle interrupted, scenting derogation in her tone.

"You weren't ready for them. And the attack *this* time caught you out as well. It seems that whoever is or was responsible for that base is as adept at keeping out of sight and detector range as the ships you faced. Is it any wonder nobody spotted anything?"

"Where are these reps that asked for this meeting? I don't have all day to wait," Fleetskup prevaricated, looking round.

Noises at the door announced the arrival of a body of individuals that seemed to represent the Delta Iridium Defence Division.

"They've come mob-handed," Apnis whispered to her captain. "How do we keep Fleetskup quiet with all those ears to bend?"

"Watch and learn," Ahxenta replied in the same low tone.

The captain of the *Arianrhod* was ruthless, sparing of words and sharp in tone. She had improved the report already submitted with material garnered by her tactical and science stations and edited by Azular, which she handed as a data shard to the leading rep. Her cut-off of Tommy Buntle at every step caused perplexity in her hosts and annoyance in Fleetskup, but she pacified the latter by supplying him with a copy of the data she had given the defence reps and reminded him of her assistance to aid the *Tallulah* out of trouble and into port. He had few defences.

"And that's how you do it," Ahxenta informed her first mate as the two were escorted off the premises after the meeting. "Fleetskup and Tallulah Tommy can chew their ears off for the rest of the day if they like – although he did say he didn't *have* all day."

"All day to wait – all day to talk is another matter."

"You're right. It's probably as well: Jesse Inks will get the ship in order more efficiently without Fleetskup on his back. He should have been promoted long ago as he's more than able. But let's go get our shuttle and see what Earbleat and Lindell have been up to."

Her officers having been efficient and with cargo drop completed to the approval of all parties, the *Arianrhod* held orbit only as long as it took to finalise local clearances. The captain had sanctioned minor repairs; replacement arms could wait until they had reached Freskat Six as she had contacts there that would give them a good deal.

The trip out to Delta's nearby colony of Iris Three was short and a rapid about-turn there had those of the crew who had missed shore leave at Merkat hoping it would be authorised on Freskat. It was a sunny and friendly place at the best of times and the settlement for which they were destined was still enjoying a late summer, Lieutenant Box informed his sidekick Dox in a voice just audible enough to be picked up by Commander Apnis in the command chair.

"You'll be lucky," was the latter's response. "And you'll be at the end of my rota for leave if you don't keep your eyes on your boards."

The captain had been in her office organising her schedule. She had put in a request for a private meeting with Admiral Zillah of the Freskat Navy and had sent on the data from Elf One, as that tale was already crossing the space lanes.

Arianrhod had been ordered on a direct line through zone Delta to zone Lambda and via Lamella Four to Freskat Six. That entailed a course through Non-Treaty Alliance space, but there had been no reports of unrest in any sectors on their route. As Apnis pointed out, that had also been the case for the area near Delta Iridium but their little altercation at Elf One had given the lie to that.

"I've already had Lindell and his team start to source armaments out Freskat way," was the dry response. "And I'm planning to stop off after Freskat at Aoria Six as some of our hull emplacements took a pounding and could do with upgrading."

"Best place," the first mate agreed. "Any chance of a market there for comms components, if we've any spare?"

"Lindell's looking into it. They have a few comms concerns."

"And then?"

"And then the Web, unless there's more business out this way."

"Another thing about our current route, Cinnabar…"

"Hostiles at Elf One again, a hidden station?" guessed the captain. "Handy for the Delta Iridium bypass, which leads direct into Lambda zone and NTA and ISP territory, *and* the Ginseng Nebula, where an alien fleet hid out in that energy field irregularity during the war and we were damn lucky they didn't take us out when we found it."

"*We* were lucky you knew the area so well that you could tell that something was off and wouldn't let Azular out in a shuttle for a close look. He gets far too curious about things. He's still assaulting your earholes about getting back to work full time, I take it?"

"As ever, now he's been loosed from medbay on the proviso that he takes it easy. He can fiddle with the data we got from Elf One and Kerrix and update the decoy; that should keep him tied to his desk."

"You wish. He'll be down in engineering haranguing Crizz."

"But we have another problem: there were no traces of zukivianite in those ships that attacked the *Tallulah*, so new-style raiders and not the hostiles we faced in the war. Maybe the usual scumbag raider packs are back in action and taking on anything they can find that was once used by hostiles. It *had* crossed my mind that there might be a hidden outpost or two that survived along our route, but we can't do business or live our lives on the risk of might be. And I won't run cloaked as there will be some out there know our heading. But we'll stick at alert status until we make Freskat."

"Then we tell Zillah and then it's her problem, hers and the ISP's and their mates. But if it *is* those ex-victims and ex-raiders branching out now that the Alliance has chased off the hostiles, I don't get how they can just find deserted hostile holes and take them over."

"I'll have words with Azular – I may as well give his brain a puzzle to mull over on the way to Freskat."

The captain spent half an hour with her science officer soon after and was not surprised that he came up with an idea that seemed to make sense. It was known that some victims of the hostiles that had begun the late war had been able to disable and remove enough of their implanted cyber-ware to free themselves. They included many ex-raiders, some of Friskianx origin and as Azular reminded Ahxenta, the commander of the rear vessel heading to Skyrtek had told them that their kind had been drawn to each other by a subtle organic empathy that their alterations had caused in them and had collectively sought sanctuary away from the usual space lanes. Their hideaway in sector sixteen of zone Beta had remained undetected, and was so still, as far as Azular was aware. It was possible that later victims knew of other hidden outposts. Their unwelcome associate Bick Micklemouse was also able to recognise not only the subtle signals given out by those adjusted by the hostiles, but agents of the hostiles and even the beings themselves, *and* he had been sensitive to the energy lifeforms of Kelfennig. It was also not beyond the bounds of possibility that such elusive organic signals were inherent in the hostile installations themselves and could be detected at distance by some means, but that was far less likely in the science officer's estimation.

"Either way we can't prove it, so I won't be tickling Zillah's ears with speculations. Nor will I be quizzing that Friskianx commander we met in the Web if ever I see him again – that was a coincidence I didn't need and I'm still antsy about it."

"Given Ms Kerrix' data, it *is* concerning," admitted Azular.

"You've gone over all we got from her, so do you think most of it is straight up and some of it isn't fabricated?"

"I'm more or less convinced, yes. For why would she go to such lengths for no reason? She could not have predicted that she would meet up with us as she did. But you still have doubts, Captain?"

"She doesn't add up. I'd like to know exactly what she is that she was able to accomplish so much and get away with it."

"The *Gadfly* was not interfered with, Captain, we're sure of it."

"So I heard. Crizz told me she had to chase you out of the *Gadfly's* bay because you were disturbing her team down there."

"I was interested," the science officer smiled.

"I know: *that's* what gets you into trouble. I'll see you later. Take it easy or I'll move your office to the brig, with no access elsewhere."

The *Arianrhod* made Freskat Six with no further difficulty and once in orbit the captain made a couple of links and then shuttled down to meet her usual contact to discuss pick-up of the thin diamond wafers that were vital components in comm linkages. Her supercargo she left to arrange their disposal to the Freskat defence department's main comms company. Zillah, admiral-in-chief of the Freskat home fleet and an old acquaintance, had been told of their trade mission and of the need for an urgent meeting.

Her business concluded, Ahxenta met Apnis and Azular for the trip to the admiral's office. Zillah had been updated on the action at Elf One and was seriously concerned, for although relatively far from her own neck of the woods, the world was firmly within ISP territory and close to the major population centre of Delta Iridium. That it had hosted a covert station was an added anxiety. An ISP destroyer from the dockyard of that body's new main HQ at Alto Finglas in zone Beta had been despatched to investigate.

The issue of the revival of one of the late hostile bases as a hub of shipbuilding and as a centre from which to launch forays into other territories was also causing Zillah unease. She was aware of a loose league of ex-raiders and ex-victims, but that they were already primed for action and had possibly launched at least one ship claiming to be a legitimate trader surprised her. Ahxenta handed on the shard of data derived by Azular. The admiral knew Ahxenta well enough not to demand her sources, particularly of the visual material, but as she scanned part of the record she saw sufficient to alarm her.

They parted with mutual goodwill and promises that Zillah would notify Ahxenta of anything that came to her notice from around the Enigma Nebula. The ISP had a small sector within zone Kappa that hosted the military station of Kellybar One as well as territory in the far reaches of zone Zeta, beyond which another once-hostile base was known to exist, close by the Starglass Nebula.

"So we check on how Lindell's getting on and then we head out to Aoria for our emplacement upgrades?" Tallica Apnis asked as the three officers from *Arianrhod* made their way to their shuttle.

"We do. We've nothing else to keep us here, apart from local links I have to make. Azular, what's your take on the admiral's reaction to our news of that raider base by the Enigma?" Ahxenta enquired.

"You've worried her, Captain, though I *did* get the impression that she wasn't overly shocked, as if she suspected that we'd not heard the last of the hostiles or their impacts. But if the ISP *is* exploring beyond zone Mu's boundary, it will have to know. The anomaly that was Ms Kerrix' entry into that part of space was in a system close to the Enigma and close to the base to which she was then taken."

"Hmm… a massive piece of defunct technology that looked like a bypass node, she said, and it came out in a planetary system that these ex-raiders knew, if they'd chased a hostile that far."

"I can't imagine the ISP or its allies are pushing exploration right now," Apnis stated. "For one, they lost a lot of ships in the war, *and* the main ISP shipyard at Skyrtek and everything in it, including ISP's

HQ. Everybody's probably hard pushed just to keep what they have afloat and get their fleets back up to workable levels."

"But they have to remain mindful of those hostile bases and they *are* in uncharted space, Commander," Azular reminded her. "If they are nuclei of aggressive activity, they'll have to be curtailed."

"I wish them the joy of that," Apnis returned as they reached their craft. "You taking her up, Cap, or would you like me to pilot her?"

"I'll take the helm. You check with Lindell and see what's what."

On the way back to their vessel, Apnis learnt that all the comms linkage wafers available from Ahxenta's contact would be needed by Greskitty Comms to fulfil their military orders and the supercargo had already agreed a price and a delivery schedule.

"Short stop-off here, then," she commented, closing the link. "So we won't have time to authorise shore leave. Maybe on Aoria, Cap?"

"I'll consider it. The crew will have plenty to do aboard."

The turnaround on Freskat Six took less than a planetary day and *Arianrhod* was soon set for Aoria Six, upgrades to their titanium-alloy based hull weapons emplacements spoken for. The ship made good time, their only interlude a courtesy call from one of their sister ships as they passed the sparsely-settled Nyx en route to their destination.

"Nat Hotshot calling in at home, then," Tallica Apnis said with a satirical smile as the *Nyx Warrior* closed comms after the exchange. "And not giving anything away about his missing cargo pod, meaning it hasn't been found yet, so he hasn't gotten to the bottom of it."

The Aorian system was close to zone Lambda outer edge and thus uncharted space, but the authorities there had no news of incursions by unknowns from outside. The small though distant Curtain Nebula was a source of the usual tales of dead planets that had once had life and strange signals, but nothing new had arisen. *Arianrhod* docked at an orbiting port close to the base of the company that would carry out her upgrades. Ahxenta, knowing the reps of Elytra Engineering, expected no problems. Such being the case, she sanctioned limited shore leave for as many of the crew as could be spared from the internal modifications needed to integrate the improved emplacement ops systems.

Shiny as a new pin, *Arianrhod* began to power up in preparation for releasing docking traces and heading out. Lindell had been busy and had secured a deal from Elytra to deliver a batch of upgrade systems to the ISP's construction dock at Alto Finglas. From there it was a short hop to Merkat. A smaller contract for the yard was in process, and having checked the status of the *PSS Emerald*, the ex-passenger liner owned by Ahxenta and captained by Melly Goodsocks, Lindell had captured that deal and organised the *Emerald* as pick up.

"Earbleat's chirping like a songbird," Apnis noted as the captain ordered their route to the bypass. "She had fun on shore leave?"

"Huh! She didn't take shore leave. She spent her time scouring the orbital premises of Elytra, chatting up the techs and reps for bits she could scavenge or snap up for what she called next to nothing."

"*Loki VI*," the commander responded briefly.

"What else. And her idea of next to nothing isn't. Lindell's sent me a formal complaint about the bill," Ahxenta grumbled.

"Take it out of her next bonus," advised Apnis. "Though I doubt that'll stop her. It might halt her endless carping about outfitting the damn thing, which would be an advantage."

"I should be so lucky. She's been at Azular to see what he's picked up from the data we got from Kerrix. She wants to develop some sort of cloaking or camouflage system for it, and bigger guns."

"Hell, at that rate she'll turn it into a mini *Arianrhod*!"

"Not on my watch she won't," Ahxenta retorted grimly. "Steady as she goes, Ms Dox. Time to bypass entry?"

"Hour and a half, ma'am."

The hours sped by, the only interlude coming after a model cargo drop at Alto Finglas. There was a call on the Ultraviolet III for the captain from Captain Jikelleli of the *PSS Green Comet*, to be taken in private. Ahxenta's face was serious on her return to the bridge.

"What's happened, Cap?" Apnis enquired.

"*Comet* saw some action just off the beacon at Kifferbuck. She handled it and Sarie's tactical team figured it was a small interceptor-type ship close to the new raider designs that we seem to be seeing more often – she's sent through the data but it's sparse."

"Kifferbuck? That's a place *we* know only too well."

"And close enough to Mellifly – the *Comet* had a drop-off there of parts she'd picked up at Merkat. But that wasn't the main reason for the link. There's a lot of activity near Mellifly, over its northern polar region. Scavengers picking up what's left of that hostile shipbuilding yard it seems. Planetary security hasn't enough clout to deal with it – or doesn't want to. Some contact in the Port Authority told Sarie that rumour says that several parties that lost out over the war are starting back in business and our name's being bandied about with a hint that we and our associates are in for a rough time if we get in the way."

"Posturing," the first mate suggested.

Ahxenta shook her head. "Two of the *Comet's* crew were jumped in the ground HQ of the firm that had ordered the gear from Merkat. They weren't robbed, just told it was a taste of the payback for what *Arianrhod* did at Mellifly. Sarie's alerted the rest of the fleet but it looks like our associates are now targets. Though Sarie also said that as far as she knew, there had been no more big bangs in the Web."

"Hell! But what do these bozos gain, apart from satisfaction? They must know we'll take them apart if we catch them?"

"Given what's happened thus far, they're dangerous, well-armed and well-organised and there are plenty of them. We watch our backs until we work out what in hell their agenda is. So no shore leave at Merkat until we've made sure it's safe."

"Crew will thank you for that," was the tart rejoinder.

Arianrhod made port well into the usual business day to the news that a contract Lindell had set up had been rescinded for no good reason. Ahxenta called for an immediate meet with the company reps and she, her supercargo and her security escort shuttled over. Azular had decided to accompany his colleagues and was quick to desert them outside their shuttle bay: he had business in the *Half Moon*.

"You clean up well," Kerrix informed the Berzic science officer as she placed the two drinks he had ordered firmly down on his chosen table, where he sat alone.

He stood. "I don't think we were formally introduced, Ms Kerrix. I'm Dr Azular, senior science officer, *PSS Arianrhod*," he grinned, his dark eyes crinkling up as he scanned her face for signs of a reaction.

He found no irritation but he sensed guarded curiosity and a slight suspicion, possibly that he was leading her on for his own purposes. So she didn't quite trust him, he inferred, despite all the stories about the *Arianrhod* and her crew that she must have heard over her stay in the Web. He turned on his courteous charm, inviting her to sit. She treated that gallantry with a sardonically raised eyebrow, but nodded.

"I figured your ship from the badge," she told him as she levered herself into a chair. "And you I *have* met before, obviously."

"So you don't forget a face?" he asked as he sat down again.

"I try to, some of the time. Yours I didn't – though it *was* in a bit of a mess last time I saw it."

He nodded in agreement. "I'm better now," he told her.

"Good. Expecting company?" she asked, indicating the extra mug. "That's for you."

The response to that was a half-laugh, an intense glance and the information that she did not drink on duty.

"Surely you can make an exception? The place isn't busy."

"You want a word," Kerrix deduced. "About what?"

"I merely wanted to thank you personally for your assistance," he said smoothly. "And to explain why I left precipitately afterwards."

She leant back in the chair, folded her arms and shook her head. "No you don't. Try switching off the fake charisma and switching on the honesty. You'll find it'll get you further."

He smiled at that. "You have a very suspicious mind, Ms Kerrix."

"Correct. And it's kept me alive thus far. What *do* you want?"

"A closer look at your shuttle."

"Your captain's seen it – and taken very accurate scans of it."

"Yes; I have the data and it intrigued me. I'd like to know more. And despite your scepticism, I *do* want to thank you for saving my skin and to make clear why I made off so quickly."

At her invitation, he explained his actions at the time. She seemed to understand and accept his justification but he had no prospect of finding out more about her shuttle, for Ally hove to and demanded her return to duty, as more customers had appeared.

"You'll consider my request, Ms Kerrix?" the science officer asked quietly as she rose.

"I'll consider it," she murmured as she sailed off to the bar.

It was four days before Azular was able to return to the *Half Moon*. He was with the captain; they had been holed up in marketing to discuss the deal that had been dropped and it had left a sour taste in both their mouths. The place was relatively quiet, as the lunchtime crowd had gone and the afternoon regulars had not yet appeared. Merry and two others were busy around the tables. Ally's young aide Evrett was behind the bar. The boss was busy rearranging shifts, the two officers of the *Arianrhod* were told upon enquiry.

"No Ms Kerrix?" the science officer asked nonchalantly.

Evrett raised his eyes skyward. "She's sick, seemingly. That's why Ally's rearranging staff rotas and he's pretty annoyed about it, as she's missed a few days. Merry knows what's up but she won't say. Took my head off when I asked nicely. What can I get you?"

The two ordered ales and scanned the place. Merry spotted them but turned her back to carry on clearing tables. They were interrupted by Ally, who had appeared from beyond the bar complaining about keeping a place manned when your workers failed to appear and you had no idea of why they were off or when they would be back. The captain disclosed that she had hoped for a quiet word with the elusive Ms Kerrix and was told shortly that she was the main reason for the problem. She had gone to ground and could not be contacted.

"Merry knows something," he hinted darkly. "They seem to have hit it off and I know she took some leftovers away for her the other day. Figure she maybe got into another fight and is nursing her hurts, but I don't know. Hey, Merry! Over here!"

The girl looked highly reluctant to approach. Her usual smile was strained as she slowly set down her tray on the counter rather than facing the three. Ally made it plain that Captain Ahxenta was there to have a word with Xanna Kerrix and insisted that his assistant reveal what she knew. Merry swallowed and refused point blank. She had given her word, and her word she would keep.

"You'll tell the captain what's going on or you won't have a job to come in to," Ally threatened.

The pause could be cut with a knife as Merry looked him in the face, shocked, her lips apart. She looked close to tears.

"I didn't think blackmail was your style, Ally, but have it your way," she said hoarsely as she undid her apron and cast a reproachful glance at the two officers. "I don't have a job to come in to."

She flung the apron in his face, stalked to the end of the counter and turned in, passing him on her way to the staff room. She looked straight ahead, ice-cold in hurt and anger.

As Ally gaped, open-mouthed, Ahxenta advised that he follow her quickly, apologise and reinstate her. She was the best assistant he had ever had and he knew it. He could not afford to lose her.

Azular was puzzled. "Merry's *frightened*, Captain," he said in a low voice. "She was not happy to see us. I suggest we do *not* probe, but find out what's happened to Ms Kerrix. You know her quarters?"

"Yes; it's a dive on green twelve close to Azure Belle's Nightclub and near the outer twelve shuttle berths. Section one, one, four, if I remember aright and it's a blue door. I'll recognise it. Drink up and let's head off. I'll settle the tab later."

The two left quickly, nodding to Evrett in passing. The trip down several levels to green twelve was uneventful, the few people passing giving them nary a look. The dingy corridor was as Ahxenta recalled, poorly-lit, lined with grey doors and empty of foot traffic. Apartment thirty one, its blue door as dull as the others, was blank and closed. Azular hauled out his scanner to probe the area and the entry.

"The lock's not particularly secure," he noted. "There's some sort of encoding but it can be breached."

"You can pick it, you mean," said Ahxenta. "Anyone at home?"

"One lifeform registering, but no movement."

The captain buzzed the entry panel and they waited. There was no response and she buzzed again.

"Still no movement, Captain."

"Then let's get in before somebody turns up," Ahxenta said as she drew out her phase rifle and released its catch.

The place was dim but not dark. The captain called out a greeting and then called for more light. As the shadows fled the two could see that the place was obviously lived in, with loose clothing on the sofa, a rumpled bed and a light winking on the comms console at the wall. Ahxenta called again as her science officer ran a perimeter scan.

"In there, Captain," he said, indicating the hygiene cubicle, where a brighter glow could be seen through the partly-closed screen.

Rifle raised, Ahxenta strode across and slid the panel back. She uttered a curse and passed her gun back to Azular with the order to hold onto it. The space was compact and after rapid visual appraisal the captain snatched up a towel and knelt down. Kerrix was crouched in a foetal position at the edge of the shower space, eyes closed. She was damp and cold. She was also a mass of welts and bruises, a large dressing was moulded across her upper back and shoulders and one leg was strapped. The captain draped the cloth over her, calling her name. A slight, muted groan indicated that she was conscious.

"This place is sodden. Is there a robe or towel out there, Azular?"

"Here, Captain. What's happened?"

"Hell knows, but she's been badly kicked about and cut up, a couple of days ago by the look of it. Why she's been left like this…" Ahxenta said grimly as she wrapped the second towel around the woman and helped her up. "Clear that sofa, I'll sit her there."

With an effort, the two assisted Kerrix to the dingy seating and set her down. Ahxenta sat alongside, readjusting the towels for decency, and was rewarded by a whimper and a few disjointed words.

"Get more heat in here, Azular, she's chilled. Says she slipped but she's got med-patches on both arms: sedatives I guess, which is why she's so out of it. She couldn't have got those third-rate dressings on without help either, so someone damn well knows about this."

"Merry," he surmised as he returned to sit down at the woman's other side. "But I don't understand, Captain. Why didn't she call in medical aid and get her to medbay?"

"Last time she was in medbay she was attacked by a maniac with a med-extractor, so I'm not surprised she wouldn't go back."

"Captain!" the science officer's voice was low but it cut the air so sharply that Kerrix turned her head in his direction at the sound, an inarticulate question on her lips as her eyes tried to focus on his face.

The Berzic looked intently at her, a flicker of curiosity lighting his eyes, before exchanging an anxious glance with the captain. Ahxenta slid one towel down to inspect the place at the woman's left shoulder. The site where her language analyser-translator was implanted still showed the marks of the last attempt on it, but there was no evidence of recent overt violence.

"So that wasn't the motive," Ahxenta inferred with a sigh. "And they appear to have left most of her face alone. Her other implants seem to be still intact as well. But why didn't Merry just tell us about this? There's something odd going on here."

"Very odd," Azular agreed as his keen eyes raked her visible hurts and his face creased in pity and disgust. "Captain, why would anyone do such a thing? Surely…" His voice trailed off as again Kerrix stared at him, eyes unfocussed, as if trying to fathom his meaning.

"What?" she asked faintly.

His gaze fixed on her eyes as he tried to read her, a subtle intuition within him increasing to conviction. "Why would anyone do such a thing?" he repeated, looking directly at her.

"What?"

"Captain? Is there anything you can tell us," he asked softly but distinctly.

A confused frown creased her brow as Kerrix repeated her muted query. Ahxenta looked on shrewdly, realising that Azular was playing some kind of game.

"Captain? Ma'am?" the Berzic officer continued.

"What? What is it? What do you…" her voice was low, hoarse and hesitant but the words were clear and Ahxenta's eyes widened as she looked at her science officer.

Azular repeated the salutation, his eyes crinkling in something akin to satisfaction as he articulated, "Captain Kerrix?"

"What in blazes are you playing at?" Ahxenta demanded in a quiet tone as once more the woman responded with a slurred question.

"I noted her response when I used your title," he said very softly. "I sensed a degree of familiarity…"

It was perhaps his rising air of gratification at a point scored, allied to the declining effects of sedation, that shook Kerrix into realisation. She took a deep breath, reviving a little, a puzzled look on her face.

"What is it?" she repeated more firmly, her eyes blinking rapidly.

"Captain Kerrix," Azular said calmly but firmly.

There was a pause as she eyed him and took in the implications of his half-smile and his quick glance at Ahxenta. She shook her head to clear it and freeing her arms from the constricting towelling, drew a corner of the fabric across her eyes and down her cheeks. She gazed at him still as emotions chased each other across her face, her breath coming in short gasps. Her eyes slid down to the badge he wore and then back to his face. He looked complacent as his eyes quizzed hers, one eyebrow raised interrogatively. She shook her head again slowly, jaw dropping.

"You utter bastard!" she hissed in a low, harsh whisper.

That wiped the smile from his face but he continued his scrutiny, trying to gauge her emotional reactions. He felt her anger rising and was prepared for it but he was not prepared for the hand that shot out to deliver a resounding slap across his cheek. The exertion cost a searing spasm of pain and she huddled into herself, softly swearing to cover her weakness. "Get the hell out!" she whispered. "Get out, both of you!"

"I probably deserved that," Azular admitted contritely, rubbing his afflicted jaw.

"I agree. I'd have given you more than that if you'd tried it on me," Ahxenta informed him crisply. "But now we'll have to…"

She was interrupted by an insistent buzz at the entry and a voice that came over quietly but clearly. "Xanna? It's me, can I come in?"

The request was repeated more urgently. "Are you okay? I've brought your stuff," the voice added in an urgent whisper.

A muttered swearing was followed by the sound of the lock being activated. Whoever it was had a key. Azular rose, rifle in hand, to block the entry. The voice was certainly not that of Merry.

The armed woman who stood on the threshold was almost as tall as Azular, and she swiftly raised her handgun in reply to the phase rifle that the science officer had trained on her. He did not recognise her, but her garb was out of step with her hard eyes and steely expression. She was dressed in a fusion of tightly-wrapped tinted gauzes over a short, dark under-dress, her face was heavily made up and she wore cheap jewellery. Her free hand clasped a large case.

"Who are you and what are you doing in here?" she demanded. "Where's Xanna? What's going on?"

"We're friends of Ms Kerrix," he replied briefly, standing back to let her see within, trying to gauge her.

She was clearly unafraid of him and her cold gaze defied his as she swiftly scanned what she could see of the interior. She stepped in, not waiting invitation, her gun still ready. She let go her case, slapping the door closure behind her without turning. His badge arrested her.

"*Arianrhod?*" she said shortly. "I hope the hell no-one saw you come in. With friends like you, she's no need of enemies."

Retrieving her case, she pushed past him to sit by Kerrix, treating the captain to an intense stare. "What happened? Why are *you* here?"

Ahxenta was mildly irritated by her tone but gave a rapid rundown of events from the time she and Azular left the *Half Moon*. She then enquired the identity of the visitor.

"Vettarista, Vetta for short. I'm a friend of Xanna, I live next door and I work at Azure Belle's. Why didn't you wait 'til I turned up, you fool?" she asked her friend softly. "And you haven't told me who *you* are," she said to the captain as she slid the towel off Kerrix' shoulder to examine a med-patch. "Are either of you medics?"

On receiving a negative and the names and ranks of the two, she cast an irate glance at Azular. "You can put that scanner down," she called over. "I'm Berzic, same as you."

"Hardly," Ahxenta stated. "And why are *you* here? It's not a social call: you know what happened. When, where, why and who?"

Vetta ignored her, opened her case and took out various articles. Deftly she stripped the med-patch off the woman's right arm, noting it was out as she slid it into a steri-bag and undid a fresh patch. That in place, she looked round, her eyes lighting on a two-piece sleep suit.

"Throw that in the thermo-clean for twenty seconds," she ordered Azular. "*If* you please," she added, noting Ahxenta's annoyed glance.

Kerrix had meanwhile made no sound other than harsh breathing but her eyes were sharp as she endured Vetta's dabbing of her hurts with a medicated pad until Azular handed over the warmed clothing.

"Thank you; perhaps you'd face the wall until I get her dressed?"

The science officer complied until the process was complete. The Berzic woman had applied a replacement med-patch to her friend's other arm and was examining the strapped leg with a med-scanner.

"That'll do, but I *will* have to change this," she said with a grimace of concern as she drew the scanner across Kerrix' back and read the result. "The new meds should kick in and take the edge off."

She was answered by a shake of the head and a muttered protest.

"Come on. Let's get you sat down where I can see what's to do," Vetta encouraged, picking up her bits and pieces as she stood.

She made for the kitchen space, pulled out a chair, set her case flat on the counter, dug out more items and realigned an upper task light. The two officers traded glances at what looked to be a regular drill. Means in place, the Berzic woman returned to the sofa where Kerrix sat quiescent, her head bent and her eyes fixed on her own knees.

"Come on, Xanna, let's get this done," Vetta urged as she assisted her friend to her feet and gently propelled her to the kitchen area.

Ahxenta had also risen, and watched as Kerrix was set astride the chair, her arms folded across its back and her head bent over them, her shirt slipped well down to expose the taped dressing. The part-healed stripes and bruised, discoloured patches that marred her back were an indication of assault with more than one implement.

"Who did that to her?" the captain demanded once more.

"If you're staying, Captain, you could assist," was the gruff reply. "Pull up the other chair; it would help if you held the waste bag open. Please keep back," she added pointedly to Azular.

He frowned but complied as the captain turned the second chair and sat, accepting the bag. Kerrix, now objecting mildly, was ordered to grip tightly to the back of her chair.

"I'll be quick. I'll *have* to strip this off, it's badly soiled," she was told. "The captain isn't squeamish, I'm sure."

"I won't see anything I haven't seen before," Ahxenta stated dryly.

"I wouldn't bet on that," was the acid reply as Vetta pinned her friend's hair back, pulled on medi-gloves and began the delicate task of detaching the adhesive edges of the padded dressing.

Once loosed, she found the pad stuck and swore softly as she dug out a syringe to force liquid into it. Kerrix stifled oaths as her Berzic friend finally stripped the pad back and inspected its putrid staining. With a worried frown, she folded the dressing and dropped it in the waste bag. Her gloves followed and she hauled on a new pair.

"Who the hell did that to her?" Ahxenta spat in fury, realising that she would have lost the bet as she stared at the crusted red and angry marks that bit bone-deep across Kerrix' upper back.

"You think they'd still be standing if I knew?" was the hot retort as Vetta drew out a fresh pad. "*You* may know better than I do."

"She needs skilled medical care, Captain," Azular said, shaken.

"We do the best with what we've got," the Berzic woman snapped viciously as she continued her task. "And that's not much. This isn't a fancy starship, it's the bowels of the back of beyond. Down here we look after our own. Nobody else will; nobody else gives a damn."

"I want to know all you *do* know about this," the captain informed her coldly and firmly. "Now."

The details Vetta ran through as she worked. She had got in from work in the early hours around three days before to find her friend huddled at her door, beaten and bloody, her clothing in rags, clearly having been viciously assaulted. Vetta had no idea how she had made it there, but roused a paramedic friend and they did what they could. All they could find out was that the woman had been jumped near the green twelve shuttle bays during a run after her shift in the *Half Moon*. There had been three, she had been dragged into a small bay and the injuries were the result. She had apparently been grilled but refused to say more and had rejected all efforts to get her to medbay.

"The bastards said they didn't like the friends she was keeping," the woman said as she fastened Kerrix' shirt.

"You give a hand here, Azular; I have a link to make," Ahxenta told her science officer as she rose and made for the door.

"What?" Vetta demanded of the man once she had roused her friend and with his assistance helped her into bed.

Azular studied the gaudily-dressed woman curiously, trying to read her. She was blocking him, leading him to suspect that her intuitive talent was akin to his and very strong even for his own people.

"You're Berzic and very smart. A seedy nightclub in Merkat's Web isn't your natural habitat. Who and what are you?"

"Nobody's what they seem to be; not me, not her, certainly not you. I suggest you mind your own damn business and think what's to be done here. Though I suspect your captain has her own ideas."

Ahxenta had. "My chief medic's on her way," she explained on her return. "I'll meet her when she gets in. I'm taking Ms Kerrix back to the *Arianrhod*. She'll be given the care she needs and she'll be a helluva lot safer up there than down here."

Vetta nodded as if expecting the move. "Please lock up before you leave. I'll let Merry Jetty at the *Half Moon* know. She usually comes by later with supplies. And I'd better deal with *that* before I go."

That was the flashing light at the comm.

"What are you at?" the captain asked as Vetta sat, ran her fingers over the console and removed a credit slip from a drawer.

"Paying her rent; that's what the notice is about. It's not paid, the landlord's agents will be in here to clear out everything, including personal stuff. You get no leeway around here for overdue bills."

Collecting her gear and the waste, Vetta asked the captain to keep her informed, passed on her link and promised to hand on anything she found out. She nodded briefly and was gone.

"What's her game and her link to Kerrix?" Ahxenta questioned.

Azular related what he had learnt. "I recall you saying that Merry told you that Ms Kerrix recognised one of my attackers as a dock-rat who'd beaten up her friend Vetta. I assume that was the same Vetta."

"She likes a fight, then," the captain grimaced, looking over at the woman. "But I wish I knew what it's all about. They didn't like the friends she was keeping? It seems that anyone linked to us is a target and if that's the kind of damage they're liable for… But they didn't target her implants, so it's us and not what *she* is."

"Or they're under orders and haven't been given the full story."

"Possibly. Scour this place for data shards, keys, personal stuff – we'd better take it with us if others can get in. And bring her boots: they hide one or two surprises. I hope her ship's all right, though you may have lost any chance you had of getting a closer look at it."

Azular looked over and sighed. "I realise now that I *did* go too far, but I was intrigued. But Captain, she was attacked after I spoke with her in the *Half Moon*. If *that* was what provoked the assault…"

"Don't go blaming yourself for this. She was hit in medbay not long after Tallica and I had a chat with her. But here's the call from the doc: she made good time. You finish here and I'll be back. We'll go up with *her* and Lieutenant Reef can pilot our shuttle back."

The woman was soon locked into the med trolley. The captain had taken the precaution of ordering her people to wear plain scrubs and not a uniform. In the event, their trip to the bay was unseen. With Azular scanning every micron of the route, it was with relief that the party made their shuttle. Ahxenta took the pilot's seat and once back aboard, she left final checks to her engineers and attended the gurney to medbay to brief her chief medical officer and to schedule a senior staff briefing after Kerrix had been assessed and treated.

Apnis was sufficiently curious about events portside that she made her way to Azular's lair to find out what had happened. That talk led her to medbay, where she caught the captain on her way out.

"What gives, Cinnabar?" she began in a low tone. "I recall hearing a rumour that you swore never to allow Kerrix aboard *Arianrhod* but here she is. And Azular's being tight-lipped about what went down. In fact I'd go as far as to say he's upset, which is not like him at all."

"Guilty conscience," Ahxenta said shortly. "I'll tell you later. For now, contact Kit Biernop on the QT and arrange a meet with him for after our briefing. See if he can shed any light on what's been going on. You'll go down in mufti and you'll have two guards at your back. Have we heard any more on Lokterix or the breakout from security?"

"No, Merkat security's being cagey. But Lindell *has* secured a new contract which will take us away from here. Redship Industrial hasn't been bullied into ducking deals with us and it's a good one. Stuff that Djassi of the *Equinox* brought in for processing that should be ready in a couple of days – *Equinox* can't hang around that long."

"Good; let Lindell handle it. I'm for the bridge as I've comms to make. If the *Equinox* is in I'll start there. Any more of the fleet in?"

"*Tallulah's* just berthed and *Quarkstorm's* due in, but that's it. But I don't like the sound of this – you're edgy and that's not like you."

Ahxenta did not disagree and two hours later, after a talk with her chief medic, she called the briefing. There was little PSS news but she had heard from Admiral Zillah that one of her ships on stop-off at the ISP's Kellybar One station had heard of debris trails beyond the edge of the triple point where zones Zeta, Kappa and Mu met and an unverified report of sightings of a huge ship near Wester 287 that did not engage and that was on a heading for uncharted space.

Azular's ears pricked at that. "Where there's strong evidence for an ex-hostile base and where Ms Kerrix was intercepted and taken – close to that hyperspace node she recorded as Starfall Exit."

"That struck me, but that's all I have on it. As for what happened after we left marketing…"

She outlined the events earlier, after she and Azular had breached Kerrix' billet, omitting the exchange between Azular and their guest.

"That doesn't explain why you believe the attack was linked to us, Cap, or why you brought her aboard, despite what that Vetta said," Apnis noted shrewdly. "You think the ante's been upped big time?"

"You have the holo of Ms Kerrix' injuries, Doctor?" the captain asked, to the puzzlement of most of her senior officers.

Flintlock grimly set up and activated her info-pad. "Not the full extent naturally: there *is* such a thing as patient privacy."

"Not where my ship is concerned," Ahxenta informed her flatly.

The bruising and slashes caused appalled intakes of breath, but as the holo homed in on the area of scored flesh across the woman's upper back and shoulders, one or two expletives hit the air.

"Bloody hell, that's quite a tattoo!" Earbleat barked. "They even spelled our name right!"

"That's seriously not funny, Whisper," Azular flared at her.

"Belay!" Ahxenta growled at the two. "As far as the doc can work out, *that* was carved using an etching tool with a heating element."

"And I bet it damn well hurt," Cottontail hissed as she took in the word *Arianrhod* crudely incised, with scoring that may have meant to convey more. "Bunch of bastards. But why carve her up like that?"

"To send us and anyone close to us a message. As far as Vettarista is aware there was a grilling, but she didn't know the topic: possibly her dealings with us. They didn't like the friends she was keeping. It smacks of this payback for *Arianrhod's* actions at Mellifly that Jikelleli told us of. So we're being watched if they pick up on who we speak to, but no word of *this* to the crew. Bellfish, keep tabs on security, business and military nets for any mention of us. Goldwash, trips off ship will need security back-up. Commander Apnis has a meet soon, so start there. Gliss, keep our tactical eyes and ears online at all times, maximum scan. Dismissed."

"A word if you please, Captain, Doctor," Azular requested as the others, visibly concerned, filed out of the briefing room.

"You're not happy I showed them that," Ahxenta surmised.

"Was it necessary?" the senior science officer questioned.

"I think so. Telling's one thing, seeing's another. What else? That's not all that's biting you."

"I'd like a word with Ms Kerrix," was the quiet response.

"I'm sure you would," Ahxenta said as Flintlock declared curtly that no-one would be having a word until she gave the green light.

"And if you're thinking of pestering her about taking her shuttle apart bolt by bolt, you can think again," the doctor told him. "I've already told the Cap that she can't quiz her on what went down for at least twelve hours. Enough is enough."

"You're sounding over-precious about Kerrix," Ahxenta noted.

"She saved my butt and Azular's from serious kicking, Cinnabar."

"Bet she's regretting it now," was the laconic retort. "And what do *you* want to talk to Ms Kerrix about, Azular?"

He regarded her intently. "I think you're very well aware of what I want to speak to her about, Captain."

"I'll be having words with her about *that*," Ahxenta warned.

"Captain, I would respectfully…"

"No. You've caused enough trouble and if she's savvy about that shady Berzic friend of hers, she'll have figured *you* out."

"Will you two start making sense? What didn't you tell us at the briefing?" Flintlock demanded, looking from one to the other.

Ahxenta was spared a reply by a call from a puzzled Lynxi Bellfish to apprise her of an urgent link from a Ms Vettarista, who seemed to be calling from a protected site somewhere in the Web's outer belts.

"I'll take it in my office," was the terse response.

"And I want words with you in *my* office," Azular was told by the chief medic as their commanding officer set off at speed.

"What's happened, Captain?" the senior science officer enquired in concern, standing as Ahxenta stepped into his office a little later.

"The three that hit Kerrix are in custody, a tad worse for wear."

"Please sit, ma'am. Ms Vettarista?"

Ahxenta nodded. "I'd like to know who and what *she* is. The perps were worked over by persons unknown before their arrest. Two are repair shed dock-rats, the other's security."

"But that means that Ms Kerrix will be required to give evidence. She won't, I suspect."

"They've been got on other charges and two more were caught: a covert op to dig out crooks responsible for breaches in security has been ongoing, I was told. The three that got Kerrix *will* be charged with assault. Vetta said that visual data found on one of them could be used to ID all three even if the victim doesn't come forward."

"Visual data?" repeated Azular. "But that would suggest that the incident was recorded."

"Part of it was, for the sadistic pleasure of several pairs of eyes later – a little lucrative side-line of two of the bastards."

"That's obscene!" Azular exploded, outraged.

"I strongly suspect that Vettarista's involved in this undercover op as part of a bigger set-up, but she's giving nothing away. If she has anything like *your* talents, she'd make a formidable agent. That doesn't explain why we're part of the equation but she hinted that our actions during the war are triggering reprisals and whoever's behind it and other incidents out there are using known petty criminals as pawns."

"Which is in keeping with what the hostiles did on a much larger scale; they often preyed on raiders and others of a similar bent, using their victims' existing propensities to further their own ends."

"Good point and I don't like where it's going. Tallica will be back soon but I'll leave the briefing on her mission until tomorrow as it's late. Lindell is finalising our contract with Redship so we'll be set to load cargo in another day or two. And then we're for Stinward. The load's ISP, which is why using *Arianrhod* doesn't worry Redship. We may be able to dig up a few things in the ISP office there. I take it the doc wanted to bend your ears about Kerrix? You told her?"

"Yes I did and she was annoyed," he admitted.

"I'll be filling Commander Apnis in as well, but it goes no further and she'll continue to be Ms Kerrix until we find out more."

"Yes ma'am. But if we ship out shortly, where does that leave Ms Kerrix? We keep her aboard and leave her shuttle in the Web?"

"No we do not. Not that I imagine *she'd* agree. But *you* still want your hands on her shuttle, don't you? You're running the data again."

"For all her impressive shielding and cloaking, she *can* be detected, I'm sure of it," he answered. "And if I've worked that out…"

"So could others; there were evidently eyes on Kerrix as well as us and maybe she's been tailed to that dock."

"Exactly, although no-one else has the data on the shuttle that we do. But we should pass on those concerns to her."

"Which *I* will do when I talk to her tomorrow. You'll have to wait your turn and only on Flintlock's say-so."

Ahxenta had updated her first mate on Kerrix in private when Apnis returned to *Arianrhod* after her talk with Biernop. The briefing over breakfast next day began with the news from Vettarista. A note of the arrests had in fact reached Biernop, who had been until then in the dark over covert ops in security. He *had* been aware of a parallel process to rout out rogues among the vast army of dock workers and others in his neck of the woods: the need for such a huge workforce made security there a major headache and incidents had reached epic proportions. That Guild and Merkat security *were* running inquiries independently had not come as a surprise to him, for with so many issues in common, joint corruption was highly likely.

The report Apnis made to the Guild security liaison of the attack on Kerrix and its link to *Arianrhod* had troubled him. As for his news, Lokterix' whereabouts was still a mystery and it was not clear how he had escaped or who his allies were. Investigations into his contacts had drawn a blank but it was known that Froyd Melson had beat a hasty retreat only hours after *his* talk with Ahxenta and Apnis. And no stashes of explosives similar to those used in the docking bay explosion been found, despite thorough searching.

One thing that had been clear from the first mate's talk with her friend was that he had no idea of the identities of the agents dealing with the problems in his Guild and in security. All he knew was that a covert group from the Interstellar Systems Protectorate's Intelligence Division had been called in, Merkat being firmly in an ISP-run sector straddling galactic zones Alpha, Beta and Delta. Anonymous agents dealt with single contacts from Guild and Merkat security, who then reported back to their relevant teams.

Ahxenta gave out very little of what she had learnt to Kerrix when she visited her. Flintlock had vetoed much talk as her patient was still weak and under sedation, but as the captain was curious about certain matters relating to her guest, she asked briefly after her health, gave her a bare outline of the recent arrests and passed on Azular's qualms over her shuttle's security. With an astute look at the weary but wary eyes, Ahxenta then began abruptly on her own agenda.

"What do you do with the IDs, weapons and other stuff that you lift from the villains you tangle with? They're not in your quarters."

"And I bet you had a good look," was the sarcastic retort. "I hand most of them on to someone who can dispose of them, and not for illegal purposes, Captain, if that's perturbing you."

"Your friend Ms Vettarista, I bet. She's a helluva lot more than a hand at Azure Belle's Nightclub."

"I don't pry into her life and she doesn't pry into mine."

If that was a hint the captain ignored it. "And now, *Captain* Kerrix, I'd like more of your story, if you please."

"And you've got me where you have the upper hand. Clever."

"I brought you here for proper medical attention and for your own protection, as you're damn well aware, so cut it."

"Thanks," was the bitter aside.

"Well? Who exactly were you, before you ended up here?"

She laughed shortly. "I *was* in command of a small survey ship out of Norvalla Three, exploring areas of little-known space. And I've told you how I got here. That's about all there is to it."

"I doubt *that*. The commander of a vessel doesn't leave her ship to investigate an anomaly, however fascinating it might be. That's a job for the science officer. I assume you *had* a science officer?"

"I did, one that was inexperienced and not cleared for piloting a sci-shuttle. Our mission was thrown together rather hastily."

"And you didn't send out a recon probe, or call in your findings? No-one else could go and your first mate raised no objections?"

"Our probes only told us there was an energy source at the centre of what we thought must be an obsolete bypass node of an unknown configuration and *that* implied an advanced civilisation that was new to us. Wouldn't you have wanted a closer look?"

Azular certainly would have in Ahxenta's opinion but all she said was, "Your first mate, your senior officers?"

"We were a small crew of thirty eight and my first officer did not object. *You* are able to choose your crew, Captain; that luxury I didn't have. I suspect my first officer was glad to see the back of me."

"And *you're* used to having your way," Ahxenta stated, aware that sedation had reduced her guest's caution. "Rank has its privileges."

"Not in the Norvallan fleet it doesn't. There, privilege has its rank, which annoys many of lower social standing who have had to work their butts off to get to senior positions," Kerrix told her.

"And how hard did *you* have to work, Captain?"

"Hard enough: such shortcuts don't pay in the end. But a system like that creates discord among those that think they've been passed over because of their inferior social status. And *you're* not interested in Norvallan societal structure."

"Neither are you," Ahxenta observed acutely.

"I don't give a damn," Kerrix said drowsily. "Fleet's for planetary and colony protection and scientific exploration, not for propping up egos and handing out titles to those that have them already."

"Tell me what happened to you down on green twelve, after your last shift in the *Half Moon*."

Kerrix looked away, her jaw tightening, her hand clutching at her thermal covering. "Go to hell," she said.

"What were you quizzed about? If it concerns my ship or my crew, I need to know!" Ahxenta spat in a low, angry voice.

"Or what?"

"Or we change your quarters to my brig and we talk there."

"With your pet telepath in attendance, no doubt."

"That's enough!" the captain snapped.

"You're damn straight it is!" a voice at the bay entry said sharply.

"This is a private conversation, Doctor," Ahxenta told her CMO.

"Not when my med-sensors are hitting danger levels it isn't. It stops now," announced Flintlock.

"*I'm* in command here, Doctor," Ahxenta said as she rose to face her officer. "You can stay, but I want answers."

"She's my patient and I have a duty of care towards her. I will *not* allow her health to be compromised."

"And *I* have a duty to…"

"Shut up, the pair of you!" screeched Kerrix, her hands at her face and tensed into claws. "I can't hear myself think!"

The two looked down for an instant and then exchanged glances, the silence lengthening as they watched. Flintlock hauled up a hand-held and began to scan. Kerrix had twisted away and into her pillows, swearing softly and angrily, but was aware enough to half-turn as the doctor advanced with a hypo she had dug out of a nearby cabinet.

"No more medication, Doctor, my brain's turning to mud as it is." She gave a juddering sigh, shaking her head to clear it. "Apologies, Captain, I was out of order. What can I tell you?"

The woman would not look at the two as she recalled as much as she could of her cross-examination by her captors at Ahxenta's quiet insistence. They wanted to know her links to *Arianrhod*, the subject of her dialogues with the officers with whom she had come into contact and details of her trip to outer nine. They were also keen to know her endpoint then, leading her to suspect that whatever tail had been in place had *not* led to bay six eight alpha two. And they had used other tactics, as the cutting they had administered had not been sufficient to provide the answers they so relentlessly sought.

"Let's just say they ended by inserting a stun-stick where the sun doesn't shine; and one of those will deliver a nasty kick, as I'm sure you know. But I suspect that *that* was as much for their enjoyment as to extract more information from me." She grimaced at the memory. "I was so out of it by then, I *could* say nothing."

"No more, Cinnabar," Flintlock cautioned in extreme distaste as Ahxenta mouthed "Bastards!" under her breath.

"Don't look so shocked, Doctor; believe me, I've faced worse," Kerrix said wryly as she at last turned. "I played dumb. I work in a bar, it's my job to sweet-talk customers, they say go, I go. They didn't believe me but time was slipping and by their talk, I guessed they had to be elsewhere. I don't know how I got away. They picked me up and dumped me outside, I think, and I started to crawl."

"This does not leave this room," Flintlock said harshly. "I'm not surprised Vettarista took them apart."

"What?" Kerrix demanded, looking from one to the other.

Ahxenta cursed inwardly at the chief medic's slip, but told her that three of five thugs who had been arrested bore injuries that had been inflicted by *unknown* assailants, possibly those issuing their orders, as the attack on Kerrix had not produced the answers they wanted.

The doctor by this time had thoroughly scanned her patient again and realised that she was exhausted. "Sleep," she ordered. "No more visitors until I say. After you, Captain," she added emphatically.

"One thing, Ms Kerrix," Ahxenta said. "That translation device you have implanted: someone knows about it and wants it badly enough to cut it out of you. Not the three that attacked you or they'd have it by now. Any idea of whom and how they know?"

The woman shook her head. "No. And that disturbs me."

"I imagine it does. Your friend Ms Vettarista?"

The eyes looking at her narrowed in anger. "If you think she's had a hand in it, you're wrong. But she's no fool and she knows about it."

"I'm sure she does. I'll see you later."

Once clear of the iso-bay Flintlock motioned towards her office, but halted to advise her duty medic that no-one bar medical staff was to approach the patient.

"She won't be out of here anytime soon," the doctor informed the captain the second her door slid shut. "She's still on pain meds, anti-inflammatories and skin salve and can't put weight on that bad leg."

"I've already had this out with Azular and she's not staying aboard my ship. She won't be coerced and we've no cause to hold her against her will. What else?"

"If this Vettarista is as smart as you think, she may have got some samples from Kerrix that could be related to her attackers."

"*That* I hadn't considered, though she probably has data she didn't link through and I *was* going to contact her on the QT. I'm heading down later anyway. I'll take Azular."

"He still wants to speak to her – he left me a comm."

"Your call, Doc. Keep me updated on her progress."

The persistent Azular arrived at the chief medic's door an hour and a half later. He had received his orders from the captain and wanted a dialogue with Kerrix before they set out. Flintlock was unwilling, but as her patient was stable and awake, she would allow him ten minutes *if* Kerrix agreed. The shrug and cynical gaze indicated that Kerrix had guessed that the science officer would put in an appearance at some point, but she made no objection when the request was made.

Azular had been warned not to allude to his eagerness to see her shuttle, or to the events that had led to her presence aboard and was careful not to use his talents to read her. That she was chary of him he could tell when she gestured him to sit. As his enquiry after her health raised only a silent nod, he launched into his apology for using his intuitive skills unfairly. She broke the awkward pause at the end.

"You're telepathic," she challenged. "You were *so* pleased with yourself that you'd got the measure of me, weren't you?"

"That *is* a little unfair…"

"No it damn well isn't. *You* didn't see the look on your face," she told him as she searched his dark eyes. "You know you come across as a smug bastard? Clearly not," she grinned at his expression. "And an irritating one at that. Just when I was beginning to believe there were people out there I could trust. No honour among pirates then: you're just a bunch of scallywags, if that's the right word."

She looked down as he reiterated his regrets, but her head reared up as he took leave. "As a scientist, I *do* understand your interest in an enigma. So, one thing: I *did* promise to consider your request for a look round my shuttle before this… trouble. I did and had already made up my mind to agree. I stand by my promises, even if I haven't articulated them. You *can* have a look, but only if I'm on hand."

Taken aback, he stood still for a second before voicing his thanks.

"Another thing: scallywag or not, I should not have struck you. If you'd been an officer of *my* fleet, I'd have been up on charges for it. I apologise for that. But not for the name-calling – you deserved that."

"I accept your apology, Ms Kerrix," he said quietly as he turned to go, a slightly quirky smile playing about his lips.

"And I accept yours," she said equally softly to his back view.

Flintlock was on her way over to tell the science officer his time was up. His face alerted her that something had occurred.

"What's up? You look like you've just swallowed a bug and you're wondering if you like the taste."

"I'm puzzled. There's more to Ms Kerrix than meets the eye."

"I could have told you that."

"I would like to know the specifics of her talk with the captain."

The doctor eyed him, shaking her head. "No you wouldn't," she advised him soberly. "But what's got you in a fizz?"

The captain was as perplexed as Flintlock had been when she heard the details of Azular's chat with their visitor. The two were on the way to marketing and a meeting with Vettarista in the *Sunlight Subspace Diner*, their security escort maintaining a discreet distance.

The Berzic woman was there when they made the diner. She was attired formally and wore much less make-up than she had when last the two had seen her. In a business suit, with plainly-dressed hair and toting an info-pad, she would pass as a trade rep, which no doubt was her intention. The three found a corner table. The captain invoked privacy, setting up her personal jammer cum bug detector, and ordered light lunches as a foil to outflank potential snoopers.

Preparations complete, Ahxenta was blunt. "You're part of covert ops to sniff out the crime and corruption going on in Merkat security and the Guild. You belong to ISP's Intelligence Division don't you? And with your interest in Kerrix and what *she* is and your readiness to keep me in the loop with what's happening, your remit has got to be much wider. Alien infiltration that's still ongoing?"

"Smart, Captain. I will not clarify, nor do I recommend you press the issue. You asked for this meeting: what do you want to know?"

"I want to know why my people are being targeted and by whom; and why the hostility seems to extend to people that have little to do with us. Its ferocity and extent are increasing. Even other PSS crews have been hit and the trail leads to the *Arianrhod*."

"Other PSS crews?" Vettarista questioned.

Ahxenta briefly told her of the attack on the *Green Comet's* crew. Scavenger activity over Mellifly Vetta knew of: it had led to clashes with official agencies, she told them. There were also rumours that bands of hostiles that had made it out after their bases were overrun were setting up ops again. One such was said to be outside Coalition space in zone Beta and sufficiently close to Mellifly to be useful as a stepping-off point for raids there and near Kifferbuck, places where *Arianrhod* had wreaked such havoc during the late war.

"There's more to it than retribution," the captain declared. "Why waste their time and energy chasing us up?"

"Hardly a waste if they *do* take you down," Vettarista pointed out. "Or if they can persuade others that any links to you are best cut. But you'd know more about who *they* are than I would — I have very few leads. And I imagine there are parties who want to know how you did it, what makes *your* ship so special that it could take on their best and win. And if they succeed in bringing you down, it'll promote fear, which allows the criminals that thrive in such conditions to prosper."

"What about Kerrix? Where does she fit in?"

"She was in trouble before she met you, Captain, with ruthless people who'd figured she was alien and probably had novel tech that would be useful to those that operate on the dark side of the law."

"Alien?"

"Not local to the charted zones; as far as I've been able to tell, her physiology would put her beyond zone Mu."

"Close to the Enigma Nebula?" interrupted Ahxenta.

"No, in the opposite direction; the closest inhabited world in Mu on that route is Kollaskin Ambit. It's on zone edge and few missions have pushed beyond it. Her biosigns suggest an origin out that way."

"But how did you deduce that?" Azular asked inquisitively.

"There *have* been derelicts found near to and beyond charted zone edges over the ages; investigations have given rise to a restricted body of data to which I have access. It includes biosigns."

"I've never heard of that," the science officer declared. "Rumours of derelict ships and deserted worlds abound of course, but I didn't realise someone was keeping a tally. ISP?"

The answer was a slight nod, but that was all she was prepared to impart. The antagonism that had clothed her during their previous encounter was gone and Azular was now more than convinced that she was a very clever and devious operator.

"On the subject of biosigns," Ahxenta put in. "You found Kerrix just after she was attacked and you're no fool. Were you able to get samples from her that might give more clues to her attackers?"

"No: she was in no fit state and given what she'd been through I didn't try. I checked her clothes and got traces of blood, which *did* match one of the perps who's been got for it, but it won't be used as evidence. The guy's from Salt Three and is wanted for gun-running there. The other two are local, pawns in it for credit and their own warped gratification. Whoever recruited them knew what they were. Their contacts are being traced to see if their string-pullers can be located but so far nothing. They're too good at hiding their tracks."

"You know how Kerrix got here." It was a statement.

"Let's say I worked it out and she didn't deny it. But now people have linked her to you, she's a target of those that are out to get you as well as those that have worked out what she is and has: her tech, implanted and otherwise, that you're no doubt aware of."

The captain agreed. "Her implanted translator *is* known about and some people want it so badly they'll risk her life to get it. My CMO has heard of similar devices but reckons they're experimental and so rare you'd never source one. But that means *they* know what it is and could make use of it: duplicate it or implant it in another host maybe.

And *that* implies a high degree of medical and technical know-how.”

“Advanced capability, such as that possessed by the hostiles who altered others for their own purposes, Captain,” mused Azular. “It suggests that some are still out there operating.”

“They had that medical facility on Mellifly,” Ahxenta said shortly. “But given the exodus from there after our take-down of their covert shipbuilding base, *that* place may have been shut down.”

“Ah, where your friend Micklemouse was subverted to become an info-sent in the pay of the hostiles,” Vettarista commented.

“What do you know of him and his dealings with us?” the captain demanded dangerously.

“Enough to know he’s trouble, though you seem to have handled him without hurt to yourselves. That’ll be another reason you seem to be popular with certain factions who want to know how you did it. He wasn’t the only one and the complex is under investigation.”

“Because it may be useful to the ISP?”

“I can’t tell you that. But as to what you want to know: *I* believe you’re being targeted because you bested a number of superior forces before and during the late war, you developed a probe that could detect hostiles and certain lackeys under their direct control – how you worked out that zukivianite was the giveaway no one knows – *and* it’s been said that your ship possesses rather more tech than a typical PSS. As far as I’m aware your gear’s nothing too far out, but there *is* speculation that you have sources that others don’t, perhaps alien. One thing: it was noted that in the aftermath of Skyrtek your ship was breached by a strange energy mass that had previously been attached to one of the renegade ships that lent their haphazard support to the Allied forces. What was it?”

“How the hell did you know about that?” Ahxenta asked sharply. “Isn’t it time you told me exactly who and what you are and what you’re involved in? And why it now seems to involve me?”

A hiss from Azular caused the others to turn. The science officer indicated the jammer and bug sensor that Ahxenta had set upon their table. It had begun to pulsate, emitting a slowly growing blue glow.

11: THE SCI-SHUTTLE

Ahxenta sat back, her eyes scanning the space around her and flicking to the security device on the table. Vettarista was doing the same as she fingered her communit and Azular was taking readings with his pet scanner. A holo-note from the jammer lit up and the captain took in the detail: the source of the targeted beam was the table opposite. It was occupied by two people, one in PSS uniform.

Ahxenta's face darkened in anger as she deactivated her jammer and cleared the table's privacy shield. "You have exactly five seconds to turn off that recording device, Mr Buntle, or you and your buddy are toast," she articulated as she rose. "Stay," she ordered the others.

Tommy Buntle of the *Tallulah* sat frozen to the spot as the captain made her way over. His companion Ahxenta did not recognise but his smart clothing oozed affluence. Both men noted that the captain had loosed her phase rifle and Buntle at least knew that she would have no hesitation in using it.

The exec of the *Tallulah* licked his lips as he looked up. "Captain?" he asked nervously as he cut the privacy shield. "You want a word?"

"Several words, Mr Buntle. Why are you attempting to listen in on my private business?" she queried quietly but ominously.

The man blustered irately as he denied the charge, but was careful to keep his voice low. His associate's hand crawling towards what looked like a standard info-pad caused Ahxenta's jaw to tighten and her hand dropped onto the device.

"Who's your friend?" she demanded of Buntle.

"That's confidential."

"Please yourself. My science officer *is* recording every word, so I *will* find out when I press charges. This I'm confiscating as evidence."

"That's private property!" the stranger snarled angrily, trying to regain control of his info-pad.

"Not when it's been used for criminal activity it isn't. Now do you hand it over to me or do I call security and you hand it to them?"

She had taken in something else as the unknown began a denial of any wrongdoing. A twitching vein close to his hairline caused a glint that caught her eye and she made out a tiny metallic fitment. A noise at her side distracted her but her eyes did not leave her quarry's face. He on the other hand looked up and past her and gave a quickly-stilled flinch of surprise. As two shapes at the edge of sight closed in, the quiet voice of Azular caught her ear.

"We appear to have company, Captain." The science officer had come up silently and had his phase rifle at the ready.

Ahxenta turned to find two tall figures. Both wore dark, burnished uniforms and were armed. She had seen them before, as had Azular, which had no doubt led him to disobey her order to remain seated.

"Our quarrel is not with you, Captain Ahxenta," the taller of the two said calmly.

"So you told me before," she returned. "I didn't believe you."

A frown crossed his face as he conceded with a nod. "We're here for him." He indicated the stranger. "He's coming with us."

"Why?"

"That's our concern. He won't bother you again."

The man stood in alarm: he had evidently recognised the pair and did not like what he was hearing. Neither did many diners nearby and a soft shuffling ensued as several tried to make their way elsewhere. The advent of *Arianrhod's* security guards did little to ease the tension.

"You *will* come with us," the leader of the two said as he placed a hand under Buntle's friend's armpit and aimed his hand-held weapon at the man's neck. "Take his gear," he instructed his associate.

"That's evidence of his bugging of my business and I want it," Ahxenta said quietly as she indicated the info-pad.

"As you wish, Captain," the man responded, eyeing a phase rifle that one of *Arianrhod's* guards had directed at his ear. "But this one's ours. Have a profitable day."

As quickly as they had come, the two and their prey were gone.

"Stand down," Ahxenta ordered her guards. "Azular, get back to our table and carry on our business. I want words with Mr Buntle."

Tommy Buntle looked acutely uneasy as the captain slid into the chair opposite him. Her eyes were not kind and she wanted answers. The *Tallulah's* exec was too fond of his own skin to hedge overmuch and admitted that the man, Flatt, was a new contact that he had met that morning who had promised him a bonus if he would swing the transfer of a small cargo pod from Merkat to Minch Fettin, a world on zone Mu edge, with no questions asked. Buntle would not agree without his captain's say-so, he glibly assured her. He was probing for details of the cargo when Flatt spotted the *Arianrhod's* officers and began to ask questions about her and her crew. Buntle had told him nothing and was oblivious that he was bugging Ahxenta's table.

The captain tapped the info-pad under her hand. "Really? Well I'm sure Flatt was recording every syllable of what you discussed and it'll be here. And I *will* check before I contact your captain. And I'd like *your* covert recorder, the one in your pocket; though I suspect your wily friend Flatt disabled it remotely before he said anything. *Now*, Mr Buntle: I don't have all day."

The man wordlessly pulled out a small bug and placed it on the table. He licked his lips nervously. "If I may ask, Captain… those two that took him… you seemed to know them?"

"You may not ask. I suggest you ship out. Good day."

Aware of Ahxenta's barely-masked fury, Buntle hauled himself up to leave, his way barred by an attendant requesting payment.

Back at her table the captain found Azular and Vettarista in polite debate. The woman had caught most of what had been said and had seen the two ex-raiders before. And she knew of the ship in which they had come into the Web two days before *Arianrhod*: a massive cargo of intricate design that seemed brand-new but had a hull spec hardly a hairsbreadth off that used by the hostile fleet that had caused such havoc up until a few months previously. It was also very close in design to the one on which Kerrix had hitched a lift and may have hailed from the same place, or even be the same one.

"Which brings me back to my previous questions," Ahxenta said sardonically. "Isn't it time you told me who and what you are, what you're up to and why your business seems to involve me and mine?"

"You don't give up, Captain."

"Neither do you. What's the score?"

After a scrutiny of both officers, Vettarista gave a guarded account of her credentials. An agent of ISP's Intelligence Division, her remit covered hostile intrusion. She had been brought in at an early stage to sniff out corruption in Merkat security, some of which related to the late war that had left many systems close to collapse. Agents of chaos were still out there, as Ahxenta and many others were aware. Part of her mission was to investigate those. And Merkat being what it was, it was an obvious hub of clandestine ops. As *Arianrhod* and her crew still seemed to be of interest to those who had lost the war and were trying to regain a toehold, they came under her sphere of activity.

"And Ms Kerrix?" That was Azular.

The agent eyed him acutely. "A colleague alerted me to her arrival. A fugitive pursued by the kind on her tail *and* who could avoid them was of interest. She knows," she added at his sharp gaze. "I *did* fix her the berth next to mine after she washed up in the *Half Moon* some time ago, not realising I'd be grateful to her shortly after."

"You know about her and you know more about these ex-raiders or whoever they are than you're telling: where they're holed up for one," the captain said. "But what's their game? One day they're taking ships out, the next they're saying they've no quarrel with me and are mopping up mischief-makers like Flatt, whatever *he* is."

"As far as I know, many hostile victims *were* raiders, but most were people that were in the wrong place at the wrong time – abductions have been going on for decades. Those that had freed themselves or had been freed were drawn together at the start for mutual defence and the need to find normality. Most would have lost home, family, identity, you name it and there was no way back. So some are out for revenge on those who did it and on any they think still freely work for them. There has to be several large groups and given their diverse origins, there will be internal conflicts. It may be that one driving force is a need for stability, a future that guarantees a living that's not going to kill them; in other words, most are *not* likely to be setting up as the raiders that were the curse of the spaceways before the war tore half the known galactic sectors apart."

"That doesn't explain the brutality of some towards my crew and others," Ahxenta stated. "It can't all be down to what they suffered. And we know there *are* entirely hostile ships out there that are not the ones that caused most of the damage in the war – no zukivianite."

"You know that?" Vettarista said quickly. "But I strongly suspect a few bands still harbour backsliders like your ex-associate Lokterix – and some who are out for payback at any price."

"Lokterix!" Ahxenta exploded. "What do you know about him?"

"That he's skipped the Web, probably with help. But it looks as if the two we had in here are part of a bigger game. The spec of their ship is hard to get: effective surface jammers and interior shielding. But her manifest is standard and she's released no cargo that's caused concern. Don't ask," she cautioned. "They're not allied to any known trading group. Their home port is listed as a number in zone Mu, but that's not against the rules. And who'll argue against a ship *that* size?"

"That size," Ahxenta repeated crisply. "What does this ship of theirs look like and where's it berthed?"

Vettarista gave an incisive look as she began a rapid tapping of her info-pad, and then turned the device to allow the captain to view the result: a huge ship, larger than *Arianrhod* and in a berth at the far side of the Web. Ahxenta traded glances with Azular: the images and data were sparse but the design was similar in detail to the visuals Kerrix had captured of the vessel in which she had hitched a lift to Merkat.

"It's not like any ship we've met, at least superficially, even in the war," Azular said diplomatically. "But the spec *is* similar to the ships used by the hostiles, at least in hull structure. And these weapons are in keeping with the type and the extent of the firepower we faced."

The ISP agent jumped on that. "You're saying that these weapons match those used against you by the hostiles in the war?"

"No," the science officer returned shortly. "You surmise as we do that these emergent groups have grown out of what were bands of ex-captives of the hostiles that had amassed sufficient arms and ships to aid the Alliance near the end of the war. And they seem to include a number of subversives that have their own agendas. It appears that they're seizing left-over hostile technology, which no doubt includes bases and hardware. Do you believe *this* ship is part of that process?"

"It's more than possible," Vettarista agreed. "What's on that info-pad you took from the man Flatt, Captain?"

Ahxenta was sure that was a ploy to deflect more probing but she turned the pad and flipped it up. "It won't let me access it. I have your link info so I'll let you know if we dig up anything. And now I'd like the data you have on that ship."

That done, she paid the bill, gathered her gear and took her leave, a tacit agreement that nothing would be divulged of anything that had passed agreed by an exchange of nods. She and Azular collected their guards and made for the nearest ride to their shuttle bay. The captain left the piloting to her science officer. She had an immediate meeting with Captain Murmur Fleetskup of the *Tallulah* to arrange.

Arianrhod's senior officers were as furious as the captain over Buntle's actions, but Fleetskup held that his exec had been the victim of fraud, and called for the return of his recorder, which as expected had been wiped. Buntle had got in first with his story was the general view, but Ahxenta shelved the threat of legal action: Fleetskup was fond of his own voice and the process would take more time and trouble than it or he was worth. She did pass an edited report to the Trades Alliance and the PSS fleet but she had more vital matters. With talks complete and cargo pods security-tagged, the payload for ISP Stinward would be ready for early loading the day after next and shipping out was scheduled for twelve hundred on that day.

Most of the crew were happy at the prospect of quitting the Web, as the current spell had not been relaxed. The only two put out were the chief medical officer and the senior science officer. Flintlock had issues with tipping their guest back into her former den and Azular saw his chances of a tour of her shuttle receding. The captain was not sorry, reckoning that the science officer would have enough to keep him busy taking the info-pad she had liberated from Flatt to pieces. That had proved tough to unlock and very little had been gleaned, apart from an origin for part of its integral casing. *That* had come from Keystone Kell, the third planet of a system bridging zones Eta and Zeta, whose residents were artificers and suppliers of superior small arms. The data had been passed to Vettarista, along with scans that Azular had netted of Flatt's physiology. The man definitely bore alien tech, although there were no signs of recent genetic tampering.

The captain had taken it upon herself to inform Kerrix that she would be headed back to her own berth the following day. Ahxenta thought it prudent that she be relocated late at night, when there would be fewer eyes about. That was met with an amused look.

"You've not been along lower green twelve near Azure Belle's in the late to early hours, have you, Captain?"

She thanked Ahxenta nonetheless for her care and for the return of the property removed from her quarters, as well as the pieces that Greffy had found on the *Gadfly*. He had repaired the fragile chain bearing the tiny locket. Kerrix was grateful: it had been her mother's, she told the captain as she fastened the trinket around her neck.

Ahxenta left her to walk into a storm. An irate Earbleat, an info-pad in one hand and a scanner in the other, was facing the CMO.

"No you damn well can't!" Flintlock was saying. "Medbay isn't an amusement park and she's not a visitor attraction."

"What in hell is going on?"

"You've only been in there ten minutes, Cap, and this is the *third* request for a talk with Ms Kerrix! First Crizz Cottontail, then Azular and now Earbleat; though the other two had the decency to call and not march in here," she added wrathfully to the second mate.

"What did Cottontail want a talk about?" Ahxenta asked curiously.

"Something about fixing her shuttle's drive system: Azular's been bending the chief's ear about an energy cell that would work. You'd best ask her, I'm no expert. And Azular said similar, though I bet *he's* still after a guided tour. But you're not going to be picking her brains about her ship's cloaking and weapons any time soon," she told Earbleat curtly. "Hell's teeth, she's not an info-point!"

"But I've gone over the stuff that Azular pulled out and Greffy brought back and if I could get some more info we might be able to retrofit our systems and improve efficiency! I could try it small scale to see how it would work, Cap," the second mate went on eagerly.

"On *Loki VI* you mean," Ahxenta said acerbically. "In here it's the Doc's call. If she says no, then it's no," Earbleat was informed.

"That's not what you said the other day," Flintlock murmured to the captain as the disappointed weapons officer walked off, peeved.

"Cut it," the chief medic was advised. "She'll need to be ready to ship out late tomorrow. Make sure she has sufficient meds to see her through the next few days, though I suspect her buddy Vetta will see to that. Or young Merry: strange friends she's picked up."

"You can talk," Flintlock retorted as a call came for Ahxenta from the bridge that Captain Adhara Peakfrost of the *Quarkstorm* was on line and wanted a word in relation to the report she had circulated.

"What's new, Cinnabar?" Apnis asked when the captain returned to the bridge after her dialogue with Peakfrost.

"Looks like the guy Flatt had a busy day before we ran into him. He met with the *Quarkstorm's* supercargo before he saw Buntle, with the same deal of shipping a small cargo pod on the QT from Merkat to Minch Fettin. It smelt like a tub of trouble, Peakfrost's supercargo said. Flatt wouldn't give details of the cargo so the super insisted his captain be brought in. Flatt refused and threatened him with violence if any details of their chat leaked out. I wonder where this cargo pod is now, if Flatt's with the two that spirited him off."

"Bet Ms Vettarista's looking into it," the first mate guessed.

"So do I. I'll let her know about the *Quarkstorm*. Minch Fettin? It's a short day's ride from there into unmapped space and that ex-hostile base off the Enigma that's the probable home of those two that took Flatt. Anything new on the Web's security and business channels?"

"Nary a thing, but Bellfish picked up a reference on a PSS channel to some ship of unknown configuration beyond Wester 287 that was keen to keep out of range and didn't respond to hails. Limited data but it's maybe linked to the one that Zillah's people called in, the one heading into uncharted space last time it was spotted."

"Who reported it?" the captain enquired.

"The *Nyx Warrior*; think we should pass it on to Zillah?"

"I do. Patch the details through to my office and I'll get on it now. I see the *Comet* and the *Urania* got in, so I'll have a quick word with Sarie Jikelleli and Cobalt Mikbeam to see if they have anything that they haven't put out on the Ultra-V III."

"*Firedrake's* due in an hour so you could try Pa Ma'Lappis as well."

"Good call. Where's Azular? He should be on bridge duty."

"Try medbay," was the first mate's dry retort.

The senior science officer *was* there and talking to Kerrix. He had created an interface he believed could link one of the smaller energy cells used as fuel sources for engineering and other modules to her shuttle's drive, he told her. It would have to be tested in situ but if it worked it might deliver sufficient power to allow flight to a safer berth. He had also sought advice from Cottontail on hull repair and on the starboard tilt. The latter required examination to pinpoint the cause but a buckled landing extensor was likely. Repairs *would* have to be carried out in a well-resourced bay but temporary patches could be applied to the hull in the interim. Unfortunately, *Arianrhod* was due to depart soon and none of her engineers could be spared to assist.

"Your captain won't sanction repairs to my ship, given that I stole hers," Kerrix remarked wryly. "What do you *really* want out of me?"

"An in-depth analysis of your shuttle's gear, particularly your anti-detection and camouflage systems *and* samples of your technology," he disclosed candidly. "They're novel to me and seem superior to ours in many respects. They would benefit my ship."

"I've already promised you access to my shuttle, but if you think you can strip her bare you can think again," was the caustic retort.

"That would not be my intent, as I'm sure you're aware."

"So some of my tech for one of these energy cells you think I can tie into my drive? And sooner rather than later?"

The science officer scrutinised her closely, a subtle feeling that she was laughing at him growing as he nodded.

She smiled faintly as she looked away from the searching gaze. "Is that how you get what you want? The big dark eyes?"

His discomfited expression produced a real laugh as she turned back. "You should see the look on your face," she chuckled. "But let me think it over for a short time… I feel my concentration slipping."

Azular's quick glance at the bank of medi-sensors beyond her cot confirmed that her energy levels were low. He quickly took his leave, promising to stop by later. A small wave was her only response.

Ahxenta had little to report on return to the bridge. Vettarista could find no trace of Flatt's cargo pod. The lately-arrived Privates brought news of an increase in raids along trade routes, the most recent being the theft of cargo drones from a ship of the Skelp Line of Kymexa Vento, by zone Gamma edge. She had been caught on her way back from her homeworld's Botrix Colony and had dropped her drones and fled. The attacking craft was small, fast and very well-armed.

"Sarie figured it sounded like the interceptor the *Comet* ran into off Kifferbuck," the captain said. "And the hit was close to Botrix, so on the border of sector sixteen of zone Beta – interesting location."

"A few baddies still out that way then, *if* that's where the raider hailed from. But nothing close to where we're headed?" Apnis asked.

"Not recently. Zillah's had no more goings on in her backyard and tourist trips to the Ginseng Nebula have restarted, so trade's picked up. I checked with ISP Central Logistics about our cargo for them and they say they've had no fresh local troubles. So looks like the old raider rat-packs or their offshoots are gearing up for business and have newer but fewer ships, if they're sending out lone wolves."

"Or their latest version of a mothership that holds a fleet of high-tech fighters isn't off the production line yet," the first mate grinned.

"Thanks for that. Azular not back yet?"

As if on cue, the senior science officer stepped out of the bridge elevator. He made for the command chair with the request that the captain spare him a couple of minutes for a private discussion. With a raised eyebrow, Ahxenta agreed and the two made for her office.

"Bet it's about getting a look around that Ms Kerrix' shuttle," Box whispered to his mate at the navi-helm console. "Greffy says Doc Azular's desperate to see it up close."

Romanna Dox turned in disgust. "Why don't you mind your own business?" she flashed. "*That* means running systems diagnostics."

"What's eating you? Lack of shore leave?"

The two continued to bicker until Apnis bid them be silent or she would dock their next leave quota. She was checking the manifest for the cargo due from Redship Industrial and musing on the couple of minutes requested by the senior science officer. That time had gone.

It was half an hour before the captain reappeared with Azular. He made for his station with barely a nod to the first mate. His face was impassive, his usual quiet smile absent. Apnis raised enquiring brows but said nothing as Ahxenta resumed the command chair.

The next hour saw the change in duty crews. The captain and first mate were last off the bridge and as Lieutenant Pollux Gliss took the conn, Ahxenta suggested they make for the mess and their evening meal after a quick rundown of the itinerary for the morrow.

"What did Azular want?" was Apnis' first question as soon as the bridge office door closed. "He didn't look his usual sunny self."

"He wanted to take a shuttle *and* Kerrix down to outer belt nine early tomorrow with a couple of energy cells he's coaxed from Crizz.

He reckons he can plug one or both into her ship's power banks and she's half-promised him some tech in return. At least he thinks he's persuaded her to part with it: she's still thinking it over."

"What did Flintlock say to that?" the first mate asked archly.

"I called her. She spat quarks at him, so I vetoed it. We'll revisit it in the morning, but it might be a useful exchange. That berth her shuttle's in now doesn't get any safer the more that seem to know about it and she'll need power to move the thing – if it *will* shift."

The following morning saw most of the *Arianrhod's* usual bridge crew in post. The captain was in the chief MO's office facing a militant Flintlock, who was adamant that her patient was not fit for transfer. Kerrix had other ideas; realising that her presence aboard was causing conflict, she wanted a rapid removal. Even so, she was not keen on Merkat's medbay, the only berth the chief medic would approve.

Azular had also been busy. Having called on Kerrix the evening before and been given assent to the exchange of tech for energy cells, he was eager to head out. He had advised the captain earlier and then called on Dr Zaiklyn Oak, a cybernetic limb therapy expert, to whom he posited the use of a prosthetic support for their guest's injured leg. Oak had made scans and sourced the support but would not discuss it with Kerrix without his chief's and the captain's go-ahead. Ahxenta and Flintlock found the pair locked in verbal combat over the issue when they made their way out of the CMO's office.

Flintlock was up in arms, but the captain questioned both doctors closely and in the end approved the support *if* Kerrix agreed, but not on her release from care until sanctioned by the medics or until the set deadline of twenty two hundred hours was reached.

Azular spent part of the intervening time in going over the data he had extracted from the captain's scan of the Norvallan sci-shuttle. He had noted two aft shielded sections and surmised that one probably protected control boards for her cloaking gear. The other may have hidden her weapons capability, for the science officer could find little else that related to that. The main drive section was also aft but there was no more than a visual record. Other sections were impenetrable to scanning, despite the high-spec probe used. The ops boards of the shuttle were also difficult to fathom and Azular expected an exciting time when finally he was aboard, though a little anxious that it might have to be after the *Arianrhod* returned from her coming mission.

Despite his doubts Azular had prepped a shuttle, ensuring that her cargo of energy cells and hull-plate patches was safely stowed. He had chosen an old runaround that was tied up in one of *Arianrhod's* little used shuttle bays as transport, as her dented hide was already a nondescript grey. The insignia linking her to *Arianrhod* he removed. Her call-sign had to remain but as so many craft came and went at all hours across the Web, any trip could be classed as routine and a convenient docking bay picked out as needed.

Azular was thankful that he had made the arrangements, for after lengthy debate and arguments with the patient, Doctors Flintlock and Oak had agreed to discharge Kerrix at eighteen hundred hours local time. Ahxenta had informed Vettarista of part of the plan and was piloting the shuttle herself. She planned to leave the science officer and one guard with Kerrix in the Norvallan shuttle's current bay in outer nine and then head out: she had other business in inner two.

The Norvallan woman appeared to be in good trim but Flintlock had cautioned both officers that she was far from healed and would need transport back to her billet after the trip to her shuttle. Azular was warned to limit the visit to the minimum required for the matters in hand and to curtail any attempts to repair the fabric of the craft.

Bay six eight alpha two was as gloomy as Ahxenta remembered when her shuttle finally made dock. She had had no trouble in entering the bay using the codes that Kerrix used for her own craft, after close scans to ensure that no surprises awaited them on the inside. Settling her vessel in the space which had housed the *Gadfly*, Ahxenta probed the whole area before she authorised debarking. As the red-lit outline of the airlock doors grew to indicate full sealing, Ahxenta's keen eyes scanned the space. It was darker than before but she could see that the cloaking projector that had disguised the *Gadfly* was no longer attached to the wall. The Norvallan shuttle was still a mess.

Kerrix was silent as she stepped down the ramp and stood in the murk, her eyes roving around. Azular followed, his gaze drawn to the battered wedge-shape that was familiar from visuals. His scanner was soon in his hands as the captain ordered her two guards to disinter the energy cells and self-attaching hull patches from the aft cargo bay.

"Hanx, you're with me," Ahxenta instructed. "Ji, you stay with Dr Azular and Ms Kerrix. You have until twenty three hundred," she told her science officer. "At that time you'll bring our shuttle over to inner two. Commander Apnis is arranging a berth and will transfer the codes. I'll see *you* then, Ms Kerrix."

"Yes, ma'am," the woman replied equably, hitching her bag of kit more comfortably over her shoulder.

No sooner had the captain and Ensign Hanx left the bay than the Berzic began a circuit of the alien shuttle, scanning as he went. Kerrix watched, arms folded, a sardonic grin on her face. Lieutenant Ji had taken her stance off starboard, phase rifle ready. She had already set a small security hover cam to guard the inner bay door.

"You have her well-secured, despite the damage to the plating," was the science officer's estimation when he reappeared.

"You mean you can't get through her hull. Good: that's the idea."

"Would you care to show me how you do it?"

She inclined her head, turned and made for the entry panel, which gave to some manipulation and the application of her left hand to the hull. The panel slid aside and the ramp descended. Leaving Ji outside, the science officer followed Kerrix into the dark interior. Her call resulted in a soft glow that grew sufficiently to make out details.

As he had noted from the visual, the pilot's place was forr'ad, with a second seat behind. The narrow couch with its stowage was beyond that, with the flight jacket hanging above. The aft area was split into sealed units that jutted into the space, their external boards flickering with tiny lights that implied current operational readiness.

"You've cloaked the internal as well," Azular noted.

"Of course. Not standard aboard your shuttles when you leave them unmanned I take it?"

"No," he agreed. "How do you generate the cloaks?"

"From my main ops panel: these sections have response plates to accept various commands, including cloak activation. The technology is integrated into the fabric of the most sensitive areas aboard. Take a seat," she invited, pointing to the secondary position.

She slid into the pilot's chair and ran her hands over the controls. They evidently accepted her touch for light intensity rose as various ops panels came to life and began to display data. His attention was drawn to the main boards as she expanded on their active functions and then displayed the information on internal shuttle security.

"External hull plates have the same security cloaking system," she explained. "Luckily my missing plates covered already secured areas."

"So the cloaking capability is basically a part of the ship's fabric. It *can* be breached by some technologies, I guess?"

"Yes it can. And I bet you've had a good try."

"I'm working on it," he smiled. "And your shielding? It didn't prevent the removal of your plating, but it's formidable."

"My ship was already damaged and some of my ops systems were down. But again I have individual section shielding as well as overall shield generation from external generators."

"Can you camouflage this shuttle as you did the *Gadfly*, to look like something she isn't?" he asked inquisitively.

"The cloaking system *can* be encoded to do that, but the facility is non-operational at present. There's little point during normal ops, as once the cloak's up she should be invisible to most scans."

"I agree. Your engine drive system… I have the interface to link one of our energy cells to your drive module, but I'll need to see it."

"How did you come up with it in any case?" she asked curiously as she rose, indicating the aft area of her craft.

"I examined the weaponry we brought aboard with you," he wryly admitted as he made to follow.

"And my scanner and no doubt my other bits and pieces."

"Not your personal effects," he said hurriedly.

"And couldn't get into most of them, as they're coded to my ident or to my touch; you didn't scan my ident when I was out, did you?"

"Certainly not!"

"I believe you," she responded dryly as she led him to the housing covering her engineering section and deftly unlocked it.

After a full exploratory and some probing Azular pursed his lips thoughtfully, nodding at a dry cell the two had released and removed from the drive system. "Only one good way to test it, but I think it's doable. I'll need to get one of our cells in here."

"And I have one or two bits to dig out," Kerrix informed him. "We *did* have an agreement…"

Azular inclined his head, his eyes lighting fractionally as he looked her in the face. His smile faded. "Are you all right, Ms Kerrix?"

"Do I look that bad? Just tired," she sighed, flexing her shoulders and turning her back on him. "I'll be fine. Go get your cell."

He moved to go but paused in concern. "I've been rather selfish and forgotten your hurts. Why don't you sit for a moment?"

"Just go get the damn cell and leave me be."

"Not until you sit and rest," he announced firmly, compelling her gently towards the nearby couch.

"You take a lot upon yourself, Doctor," she said harshly, allowing herself to be guided nonetheless. "What *is* your rank by the way?"

"Commander," he said calmly. "Please sit."

"You can be very persistently annoying, *Commander*."

"I do my best. Please sit."

"I'm sat. Go get the cell."

With a last penetrating look, Azular turned and made for the exit.

He found Ji prowling the space beyond. He hefted one of the two energy cells that had been left on the deck, informing the lieutenant that he intended to link it to the drive of the shuttle but would warn her if initiation was to be attempted. She confirmed, watching as the science officer made his way back up the ramp and into the craft.

Kerrix had been busy for she had unlocked a storage unit by her seat and had pulled out some items. He recognised one as the device that had generated the cloak to disguise the *Gadfly*. Two small pieces sat beside it. He smiled as he continued to tow the energy cell to the rear of the shuttle. Kerrix came over and sat by him as he began the delicate task of hooking the new cell into the relevant space.

"It accepts it," Azular noted. "The interface shows power transfer but will the drive draw and transmit the energy for operation?"

"Shut the unit up and we'll find out. You'd best call your security officer in here," she advised. "There may be exhaust leakage when I attempt to power her up."

With the panel secure and Ji strapped into the couch behind him, Azular watched keenly as Kerrix set the start sequence. She was quick but kept up a commentary as her hands flicked across her boards. As far as he could see, the process was more or less regular as external scanners were primed to scan the area beyond the craft for hazards and the ship's status confirmed as safe to proceed. Warning lights and a voice alert gave notice of the hull plate damage, but externally generated shielding was set to compensate. It would be safe for a flight internal to the Web, Kerrix reported as she slowly brought the power up to sufficient for manoeuvring.

"The permission codes to allow exit are here. The bay entry key fits into this portal and it holds the external bay door codes, though they can be punched in or transmitted from a central unit. Once the codes are accepted this will light up and you're good to go."

She shut down her ops boards and as the ship powered down she sat back, half turning to look at the science officer.

"May I try the controls to initiate the start sequence?" he asked.

She shook her head with a quick smile. "You won't be able to: the ops boards are locked to my biosigns and won't recognise you."

He was surprised, his eyes widening. "Another security measure? But what if there's an emergency and someone else has to pilot her?"

"Hard luck," was the retort. She grinned at his expression. "You take my seat and I'll add you as an interim operator to her databank."

Azular's eyes lit up in lively if surprised anticipation and he quickly complied. As soon as he was seated, Kerrix leant over him to tab a control at his far side, issuing a verbal command. A panel to his right slid over to reveal a hollow in which a stylised hand was depicted.

"Put your hand into the recess and when I press down, state your name, rank and ship to record your voice print. You'll feel a prickling sensation as your biosigns are recorded and a genetic sample taken."

He looked up warily before obeying but was rewarded by the hum of operational systems as the ops boards lit up to his touch.

"You can't use voice ops as she's set to Norvallan. But you'll be able to prep her for start. I suggest you don't do anything else."

"Or?"

"Or I eat you for lunch and then take you out of the system," she said as she slid into the secondary position and tied the restraints.

"Understood."

With a frisson of elation, Azular followed the start-up sequence as far as he could recall, Kerrix watching carefully at his back. With only one or two prompts, he finalised the procedure and brought the craft to launch readiness. He felt strangely jubilant: as a skilled pilot he was familiar with a number of designs of shuttle but this ship was in many respects novel. He brought the power back down gradually, switching off the ops boards as he had seen Kerrix do, and gave a satisfied sigh.

"Well done," she congratulated. "Very good for a first attempt."

He turned to look at her, an eyebrow raised suggestively. "I *could* have a second attempt. She's capable of launch: the boards show she would make it out of the bay and into the flight-ways of the Web."

As her eyes widened in surprise and almost incredulity, he pursued his train of thought. "We could leave the *Arianrhod's* shuttle here and use yours to cross to inner belt two?"

Kerrix stared at him. His roguish smile implied that he was joking, but she was unsure. Nonetheless, her answer was sharp when it came.

"Absolutely not. We don't know if she can hover, much less fly; she's missing a sizable bit of her hull; she has a list to starboard for a reason as yet unidentified; and most importantly, your captain would shoot you – and then she'd shoot me. Get the hell out of my seat."

"Yes ma'am."

12: ORANGE 2334

Captain Ahxenta and Ensign Hanx strode into the berth in inner two directly after Azular had docked *Arianrhod's* shuttle at twenty three hundred. Apnis had arranged the green twelve bay sufficiently close that Kerrix would have a short walk home. The captain scanned her science officer's face for signs of the success of his mission when the three alighted from the shuttle and was satisfied that all seemed well. She was less happy with her perusal of their visitor. She looked drawn and tired and stumbled as Azular guided her off the ramp, her leg brace plainly not sufficient support. Ji carried her kit bag.

The science officer quickly verified the positive results of his task: the novel shuttle now had a power source and was capable of limited operation. He had left the second cell and the self-fixing hull patches and had taken charge of the shuttle's empty energy cell, which he hoped to re-energise. He would return it when next *Arianrhod* was in the Web. Ahxenta gave him a searching glance at that but let it pass.

"I'll accompany Ms Kerrix to her quarters to make sure she gets there safely," he continued, smiling at the Norvallan woman.

"You won't," she retorted. "I can make my own way, thank you. And you'll want to get back to your ship to play with your new toys."

Ahxenta could see Ji grinning at that but ignored it as she accepted Kerrix' thanks for her care aboard ship and her hopes that *Arianrhod* would have a safe and pleasant flight. The captain *did* sanction the science officer as escort however, and sent Hanx with the two, as she had a number of questions to ask Ji about the activities aboard the Norvallan shuttle. She also wanted to check out the gear that Azular had exchanged for the energy cells and hull patches.

The young lieutenant narrated events as far as she was able. That Kerrix had configured her shuttle to accept Azular's control surprised the captain; that her science officer had proposed trying to fly the craft out of her berth did not. Kerrix' response was likewise much as Ahxenta would have expected. She left Ji in the bay to keep watch and stepped up to examine the booty that Azular had collected.

The external cloak generator that had been used to camouflage the *Gadfly* Ahxenta recognised. As it seemed such a useful piece of kit she wondered that Kerrix had parted with it. One small object looked like a scanner but did not respond to her touch. A larger item the captain knew must be the energy cell from the damaged shuttle as it matched *Arianrhod's* in size. The final piece was a handgun. She picked it up, trying it for size. It was small and light, but a quick scan showed it was energised and packed a hefty punch. Ahxenta suspected that her second mate would be super-interested once she heard about it.

The captain called the ship to let Apnis know that they would be heading up soon. It had been a long day and unless there was urgent business, mission briefings would be held over until morning, after the loading of their cargo for ISP Stinward. By the time Ahxenta had done, Azular and Hanx had made it back with word that Kerrix was now home. The science officer had scanned the place and it was safe. His only concern was that their presence had been noted by people in the area – *Arianrhod's* insignia always seemed to attract attention.

"Vettarista knew she was headed back," Ahxenta told him. "And Ally's now aware of where she's been, though not the full extent of her injuries. She still has a job."

"Ah," Azular said, realising that that was part of the business that had taken the captain into inner two earlier. "Good."

The next day was busy, with early loading stretching as the captain had insisted that two of her fighters escort the cargo pods from their storage at Redship to *Arianrhod's* bays: she had no intention of losing any in the way that the *Nyx Warrior* had lost hers. She also had her tactical stations track the load at every step. With departure planned for twelve hundred, there was no time for slip-ups.

The briefings were held at ten thirty and Ahxenta had stipulated one hour. Her own mission had been an unscheduled visit to Merkat security to be updated on the situation over Lokterix and the attacks on her crew and on Kerrix. The duty officer had routed out a senior official to talk to her. There was nothing new on the fugitive, or on the later attempted assault on Kerrix in medbay. As for the device set to take out *Arianrhod's* shuttle on her earlier visit, a stash of explosive *had* been found but SSO Parket refused to say where. The captain had then called in at the *Half Moon* for words with Ally. Kerrix would be retained on his staff.

Lieutenant Commander Earbleat had been atypically silent during the captain's update, her eyes repeatedly drawn to the pieces that Azular had brought. She was eager to have a close look at the cloak generator but he would only describe its basics and refused to hand it over. It was one of two that Kerrix had aboard her shuttle and it was capable of holo-projection, much like their own decoy, which would make it useful to him and Chief Cottontail as they were the two most involved with decoy operation. The scanner was a curious piece. It was Norvallan fleet issue, Azular explained. Kerrix had adjusted it to accept his biosigns but no-one else would be able to operate it. One of his tasks was to change that. The device had a quirk that would make it invaluable, even though it was a hand-held: it was capable of linking to relevant databases and self-updating *if* it was in range of said databases or already-updated control units or scanners.

"And just where are these databases, units or whatever?" Ahxenta demanded sceptically.

"These types of unit are standard aboard Norvallan fleet vessels, ma'am. Relevant updates are sent out from source to bases and ships of the line, and linked scanning systems can be set to rove for new data and be upgraded by accessing already-updated units."

"So you set that thing to rove for a relevant Norvallan data source in range, and you'll know there's a ship or similar out there? Which will no doubt figure you're trying to access its data?"

"That's about the gist, ma'am, but the range is limited and security measures are in place to prevent unauthorised access to revised or novel data. *And* any units would have to be within our short scanning range, as far as I'm aware."

"But it's basically a way to let us know if there's a Norvallan ship out there, no doubt so that we can stop and say hello," Ahxenta said dryly. "Very astute of Ms Kerrix: using us to find her a ride home."

"That's hardly fair, Captain. The chances are slim that we would come upon such a source, but we do now have equipment that might be of great use. This handgun for example is a very powerful weapon for all its size, and can cut through hull plate – though possibly not meta-jurillium hull plate."

"Now that makes it *very* useful," Earbleat broke in, smiling widely.

"You won't be taking it to pieces," she was told curtly. "And I still have the energy cell to examine. If it could be recharged, it would be useful to pass back to Ms Kerrix when next we're in the Web."

"Assuming she's still there," Apnis added laconically. "Now tell us about your closer look at her little boat."

As the captain and first mate made their way to the bridge after the briefing, Apnis turned to Ahxenta. "Do you get the impression that our Azular is ultra-excited about everything relating to Norvallan technology and the mysterious Ms Kerrix?"

"He's like a kid in a candy store," the captain grouched. "To him it's new tech and he's keeping a tight rein on the kit he persuaded her to part with; though why she *did* give him some of it is puzzling me."

"Maybe it's bugged?"

"No; he'd have worked that out and she wouldn't dare, she knows our rep. I think she wants him to come to grips with Norvallan tech so that if we meet similar or any PSS reports it we'll recognise it. And she wants her shuttle fit to fly if she has to shift it. But he'd better be on the bridge at twelve hundred for departure or I'll have his ears."

Both science officers were in post, as were most of *Arianrhod's* senior officers, and the emergency bridge was on standby. Ahxenta was leaving nothing to chance. Their ISP cargo was vital for the new fleet shipyard being built at Stinward, it was costly and their endpoint was known. Given their recent troubles and news of other incidents out in the spaceways, she wanted no glitches. She gave the order to loose *Arianrhod's* docking struts and the ship slipped her traces. The final farewell from Port Control echoed across the bridge as she slowly backed out of the Web and into free space.

"ISP Central Logistics Stinward, Captain?" Navigator Box asked.

"ISP Stinward," Ahxenta confirmed. "Best speed, helm."

"Aye, ma'am," Dox called from her station as she set her boards.

"Didn't Grey Bluejohn tell us that the *Hexameter* met trouble out by Stinward? Though we haven't seen Bee Lyvy Coxen to get the full story," Apnis stated. "Nothing since?"

"Not that I've heard. But we set long-range scanners at maximum and we run silent, with cloak and decoy ready to deploy. Plot a course via Lesser Kirrin and New Zegonia and then to Polstarn, Mr Box. I don't want to cross the empty spaces of Theta if I can help it."

"Aye, ma'am," the navigator sang out.

"Yes; one Coalition-controlled zone is plenty, even if they're still part of the glorious Alliance," Apnis agreed. "We can cut across the bypass by Lesser Kirrin but give Cygilla Prime a miss. Wasn't that where the *Obsidian's* loading gear was damaged?"

"It was. But we shouldn't need a stop-off. We resupplied in the Web and Lindell had his people check every scrap of incoming stores to make sure nobody pulled a fast one."

"I doubt they'd dare. Our suppliers are certified, they deal only in the best and none of them would risk upsetting us."

The *Arianrhod* sped on, all stations keeping a close status watch on conditions both inside and outside the ship. It was hours down the line when Bellfish picked up a patchy distress signal. Gliss was quick to reconfigure his sensors to sweep the relevant area for its source.

"Triangulating now," he called. "Signal's from a system listed as Orange 2334. It's a shielded source, Captain," he added in surprise. "Why would you shield a distress beacon?"

"To mask its nature," Azular answered him. "It might be a ruse to draw in a rescue ship. I'll see what's on file… there's a mining station on the third planet under the authority of Lesser Kirrin."

"A mining station sending out a distress?" queried Apnis. "What is it they're mining that they don't have ships running that can help?"

"No other information, Commander," Azular reported.

"Let's see what's up. Change course to Orange 2334," ordered the captain. "Cloak up, Dox. Do *not* respond to the signal, comms: until I know the score, I won't risk giving out we're in the vicinity."

Arianrhod slid off the bypass with every gun installation on her hull prepped for action. Gliss had refined the signal to locate its source as the third planet and Azular's probing had verified that it came from a collection of linked surface structures. They could detect no activity in nearby space but did not discount the possibility that something was hidden out of sensor range behind the planet or in the shadow of a moon. As the minutes ticked by and the planet came within visual range, their readings sharpened to reveal the details more clearly.

"One of the surface domes has been blown!" Greffy called out from his station. "Very recently by the look of it," he added.

Azular concurred. "Destruction from an external assault's caused a breach in the upper quadrant and I read fused construct materials. But there's old damage as well, as if *this* attack was carried out on an already-smashed dome; the others are showing signs of breach as well. There are no craft in orbit and none on the port facility pads."

"Are we close enough to detect lifesigns?" the captain demanded. "If there's nothing then this is a trap and I smell big trouble."

"This I don't believe!" Greffy said in consternation. "This has got to be a set-up. Look at these signs, Doc! We know these readings."

"What have you got?" Ahxenta called as she stood.

"An old acquaintance – this reads like a well-enhanced Comet Six hiding out in an underground silo just outside the main operational dome of the complex," Azular informed her.

"If it *is* that little runt and he's called for aid as some sort of trick then he's fried!" the captain raged.

"Check the records for Lesser Kirrin mining disasters," Azular told Greffy. "It seems to me that a former incident caused evacuation of the complex but there's been recent damage to the main dome. And *that's* the source of the distress. So where Micklemouse fits in, Captain – if that *is* his ship – I can't tell."

"In other words, a set-up! But are *we* the target or was it anyone who happened to pick up the distress and respond?"

"Unknown, Captain. What have you got, Greffy?"

"You were right, Doc: main and side dome breaches and complex evacuation. Suspected sabotage, but as ore sources were drying up it was never reinstated. Minimal salvage ops were set in place and it was rumoured to be an insurance fraud but nothing proven. It happened over a year ago, Kirrin time. The place was totally abandoned."

"Now it's not and as far as you can tell, Azular, Micklemouse or at least what looks like his ship is down there," Ahxenta surmised.

"It appears so, ma'am. Lonagan Four is in this zone and we know Micklemouse visits there; and so is Sevolb, where he told Captain Holdspan that an unidentified PSS had been hit by raiders."

"That hadn't escaped me. And the Friskianx system's not far off. So there are a few unsavoury characters in the neighbourhood. But *that* damage was not caused by his ship, in spite of her big guns."

"Agreed. From the type of damage, I estimate that we're dealing with advanced, non-local tech. I'll check against the data we got from the *Green Comet* on her incident at Kifferbuck. Ah! I have a match on trace weapons signals from the scores on the *Comet's* hull."

"Show me!" Ahxenta ordered.

"That *is* very recent damage," Greffy noted as Gliss called that his tactical sweeps of the surrounding area had come up blank but there were a number of hiding places out of sensor range.

"We could send out probes to sweep the far side and the moons, Captain," the senior science officer suggested.

"No; that would give us away. If there *is* a ship similar to the one that hit the *Comet* out there they'd know. Their tech's in advance of ours and the damned hostiles that chewed up chunks of the mapped galaxy could detect cloaked ships by their displacement shifts. Hot up the weapons, Whisper; Crizz, make sure we're ready to shift. And prepare the decoy. If we have to deploy it, I want it ready."

"Understood, Captain," Azular responded.

"Set main holo on full, Gliss," Ahxenta rapped as she resumed her chair. "Amber alert. Plot evasive routes out, Mr Box."

"Micklemouse?" queried Apnis in a low tone.

"We run into trouble and he's on his own. I'm not endangering my ship for readings that might be his."

"Incoming!" Gliss yelled as two blips shot out from the shelter of the nearest satellite of the parent body.

"Battlestations! Shields up!" the captain yelled.

The chief tactical officer had set off the red alert and calls that shields and phase weapons were operational rang around the bridge.

"They were damn quick off the mark! Full tactical! Earbleat, get a bead on those ships and get set to hit them with all you've got. Drop the cloak, Dox, it's not helping. Web in everyone!" Ahxenta sang out, tightening her own seat restraints.

"Smaller than we've seen but close to hostile spec," stated Apnis as she hauled her ops board across. "Azular?"

"Correlating with the *Comet's* data. Both resemble the ship that hit her, but shielding is hindering clear readings."

"I'd say phase cannon," the first mate put in dryly as the great ship rocked to a burst that caught her port side.

"Confirm armaments as phase cannon on the nearer ship; she also has torpedo tubes and slicer beams!" Gliss warned "The other one's trying to flank us and she's coming in with all guns blazing!"

"Get us close enough to take out main weapons on the lead ship!" Ahxenta ordered. "Tactical, pinpoint her comms arrays: I want them out. Tallica, take auxiliary weapons and deal with that second boat."

"Aye, ma'am," the first mate barked, releasing her seat restraints.

Her eyes skimming the tactical data across the bridge holo, the captain felt her webbing tighten as Dox sent the ship into an upward corkscrew to avoid an incoming stream of fire.

"They have fighter bays!" Azular reported. "No sign of launch."

"Launching deflecting drones against second ship!" bawled Apnis. "She's using wide-spread missile salvos!"

"Damn!" the captain hissed as a violent thud indicated a direct hit to *Arianrhod's* hull.

"Hell! We've lost an aft shield!" Cottontail's voice echoed across the bridge. "Repair team on it."

"Helm, compensate!"

Dox lost no time and under her skilful hands the ship shot off at a tangent to protect her exposed stern, returning in a wide sweep to the attack. As the minutes ticked by, the superior weaponry and power of *Arianrhod* began to tell. A relentless stream of firepower sent out after the leading ship caused her to veer and as a final well-aimed torpedo caught her tail she spiralled out of control to explode in a bloom of flame. The second craft, slowed by Apnis' assault, swerved abruptly and speared off into the dark of space.

"Let her go, but track her as far as you can," Ahxenta called out. "Damage reports all stations. Stand down red alert."

"So what've we got, Cap?" the first mate asked as she resumed her usual position at Ahxenta's side.

The captain was scanning her boards. "Casualties minimal; we've taken surface damage but we'll make it to Stinward and they'll have the gear to refit us. Those ships were as near as damn the spec of the one that tried to get the *Comet*. Her tactical team logged it as a small interceptor-type. I want all we have on those two. I'll send that and a report to the PSS fleet, copied to the ISP. Lesser Kirrin had better be alerted – Coalition or not, it's their jurisdiction."

"That distress is still going," Apnis remarked.

"So I see. Are we still reading that Comet Six, Azular?"

"Yes ma'am, but she's increased her shielding. That suggests that she knew that a firefight was going on overhead."

"I bet I'm going to regret this," Ahxenta growled. "Okay Dox, bring her round and into a close orbit. Gliss, keep your team at full alert and maintain a bead on everything in and out of this system. Azular, you and Greffy get everything you can on the debris floating around us. And no, Ms Earbleat, you are not going on a recce to pick up bits! We scavenge pieces the tractors can bring in but nothing else *and* they'll be held in high security until they've been verified safe."

"You can read her like a book," the first mate said with a grin. "So what do we do about it if it *is* Micklemouse?"

"Get him a link to his pal Doosbak at Lonagan Four and they can sort it out between them. I'm not having him or his ride on my ship."

"If we did, it *would* give us a chance to check what's been altered in him *and* his ship since last we were close enough to do it," the first mate hinted. "Azular can handle him and he knows he owes us for giving him the lowdown on Lokterix. We can let out we were headed for Selliden and throw him out there. He can get his ship fixed and make for Lonagan from there and it's a direct link to Polstarn and then Stinward for us. And if we want to pick up spare arms, Selliden Central can supply: it's a big place with refit yards, it's ISP *and* it has a local ISP office as it's bang on the Alpha-Epsilon border."

The captain pondered. "Several good points but it goes sorely against the grain. I'll check with Azular and see what he has so far."

She rose and made for the science stations, stretching to ease taut muscles. Both science officers were capturing and storing data from the flak beyond the ship. They had organised the hauling in of debris for close analysis later but could report that the hull of the lead ship was similar to that of hostile vessels they had scanned during earlier clashes, though they could not link ship design to known shapes.

"Using resources left over from the war or not used," guessed Ahxenta. "So they're raiders holed up in ex-hostile bases or they've stolen the stuff and are kitting out their own dens with it."

"Or they *are* hostiles and have altered their original blueprints to exploit what they've obtained or developed," Azular said.

"Or any number of other explanations. Get what you can that I can put into a report for the fleet and a diluted version to hand over to the ISP and the TA. But leave Greffy with it for now. Are we still reading traces of what seems to be Micklemouse's ship?"

"We are, ma'am: I've been keeping an eye on the signals. Whoever is down there is trying to scan to see what's gone down but as they're underground and running silent, they won't have got much."

"Too scared in case the bad guys have won and he'll be next on the menu," Ahxenta nodded. "Have you done in-depth?"

"As far as possible; it reads very much like the augmented Comet Six. I doubt there are two like it."

"So do I," the captain agreed. "Commander Apnis suggests we bring it and him aboard and comb over them to see what's changed since last we got up close and personal. Your take on that?"

"I don't like it but I see the logic. I'd be interested to see how far he is from the influence of his late masters and how far he's been able to retain their tech. And it *would* allow us a clear scrutiny of that tech, as he couldn't object. I expect he *has* succeeded in losing that inaccessible stash of high explosives planted aboard his ship, as he had no control over the trigger."

"I bet he has. But can you handle him?"

"Yes. Though I suggest he's given a systems inhibitor before he steps out of the docking bay, lest his info-tech talents are still strong."

"Agreed. I'll set it up. How far did you track that second blip, Gliss?" she called to the tactical officer.

"Her last heading would put her on a course for the Helix Cluster, Cap, but she's out of range. Nothing else."

"Interesting: there's an ex-hostile base beyond the Outer Reaches Archipelago further on and a bypass node at Vreskota Two."

"Not to mention the Orriga Asteroid Field," Azular added.

"As I said, interesting."

Micklemouse, when *Arianrhod* finally made contact, was glad to see a way out but was uncertain of his rescuers. He knew them of old and knew the means they were likely to use to limit his abilities. His options were few, Ahxenta told him: he either accepted her terms or she would leave him to find his own way out. His craft was low on fuel and had been damaged as he tunnelled his way into the silo to avoid incoming fire from an unknown ship that had burst into local space and began a direct assault on the station's main dome, he told her. He had been close enough to his vessel to jump aboard and run. What he had been doing in the burnt out station he would not say.

In the event, he and his ship were picked up as one when he had been persuaded to reverse out of his hidey-hole to a point where the *Arianrhod's* tractors could get a grip. The PSS lost no time in scanning every iota of the Comet Six and took the precaution of disabling her weapons by well-aimed pinpoint phase shots as soon as she was clear of the lower atmosphere. The sensors that Micklemouse had turned in their direction were also targeted and immobilised.

The trader was not surprised to find an armed party awaiting him when he stepped into the pressurised space arranged for his craft. He was also not surprised that no-one was smiling: his antics in scanning them had not amused the captain. He was told that his home for the trip to Selliden would be the brig and meanwhile Dr Flintlock would dispense a systems inhibitor to curtail his abilities.

"And if I refuse?" Micklemouse asked, trying to sound confident.

"You step right back aboard your ship and we put you back where we found you," Ahxenta snapped curtly. "Take it or leave it. I have contracts to fulfil and I've no time for shenanigans."

He took it. He was stripped of his armaments and scanners, dosed by the doctor, and with Azular alongside and two armed guards at his back he was frogmarched to the brig to be deposited there to enjoy his own company. The captain had left Earbleat and Greffy to probe his ship and compare the readout to their previous scans. Meanwhile, she made for her office to contact the authorities on Lesser Kirrin to apprise them of the situation and find out what they knew, and then to pass on her report, augmented by data on the attacking ships, to the PSS fleet and the ISP local office at Selliden Central.

The results of her exchanges the captain gave in a short briefing to her senior officers. The Kirrin representative that she had dealt with had voiced alarm, but as Orange 2334 had been a civilian concern, the authorities would take no further action. There had been reports of unofficial salvage ops at the site, but nothing that merited criminal investigation. No reply had come in from the ISP and of the PSS fleet, only the *Quarkstorm* and the *Emerald* had linked for clarification.

And Captain Goodsocks of the *Emerald* had news: the unnamed PSS that had lost comms gear to a raider pack near the Crimson Drapes was the *Pearl Shield*, one of the oldest and smallest vessels in the fleet. Goodsocks had met her first mate Myrica Dowris at ISP Silverglass and had been told that the *Pearl* had met three small fighters of old raider design and had seen them off without trouble, for though well-armed, no back-up had been evident. But as the *Pearl's* main comms array had been hit, she had dropped into Lonagan Four, where her chief engineer had a mate that could source them the parts.

"No back-up?" Apnis queried. "Looks like some of the old-school raiders are still operating then, but are rapidly running out of kit. The *Pearl* is small as Privates go, *Valkyrie* class, but Kurrin Tilius has been around more blocks than most. *He* wouldn't send out a warning over a few fighters at his back, and the rep of Lonagan Four wouldn't put the frighteners on him either."

"True," Ahxenta agreed. "I passed the data we have on the ship that lit out to Goodsocks – *Emerald's* heading into Dryssicon Major with gear for their repair sheds and that's not too far from the Helix. But as for our visitor in the brig, I plan to notify the authorities on Lonagan that we have a trader aboard that claims to ship out of there and goes by the name of Froyd Melson. I'll give them the bare bones of his rescue and he can weasel out of it any way he sees fit."

"Will you tell him before you dump him?" the first mate asked.

"That depends. What did you make of his current capabilities and what did you get out of him, Azular?"

"The tracking device planted by his late associates is still inactive but one cyber system that Dr Flintlock disabled is now functional, as far as I can tell. What its function *is* I've not been able to work out, although it may be related to his info-sent capabilities."

"So how did he reset it?" the chief medic interrupted. "He must have had help."

"I agree and from that I guess he's being used as a data-harvester again, perhaps with his consent, but he was not frank. All he would admit was that he was on a salvage mission on his own account. I could try to find out more, Captain, as we have two days before we reach Selliden. His abilities seem less strong than before the doctor's intervention, but with the systems inhibitor it's difficult to judge."

"See if you can get more out of him of his dealings with Doosbak and Lokterix, particularly the trading in sensitive data. I bet he held a lot back when Tallica and I grilled him in the *Port in a Storm*. If he was paid good rates for shipping highly encrypted data shards there must be a lot in it. As he talked about a hush-hush Web-based commercial interest, it strikes me that this data is more than the usual novel tech or trade-route stuff. Lean on him if you have to. Axellina can help."

"Will do, Captain."

"Captain, I object…" Flintlock interjected.

"Noted, but I want to know of anything that could impact on my ship and my people, and I suspect that this might. What did you and Greffy get on his boat, Earbleat?"

The second mate reported that the ship's shielding, weapons and comms had been upgraded, but the download and storage cyber suite where his data was extracted and where his masters reprogrammed him read the same. Two sealed storage units next to the suite that had once held explosives for remote detonation had been battened down but their contents were cloaked and thus unreadable.

Azular had been listening intently. "I could use the scanner Ms Kerrix gave me. It will only accept me as its operator, but I can try."

"I'll bet," Whisper Earbleat sniffed. "I thought you were going to fix it so it would respond to any of us?"

"It's based on biosign recognition and that's not easy to alter. And the command language is Norvallan, with which I'm *not* familiar."

"Cut it," commanded Ahxenta. "Do it," she added to Azular. "But getting info out of our pet weasel is a priority. If he doesn't come up with the goods, tell him the Lonagan authorities will be given both his names before we drop him at Selliden."

The dialogue with Micklemouse told them that he and Doosbak were involved in the transfer of encrypted files of unknown matters. There had been contact through Doosbak with others besides Mak Trebint, but he declined to name them. The Web at Merkat was only one of various stop-offs that he had made and of those he claimed to recall, Mellifly, Salt Three and Minch Fettin were the most recent.

"Little sod gets about then," Crizz Cottontail muttered when she heard during an update meeting.

"His contacts probably used false names," Azular stated. "But it will be worth questioning him on the nature of the goods behind the fascia of his storage units. I've updated the captain: my scans show a data download-retrieval system similar to that in his cyber suite but much smaller, more complex and highly shielded, possibly to avoid volatile damage if the data shard or unit undergoing extraction has self-destruct as part of its encryption cycle to prevent data theft."

"Encryption cycle?" repeated Apnis. "Are you saying he's got a purpose-built clandestine data-abstraction facility on board?"

"That's what I infer from my scans. The units hide a single space, but we don't have much time to verify it before we make Selliden."

"That scanner your friend Ms Kerrix gave you must be one smart device," the first mate observed ironically.

"It has useful elements," was the equally dry retort.

"So Micklemouse is setting himself up in the espionage business, is he?" Cottontail demanded. "Or are he and Doosbak in cahoots and Doosbak trusts him enough not to cheat?"

"That'll be the day!" Whisper Earbleat snorted. "He's out to make profit but if he's found out, it's more than trouble he'll get. I'll bet the data he's paid to shift is a lot less than legal."

"That's enough," Ahxenta cut in. "I'll be in on an interview over that data-stealing facility and it'll be now. Back to work, we have a ship to run. Tallica, you have the conn; Flintlock, you're with us."

Micklemouse could sense that the three officers had more than a pleasant chat in mind when they entered his cell. He was left in no doubt when the captain ordered him to the table, sat down opposite, unfolded an info-pad and activated its holo-projection port. Azular and Flintlock sat either side of him, both looking grim.

"The inside of your twin-fronted hold, Micklemouse, beside your still-working cyber suite: you'll tell me *exactly* what's in it, what it's used for and why, where it came from and who fitted it. You have thirty minutes or you, *without* your ship, will be handed to the Selliden authorities with a report, copied to the ISP here, on all we know of you, your activities and those of Doosbak, alias Chel Fogrun."

"How did you get that?" the trader asked in horror, gazing at the clear holo of the inside of the covert space. "It can't be scanned!"

"Wrong," Ahxenta said coolly. "You have twenty nine minutes."

Micklemouse licked his lips, unsure of what they knew but acutely aware that the captain would carry out her threat. The three could see by the fearful expressions crossing his face that various notions were warring in his mind. The safety of his skin won out and he admitted to attempting to decode and copy the data shards with which he was entrusted. Doosbak knew of it, he claimed. The gear had been fitted aboard *his* ship as several of Doosbak's sites had been probed by law officers looking for evidence of shady dealing. As the data shards that he had been passed were sealed within tamper-proof cases, he had decoded few and those few held data that had meant nothing to him.

The captain looked distastefully at the trader. A glance at Azular confirmed some truth in the tale but the man was holding back.

"Where did you get the tech, where was it fitted and who did it?"

Micklemouse bit his lip and stared at her, silent, a slight shake of his head indicating that he was extremely reluctant to say more.

Ahxenta gave him ten seconds before she went on. "Your facility will not be operational when you leave my ship. We now have the full blueprint of it and it *will* be passed to the appropriate authorities."

"You can't do that!"

"Why not?" she asked calmly.

"I'd be fried!"

"By whom and why?"

As the silence lengthened, the captain rose. "As you please. You're a crook, you keep very fishy associates and every time you come into my orbit you bring trouble. And I've had enough of it and you."

"Captain!" his shrill voice cracked. "I'll tell you what I know…"

He knew little. The refit of his Comet Six had been carried out at Mellifly at the instigation of two new contacts of Spendle Doosbak. He had flown his ship into a repair base, one of many still active, and had left it there until the job was done. He had undergone surgery in the interim to reactivate his cyber systems. Doosbak had control over the putative use of the data decode unit and the trader would be told where to be when it was needed. Thus far he had not been called. He insisted that he did not know the names of the new contacts, but he did say that one hailed from Xerophyte IV, as the man had said that he was heading back to a base there once the refit was complete.

The trader's shifty eyes and swift-flicking glances from one to the other of the three, as if gauging their reactions, caused Azular to scan him deeply. Something was tugging at the back of his mind.

"Describe this contact from Xerophyte IV, particularly in relation to his cyber-implants and his face," he directed suddenly.

That struck a nerve, for Micklemouse's eyes widened. "He didn't have cyber-implants that I was aware of, he…"

"He did. Tell us about them and him — and his name. You *had* met him before, after all."

Ahxenta glanced at her science officer, sensing that his quick brain had pieced together a puzzle. She thought back to the trouble she had met on her last trip to Xerophyte IV. One link to the sly little man rose up in her mind from a quizzing she and her people had dealt him after they had rescued him from Kelfennig. They had also had Doosbak in the brig, after that sinner had tried to coax the trader out of their clutches and into his at the behest of his manipulators.

The captain's angry eyes searched the face before her, which was trying to look innocent. "You said once before that you could almost scent the likes of him, didn't you? And your business at *that* time if I recall was covertly shifting data shards of classified stuff to different persons and places, or gate-crashing top-level meetings such as the one where Commander Apnis and I first met you and your buddy Spendle Doosbak. You were there to use your info-sent talents to abstract data and pass it on to your tricksy masters."

Micklemouse's jaw dropped. How they had figured the identity of his contact escaped him and he felt his own sense of safety taking a nosedive as he began to realise what that knowledge would mean for him should it fall into the wrong ears.

"Look, Spendle set it up. The guy had called him at Mellifly as he knew he was around. I was brought in as I'd done a few things."

"This guy – his name, his abilities," Ahxenta demanded harshly.

"He was calling himself something like Hoxith…"

"Hoxiz," Azular put in calmly. "Still using the same name then."

"His mistake. Keep talking, Micklemouse; you have very little time left to make a clean breast of it," the captain said shortly.

Completely undone, the trader described the contacts that he and Doosbak had met and with whom they had agreed terms. Ahxenta's tightening jaw as his tale advanced was hardly needed to tell him that she was utterly furious. She left him to stew when she realised that he had little left to reveal. They were close to Selliden Central and she wanted a closed session with her senior officers before they docked.

"Maybe they don't know the war's over," Apnis stated when she heard. "It looks like some of these human-looking semi-cyber villains are out there still and in the business of stirring it and using easy pickings like Micklemouse and Doosbak to do their dirty work."

"It seems so," agreed Azular. "They escaped the worst of the war and for their own reasons are using similar tactics to obtain what must be significant data. And Mellifly is still a centre of intrigue."

"You had *me* foxed," Axellina Flintlock admitted. "How did you pick up the link to Hoxiz? You'd never met the guy face to face."

"The captain, Commander Apnis and Lindell described him and their reactions to him quite concisely after their meeting with him at Thystal Comms on Xerophyte IV. Micklemouse had admitted that a man that fitted the description was one of his former operators and he was so terrified of him that he could sense him. I could feel that he was prey to similar fears as the captain was questioning him."

"Good call," Ahxenta nodded. "But it leaves us with a problem if

Hoxiz and his like are still on the loose and with a grudge against us and those that put a stop to their antics a few months back."

"Especially us; but who do we tell?" Apnis asked. "They'd want to know how we're so sure of it."

"Lokterix is still free," Earbleat put in. "Wonder if he's part of the game Micklemouse and Doosbak are involved in and if he's linked to Hoxiz? But I don't get why the two runts linked up with these scum again. They sure as hell lost out last time and nearly got cooked."

"They perhaps had little choice," Azular suggested. "Their weak points are no doubt well-known. Doosbak for example wouldn't wish to relinquish his post as part of the Coalition Central Council as he has too much in prestige and credit to gain by it."

"Much as I loathe the Coalition and what it signifies, they should know they have delinquents like Doosbak as part it," the first mate said decidedly. "It can't do their credibility or security any good."

"Not our concern," Ahxenta replied. "But we do have the tech to detect hostiles, or some of those that are linked to them: the probe that could detect their nature, particularly the zukivianite part of it."

"They may have developed a countermeasure to block such scans, Captain," Azular warned. "They're not fools and as the ISP took over our tool and put it into production, they would be aware of it. But as the commander pointed out, whom do we tell that we're sure that not only are there hostiles still active but that they've recruited others to their purposes? Perhaps you should pass it to Ms Vettarista, but not openly – a call to her from the *Arianrhod* would certainly raise a storm if it were detected."

"You're not serious?" Apnis demanded.

"Have you another suggestion, Commander?"

"Apart from Admiral Zillah, no."

"We shelve it for now," the captain notified them. "We're almost at Selliden and we're for the bridge."

"Micklemouse?"

"Can sweat, Tallica; I've better things to do than bother about him. But make sure he's still under control, Doc, as I don't want him trying his info-sent tactics from the brig. And I bet he thinks he can."

13: OBSIDIAN SKY

Captain Ahxenta was dissatisfied with the results of the meeting with agents from the Interstellar Systems Protectorate that she, Apnis and Azular had had only hours after *Arianrhod* docked at Selliden. They were reluctant to act over her report of the assault at Orange 2334, that world being in Coalition territory, but they accepted her data on the attacking vessels. Apart from a promise to send the data to their Alto Finglas HQ, no further effort was deemed necessary. That being so, Ahxenta was in no mind to pass on anything about Micklemouse and his covert activities, although he had more or less confirmed that hostiles like those faced during the late war were still at large and still very much operational.

"So what *do* we do with our rat in the brig?" Apnis asked as the three made their way out. "The ISP here's not interested in anything past its own doorstep and I can't imagine that the port or planetary authorities want him in their hair."

"We don't tell him that. We notify the PA of his ship as he'll need to get it fixed if he wants to head to Lonagan. But as soon as we're to rights, we're for Polstarn and then Stinward. I want rid of this cargo before anything else happens. Maybe the ISP office there will show more interest, or offer us a job. Lindell's trying to find us a contract but trade's slack. Azular, you and Greffy make sure you get all you can from Micklemouse's ship and inactivate anything that may cause trouble. If you *can* get into that data-abstraction suite, do it. There may be something there you can use to get to the data on Flatt's info-pad. I take it the scanner you got from Kerrix couldn't read it?"

"It registered empty, leading me to suspect that Flatt had wiped it before he handed it over, as he most likely did to Buntle's recorder."

"Do what you can. The rest of our dealings can be handled from the ship, I've had enough face-to-face. But I *will* give the PA part of the deal on Micklemouse and his Melson alter ego, as it has a right to know what it's got. I'm more inclined to run the story by Vettarista as well, once I can do it without raising hackles. Let's get home. It's almost time for that briefing I scheduled on repair and resupply."

Repairs to *Arianrhod* would be complete in two days, the captain found. The Selliden yards could fit a new aft shield, recharge her hull emplacements and restock her armoury. She ordered her supercargo to source and cost the goods but delivery and fitting she assigned to Earbleat: as a skilled scrounger, she was very able to cope with it. Her other senior officers were dealt their own problems to pass the time.

Flintlock disliked her task of ensuring that Micklemouse left them less talented than he had arrived but saw the benefit in blocking some of his active implants. It was clear that those who had altered him must be tracking him but thus far neither she nor Azular had been able to work out how, nor to what distance their influences extended.

Azular and Cottontail were ordered to probe the cloak generator that Kerrix had handed on. Like *Arianrhod's* decoy it could project a holo around itself and emit signals to simulate a ship, but it could also project a secondary holo image at distance. If such a function could be integrated into the decoy, it would make it formidable. Azular also wanted to recharge Kerrix' energy cell, seeing it as a bartering aid, but was told that his priority was to access the data-abstraction suite on the Comet Six to make sure it held nothing of harm to *Arianrhod* and to extract anything useful. How far such intrusion would cost once it reached the ears of the trader's masters, no-one would speculate.

The captain also reminded Azular of the handgun that Kerrix had given him. From his pained expression she figured that he hoped she had forgotten, but he admitted that he *had* tested it and found it very potent for so diminutive a piece. He had stored it securely for further assessment. It was awkward to use, it needed a delicate touch and was intended for someone with small hands such as its former owner. Earbleat regarded him crossly as her request to examine the gun was met with a civil but steely rebuff. Ahxenta left them to fight it out.

By the time *Arianrhod* was shipshape and ready to resume her mission the chief medic was able to report that she had been able to block the signals from two of Micklemouse's cyber-implants and had extracted what seemed to be a non-operative piece from his upper left shoulder that the man had complained was causing pain. He had made little protest as, apart from the fact that he was in no position to object, he was coming to realise that the ploys into which Doosbak and his own sense of greed had led him were spiralling ominously out of control. He had also realised that his masters would hold the captain of the *Arianrhod* and not himself responsible for any meddling.

Azular had in the interim been busy and had breached the data-abstraction system held in the Comet Six. It was shielded so heavily that he was convinced that it *was* to prevent damage if data-copying resulted in volatile self-destruct. The area also housed recorders that activated on entry. He wiped his own traces but prudently left what had already been logged. A detailed scan resulted in an in-depth spec of the interior but some systems were new to him and he had no intention of tampering, as that would warn the hostiles who had set up the suite that it had been violated. He also suspected that one intricate device was a trigger to initiate catastrophic meltdown.

Greffy had been left with Cottontail and her second Gem Ferry to begin on the workings of the Norvallan cloak-generator but they had little to report by the time *Arianrhod* was ready to depart. The chief engineer had duties in her own domain that she was loath to leave to lesser mortals, feeling that Selliden's repair teams needed watching.

It was with relief that the crew of the great PSS bid farewell to their castaway. Ahxenta shipped him to the Port Authority's office in one of her shuttles. His ship she released into one of their small bays via grapple drones sent out by a local yard. She wanted to be far away by the time the man linked to his contacts, reckoning that it would not be long before the powers that were behind his abilities and his ship would soon figure out what had occurred and who was liable. Yet again, *Arianrhod* would find herself in some firing line.

"Set for the local bypass but not to the beacon for Polstarn until we get closer," the captain ordered, scanning her boards, all of which were showing green. "No doubt there'll be a few eyes on us."

"Any more on that non-working piece of tech the doc removed from Micklemouse?" the first mate enquired softly.

"She's given it to Azular to play with, along with the med data, but he's enough to do with his other jobs. Upgrading our decoy's now his main concern, but even if he and Crizz can't alter it to project an external image using the Norvallan cloak device, *that's* a useful piece of kit – if it could be fitted into one of our shuttles it could provide cloaking at a smaller scale for the *Gadfly*."

"Or *Loki VI*," Apnis responded scathingly. "Though why what's essentially a destructive projectile needs a cloak…"

"If you can't see it coming, it might be useful," Ahxenta grinned ruefully. "But only the once – after that, it's stardust."

"Expensive stardust," was the acerbic reply. "But let's hope this leg of the mission is quieter than the last."

The succeeding days were calm. *Arianrhod's* tactical and science arrays had detected passing ships and hyperspace comms but Polstarn was gained with no hitch. Crossing three galactic zones by the most direct route was a strategy Ahxenta rarely used she but deemed speed to be crucial where an ISP contract was involved. Lindell had been active and by the time they made Stinward two other deals had been agreed. The first meant a stop at New Zegonia for a batch of meta-jurillium for the ISP's Silverglass holding station; the next would take them to the Skyrtek system for three pods of salvage that ISP recovery teams had retrieved from the wreck of the former ISP shipbuilding dock off Skyrtek Prime. These were bound for the new ISP HQ and shipyard at Alto Finglas, where laboratory and intelligence-gathering facilities had been set up to analyse wreckage from the recent conflict and to acquire data on an enemy that had caused such destruction.

ISP Stinward housed a huge centre for collection and distribution of supplies to ISP facilities all over the charted galactic zones. The cargo pods the *Arianrhod* carried were transferred to Central Logistics as soon as checks had been made and clearances issued. The captain had left the details to her first mate as she had a meeting with policy reps to discuss recent raider attacks and other illicit activity across the sectors where the ISP held sway, and its response. She also wanted to see what she could find out about any remaining hostiles and their activities, given that her crew and her associates had been subject to unprovoked violence from persons linked to them.

Ahxenta had taken Azular with her and was pleased to find that the three ISP agents were more informative than their counterparts at Selliden. She passed on her data on Orange 2334 and was informed that the ISP was aware of a recent upsurge in assaults by interceptor-like ships similar to improved raider designs and likely to be based on hostile technology. One strike in the Hellatrix system in zone Iota had involved the excision by precision fire of cargo pods from a ship owned by a gem-mining group. The ship had got out by dropping her cargo and making a run for it. She had not been pursued and it was assumed that the attackers were raiders out for booty. An attack near the world of Yistreen in zone Kappa on a loaded merchant ship had been more serious. After sending a distress the crew had made off in an escape craft, which had been destroyed. The ISP was investigating.

Ahxenta queried the strike close to Stinward on the *Hexameter* and although the reps agreed that little damage had been done to the PSS, they were reticent as to her cargo. That led the two from *Arianrhod* to conclude that it involved their own shipyard, now being built. The ISP consensus was that the raiders were creating new strongholds to replace the originals and were sourcing ships and gear their own way.

That being the case, the Alliance of the ISP, the Coalition, the NTA and others was being boosted by joint measures to combat the threat.

The ISP agents were reluctant to discuss the possibility that hostile bands still stalked the spaceways. Ahxenta was direct: the attacks on her people and contacts led to the conclusion that her ship was being targeted because of her actions in the war. Azular was certain that the reps were aware of the issues but his genial enquiries only spurred them into closing talks with the tentative promise that if more came to light, the Trades Alliance would be told.

"At least there should be more ISP ships to call on if this does escalate," the captain said ruefully as the two made their way out.

"That depends on how quickly they can be built or those damaged in the war repaired," the science officer replied. "The assembly docks at Alto Finglas weren't hit, but they're small compared to all that the ISP lost at Skyrtek Prime."

"The ISP will pull out the stops. But that doesn't help us if there are bloody great torpedoes out there with our name on them or maniacs like Lokterix that will risk a lot to take us out."

"I'm puzzled as to why this crusade against *Arianrhod* continues," Azular disclosed. "It surely can't benefit the perpetrators."

"It's maybe part of the hostile psyche or maybe it goes with cyber-alteration," the captain grimaced. "The likes of Lokterix are inclined to bear grudges. But we'd best get aboard as we've a long haul ahead of us – here to New Zegonia, then to Silverglass, Skyrtek and across to Alto Finglas. That's eight galactic zones if we take the direct routes through and we'll have to stop off for resupply at some point."

"Keystone Kell has supply depots and is close to the node linking Eta and Zeta zones," the science officer suggested with half a smile.

"And it's well-known for the excellent quality of the small arms it produces," was the wry retort. "You want to make sure Earbleat can get her hands on new toys so she'll stop pestering you into handing over that gun of Kerrix' that you're so keen to hang onto."

"No comment," he smiled.

Apnis and Lindell had settled business by the time the two made it in and the captain thus lost no time in giving the command to break orbit and head for New Zegonia. Ahxenta had ignored Azular's hint for a stop at Keystone Kell as it would take them too far off route but had decided to halt at Vrackin Twelve, a lush ISP world mid-way between Silverglass and Skyrtek. It was used by long-haul starships as a repair and resupply post and *Arianrhod* was known there.

The few days that it took to gain New Zegonia gave those tasked with specific projects time to advance. Azular had recharged Kerrix' energy cell but a means of external projection for the decoy whilst it was active had eluded him and the chief engineer. They had refined its image quality and increased its scanning resistance using insights got from testing the Norvallan cloaking device and Cottontail had delegated Gem Ferry to assess the viability of incorporating the cloak into the *Gadfly*, as he had become familiar with its operation. That project was still ongoing by the time the *Arianrhod* made orbit.

Although at the hub of a Coalition-controlled zone, the colony of New Zegonia, like the original homeworld of Beta Zegonia 68c, was independent. It was rich in the beta- and meta-jurillium ores prized as sources for the ultra-durable alloys that were standard base materials for ships' hulls. The resilience of the alloys also made them useful for numerous other applications and they were much sought after.

The cargo of meta-jurillium sheets for Silverglass had been loaded into a huge pod for insertion into an aft cargo bay. As the captain had insisted that her own teams check out the pod before transfer, the job took longer than the supply office had forecast, but the friction it incurred was smoothed over by Lindell's diplomatic tongue. Still, it was more than a standard day before the process was concluded and *Arianrhod* could set her sights towards the ISP holding station.

Ahxenta had stationed her most experienced crew on the bridge for the first leg of the trip across a Coalition-led zone. Their presence would certainly be noted by unfriendly eyes and their expensive cargo was in high demand in many trades, including cybernetics. *Arianrhod* kept an intricate course through hyperspace, she was cloaked despite the energy drain and ran at amber alert.

They were more than six hours out when a glimmer of trouble arose. They had just made zone Zeta and the changeover node at the Non-Treaty Alliance outpost Ella Nine when Gliss reported a shift in local hyperspace that heralded a cloaked ship clearly making for the same point. The tactical officer pulled in all he could with his fine probe beams. The results so perturbed him that he called for confirmation from the science arrays that the signals were real.

"What have you got?" Apnis asked as she strode over to look.

"She's big and reads as a PSS, Commander, but her signals are way weaker than they should be and I have readings that are not clear. No sign of another ship, but there's only one PSS I know apart from us that has a cloak and that's the *Obsidian*."

"Captain to the bridge!" the first mate called. "Get Azular up here, we may need him. What is it?" she asked sharply, turning to Greffy, who had let out an expletive that made most heads turn.

"Traces of zukivianite ma'am, but she *is* reading as a PSS!"

"It's bad," Ensign Ishbel Larai at second tactical reported to Gliss. "Her cloak's failing and so's her shielding. Readings are clearing… She's dropped her cloak. Lieutenant, it *is* the *Obsidian Sky*!"

"Confirm!" rapped Apnis as Ahxenta appeared from her office.

"Confirmed! She's reading as the *Obsidian Sky*," Gliss verified.

The first mate quickly brought the captain up to date as the main bridge holo spun to the ever-changing data input and the two senior officers took up their usual positions, Ahxenta ordering red alert.

"Bring us in closer to the *Obsidian* and get me a link but keep your targeting eyes on her, Earbleat, and run weapons hot. I don't want to run the risk that this is some very clever set-up."

"Targeting aye," the weapons officer confirmed. "Want me to ready *Loki VI*, Cap? She's not complete, but she'll pack a punch."

"Negative on that, Lieutenant Commander!" Ahxenta said testily. "Have you made that link, Mr Bellfish?"

"Something's blocking comms, Captain."

"Her arrays are damaged," Gliss called over. "What in the… she's sending out fine-beamed phase fire towards her *own* comms arrays!"

"Arrays reading as a strong zukivianite source!" Greffy cried as Azular sped onto the bridge and made for his station. "They've been subverted! There's something not right with them."

"Got them!" crowed Bellfish. "Captain Bluejohn for you, Cap."

The hazy outline of a grim-faced Bluejohn, his face a mass of cuts, coalesced in the main viewer and Ahxenta realised that the ship had seen serious action: red alert beacons glowed at every bulkhead, many crewmen wore wound dressings and a couple of medics were busy.

"What in hell's happened, Grey? And how can we help?"

"Later, Cinnabar; for now, if you could take out those mechanoid parasites that are infesting my hull and chewing my external systems to bits I'd appreciate it – it's some sort of limpet technology and my hull's crawling with the damn things."

"Confirmed, Captain," Azular's voice rang out. "It reads as hostile tech and discrete units are disrupting external arrays, patches of hull – and I read penetration of hull plates."

"We know they're getting through," Bluejohn spat. "I've got crew with phase-guns scouring the decks on hunt and destroy missions."

"Send us your data, Grey. You'll need to reduce your shielding to let us get at them. Earbleat, get your teams to target every single one, the finest beams you can, without damaging the *Obsidian's* hull."

"Aye, ma'am."

"A few bits of buckled hull plate I can put up with, as long as you take them out," the captain of the *Obsidian Sky* said harshly.

As the data poured into the relevant stations, Ahxenta scanned her boards and called up tactical readouts. "Dox, optimal distance, liaise with tactical on placement and weapons on timing. All hands, tighten your restraints. Get ready to run at your discretion, Earbleat!"

"Hell, I bet this is the first time you've ever had to order open fire on one of our own," Apnis breathed as the holo gyrated to the ship's forward movement and spears of energy lanced from the *Arianrhod's* weapons arrays to make landfall on the skin of her sister ship.

"Roger that. Azular, get everything you can on what's attached to *Obsidian* and use all you have to develop a response. We've more on alien tech than most and extensive expertise in how to deal with it."

"So we've something to be grateful to Micklemouse for," grinned Apnis mirthlessly as the senior science officer acknowledged.

"That far I wouldn't go," was the rejoinder as *Arianrhod* pivoted into place to deal with the pestilence that was threatening the *Obsidian Sky*. "Greffy, you keep your eyes and your gear on *Obsidian's* hull – her people have their hands full. Ensign Larai, maintain watch on the local area: if anything comes within range, I want to know."

"That's a lot of hardware!" Apnis whistled as the holo of the great black ship shifted and other parts of her hull came into view. "I hope we can pick them off before any more of her hull plate destabilises."

"How are we doing, Earbleat?" Ahxenta barked.

"Killing them Cap, but I don't want to send too much firepower over in case I take out her external arrays and sensors."

"Sensors can be replaced. Just cut them out."

It took over an hour for the hostile gadgetry to be cleared from the *Obsidian Sky's* hull. The assault had impaired her external sensory and weapons systems and her plating was far from sound. Bluejohn had taken stock of his options. That his ship would need extensive repairs was certain but until he was sure that his people had got every last one of the destructive alien units that had made it past his shielding and plating, he was reluctant to make for any port.

The *Obsidian* had been attacked by two ships just after a drop-off at Barfit, a small Coalition world just inside the NTA-majority zone Zeta. They had hit her close by the local node, having come off the bypass all guns blazing. The great PSS was very able to defend herself and both had quickly backed off, but not without inflicting a deal of damage. As a parting shot one had sent a large breaching pod at very high speed straight at them. The *Obsidian's* gunnery crews had caught it, but it had exploded into numerous tiny guided missiles that kept on course until they hit her hull. They had then spread out at speed, attached, and begun to disrupt ship's systems and weaken her plating. Bluejohn had ordered the run to Ella Nine as he had no intention of remaining an easy target for reinforcements.

His science stations had shown the small devices to be structurally cybernetic, with intricately engineered innards complexed to organic moieties. They contained traces of zukivianite and both corrosive and explosive elements as well as inbuilt propulsion and guidance gear. In the currents of the bypass Bluejohn could not deploy his hull repair bots, but he had ordered his weapons teams to target the pieces, as he had no idea if they were trackable by the ship that had fired them.

"We're for Silverglass," Ahxenta told him. "That's your best bet in this sector and they'll have the basics to get you at least operational. We'll escort you there and I suggest we don't hang about. Did you get scans of the two that attacked you?"

"I did and they looked to be a tad larger than the rogues that *you* met at Orange 2334 – I did get your report," Bluejohn grinned. "But these were subtly different. I'll pass you all our data. I'll…"

"Captain?"

Ahxenta held up her hand to halt him, realising by the sharpness of Azular's voice that something was urgent.

"What is it?"

"I've been scanning *Obsidian's* hull. I read positive for hostile tech in two of her fighter bays. Sending it to the holo now…"

As an outline projection of the relevant section emerged in the grid both Ahxenta and Apnis undid their seat ties and jumped up. Captain Bluejohn had instructed his science and tactical teams to scan the fighter bay areas but they seemed to be having trouble.

"The infiltrating pieces are masked, I think," Azular called. "Some kind of cloaking and jamming technology and they read differently to the units that we destroyed on the *Obsidian's* hull."

"How the hell are you reading them then, when I can't?" Bluejohn demanded. "We're getting interference here."

"I've linked the Norvallan scanner to our external sensor arrays," the senior science officer disclosed. "I thought it might be useful."

The captain of *Arianrhod* exchanged a look with her first mate. "In the event we come across Norvallan tech," she said in a low voice.

"I've sent armed teams to my bays to deal with them," the harsh voice of Bluejohn echoed across the bridge. "I'd appreciate ongoing scans from your end to guide them, Cinnabar."

"On it," Azular said briefly. "Patching relevant monitor readout to you, Lieutenant Bellfish; request you link it across to *Obsidian*."

"Acknowledged," the comms officer responded.

Twenty minutes later and the two hostile pieces were dust on the *Obsidian's* fighter bay decks. From the slivers left, her science officers conjectured that the units were autonomous drones and encoded for destructive infiltration through the toughest protective shells.

"So how many more have I got that I don't know about, if they're cloaked and jamming us?" Captain Bluejohn wanted to know.

"We'll run continuous scans as we go," Ahxenta said firmly. "But you know we won't be able to probe every nook and cranny of the *Obsidian*, Grey. So we run more analyses when we hit Silverglass. For now, we ship out."

"Roger that, Cinnabar. And thanks for the assist."

Instructions were given to both crews to prepare for insertion into the bypass and set directly for the beacon to Silverglass station. They ran silent, uncloaked and at red alert, with *Arianrhod* using her main tractors to stabilise the *Obsidian Sky* in the hyperspace currents.

It was almost forty hours later that the two great ships dropped off the bypass close to their destination and hard by the nebula that gave the station its name. They had met nothing on the way in, comms had been quiet and Apnis had planned the rotas to ensure that the most senior officers were on the bridge when they made Silverglass. Messages had been passed to the ISP and the PSS fleet on the two ships faced by the *Obsidian* and their new level of technology. The ISP station was a well-equipped centre and able to offer immediate emergency repairs. As a result of the late war, the place was fully-manned and supply throughput was high. Bluejohn was relieved but very aware that he would have to pay the going rates.

Azular had set up continuous scans of the hull and outer sections of their sister ship during the hyperspace trip, but those had yielded no evidence of other self-directed drones. In a short private briefing, he suggested more intense analyses from within the ship: *Obsidian* was huge and as well-protected as *Arianrhod* and his novel scanner linked into *Arianrhod's* external relays could not run scans deep within her. The scanner would have to be used in hand-held mode aboard her or linked into *Obsidian's* internal systems under Azular's guidance. An account of the device had been given to Bluejohn and it had been agreed that Ahxenta and her science officer would shuttle across.

"I haven't been aboard *Obsidian* in a while," Ahxenta observed to Bluejohn and his senior SO as she and Azular stepped off the ramp. "How bad was it, Grey?" she asked, noting his shadowed eyes and tired face.

"Bad," he conceded. "Let's head up to the bridge."

The *Obsidian* and the *Arianrhod* were both *Vanguard* class, as were most PSS craft, and structurally similar; the visitors were thus familiar with the route and the four were soon on the bridge. Azular followed his counterpart across to her station. He had explained the operation of his novel scanner to Captain Bluejohn and Dr Skolla Tann on the way up and it had been agreed to tie the device into the main science station and carry out sweeps of the interior of the ship from there.

Watched by both captains, Azular quickly linked the appliance to the internal scanning arrays and called up the results on one of the monitors. The Berzic had already pre-set the device to seek out the alien drones using the *Obsidian's* data. On Tann's advice the search began at the fighter bays where the last two devices had been found. Bluejohn's relief as sweep after sweep came up empty was palpable but the *Obsidian* was a large ship and even with her superior ops systems, the search was taking time.

It was almost an hour later that a positive signal was received. The two captains had withdrawn to Bluejohn's office to discuss the latest in relation to the PSS fleet and to check on incoming messages from their usual sources. The alert sent both racing back onto the bridge.

"It's in medbay, in an iso-lab that's under refit," first mate Ginger Stone said tartly. "I've despatched a team. As far as we can tell it's inactive. I've ordered the area cleared as far as possible but we've a few of our wounded still down there."

"I suggest you get more security teams ready," Ahxenta advised as Bluejohn acknowledged. "Taking out that one might alert any others still free that it's been caught."

"Good call," he agreed, nodding to his first mate to confirm.

The next few minutes were a waiting game as the team in medbay cornered and blasted its quarry. Azular and Tann had continued deck by deck sweeps to flush out other rogues. Three more had been detected in isolated corners by the time scanning was almost done. None were active and Bluejohn was in hopes that his ship was clear. Warnings of the types of ship that had attacked *Obsidian* and of the tech used to cripple her had been sent out to relevant agencies of the bodies that were part of the Alliance, but both captains were acutely aware that enemy agents would also have got wind that their tactics were now common knowledge and had failed on at least one PSS.

"And I'll bet they'll know that *Arianrhod* was involved," Ahxenta remarked wryly. "Another good reason to mark us, I suppose. We…"

Simultaneous cries by Azular and Tann alerted them to a problem. The Berzic science officer had jumped to his feet and seconds later part of the overhead holo-grid erupted as a missile burst out in a shower of flak. As Ahxenta drew her handgun and prepared to fire, a spear of energy shot out from the weapon in Azular's hand and the drone dropped like a stone.

"I guess that's the last," Tann remarked as she scanned the molten morsel on the deck with her hand-held probe. "That was a live one."

"Not any more," the *Arianrhod's* science officer responded as all eyes were drawn to the misshapen lump of organo-metal.

"That's quite a weapon," the *Obsidian's* captain observed. "It took sustained fire from a few of ours to take the others out."

Ahxenta looked askance at her officer. Azular was toting the small handgun that Kerrix had given him.

"And how long has that been in your pocket?" she asked.

"Almost since the day I got it. It doesn't take up much space."

"Evidently."

"Where in blazes did you pick it up?" enquired Bluejohn, his brow creasing. "For its size, it packs a heap of power."

"A long story for another time," Ahxenta replied. "Just make sure *Obsidian's* clear of whatever those things are," she told her science officer. "And then we have to get back to the ship – we're on a tight schedule and I want to source a few spare munitions as I'm here. But let me know what else we can help you with, Grey. *Obsidian's* taken a serious beating and it'll take you time to get her back up to spec."

"You're telling me. But I've a cargo in my hold, micro-engineering parts for Silshoon and they're in a transfer pod. If you could ship that for me – if my clients agree and it's not out of your way – I'd be thankful. They're old customers and I don't want to let them down."

"We're for Skyrtek via Vrackin for resupply, then Alto Finglas, so we're headed that way," Ahxenta mused. "I'll check my schedules with Lindell, but we can drop in on Silshoon on the way to Merkat. I'll get back to *Arianrhod* and let you know. If you'd send me the data your science and tactical teams have on *that* beast and the others?"

"You got it. And thanks for the assist. Especially you, Dr Azular."

"You're welcome, Captain."

The flight back to *Arianrhod* was quiet bar one or two exchanges with her bridge crew, but once their shuttle had docked and the two were heading out, Ahxenta turned to her science officer. "You were quick to jump in with that handgun so you've clearly studied it closely *and* you've used it. Anything else it does you'd care to tell me about?"

Azular acknowledged the hit with a grin. "I don't know if it was initially set up for Ms Kerrix, but it *has* bonded to me and I doubt it can be used by anyone else. It *can* pierce meta-jurillium, so I would be careful using it in anger. I suspect it also learns: it picks up on targets and stores the data. So if we meet another of those autonomous drones it will take it out, even if set to the equivalent of stun."

"It wasn't set to stun back there," Ahxenta observed trenchantly.

"No ma'am. Given what we were likely to face, I thought it wise to have it at full power – and it *can* be recharged using our facilities."

The captain sighed gustily but let it go. Azular, like many of her crew, would not seek leave for actions he deemed appropriate.

"Anything else?" she demanded.

"I'm working on it," was the enigmatic response.

"What about that device Flintlock took out of Micklemouse that you've also failed to mention?"

"I have a theory, highly unsubstantiated, but I would have to liaise with Dr Flintlock and I suspect she may be reluctant."

"Explain."

"The device is highly complex, pico-engineered, protected at many levels, capable of multiple linkages to delicate core bio-systems and meant for use in humanoids. It was perhaps inactive and causing pain in Micklemouse because his masters did not have the expertise either to encode it or to insert and attach it properly."

The captain looked at the science officer. "You're not suggesting the doctor implants it in someone else?"

"Certainly not and I doubt that Dr Flintlock has the expertise. But I *will* need access to confidential medical files and I suspect she'll argue – unless you intercede."

Ahxenta narrowed her eyes. "I think I see where you're going with this. It'll keep. I want to see how far our cargo drop and scheduling has got. You're on the bridge for the duration."

"Yes, ma'am."

Cargo handover was complete, Apnis reported as the captain took the command chair. The delivery was in ISP hands, all clearances and payments had been passed and Lindell was in process of locating and dealing for the arms that Ahxenta had specified on her way in. Data from the *Obsidian* had been received but they still waited word on the transfer of her cargo for Silshoon. The *Obsidian* herself would remain at Silverglass. The ISP office there had authorised release of sufficient resources to fit the ship to a spec that she could continue her voyage. The data passed to the ISP Council at Alto Finglas had alarmed that body to the extent that it had sent out a heavy cruiser to investigate the area near Barfit, it being close to Silverglass and ISP territory.

"You'll love this, Cinnabar," Apnis snickered. "Bellfish tracked their comms and the ship that's to be sent out is the *ISPS Repulse*. She should be here in a little over thirty six hours, top speed."

"Then let's make sure we're well on our way to Vrackin Twelve by the time she gets here," the captain returned severely.

"The unpleasant Colonel Myrtleberry may not be in charge..."

"I wouldn't put credit on it; she was in the hot seat the last couple of times we had dealings with her. But Grey can keep us up to speed as he'll still be here if the *Repulse* calls in. Yes, Lindell, what is it?"

The supercargo had found and successfully bid for the arms listed and they would be delivered in two hours. The supplies for pick up at Vrackin would be ready by the time they got there and the Silshoon clients awaiting the parts were content with the change of carrier.

Ahxenta confirmed and set her crew to prepping the ship for departure. The *Obsidian's* transfer pod was loaded into an inner hold and *Arianrhod's* huge outer bays readied for the three pods of salvage from the wreckage of the ISP's ex-shipbuilding dock at Skyrtek.

The short journey to Vrackin gave the captain time to talk to Azular over his theory relating to the implant removed from Micklemouse. As she had guessed, he was sure it was a prototype language analyser-translator, possibly parallel to the one Kerrix bore. He thus needed the medical scans Flintlock had taken of her as comparisons. If he was correct it raised a concern: whoever had inserted the device into the trader was likely to know about the one Kerrix carried. They may also have been involved in the attempt to remove it, implying that Micklemouse's contact Hoxiz was part of it and that the latter might have links to Lokterix – both had been on Xerophyte IV months before when Ahxenta had been attacked, both knew Micklemouse, and, the trader's contacts on Mellifly and Lonagan had given him, via Doosbak, the contract that had led to the meeting with Trebint.

Something else had occurred to Azular: on their visit to Xerophyte IV they had met undercover operative Commander Molli Warweft of ISP's Intelligence Division and had given her the name Hoxiz as a potential alien infiltrator. They had heard no more, but as Vettarista had in effect disclosed that she belonged to the same organisation, it was another reason to advise her of the latest as far as Micklemouse, Doosbak, their dangerous allies and their activities were concerned. Ahxenta, aware of the implications, ordered Flintlock to release the relevant medical notes. The CMO was unhappy, but realising that resolution of the mystery might help Kerrix, she complied.

By the time *Arianrhod* made Vrackin Twelve, Azular had results that impelled him to request an urgent briefing with Ahxenta and the chief MO. The device implanted in Kerrix was close to her neck in her upper left shoulder and from images the doctor had taken of the woman, Flintlock had established that it was the nexus of an intricate network of microscopic fibres that linked into diverse bio-systems, including nerves. Insertion must have entailed precise, skilled and time-consuming surgery. The appliance itself the doctor had been unable to scan as it was shielded and she had no intention at the time of putting her patient under undue stress. The piece that had been removed from the trader had been located in virtually the same place in his body and was similar in size and general shape, although not identical to the Norvallan implant. The links of the unit to tissues in Micklemouse were few but Azular had verified the presence of profuse fibres that were capable of surgical attachment.

"In other words, if it *is* a translation device, it's non-functional and they don't have the ability to implant it fully," Ahxenta said shortly. "But would it be capable of working if it *was* properly attached?"

"I can't say," Azular told her. "Given its intricacy and number of potential connectors, it may be possible, but thus far I can't say if it *is* one of these devices. Without an in-depth analysis of the one that Ms Kerrix carries and a comparison with this, I can't tell."

"*She* might," Flintlock said bluntly.

"That had occurred," he admitted. "But where did Micklemouse's masters obtain it? It was probably inserted when he was adjusted on Mellifly, at that centre that Ms Vettarista says is under surveillance by ISP. But there's a problem: we have excised this device and if he *is* being tracked by those who implanted it…"

"They'll know it's been removed and that *we* have it," the captain finished. "That hadn't escaped me. Seems like we'll be having a lot to tell Vettarista," she noted sourly.

"She *is* part of ISP's covert ops," Azular put in. "I also suggest we tell her of the Web-based commercial interest that Micklemouse told us was the end-point for the data shards he passed to Lokterix."

"We keep this under wraps for now," Ahxenta decided. "We have supplies to pick up here and then we're for Skyrtek and the cargo for Alto Finglas, and that's a long haul. We'll drop into Silshoon on the way back to the Web. You're with me for the bridge, Azular."

The bridge was in its usual ordered state when the two reached it. Their supplies were in transit, Lindell was dealing with credit transfer, *Arianrhod's* loading crews were on standby and Perla Jute was hunting for new contracts. So far naught had come in but trade channels were lively with news that a Green Flag Line cargo ship and another of the Skelp Line had been hit, allegedly by raiders, and their payloads lifted. Both vessels had made it out but commercial lines were now making waves about more protection from the ISP and other related bodies and were upping costs to cover increasing insurance levies.

"So possibly more trade for us?" the captain surmised.

"And way more trouble," Apnis sniffed in reply. "What was the meet with Azular and Flintlock about?"

"Later. Now we get the show on the road, as we lost time over the *Obsidian*. Not that I grudge it, Grey would do the same for us."

Three hours later and with all boards green, Ahxenta gave the command for departure. There had been no more reports of trouble in their immediate area or in the direction in which they were headed, but beyond Skyrtek a direct route across Alpha would bring the ship within the sphere of influence of the Friskianx system and its allied world Lonagan Four. The captain ordered all defences active for the trip. With a grin as wide as a cargo bay, Whisper Earbleat announced that *Loki VI* was now ready for use on the captain's orders. Between them, she and Lieutenants Ferry and Greffy had produced a low-level cloak for her pet gadget, using part of the Norvallan cloaking gear that had now been installed on the *Gadfly* and a few bits and pieces Earbleat had scavenged during her sortie at Elytra Engineering. She had also fitted the automotive with small-scale phase cannon.

"I don't recall authorising that," growled Ahxenta.

"It's called showing initiative," Commander Apnis soothed.

"It's called bloody-mindedness. Direct route to Skyrtek, Mr Box, and steady as she goes, Ms Dox. Everyone else, stay sharp: if there are any surprises out there, I want to get them before they get us."

14: KEL'MOTH

The *ISPS Repulse* had dropped into Silverglass Station on her way to Barfit, Bluejohn informed Ahxenta in a quick link. She must have run at top speed to have made it in so fast, in his opinion, but she had met no obstacle, though her direct path had taken her across several zones, close by the Crimson Drapes Nebula and in reach of Sevolb, Friskianx and Lonagan. *Arianrhod* had made the Skyrtek system two days earlier and was in orbit over Skyrtek Key, the third planet and former site of the Interstellar Systems Protectorate's main planetary affairs office. It was a scarred, derelict world now, with a few clear-up and science stations across its surface that had been built into the ruins of its shattered structures. Shoals of wreckage from the final battle of the late war were in orbit. A great deal more was further out, held in the gravitational fields of the system's other planets, mostly around Skyrtek Prime, the sixth, which had once been the main centre of ISP shipbuilding.

Colonel Myrtleberry was still in command of the *Repulse* and had mentioned *Arianrhod* during a briefing with officers from the *Obsidian Sky*. Bluejohn had passed on the bare minimum and had not referred to the trip by Ahxenta and Azular to his ship or the scanner used to track down the last pieces of alien tech that had infested his vessel. He had been obliged to give up some shards of the drones that had made it through his hull but he had made sure they were from those his crew had destroyed, lest any traces of damage by Azular's handgun had been left on the others.

The *Repulse* had stopped briefly at Silverglass and was long gone. The *Obsidian* was still there, her overhaul slow, for the well-equipped station had few trained repair personnel. As soon as his ship was fit, Bluejohn intended to head to Selliden Central, an ISP-affiliated planet that had a decent repair facility and a first-rate medical centre.

The gist of the comm the captain repeated to Apnis on her return to the bridge. Both were wary enough not to take the news of a clear run through the Coalition-run sector of zone Alpha at face value. Ahxenta mulled over routes that would give Friskianx a wide berth.

"We could cut across to the Elf One beacon and then up to Alto

Finglas," she said. "It would put us close to Lartzeg Trine but apart from the dust left by the Allied forces, there *should* be nothing there."

"I wouldn't count on it. I'd not go near, but make straight for Pixel Point. We'd skirt the Crimson Drapes and there's been action there but that's a reason we wouldn't be expected to go that way. We can cross directly to Alto Finglas from there."

"I'm not so sure that we wouldn't be *expected* to head that way – *Arianrhod* has a rep for unorthodox moves. And our cargo worries me. It's supposed to be what's left of the wrecks of various ships, and that includes hostile. I just wonder what debris *has* been swept up and how secure these salvage pods are, now we have them aboard."

"That's a damn good point, Cap. We've seen these autonomous drones that attacked *Obsidian*, so how much more self-directed hostile gear is capable of action after its owners have been blown to dust?"

"Precisely; I'm reminded of that defunct bypass node that Kerrix figured she'd found – unknown tech that came to life and sucked her in, once she was close enough to be noticed, presumably."

"Azular and Greffy *did* scan those pods before we brought them in and after they'd been locked down but it might be wise going over them atom by atom," Apnis suggested.

"And with Azular's new toy – we used standard scans as they were brought in as the ISP monitoring gear is top-notch and I didn't want it recording anything it shouldn't – and I bet they had eyes on us."

"Lindell and his team are completing our clearances. We'll be off within the hour," the first mate told her.

"Keep on top of it; set our initial course as Elf One but be set to change once we're en route," Ahxenta directed as she rose and made her way to Azular's station, where she found he had forestalled her and had already linked the Norvallan scanner into the ship's internal scanning relays in a sweep of the first enormous cargo pod.

"Nothing yet," he reported. "It seems largely to be wreckage from superstructure, so pieces of the orbital docks around Skyrtek Prime. I'm reading hull relics with meta-jurillium signatures and other typical materials but little that could be shielding or standard arrays. Partial ISP vessels then; larger fragments would have been scanned in situ or hauled in for testing in the facilities here."

"Have you scanned for specifics?"

"Such as zukivianite? Yes ma'am. I've also input all the data we have on alien ships and their crews. The scanner's integral archive duplicates some of our data and includes novel structures that we don't, or didn't, have. I've been able to extract some to add to our databanks, but its capacity to deep-probe eludes me at present."

Azular had set Greffy to start continuous scanning of the exterior of the salvage pods to ensure that they remained fully locked down. Coding and tamper-proof seals were in place as routine to protect the contents but he believed in caution.

"Keep me informed."

"Yes ma'am."

Clearances at that moment being granted and permission to depart received, Apnis gave the commands to ready engines, set for Elf One and break orbit. She had also ordered long-distance scans and serial weapons diagnostics runs, and the comms officer was monitoring the available channels for news of any unrest in their general direction.

Back in the captain's chair, Ahxenta scanned her boards. Still wary of Lartzeg Trine, she decided to heed her first mate's advice and set for Pixel Point via Needle Beacon, a post straddling Alpha and Delta zones, where they could switch course at any sign of trouble. Once clear of Skyrtek space, she gave the relevant orders.

Arianrhod was four hours out when a curse from Azular alerted the captain to a glitch. She made for his station, where he had told Greffy to increase scan depth on cargo pod three as an anomaly had shown. It was an organo-cybernetic fusion that matched data they had logged during hostile encounters. There was a clear zukivianite trace and the mass was slowly moving.

"Got it!" Greffy called. "It's making for the pod wall! Two metres and closing. It'll make contact in fifteen minutes at its current rate."

"Red alert! I want security suited up and in!" Ahxenta snapped. "You too, Azular. Take that scanner *and* that pocket handgun. Crizz, secure the bay and keep your eyes on the action – I'll blast that pod into space if I have to."

Ten minutes later and Azular, garbed in protective gear and toting his kit, met up at a run with Hanx and Marks, both suited and armed, at the bay doors. Lieutenant Goldwash and two others brought up the rear. They would man the airlocks to get the team out in an emergency. Tactical was following the party on local visual cams and had sent in two hover cams as back-up. Greffy was meanwhile tracking the progress of the anomaly from the bridge.

The corrupted pod was secured to the deck by locking bolts and magnetic grapples and the fine-mesh shields that were dropped when in flight protected the bay from space. If cargo checks were required, pressurised tubes could be extruded into the bay but the wary Azular had decided that the inspection ramps that criss-crossed the vast space were a safer option. Greffy had calculated the exit point of the device and Azular and his team raced for the nearest route there. The low gravity made the going tough but magnetic pads on their boots gave stability. Greffy's commentary let them know that the mass was still moving at the same rate and on the same track. As the position was reached Azular, scanner in hand, had the piece pinpointed.

"There," he instructed the two security officers, a spot of light lancing out from the fine-beamed targeting eye he carried to indicate the breach locus on the shell of the pod.

"Reading it as burning through!" Greffy called out.

"I concur," Azular agreed. "Have your rifles set to full but let me take the first shot with my handgun."

"You sure, Doc?" Hanx enquired.

"I'm sure. Just be ready to shoot if I can't stop it."

The spot on the shell had begun to glow and then buckle, bulging outwards as the pod began to give. With a spray of hot metal, what looked like a sharp-nosed corroded cylinder broke surface. Azular quickly opened fire, having no intention of attempting initial analysis. The progress of the projectile was checked slightly, but it was clear to the three on the scene that it was encoded to detect danger and take protective action. It veered upwards and away and Azular called on his team to fire. Repeated hits from three high-energy weapons took their toll and the thing began to slow but it still ducked and wove as if it were sentient. It was an extendable short grapple-arm that finally caught it and held it sufficiently long for the weapons fire to bite and eventually the piece, now little more than a distorted lump, dropped to the level of a ramp below them.

"Well done, Chief," the science officer commended as he swung down to check the thing, realising that Crizz Cottontail had activated the grapple from her bridge station.

"Nasty piece of work, Doc," Hanx observed as he dropped down beside him. "If we'd been in a tube it would have gone through it like it was paper. Is it dead?"

"It won't be going anywhere, but don't touch. I want what's left of it in my lab. Keep scanning all three pods, Greffy," he instructed. "I won't discount the likelihood of more in there ready to jump out."

"Aye sir," Greffy called as very carefully, the senior science officer scooped the remains into a sample can and locked it down.

"I recommend we seal off this area, Captain," Azular advised.

"I agree; and I'll be having words with ISP HQ and with the guy on Skyrtek who set the final approval on that damn pod. It could have cost us one hell of a lot more damage if we hadn't been on it," Ahxenta rasped. "You three get out of there. Engineering, secure the bay. Cancel the red alert but keep us on heightened status."

The captain pondered, checking her boards. "Head direct to Alto Finglas via Needle Beacon, priority speed helm. It means less time in Coalition space and keeps us in ISP space until Beta. I want rid of that garbage in my cargo bay lest it's hiding more lethal surprises."

"The Skyrtek teams may not have detected that gadget among the junk," Apnis said as acknowledgements rang out.

"They should have. They have the tech to detect zukivianite linked to hostile organic material in ratios that indicate hostile physiology at any rate – *we* gave it to them, remember?"

"Sold them the designs and the first sensors Azular, Flintlock and Cottontail ran up, you mean," the first mate corrected. "But good point. There is of course another explanation."

"More than one I should think. But you mean that *that* device may have been planted intentionally when it was known that we would be carrying that particular cargo pod," the captain replied grimly.

"Precisely. The charted zones aren't free of hostile influence and there's no saying how many agents are incognito and still out there, despite the probes we passed to Myrtleberry after the end of major hostilities. Even with ISP's production and distribution, I doubt they flushed out every infiltrator from every ISP and other treaty group."

"Roger that. I'll send an alert on the U-V III to the fleet and warn Goodsocks to steer clear of ISP deals involving salvage. But first I'll see what's new with Azular. After that, I'll be in my office setting fire to ISP ears. You take the conn but alert me if anything shows."

"Aye, ma'am. But I can't imagine the *Emerald* would be contracted to haul those pods – she's not a big ship as cargo carriers go."

"I'm not taking the chance: she's ours and as such she's more of a target than most other ships. If there *was* malice in mind with the cargo in our aft bays, the bandits would find a way."

Ahxenta made for *Arianrhod's* science labs to find both officers busy. Greffy's continuing scans were clear and no other active unit had come to light in close remote probing of the three cargo pods. Azular's analysis of the shards of missile left implied that it once had shielding. The power needed to take it down had destroyed most of its form and little else could be learnt other than that it was certainly hostile in origin. Azular's best guess was that the object had been ejected from its parent ship and had drifted among the wreckage or it had been deliberately planted within the pod.

The HQ officials at Alto Finglas to whom Ahxenta spoke were disturbed but firmly refuted deliberate intent. She could not reach the relevant cargo release officer at Skyrtek but his deputy vowed more care in future. Ahxenta was annoyed but could do little but warn her fellow PSS captains of the latent dangers of taking on similar cargoes. She had no sooner sent that link when Bellfish broke in with word of an urgent comm from an ISP starship on active duty. The captain was not surprised to see Colonel Ellin Myrtleberry.

"So what did our old chum the colonel want, Cinnabar?" Apnis asked when at last Ahxenta reappeared.

"She'd gone over what she got from the *Obsidian* and from her people at Skyrtek and she contacted Admiral Zillah. She thought we may have passed *her* the gen, as she knows we're acquainted."

"And we trust Zillah a sight further than we trust Myrtleberry or most others in authority."

"You bet. She wanted to know more on how we detected and cut out the drones on the *Obsidian's* hull and how we had the nous to scan the ISP cargo and to find what we did, but she's little wiser – it's none of her damn business. But those salvage bins were designed to the highest spec to prevent covert scans, apparently."

"So the ISP's highest spec isn't as high as it thinks it is," snorted Apnis. "She should know by now that we trust no-one, no matter how nice they are to us in hiring our services. Did you mention our suspicion that the missile was deliberately planted?"

"I did. She was narked but not as surprised as she could have been which leads me to suspect that she's aware that some of her own are less than squeaky clean. She'd also had reports from the ISP offices at Selliden and Stinward on Orange 2334 and these new-design raider ships. And she knew we picked up a stranded trader and who it was – I figure she dug around and spoke to Selliden Port Authority."

"But did she link him with the trader we picked off Kelfennig all those months back?" Apnis asked. "He was using another name then. He seems to change his name as often as he changes his socks."

"She was being close but I bet she has. We know she's the ISP's equivalent of an info-sent, not as complex as Micklemouse but with genetic and physical upgrades that include extrasensory capabilities *and* she may have data recording facilities for all we know."

"Has she got her people alerted to the mouse and his wily pals?"

"More than likely, but they can hardly tail him across the mapped galaxy. Vettarista knew about him and his alteration at that med place on Mellifly but the ISP is keeping that open for its own ends."

"Maybe to produce a few more Colonel Myrtleberries," Box piped up brightly from the navi-helm console. "We could ask around?"

"One peep out of you about anything you overhear on the bridge Mr Box, and you'll be running nav simulations from the brig for the foreseeable future. Is that clear?"

"Yes, Captain, as glass," was the chastened response.

"Fool!" muttered Dox alongside. "The ISP will have its own med facilities for turning folks like Myrtleberry into annoying pests."

"Can't keep a good crew down, Cap," Apnis chuckled. "But we're all clear, so time to change the watch. We've all done over hours."

Needle Beacon was reached and the bypass switch for a route across Delta to zone Beta margin made without mishap. *Arianrhod* was now within an area where most habited worlds were allied to the ISP, but her path would take her near the Crimson Drapes Nebula. Ahxenta thus ordered silent running, planning to deploy her cloak as she came close to the nebula's outer zone, although the raider assault on the *Pearl Shield* had been off from their route, on the far side.

Comms nets had been alive with news, including a report of a raid near where the *Pearl* had been hit. The victim had escaped minus her cargo, leading Apnis to suggest that raider tactics were improving: the old raiders destroyed all rather than leave witnesses. An update from Bluejohn told them that with *Obsidian's* most urgent repairs complete, he was making for Selliden. He had found no more hostile tech.

As hours became days and progress remained steady, Ahxenta was beginning to think that they would reach their next stop trouble-free. Lindell had agreed a contract to ship a batch of medical gear from Berzic to Merkat medbay; as they were due to nearby Silshoon, it was a good deal. The ship had made the far edge of the Crimson Drapes and was heading for the zone Beta crossing point when the alarm sounded. The captain and first mate had just come on duty and were preparing for the final five hour stage into Alto Finglas.

"We have another ship on the grid, Captain!" Pollux Gliss called out. "She's big, bigger than any PSS I know," he added.

"Call-sign?"

"None detected. She's not cloaked but I only get surface readings. She's changing her heading to match ours…"

"What! Red alert! Shields up! Weapons on line!"

"I don't read her as targeting us or her external weapons powering up," the tactical officer bellowed above the sound of the siren.

"Mute the noise!" Ahxenta ordered as hurrying feet heralded the advent of officers to stations and the overhead holo-grid expanded to show the latest on the new arrival. "Can you get a visual?"

"On it," Gliss replied briefly.

"She must be able to read us despite our cloak, Captain," Azular stated as he scanned the incomer. "Ah! That's interesting…"

"What have you got?"

"You recall Ms Vettarista's data on the ship that brought in those ex-raiders we met in the Web? She was huge, with a structure similar to hostile specs and to the ship Ms Kerrix stowed aboard? Vettarista said her surface jammers and interior shielding blocked scanning."

"What about your Norvallan scanner?"

"Partly blocked, but my readings show similarities. The visual *is* a match," he continued as Gliss pulled the image up.

"She's matching speed but not closing," Apnis observed, tapping her board. "She's holding off our starboard then. Looking to chat?"

"*I* won't be opening a dialogue," Ahxenta said shortly. "Maintain present course and speed. Drop the cloak, she knows we're here, but keep weapons hot and do not drop our targeting eyes."

The two vessels continued on, taking the measure of each other, as Azular reported that *Arianrhod* was being scanned but her jammers were effectively foiling the probe beams. Fifteen minutes passed.

"Incoming message for you, Captain," Bellfish announced. "No name, but he's asked for *you* by name."

"Time we found out his, then," Ahxenta said dryly. "Put him on."

The face in the viewer was familiar. It belonged to one of the trio who had trailed the captain and her team to her shuttle's berth weeks before and had then turned up later in the *Sunlight Subspace Diner.*

"Maybe he's decided now's the time to pick the quarrel he doesn't have with you," suggested Apnis.

"Captain Ahxenta," said the man.

"And you are?"

"My name isn't important."

"That's your problem, not mine. But until I get some sort of ID on you and your ship, this chat is at an end. Ahxenta out."

"Captain! I'm Commander Vexin Thal," he disclosed. "My ship is the *Kel'Moth.* We're based close to the border of galactic zone Mu."

"Zone Mu has a long border."

He scowled, eyeing her sourly. "We call our base Starfall."

"You're a long way from home."

"I suspect you know quite well who and what we are and where we come from," he starkly observed.

"I know what you *were*," Ahxenta replied. "So what are you now and what's your business with me?"

"We operate as traders. My business is a man you call Lokterix."

Several sharp glances were traded around *Arianrhod's* bridge but her captain was giving nothing away, despite her surprise. "Go on."

"We know you had dealings with him. In fact you warned me against him when we first met, at Skyrtek. I didn't heed you then."

Ahxenta sat in silence, smiling sceptically, aware that her officers were scanning everything they could of their opposite numbers.

"He didn't have our cause in mind when he joined us, he and others. They had their own agendas or were covert supporters of our enemies. They've done us harm and plan more. We're identifying them and routing them out. They're interfering with our business."

"Which is?"

"Trading," he replied levelly.

"Lokterix?" Ahxenta asked as Apnis let out a disbelieving oath.

"We're aware of his vindictive nature, his grudge against you and that he has alien contacts. They're out to get us; we *have* after all taken over bases they once held. He was at Starfall when the war ended, and until recently. We'd *had* doubts of his intent but he guessed and fled. We assumed he'd make for Mellifly and then for a newly set up hostile post off zone Beta, near Coalition space, but one of my officers spotted him when we were in Merkat. We'd picked up his trail when we met you. After his clash with you he ran and we lost him. Others like him are still part of our structure, as we've found to our cost. They're undermining us and we want rid of them."

"Really? And now you're chasing him down in your very high spec ship, which is a tad superior to the one you had at Skyrtek – which hailed from sector sixteen in zone Beta, if I recall."

"We're upgrading our fleet," Thal said shortly. "Our base in sector sixteen is no longer secure and we have other business. But as you've dealt with Lokterix, I want to know if *you* know where he is."

"So you just drop by and ask. How did you know I was here?"

"I have contacts. I knew you were on a track from Skyrtek to Alto Finglas and this is one of the obvious routes."

"You don't add up, mister, not by a long way. How did you know what I'd been doing and where I was headed?"

"Do you know the phrase 'the enemy of my enemy is my friend'?"

"Yes, and I don't set store by it. And you have not answered my questions." Ahxenta paused. "You tell me why you're really so keen to clean the spaceways of these hostiles *and* how you tracked me and then maybe I'll be more disposed to assist you with your enquiries."

Thal's second muttered something, to which he reacted by raising his hand, his jaw tightening; he was obviously weighing his options.

"These hostiles have taken out two of my ships in the past month. They overran a base we had set up outside sector sixteen of Beta and destroyed everything and everyone. They anticipate our every move and are growing stronger. So they have allies and they have spies. *I* have allies and I know that you headed out of Skyrtek with a cargo for Alto Finglas. Who and where my allies are I will *not* tell you."

"The last I heard, Lokterix had escaped Merkat, with help. Two likely but unproven routes were ships bound for Sevolb or Mellifly. That's all I have," Ahxenta said evenly. "By the way, we had trouble after Skyrtek. I don't suppose you know anything about that?"

"No Captain, I do not. Thank you for your information. Have a profitable trip. Thal out."

As the image faded, the holo-grid displayed the *Kel'Moth* bank and turn. Ahxenta let out a sigh. "Track that ship. He doesn't stack. His old den in sector sixteen isn't secure? It sounds like his ex-masters knew about it and maybe it's how they got their moles into his outfit. He set up a new base further out and *that's* been taken out? His lot had taken down that ex-hostile base by the Enigma as part of the payback for the hostiles' treatment of them and found it was full of useful hardware *and* close to a defunct bypass that was a route to other strange places? His allies are keeping their eyes and ears open for us? He's rounding up strays like Lokterix and Flatt? And he trails us, stops for a chat on some spurious excuse and then makes off?"

"Too many questions, Cap, but it tells us one or two things," the first mate pointed out. "Two of *his* ships were taken out? Not two of ours, or our fleet's. Has he got clout or is he pretending he has?"

"He *is* in command of a damn big ship with more armaments than two of ISP's finest. And if his enemies anticipate his every move, they now know he's contacted us," Ahxenta stated dourly. "Just dandy."

"I note you didn't mention that his ship or one of his ships had a stowaway aboard when it left this Starfall place? A fugitive they tried to shoot down that had a lot of trouble from persons unknown when she did get out at Merkat?"

"I didn't mention a lot of things. Azular, what's your take on this Commander Thal and his crew?"

"My readings are limited but I didn't read zukivianite, possibly as their bridge is shielded. We know that Thal is part-Friskianx but that may not be the case for his crew. From the visuals, there *are* a few that have remnants of what look like hostile implants. I noted that not all bridge stations were crewed and from my scans of the ship, huge as she is, she's poorly manned. Thal seems cool, but I sense he's frustrated, possibly over the problems that are bedevilling him."

"Or because you seem to be having trouble believing that he's a trader, Cap," Apnis put in. "Any clues as to his cargo, Azular?"

"None, Commander. But the ship has four detachable cargo pods parallel in spec to her hull and matched to her external bays. I hence conclude that they came off the same production line. Thal talked about a fleet: I wonder if he has more of the same at home?"

"Thanks for that," Ahxenta growled. "But if he's a trader, why's he chasing down villains like Lokterix?"

"They're getting in the way of his trading," the first mate said cynically. "Though I'd think he'd be better paying an assassin if he's so keen. It seems a waste to use a ship that size for such a mission."

"He has another agenda is what he has," the captain said sternly. "Who the hell gave him the lowdown on us?"

"Friends in key places, Cap; and that's a worry if they're part of the ISP or any other frigging concern that's liable to trade with us."

"Well, he's out of sensor range now," Ahxenta noted. "Straight to Alto Finglas, Mr Box, and all speed, helm. There's no point in taking a devious route if Thal and his like know our heading."

As soon as *Arianrhod* made port a request came in from ISP HQ for a session to discuss the rogue cargo pod. The captain agreed, lest more evidence had emerged. She took Apnis, Azular and two guards – her tactical station had noted a Coalition ship with diplomatic insignia in orbit and she anticipated a large party, as the Trades Alliance had also sent reps from its own nearby HQ.

In the event no Coalition agent was present but the captain was advised that the results of the meeting would be circulated to relevant bodies. She took her own measures and had Azular set up the means to relay the event to her ship. The lead ISP rep was seething but could do little but call for a recap of the incident aboard *Arianrhod*.

Ahxenta was curt, given that she had already sent in a report, and pressed for a response. There was little: the ISP was still adamant that there was no indication of deliberate sabotage. The op in control of final cargo clearance at Skyrtek had been removed from post and upgraded screening routines were now in place but that was it. The upper echelons of ISP *did* want the remains of the device as it *had* been in their cargo pod. The captain shot a glance at Azular. At his slight nod, she agreed. It was a lump of metal in his lab and nothing more could be got from it. She would hand it over once her dealings at Alto Finglas were complete, she told them, although the specific readings her team had taken during and after the event she refused to give. The net results and conclusions had been supplied in the report passed to the ISP and to the Trades Alliance, amongst others.

Such bluntness did not go down well but the chief ISP rep insisted on an account of why she had seen fit to scan the load and how she found the device, as the pod's ultra-high spec should have foiled any probe. Ahxenta was in no mood to repeat the answers she had given Myrtleberry, but pointed out that if the ISP's anti-scanning tech was so smart, her team should not have been able to carry out the process – which was standard aboard her ship in any case. She cut the talks at that juncture, refusing to go over the aftermath of the assault on the *Obsidian* apart from advising that the ISP and the TA take note of the technology that allowed such a long-distance attack to take place.

"You pissed them off," Tallica Apnis noted as the five from the *Arianrhod* made their way back to their shuttle. "We may have messed up our chances of more ISP contracts."

"Contracts like that last we can do without," was the retort. "But without our vigilance, the ISP would be more subverted than it seems to be, as Myrtleberry is aware. *Are* those reps as sure as they want to appear that there wasn't underhand dealing with that cargo?"

This last was addressed to Azular, who ruminated for a moment. "There were undercurrents, but nothing specific, Captain," he said at last. "The incident has them rattled at any rate."

"Good: it might improve their attitude."

Their return trip was routine and by the time the craft had docked and the captain and first mate had made the bridge, all accounts had been settled. That being the case, Ahxenta decreed that the residue of the hostile piece be given up. Azular was sent over. He was to pass it to the chief scientist and hoped to find out more. He was told little, but the chief did admit that news of the device had given the science team a jolt, despite the incident being played down by the authorities. The man was curious as to how the device had been detected, leading Azular to suspect that he had been primed, but the Berzic officer gave nothing away and as soon as his shuttle had regained *Arianrhod*, the captain gave orders to break orbit and set for Silshoon.

The trip across the minor sector of zone Beta and into Delta was relatively short. The *Obsidian's* clients at Silshoon were ready for their transfer pod and had a ferry on standby. The firm itself had an orbital lab for which the parts were destined. After essential business and an exchange of civilities, *Arianrhod* set for neighbouring Berzic. Ahxenta had sent on the details of the transaction to Bluejohn, who was still at Selliden, his ship as yet in no fit state for active service.

The Berzicon medical company, based in a site on the outskirts of one of the major cities, had no facilities to send cargo into orbit. Ahxenta thus took the *Gadfly* down for pick up, with Azular and two armed guards as escort for the valuable consignment. Lindell was on hand back aboard to complete the obligatory paperwork.

The shuttle docked in an allotted bay and was left with the pilot whilst the others made their way to the Medi-Tech offices in an auto-car sent for them. An escort waited to lead them into the main block and thus to the trade bureau. Business speedily settled with the reps, the quartet was led to a despatch bay. Azular probed the large crate in detail and found nothing amiss. His calm smile may have misled their hosts but his captain knew him well and sensed that he was edgy. She declined refreshments and, cargo in tow, she led the way out to their car. A look at her science officer caused him to haul out his scanner to sweep the vehicle, to the dismay of the two reps at their tail.

"A hurried attempt, Captain, as it's not secure: we were expected to accept hospitality, I think. I've no doubt it's set to blow as we head off site," he stated, crouching down to pull a packet off the underside of the car. "Nasty, and we've met similar. It reads like the explosive used in the attack on our shuttle's bay in the Web and it has a cloak setting, but that's inactive. Perhaps whoever planted it thought we wouldn't notice it. Or they weren't familiar with the device."

Ahxenta swiftly hauled up her communit and ordered her pilot to carry out a local scan. She then linked to *Arianrhod* to report, her eyes scorching the shocked reps. One began a call to his company security and moments later, three pairs of heavy boots thundered up. Azular had been turning the object in his hands but halted to peruse the trio as the rep who had made the call gave a garbled account.

"May I see it, sir?" one of the three guards asked politely, his over-eager eyes skipping back and forth from the pack to Azular's face.

"No," the Berzic officer responded equally civilly, and shot him.

The other guards were stunned but quickly pulled their weapons to aim at the science officer's head as their team-mate dropped like a stone. Ahxenta and her own security were as fast and all three had phase rifles unsheathed and ready.

"Drop them!" the captain warned.

As the guards complied, Azular advised them to check their mate. "He's not Berzic, in spite of the signals his suit emits. And his cyber implants pack a punch. You two *are* entirely Berzic, which does not of course mean that you're innocent of attempting to murder us."

In spite of instant and voluble denials, Ahxenta had no scruple in ending the exchange, deeming it wiser to hold further talks from her bridge. The threat of legal action effectively closed negotiations and with their cargo secured to the car, the team quickly boarded. They drove in silence until they made the *Gadfly*, where pilot Elsey Gunn reported that no other concerns had arisen.

"That damned Norvallan handgun's a useful tool. I didn't see you draw it," the captain remarked wryly to the science officer.

"It's sufficiently small to hide up my sleeve. But I'd set my scanner on the approaching security and spotted that something was off."

"You were expecting trouble." It was a statement.

"Yes, ma'am. There were a lot of eyes on us in the despatch area, not all of which were in the immediate vicinity."

"We were being watched?"

"I suspect we were watched from the instant our shuttle landed," he replied dryly. "I took steps."

"The two reps?"

"Were nervous, but that may have been our reputation rather than an inkling that all was not well," he grinned. "Perhaps there are some out there who anticipate our every move and are growing stronger?"

"Very funny. But people *are* finding out about us and our business too easily, the cranky Thal for one. You're sure our cargo's okay?"

"Positive, Captain. Medi-Tech is an established company of sound reputation. Though I *am* curious to know how long that guard has been on the payroll and how many other new recruits they have."

"I'll find out when I singe the ears off their legal unit, *and* I'll report it to the local crime squad," Ahxenta promised grimly. "I'll be glad to get back to the Web: at least *there*, I know to expect trouble."

The upshot of the captain's enquiries brought to light the fact that the rogue guard, with others, had been recruited only days before; all were now being investigated. Business completed and with no more time to pursue the attempted assault on her team, Ahxenta gave the order to quit Berzic planetary space and make for the Web.

The delivery to Merkat's medbay was swift once approvals had been granted. Flintlock and Azular had been sent with the cargo to ensure its safe arrival. The deal had been lucrative in spite of obstacles and the crew was happy to be assured of bonuses and shore leave for those who had missed it previously. There had been a lull in the spate of violent crimes that had plagued Merkat security, according to the latest that Bellfish had heard on the way in, that had been confirmed by the Port Authority. In Apnis' view, she and the captain could find out how the land lay by a visit to the *Half Moon*: Ally always had his finger on the button of local affairs and was likely to know more than many about ongoing covert operations, both legal and illegal.

Ahxenta had laughed quietly but agreed, as their next contract of another pick-up from Redship Industrial would not be ready for a few days. The captain had called Vettarista to request a meeting and a lunch was set for the next day in the *Sunlight Subspace Diner*. The two senior officers then headed in for a talk to Kit Biernop to check how things were with the Dockers' Guild, and then to join Flintlock and Azular to hear what they had picked up in medbay.

The science officer was already in the *Half Moon*, having left the recharged Norvallan energy cell in the shuttle he had flown over. He was hoping to see Kerrix to let her know and to request another look at her craft, being curious as to how far she had been able to repair it with the gear he had left. He walked into a tiff between Merry and her boss. Merry had achieved the top grade in the psychology degree on which she had worked in her free time over the last few years and Ally was fearful that he was about to lose her skills. A promise that she was not set to decamp, as she hoped to begin her Master's degree and would need to work to fund it, did not reassure him.

"Why she thinks she needs a Master's degree!" Ally complained as Merry stalked off. "What good does it do?"

"It'll get her out of here and into better company – the kind that congratulates her on her achievement instead of moaning about their own concerns," remarked Kerrix, who had appeared at his side with a tray of glassware. "She's smart enough to get an even higher degree, if only someone would realise it. As *Dr* Jetty, she'd make an excellent ship's counsellor," she added pointedly to Azular.

"*Arianrhod* has a very able ship's counsellor," he stated equably, his eyes lighting – Kerrix was obviously well and back on form.

"You attend to Dr Azular," Ally instructed. "I've orders to finish."

"Aye sir," she retorted. "Miserable grouch," she muttered to the Berzic officer, glowering at Ally's retreating back.

"Dr Jetty? You think a title makes a difference *Dr* Kerrix?"

"What is that supposed to mean?"

"I assume that *you* reached doctoral status or the equivalent as a high-ranking science officer in your fleet?" he said quietly, leaning his elbows on the counter as he cocked a playful eyebrow at her.

"I suggest you mind your own business *Dr* Azular. What would you like to drink?"

"What do you recommend?" he responded archly.

"Water," was the laconic rejoinder.

"I'll have ale and please put it on a tab. I find you a little prickly at times, Ms Kerrix."

"And I find you damn annoying all the time, but I can put up with it," she replied as she filled and passed over the beaker. "Your drink, sir. I'll put it on a tab; anything else?"

"No ma'am."

"Then go sit down."

"I'd like a quiet word, if you don't mind," he continued softly and in a more serious tone.

"Later," she murmured. "Here are more customers. Go sit."

"Yes ma'am," he smiled, scooping up his beaker.

She dealt with the duo that had just come in, pointing them to a seat by a far wall. She knew their ways and as she had spotted the captain and first mate of the *Arianrhod* slip through the holo-door, she suspected that the two barflies would be intent on eavesdropping. Malty and Jurry took one look at her inflexible face and decided that obedience was probably the better part of valour. They slunk off.

"Good afternoon, Captain, Commander; what can I get you?"

"Two ales, and put it on a tab," Ahxenta said, looking around.

"Aye, Captain," the woman acknowledged.

"Azular's over there but no Flintlock," Apnis noted, scanning the place likewise. "Don't see anyone else we have to chat to. Those two by the door hail from the *Tallulah* – I saw she was in. Don't recognise them, though. New blood, maybe."

"Maybe," Ahxenta agreed, turning as Kerrix placed two schooners of ale on the countertop.

"Your drinks, Captain," the woman announced with an enigmatic smile. "I *have* put them on a tab: Dr Azular's tab. Perhaps you'd let him know. Have a good day."

She turned to serve a newly-arrived quartet. The two PSS officers swapped wry glances as they collected their drinks and walked off.

Apnis was still laughing as they joined Azular at his table. "Have you and Ms Kerrix had a spat?" the first mate asked as she sat.

"Not exactly," he responded. "Why?"

"Cap'll tell you. But where's Axellina?"

"The *Karillion's* in – she was intercepted by Captain Flintlock."

"She'll be a while in that case: Race Flintlock can talk the paint off a ship's hull."

"Cargo drop went smoothly?" was the captain's greeting.

It had, Azular assured her. He went on to list the scanty news that he and the CMO had picked up. Emergency admissions were down as violent crime was easing. There had been no attacks on patients, as far as the reps they had met knew. There *had* been injured crewmen brought in by visiting ships but details there were confidential.

Ahxenta nodded. That tallied with Biernop's news. The crime rate had fallen, there had been no further explosions in areas under Guild control and no arrests related to previous incidents. The Guild was sifting out culprits of local violations and two ships that had been attacked had hauled in for repair. Both were Friskianx, out of Jurgall Three and the details had not been broadcast widely.

"You may as well get us all another ale," the captain told Azular when she had done. "Your friend Ms Kerrix put ours on your tab."

She chuckled at his scandalised expression. "And as we came here to talk to Ally, see if you can rout him out. The place seems quiet."

As the science officer made for the bar, he spotted Dr Flintlock at the door minus her brother. He waved and mimed that he would buy her a drink, as he had spied Kerrix on her own behind the counter and hoped to broach the subject of her shuttle. The drinks ordered, Azular began by mentioning her recharged energy cell.

"So what's the exchange *this* time?" she smiled expressively.

"You don't miss a trick, do you, Ms Kerrix?"

"Answer the question, Dr Azular."

He was honest and admitted that he was curious about her shuttle and the upgrades he was sure she had carried out. She conceded with a nod. That being the case, Azular offered to bring the energy cell over to her shuttle's berth in outer belt nine in his own craft.

"Won't do you any good," she apprised him. "She's not there. I moved her. And your colleagues are waiting for these drinks."

"Where's Ally?" he asked to hide his surprise.

"Still sulking in his office."

"I'll carry the drinks over. Please ask him if Captain Ahxenta can have a word, if he's not busy."

"Will do. Drinks are still on your tab, by the way."

"So noted. Please have a drink on me."

"Not while I'm on duty. And I'll speak to you again later."

"I'll take that as a promise."

"Or a threat," she rejoined as she set off.

Back at their table, Azular found his crewmates talking over the latest gleaned by Dr Flintlock. Captain Flintlock had told of trouble at his last stop of Delta Iridium of serious attacks by what looked like raiders on small traders plying routes between Delta and its outposts of Iris Three, Flag Delta and Blue Delta. There had been precision hits to cut out cargo pods, demands for transfer of in-hold cargo and the spiking of ship's systems. The three prey vessels had loosed their loads and run. All were rescued but all had suffered fatalities. The *Karillion* had not met trouble but had been given the attacking ships' specs by worried Delta authorities. The specs matched those of the small interceptor-like types that had been reported elsewhere.

"Raiders are back on track again, then," Ahxenta concluded. "But they're less deadly than before if they're leaving survivors."

"They're using very different ships and tactics," the science officer pointed out. "They have better and faster ships but they *are* smaller and fewer. The mothership plus fighters and sweepers that took out everything and cleared the evidence was a clumsy operation, which is possibly why they were so easily exploited by the hostiles that took over most of their operations – if that *is* what happened."

"Clumsy but deadly," Tallica Apnis remarked. "But here's Ally, so I guess business is slack at the moment."

Business *was* slack, Ally agreed, but it would pick up later. The recent disruption in the Web might seem to be over but it had not gone, and as the *Half Moon* had come in for a larger share than most, it was oddly good for trade. They had had some odd customers in asking about ships and crews, types of cargo moved and other business ventures around the place. *Arianrhod* had come in for a fair share of the gossip, he admitted. Not that his people would say anything out of place: they knew better. As he began to describe one or two of the strangers that had recently surfaced, an altercation at the bar distracted them. It was Kerrix and she was spitting mad at a loud-mouthed individual who seemed to be threatening her.

Ahxenta jumped to her feet with an oath. She recognised the man at distance. She had seen him last in the offices of Thystal Comms on Xerophyte IV. It was Hoxiz.

15: A LITTLE TROUBLE

The man at the bar had raised a menacing arm but Kerrix was having none of it. She began to make her way around the counter as Merry emerged from the rear and another two staff hove up. Ally muttered that the guy had been in twice before asking about the *Arianrhod* and other things but Kerrix had not been on duty on either occasion. The officers had other concerns, as the highly-cyber Hoxiz was physically superior, vicious and capable of causing much damage. Apnis drew her rifle as she and the others raced after the captain.

Hoxiz' inbuilt systems alerted him to the group and he turned round, his head rearing up. He recognised Ahxenta and Apnis and sneered defiantly before turning to run. Kerrix made to go after him but her arm was caught by Azular, sprinting up from the back.

"No," he cautioned quietly. "He's a bad piece of work and he's more than he seems – he could tear you apart."

She halted at that. "You *know* him?"

"Not personally. I've never met him, but believe me you wouldn't want to."

She laughed harshly. "Too late for that, I already have," she shot back with a look on her face that pulled them all up short.

"But you weren't here the last twice he was in," Ally said, baffled.

"Where *did* you meet him?" the practical Azular asked curiously.

"In medbay – *he* was the bastard that tried to surgically extract one of my implants." She rubbed her left shoulder at the memory. "He's changed a bit but the arrogance and the creepy eyes are the same."

"Hell, you were damn lucky the duty meds rushed in and he didn't blast you for the hell of it," Apnis grunted. "But he's here now, he's no friend to us and I assume he's found out a thing or two about our recent activities. So what do we do about it, Cap?" she asked.

"What do you know about him and his dealings and what did he want to know about my ship?" the captain demanded of Ally.

The man had not been around long, Ally was sure. He had been in twice in the past four days, had said he was new to Merkat and was there on business, which he claimed was medical applications. His markets were clinically-related, such as drugs companies, developers and suppliers of surgical devices and similar. He was there to set up a network of new clients and trade carriers. He had heard of *Arianrhod* and his enquiries related to the regularity with which her crew used the *Half Moon*, where the ship berthed and when she had last been in. His manner, however, tended to repel everyone to whom he spoke.

"I'll bet," the first mate opined. "He's an aggressive type that has definitely not got the hang of civility. Wonder where *he's* berthed?"

"We're not likely to find out, he'll have covered his tracks and he'll be well-protected," Ahxenta replied. "And you'd better make sure he hasn't found out where your place is, Ms Kerrix."

"I've upped security. My place was too easy to crack for some," she said pointedly, with a side-glance at Azular. "But what was your contact with him, Captain, if you don't mind me asking?"

"I do. It's none of your concern. But I suggest you don't go near him unless you're prepared to shoot first and ask questions later."

"I'll remember," was the short rejoinder.

As the captain and her team made their way back to their table to finish their drinks, most of the curious eyes upon them were rapidly withdrawn. A couple of pairs lingered.

"Wonder what that was about, mate," Malty remarked to his pal, over in the corner booth where they had taken roost.

"Don't ask," Jurry advised. "Ahxenta will only come over and box your ears for you. We can maybe get it out of young Evrett later. He was earwigging behind the bar where he thought it was safe."

"Fair enough. But what's Dr Azular whispering to Kerrix about?"

"Search me, I can't lip-read. But I wouldn't go asking *her* – she'll tear your head off, after she's punched out your lights."

The result of his quiet word with Kerrix was evidently favourable for Azular sported a soft smile as he made his way back to his table. He was greeted by a smirk from Apnis.

"Got your own way, then?" she asked archly as he sat.

"Very droll, Commander. I've informed Ms Kerrix that I'll pass her energy cell over at a suitable point. She's moved her shuttle to inner three, although she won't say which level. But she *has* agreed to let me see the changes."

"She was able to fix it up enough to move it? How in blazes did she manage that?" the captain asked.

"That's one of the things I'd like to find out, *and* how she was able to find a new berth. She's on duty until late, but is free tomorrow after fourteen hundred. As we have our meeting at twelve thirty, I've arranged to catch up with her after that. I can use one of our small shuttles to transport the cell if you have other plans, Captain."

"Lindell, Tallica and I will be in talks with Redship after we've met our contact for lunch, so we'll still be here," Ahxenta informed him firmly. "We'll come over in the *Gadfly*, she needs an outing. I assume your rendezvous with Ms Kerrix will only take a couple of hours?"

"I expect so, Captain."

"Then that's settled. But drink up all, and we'll head home. You can put in a call to your chum Biernop and see what he knows about Hoxiz, Tallica — he must have come in on a ship about four or five days ago and if he's posing as a medical rep looking for business, there may be a record of his slime trail. And you may get something on that angle from your contacts in medbay, Axellina. But we'd best mind our backs on the way to green twelve: he may have some nasty friends that have our number."

There was much to talk over on the following day when Ahxenta, Apnis and Azular met with up the Berzic agent. As before, Vettarista was dressed for business. The *Sunlight Subspace Diner* was quiet, with privacy shields in operation around most tables. The captain brought up her main points quickly, her first one being the reappearance of the hostile agent Hoxiz in the Web, his links to both Doosbak of the Coalition Central Council and Micklemouse, and his direct complicity in the attack on Kerrix. The hostile influence was thus far from over, it was growing and others were still being coerced into supporting it. Much of the activity appeared to involve information transfer, with data shards heading for places including Minch Fettin, Mellifly, Salt Three and the Web; and a base in the latter for a clandestine business, probably technical, that made use of the data. Kit Biernop had been unable to find anything on Hoxiz, which probably meant that he was using an alias. Vettarista's eyes blazed when she heard of the language analyser-translator that Micklemouse had had inserted at Mellifly.

"So that *is* what they're at, amongst other things. We figured."

She explained her logic. She and her colleagues had been keeping watch on several suspect outfits in the Web, one of which was a tech-med concern that dealt in the creation of rare and highly expensive micro-medical devices. They had linked Hoxiz to that as well as to another comms operation on Xerophyte IV.

"Thystal," Azular interposed. "Ms Warweft was your agent there."

"Yes. You met her there months ago, when you ran into trouble with Lokterix and a couple of heavies. You passed the name Hoxiz to her. Nothing could be pinned on him then and she couldn't dig too deeply or update you: as a native of Xeroph Township One and with history there, she had had to use her own name even though she was undercover. You've got details on that device Micklemouse has?"

"Had – Dr Flintlock extracted it. It wasn't complexed into his bio-systems in the way it should have been," the science officer clarified. "You suspect a covert operation here is producing such things?"

"I do. You can imagine the profits to be made, but they'd need to be capable of implanting it. That was the likely reason for the attack on Xanna Kerrix in medbay. We now have data on the prototypes we think they're trying to create. I'd like that device."

Azular looked questioningly at Ahxenta, his frown suggesting he was not happy to hand it over, but she nodded.

"We'll get it to you," the captain agreed. "I take it you've been briefed on what happened to the *Obsidian Sky*?"

"And to you en route to Alto Finglas; I have. Another thing: the volatiles used in the affair with your shuttle. You know that explosive delivery systems are part of medical tools like hypos? We *have* found traces of similar elements in the premises of the outfit we think is at bottom of attempts to replicate the language analyser or produce one *and* create other stealth-tech for implantation. And we're sure that the man Lokterix was behind the explosions, but he's still at large."

"Maybe not for much longer," Apnis cut in with a quirky glance.

In response to Vettarista's enquiries, Ahxenta told of the meeting with the *Kel'Moth*, Thal's overtures of amity and his avowed mission to find Lokterix, but the agent warned her not to assume that trouble in the Web was over. Intelligence suspected that groups were around whose aim was to foster chaos and wreak reprisals for what they saw as the actions of *Arianrhod* and others in spoking their wheels during the war. Some bore specific grudges and would stop at little to deal revenge in any form, including striking at contacts of their targets.

"That would be ours," Ahxenta frowned. "We know they're trying to undermine our trade by making contractors wary of using us and they *have* hit our fellow Privates."

"There *is* more than one way of putting you out of business than blowing you to hell," Vettarista agreed as the captain wrapped up her info-pad. "But I suggest you warn your people to mind their backs."

"They usually do," Ahxenta stated. "I'll leave Dr Azular to discuss the handover of the language analyser – I'm sure he'll have his own ideas. Commander Apnis and I have to go. I'll settle up on the way out," she added to her senior science officer.

She and her first mate set off to find Lindell for their meeting with

Redship, leaving the science officer with the agent, who was aware of his reluctance to part with the device. They sat on, Azular assenting at last on the proviso that he was given the data on the prototypes of similar. He agreed to complete the handover the next day at about the same time – he had other business now, he told her.

"Yes, your meet with Xanna Kerrix – I saw her last night and she spoke of it. She's one reason you don't want to let that translator out of your hands, isn't she? You think she'll know more about its ops than you. She won't," Vettarista went on, smiling at his discomfiture. "I've already asked about hers. But what's so fascinating about her ship that you want to look it over so badly?"

"It's in advance of the normal run of shuttles available, as I'm sure you're aware," he replied. "Much of the technology underpinning it is novel to me and I believe it might be useful."

"To give the *Arianrhod* the edge, you mean. That's why your ship has the reputation it has: the best of everything and a crew expert in taking advantage of every trick in every book. Good luck with Xanna Kerrix – she'll give you a run for your credit."

"That I know. She already has."

"Oh?"

"Nothing important," he said hurriedly. "And as Ms Kerrix finds me annoying, although she tolerates me – she told me so – I doubt I'll find myself ahead in any exchange."

"She finds you annoying but tolerates you?" Vettarista reiterated, shaking her head with a sly grin. "For all you're a Berzic telepath, and a damn good one, sometimes you can't see a fly until it spits in your eye. Enjoy the rest of your day. I'll see you tomorrow."

Leaving him in some perplexity, she rose and made off. He sat on to collect his thoughts and then set off for a tube that would take him to green twelve, where he had arranged to find Kerrix.

Ahxenta, Apnis and Lindell made their assigned shuttle bay on green four around two hours later, the first mate betting that the science officer would not have returned from his rendezvous. She was right as there was no sign of him. The bay read clear and opened to the security key that Ahxenta proffered. The three stepped across: the *Gadfly* was where they had left her, shining in the dim light.

"I'll remind him we're waiting once we're aboard," the captain said scathingly to Apnis as the ramp descended and she stepped up to the entry of her favourite shuttle.

As she looked around, her brow creased. The energy cell was still strapped into the seat where Azular had placed it for ease of removal. She examined it and then called up the log of her vessel.

"He's not been back here since we saw him in the *Subspace*," she said tensely. "I don't like it. Something's up."

A link to the science officer produced no response. The captain called the *Arianrhod* to alert the duty officer: Azular had not contacted the ship. A quick round of local comms indicated that there had been no report of unrest in their neck of the Web, but that meant little.

"Lindell, stay here," the captain ordered. "Tallica and I'll check the local area. Kerrix I won't link to, but her billet's on green twelve."

As she was speaking, her wrist communit vibrated and she tabbed it to receive, the holo alerting her to the source. "Azular, where the hell have you been? Are you all right?"

"Later, Captain. We're on our way and will be with you in fifteen minutes or so. We had a little trouble but all's more or less well."

"Wonder what he classes as a little trouble?" asked the first mate.

The little trouble had started on the way to a series of inferior bays in the nether reaches of inner three's blue level sixteen. Azular knew the area as the *Anchor's Rest* was a well-known bar on blue six where dock workers were wont to hang out after their shifts. Kerrix' shuttle was in section delta, bay ninety five, a work space with heavy engineering and technical facilities where craft could be left long-term for a large deposit but small weekly fee. Vetta had supplied company codes to allow entry and exit and these had been set into the shuttle, and the craft cloaked to resemble a typical runabout, Kerrix told Azular. He was curious to see the result, as Kerrix was dressed in flight fatigues, which implied that she was planning a trip. She was also armed.

The two had reached section delta without a hitch, the agreed plan being that the shuttle would be moved to inner two's docking area on green twelve where, with relevant credentials, it was simple to arrange a short-stay company berth. That would allow the Berzic officer to see her fly and simplify the transfer of the energy cell. The bulkheads of the poorly lit and dark corridors of level sixteen bulged with waste removal pipes, cooling tubes and other signs of heavy industry. Safety refuges lined the walls and the passages were divided by solid hatches that would seal automatically in the event of the escape of dangerous substances. Azular found that his usual scanner, useful as it normally was, had trouble penetrating some of the surrounding structures.

"I left the scanner you gave me linked to my bridge station," he informed Kerrix quietly when he caught her looking.

"Just as well I brought one of mine," she said. "It… what the…"

"Two, heading this way!" he interrupted. "Armed and in a hurry."

They had hardly turned to seek shelter in an info-recess when the sound of heavy feet caught their ears and a searing burst of phase-fire ripped past their hideout. The gunmen knew exactly where they were, they were obviously the targets and the shots were deadly. Azular's phase rifle was in his hands and at the ready in seconds. He leant out to fire at the source of the bolts, pulling back as return fire ricocheted off the edge of the recess. Kerrix had primed her own gun and dropped to her knees. She let loose with a shot and slid back, only to dive out again, roll quickly behind a projection in the opposite wall and take cover as a blast of weaponry echoed around the space.

Azular had taken stock of their situation and had noted a side way guarded by a safety door release switch just down from the woman's position. He gesticulated and she nodded, understanding. Both made the lunge at once, firing blindly along the passage to where their two assailants were in hiding behind jutting industrial blocks. The science officer drew the door release over as he pushed his companion ahead of him and into the space. The door zipped across with a whoosh and he pulled down a securing lever.

"It won't hold, they can get through from their side," he said, his breath coming in ragged gasps. "Where to now?"

He made for an open access panel ahead, from which another dim passage extended. His eyes took in the area beyond as the boom of weaponry against the door behind them echoed. Swiftly, he blasted an area of wall close to the panel's ops plate, repeating the action on the opposite side. He then hit the lock and the panel slid across.

"This way!" Azular ordered, leading back the way they had come.

He halted at the entry to a safety refuge in the wall, undid its ops plate, hit a switch, disabled the occupied sign and reclosed the plate. With a dull grinding, the massively heavy door swung out. He pushed her into the tight space, squeezing in alongside as he hauled the door in and twisted the lock wheel. A hiss confirmed an effective seal. The illuminated ops panel was tough to decipher in the near-dark but an escape hatch in the opposite side of their space was outlined in red.

"Controlled space on the other side," Azular panted. "Entry only when authorised as there could be radiation leakage or other hazards. This space is protected plate that they shouldn't be able to scan."

"Which means you can't either," she retorted in a sibilant whisper, trying to twist into a comfortable position. "I can't reach *my* scanner. In fact I can hardly move. You realise I'll have a reverse impression of a *PSS Arianrhod* badge on my face when we do get out of here?"

"Hush," he warned. "Listen…"

"To what? I can't hear a thing except your breath in my ear."

"Will you be *quiet*, Ms Kerrix?"

"*If* you get your rifle out of my hair," was the muted retort. "I'll try to reach my leg pocket – my scanner's there."

"Shhh!" he hissed in exasperation, reaching around her to set the safety catch of his firearm.

With some trouble, Kerrix was able to free her scanner and slide it into a position in which she could operate it. Azular watched intently as she held it up against the outer wall of their refuge, twisted it and then let go. It held fast and her finger traced some complex pattern on its face as she uttered a series of low-voiced commands. A holo of the bulkhead to which the device was attached was extruded into the space before it and the science officer could see a filmy image of the dim passage beyond. Two shadowy forms were visible and they were close. One was perusing a hand-held probe.

As their pursuers drew nearer, Azular felt her hand tighten on his arm. They waited, still, watching as the pair reached their refuge. The leader ran his probe over its door; the other cocked his rifle and eyed his crony's scanner. A few words and a nod were exchanged and the two moved off slowly, probing their surroundings as they went. They repeated the action on the two refuges opposite and then made for those further on, to fade as the Norvallan scanner's range cut.

Kerrix released her grip on Azular's arm and exhaled gently. "So they couldn't get through the plating," she said softly.

"Apparently not," he replied equally quietly. "But *you* could."

"*My* technology," she responded, reaching up to catch the hand he had extended to touch the still-operating device.

"It's not like the one you gave to me. I *would* like to examine it."

"I bet you would," was the ironic return as she pulled the science officer's hand gently away from the wall.

He could feel laughter welling up in her, but he could also feel an almost-electric quiver as she loosed his hand and drew hers away, her fingers lingering. For an indefinable reason Vettarista's dry remark on his lack of clear-sightedness over Kerrix resurfaced and he captured her hand, his long fingers contracting around hers. She stood frozen for an instant but slowly her grip tightened in response as she looked up at his eyes glinting in the dark. Propelled by an irresistible instinct, he bent his head to reach her lips.

"Hell, that was stupid," she murmured moments later as she slid her arms from around his back to rest against his chest.

"I concur," Azular agreed softly, his grip slackening. "I apologise; I – forgot myself."

"We'd both best forget it, perhaps?" she said in a rough tone, one of her hands moving inexorably around his waist and up his back.

"Indeed," he responded. "Ms Kerrix…"

"Call me Xanna, for pity's sake. My name's Xanna. What's yours, apart from Azular?"

"Azular," he said.

"Azular Azular? That's novel."

He gave a low, throaty chuckle. "Just Azular."

"I commend your kin. I was burdened with too many names to be practical, so I chose two that didn't tie me to relatives or ancestors I didn't know or didn't like."

"Indeed?"

"Indeed," she repeated huskily, aware that his arms were seeking her again, tightening, his face coming closer.

"Oh hell!" was all she had time to say.

A minute ticked by before she pulled away to rest her head against his chest. She let out a sigh. "Thank you," she said.

"For what?" he asked gently.

"For making me feel alive again. It's been a long time since…"

"Likewise," he disclosed into the pause.

"Azular…?"

"Yes?"

"Get your rifle out of my back, it's digging in."

"Yes ma'am," he laughed quietly. "Your scanner's still showing clear. I expect we should move before those two think of returning."

"Good idea," she agreed, retrieving her device.

Extremely warily, Azular released the airtight hatch to the passage outside. They could hear a faint susurration from the systems around them but nothing else. Scans of the immediate area were clear of any foot traffic bar themselves. He shut the panel behind them.

"I read no secure cams," Kerrix whispered. "I expect they're only in central areas and at sensitive sites. Blue sixteen isn't a popular place but I guess security has a presence. We head for bay ninety five?"

"It seems the best option," he agreed. "I suggest an indirect route lest those thugs were aware of our endpoint or are still searching."

"Or there are more out there," she added impishly.

They made their way slowly, passing a few others on the way but no-one who gave more than a second look at the uniform worn by the Berzic officer. As far as they could tell they were not followed. The bay was nondescript, small and quickly opened by the access key that Kerrix held. The one local secure cam high up in the bulkhead wall outside was non-functional. The ship was exactly as Kerrix had left her, she told him, and the safety systems she had set in operation showed that no one had been anywhere near her – although the entry panel to the bay had been attempted unsuccessfully.

Azular regarded the craft in surprised interest. The starboard list was present but less evident, he needed his scanner to detect the hull section that had been patched and the instrument could not penetrate the plating. The craft looked like an atypical runabout, her wedge shape lessened but not lost. There was no external projector of the type that had disguised the *Gadfly*, leaving him to assume that Kerrix had restored her on-board cloaking and coded for camouflage. As before, her inserted ID allowed access and as the light grew Azular could see that the internal spec was the same. As she slid into the pilot's chair to start her systems, inviting him to sit behind, he noted that her flight jacket had gone.

"Let's check the drive," she said, rising a little awkwardly.

They made for the aft engineering section, where Kerrix unlatched the casing to reveal the drive unit. The cell that Azular had plugged in on his prior visit was there at eighty four percent capacity, the active power transfer shown by a series of pulsating light points.

"Still functioning effectively," he said. "You boosted the power?"

"Yes, using small energy packs rather than the second energy cell. I didn't want to dislodge *this* in case the interface shifted. I'll close up. We'd best check those records my scanner got of those two thugs."

She locked the unit, sighing. As she stood her leg gave way and she stumbled. She cursed quietly but he caught the small hiss of pain.

"What is it, what's wrong?" he demanded.

"Nothing; just caught my foot."

"You're not a good liar, Xanna."

"You know that's the first time you've used my name?"

"Stop it," he ordered, turning his scanner on her. "What is it?"

"I took a couple of creases – my foot and my arm," she admitted.

"Why in hell didn't you say?" he said sharply, concerned.

"We had other priorities, remember? They're minor."

"Get your boot and jacket off. Where's your emergency med kit?"

The injuries were beyond minor but not serious and Azular did his best with the depleted kit Kerrix dug up, irritated at himself that he had not noticed earlier and irritated at her that she had not trusted him enough to tell him. He helped her back into her jacket, enquiring gruffly if she felt able to fly the craft. Her answer staggered him.

"I won't be flying her: you will."

After his initial shock Azular settled her into the secondary seat and with a thrill of expectancy took the pilot's chair, knowing she was watching every move. To his surprise he found that she had recoded her systems to respond to verbal commands in Inter-Lan. He was still in the database and good to go, she told him, but their first task was a skim over of the holo that her scanner had picked up. She talked him through linkage of the device to the holo-generator port and the run was projected, with relevant data shown as a list alongside.

Neither of the two men seemed familiar, but Azular could tell that they were well-built, were cyber-enhanced and were toting advanced firearms. The Norvallan system had no standards against which to match their biosigns, but Kerrix copied the file to a shard that Azular could take with him. His main concerns were how their trail had been picked up and who had been the target, himself, Kerrix or both. As secure cams operated on almost every level of inner three blue, it was possible that those behind the hit could link into security's records or had a mole who had spotted them. Or there may have been eyes on them both for a while and their meeting had triggered the tail. As the data transferred to the receiving shard, it occurred to Azular that he and Kerrix had been absent for over two hours and his shipmates might conceivably be concerned that his mission with the energy cell had failed. It was at that point he linked to Captain Ahxenta.

Azular recalled the ops sequence he had set for start-up the last time he had sat in the chair. Aware that Kerrix was observing closely, he primed and set external scanners, checking for hazards within and beyond both sets of bay doors. He fitted the entry key Kerrix had given him into its portal, watching as permission codes were verified. Having ascertained ship's status as flight-ready, he took note of the visual and voice alerts that hull plating was patchy and full cloaking could not be achieved and ordered added shielding. He also carried out a weapons check and was pleased to see that the craft had ample for her size. Slowly he brought her up to readiness, feeling the thrust as she began to move. A strange familiarity with the ops boards crept over him as he made for the extern door and slid into free space.

This was known territory but he felt elated as he scanned his chart and set for inner two and their destination bay on green twelve, the hazy 'tween-belt space sliding by. With Kerrix on tactical watch at his back, he made inner two and quickly found his target bay. He sent in the relevant entry codes and watched as the door slid across.

"No hazards detected," she said gently. "You're safe to proceed."

He made entry safely and set down, sequentially switching off his ops. Leaning back, he smiled to himself, satisfied, and then turned to look at her, a raised eyebrow daring her to comment.

"Good job, you did very well," she smiled back, nodding. "You should be proud of yourself. That was a near-perfect landing."

"Near-perfect?"

"Stop virtually patting yourself on the back and get the hell out of my seat. Your captain will no doubt be simmering until we show. And we'd better scan every atom of the way up to green four."

By the time they reached the bay in which the *Gadfly* was docked, the estimated fifteen minute limit had come and gone and the captain was waiting for them on the outside, her irritation rising. She greeted the pair tartly but her relief was patent.

"You two took your time."

Kerrix eyed her quizzically. "Blame the pilot," she said, cocking a thumb at Azular.

With a startled look at her clearly gratified science officer, Ahxenta gestured them through the bay door, securing it as she ordered them to make for the shuttle. It was only when the three had joined Apnis and Lindell inside that she demanded the details of their trouble.

Azular pulled out the data shard and slid it into a port on the ops board as he briefly described the events and their sequel. None of the others recognised the dim figures. Kerrix remained silent and shook her head when asked for her views, shrugging equivocally.

"What in hell's that supposed to mean?" Ahxenta snapped.

"I've nothing to add. I'll take my cell and leave you to it. I'm sure you want to get back up to your ship. I want to get back to mine."

"You're not thinking of heading back to inner three?" interrupted Azular. "You're not fit to carry that cell, much less fly a shuttle."

"No. I'll leave her where she is, at least overnight," the woman sighed, raising her shoulders to release the tension.

He nodded. "I'll help you with the cell. And as I'm here tomorrow on business, I'll bring a new emergency medical kit for your shuttle."

As the captain's eyes blazed and she exchanged a look with Apnis, Azular blithely continued, "It'll be a sight better than the excuse for a one you have. And I suggest you visit the emergency medical station on twelve: you need treatment. Ms Kerrix was injured," he explained.

"The med kit I'll take. But if you think I'm taking phase-burn to a med station, think again. They'll ask questions that I'm in no mind to answer. And *I* suggest you take your own advice, *Doctor*: think I didn't notice the crease at the top of your left shoulder? Nips, doesn't it?"

"You don't miss a trick, do you?" he sighed, grimacing.

"So you keep telling me. And if you're down here tomorrow, ditch the uniform: that badge attracts attention wherever you go."

"When you two have quite finished," Ahxenta broke in, folding her arms. "I'd like the details you missed out, all of them, and more from you Ms Kerrix, speculations included, on how and why you think you were trailed and shot at. And then Commander Apnis will escort you to your ship with that cell. You'll stay here, mister."

In the event, with very few omissions, the two recalled every point they could before the captain called a halt.

Flintlock had verified that the graze on Azular's shoulder was minor, requiring no more than a pain shot and a dressing in place of the temporary patch that Ahxenta had applied aboard the *Gadfly*. The chief medic was, however, vexed that Kerrix had been left to fend for herself. Apnis had attended her to her ship and then her quarters and had reported that she seemed calm but was adamant that she would not seek medical aid. The upshot the next morning was that Flintlock decided to catch an early ride with Azular to check on the woman, as she also had business Web-side set for later in the day.

From the data on the shard Kerrix had given him, Azular had worked out that both assailants bore hostile cyber-enhancements and had biosigns that indicated Xerophyte or Salt Three as their origin. That implied a link to Hoxiz, prompting the captain to order escorts down with Flintlock and Azular, to their joint irritation. The CMO had private meetings with old friends who, she hoped, might give her a lead into companies promoting high-spec medical devices and the reps allied to them. Her evening dinner date was in a quiet restaurant, she had reserved overnight lodging, and a minder she did not need, she told Ahxenta. Azular had plans that he was unwilling to divulge, but he stated that he too would remain Web-side. The strategy agreed was that uniforms would not be worn and the guards, also in mufti, would maintain watch until the close of business hours, after which they would be free but would remain on call until *Arianrhod's* shuttle returned them to the ship at twenty two hundred hours.

A high security shuttle bay on green four had been taken as it was close to many prime amenities in inner two. The team's first stop Web-side was the *Half Moon*, where Kerrix was on early shift. As the breakfast crowd had gone and the next influx had not yet begun, she would be relatively free to talk. The two found their quarry recoding a menu pad that some joker had altered and requested a private chat.

She nodded and began to pour a couple of drinks. "Ale okay?"

"Nothing for me," Flintlock told her.

"You come here to drink," she told her. "This place isn't a public park and Ally won't stand for people using it to hold meetings. These are small and fairly mild. Your tab, Doctor?" she grinned at Azular.

"I expect so," he responded wryly. "Please have one yourself."

"Not on duty," she rejoined, setting out the drinks. "Even when you're not in uniform you look like you're in uniform," she went on, eyeing him up and down. "And I see you're armed – very wise. Take the quiet table over by that out of action holo-station and I'll bring these over. Your bodyguards want a drink as well?" she asked, tilting her head at Ji and Hanx holding up the far end of the bar.

"Not on my tab they don't," Azular informed her.

"They look odd out of uniform as well; civilian clothing evidently doesn't sit well with the crew of the *Arianrhod*. Expecting trouble?"

"Just bring the drinks over *if* you please, Ms Kerrix."

"Aye sir. After you."

She sat down equably enough although she regarded the doctor askance as, with privacy set, Flintlock hauled out her medi-scanner.

"You'll find med-patches for phase-burn in the medical kit Azular brought in," the chief medic told her. "Use them. Your other injuries are progressing satisfactorily but I *would* like a visual check."

"You're not going to get one out here and I'm not taking you into the staff room. Too many eyes about, though I know most of them. And I suspect one or two of the regulars have recognised you two."

"So do I," the science officer noted wearily. "I'll pass the med-kit to you later. What time are you off-duty?"

"I'm free from fourteen hundred. After that, I'll be in my place. You know where it is."

"And if you don't mind, Ms Kerrix, as I didn't have time to see all the alterations to your shuttle, I would be grateful for a look. I take it you haven't attempted to fit your energy cell yet?"

"I haven't. She's still on green twelve, but I'll arrange a new berth. I don't want to go back to inner three in case there's a record of her there. Anything else?"

"Not in here," Azular returned. "I have a meeting shortly, but I *will* call on you after fourteen hundred. Doctor?" he asked, turning to Flintlock, who had been watching her fellow officer closely.

"Just apply those meds," she advised. "I have several meets, so I won't see you later; or you, Azular. I'll collect Ji on the way out."

As soon as the chief medic had gone, the science officer turned to the woman. "One more thing, Ms Kerrix… Xanna. I'd like to thank you for the technology and the data you've shared with me: it's been of great help. Perhaps you'd join me for dinner this evening?"

As her eyes widened, he assured her that it would be a quiet place. She inclined her head in wary agreement. He promised to finalise the details later and rose to leave. Two pairs of eyes watched shrewdly from a side booth with a good all-round view. They could not hear but with years of people-watching behind them, both were adept at reading body language and making profit thereby.

"What d'you make of that, Jurry lad? Dr Azular soft on Kerrix?"

"Might be, Malty. More fool him: her left hook's nowhere near as fast and hard as Ahxenta's I'll warrant, but she packs a nasty punch."

The senior science officer had been joined by Ensign Hanx. He had an hour before he was to meet Vettarista and had decided that a trip to the *Port in a Storm* on green six might be profitable.

By the time of his meeting Azular had learnt that he and Kerrix had not been the only assault victims on inner three blue sixteen the day before. Kit Biernop, whom Azular and Hanx had met in the *Port*, told them that a repair op servicing faulty secure cams close to bay ninety five had been hit. That implied to Azular that Kerrix had been the target and whoever was behind it knew of her shuttle. He kept his own counsel, and having left Hanx at the door of the *Sunlight*, he made his way to the table where Vettarista was waiting.

Azular wasted no time, ordering a meal and prepping his info-pad as if for business. The woman had sensed his anxiety but waited until privacy was active and both had set their bug detectors. As he passed the language analyser-translator across the table, she slid the shard of data on the parallel devices to him and bluntly asked what the trouble was. He told her of his meeting with Biernop and his news and she nodded. She had been digging, and having heard of the attack had guessed that Kerrix' intimately-linked translator was not only known about but the stakes were being upped to obtain it.

Azular was cogitating on just how much the agent knew. "She said someone aboard the ship she used to reach Merkat tracked her when she jumped ship. They had clearly captured her ID signal."

"I know. It was probably inferred that she'd come through that obsolete bypass node, so she had to be alien and would likely have novel tech. Some bright sparks figured her biosigns as humanoid and guessed what her implants could be. Tech labs have been trying to develop gadgets like the translator for years and I'll bet these hostiles had advanced models, implanted or at least attached. How else could they have infiltrated so quickly once they started? But *they* were cyber. So the bright sparks scented profit *and* advantage. And they had to be part of the set-up at that ex-hostile base off Mu and near the Enigma, Starfall they call it. So Xanna was the main target yesterday?"

"That's what I deduce."

"And you?"

"Possibly, as I belong to the *Arianrhod*. I take it you've seen the recording of the perpetrators?"

"Yes; I didn't recognise them but the scan was fuzzy. The readings pointed to an origin on the far side of Eta, maybe Xerophyte. I've got people checking. But if these traders that operate out of that Starfall base are friendly, why are they still on her tail – and on yours?"

"You said there were other groups here that may be hostile to us. As for Xanna… Ms Kerrix, it was perhaps inferred that she would try to get away on that ship that was due to leave and *that* was taken into account by the infiltrators that Thal is trying to find and remove. Thal said that Lokterix *was* there until recently but fled when he realised they were onto him, he thought to Mellifly. Thal's certain that his operation's still being sabotaged. He's very bitter about two ships he's lost and a base that his enemies had attacked and destroyed. But if that's the case and one infiltrator *was* aboard the ship that Xanna got away on, that would account for the shot at her shuttle and would alert whoever was aboard to her whereabouts."

Vettarista nodded. "And then tell others. But it still doesn't mean that this Thal would be a friend to her. Your captain didn't mention Xanna in her dealings with him?"

"Of course not!"

Apart from a smile at his tone, she continued calmly. "Thal must be aware of Xanna and know she skipped from his base."

"I doubt she's his current priority, nor is he ours. Have you more on the other factions that may be agents of chaos and hostile to us?"

"Hoxiz must be part of one. He's certainly linked to Lokterix and he's had dealings with the tech-med company that's trying to develop implanted language decoders, though I think they're a separate outfit and may have their own operatives. There's a band that trafficked out of Mellifly in suspect goods that left in a hurry when *Arianrhod* took out that hostile shipyard… they're trying to get back in business and they've chosen to do that here, though we think they made originally for their home port after the firefight: Treskk Primus."

"Treskk Primus?" Azular hissed.

"Yes, I knew you'd recognise the name. *Arianrhod's* not liked there and I imagine they bear grudges."

"They're little more than pirates and dangerous at that. They did us very serious damage a few years ago."

"I know – half the galaxy knows, as you paid them back and then some," Vettarista remarked. "But your ship will certainly be on their hit list. So there are potentially two groups that are no friends to your people. It *is* possible that Lokterix has his own gang but he strikes me as a loner who uses others. There *are* other lone operators that we're keeping tabs on but they're small fry and not likely to be involved in all this. I'd pass you a data shard of the relevant details but there are a couple of pairs of eyes watching us – or should I say watching you – from a table in the far corner, behind you."

As her eyes flicked to his left, her tone warned of something out of kilter. He shifted round as he turned his info-pad towards her as if to show something and caught a glimpse.

"They've not long come in," she went on. "Recognise them?"

"I'm capturing visuals; I won't scan as they'd notice. And yes I do. As do you. They're the two who tailed me and Ms Kerrix yesterday."

16: CONSPIRACIES

Vettarista, with a fixed smile on her face, rapidly tapped text into her info-pad as Azular tuned his visual of the two at the far table to high definition. As he zeroed in on the one who had held the probe during the episode on inner three, he spied a glint close to the man's hairline that implied a prosthetic implant. The duo appeared to be dressed in regular business attire, but its glossy sheen evoked armour plating. That, with cyber-enhancement and the weapons that the two would surely be carrying, indicated that it would be unwise to engage them. He advised the ISP agent of the issues, aware that the pair had begun to set up a small piece of equipment on their table.

"I don't know what that is they're handling but they may be set to bug our conversation," he warned Vettarista.

"I've put things in place. We leave now and head for marketing: there should be plenty going on at this time of day. Tell your security not to join us. I'd like to know how they knew you were in here."

"There may be other eyes that noted me and passed on the news," he said in a low voice as he circumspectly scanned around the space while wrapping up his info-pad and calling up the bill.

"Or you and your buddy were followed from the *Port in a Storm*, or even before that," she posited.

"That's feasible. I'm beginning to believe that the ones causing us trouble can link into security's cams or moles in security tip them off, or they have a dedicated spy-cam net."

"Possibly," replied Vettarista as they left. "Those two won't follow as their food's just turned up but there may be more out here."

"I'm aware of that, believe me. I'll tell Ensign Hanx to head back to our shuttle but to take care. However, it *is* a remote possibility that you're the subject of their scrutiny."

The woman laughed but agreed. Marketing was a short hop away and the two reached it quickly. Azular had linked to Hanx to apprise him of trouble and instructed him to contact *Arianrhod* and Ji from the shuttle, but gave no details. Vettarista refused to reveal her plans but passed over the data shard of suspected hostile ops and the two parted. Azular made his way to the bay on green four and called the ship to update the captain. If his hunch that their enemies had access to security's cams or had plants in security that *had* such access were accurate, it might be wise to alert Biernop. He also loaded the data he had been given to the shuttle's banks for relay to the *Arianrhod*.

The science officer's next stop was green twelve, section one, one, four. He recalled thirty one's grubby blue door. The last time he had seen it had been when he had escorted Kerrix back after having tied one of *Arianrhod's* energy cells into her shuttle-drive. His scan showed one lifeform and he pressed the comm. She must have called up the external vis-screen, for as the door panel slid aside she greeted him formally and invited him in.

"Ms Kerrix: your med kit," he smiled as he held up the pack.

The door closed behind him and she gestured to the sofa, asked him to sit and offered coffee. He accepted and set his burden on the low table, deftly opening the kit and disinterring part of the contents.

"Phase-burn patches," he told her as she set two mugs down and sat opposite him. "I can assist in their application, if you like."

She made a face at that effrontery, smiling even so. "I *can* manage, thank you all the same."

"This coffee's good."

"No it isn't, it's insipid. And you didn't come all this way to pass on a med kit and insincere compliments. What's the matter?"

"You think there's something amiss?"

"Azular, will you stop playing games and cut to the point. I can see by your face that there's been a development. I know you met with Vetta. I don't want to know the content but how did it go?"

His grin faded and he gave her the barest outline of events.

She nodded. "It adds up that security's inner ops are subverted to the extent that an outfit can have a finger on secure cams and can follow who they want. My shuttle's not going near inner three again. But you're safe in this part of green twelve – the cams along this way don't work and if they're fixed, they're soon broken. What else?"

Azular repeated his dinner invitation. He would call in at nineteen hundred, their objective being the *Milky Pearl*, a small place on green seven. With a quirky smile he also requested a visit to her shuttle in its current berth. He wanted to know how she had carried out the repairs before she had moved the craft from outer nine.

"You don't give up, do you? But I was expecting it. And as you're not in uniform, you'll probably pass muster from here to there. Drink up and we'll head out. But only an hour as I *have* other things to do."

"Like what?"

"Mind your own business."

"Yes ma'am."

Azular found out about the other things when he called at apartment thirty one at nineteen hundred. Kerrix had been busy. She was garbed in a simple dark blue gown with a short fine lace jacket that hid the scarring that no doubt still disfigured her. She had also been in the hands of a personal enhancement therapist.

"You look… different," Azular greeted her. He had been about to say "striking" but reckoned it would most certainly be met with a barbed comment. He suspected the hand of Vettarista in the change.

"Borrowed finery," she admitted, gathering up a small lacy purse. "A friend of Vetta's. By the way, before we go, she asked me to pass on some news that she did not want to trust to any comms link."

The summary was that the ISP agent had an undercover colleague in the *Subspace* who had spiked the suspects' drinks, slipped a tracker into each of their pockets and had them followed. They had then been arrested on charges of theft and causing affray whilst under the influence of alcohol. They were now in custody, where enquiries into their backgrounds and their physiology would be made.

"A set-up? That won't stand up in a court of law."

"*If* it's uncovered and it depends on the court. Vetta's trade allows such latitude, I imagine. And you're telling me that you and yours don't use such tactics if they suit?"

"No comment," he grinned. "Shall we go?"

The *Milky Pearl* was small but had a buzz that would increase as the evening wore on. Azular had booked a table and they were shown to a private corner. As he quickly set up his scanner-jammer, his gaze raked the nearby tables. His brow knit and a resigned look replaced his relaxed smile. Kerrix turned her head to see what had caused the change and began to laugh. Realising she had been seen, Dr Flintlock nodded over, grinning knowingly.

"Popular place with the crew of the *Arianrhod*," Kerrix observed.

"So it appears."

"What does your security escort do when you're on a date? Stand outside the door?"

"Ms Kerrix…"

"You've forgotten my name again."

He shook his head, laughing. "Xanna. I'm beginning to find you as annoying as you find me. *Do* you still find me annoying?" he asked half-jokingly, his mind flitting back to earlier in the day and the short trip to her shuttle. There had been no more than an exchange of light banter until she had shooed him out and onto the extended ramp at the end of the visit. Her hand on his arm to haul him away from the lit ramp and into the semi-darkness had been enough to shake him into a repeat of the kiss he had given her in the safety refuge. He had surprised himself and startled her, but she had not drawn away.

"Hell, yes," she smiled into his face. "Don't you think you are?"

"Let's look at the menu," he parried, a warm flush suffusing his face, his normal calm strangely ruffled.

The meal proceeded amicably, with Azular learning more of the aspects of a Norvallan sci-shuttle, including inbuilt self-repair systems and partly self-healing skin. Kerrix' interest lay in life aboard a PSS and the problems that beset trading in the mapped galaxy. She had met several crewmembers of private starships in her time in the *Half Moon*; some had impressed her and some certainly had not.

The two had almost forgotten their surroundings and Azular was urging his companion to try a honeyed fruit he had pinned on a fork when her eyes froze at something out of his line of sight. Her hand slid up to grasp his, warning him not to turn or to draw attention.

"It's that thug that tried to get at my implant in medbay, the one we met recently in the *Half Moon*," she murmured.

"Hoxiz?" Azular whispered in return. "What's he doing?"

"He's not looking our way. He and an associate are in a side booth and they've got their eyes on Dr Flintlock and her friend."

"Associate?" he repeated, noting a nuance in her tone.

"Another face I know: medbay's senior surgical officer Dr Herta."

"Are you sure?"

"I am. I've had a few harsh words with Dr Mazy Herta."

Azular was aware of the aims of Flintlock's talks and with Hoxiz as a key suspect linked to front-line medical tech, some of it for illegal use, he had no illusions but that the man's presence meant trouble.

"Damn! What are Dr Flintlock and her friend doing?"

"Looking and laughing at us; and *that* will alert that maniac to our presence here. What do we do?" she asked.

"What do you suggest?"

"Pay up, ship out, come in again by the back door and take them out. Or face them right now. Though I still suggest you pay the bill or you'll never be allowed back in here with a date."

"Xanna, why must you be so flippant? This is serious."

"Believe me, I am," she said, releasing his hand. "Ah! He's spotted us and so has Herta. I'm going over there to call his bluff."

"You're going nowhere: that man is part-cyber, dangerous and has little sense of the appropriate. He won't hesitate to lash out," she was told as Azular looked over to see that she was correct: it *was* Hoxiz.

She eyed him intensely. "You're not in command of *me*, Azular, Azular. And you're cute when you're angry," she added with a smile.

"I hope Dr Flintlock has taken steps to detect scanning," he said, ignoring the comment as he set his own scanner to directional mode to confirm that they were not the subject of bugging.

"How did he know she'd be here?" Kerrix questioned.

"Possibly through Dr Herta. Dr Flintlock would know her."

"She does. She was with me when I clashed with Herta some time ago and did not hold back."

Azular had been mentally revolving strategy and had decided on a direct approach. He hit his wrist communit. The doctor answered, amused rather than surprised, but was quickly alert when he told her that she was the object of Hoxiz' scan. As she and her friend turned to the wall booth, Azular was disturbed by motion at his side. Kerrix had dug a small handgun out of her bag and was coolly setting it up.

"I've got another attached to my leg," she informed him briefly. "One wrong move from either of those two and I *will* let loose. That bastard would have killed me without a scruple to get my implant."

"No doubt, but I suggest you do *not* try anything in here. The staff are already aware that something's going on."

As Flintlock rose, Kerrix stood likewise, her hand on Azular's arm with the order to stay. She made for the doctor's table, her eyes on Hoxiz and Herta all the way. Azular extracted his handgun, aware of curious glances and a rising hum of conversation.

Kerrix' nod and her smile may have suggested to other diners that she had merely gone to talk to a friend, but her deliberate stare at the two over at the wall told *them* that she was well aware of their ploys.

"Are Dr Herta and Mr Hoxiz – or whatever he's calling himself – listening in on you, Doctor?" she asked Flintlock.

"I don't know," was the grim reply. "When did they get in?"

"They have their food, so I guess a little while ago. I'll enquire. My companion *is* covering me from his table, so any trouble from either of them and he *will* shoot first and ask questions later," she went on. "We *have* called security and I am armed."

Deliberately slowly, Kerrix walked over to their table. "Dr Herta," she greeted the woman with a courteous nod. "Do you know you've taken up with a known felon? And are you aware that he's bugging Dr Flintlock? You must be: that *is* clearly a recording device. Lest you didn't hear my remarks to Dr Flintlock, let me repeat them. I'm being covered by someone who is armed and prepared to fire at any sign of trouble, security is on the way, and *my* firearm is primed."

She raised the small gun to show them, her aim clearly Hoxiz. Her free hand slid across to clasp a small conical appliance that sat on the table near the man. "You try it and you're toast," she warned as his lips curled into a sneer and his hand began to move forwards.

Herta's attempted smile was as false as her denial of illegal activity. The bug was a privacy guard, her colleague was a company rep and they were discussing private business, she stated in a hard, icy voice, before cautioning Kerrix to back off.

The woman ignored her, her eyes on Hoxiz, whose hand flew out to smack down on the bug and on the hand that held it.

Kerrix fired. "I warned you," she hissed through clenched teeth.

There was no noise, no flash, but the man visibly jerked as a stun bolt hit him amidships, pushing him against the back of his seat. His eyes glazed and he slumped loosely.

"You want the same, *Doctor*?" Kerrix asked, nursing her damaged hand, which still held the bug, under her arm.

"You get the hell out of here!" Herta snarled.

"No. I want answers *now*, or you'll be under arrest for attempted murder. You know damn well he was the bastard that tried to remove one of my implants when I was in medbay and under *your* care."

Herta gave a sham gasp. "No! And what've you done to him?"

"He's stunned. You *will* tell me what you were talking about and why you aided his attack on me. Or you're answerable to the law and to my friends. And my friends are not friendly, believe me."

"She's already answerable to the Interstellar Medical Council," the cold voice of Axellina Flintlock said at her back as the *Milky Pearl's* duty manager hove up to see what was going on.

The *Arianrhod's* chief medic was blunt. "They were monitoring my conversation and both are involved in criminal activity. I want them under arrest now or I'll create a scene you won't get over for a year."

"You can prove nothing!" Herta barked at her.

The duty manager raised his wrist comm, called in orders and then eyed both Flintlock and Herta. "I don't want a fuss," he said. "There are other diners here. I'd be obliged if you'd come over to my office and we'll deal with this. What's wrong with that gentleman?"

"I shot him," Kerrix said. "And he's no gentleman."

"I'll get a medic!" the man gaped, staring at her.

"We've got several of those," she grimaced in return.

"He's only stunned, he'll be fine. I'm the chief medical officer of the *PSS Arianrhod. She's* the senior surgical officer of Merkat medbay, but not for much longer," Flintlock rapped as three Merkat security officers sped over, having been directed by an aide at the door. Hanx and Ji were behind them, still out of uniform but both armed.

The matter was repeated and the suspects readied for escort to the manager's office. Flintlock, having studied Kerrix' hand, steered her back to Azular with the order to get it strapped up promptly and she would deal with Herta and Hoxiz.

"After dinner," was the short reply as Kerrix sat, dropping the bug onto the table. "It's fine."

"You'll do as the doctor advises," Azular said calmly. "Dinner is finished anyway. I'll see to it," he added, looking up at his colleague.

"Good; I'd better let my friend know what gives. I take it you got Hanks and Ji back here?"

"I did. The captain knows the score. I'm staying here overnight, so I'll look after Ms Kerrix."

"You'd better."

"Remember to pay your bill," he retorted with some irony.

"Not that you'll be allowed back in here, either of you," put in Kerrix with a painful smile. "Or me."

"Let's get to the emergency room in medbay," Azular said gently, realising that she was in distress. "Let me take that gun and the bug."

"I'll need that as evidence," Flintlock declared, snatching the latter away. "Don't worry, I'll get everything off it before I hand it over."

She turned on her heel, leaving Azular to deal with his own affairs, which meant paying his bill, collecting their property and helping Kerrix to her feet. An aide was there to see them off the premises.

"Back to mine," she said quietly. "I'm not heading anywhere near medbay. I'll get out of this outfit and then head for the emergency med station on green twelve – it should be open at this hour."

"*We'll* head there," he corrected.

In the interim, Ahxenta had asked Apnis to contact Kit Biernop to advise him of the incident, left an urgent link for Vettarista and set up an early briefing with the most highly-ranked person she could trust in Merkat security. With two days left in dock, she wanted to ensure that as many threats to her people as possible were neutralised. By the time she had done and had been updated on ship's business, Flintlock had called. Analysis of the bug had proved that part of her dialogue with her friend in the *Milky Pearl* had been recorded. They had luckily almost done but the names of concerns selling advanced tech for specialist applications and the reps pushing the products had been part of it. They had then moved onto personal matters, the doctor was forced to confess, including Azular and Kerrix, which had no doubt alerted Hoxiz to the two at the nearby table.

The security outcome was less positive as the covert bugging was the only charge that had been pressed, but Hoxiz and Herta had both been held, Hoxiz under the name Berg Brack. He claimed to be a rep for a firm called Noygul Medtech. Flintlock had checked and found that it had an office and lab in the Web. It was registered as dealing in small medical devices and had operated for a year, but one of the doctor's earlier contacts had heard that the firm was linked to the transfer of suspect medical supplies. Merkat security would only say that enquiries were ongoing and relevant searches would be carried out if necessary. The visit by the captain of the *Arianrhod* set for early next day had raised hackles when the news filtered down but had resulted in no more information. Flintlock had refused to be drawn on any of the content of the recording made by Hoxiz and dared the security officers to detain her. They didn't.

The following morning saw a flurry of activity aboard ship as several officers were headed out. Ahxenta had left word for Azular to meet her in the *Half Moon* for breakfast as she wanted him for her meetings with security and then with Vettarista. Apnis had arranged to meet Kit Biernop for her early meal and would catch up with the others later. The captain had insisted on her own back-up for the meet in security's HQ and had assigned Lieutenants Ji Lerro and Jen Airy. Flintlock had her own agenda and had a tryst with her friend of the evening before in Merkat medbay's dining hall.

The captain judged it best that the *Gadfly* be used to transport the party from the *Arianrhod*. She piloted the shuttle and berthed her in the most secure bay available on green eleven of inner two. The crew went their separate ways, Ahxenta and the security escort making for the *Half Moon in a Puddle* up on green two.

"Early this morning, Captain," Ally greeted her as Ahxenta came in through the door, looking around for her senior science officer.

"Breakfast," she said. "You two order what you want and put it on my tab," she instructed her guards. "I'll wait for Azular, he should be here shortly. Meanwhile, coffee would be good, Ally."

"I'll see to it, ma'am. Merry!" he called over to his young acolyte. "Get the captain some coffee. Where are Xanna and Jez?"

"Xanna's in the back sorting stuff," was the reply as Merry's head slewed round. "I've not seen Jez, but he's maybe in the kitchen."

Ahxenta chose a table with a good view of the door and sat down. The young assistant was quick to come over with the coffee.

"How *is* Ms Kerrix this morning?" the captain asked her.

"Fine, ma'am," was the guarded response. "I'll tell her you asked."

Ahxenta nodded and Merry made for the bar, where her friend had appeared from the private space behind. The captain could see them talking and Kerrix had her left hand strapped. The two were still chatting when Azular, smart in his uniform, strode in. His advent prompted Merry to disappear with a quick word, the result of which was more coffee at Ahxenta's table. That ended the science officer's tête-à-tête at the bar and he made his way over to the captain.

"Ma'am," he greeted her. "You've not ordered?"

"I was waiting for you. I've called up the menu. How's your friend Ms Kerrix today? I see her hand's bound up."

"A small fracture and bruising," he responded briefly. "It should heal cleanly. But perhaps we should talk privately?"

The two ordered their meals and invoked privacy. The captain was given a detailed account of the events of the previous evening. She then brought her science officer up to date on what had transpired after he had left the *Milky Pearl*.

After the meal Ahxenta, Azular and the escort met up with Apnis on the way to Merkat security to hear what she had to say after her talk with Kit Biernop. That the Web's secure cam net may have been infiltrated had fired his own suspicions that operatives in security's visual recording section had been passing on information for credit as part of a small-time corruption ring. If, as it now seemed likely, it was being used to identify targets, it meant that those guilty had full-time access and a detailed knowledge of what ships were in the Web, given the attempts on the *Arianrhod's* crew and others. Biernop was sure that workers in the maintenance crews tasked with secure cam repair had to be in the loop. They did not belong to security but had their own Guild and were called in as needed. He had asked around and dug up two names but had been warned off by a contact who had been beaten up for talking to a senior security officer.

"He wouldn't give me the names as he'd no proof and didn't want to implicate anyone," Apnis said. "But he set up a jammer-scanner and that's not his style. The attack on the op in inner three is making him antsy: why target a repair guy? Because he might spot something out of place or that fiddling with cams *is* going on, is Kit's take on it."

"Or some outfit has set up a covert cam network and tied it into security's to make use of *its* systems," Azular mused. "That implies security complicity, or there's some base that links to the system."

"I don't like the sound of it," the first mate said. "But Kit figures that the ISP Intelligence people brought in over Guild and security issues are upping the ante, as he's finding a lot more checks popping up that are classed as routine. He's too old a hand to believe *that*, but faces are turning up that he's not seen before. There's one I spotted in the *Pink Kettle* before he came in that supports his views," Apnis whispered as she looked around warily. "They have a new table hand, who also moonlights in the *Green Diamond* in the evenings. She goes by the name Wekki Munnet and the last time *we* saw her she was working a long way away from here, in the *Red Sunset*."

"Warweft?" the captain breathed.

"The same. She recognised me right away, probably from that link we had with her months ago when we passed on Hoxiz' name, but we both pretended we'd never met before. Maybe she's been brought in because of the link to Hoxiz?"

"Later. We're here," Ahxenta stated. "Hills had better have more news on the table or there'll be trouble. Ji and Airy, stay sharp."

Senior Security Officer Jiff Hills had news: he knew the captain of the *Arianrhod* sufficiently well that he had exerted himself. The billets signed out to Berg Brack and Mazy Herta had been searched. Brack's place was clean but Herta's held surprises, including technical pieces now with security. There were facts that Hills would not reveal about Herta's private life but that had resulted in her suspension from duty. Both were still being held for more questioning. Noygul Medtech had confirmed that Brack had been recruited as a rep two months before but would say nothing more than that. Medical tests had confirmed that he was highly cyber-enhanced and his biosigns implied an origin of outer zone Mu, where Minch Fettin was the most populous planet, but results were inconclusive. As for security's cam system, Hills was shocked at the idea of its possible subversion, but did say that there had been problems involving its misuse in the past.

The officer had his own questions in relation to Dr Azular and his friend, as it was conceivable that Brack would file charges against her for stunning him. The science officer was curt: it was self-defence for his assault on her and if she chose not to press charges then that was her affair. Ahxenta was far from satisfied that no further legal action was to be brought against the two but there was little she could do other than warn Hills of the dangers posed by Hoxiz and of the potential of high-level infiltration in his own backyard.

"He's honest," the captain told the other two as they made their way out, their escort stepping in behind. "And he has some clout, but his hands are tied by what he doesn't know. But it's time things were done about the leaks in security, the drips are becoming cascades. On another note, we're due out by nineteen hundred tomorrow and the cargo pods will be brought in at sixteen hundred. Lindell will get the clearances in place. I've ordered fighter escort from Redship's storage across, as it's classified cargo for Silverglass. But Lindell's left me a link so I'd best check it as it may be about the payload. As we're due to meet our other contact in marketing in fifteen minutes, we'll head down now and I'll make the call from there."

A small meeting room had been reserved for the talks in the main suite on green four under Ahxenta's name. The captain ordered Airy and Ji to remain on watch outside, locked the door and scanned the area. She then linked to her supercargo aboard *Arianrhod.* It was news of another deal that Lindell reckoned would interest the captain: several small batches of high-quality raw crystals had been put up for quick sale at gem mining station Brown Amber, on the edge of zone Beta. The original contract had fallen through and the miners wanted a rapid turnover to bring in much-needed credit for upgrades to their badly-damaged mining fleet as a result of the hostile take-over early in the galactic conflict that had almost put paid to their operations. Once the gems were cut, polished and array-set, there were various markets, mostly comms-related, that would pay a high price for them. It would mean decent profits for the *Arianrhod* and for Ahxenta's contact on Freskat Six, if he could carry out the work. The drawbacks were that the ship would have to pick up the goods on her way out with the Redship merchandise for Silverglass Station, which was in the opposite direction, and the cargo for ISP Silverglass was costly and classified and not something that should be brought within spitting distance of a well-known trouble hotspot.

The captain weighed the news as she ran over the accounts that the supercargo had sent. "We'll take it," she decided. "It's a good deal, we're known at Brown Amber and they wouldn't dare pull a fast one. If we speed up the Redship deal we can make headway sooner than nineteen hundred. Put me through to the bridge. The engines will have to be set for speed and all our shields and weapons primed and ready for action. We'll need the decoy set to deploy as well. Did you and Crizz carry out any more on it, apart from upgrading its image quality and scan resistance?" she asked Azular.

"No, Captain. We had other priorities," he responded smoothly.

"I'll bet," Ahxenta said dryly. "You'd better make sure all our crew on leave know that our schedule's tightened up, Tallica. They'll have to be back up and ready for duty before sixteen hundred tomorrow."

"Aye, Captain. That buzz will be our contact, I guess," the first mate added as a noise at the entry cut the conversation.

It was Vettarista. She had been filled in and updated on the events of the previous evening by her contacts. Noygul Medtech was not the firm involved in developing novel and costly micro-medical devices and to which Hoxiz had links, as the agent had warned in the data she had passed to Azular; *that* firm was listed as Kasinnick. But the net was tightening and ISP's senior command, alarmed that another serious war was brewing, had taken steps to break the criminal rings that thrived on disorder and to track down their allies. The Alliance of ISP, Coalition, Non-Treaty and Independent bodies was holding but rows over whose ships would patrol what sectors was impeding progress, as was the presence of criminal elements in Allied ruling councils. Doosbak was one, but his Coalition Council membership had been suspended pending inquiry into his businesses for fraud.

Ahxenta on her part passed on what she had recently learned and was heartened to be told that more charges would be brought against Herta. As for the Treskk outfit now set up in the Web that had once obtained and supplied dubious goods to criminal and possibly hostile clients from their hidey-hole on Mellifly, they were under surveillance by security, not the ISP. Apnis dared to mention Commander Molli Warweft and was told tartly that it was not her concern.

Azular had been silent during the latter part of the discussion and the captain could tell by his face that he was brooding on some topic. "Minch Fettin," he said at last. "Hoxiz' and Herta's joint interest in the creation and implantation of complex, rare and very costly micro-medical devices, as well as their theft by brutal means, the attempt on Ms Kerrix in medbay being an example, the prototypes developed by a company linked to Hoxiz and the non-active device extracted from Micklemouse. Merkat can't be the only base for these activities and with recent troubles at the suspect medical facility on Mellifly, there must be another that's testing the devices in situ. Micklemouse listed Minch Fettin as one of his stops for the delivery of highly encrypted data; indeed we know he had similar to deliver here via Lokterix for a commercial interest. Minch Fettin has been posited as an origin for Hoxiz *and* it's the place that Flatt gave as the destination for the transfer from here of a small cargo pod with secret contents. You recall Flatt was taken by Thal during his dialogue with Mr Buntle?"

"I do," Ahxenta replied. "Your point?"

"I wonder if Minch Fettin might be the base for a medical facility, akin to Mellifly, for altering humanoids to serve hostile purposes. It's out of the way but close to ex-hostile territory. They may have had a facility there, at the other side of the mapped galaxy to Mellifly."

Vettarista nodded slowly. "That's a good point," she agreed. "We know that there were and still seem to be a number of agents of chaos out there – a centre other than Mellifly would make sense."

The meeting was concluded shortly afterwards and Vettarista left as circumspectly as she had arrived. The officers dissected what had been discussed, but Ahxenta wanted a rapid end to all business in the Web, as the ship's next mission was her priority.

"We'll meet up with Axellina for a late lunch and find out what she's got from her talks in medbay," the captain decided. "Then we'll head back up to the ship."

The senior science officer excused himself from lunch as he had other matters on hand. As he explained his reasoning, he was treated to a sardonic gaze from his commanding officer.

"In that case, Tallica and I will head to the *Half Moon*," she said. "I *will* see you later," she added pointedly.

Dr Flintlock was timely and was standing at the bar when Ahxenta and Apnis, minus their guards, arrived. The three were quick to find a private table. The doctor had news that she had got from friends on the arrest of the senior surgical officer. Security was swarming over her office and quizzing her contacts. Not before time, according to some, as Herta was known to push her own interests ruthlessly and had a name for accepting favours to endorse products or services.

"A bribe-taker," Ahxenta commented acidly.

"Exactly, so more charges are likely to be brought. She was also an innovator and liked to introduce new methods on her watch, as long as it was a project she'd had a hand in," Flintlock disclosed. "She was particularly involved in high-end tech, one of my contacts told me. But where's Azular, Cap? He'd be interested in this."

"Azular's busy," was the scathing reply. "He's staying over again tonight. He *says* he's got more to discuss with Kerrix, given what they didn't cover yesterday because of the shenanigans with Hoxiz. I note *she's* not here, so I figure what *he* wants is another in-depth look-see around that damn shuttle," Ahxenta guessed resignedly.

"No he doesn't," the doctor explained in a sibilant whisper. "What *he* wants is another in-depth look-see around Kerrix."

"What!?"

Flintlock winked conspiratorially. "He was berthed next to me in the dorm quarter of green four. He wasn't there when I made it in very late last night and I *did* buzz – and scanned, truth be told. I met him on his way back this morning as I was on the way out to an early breakfast meet with the first of my buddies to see how things were in medbay after Herta's arrest. He was still in mufti and you should have seen the smile on his face."

"Our Azular?" laughed Apnis. "Last time he got involved was a very long time ago and that all ended in tears. Let's face it, Cap, it's the uniform of the *Arianrhod* that's the attraction; and being what *he* is, Azular can work out when people are more interested in what they can get than in him. But I thought he and Kerrix didn't hit it off."

"You're wrong," Flintlock chuckled. "I saw *her* giving him the eye on the sly when she was in my medbay – my med scanners don't lie. And I caught *him* peeking in at her now and again when he thought she wasn't looking. I felt like banging their heads together and telling them to get on with it."

"You didn't tell *me* that," the captain remarked.

"None of your business, Cap."

"He'd better be back on board by sixteen hundred tomorrow is all, or I'll have his hide," Ahxenta announced darkly.

Azular was not only back aboard before the allotted time, he had brought back one of the energy cells that he had given Kerrix and the spec of the response plate technology that was integral to various units aboard her shuttle and that enabled specific instructions to be acted upon. This could include cloaking where the facility was part of the relevant unit. He hoped to replicate the mechanics of the system, partly at least, to the benefit of *Arianrhod*, he told the captain when she stopped by his main lab just before they were due to leave.

"What was the trade, apart from your company and a good feed?" she demanded suspiciously as she looked at the graphics on his main console. "I can't imagine you got *that* for nothing."

He looked abashed. "I helped her fit her own energy cell back into her drive system and arranged to have that damaged landing extensor realigned. It's almost spot-on," he added artlessly, looking up at her.

"How?" Ahxenta continued dangerously, folding her arms. "It needed specialist repair."

"I made a fine adjustment to the shuttle's exterior to enable her to move more freely in the Web and we relocated her to a secure berth by the inner six repair sheds. I then asked Commander Apnis' friend Kit Biernop to help. He and a couple of reliable mates carried out the work very quickly on the QT. And then we moved her again."

The captain knew her senior science officer very well and knew when he was using his calm civility as a mask. "What fine adjustment did you carry out that would help *that* shuttle, with all its camouflage and cloaking capability, move freely around the Web?"

"I integrated *Arianrhod's* call-sign into one of the hull patches that are holding her plating together," he admitted.

"You did *what?* You are way out of line, mister!"

Azular's explanation that he judged it necessary for Kerrix' safety given what had happened and that *Arianrhod's* own shuttle, the source of the signal, had not been compromised did not satisfy the captain.

"That Norvallan boat now reads as one of ours! And when we're not here, she'll still read as one of ours!"

"She won't, ma'am," he differed. "Ms Kerrix did not exactly agree with the modification, anticipating your reaction I think, and insisted it be reversible; and it *has* been deactivated. But she *did* see that it would be useful to move the shuttle for repair."

"And who'll be getting the bill for this repair?"

"Mr Biernop did not charge for it – and as far as he's aware, the shuttle is an old and little-used one of ours. I piloted her and he and his crew did not see Ms Kerrix."

"You've still got one hell of a lot of explaining to do, Doctor, and it had better make sense or you'll be spending this trip in the brig!"

"That's what Xanna – Ms Kerrix – said," Azular remembered with a grin, but his amusement faded as other memories intruded. "That scarring on her back – I saw it as I helped remove her jacket after the *Milky Pearl* incident had left her with that broken hand – it's still bad and causing her pain. If we had had less contact with her…"

"That's your hormones talking, not your head," Ahxenta told him astringently. "She's been followed since she got here, so it's obvious to a few that she's got tech that's worth stealing and they're pulling out all the stops to get it. What else?"

"I *did* get other data, with which I'll augment our databanks. I now have specs of the main classes of Norvallan ship, and of other vessels and technology that have proved hostile to her people. It's far from complete, but it may just give us an advantage at some point."

"So if we come across an alien ship, we'll be able to tell if it's one of hers? Exploiting us to find her people again?"

"*I* requested the data, ma'am. There was the report by the *Nyx Warrior* of a vessel of unknown spec beyond Wester 287, which puts it close to that raider base that seems to be called Starfall. There may be the remote possibility that it was Norvallan – or an unknown but hostile ship. *We* are unlikely to come across a Norvallan ship, but we may hear reports of other encounters where a spec has been got. I also have some of the navigational data from the area of space at the other side of the anomaly through which her ship came," he added. "Though I doubt I'll be able to make much of it."

"And you'll have enough to do here without spending your time on that," he was told curtly. "There's the decoy device for a start. I want you and Crizz on it as soon as we're away from Brown Amber. For now, you're on the bridge, as Greffy's had a long spell."

After a short homily on the liberties he should not be taking with her technology, the captain left him to finish up a few tasks and made her way to the bridge, as *Arianrhod* was in the final throes of making ready to leave the Web.

"Azular on his way up?" the first mate greeted her as Ahxenta sat down heavily in the command chair and began to call up ship's status on her boards.

"He is," she growled.

"What gives, Cap?"

"If I didn't need him on the bridge he'd be in the brig," was the harsh and clearly audible response.

A few startled glances swept the other bridge stations as the duty officers glanced at one another. The two at the navi-helm console were no exception.

"Not a word," Dox ordered her sidekick in a stage whisper.

Commander Apnis was equally as curious but knew better than to question her captain when every ear in the place was attuned. As the senior science officer entered the bridge and made his way to his own station he was treated to several inquisitive stares, not least from his junior, Greffy, whom he relieved of duty with only a nod. But as he sat down with a smile and set his instruments, a raised eyebrow dared any of his colleagues who caught his eye to comment.

17: THE FIREWAVE

The great starship raced through the dark, her outer aft cargo bays sealed by locked, fine-meshed safety shielding. The pods of classified freight for Silverglass were fixed to the deck under constant scan by tactical and science stations. *Arianrhod's* endpoint was Brown Amber, an insalubrious mining station orbiting an asteroid on the edge of Beta zone. Amber was just within the outer edge of The Belts, a vast asteroidal accretion revolving at huge distances around parent stars in a region known as the Outer Zone, a remote sector beyond patrolled areas of the mapped galaxy.

Lindell had arranged a rapid pick-up, time being crucial. The team was expected and as the copper glow of the station grew in the grid, Dox expertly brought the ship into dock. The first mate had insisted on locating pins and Ahxenta had two security guards as escort for her, Azular and Lindell. Tactical and weapons were at the ready, with comms primed to keep tabs on the crew whilst they were on station.

Apnis had set comms to monitor trade and off-ship channels, as several unknown vessels were in orbit. These included two freighters, one unregistered and another bearing Friskianx insignia. Greffy was directed to keep a close watch on the latter, which had begun to alter her position when the *Arianrhod's* shuttle had departed the ship. The science officer soon found out why: by the time business was done and the team was on its way back aboard, the ship had pulled into a berth one over from *Arianrhod* and Greffy had worked out that the hull signature of part of her plating read positive for zukivianite. The suspect section of plate also sported a fleet of discrete units that read uncannily like the limpet drones that had attached and pierced the hull of the *Obsidian Sky*, that ship's data having been linked into *Arianrhod's* scanning arrays.

Apnis alerted the captain and then tried to contact the Friskianx. Receiving no response, she ordered Earbleat to fix targeting eyes, ready weapons and prepare fine-beamed phase-fire if the presently-quiescent drones so much as stirred. That elicited an irate demand from the Friskianx captain to know why *Arianrhod* was targeting him.

The first mate was frank as the unknown face appeared hazily on the holo, making no bones about the fact that she knew of the hostile tech attached to his hull and its capabilities. She also knew how to disable it, she told him, and asked if he required that service as a note on her board reported the safe return of their shuttle. He was furious, told her it was none of her concern and demanded that she cease targeting. She refused equally as icily, warning that she would open fire should any of the drones even blink in her direction.

Greffy had meantime been busy. The ship bore a Friskianx device and her call-sign implied that she was Friskianx and named *Firewave* but she was not of any standard spec in his databanks. Her hull was shielded and he could not get clear scans but he had found enough to convince him that it was either a new design or an old one: *Arianrhod* had met similar during the recent war that had threatened to overtake the known galaxy. He studied the captain in the visual link and asked Bellfish to send his comms signals to the science station to enhance his own readings of the freighter's bridge.

It was as the *Firewave* was powering up weapons in response to the threat from the PSS that Ahxenta made it onto the bridge, her senior science officer at her heels. Azular made for his own post, calling for an urgent update. Quickly in possession of the data, he expanded the holo to bring in more of the background of the Friskianx bridge. As far as they could see, the few visible crewmen were all uniformed similarly. It was sharp-eyed Greffy who spotted something odd.

"They're all wearing the same ranking insignia," he said, puzzled, as Ahxenta gave the order for shields up and all weapons on line.

"Good call," Azular replied. "I'll link my Norvallan scanner to our external arrays… I *can* get through her hull! Gliss, get this up on the holo. Greffy, see what else you can get from your holo of their bridge crew. There's something way off beam."

"What have you got?" the captain demanded as the link to the Friskianx ship was cut from the other side.

"She's not typical Friskianx, Captain. She's more like a hostile and her shielding impedes close scanning. Those drones are not fused to her hull, they can be loosed – on command, I'd guess. The crew are not purely Friskianx *and* I'm getting substantial cyber augmentation."

"Hell! Are you sure?"

"Positive."

"Battlestations! Bellfish, warn Amber that they may have a hostile on their doorstep. Full tactical readout on that ship!"

"Drones are being loosed!" Gliss spat as the red alert rang out.

"Earbleat, have your teams take them down! Tallica, take auxiliary weapons and target whatever else looks at us. Helm, loose us, come about and get me manoeuvring room – this is a helluva tight space."

The main holo expanded and calls that shields were at maximum and phase cannons were powering up rang out. The crew hung on as the ship forcibly loosed her restraining struts to gain free space.

"She's got phase cannon, slicers and torpedoes!" Gliss called as a blast shook the ship and Cottontail cursed that her plating had taken a direct hit.

Brown Amber, anchored to an asteroid, was a confined area of close-packed docks where fast manoeuvring was risky. Local comms sang out with voices asking what in hell was going on, an adjacent vessel attempted to leave and Ahxenta's commands rang around the bridge as Dox sent *Arianrhod* into a tight arc to avoid incoming fire.

Earbleat was in full flow, crowing over every hit and tallying her teams' targets. "Got 'em all, Cap! That's the last as far as I can see!"

"Just make damn sure!" was the sharp retort as *Arianrhod* shook to another blast. "Some of their hits are getting through."

"Other unknown's undocking!" Larai cut in. "She's coming about! Trying to get readings, but she's shielded… weapons are powering!"

"Tallica, mark her!" the captain ordered.

"On it!" Apnis yelled.

"Amber is powering her main defence emplacements and readying defence craft!" another voice broke through the noise as a searing flash dazzled the eyes of those looking at the holo.

"Hostile is turning about!" roared Gliss. "She's making a run for it! The second ship's sent a bolt across her bows!"

As the hostile shrunk to a blip, *Arianrhod's* status reports updated. She had taken several hits but was intact. Medbay reported minimal casualties and all main ship's sections were stable but shields needed repair and weapons replaced. The captain called for a reduced alert, ordered tracking on the hostile and data on the intervening ship as Bellfish notified her that Security Chief Silkie wanted answers about the damage to Amber's structures and the firefight.

"He wants answers!" Ahxenta fumed. "His station allows a fizzing hostile to dock and *he* wants answers! Get him on the comm!"

The man was unprepared for the scorching volley of criticism that the *Arianrhod's* captain launched at him. His argument that her ship had targeted another vessel without provocation sunk without trace as Ahxenta pointed out that the ship was clearly not Friskianx despite its badge, that it carried hostile and highly dangerous technology and it had energised weapons and loosed attack drones at her ship. Silkie's threat to file a complaint about her behaviour with Brown Amber management committee met with incredulity.

"*They* took the first shot," the captain reminded him grimly. "And you're damn lucky they didn't turn on you! I take it you *do* remember the take-over of your station by hostiles not a hairsbreadth off the spec of that frigging boat that *your* people allowed to dock here. I want to know what she was doing here and if you won't tell me then your management committee's going to have its ears torn off!"

Shaken, Silkie broke the link with the promise to get back to her.

"We don't actually have time for this, Cinnabar," Apnis reminded her quietly as she settled back into her usual seat. "We have our cargo for Silverglass that won't wait. And now we need repairs."

"Tell me about it. And what about that unregistered carrier that jumped in? Where's she got to?"

"She's hanging fire just off station. She may want a word. What have you got on her, Azular?"

The science officer looked mildly amused as he reported. The ship was a good deal smaller than *Arianrhod*, she appeared to be of recent construction, she bore external cargo pods and she was well-shielded both externally and internally. She had surface jammers that thwarted scanning and a complex hull structure with no trace of zukivianite.

"And?" Ahxenta demanded, scenting something.

"In style and structurally, she resembles Commander Thal's ship – I would hazard a guess that she's off the same production line."

"Are you sure?"

"By no means, but the readings I *can* get are pointing to that."

"Unregistered freighter is hailing us, Captain," Bellfish alerted her.

"We might be about to find out," the first mate said in a low voice as Ahxenta gave the order to put the link through.

"Belay, Captain!"

"You what?" Ahxenta was startled at Azular's loud hail from his station. "Hold!" she ordered. "This had better be good, mister!"

"Apologies, Captain. But we have just refined some data that may be an issue. Greffy, get it up on the grid and expand," he instructed.

"What is it?"

"It's enhanced details of the *Firewave's* bridge," explicated Azular. "Greffy caught it from the chat we had with them. Note that they're wearing identical uniforms, including ranking pips, and there are few of them. That struck me, but recognise *that* face, ma'am?"

"Bloody hell!" Ahxenta stared.

"Lokterix!" Apnis breathed. "Looks like Thal missed him then."

"Put through the link from that freighter."

"Aye, ma'am. You're on line," Bellfish advised her.

The face that materialised in the holo-grid viewer was not familiar but the uniform was: Azular had been right. The woman introduced herself as Commander Kismulin Ver of the cargo ship *Kel'Beth*.

"Out of Starfall, I presume. I'm Cinnabar Ahxenta, captain of the *PSS Arianrhod*, as I'm sure you're aware."

"I am. The ship that attacked you – what do you know of it?"

Ahxenta frowned at the cool tone but answered that she'd never met it before but as it was posing as Friskianx and had changed berth to launch an attack on her, she deemed it hostile. She then turned the question, asking why the *Kel'Beth* had fired on it. The reply that it was one of several craft suspected of attacks on her people's bases and ships made sense but Ahxenta felt that Ver was holding back and said so. The woman eyed the captain warily before telling her that though Friskianx in design, the *Firewave* was structurally dissimilar. Her origin was unknown and the *Kel'Beth* had trailed her from Kelpin to Mellifly in the hope that she was make for her base. She had struck out for Amber, perhaps spotting the tail. Ver's plan had been finally sunk by the *Firewave's* attack on *Arianrhod*, for which there seemed no reason.

Ahxenta shook her head. Something was still not adding up. "If you were tailing her, why draw attention by firing on her? You could have followed her out of here if you wanted her so badly. We had her on the run and Amber was readying defences, so she'd hardly stand and fight. Why she thought she could take us on is something else."

"Some of her crew perhaps harbour resentment towards you?"

"You know damn well Lokterix is aboard that ship, don't you?"

Ver's eyes blazed. "How did you know that?"

"He was on the bridge when they linked. Stupid move, but as the ship's poorly crewed maybe he has to be. *Your* people want him, so why let him run? Your ship is probably capable of taking theirs out."

"We want to find their base."

"So you can do to it what they did to yours?"

That bit and Ahxenta continued relentlessly, "Your hit was meant to cripple, not destroy. She'll have to go somewhere for repairs."

"Yes, she will." Ver's jaw tensed as her steely gaze held Ahxenta's. "If I send you an encoded comms link, will you let me know if you hear more about her or any ship like her? She *is* also your enemy."

Ahxenta was grim. "I'll take your link, but I make no promises."

There was a pause before Ver replied. "Understood. Transmitting now," she continued, gesturing over to some station beyond.

"Data received," Bellfish confirmed.

"Have a pleasant and uneventful onward trip, Captain."

"And you. Ahxenta out."

The captain had no need to order scanning and tracking of the *Kel'Beth* as she made her way out of Amber space for her spec was clear in the view-grid as *Arianrhod's* tactical team got to work.

"She's probably doing the same to us," Apnis stated caustically.

"She is *not* scanning us overtly, Commander," Azular apprised her. "Although a few of our fellow ships *and* Amber are trying to."

"Security Chief Silkie on line for you, Cap," interrupted Bellfish.

"Put him through," Ahxenta grunted. "Seems I'm popular."

The chief had spoken to the management committee chairman, who had been shaken by the exposure of the *Firewave* as a hostile. An immediate inquiry would take place and Ahxenta was invited to give evidence. The captain's wrath at that request was patent. Her succinct reply sent the man off with chastened features and gratitude that she would not be stopping by his office any time soon.

"They may not let us back in here," the first mate commented as the order was given to prepare for departure.

"Their loss," was the tart rejoinder. "This escapade's cost us more than scratched paint and wasted time. Let's get the hell out of here."

The captain had decided to hold off halting for repair and ordered all speed to Silverglass. They had a long haul across a number of zones, and she did not intend to miss her deadline. Her route skirted zone Beta edges to ISP's Linza Base, across Delta and Alpha to Selliden and then directly across Epsilon. An update from Bluejohn advised that Selliden space was clear. The *Obsidian*, repairs complete, was on the way to Marridan with a cargo, after which she was for the Web.

Despite the quietness of the spaceways, the usual chatter giving no indication of major action anywhere, Ahxenta was cautious. She had passed on most of the data from her encounter at Brown Amber to the PSS fleet, with a moderated version sent to the ISP via Admiral Zillah. She then pressed Azular and Cottontail for the latest on their work on *Arianrhod's* decoy, as she had received an advisory from the science officer days before that he had ideas for an external image projector unit based on Norvallan design. Having heard naught since, the captain cornered Cottontail, whom she and Apnis had joined in the mess for lunch.

The chief engineer was irritated. "I don't know why you're asking me, Cap, I'm not his damned keeper. What *is* it with Azular anyway?

You can never find him when you want work done and when you do he's always got a smile on his face. Who's been oiling his engine?"

"I don't think I want to answer that," Apnis chortled, with a sly look at the captain.

Ahxenta only grinned. Cottontail was known to have little time for dalliance: an ill-fated liaison during her compulsory military service many years before had left her with a son, Sim, who was now a senior engineer aboard the *PSS Tektite*, and the conviction that her engines were much better company anyway.

"It's that damn Norvallan tech. I bet he's got a lot more than he's telling. Earbleat's still sore she couldn't get her hands on that scanner or that pint-sized handgun he keeps in his pocket. And when he *is* in his lab, the keep out sign's always on. Greffy's no help, he just says it's essential work. And what are you laughing at, Tallica Apnis?"

"Sorry, Crizz, it's not you, it *is* our overly cheerful Azular. But as he's just come in, maybe we can capture him and get a few answers."

"Hah! You'll be lucky – he always knows damn well when you're trying to outflank him."

The captain called Azular over even so and once he and his plate were at the table she ordered an update. He *had* been working on the decoy and had come up with a prototype add-on that could project a secondary image beyond the decoy's own generated image. He had fine-tuned it to improve its self-defence and to simulate cloaking. The latter would suggest to an enemy that the device was a cloaked ship and hence any scan of her would be largely unproductive.

"In other words, it makes the decoy more believable to enemy tech close up," Apnis surmised.

"Exactly, Commander. It still has to be tested in use but that's not feasible at present as we're moving at speed through hyperspace."

"I thought we were supposed to be working jointly on the decoy," Cottontail griped. "We both of us did develop it after all. And what's this image projection add-on about?"

"The last time I called you about working on it, you said you were busy," Azular said blandly. "And as for the add-on, it could be used to project a detached cargo pod, an escape transport or fighters."

"It seems more trouble than it's worth," asserted Ahxenta. "It needs controlled from the bridge and you'll both have your hands full there if we do meet trouble."

"I could programme it to run a specified sequence whilst we take any action necessary to protect the ship. As it is, our tactical stations can track it. One of our main problems in its use has always been the need to drop our cloak to let it go. If we could solve *that*, the decoy would be more than just a useful piece of kit."

"Then we could sell it on the open market and retire," the chief engineer told him sarcastically. "Would that suit you, whatever it is you've been doing off-ship lately?"

"That's not your concern, Chief," he grinned at her.

"Cut it, both of you," the captain ordered. "Keep working on the decoy when you have time, but our mission comes first and you'll both be needed on the bridge. We've a few days and course changes before we get to Silverglass and a lot can happen in that time."

"Yes ma'am," the two officers responded, but Azular still had a quiet smile on his face as Cottontail made her farewells.

"I note you've been upgrading our databanks as well," the captain said to him. "So we can now spot a Norvallan ship a sector away?"

"Hardly, ma'am. But if we do come across one, or hear news of an unknown that might be one, we have the means to identify it."

"And make profit of the upgrades to Norvallan tech that any such ship might carry if it corresponds to that precious scanner of yours that you link into the main bridge science station when it suits you?"

"I have reservations that such would be the case, Captain. And I only link the scanner in while I'm there as I'm the only one who can operate it – Ms Kerrix made sure of that when she gave it to me."

"Ms Kerrix seems to have made sure of a lot of things," Apnis commented dryly.

"Excuse me?"

The first mate laughed at his expression. "No offence Azular, but you seem to spend a lot of time these days with your mind elsewhere than on your business and it's noticeable."

"Thinking is a requisite part of the scientific process, as I'm sure you're aware, Commander. And as my results testify."

"I'm off to do the rounds," the captain said as she stood, scenting an argument. "I'll see you both on the bridge later."

"And I'll let you get back to your daydreaming," Apnis remarked, slotting her crockery into the recyc hatch. "I've also got work to do."

He watched the two leave the mess, the piqued look on his face turning into a smile that faded as memories arose. Perhaps he *had* let thoughts of Xanna Kerrix intrude more than they should. Yet still he could not shake the vision of the crude scarring on her back spelling out *Arianrhod*, a flinch of pain as he helped her remove the screening jacket, her bitter "ugly, isn't it?" when she realised his intense scrutiny of the disfigurement and the other scars that were fading. Despite her hard-bitten veneer, the cuts went more than skin deep. And the guilt was still there that but for him, she may have been spared that. He shook his head, knowing that the captain was right: no matter which way the wind blew she was a target. And the aftermath of that fateful face-off with Hoxiz in the *Milky Pearl* had been extremely pleasant.

Azular had tried to assure Kerrix that her mutilations did not repel him as he had helped her into comfortable kit for the short trip to the emergency station. Her scepticism was obvious, he remembered, but she had accepted his assistance. The station medics, not pushing for answers, had repaired her hurts, dispensed pain relief and sent them off. It was perhaps the analgesia, or her awareness of his real concern as he made her sit, prepared hot drinks and talked to her that undid her adopted cynicism and let him sense the strong attraction for him that she was trying to hide. And that had undone him: moved by the irresistible impulse to express his own feelings, he had drawn her close and kissed her long. She made no protest.

A frisson of pleasure ran through him as Azular re-experienced his sensations. Awareness of his position and hers had clicked into place shortly afterwards and with no wish of exploiting her weakness again, he had made a reluctant move to leave for his own lodgings. And she had asked him to stay the night. His indecision was fleeting. He did.

Azular had awoken to the sounds of action as she readied herself for her very early shift in the *Half Moon in a Puddle*. Realising that she was being watched, she came over and tweaked his nose as she told him to help himself to coffee and reminded him to lock up before he left. His request for a kiss was met with an embrace that left him in no doubt of her regard, despite the fact that she bit his nose as an encore and chided him for making her late for work.

"May I join you?" the rather sarcastic voice of Axellina Flintlock cut through his reverie. "Or are you busy?"

"Not at all," he sighed. "Please sit."

"Cap's been bending your ear, then?" she began. "About what?"

"Work," he said shortly.

"And?" Flintlock probed quietly. "I haven't had a chance to talk to you about what happened after the Hoxiz affair: you weren't there next day when I met up with the Cap and Tallica in the *Half Moon* for lunch. You were busy – you and Ms Kerrix."

"If you have something to say, Doctor, I suggest you cut to the point," he told her wearily.

"A few have noticed that you've been a happy bunny since we left the Web, and given the company you were keeping there, one or two have made a guess as to why. But *what* you got up to is a tad more unclear: the captain *did* threaten to throw you in the brig just before we left for Amber and the crew's keen to find out the reason."

"The crew can mind its own business," Azular snapped. "I don't see why my personal life should be anyone's concern but mine."

"Don't get het up – it's natural curiosity."

"Nosiness, you mean."

"Maybe. Did she stay at yours or did you stay at hers the last night you were in the Web?"

He stared sharply at her. "Is there a point to this chat, Doctor, or are you merely gratifying your own salacious curiosity?"

"Touchy," Flintlock noted. "But seriously, Azular," she continued softly, "She took a lot of rough usage at the hands of those thugs and it's had emotional, mental *and* physical effects. And you've both had troubles since. She's vulnerable, even if she doesn't show it."

"I know that and I have *not* taken advantage, if that *is* what you're inferring. And this isn't the place to discuss these matters, Doctor."

"I call you into my inner sanctum for a cosy chat and the crew *will* wonder what's going on," she told him. "But you're my colleague and I hope my friend, and I have to think of your wellbeing too – I'm the one ultimately responsible for the health of all the crew after all. You realise she won't stay at Merkat forever? She wants to get back to what she was and you're helping her do that, with all these exchanges of tech and such. And once she's gone, where does that leave you?"

"That has crossed both our minds, believe me, Axellina; but we face it when we come to it."

"You're *that* serious about each other? I'm here if you need to talk about it," Flintlock added hurriedly, seeing the look on his face.

"Thank you for your concern, Doctor. I have to go."

"You haven't finished your lunch so sit still. Whisper Earbleat still bending your ear about the latest stuff you brought back?"

"As ever," he sighed, shaking his head. "What *is* at the bottom of all this interest in me and what I do?"

"This is the *Arianrhod*, Azular: the crew are sharp, smart and nosey as hell. And if they can't find answers, they'll make some up."

The lengthy ride to Silverglass was standard and allowed time for the crew to carry out regular tasks. The captain was likewise engaged and in a routine briefing with her chief medic on the crew's state of health she brought up the subject of her senior science officer.

"He's as capable as the rest of us of making a fool of himself even if he is a bit long in the tooth, Cinnabar."

"Speak for yourself," Ahxenta retorted. "He's not much older than I am and I've been around a few blocks in my time."

"No comment, Cap. But you've no need to worry about Azular. He knows his first duty is to this ship and her crew and I suspect *she* knows it too and would expect no different."

"You know her better than I do and I can't say that I found her the easiest to get along with."

"Too like you, you mean; she may not have a lethal left hook but she's got a few moves and a mouth that gives as good as it gets."

"You're sailing close to the wind, Doctor. But as Azular and Crizz have come up with the fixes for the decoy, as far as we know without testing it in action, then he's pulling his weight. What he's doing with the other stuff he has in hand he's keeping to himself."

"Huh! He's been in here asking for access to more of *her* medical data, since last time I only gave him enough to check out the linkages to that implant that Micklemouse had. He says it's to do with biosign recognition for a database he's setting up and he's only got Norvallan and other typical species readings from her shuttle's info banks."

"So what does he need her medical data for?"

"She's not pure Norvallan, apparently – her mother was from an allied world with subtly diverse genetics. So she's a hybrid and he says her data will enhance the recognition codes. I told him to get lost and that he'd be better trying to add in more of the readings he got from those ships that are pretending to be our buddies but are full of ex-raiders and all sorts of other vermin."

"And?" the captain demanded.

"Says he's done that already *and* he's figured how to cut the energy burden and improve the cloak of Earbleat's pet guided missile. I bet he's only helping with *Loki* to stop her nagging over the stuff he's got his paws on. And once *she* figures what he and Crizz have done for the decoy, she'll be blazing mad he didn't pass that on. But how long are we stopping at Silverglass and where are we headed for repair?"

"We'll be long enough at Silverglass to drop our cargo and take on arms supplies. Lindell is liaising with local command to provide what we need but they won't do it at bargain prices. Hull repairs will have to wait until we get to Delta Iridium's repair centre, but we can get good rates there and it's on our flightpath to Freskat. Provided that's not trouble," Ahxenta added as her wrist communit buzzed and the first mate's voice requested her presence on the bridge.

"No red alert," Flintlock called after her as she sped off.

"Not yet," the captain shot back as she raced for the elevator, aware from the first mate's voice that something was going on.

Even as Ahxenta entered the bridge, Apnis had upped alert status to red, called battlestations and was demanding details from the voice that was crackling out of the comm. The captain recognised the less than dulcet tones. It was Captain Murmur Fleetskup.

"So what's the *Tallulah* got into now?" she inquired with asperity as she tied herself into her command chair.

"Two high-speed ships burst out on top of her off the beacon at Idledott. One's sliced off an external cargo pod. Getting data now…"

As Ahxenta scanned the holo-grid that had expanded into the well of the bridge, Gliss confirmed that the readout matched the data the *Obsidian* had sent them of the two that had attacked her off Barfit.

The captain swore loudly. "Dammit, I thought so! *Tallulah*, back off! Let your pod go – that ship's got more than just big guns!"

"We can take her! She's started to retreat!" Fleetskup barked as he continued to spit out orders to his gunnery crews.

As the grid spun and enlarged, Ahxenta swore again. "Shields up! Weapons online! Dox, evasive! Protect our damaged hull plates: that other blip's got our mark! Earbleat, ready torpedoes to target what's coming out of her! "

"Got her in my sights, Cap! She's up for a fight!"

"Here she comes!" Apnis roared as Earbleat set her crews to their targets and Gliss yelled that another ship had come off the bypass.

"*Tallulah*, get that breaching pod! Take her down with all you've got *now*! We've got our hands full here!"

Fleetskup ignored her, ordering his ship into a tight arc to target his quarry. Even as he did so, the huge ship that had come storming off the bypass was on them. It swept up and over *Arianrhod*, banking and swerving to loose a stream of fire at the hostile that was pressing its advantage against *Arianrhod's* damaged hull plating.

"Damn! Aft shielding hit! We've lost a chunk!" came the voice of Crizz Cottontail at engineering. "Risk of hull breach!"

"Helm, compensate! Get us out of the way of her phase cannon! *Warrior's* got her on the run. Earbleat, get that damn breaching pod or Fleetskup will have a ship full of holes!"

The *Tallulah* had already drawn back to lock weapons onto the breaching pod, but immediately she did so it burst apart to release a deadly phalanx of tiny projectiles. The swarm turned as one to home in on the PSS. Instantly aware, Earbleat called for precision targeting of each missile. One tiny explosion after another lit the dark, but the depleted and slowing cloud continued inexorably on course.

"I read at least ten that have made it through and are settling on *Tallulah's* hull!" Azular warned. "I'm getting zukivianite traces! Data on grid: they're beginning to spread out!"

"Come around and position us to take them out!" Ahxenta roared. "Fine-beam targeting and make sure you kill each one! Where the hell's their mothership?"

"Run off with *Tallulah's* cargo pod," responded Apnis. "*Warrior's* sent the other one packing – it's racing for the bypass."

"I have Captain Holdspan for you, Captain!" Bellfish sang out as Earbleat confirmed that ten attaching drones had been destroyed and Azular announced that no more had been detected.

"Put him on grid… Thanks for the assist, Captain," Ahxenta told him. "We're in a little less than fighting trim."

"I'd noticed," he said tranquilly. "Your trouble at Brown Amber?"

"I see you read my report. I'd no time to stop for refit as I was on a tight schedule. What are you doing in this neck of the galaxy?"

"We were heading for Vrackin from Cygilla Prime and picked up the *Tallulah's* distress. Those ships looked like the ones that shot the *Obsidian* to hell off Barfit," he mused.

"Out of the same mould, if not the same ones," Ahxenta agreed. "You got the data on that as well."

Holdspan nodded. "I did; and I met Captain Bluejohn at Selliden on a stop-off there, so he gave me more of the story."

"Got Captain Fleetskup on the comm, Captain," Bellfish called.

Apnis looked skyward. "Here come the complaints."

"Put him on hold," instructed Ahxenta. "I'm for Silverglass with a cargo," she told Captain Holdspan. "I should be able to make it."

"I'll escort you and the *Tallulah*. It's on my way in any case."

The link to the *Nyx Warrior* was cut civilly. Ahxenta then faced the captain of the *Tallulah*. As Apnis had surmised, he was upset that his ship had been hit by friendly fire, even if it had cleared the drones.

"We could have coped, Captain. We *were* dealing with the hostile who'd cut off our cargo pod and now we've lost *that*," he said sourly.

"I very much doubt you could have coped," she countered. "It took *Arianrhod's* and *Obsidian's* joint firepower to clear the drones that had infested *Obsidian's* hull and still they were breached. I take it you *did* read the full report I sent through on the UV-III, and the data from Captain Bluejohn on the attack at Barfit and its results?"

"I glanced over it," was the evasive reply. "However, your fire has caused damage to my hull and I require reparations."

"You won't get them from me. Your hull was already damaged, and if the *Arianrhod* and the *Warrior* had not answered your distress, you wouldn't be here. I suggest you count your lucky stars and get on with your business. What was in your lost cargo pod anyway?"

"That is classified information."

"Please yourself; I intend to send a note on this action to the fleet, copied to the TA and the ISP. Captain Holdspan will do the same. I expect you *will* contact the *Nyx Warrior* to express your thanks for her help?" she added ironically. "*Arianrhod* out."

As Bellfish cut comms, Apnis grinned at her captain. "So no sign of Tommy Buntle on the bridge and Jesse Inks is still acting first mate. I guess Fleetskup's not found a replacement he likes?"

"Looks like. I can't imagine who'd take the job, unless he puts up a heap or any hopefuls don't know him. But we're for Silverglass and then we'll have to hot ship it to Delta. List what we need once the damage reports are in, and liaise with Nat Holdspan on escort. I'll go draft the report. And keep a beady eye on Fleetskup – I bet *he'll* stop off at Silverglass to see what he can wheedle out of them."

"Aye, aye, Cap."

The ISP authorities at Silverglass were so perturbed by the attack that they called for talks with the captains involved. Ahxenta left her first mate to handle cargo delivery and refit and made her way over to the ISP office to meet Captains Holdspan and Fleetskup. The data had been speedily passed onto ISP's HQ at Alto Finglas, for as thorough enquiry into the previous attack near Barfit by the *ISPS Repulse* had found no more than debris and the area had been quiet since, the matter had been considered a one-off.

"Premature," Ahxenta stated before giving such a crisp account of her actions before and during the hit on the *Tallulah*, as well as in-depth details of the assault on the *Obsidian*, that Fleetskup was forced to admit that her strike on his ship's hull was perhaps justified. She also learnt that the *Tallulah's* missing cargo pod had contained top secret cargo for Silverglass and the ISP was rather put out at its loss.

"Someone knew about your cargo," was Captain Holdspan's quick response to the captain of the *Tallulah* and the two ISP reps.

"That's ridiculous, Nat," Fleetskup argued. "Everything was set in place under tight security and my pod was highly protected. And as the pod was blasted off, it was more likely that those raiders were just intent on grabbing what they could, whatever it was."

"Hardly," Ahxenta pointed out. "The aim was to disable you using limpet drones. And they're complex tech, as my science team's data, which was in my report, shows. It seems there's a return to hostilities with enemies in smaller and maybe less deadly ships than before, but with improved, more insidious tech, which they leave behind when they run. And as far as we know the tech is self-directed. It could be that if it's missed, it latches on to what it finds, takes it out and then alerts its owners to its whereabouts. And that means that *they* must have highly-equipped bases of operation, probably several."

"Pure speculation!" scoffed Fleetskup.

"But the prospect's worrying," the senior rep said. "Several drones *did* attach to your ship, Captain, and as Captain Ahxenta has said, the units are based on hostile tech, they're independent, and they disrupt external ship's systems and penetrate hull structure. And this is the third attack in which we know they were used."

"I want to know who and what the crews of these ships are," said Ahxenta sharply. "They *can't* be the hive-brained aliens that took out everything and everyone during the war, no matter the cost to them – *they* had detectable zukivianite in their makeup. This lot don't, or it's so well shielded we can't detect it. I'd figured they were our ex-raider packs that had stolen enough hostile tech to set up in trade again, but with elements that bore grudges, especially against us. But how did they do it so fast? They were never as savvy as that."

"If I recall various reports during the war, Captain," Holdspan put in, "The hostiles used humanoids not only as pawns but as a means of altering their own to pass as human and thus infiltrate a number of galactic institutions. That's why they got so far. It may be that they've advanced the process and these new-style crews are the result, in redesigned ships and with new hideouts but still hostile in nature."

"I don't like where this is going, Nat," Ahxenta said, recalling the language analyser that Micklemouse had lately sported, as well as his original alteration into an info-sent at a facility on Mellifly. "But you have a point. We took out that shipbuilding yard at Mellifly and it put lots of backs up. We maybe wrecked a lot of other things going on locally and that's why we're a popular target now. There are still numerous vindictive elements that want to get back at us."

"An intact ship and crew would have to be captured," he posited. "But that's a job for the ISP and its allies, not for the likes of us."

"Too true," Fleetskup interjected. "But I have repairs to organise and business to transact and I'd like to discuss it with you," he said to the senior ISP rep, who looked less than enthralled at the prospect.

"I also have repairs and business to organise," Ahxenta said. "But

I'll be doing it from the bridge of my ship."

The captain made her farewells, asking to be kept informed of any ISP actions in respect of the situation, and turned to go. She found Holdspan at her back, the captain of the *Warrior* having no wish to have his ears further assaulted by Fleetskup. She took the opportunity to repeat her thanks for his aid and for his escort in, suspecting that he had heard none from the captain of the *Tallulah*.

Once back aboard, Ahxenta made her way directly to the bridge. She had noted a lot of activity around *Arianrhod's* hull during her ride up and was hoping that most of her arsenal was back on line. There was news: Lindell had not only acquired the arms they needed but he had found a local market on Freskat for some of the comms arrays that her associate there could produce. As the supply and fit teams of Silverglass were not pushed, refit was going ahead rapidly. Apnis had authorised emergency repairs to the most damaged aft shielding units and *Arianrhod* would be ready to ship out in just over two days.

The delay was less than expected given the damage sustained, but the captain fretted at its necessity. There was plenty to occupy the crew, but she felt that the current state of the spaceways was making trade more difficult as well as more costly.

A link from Melly Goodsocks the day before *Arianrhod* was due to depart told of a clash with an interceptor off Lamella Four in zone Lambda. The raider had hit a carrier from Nyx. *Emerald* had answered her distress, seen off the rogue and towed the ship to Freskat, where Goodsocks reported the conflict to the ISP authorities. The raider had escaped but *Emerald* had captured its complete spec.

"It matches what we have but is more comprehensive," observed Azular at a briefing that Ahxenta had called over the incident and the results of her meeting with the ISP. "Yellowfork is earning his keep."

"So's Helly Pinkhorn," was the wry response. "The Nyx transport company was very grateful, so she persuaded them to put a couple of urgent cargoes her way to express the gratitude. *Emerald's* heading to Nyx for pick-up. And Erinna Bottle's every bit as sharp as you when it comes to cadging bits for weapons systems," she added to Earbleat. "She's fitted their aft phase cannon guidance arrays with stabilisers she bagged from the Freskat Navy's scrapyard."

"Speaking of weapons, Cap," Earbleat chimed in with a glance at Azular. "When do I get a closer look at that teeny handgun that Ms Kerrix gave us? Given what happened aboard the *Obsidian Sky*, we need to work out how it packs the punch it does."

"Gave *me*," the senior science officer corrected. "And I've told you before that you will not be taking it to pieces."

"What about its spec? I bet you've worked it out. And what did you and Crizz do to the decoy? It's now got an image projector, it can defend itself and it has a cloak sim. That's the kind of things I need for *Loki*. We serve aboard the same ship and work for the same ends, or hadn't you noticed? And there's that Norvallan scanner…"

"That's enough," Ahxenta warned. "We're shipping out shortly and you'll both have plenty to do before that and on the road to Delta. If there *are* more of those interceptors that loosed drones at the *Tallulah* out there, I want to know about it before they hit us. And if Holdspan's notion *is* how it is and they *are* crewed by Hoxiz-like scum that are as sinister as him, then every galactic zone's in trouble."

"Only two of these new-style ships have launched drones, as far as we know, as did the *Firewave*. But there must be far fewer individuals aboard them than made up the highly cybernetic crews of the huge ships used in the war," Azular frowned. "And I don't see how these hostiles could have handled a series of centres capable of the physical and genetic manipulations that result in beings like Hoxiz."

"Really? Remember Micklemouse and our talks with him after we lifted him off Kelfennig the first time? He said he'd had contact with others like Hoxiz that were more than info-sents, strongly cybernetic, powerful and that scared the living daylights out of him. And Hoxiz appeared humanoid enough to him at the start."

Azular nodded slowly. "I feel as if I'm missing something."

Ahxenta let him think for a minute or two, knowing that his sharp mind was piecing together the clues that would produce hypotheses.

"The drones," he said. "We detected zukivianite in all three cases of their presence but not in other hostile vessels we've met recently. You recall the probe we built to detect traces of zukivianite allied to cyber-organic bodies in ratios that indicated hostile physiology? It allowed the ISP to flush out plants that were alien in origin, although not their subverted agents or allies. *We* used it to identify a few in the Web while we were testing it. But we didn't have the opportunity to use it on Hoxiz. I now wonder if it would have come up positive."

"What do you think?" the captain asked.

"I suspect not, even close range, though he *is* a hostile agent. But zukivianite is used aboard certain of these ships at levels our scanners can detect at distance, so it must be crucial in some hostile tech and possibly also in their physiology. But then there are beings like Hoxiz, to all intents humanoid, whose mindset seems to be at variance with their purported persona."

"Some sort of fusion or hybrid?" Flintlock interrupted.

"Possibly, but I doubt it. As he and his like were about before and during the war *and* altering others for their own ends, it could be that the hostiles had already produced human-like types *not* as reliant on zukivianite as they and many of their moles were. Zukivianite *is* rare, so it would make sense. But we found evidence that they were using humans as sources of organic matter to integrate into their own bodies during hostilities, which suggests that those larger ships were crewed with a different kind of being and the Hoxiz-like types were used elsewhere or were perhaps more in control positions."

"Hive-brained," the captain said. "Zillah first noted that the tactics used by the ships attacking Freskat implied that the crews had a hive mentality: they took huge losses without retreating and didn't seem to care what happened to them. The hostiles lost much of their fleet and must have lost vast numbers of their mostly-cybernetic crews. In the fight for control of every sector, were the crews deemed expendable? Only they didn't win, they were defeated by the Allied fleet. And their known bases as far as we know were taken over by the ones that they had tried to subvert but who'd got out and fought back. Though Thal said a base of his had been attacked and destroyed."

"Thal," repeated Azular. "I recall that meeting with Ms Vettarista in the *Subspace*, when he took custody of Buntle's associate Flatt. She gave us possible reasons as to why Thal and his like are out there and posited that there must be several disparate groups that are the by-products of what the hostiles *did* accomplish – they had been seizing and manipulating victims both physically and genetically for years before they erupted from their enclaves to cause the war that nearly tore the known galaxy apart. We know that one result of the victims' alterations is their ability to identify and be drawn to others of their kind, hence Thal and his people. But there must have been several and varied genetic effects, not all of which were predicted or even recognised by their creators. And one or more such outcomes may have produced beings like Hoxiz: not reliant on zukivianite but as malicious and bent on destruction as the hostiles; not hive-brained; perhaps more intelligent; and with an instinct for self-preservation that would make protecting themselves their priority."

"And savvy enough to hide it from their creators?" queried Apnis.

"I wonder if Hoxiz and his like were earlier types and *they* were the ones who began the capture and alteration of Thal and *his* like. They would be shrewd enough to ensure that their dupes could never do what *they* had done: in essence take over the operation and use their former directors as cannon fodder whilst keeping themselves safe."

"That's a big can of worms, Azular, but there's sense in it," agreed the captain. "And when their tactics didn't work and their huge ships and guns failed to achieve their goals *and* they had lost most of them, they decided to carry on with the smaller, faster and smarter tech that they had or could get and with crews more like themselves."

"And still having that vindictiveness as part of their make-up, they'd remember who had helped ensure their failure and take their revenge," Apnis put in. "That would be us. But where does Lokterix fit in? He'd only been recently genetically altered when you first met him on Xerophyte IV, Cinnabar, judging by the samples Warweft got, and *he* was originally Friskianx. But Hoxiz was on Xerophyte at the same time and I don't recall that we got a scan of *him*, though Merkat security's scans of him as Brack said his biosigns implied that he hailed from the edge of zone Mu…"

The first mate was interrupted by a call that an urgent link for the captain had come in from Captain Jikelleli of the *Green Comet*, to be taken in private and immediately. Ahxenta quickly adjourned next door whilst the others speculated in low voices as to the nature of the message. It must have been short for it was only moments later that the captain returned. She was grim-faced as she took her seat.

"Cap?" Apnis queried.

"There's been another attack by raider interceptors, three of them off the beacon at Kanelian Juxta. No limpet drones but a helluva lot of firepower. And they've hit one of ours. *Green Comet* answered the distress and got there in time to see them off but not before they'd done a lot of damage *and* caused a lot of casualties, some fatal. *Comet* loosed half of her armoury at the bastards."

"Which ship, Cinnabar?" the first mate urged, aware that the news had disturbed the captain.

"The *Firedrake*."

"Oh hell!" the chief medic gasped, to a collective sharp intake of breath.

Flintlock looked at Ahxenta, her brow creasing. The *Firedrake* was a *Vanguard* class ship, as was *Arianrhod*, and as well-equipped as any in the fleet, and she had a crew hardened to action. Her captain was a veteran of both mercantile and military lines and was known for his shrewdness and his tenacity. He would stand and fight but he would not take reckless action that would endanger his ship or his crew. The officers around the table looked at one another in silence.

"When?" asked Apnis softly.

"Less than three hours ago."

"Why did Sarie Jikelleli call you, Cinnabar? Pa?"

"Captain Ma'Lappis has been badly injured but he'll make it, Flick Poppet told Sarie. But his son was one of the fatalities," Ahxenta said harshly. "His station blew when main engineering took a direct hit."

"Oh damn!" the doctor whispered. "Who'll tell Flish?"

"I'll have to, before it goes out on the fleet channel. Flick Poppet asked Sarie to contact me as his comms are shot and he's picking up the pieces and holding his crew together. And Pa Ma'Lappis isn't in a fit state, though he knows about Patt. Poppet will have to contact the families, but his hands are full just now. Is Dr Ma'Lappis on duty?"

"Yes; I'll call her into my office and you can talk there. Tell her to take all the time out she needs. Knowing Flish, she'll want to carry on – just like she and the family did after they lost her mother a couple of years back. But what's happening to the *Firedrake* now?"

"*Comet's* towing her to Marridan; it's a straight run, they've got the best med facilities in the sector and good repair yards. Poppet doesn't want to hang around any longer than he has to and his crew needs support. *Firedrake's* still got the cargo she took on at Kanelian. It was for Merkat, so the *Comet* may take it as she's headed there. But how badly she's been hit I don't know. They have five fatalities including Patt Ma'Lappis and others with very serious injuries. But no word to ours as yet," the captain warned. "I'll put it out ship-wide once I've spoken to Flish. Dismissed. Let's go, Doctor."

"Felipe Poppet okay?" the doctor enquired as she and the captain made their way down to medbay in the transport tube.

"Minimal injuries, so Sarie says. And he's coping for all he's quite young. Mora Ma'Lappis was a hard act to follow. Why?"

"He and Flish have an accord," Flintlock explained delicately.

"I didn't know that."

"And I didn't tell you, but just be aware."

Dr Felicity Ma'Lappis was no fool and had sensed a serious matter when ordered to her chief's office for a talk with the captain. As the commanding officer of a starship that often saw action, Ahxenta had had to break bad news before but it was never easy as reactions were difficult to predict. She found the words and faced the resultant stony grief of her young medic calmly.

As Flintlock had foretold, Dr Ma'Lappis insisted on going straight back to work. The captain thus left her with the CMO and set off to her bridge office to inform the rest of the crew and to send out word to every other ship in the PSS fleet of the attack by Lamella Four and the complete spec of the raider that the *Emerald* had captured.

On Ahxenta's return to the bridge she was greeted with word that emergency repairs were proceeding more quickly than scheduled and that arms resupply was nearly complete. Apnis had set the crew to stress-testing the patchwork on the hull and applying sims to the new weapons. *Arianrhod* would be ready to depart early the next day.

The bridge crew was uncommonly quiet, shaken by the news. Box spoke softly as he remarked to his partner that one catch with a ship like the *Firedrake* was that more than one member of the same family served aboard. The PSS trade was in the blood and ships were often owned by serving officers or their kin. Look at the *Tallulah*: Captain Fleetskup's mother was the main investor, though she lived in luxury on Milkit Major whilst the *Tallulah* was based at Merkat. Then there was the *Tektite*, a family-run concern out of Stella Triplet. Her captain and first mate were siblings known as the Teakettle Twins.

"You go calling the *Tektite* the *Teakettle* within ear-range of any of her crew and they'll pin *your* ears to the nearest hard surface," Dox cautioned her colleague.

"Have you seen her? She's the only *Skylance* class ship in the PSS fleet and she looks like a bucket."

"A bucket with more guns than an ISP warship and a crew that's crankier than a cat with ten ornery kittens," Dox said sharply. "I want you to run a sequence of jump line plots so that I can calculate the pressures on various parts of the hull. I don't want to stress the weak spots if I can help it and it's a big trek to Delta Iridium. So get to it."

"Aye ma'am," was the crestfallen reply.

Commander Apnis shook her head wryly as the captain resumed her seat after a quiet word with Lynxi Bellfish at comms.

"Nothing for Flish as yet, but I expect Poppet will link in as soon as he's able," Ahxenta reported. "Bellfish will keep his ears on local nets as well as the usual. Nat Holdspan sent an advisory that a trader hauling goods to Vrackin from Fyvie Major was buzzed by a shot-up Friskianx freighter that tried to slice off a cargo pod. The trader crew were all ex-marines, so the ship was armed to the teeth and quick off the mark and saw the rogue off. They didn't get much of a spec, but Nat asked for a look and he figures it may have been the *Firewave*."

"If it was, she's come a frigging long way," the first mate said. "You going to call it in to Ver of the *Kel'Beth*?"

Ahxenta sighed. "Yes I am. It's no loss to us and if her people are keen to take her out, I'm not going to stop them. I'll do it now."

The link was long, for thirty minutes had gone before the captain returned. Ver had been surprised but civil and had news that Ahxenta thought best to pass to the PSS fleet and the ISP. Thal's people had reason to believe that their enemies had set up an ops base on Zeta Dixt, the third planet in the system of the same name, close by the Silverglass Nebula and almost in the centre of NTA zone Zeta. As an isolated sector with no settled planets it was untravelled and any base there was unlikely to be spotted by regular shipping. In Ver's opinion, Ahxenta's news of a possible sighting of the *Firewave* supported their suspicions, as Zeta Dixt would be a logical place for her to head.

"She wouldn't tell me why they suspected that the hostiles had set up on Zeta Dixt, but I passed it to Admiral Zillah. She'll see the story gets sent in the relevant directions."

"Maybe Thal squeezed it out of the menacing Mr Flatt, once he'd got him where he couldn't argue," the first mate suggested.

"He may have. At any rate it's another piece in the puzzle of how these hostiles seem to keep popping up. If there *is* a new hostile ops base at Zeta Dixt, you can bet there will be others."

"Oh joy!" Apnis sighed. "Let's hope we don't find one. But I'd best get the rotas redone, given our rescheduled leaving spot."

The *Arianrhod* had made out of Silverglass for Needle Beacon and set as directly as possible for Delta Iridium. Despite the energy cost, she had run cloaked, as with her ship far from tiptop shape, the captain reckoned it wise. By the time they reached their endpoint, all was in place to render the ship sound. News from the *Firedrake* was positive: there had been no further fatalities and of those seriously hurt, most would make a full recovery. The latter included Captain Pa Ma'Lappis and Flintlock was relieved to hear that she would not lose one of her most competent medics, as Flish Ma'Lappis had elected to stay on.

As work on the ship advanced in Delta Iridium's repair docks, the *Gadfly* was pressed into service as a short-run small cargo transport. There was reluctance by local traders to take on contracts for fear of raiders but as the area had been calm, Ahxenta had sanctioned the missions. They brought in much-needed revenue and gave her crew work to do as a change from gear testing and other mundane tasks.

"I'll be glad to feel space under us again," Apnis said feelingly when, repairs complete, *Arianrhod* was ordered to prep for departure.

"You and me both," Ahxenta agreed as she checked her boards. "Zillah wants a meet when we haul in. She's sent a list of topics, so I've set Azular to sifting data. We'll head across once business is in train. The contract Lindell arranged with Greskitty Comms will use about a third of the array-set stuff we're having done and the rest he's trying to trade locally. Coronis here may take some as they know us and the usual quality of the goods. If we can shift it quickly and can get more orders, there's profit in it. The crew may as well catch some shore leave when we make Freskat as we'll be there a few days."

"Sunshine here we come," Box muttered to his mate. "And maybe a bonus, if we get the shiny stuff set quickly and sold to the Freskat Navy. It must need stacks of comms gear for its new ships."

"He lives in hope," the first mate remarked to the captain.

"The Navy doesn't make its own comms linkages," explained Dox wearily. "It buys them in from companies that do and it'll have its own contracted suppliers. You'd never make a supercargo."

"Wouldn't want to; I'd rather fly the ship."

"*I* fly the ship," she pointed out. "*You* work out various ways to get where we're going. You can start by plotting us an efficient course across Lambda to Lamella without running afoul of no-go sectors or border patrols at crossing points, or coming anywhere near Zingle: the gravity wells of that worm-pocket play havoc with my stabilisers."

"You got it," was the adroit reply. "If we head for Hespera Two and avoid Lamella, we can make Freskat three hours sooner *and* get a good view of the Ginseng. It's summer in the central settlement," he added. "What say we hit the *Bowsprit* once we're on leave? There's a handy lodge-house just over the way we could stay in."

"You'll be on your own," Dox told him frostily. "We stayed there last leave here and impressed I was not. And you still owe me for it."

"Well how about the *Warped Space Inn* off Route A1? I'll pay."

"The *Warped Spoon*? Who you kidding? *Warped* about sums up that place, silverware and staff included. It's the *Halcyon* or nothing."

"Will you two attend to your jobs and keep your personal lives out of it?" Apnis directed.

"Aye, Commander," a downcast Box responded. "*Halcyon* costs," he added to the helmswoman in an undertone.

"Exactly. I'm worth it. Plug in the coordinates and stop whining."

"Coordinates, aye."

The first mate caught the captain's eye and grinned.

The Ginseng Nebula was as spectacular as ever as *Arianrhod* made her final approach to Freskat Six. Having met no hitch on the way in and knowing that a market on Nyx had been found for the spare comms-link wafers, the crew anticipated a good time. The captain's shuttle was loaded and set to head out once orbit was achieved. As *Arianrhod* was a frequent visitor to Freskat and her people well-known, little in the way of formalities were required.

"Wonder why the Cap always goes down alone to do business?" Box speculated quietly as Ahxenta made her way off the bridge.

Dox sighed. "Where's the point of a troop going down when the cargo's in a bag and there's no negotiation? And he's a buddy. Would you want somebody earwigging if you were meeting an old friend?"

"I suppose not."

The first mate could have told the two why Ahxenta was chary of introducing her contact or giving any hint of his links. Apnis was the only person who knew that the captain's friend was her nephew. Her only relative, she had legally adopted him as a baby after his parents were killed to prevent him being taken away. As she had been young at the time and in statutory military service, he had been put into care and she had visited when possible. Now he was an adult, she had no wish of his tie to her to be known: the captain of the *Arianrhod* had a reputation that was liable to make anyone close to her a target.

By the time Ahxenta returned, Apnis and Azular were aboard the shuttle that would take all three down to the HQ of the Freskat home fleet. The captain took the helm and shortly after, the three officers were seated in the admiral's office. Zillah, concise as always, wanted a verbal report on recent events. She was also curious as to how the captain had found out about the probable hostile base at Zeta Dixt. It was far enough distant not to pose a direct threat to the Freski but its existence implied the presence of others which could well be closer.

Ahxenta gave little away, but Zillah understood that there seemed to be allies as well as enemies in ships that resembled raider craft. The existence of bogus freighters like the *Firewave* that bore limpet drones was more worrying, as there was no way to know what would happen to a ship that had been totally infiltrated and the power needed to take the drones down was formidable.

Azular handed over his shard of the tactical and technical data on the hostile ships. Zillah's input was more on the debris trails beyond the junction point of zones Zeta, Kappa and Mu. Another ISP ship sent out had found sufficient residue to figure that at least one source ship was hostile but there was little to retrieve, as scavengers had got in first. The military ship *had* spotted a huge novel vessel and made scans, but the shielding on the craft had baffled them. It had not engaged but had headed off on a bearing for Minch Fettin. The data recorded *did* however match the readings that Ahxenta had passed to Zillah earlier of the huge transport that had been berthed in the Web and was believed to be based in the former hostile bolthole by the Enigma. That the ship had not turned to fight was one point in its favour and its heading of Minch Fettin, in the opposite direction to its suspected home base, was in Zillah's opinion probably a blind.

"What?" the admiral demanded as the captain exchanged glances with her science officer, who was looking somewhat serious.

In response, Ahxenta gave her guarded details of her dealings with Flatt and Micklemouse, the link of chief surgical officer Herta to a hostile agent and their shared pursuit of innovative medical tech with obvious illegal uses. Minch Fettin was a common factor that had led Azular to speculate that the world might hold a covert medical centre for adapting people for alien use, or of another hub of hostile ops. If the large ship spotted *was* one of the recently-built craft that Thal and his allies used, then there was maybe another motive for her heading.

"Or it's coincidence," Zillah broke in. "Minch Fettin isn't the only planet in the sector. Canna and Brittle are independents and close by, though there's not much worth looking at on either of them."

With no more to discuss, a halt was called and the meeting ended. Azular intended to head back to the ship. The captain and first mate had other business with local concerns that had expressed interest in trade and were to meet Lindell. As the party split up, Apnis looked after their colleague shrewdly.

"He's refused shore leave. He's saving it up for Merkat, I'll bet."

"In which case, he'd better be headed to his lab and the work he has to do," Ahxenta retorted. "He's sure that response plate stuff he picked up from Kerrix can be used to camouflage certain sections or units on command; he thinks it might be handy to hide our tech from prying eyes if we have visitors or repair crews aboard. *And* he reckons he can use it to part-cloak our hull in sensitive areas – jammers are all very well but against advanced tech they're only partially effective."

"Nice if it works but it'll cost," the first mate forecast. "But it looks like it's one of Thal's ships cruising out there in the far reaches and not a Norvallan and I bet that's not escaped him either."

Apnis inferred correctly that Azular had concluded that none of the recently-sighted unknowns could be Norvallan. But he now had the specs of the main classes of Norvallan ship and he intended to compare that data to everything that he had amassed on all the ships linked to Thal, as well as to recent raider interceptor designs and to the various hostiles they had met. Some time later Greffy found him in his lab, chin on hands and gazing intently at a holo projection.

"What's that, Doc?"

"*That* is a Norvallan heavy cruiser. You'll note these gun ports are set in a ring around this central hub. The data indicate that the phase beams can be brought together to produce a focussed burst of fire. Short but highly effective in a tight spot."

"Ms Earbleat would be interested. I've never seen a weapons set-up like it. Or a ship that looks like a fish with its tailfin in reverse."

"Hardly. But her hull fabric interests me. It's complex and the fine detail shows that the surfaces of the cross linkages are covered in tiny projections, possibly to dampen vibration due to movement."

"Or external impacts like phase bolts. But what else? The signage I can't read, but the molecular structure reads as metal alloy plating."

"Yes, that's what I think. I have the data from Ms Kerrix' shuttle and *its* hull plating is a variant of meta-jurillium that I wasn't able to pin down to any known sources."

"This isn't the same?" questioned Greffy.

"*This* is a standard design spec; *this* lists the molecular signatures of optional plating materials and this one matches a signal in our files of a piece of hostile hull plate we found in the debris around Freskat in the aftermath of that conflict during the war. It was a unique result and I didn't capture any others the same."

"What you're saying is that the Norvallans use some type of meta-jurillium alloy that we've come across before, only it was on the hull of one hostile ship that was taken out at Freskat?"

"That *is* the implication, yes."

"The Norvallan scanner…" began Greffy.

Azular shook his head. "No, not yet. I have limited data on vessels and technology that the Norvallans deem aggressive and I'm about to run comparisons with that. *They* may have met the hostiles before."

The two sat, brows wrinkled, as the data cycled through.

"Well," Greffy noted at last. "There's a match for the huge ships the hostiles used early in the war. But if the Norvallans *have* met them and logged them as dangerous, it suggests that hostile range went well beyond the edges of mapped space off zone Mu."

"We know of at least four hostile bases in uncharted space. The one beyond Mu at the border of Zeta is now Thal's Starfall HQ. The beings on Kelfennig who gave us the data did *not* mention another base on the opposite side of Mu," Azular stated.

"Maybe they didn't know, if it was quite far out?"

"Possibly. But I'm sure I'm missing a piece of the puzzle."

"Why don't we check *all* the data on that shard of hull plating you mentioned? It's in the system after all," Greffy suggested.

"Good call. I'll pull up a detailed scan. Most hostile ships were piece-built of an amalgam of plating materials, as they preyed on any ships they could to exploit their materials."

"And their crews," Greffy recalled with distaste as data extraction began. "Two meta-jurillium signatures," he continued.

"This one's the same as one on the Norvallan list that's deemed suitable for their heavy cruisers," Azular noted. "But *this* one is from a minor ore source on Kirtish, according to our records."

"Kirtish?"

"A small mining planet on the outermost edge of Mu; call up the nav-charts from that area on the auxiliary and let's see exactly where it is. There's something still niggling me."

Azular studied the holo for a little, realigning the image to obtain various views. "Look here: Kirtish is just slightly off an almost direct line from Starfall Exit. If Kirtish *was* on a straight bypass route across this sector of Mu, such a route could cut through Canna and extend into uncharted space to an exit that would match the position of that bypass node through which Ms Kerrix came out, near Starfall. If we extend this hypothetical bypass route in a straight line the *other* way, past Kirtish, it may lead to the defunct bypass node that was her entry — or an exit for any hostile ships to go scavenging beyond the mapped galaxy on the *far* side of Mu."

Greffy sucked in his breath. "That's a *lot* of speculation, Doc."

"I realise that, but it's a start. It would explain how an alien ship could obtain meta-jurillium from a source unknown to us but known to the Norvallans. And if the hostiles have exploited *them*, they'll have tech in advance of ours, which is a concern, especially if they have a way to resupply using a bypass into unmapped space. It also suggests that Norvalla is beyond Mu but not so far beyond to be out of hostile reach. I recall a meeting with Ms Vettarista a while ago when she told us that Xanna's biosigns indicated an origin around Kollaskin Ambit. The logic was that her biosigns had a similarity to some found among data the ISP has amassed over a long period on derelict ships drifting close to and outside recorded zone edges at that side."

"But the data doesn't point to Norvalla. All we've got is that the hostiles look to have gone further beyond the mapped zones this side than was thought *and* look to have hit planets there. There may be an old bypass they used. There *was* speculation that they had their own routes beyond zone Beta and probably Alpha, to get them to their bases there. But if there *is* a bypass here close to that Starfall base… ah! Thal would know about it, surely? He was a hostile."

"I believe he escaped them before he was fully integrated, but he's clever and from what he and his have done thus far, he must know: one of his ships *was* pursuing a hostile there when Ms Kerrix first met him. And he's been plagued by infiltrators that… I wonder…"

"What is it, Doc?"

Azular tapped his fingertips together, thinking deeply. Greffy sat by puzzled, but awaiting the outcome.

"Her shuttle was seized and taken to Starfall base. Someone *there*, an infiltrator maybe, must have realised that the shuttle had come through the Starfall Exit node and figured her origin by her design. *And* she was crewed. If such a spy knew of Norvalla and its level of tech, they may also have worked out why a live victim would be very useful. I'm beginning to think that whoever it was must have known that Xanna would try to escape, and the ship making for the Web at Merkat would be an obvious means."

Much of this information was new to Greffy. As a junior officer he had been kept out of the loop as far as most of Kerrix' history was concerned. "They let her go?"

"No," Azular smiled. "Believe me, she made her own escape. But she wasn't perhaps hindered. It would explain the trouble she's had ever since. Her pursuers no doubt thought she could be tracked more easily in the Web without Thal's people on the watch. And they could count on more of their own kind there. But they did *not* count on her tenacity or that ISP agents were watching *them* and had realised the score; hence Ms Vettarista's awareness of her from the moment she arrived. Xanna said that her captors had read her implanted ID *and* got her spec. A hostile plant could have worked out from *that* that she also had an implanted language analyser and translation device."

"It's feasible and interesting I guess," Greffy said. "But shouldn't we be working on integrating that response plate tech into restricted areas and part-cloaking the hull to hide our auxiliary torpedo tubes?"

Azular looked askance. "Aren't you taking shore leave?"

"No sir. I'm saving it until we make the Web at Merkat."

"Why?"

Greffy squirmed, blushing. "I'm seeing someone there."

Azular's eyes widened. He had had no idea, but recalling his own interest in Merkat, only nodded. "None of my business and you have a point. But I'll report *this* to the captain, and I'd best pass on the data on the circular gun-port layout for focussed phase-bursts to Ms Earbleat or I'll never hear the end of it."

"Only if she finds out," Greffy grinned. "You could keep it under wraps to beat her with later."

Ahxenta and her team had come back with a contract to ship a heavy load to Molly One, a colony of Aoria Six. The cargo would be ready in two days. As the colony was a short ride from Nyx, the captain had chosen to drop the batch of comms links first as it was small and could be shuttled over. The logistics of that and another contract that involved a trip to Stella Marina to pick up three desalination rigs for Zidexall Primary kept Ahxenta and Lindell busy for the next thirty six hours, by which time Azular's ideas had crystallised on the siting of a trial response plate he had created. As one of his other projects was the decoy, he had decided that a response plate would be useful in partially uncloaking the section of *Arianrhod's* hull that held the decoy unit. He was adjusting a signal initiator that he would have to install in the bridge's main science station to send the drop cloak command to the plating over the decoy's bay when an insistent buzz at the lab door disturbed him: most visitors would respect the 'No Entry' sign. He cursed as he ordered it open.

"*What* do you… apologies, Captain, I thought it was Lieutenant Commander Earbleat again."

"You're forgiven," Ahxenta replied shortly, stepping in. "She's in engineering playing with guns. I've read over your speculative report on this hidden bypass and the forays of hostiles into unmapped space beyond Kollaskin Ambit. That's not what you were supposed to be doing and I don't plan to take it to Zillah."

"All knowledge is to the benefit of the *Arianrhod,* ma'am."

"Stop making excuses. What else have you been up to?"

In response, the senior science officer outlined his project and the alterations needed to the plating in the aft section housing the decoy.

"We'll need the plating off ma'am, but our own people can do the work. My model works and as the main snag in deploying the decoy *is* the need to drop our cloak, it would leave only a tiny fraction of *Arianrhod's* flanks exposed. Once complete, the decloaking response could be tested without launching the decoy."

"You have two days Freskat time to source what you need and get the work done. Greffy and Gem Ferry can help as Crizz is busy. And I know that look. What else?"

"Admiral Zillah commands the Freskat home fleet but she has ISP links. She may have access to the data that Ms Vettarista told us of, on the derelicts that have been found drifting at zone edges. And as the ISP *is* exploring space beyond the zone Mu boundary, I assume there must be preliminary star charts, raw maybe, but usable. I would like to compare them to the data that Ms Kerrix gave us of the stellar alignments on *her* side of the bypass, before she was pulled through to come out by Starfall. Or perhaps Thal would have such data?"

Ahxenta looked at him in exasperation. "I should have anticipated that. You tread a mighty fine line, mister. But leave it with me: if the potential exists that hostiles are active beyond Kollaskin Ambit or Kirtish as well as at Zeta Dixt then the ISP should be informed."

"Thank you ma'am."

"And I expect to see that response plate tech operational before we leave orbit," she told him as she left.

Apnis overtook the captain on the way to the bridge. "You look down in the mouth, Cap. What is it? Azular up to no good again?"

"He's obsessed! But at least he's done something on the decoy."

"He's not the only one. Have you seen the small-scale phase-beam cluster gun that Whisper's got in Crizz's side lab? The bloody thing fires. She took out Gem Ferry's pet model warship and he's livid."

"We've got a crew of damn unruly kids!" Ahxenta snapped. "It's time we rounded them up and got them back on duty."

"We've got two more days until we ship out, Cap. Let them wear themselves out on shore leave and *then* kick them up the pants," the first mate advised. "But what else has got you in a frizz?"

The material gave the first mate food for thought and led to the conclusion that Thal had left out much in what he had told them. It was likely that his people were hitting ships that came off what now looked to be an operational bypass that the hostiles used to cross into and out of uncharted space. On balance, Ahxenta believed she could take part of it to Zillah, the payback being the data that Azular was keen to have. She left him behind, however, when she shipped down.

When the order was given to break orbit and make best speed for Nyx, most of the crew bar Whisper Earbleat were keen to be back on duty. The refusal for more time to source parts for her new project had left the second mate grouchy. The run to Nyx was short and the cargo dropped within half a day. The only ship met en route was the *Nyx Warrior*. She had stopped off at her homeworld to pick up a load of heavy engineering for Wild, for the end node of the new zone Mu bypass. They parted company at Molly One, with the *Warrior* heading off for a long trip across five galactic zones.

The large shipment for Molly One took the best part of two days to unload, giving *Arianrhod's* senior science officer time to integrate the star charts that Zillah had been persuaded into handing over into his own databases. From comparisons he had run with data from the Norvallan shuttle, he had found a few stars in common that gave a positive alignment for the location of the implied bypass entry on the far side. Kerrix had told them that the anomaly her craft had been sucked into was in an isolated planetary system with a red-orange star of high lithium content and Azular found a match with one logged by an ISP mission to the general area years before. The star had been tagged K457:003, but the ship had done no more than record its type and position within the starfield and its proximity to a region of high negative mass-energy density that extended on a direct line to Kirtish. Thus, if his calculations were correct, there was an unknown bypass that stretched from Starfall Exit straight across zone Mu and beyond Kirtish to the unexplored region containing star system K457:003.

"My reading is that the hostiles know this bypass and can use it, and the same may be said of Thal's people," Azular explained in a short senior staff briefing. "Ms Kerrix said that the first ship she met in what she saw as alien space was being pursued by what we know was one of Thal's. It was perhaps heading for the bypass to escape. From the data I have, I suspect that this bypass, and possibly others used by the hostiles, belongs to an earlier phase of galactic expansion. The entity we met on Kelfennig led us to believe that the enemies we faced in the war were descendants of colonists they had sent out eons ago. *Those* colonists must have had hyperspace travel systems. Their successors, the hostiles still here, may have reactivated them. *That* would explain why they seemed to come from nowhere in such a short time and why they could remain hidden for the years it must have taken to build their ships and recruit or abduct their lackeys."

The captain mused, tapping her lip as she perused Azular's holo. "Minch Fettin: you suggested there might be a medical facility there like the one at Mellifly. Handy for Thal's Starfall base and not above a hop from what you think may be a hidden bypass. And Mellifly's handy for that other hostile base off the edge of Beta."

Azular's brow wrinkled. "Interesting. We were told that ships were spotted leaving Mellifly in large numbers after *Arianrhod* took out that huge hostile shipbuilding yard over the northern polar area. There's been nary a word or a sighting of them since."

"They probably scattered," the first mate interrupted.

"Or made for another hidden or ancient bypass off that sector of mapped space," the science officer postulated.

"Unlikely. They can't *all* have been hostile," Apnis argued. "Most were probably regular crooks in the pay of bigger villains trading with the hostiles and realised that not only were their livings going up in smoke but they were liable to be spotted and arrested. And since then *Arianrhod's* been a target of violence against our goods, our crew and our associates. So they've started another war – against us."

"Not only us," Azular differed. "But if there are ancient bypasses that few bar hostiles know, it would explain why Thal's people keep being outfoxed by them – he *did* say that he had lost two ships and a new base off sector sixteen on the Gamma-Beta border. If hostiles or their spies can jump in and out, they would be difficult to track."

"Conjecture, and there's zip we can do about it," the captain said. "We have a ship to ready for the trip back across Lambda and up to Gamma. That'll give us a chance to test the decoy bay's decloaking response plate. So Azular, you'd better tie it into the science stations and link the results to the helm, as that controls the cloak."

"It's in hand, ma'am. It'll be in place before we leave orbit."

It was and by the time *Arianrhod* left Molly One, the system was primed. Ahxenta had decided to make for Stella Marina via Freskat and Lamella to keep within populated sectors. The decloaking test was set for an open area where the only inhabited system, Umbel, hosted Umbel Station, an agricultural outpost of Lamella Four.

Several days had passed and Freskat was behind them. It was as Box was griping about having little to do but plot their onward route that Bellfish alerted the on-duty bridge crew to possible trouble ahead.

"Distress call! *SS Watersprite*, a small cargo out of Lamella! She's close to the Kolly Beacon asteroid field and has two raiders on her!"

"On it!" Ensign Larai responded, sending her tactical output to the bridge holo. "Too far yet but I've got the outlines of three ships."

"Red alert! Captain to the bridge! Crew to battlestations!" roared duty officer Pollux Gliss. "Shields up and ready weapons! Cloak on line, helm, but do *not* deploy. Ready to come about on my mark!"

"Lieutenant!" Larai exclaimed. "Spec matches the interceptor-like raiders we've met before but these are way bigger than the ones that hit us at Orange 2334!"

"Confirm!"

"Confirmed. Readings definitely match those of new interceptor design but these things are huge."

Ahxenta and Apnis raced onto the bridge. Gliss had given the command to come off the bypass and make direct to Kolly Beacon but not to respond to the distress to reduce the likelihood of alerting the enemy to their approach. He brought the captain and first mate up to speed as three others shot in to take up salient positions.

As the *Arianrhod* sped on, the captain took quick stock and called for the cloak. She ordered Azular to ready the decoy for launch and set Gliss to capturing full tactical scans of all three ships. Her weapons officers she bid target the attackers and prepare to fire.

"Web in!" Ahxenta called out as she tightened her seat restraints. "Azular, what have you got on those blips?"

"Trying to get clear readings, Captain. Both ships match raider interceptor design but they're more heavily armed: phase cannon, multiple torpedo tubes, what look like slicer beam ports. Hulls are heavily shielded. They're aware of us despite our cloak," he warned as Gliss called out that one was turning in their direction.

"What in blazes is going on?" Apnis demanded as the tactical holo in the overhead grid rotated to let them see that the second hostile and the *Watersprite* had also changed course.

It was as Bellfish announced that the *Watersprite's* distress call had ceased that Azular let out a harsh expletive.

"It's a trap!" he bellowed. "All three are hostile! Repeat, all three are hostile!"

19: THE MINCH FETTIN CONNECTION

Arianrhod speared off in an explosive spiral, pinning everyone in their seats. Dox had reacted before the captain had given the order and as the ship swept off course and into a jump that would take her back towards ISP space, a sonic shock against her hull caused her fabric to shudder. She reeled to another blast as Ahxenta ordered the cloak down and the launch of deflecting drones to baffle incoming fire. Whatever the new ships were, they had got *Arianrhod* in their sights and were intent on taking her down.

The lead ship swept across the field of view at a near-incredible speed, letting loose a stream of phase-missiles. *Arianrhod's* gunnery crews had opened fire and were raining bolts at the enemy. The great PSS banked and swerved but turned to outface the hostile and bring her into the sights of her forr'ad phase arrays.

"Ready *Loki* but do not deploy!" Ahxenta ordered as she scanned the huge shape and the tactical output from her bridge stations that fed into the main holo. "Tallica, take auxiliary weapons and focus on her fighter bays; weapons station two, mark her comms and scanning arrays; Earbleat, target hull emplacements. Azular, ready the decoy: this is where we'll need it. Comms, send out a distress, all channels."

"She's got most of our drones!" Whisper Earbleat yelled. "And here comes the other one! But she's not as fast."

"Decoy ready to go on your mark, Captain. Location?"

"Hold for now! Helm, hard to starboard – bring us out above her! All weapons stations, full salvo and then *hold*… Helm, get us out of here! I want that thick patch of asteroid debris between us and them. Azular, prepare to release the decoy aft of us and leave it to run the programmed sequence."

Weapons fire lanced across the space between *Arianrhod* and her nemesis and her hull shook to the shock of return fire as she rose like a firebird and then dove beyond the thickening mass that marked a dense patch of dust where colliding asteroids had fragmented. On command, the decoy shot out of its bay to take up a spot astern.

"Gunnery teams, chose your shots and make them count!" spat the captain. "Fine beam through that debris!"

"That second beast's picked up speed and is coming round!" Gliss alerted her. "She's making for the decoy!"

"Launching more deflecting drones!" Apnis called. "She's cutting across the debris field! Is she crazy?"

"*Watersprite* is heading in but she's staying out of the line of fire!" bawled Ensign Larai at second tactical.

Azular had been puzzling the activity of the cargo vessel and had locked his Norvallan scanner in to boost his own station's capacity. "Suggest long-range torpedoes to disable *Watersprite*!" he called at the top of his lungs. "She's controlling the other two!"

"Cook it, Earbleat!" ordered Ahxenta.

"She's moving out of torpedo range, Cap! She's onto us!"

"Then send *Loki* on her tail! I want her gone!"

"*Loki VI* ready to launch… there she goes! On her, on her…" The weapons officer kept up a running commentary as her beloved small craft ate up the distance to her target. "Hit her!" she screamed at last. "She's out of commission. Now these two pay the price!"

"A ship coming off the bypass! It's huge and it's not one of ours! It reads as hostile! Just a sec…" Gliss paused. "It's the *Kel'Moth*!"

"*Kel'Moth* is targeting lead hostile… but *she's* still raining fire in our direction!" cried Larai. "Why isn't she covering her own flanks?"

"Second hostile is still trying to take out our decoy," Azular stated calmly. "Sending the command to cloak and return."

"*Kel'Moth* has disabled hostile's main engines and she's spiralling out of control," Larai reported. "She'll collide with that asteroid!"

"Tallica, throw all you've got at that second ship! Hold! Thal's going for her," Ahxenta noted, breathing heavily. "Azular, get our decoy back into her bay before they spot her."

"Thal seems to have one helluva grudge against whoever *they* are," the first mate said harshly. "He's targeting the main engines on that as well! He's got them. His gunnery crews are damn good."

"Cancel distress and stand down weapons but keep them hot. All stations, stay sharp. Tactical, keep your eyes on the *Kel'Moth*," the captain instructed as Apnis made her way over.

"Reckon he'll want to chat?" the first mate asked as she sat.

"I damn well want to chat," Ahxenta replied. "Where did he come from and why? I can't imagine he answered our distress."

The science officers were examining the debris field and the four vessels around them. Thal's ship had left the two great hulks to make for the disabled *Watersprite*, a move that had Earbleat spitting as she was fretful that the remains of *Loki VI* would be on his menu.

"What's he doing?" Apnis asked. "Is he sure there's no life left in those two beasts?"

"There may never have been life in them," Azular declared. "They were heavily shielded and I could get no life readings. Now that their shielding is down, I *still* get no life readings. That may be the reason they were controlled by the *Watersprite*."

"What *have* you got on them?" the captain demanded. "And how did you figure those two great things were under outside control?"

"Their line evoked hostile tactics at the battle for Freskat: a trio of ships with one in control. The *Watersprite* held back, so she had to be in control. But as the tactics of the other two gave no hint of instant counter-response, I suspect the *Watersprite* must be short-handed. Her structure's akin to the *Firewave*: trace zukivianite but no limpet drones. As for the other two, they're similar to the interceptors we've met but their lines and hull inclusions point to an origin beyond Kirtish and Kollaskin Ambit *and* they match data I have of vessels the Norvallans deem unfriendly. Thal may be able to enlighten us."

As he spoke, Bellfish called that Thal was online. The *Kel'Moth* had come about with the *Watersprite* in tow. Thal was short in his terms of concern for *Arianrhod* and her crew but replied to Ahxenta's queries. One of his scouts had been in pursuit of the *Watersprite* but she had eluded them at Fenik Moot, by the Garnet Nebula. The *Kel'Moth* had picked up the trail days later when following a lead that a hostile base had been set up at Peden Post, the third, very bleak planet of the star Peden that sat on the edge of the Garnet, close to the Delta-Lambda border. The *Watersprite* had by that time picked up her two attendant vessels, probably at Peden. As *Arianrhod* had been intercepted, it was likely that she was the target to be lured in by the fake distress call.

Ahxenta was not satisfied by that. "Why my ship?" she demanded.

"You may recognise one of the crew aboard the *Watersprite*," Thal told her darkly. "Your old contact Lokterix. I want him. Now I have him. I suspect his ship was on another errand but had come to hear of your presence locally. As I told you before, their kind has spies."

"Why Peden Post? There's nothing there."

"Except an old listening post used once by raiders and then by the aggressors that preyed on my kind – and yours."

"The hostiles," Ahxenta reminded him. "And we figured long ago that they must have had listening posts to pass messages between the two main arms of their forces in the war. Where did those two great battleships that you took down so quickly originally come from?"

"And with which you seemed to cope very well," he observed.

"Answer the question."

"I suspect you've worked out that they hail from beyond settled galactic regions. They came from a base set up by force years ago in a remote area of a planet called Telzilt, the third in the Telzilt system. It's beyond zone Mu on the Kirtish side."

"Through that hidden bypass, I guess," the captain said. "The one that runs from an uninhabited planet close by your Starfall base to at least as far as a deserted system with a red-orange star in uncharted space that the ISP has labelled K457:003. Is that this Telzilt place?"

Whatever Thal suspected that Ahxenta had guessed *that* was not it. "How did…? You *are* smart, as I said long ago. No, that's *not* Telzilt," he said, his grim face twisting in emotion. "The Telzilt system is a way beyond the bypass and its third planet is populated. I will say no more on that, but our joint enemies still have active bases outside charted zones and in isolated regions inside. We don't know how many are left of the original hostiles. I'd guess few, as their ships are under-crewed, but their hostile propensities will still be great."

That raised other issues of interest to Ahxenta. "Are these hostiles that seem to be readying for action again the original highly-cyber types that crewed the huge ships that began the war by blasting everything in their way, or the more human-like ones that infiltrated galactic concerns like the Coalition Council? And who *were* the aliens that abducted and physically and genetically altered you and yours? At our first meeting you said you were *authorised* to tell me that your people were former captives of the scum hitting Skyrtek and you'd escaped their control. You and your ragtag fleet were out to take back what you said was yours, their bases in fact, which many suspect were once raider bases. Now you're here in control of a heap of hardware and don't need authorisation from anyone. Care to explain?"

Thal was clearly irate, but evidently deeming that openness was his best option, he conceded that some of his people had been involved with the raider fleets that had harassed the known galactic zones for decades, although he himself had not. He claimed to have been an agent infiltrating raider circles, but his agency he refused to disclose.

As far as he was aware the mainly highly-cyber hostile crews had erupted out of their dens in radical ships many years before to begin a takeover of scattered raider bases operating outside settled sectors. Some of the aliens *were* human-like and several forms existed that had developed over centuries. They had initially seized their raider victims to carry out alterations that would make them useful agents to foster the hostile aims of control. Others vanished and it later became clear that the aliens were assimilating organic matter into their own bodies. By the time Thal had been taken, human-like hostiles were dominant in the command chain, their fleet was huge and there was at least one facility in charted space for physical and genetic manipulation. The underground of escaped victims who had shaken off alien influence had by then been set up and Thal had been drawn into it.

Ahxenta was hesitant to believe what she was hearing but it had a ring of truth. As Thal had been in military service and had lost most of the impacts of his captivity, he had come to command the ship at Skyrtek. Many of his people had been lost during the war and many more in the aftermath, when their priority had been the take-down of the known alien bases. Some of his kind had been out for revenge at all costs and it had cost them. He and those of his people that *had* made it through set up at Starfall, as it had been the least damaged of the known hostile bases and was equipped with the cream of hostile hardware *and* software, including the means to continue assembly of what became the *Kel'Moth*. As he was one of the most experienced and senior people left, he had succeeded to the command of the fleet.

"I see," the captain said when he had ceased. "Thank you for that. But you called me. Was there something specific you wanted?"

"To thank you for passing the news about the possible sighting of the *Firewave* to Commander Ver," he responded curtly. "The *Kel'Beth* followed it up. Your source was accurate and the *Firewave* is out of commission. Lokterix escaped her but now I have him and this ship."

"Ver told me of a hostile base on Zeta Dixt so we're even on that score," Ahxenta said equally bluntly. "I have another question. Minch Fettin: do you know what's going on there? The man Flatt you took from the *Subspace Diner* a while ago claimed to have a covert cargo he wanted transported to that place. The cargo vanished."

Thal stared at Ahxenta, trying to gauge what she knew. "What do you suspect?" he asked at last.

"Things suggest that it might be a centre for surgical and genetic ops that involve high-tech surgical intrusion, very complex and highly advanced medical devices and huge amounts of novel data."

"What things?"

Ahxenta shook her head. "What do you know?" she persisted.

"We know there's a centre for genetic alteration and cyber implant that's long been undermined by alien influence," he said after a pause. "As far as I know it still exists. Still, the planetary authority there does not take interference kindly. But you seem to suggest that there might be more to the place and the agent Flatt is involved?"

"Is?" repeated the captain. "He's still around then?"

"We're not barbarians, Captain," Thal said acidly. "He's alive and has been questioned but we know nothing of this cargo you mention. It's possible that he wiped the knowledge of it from his own memory systems. He's a variant of an info-sent, less strong than some but able enough to do us a lot of mischief. He was involved in infiltrating one of our groups and passing data to his operators. He was exposed and is now in our custody, in a secure holding place."

"If you're going to do the same to Lokterix, I suggest you make your holding place super-secure. He's not an info-sent but he's a nasty piece of work and smart with it."

"Yes I know; he was enlisted late and was malicious to begin with. But you're interested in Minch Fettin?"

"It's a name that keeps coming up in relation to high-spec medical gear that's likely to be subverted for hostile use by corrupt outfits. An agent of theirs that uses the names Hoxiz and Berg Brack is involved. As Hoxiz he had links to Lokterix and to a covert medical centre on Mellifly used for cyber and genetic ops. Have you heard of Hoxiz?"

Thal inclined his head. "Yes. Do you know where he is now?"

"The last I heard, some while ago, he was in custody in the Web at Merkat under the name of Brack."

Thal nodded again but did no more than make his farewells and cut comms. As the bridge crew of *Arianrhod* watched, the huge ship, her captive in tow, made off towards the bypass.

Apnis sighed gustily. "No offer to help us back on line, no thanks for saving him some stress in taking out those bandits," she noted.

"His thanks we don't need and he knows I'll not accept his help. But he's verified that the hostiles got far enough beyond the charted zones to know Norvalla. That'll be a fact for your friend Kerrix when we haul into the Web, Azular, if she's still there. She's maybe heard of this Telzilt place that Thal's so cagey about. But he and his took heavy losses hunting the hostiles after Skyrtek? Did they do it of their own accord or were they pushed, I wonder?"

"You mean the beings of Kelfennig, ma'am," he replied. "They *did* say they would try to influence the take-down of hostile places of power by Thal's band. They may have induced some of them to act, as they *did* exert influence on Micklemouse while he was down there and we certainly experienced an emotional reaction to them."

"They creeped us out you mean," the first mate reminded him.

"Indeed, Commander."

"D'you think it was wise to mention Hoxiz, Cap?" asked Apnis.

"If he's inclined to put a stop to him, he's welcome," Ahxenta said. "But for now we've a ship to get to rights. Lamella's the closest but it's no great shakes as far as top-class weaponry's concerned."

"Our updated decoy performed well, though – it foxed the second hostile. I suppose it was worth it to get Lokterix off our backs and that's two hostiles posing as freighters out of the picture, if Thal was right about the *Firewave*. But how many more are out there?"

"Thal's still holding a lot back and it strikes me he's going out of his way to make us think he's friendly. What *are* his dealings beyond Kirtish? I bet he uses that bypass and I bet it's not for cleansing the galaxy of the aliens that targeted him and his."

"*How* does he use the bypass?" Greffy wanted to know. "He must be able to get it online when he wants, but it must stay quiescent the rest of the time. If not, it would have been picked up long since. Not many head out that way, but the ISP exploratory fleet has and I'm sure some of the zone Mu independents must have as well."

"It may have to be tackled in a specific way, to activate a node or a beacon," Azular guessed. "As derelicts have been noted close by and in nearby space over the years, it may be that some have inadvertently triggered it, been pulled in and been unable to get out or have been forced to abandon ship when they did get off into unmapped space."

"There may be a few still on the bypass that didn't escape and are drifting," Greffy said.

"I suspect they'd have been found and scavenged."

"Speculation," the captain interrupted. "And it's not our concern. That the last of the reports in, Tallica?"

"Aye, Cap: we've lost three energy cells, our shields need work, a few hull plates want realigning and we're down deflecting drones and torpedoes. Minimal ship damage otherwise and only minor injuries to crew. But it'll still cost and our insurance reps will no doubt squeal."

"The *Kel'Moth* must be well on her way by now so we head back to the bypass. Make straight to Lamella Four, helm. We can pick up a few necessary bits there. I'll let Zillah know about the action as there may be more bad guys out there. And if Thal's news on Peden Post is accurate, the ISP should be told, as will the Non-Treaty Alliance – it borders their space. I'll put it out on the PSS channel as well, as the *Warrior's* headed across Delta, though she should be far enough away from Peden to avoid local trouble."

Arianrhod made a short stop at Lamella Four to have her hull patched and to take on arms. With no news of other attacks on shipping, the cynics of her crew were left to assume that she was being explicitly targeted by people with grudges against her. The decoy's decloaking test had been shelved as the captain felt that speed was crucial and the device had proved its worth. The downside of that for Azular was that he had Earbleat at his elbow more often than usual with appeals for the means of outfitting a new cargo pod as *Loki VII* with the tech he had refused to part with for *Loki VI*. She had also suggested he upgrade the decoy to resemble a new PSS, name her the *Red Herring* and register her with the Trades Alliance. Azular was not amused.

The science officer spent his spare time during the flight to Stella Marina in searching the star charts he had upgraded with the data from Zillah and the Norvallan shuttle. If Kerrix' craft *was* equipped with the navigational data that had led her ship to K457:003, it should be possible to link that to the charts he now had and find a route to Norvalla. With the little got from Thal he had no means of deducing the coordinates of the Telzilt system but if Kerrix *had* heard of the place by that name, it could also be located.

The engineering company on Stella Marina that had produced the desalination rigs had moved them to an orbital transfer station, which meant a quick about-turn. The trip to Zidexall Primary involved a run across zone Gamma and into Beta, a well-travelled route in ISP space most of the way and no surprises were expected. *Arianrhod* sped on, her only halt at the lush world of Millet to pick up a cargo of rare pharmaceuticals for Kelpin. The captain had heard nothing from her contacts over her recent report but there had been a hit on a carrier making from Keystone Kell to Larrikon Seven with a cargo of small arms. Both ship and cargo had been wrecked. The general view was that the incident smacked of desperation on the part of the hostiles.

"Only hope the Zidexallians cough up the credit as soon as they have the gear," Box said to his partner in a low voice as she brought the ship into a close orbit. "They've a rep for not parting with credit until they can't help it, and sometimes not even then."

"No credit, no cargo," Dox told him. "We've been here before. Docking achieved, Captain, all boards show green," she added loudly.

"Roger that," acknowledged Ahxenta. "Now for fun with the Sea Rigs trade reps," she said to Apnis. "Lindell's told them we're on a tight schedule so they'd better not try any back-pedalling over price."

"Yes, we'll get a fast delivery bonus if we make Kelpin with their goods within the next few days," she agreed. "It was lucky we were close enough to detour to Millet at short notice; it helped us win the contract. And then we make for Merkat?"

"We do. Lindell's got a couple of meets set up there that might lead to a couple more deals."

The *Arianrhod* was well enough known at Zidexall Primary that the threat of a visit by her captain was sufficient to ensure that the trade reps at the company in want of the rigs made sure the transfer was completed smoothly and to time. The ship was soon on a heading for Kelpin. The only vexing news en route came in via a nameless source that Ahxenta guessed to be Vettarista. Hoxiz and Herta, having been allowed bail, had fled, their implanted security tags extracted and inserted into unwary and extremely cross locals. As Hoxiz had been arrested as Brack, a name without a criminal history, he had not been classed as high risk. The captain vented her ire by passing the news to Ver with the request that she send it to Thal.

The cargo for Kelpin was dropped quickly and *Arianrhod* made good time back to the bypass. It was a short haul to Merkat and the Web, with the crew warm in the knowledge that bonuses were on the way and with hard negotiation ahead, shore leave was assured.

As the huge net of docking struts of one of the largest bays of the outer belts began to lock into place and the restraining cross-pieces glowed red to indicate a secure hold, the helmswoman eased back on the power to bring the great ship to station-keeping.

"Boards all green, Captain, docking complete," Dox announced as the main bridge holo reflected the external lights of the glittering net in which *Arianrhod* sat.

"Roger that, helm. I'll head to the harbour office and check what's what," the captain said to her first mate. "The *Zephyr* and the *Nova Stella* are in, so I may get their news. I see the docking fees have been upped, which may mean there's been trouble since last we were in."

"Or it's just greed," Apnis remarked.

"True. I'll link if I hear anything. We're well into business hours, so Lindell can start setting up meets. You sort duty rotas and check what we need in supplies and minor refit. Use our own repair drones if you can. Ms Earbleat, run an armaments inventory and make sure we're up to full spec on high energy torpedoes, pulse cannon energy bolts and deflecting drones. If we're short or need spare parts for the arrays, make a list and run it by Commander Apnis. Tallica, see what Axellina and Crizz need for their departments. I'll see you later."

Later turned into much later as the captain was caught up in a debate with the Port Authority over added levies incurred as a result of the trouble *Arianrhod* had attracted during her previous visits. Ahxenta had headed inwards to the PA's HQ by the main marketing suite on green four of inner belt two after her stormy visit to the harbour office, and after telling the Authority reps there what to do with their charges, she called her first mate for an update on ship's news. All was proceeding satisfactorily, she was told.

"Then I'll head to security to see if Jiff Hills has anything new on Hoxiz and Herta. I heard in the harbour office that things are quieter here than when last we were in, but Jennik Kilmaur told me that the *Zephyr* had a run-in with raiders near Quartic Cross. He got away with buckled hull plates but he's passed it on to the ISP: Quartic's close enough to Alto Finglas to cause concern. *Nova's* due to ship out soon but the *Firedrake's* on her way in for more repairs – she'll be here in twelve hours so make sure Ma'Lappis is at the top of the leave list. I'll head for the *Half Moon* after security, as I expect I'll get more out of Ally and his hangers-on than I will out of SSO Hills."

The captain was not surprised to hear that little had gone forward with regard to the fugitives. Hills could offer nothing other than that an all-points bulletin was out in every port locally and every ISP and Allied main office had been notified. But the mapped galaxy was vast and every regulatory body was at liberty to ignore anything beyond its own borders. Hill's other news was more relevant: a shielded hub close by his own data surveillance suite had been found that tracked not only the visual yield from security's cam network but that from a smaller net of illegal hidden cams that had been tied into the official system at junction points. The SSO would only say that the matter was pending. Ahxenta scented the hand of ISP's Intelligence Division and put in a link to Vettarista as soon as she cleared Hill's office.

The *Half Moon in a Puddle* was gearing up for the usual influx of regulars at the close of Web business hours but Ally was on hand to set out a pot of his finest brew. The arrival of *Arianrhod* had not gone unmarked on the bar's local external channels and the advent of the captain was no surprise, he told her. Ahxenta realised that her first mate had been active in organising leave, for several of her crew had also made it down and into the *Half Moon*. She nodded over and turned back to the bar to find that Captain Maris Fleete of the *Nova Stella* and her first mate Lyannis Merzin had hauled in alongside.

"Captain," Fleete greeted her. "Busy time out there for *Arianrhod*, I hear. We're due out shortly so we thought we'd grab a last jar."

The *Nova* was headed for Stinward with a small cargo for the ISP, Fleete told her. There had been no trouble in that neck of the galaxy since the *Hexameter* but she was wary: her vessel was of a smaller and less well-armed design than the *Vanguard* class that made up most of the PSS fleet and she did not intend to attract attention. At Fleete's request Ahxenta began to tell of the *Arianrhod's* last trip there but the cheep of her wrist communit interrupted her. A holo-note flowed out, short and to the point. She grimaced.

"I have to go," she announced, swallowing the last of her ale.

The captain took her leave and made for level four. She found Vettarista at the *Sunlight Subspace Diner* and the two made their way in. The agent had little on Hoxiz and Herta but her people were tracing local links and potential escape routes. As for an illegal secure cam net, a sharp-eyed repair op had spotted a linkage junction node close to a cam she was fixing and alerted her division *and* Merkat security. An officer there informed an Intelligence contact and the ensuing search turned up the intrusion and its extent, which was great.

"It's no wonder they could follow practically anyone they wanted; we've now to find the eyes that were on watch. Security got a few and we turned up a couple, but there has to be more out there *and* people in control," Vettarista said. "A shake-up's ongoing, the complete spy-cam net is down as far as we know and arrests have included security and repair people. The news isn't out as it would cause chaos. From what we've figured, their set-up was developing and was the work of months not years, which means that most major businesses wouldn't have been compromised. But we don't know if there's another net out there *not* linked to the security system."

Ahxenta in turn advised the woman that she had told Thal of the absent pair, giving her reasons and more in-depth on the dealings she had had with him and his. She was taken aback when Vettarista told her that Thal's doings were under ISP investigation, as he seemed to have built up a large fleet. They knew of his Starfall base and others of his off the edges of the settled zones but he had not taken over the central ex-hostile base on Lartzeg Trine. Vettarista was party to the details given to Zillah on the suspected bypass used by Thal and brought the topic up. She had heard that the data from derelicts and from the ISP's forays into uncharted space had been the exchange but that Azular had worked out a route for the likely archaic but now active bypass across zone Mu used by the aliens surprised her. A little reflection supplied the answer and she taxed Ahxenta with the use of Norvallan data. The captain confirmed it but would say no more. The agent did not press her but asked if there was anything else about the hostiles or Thal's alliance of which the ISP should be aware.

"Did you know about his new base just off the border of Gamma and Beta in unmapped space?" was Ahxenta's response.

"What new base?" the Berzic woman asked sharply.

"His ex-new base," she amended. "He said his people had set one up off the edge of sector sixteen but hostiles took out everything and everyone. He was very bitter over it. He's also recently lost two ships. He blamed it on the hostiles' rising power and their spies and allies all over the place. He thinks it's how they figure his every move. And ours, come to that," Ahxenta frowned. "He reckons *he* has allies as well, though who the hell they are and where they are I don't know."

"So it *was* a base then. I'd heard of the destruction of what was taken to be a hidden outpost on the borders of the Skipper Nebula, near Kelfar Keeth. As that place is on the edge of nowhere, we'd figured it was some old raider hidey hole. Anything else?"

There was nothing else that the captain intended to share but she did enquire after their joint acquaintance Kerrix, as she had not been visible in the *Half Moon*. She still worked there, Vettarista disclosed.

"Which will no doubt put a smile on your senior science officer's face," the agent remarked archly. "But as I'm still a humble hostess at Azure Belle's, I have to go. Good to see you again, Captain."

The captain finished her drink, paid her bill and left. It had been a long day and her shuttle beckoned.

The first mate was still on duty when Ahxenta made the bridge. It was quiet, the dark watch in place. The two logged off and headed to the crew's mess, where the captain passed on her news and learnt what had gone down ship-wise. Lindell had set up meetings for early the next morning for two deals, one of which involved heavy gear for the ISP's new shipyard at Stinward. He had a couple more leads he was following up, the first group of crew to be assigned shore leave was safely in the Web and a second lot were due down next day.

"Azular among them?" the captain queried.

Apnis smiled. "No. I figured you'd want him for the meets port-side. I think he did too as he didn't request. But Greffy did. I sensed something going on, but they weren't saying. Kerrix still around?"

"She is, according to Vettarista. I didn't see her but I'd no time for a private word with Ally as Maris Fleete crept up on me and bent my ear for a bit. Let's go over the timetable for the meetings. If they take us up to lunchtime we can head to the *Half Moon* after them."

The next morning ran to schedule, the talks ending just after noon. Lindell and Azular joined Ahxenta and Apnis in the *Half Moon*, where Ally was at the bar. Kerrix was at the far side rounding up used wares and two other attendants were busy serving. Several heads turned as the four stepped in, including a couple of their own crew.

"Nice to have you back in, Captain," Ally greeted her. "Lunch?"

"Lunch it is. I didn't get a chance to talk to you yesterday. What's new Web-side that I should know about?"

"Apart from the upped docking fees? We've had complaints," he chuckled. "Then there was the arrest of one of medbay's chief medics who'd been on the take *and* involved with trade reps peddling high-tech, or so two paramedics who drink in here told me. She skipped the Web with a rep who'd been arrested with her. Medbay's shook up as more have been dismissed with no testimonials. A few in security are seeing the inside of their own cells too but nobody's sure why; rumour says they were paid to look the other way. Crime rate's gone down since and we haven't had any new bangs put down to sabotage rather than stupidity. I haven't heard of any serious assaults round the inner belts but the usual punch-ups still upset the locals. A few Privates have been and gone, including the *Tallulah*. She made off to Cassary with a cargo weeks ago but she's due back about now. The *Hexameter* and the *Labyrinth* left two days ago but I don't know where. I heard about the *Firedrake*. Shame, she's been around the block a few times but she always made it through. No shuttles have been mislaid either," he went on slyly. "Anything new your end, Captain?"

"No," Ahxenta said shortly as she punched in her selection on the menu pad. "We'll sit by the wall," she added.

"Separate tabs?" Ally asked.

"Put them on mine and charge it as a business lunch. After the talking we had to do this morning, we deserve it."

"Trade's been tough with this raiding on the up again, so I hear," he agreed. "But not for the PSS fleet I imagine, as you lot have always stepped in where the usual transports fear to fly."

"What have you heard about that, Ally?" Apnis asked curiously.

"Some of the pilots that haul in here reckon that this war we've all been through hasn't ended yet; a lot of the attacks on freight lines we hear about have been put down to the antics of a few camps of aliens still left. The old raiders are said to be back in action as well but we haven't seen it here," he shrugged. "It hasn't affected my trade."

"Let's sit, if you've all ordered," Ahxenta told her crewmen. "Too many ears are tuned in to what we're saying. You coming, Azular?"

"Yes ma'am," he responded, tearing his eyes away from the spot in the distance where he had been trading glances with Kerrix.

Ally brought their drinks order over and told them that their food was on the way. Their chat to that point had centred on the news from the *Half Moon* and their own successful business talks that had resulted in two more contracts that would see them clear of the Web in ten days, leaving ample time for shore leave for most of the crew. Lindell had set up another meeting for later in the day, but as it was with an old customer, he was optimistic that it would be short.

After their meal, Apnis sought privacy to contact her friend Kit to arrange a short tryst to get his news on the latest goings-on Web-side. She returned to the table to find the captain and Lindell alone.

"So where's he gone, or need I ask?" she demanded as she slid in.

Ahxenta inclined her head to a far corner of the bar, where Azular and Kerrix were deep in conversation. The first mate raised her eyes to the ceiling and shook her head slightly but made no comment. The science officer returned minutes later, a look of content on his face.

"Got a date?" Apnis asked.

"Very funny, Commander. I've ordered us some more drinks – on my tab," he grinned satirically. "We have time before we meet with the reps from Agrotech Stellar."

Kerrix brought the drinks, looking a tad serious as she gave them out. She said no more than necessary for the service but smiled as she caught Azular's eye. Ahxenta noted the return to a pained expression as the woman turned away and drew her own conclusions.

A little later, when the quartet had made marketing to set up for their next meeting, the captain drew her science officer aside.

"You've told Kerrix that you might be able to use the charts you now have and her nav data to find her a route home haven't you?"

He paused a second, considering, before nodding. "Yes ma'am."

"She didn't exactly look overjoyed."

"I sensed she was equivocal," he agreed. "Although once there is a known route *to* Norvalla, the reverse route should also be possible."

"Through possibly hostile space and using a hostile bypass that we don't know how to access?" queried the captain.

"Now that *is* the problem."

"One of the problems I would imagine," was the dry response as the two rejoined their colleagues.

The talks with Agrotech Stellar were brief and a contract for the transport of a large load for the agricultural colony of Vreskota Two was soon drawn up. It was a short trip across zone Alpha and could be fitted in during *Arianrhod's* wait in the Web for her other two cargoes. Flexing her shoulders, Ahxenta led the way to the local dock and their shuttle. Apnis planned to change into civilian clothing for her date in the *Port in a Storm* with Kit Biernop. Lindell had his team already working on the details required for the business agreed, as the captain had called for all the pieces to be in place in short order.

"I'll want you for the trip across to Vreskota," Ahxenta notified Azular once they had docked aboard. "If you want shore leave before we go you'd best make it soon."

"Aye, Captain. I have one or two things to arrange first, so I'll do that now and leave with Commander Apnis," he told her.

"I'm leaving in an hour," Apnis said, smirking. "I'll see you then."

The departing shuttle was busy as several others were heading down, including Flintlock, who had a reunion with a friend in medbay. The craft made into her dock in inner two and the first mate, chief medic and senior science officer left together; all three were out of uniform.

"Heading for apartment thirty one in section one, one, four with your luggage?" the doctor asked Azular jocularly.

"No," he answered testily. "It's none of your concern where I'm headed, Doctor."

"*Half Moon,*" she chuckled as they stepped into a transport tube.

Apnis skipped out at green six and Flintlock at three, leaving the science officer to alight at green two. He strode along confidently and soon reached his goal. From a booth in one of the far recesses of the *Half Moon in a Puddle*, two pairs of eyes followed his every move.

"That's Dr Azular back again," Malty observed to his buddy in a low voice. "Second time today but this time in disguise."

"It's a poor disguise if we know it's him," Jurry pointed out. "His uniform will be in the kitbag. Here to see Kerrix do you think?"

"He might be. Something's definitely going on there, Jurry my lad. Maybe it's something in the ale."

"Doubt it; we've been coming here for years and nobody's given *us* the glad eye," his friend lamented.

"Just as well – it would cost us. But his sidekick Greffy was in just before lunchtime and he and young Merry haven't been back since. Something there as well, I'd wager," his friend nodded sagely. "Aye: he's headed straight over and *her* face has lit up like sunrise over a hill. I'll slope up to the bar and see if I can hear anything."

Malty returned within the space of three minutes, two small pots of bargain ale in his hands. "*She* was in a sharp mood," he told Jurry as he slid into his space. "Asked me if I needed assistance to find my way back here and threatened to call that pot-bellied security bod Jox to give me a hand. She's taller behind the bar. *He* looked a bit glum.

Don't know if it was me or they were having a spat."

"It was you," he was informed. "Evrett's been here for an hour and Jez and Lotty have just come in, so I bet *she* heads off with him."

Jurry had read his birds correctly and was gratified to see the two make off through the holo-doors of the *Half Moon*. He was also at pains to point out to his companion that theirs were not the only eyes following the pair: a table of crewmen in the uniform of the *Arianrhod* had also marked their exit and were nudging one another.

"Can't keep anything in the dark around here," Malty hiccuped. "He'll be having his leg pulled back aboard and no mistake. But look who's just come in: if that's not Tallulah Tommy then it's his twin. So where's Fleetskup? They're hardly ever apart."

"Probably at his back; I bet he's waylaid Azular to fill his ears with noise. I heard *Tallulah's* still not up to full strength but she's got a new first mate. Don't know who."

"Might be the uniform that's come in with Fleetskup, whoever she is. She looks a handful," Malty observed.

Captain Murmur Fleetskup had a resonant voice and was quick to introduce his new first mate, Commander Modis Dyne-Bek. Nodding affably, Ally eyed the new arrival. She was sturdily-built, with flaring nostrils that looked as though they scented bad beer. Dyne-Bek had seemingly last served aboard the ISP vessel *Steel Guardian*, a prison ship based at the Sekward Central adjudication facility.

"She speaks to you as if you're a public meeting," Jurry noted as he listened. "Bet Jesse Inks is majorly pissed at being passed over yet again. What's Fleetskup got against him, apart from the facts that he's younger, better looking and far more talented than his captain?"

"Search me," Malty said. "But drink up. If we introduce ourselves nicely to the lady she may stand us a jar one of these days."

The unimposing Captain Fleetskup had indeed caught the senior science officer of the *Arianrhod* on his way out and had stopped to present his new first mate. Kerrix had kept walking, stopping a little along to examine her communit in great detail until he rejoined her.

"Captain Fleetskup's new first mate," Azular said, deadpan.

"I'd worked that out. She looks like she'll keep him in order," was the rejoinder. "I wonder if he's dredged up more of similar. He was short on a few positions the last I heard."

"Not our concern," he told her. "We have other things on hand. I need to book a room. And take you to dinner."

"As long as it's not the *Milky Pearl* I'll follow you anywhere. But why don't you stay at mine? It's not paradise but it's handy."

"Handy for what?"

"My shuttle: she's back in green twelve, in one of the near bays."

His eyebrows shot up. "You moved her again?"

"She needed the exercise, as did I. Vetta warned me that security had broken a secure cam spy ring and it was possible that my last berth had been put at risk, so I moved her."

"Good. But I'll still reserve a suite. And I hope you'll be my guest tonight?" he asked, looking down teasingly, if a little unsure.

"You know I can't resist the big dark eyes. But I'm going to have a shower and change: it's been a long day and it's not over yet."

He left her at her quarters and set off to reserve a room and catch up with matters. By the time he returned she was ready. Their plan had been to head to her shuttle and then to dinner. One long look at her changed his mind and he reached out to gather her into his arms.

Several minutes later, Kerrix extricated herself. "We carry on like this and nothing will get done," she laughed softly. "Come along."

Locking her apartment carefully, she turned, took his hand and led him along the passage. Both were still stirred by the emotion that had drawn them together and with senses super-sharpened, a moving light high on the wall simultaneously drew their eyes. Azular felt her grip tense and then relax as she let go his hand to reach into a pocket. He was equally fast and made for the small handgun she had given him. He had recognised the device as a miniature hunter-drone and it was deadly. They may not have been its target, but that it was there at all meant trouble. He dropped to one knee and fired, hearing her throw herself to one side as she took aim. As a single bolt shot from the drone, two spears of light hit their mark and it exploded, the pieces scattering like stars.

The sound of running feet caught his ears and Azular leapt up, his gun ready. Two uniformed men rounded the corner with weapons in hand but as he took in the flak on the deck, the leader pulled up, his grip on his phase rifle relaxing. Azular's sigh of relief was palpable as he straightened and nodded.

20: A NORVALLAN CONNECTION

The most recent goings-on in relation to law and order as far as they affected security and the Dockers' Guild were trying the mind of the *Arianrhod's* first mate. Tallica Apnis was seated in a private booth in the *Port in a Storm* on green six, her meal before her. Kit Biernop sat opposite, his face serious in the dim light. As a Guild liaison with Merkat security, he was deep in the matter of the misuse of a great part of the secure cam network for criminal activity. Much of it had led to violence, the degree of which would likely never be known. As he outlined the extent of the infiltration, his main concern was that a parallel cam set-up might exist. He was sure that felons were still at work in both security and the Guild, but the crime rate *had* reduced and his people were breathing more easily.

Apnis also found out that a major crime ring, recently exposed by a plant, had been boosting their operations in the Web. Their initial speciality had been the acquisition and supply of highly illicit goods, using remote docking bays and the help of Dockers' Guild personnel, but they had now set up in extortion and other trades. Their weapons of choice were micro-explosive units, elements of which were based on the hostile tech that had formed part of the devices that had been used for the attempt on *Arianrhod's* shuttle. Biernop was concerned that after *that* episode and the subsequent explosion, Merkat security had hunted exhaustively but found no big stores of the high-grade explosives integral to the devices, but two very recent crimes had used similar materials. The other point in the break-up of the gang was that amongst a list of potential targets, one stood out – the *PSS Arianrhod*. Apnis asked for details and Biernop promised to obtain and send them on but there were two elements of the matter he thought she should be aware of: the origin of most of the gang members and the fact that some were still at large.

The commander made for her shuttle on green twelve soon after. Having no intention of calling from any public space and as Flintlock and Azular were remaining Web-side, she decided to head up directly. The captain was in her office when the memo that Apnis was on her way in and wanted an urgent word was sent in by the comms officer.

It was a grim-faced commanding officer that waited on the inner side of the small docking bay.

"What's up, Cinnabar? I didn't expect you to come down here to find me. What's happened?"

"Let's hear your news first," the captain said shortly.

As the two made their way up to the bridge, Apnis reiterated the details of her conversation with Biernop.

"Treskk!" Ahxenta burst out when she heard of the criminal outfit broken by Merkat security. "That clarifies a damn lot! Vettarista said that security had that bunch under surveillance a while back. So they busted them but Biernop thinks some might still be in business?"

"He thinks they've skipped the Web as their IDs are out, but there have been incidents since using the stuff that they'd been peddling and using themselves. But what's got you rattled?"

"Azular and Kerrix were targeted by a mini hunter-drone carrying some damn high-tech explosive bolts."

"Are they okay?" Apnis demanded.

"They downed it first but one of the pieces was still active after it hit ground. Luckily Nat Holdspan has a quick eye and a fast gun. He and Sol Treskitt heard the bang and raced in. Nat spotted one piece still on the move and blasted it to hell before it could lock on. So it looks like it *was* targeted and one of ours was the target."

"That's pretty circumstantial, Cinnabar; and someone would have had to know where Azular was and tracked him."

"Didn't you just say that Biernop was worried that another illegal secure cam op might still be out there?"

"He did. I'd better call and warn him he may be right. So the *Warrior's* in then? She must have made good time from Wild."

"She docked a few hours ago and Holdspan and Treskitt made for inner two after the harbour office. Nat's been hit with extra levies as well and he demanded an out-of-hours meet with the Authority to argue it. They'd docked their shuttle in green twelve and Azular and Kerrix were headed to *her* boat, as it's now in green twelve. Nat called security and they sent a team to pick up the drone pieces as evidence and take statements. Azular pled ignorance. He and Kerrix got scans of the bits before the team got there but if *Arianrhod* is on some sort of Treskk hit list then our people *are* targets. But whether Azular was tracked from the time he set foot in the Web or after he'd been to the *Half Moon*, or he was seen after that, I don't know."

"He would have had to be recognised," Apnis pointed out. "He wasn't in uniform. And nobody followed me, and Axellina and the rest of our people are okay, I take it?"

"They're all fine and have been warned. But face recognition is easy to code into a remote surveillance net even if there's no-one on hand with the faces of my senior officers imprinted in their brains."

Ahxenta was interrupted by her wrist comm. It was the comms officer announcing an incoming for her from Captain Holdspan.

"I'll take it in my bridge office," she responded. "I'm almost there now. You may as well sit in, Tallica."

Holdspan and his first mate had had a dialogue with reps from the Port Authority and had put them straight before heading to security for an update. There, they had overheard Hills taking a report from an officer on green twelve who had responded to an anonymous report of weapons fire near the entry to the local shuttle section and had found two wrecked surveillance cams along the main passage. They were not security's cams. Hills ordered the despatch of a team of investigators and then told Holdspan that the flak of the hunter-drone was being analysed, but as there was so little left they could not pinpoint its origin or say how and where it had been put together. Hills would keep him and Ahxenta abreast of any further news on the case. Ahxenta quickly thanked her opposite number and linked off. She could hear her first mate shifting restlessly at her side.

"Anonymous report?" remarked Apnis as soon as the link cut. "I wonder who made that and took out the cams. Maybe you should call Azular for more news – though he and Kerrix might be busy."

The captain had had the same idea and quickly ordered comms to make the link. The two were on board the Norvallan shuttle, having made it there after their lively adventure. Once the science officer had heard the gist of Captain Holdspan's message, he admitted that he and Kerrix had been sufficiently suspicious that they had retraced their steps to check the area and had spotted cams where no cams usually were. Azular had thus made sure that he and Kerrix were out of vis-range and had put both out of action before using a local comm station to make the call to security.

Once Ahxenta had passed on Kit Biernop's news, she cut the link and looked over at her first mate. "Does it strike you that Azular isn't his usual calm and collected scientific self?"

"If you mean he's getting crazy, yes. I suspect half the crew's aware of it. I also noticed that Kerrix was looking a little low. Think she's figured the way home and now doesn't want to go?"

"No I don't. She's probably just wondering how she'll get there – if she *has* worked it out."

"We won't be giving her a ride then?"

"Like hell!" was the captain's immediate retort.

Kerrix and Azular had indeed merged the data that Azular held on the area beyond zone Mu to star system K457:003 and the star charts in her shuttle's nav-system that gave a route from Norvallan space to that point. There were many gaps in the final product but they had calculated a route to Norvalla. And Kerrix knew of the Telzilt system: *that* had been the reason for the serious look noted by Apnis.

Azular turned round to face her once he had cut the link. "What is it, Xanna?" he asked, anxious at the sharp intake of breath and the silent nod that had greeted his query just before the captain's call. "What's disturbed you about the Telzilt system?"

She shrugged, a quirky smile on her face as she looked into his eyes. "You know I'm only part-Norvallan. My mother was Telziltic."

"What!? Tell me," he entreated.

"My father's ship was part of a long-stay deputation to cement an alliance and launch treaties between Norvalla and Telzilt. It took months. He met my mother at a tech-trade event: instant attraction, hasty betrothal and legal union aboard his ship. As far I know, she was a scientist on an orbital research station and belonged to one of the elite clans, though she was later held to be an upstart. The Telzilt system's here," she grinned crookedly, pointing. "About half way between Norvalla Three and the planet you call Kirtish."

"An upstart? Why?" Azular asked.

"The match was deplored by his family, once he'd had the nerve to tell them. He'd been expected to add to their social standing by taking a high-ranking Norvallan mate, not an outworld unknown."

"What happened?"

Again she shrugged. "Telzilt was invaded by an alien group intent on takeover. My mother was serving aboard a Norvallan cruiser – I suspect to keep her in-laws at distance. Her ship was one of three sent out to answer the distress that Telzilt put out to its allies. All three were lost. I was too young to know."

"What happened to you after that?" asked Azular inquisitively.

"My father's family had already tried to invalidate his marriage as it had taken place under archaic Fleet law. But his very highly-ranked best friend was a Fleet legal expert and took on the case to prove its validity and thus my legitimacy. None of his associates would touch it as the family wanted it swept away and forgotten. He won, but most of my blood kin still regard me as a bastard in more than one sense."

"And then?"

"My father was strong-armed into a union with a suitably-ranked mate who spawned a litter of four to ensure that the titled line was secured," she replied mordantly. "He then inherited the protectorship of the Norvallan colony of Valla Key, though I suspect his wife and sons had more of a say in running it than he ever did."

"And you?"

"I passed through the best scholastic facilities in the most distant places, gained the credentials to become a science officer and joined the fleet to make sure I got even further away from home."

"And you've been on the run more or less ever since?"

"More or less," she smiled. "But what's this about Telzilt?"

All that Azular could tell her was the very little that Thal had said but in light of her information it seemed that the hostiles had made it well beyond the edges of zone Mu.

"I think we've done sufficient for one evening," he concluded. "So now I'm taking you to dinner. No more adventures."

"Until the next one," she smiled at him. "I'm beginning to think that the jokers that always seem to know where we are have trained the local rats to track our scent."

Ahxenta had a session with Hills over the drone attack set for mid-morning the next day. She took Azular; he was on leave but as Kerrix was at work he was free. The captain was not satisfied with progress. Hills, loath to admit that the *Arianrhod's* officer had been the target, had done no more than examine the site and take samples of deck where the thing had crashed. The only clue from that and drone flak was that the trace explosive found was akin to that used in the bomb that had been set to blow up *Arianrhod's* shuttle. The drone's tracking and other ops and its original number of bolts could not be verified. Irritated, Ahxenta had brought up what Holdspan had heard of the weapons fire and wrecked cams on green twelve. The peeved SSO then admitted that there was still a problem in certain areas but he had not linked the drone incident with the illegal cams. In the face of the captain's ill-concealed wrath, he had promised to look into it.

Apnis and Lindell, fresh from trade talks, were having drinks with Nat Holdspan and his first mate, whom they had met in marketing, when Ahxenta and Azular walked into the *Half Moon* later. The two joined them and after greetings and gripes over raised docking fees and the lack of diligence by security over the hunter-drone, Ahxenta turned to the captain of the *Nyx Warrior*.

"You made good time from Wild, Nat."

"No trouble on the way out *or* back as the *Warrior's* big enough to deter most of those that prey on shipping. And she's a fast ship."

"Though we had one unusual incident that left us puzzled," Sol Treskitt disclosed.

"Really?" Azular put in, sipping his ale. "What happened?"

"We'd dropped our cargo at Wild, loaded up another there and set for the ISP station at Kellybar One to offload part of it. There were two ISP cruisers in and one had been out by Wester 287, near the ex-hostile base that you alerted us to, Captain, a while ago," Treskitt said to Ahxenta. "Well, they'd heard rumours of a ship unlike anything seen before that had jumped out of hyperspace as if it had come off a bypass in uncharted space near the edge of Kappa. We thought it was one of the usual tales, but as we were due into Wester 287 with more of the food supplies we'd loaded at Wild, we scanned long-distance after our drop-off – we came off at Kappa edge. And we spotted it, or at least some ship we'd never seen before," he concluded.

"Well, don't keep us in suspense," Apnis smiled. "What was it?"

"We logged a moving object in orbit around a planet in a system on a line from that base, on our side. We didn't head in close as we had a tight about-turn, but it was there and it was active. Cap ordered visuals and scans in passing but we didn't want to risk it seeing us in case it was hostile. But it *was* a ship – a big ship – that's never been recorded before." Treskitt sat back, smiling. "It's a mystery."

"You called it in?" Ahxenta asked.

"We passed our data to the ISP at Kellybar," Holdspan told her. "If they want to investigate, they can. I had schedules to keep."

Azular exchanged a quick glance with his captain and asked if the young captain had the evidence to hand, particularly the visual. He had: Holdspan believed in having as much as possible relating to his ship within reach and could call it up from the *Warrior* onto his info-pad. He set the unit up where they could all see the holo of a strange double-hulled vessel, an outline of a *Vanguard* class ship alongside.

"She *is* huge but nothing like a cargo carrier in design," Ahxenta pondered. "Have you seen anything like it, Azular?"

"Bloody hell!" a soft voice said at his back and the science officer turned to see Kerrix staring at the distorted shape.

"Ms Kerrix," he said formally, but changed his greeting as he saw the expression on her face. "Xanna, are you all right?"

Azular glanced back at the image and then looked up again. "It may have come off at Starfall Exit. You recognise it?" he said softly.

By this time all the officers at the table had turned to look at her and one or two regulars seated nearby were trading curious glances.

Kerrix came closer, placing a hand on Azular's shoulder as she leaned in to see more clearly. "It's a *Norvallan* ship…" she breathed.

"What! Are you sure?" Ahxenta questioned.

Kerrix nodded slowly. "It's an old spec; they haven't built a heavy cruiser like that in years. It wasn't practical," she clarified. "If I could make out these markings… can you refine the image, Captain?"

Holdspan homed in to focus down on the holo of the twin-hulled ship. The result was hazy, but an outline of a large crest that took up a fair part of a flank of one of the twin hulls sharpened.

"May I see the whole image again, Captain, if you don't mind…"

Azular had risen to his feet. "Sit," he invited, aware that tension was sheeting her like a film.

He guided her into his chair as Ahxenta traded glances with Apnis and Lindell. The captain of the *Warrior*, intrigued, complied quickly and soon a complete holo of the odd form hung above the pad.

Kerrix stared dazedly at the rotating shape. Azular's hand tensed on her shoulder and she reached up absently to make contact, her other hand sliding up to her face as she sat back deep in thought. She sat up again, freeing her hands to commandeer Holdspan's info-pad, to that captain's evident surprise. With swift fingers she began to work on the image, raising more puzzled glances from those around her, and from Ally, who, curious, had come up to have a look.

"You've got first-rate scanners, Captain," she told Holdspan. "I'd swear it's the… it's definitely an old design. These markings show it's a flagship," she said, looking up at Azular, who was watching intently.

The science officer tightened his lips and regarded her in concern. "You recognise it," he said. It was a statement, and as she affirmed with a nod, he quietly added, "Rescue party?"

"Like hell," was the swiftly ironic retort as she shook herself back to reality. "I can't imagine why they'd send a ship like that to… *how* did it get through that ancient bypass without being shaken to pieces anyway?" she asked him. "Or without some help," she added a little more dryly, leaning back again to examine the holo.

"What ancient bypass?" Sol Treskitt asked inquisitively.

"Later," Kerrix replied. "The Norvallans are quick to scent profit and any gateway into new and potentially lucrative markets would appeal big time to some. But that's a military ship even if it *is* old."

She manipulated the info-pad again to bring up some of the readings associated with the holo, to the extreme mystification of Holdspan and Treskitt, who were swapping baffled looks.

"That's quite a power output so she's operative and as far as I can see she's not had a run in with anything she couldn't handle," was the result of the inspection. "No readings of weaponry, hull structure or drive systems but as she's shielded you wouldn't get that."

"She's not a standard spec," Azular put in from behind her as he leaned in more closely. "I don't recall seeing that outline before."

"She's not standard, no: she was a new design half a lifetime ago and only a few were built. It seemed a good idea to have self-reliant single hulls but it was found in extended trials that the design was inefficient and not practical as one entity. So they split them and used the separate hulls as training ships. The class ship was kept as a fleet flagship for state and diplomatic use and I think that's it."

"How do you know all that about what to me and my officers is an *alien* ship?" Holdspan asked enquiringly.

"We'd all like to know *that*, Ms Kerrix," Ahxenta said sharply.

The woman turned to face the commander of the *Arianrhod*. "You know damn well how I know," was the less than courteous retort.

"Xanna!" The quiet voice of Azular behind her was heavy with warning. "Other ears are out there," he reminded her in a whisper. "And you do *not* speak to Captain Ahxenta in that tone."

"I'll speak how I damn well like! And you can mind your own business! Damn! Apologies, Captain," she amended after a pause and a glance around. "I'm out of order. She's a Norvallan heavy cruiser, the *NFS Twin Star*. But she hasn't seen active service in years. She's brought out for state events and the odd political mission, but she still packs a punch. Her arms were state of the art once and her titular commander keeps them shiny. But why she's out there…"

"Captain Ahxenta may be party to this mystery, but I'm not. Will someone please tell me what the heck is going on?" Nat Holdspan demanded, looking at the officers of the *Arianrhod* and then back at Kerrix, whose hands were still poised over his info-pad.

Ahxenta sat back, her cynical expression clearly denoting that the obligation was most definitely on Kerrix to explain. The woman read the look and shot one back that was as challenging.

"That, Captain Holdspan, is a ship of the Norvallan fleet. And as I've lately found out, Norvalla is outside the charted zones, beyond the edge of Mu. It's past Kirtish, but not as far past as I'd thought," she added ruefully. "And I'm Norvallan – well, part-Norvallan."

Holdspan looked at her with probing intensity. "You're an alien?"

"You look surprised," she retorted, amused at his expression.

"Interested," he parried as Ally, whose mouth had dropped open at what he was hearing, gave an audible gasp.

The young captain turned his puzzled and somewhat wary eyes on Cinnabar Ahxenta. "You knew, Captain?" he asked.

"I've been aware for some time that Ms Kerrix was not all that she appeared," she answered wryly. "But she's humanoid enough to pass muster around here. What more do you know or suspect about that ship, *Ms* Kerrix?" she asked, turning to the woman.

"I think she's the *Twin Star*, an old Norvallan flagship. Her titular commander is Admiral Pertik Posettix, but why he'd be sent so far out, to a recently discovered anomaly on the far side of *our* charted space sectors, I don't know. Unless that wasn't his mission – he's a canny space veteran and not a fool."

She paused. "I wonder… if the Norvallans got to the site of the anomaly that brought me across zone Mu and out at the node those raiders call Starfall Exit… if there was contact between the ones that captured my shuttle and *my* people? That somehow between them they've managed to negotiate a passage through that ancient bypass?"

"Would your people negotiate with strangers that had abducted one of their own?" Azular asked.

"Point one, how would they know that I'd been taken? I imagine the report that got home was that my shuttle had been destroyed. That would please some and check any rescue mission. And point two, if there's profit to be made, *some* of my kind would negotiate the shirts off their own backs to make it. The main reason they make alliances is so that they can gain from them."

"You're a cynic," Azular grinned down.

"With good reason: my loss has likely contented a few of my kin."

"When you've both quite finished," Ahxenta cut in. "What *is* a Norvallan heavy cruiser looking for out by zone Mu if it's not you?"

Kerrix bit back the retort that was rising and raised her shoulders in doubt. "That's a very good question and I don't have an answer, but I'm convinced she's the *Twin Star*. Why she's been pulled into active service and sent so far out eludes me, unless it's a political or trade mission. I'd sure as hell like to find out, but…"

"But what?" Ahxenta persisted.

"I don't like it: it feels… wrong."

"Did you get lifesigns, Captain Holdspan?" Azular asked sagely.

It was Kerrix who replied. "No; but if you're hinting she's been taken over, it's unlikely. She'd make a fight of it and that ship has not been in a fight. And anyone taking her over isn't likely to repair her and go cruising: a ship that her own crew finds hard to handle at best and out-and-out frustrating at worst? And here she is, in the back of beyond. Or perhaps there's another bypass not related to the one by that red-orange star that sucked me in."

"You're in the realm of speculation," Azular scolded her gently.

"So who exactly *are* you?" Sol Treskitt asked the question that was no doubt in one or two of the surrounding minds.

"No offence, Commander, but that's my business, not yours."

"But you *have* been cut up over it," Ally put in from the sidelines. "You're not telling me those attacks on you were random and that there aren't people out there after you for one thing or another?"

Kerrix looked up at him as he continued in the same vein, listing the incidents for the edification of the two from the *Nyx Warrior*.

"I'm grateful for what you did for me, of course," he ended. "But trouble seems to follow you around like a dog on a string."

"Are you telling me that my services are no longer required and I should find myself another job?" she demanded.

"Well you're not working now are you? You're talking. And no," he went on at the glint in her eye. "You're welcome to stay on here as long as you do a good job," he told her, now unsure of her status.

"Then I'd better get on," she grinned maliciously. "Thank you for the use of your info-pad Captain Holdspan, and for the information. I'll need time to digest it."

"I think we all will," the captain returned, eyeing her as she rose and stalked off.

"May I have a copy of all your data on the incident, Captain?" Azular put in politely as he resumed his seat.

"Of course," was the civil reply, "And perhaps you'll let me in on what you know of Ms Kerrix? I *did* think she was an odd sort for the *Half Moon*, from what I've seen of her, but this…" His words failed.

"We can't tell you what we don't know, Nat and we can't tell you all we do," Ahxenta apprised him. "We *had* figured she was not quite usual but she's aided a couple of my officers out of trouble and for that I owe her. If you must know more, you'll have to ask her."

"And you can bet she won't tell you, Cap," Treskitt winked. "But there's nothing like a mystery to make life interesting."

"Trust me, she's not a mystery you'd like on your hands," Ahxenta stated. "But I need sustenance. You here for the duration, Nat?"

"No, I have another marketing meeting, so if you'll excuse me, I'll have to head down and find my supercargo. I expect I'll see you later at the memorial service, Captain. Here's the data, Dr Azular."

"Thank you, sir," the science officer replied, accepting the shard.

"I expect you'll be going over that with Ms Kerrix once she gets off duty?" Apnis said slyly as Holdspan and his first mate made off.

"Obviously, Commander," was the equable reply. "I'll see what else I can find out about this mysterious ship and let you know."

"Don't forget our Agrotech deal," the captain warned. "We'll be loaded by late tomorrow, we set off after that and you'd better be on board. The trip to Vreskota won't take long, only a couple of days."

"Aye, ma'am," he agreed, aware of Apnis and Lindell smirking at one another across the table.

Lunch was quickly despatched as the captain and first mate, with other senior PSS officers, had been invited to a memorial service for the five crew lost aboard the *Firedrake*. It was to take place in a small sanctuary next to the garden area of green seven of inner belt one. Captain Ahxenta had sent her condolences to Captain Ma'Lappis but had not seen him since his ship had docked.

"Who else is in?" Apnis asked as they slid into a transport tube. "The news of the service was sent out on the UV-III and as it's a rare event, I expect any PSS in the area will try to make it."

"The *Sardonyx* is in at any rate: JJ Stonecross and his first mate are just down the tube there. JJ and Pa Ma'Lappis go back a long way," the captain said, inclining her head in the relevant direction. "*Zephyr's* still around, so Jennik Kilmaur and Bo Brass will be there. And if the *Tektite's* anywhere within shooting distance, the Buckle twins will try to make it – Mora Ma'Lappis was a Buckle before she met Pa."

"Hope to hell the bunch that are targeting us and our associates don't get wind of it. They'd have a field day."

"Thanks for that," Ahxenta grunted.

The room was half-full by the time the two arrived. They nodded to colleagues in passing but made first for Captain Pa Ma'Lappis to pay their respects. Flish Ma'Lappis was with her father, Flick Poppet and several of the *Firedrake's* crew. In the distance Ahxenta could see Fleetskup, who was introducing his first mate around. She indicated the opposite side of the room and she and Apnis set off to where the captain and first mate of the *Nyx Warrior* were standing to attention.

"It's a good turnout," Captain Holdspan remarked as several more familiar faces appeared. "I see Teal and Zoa Buckle of the *Tektite* are in and there's Captain Peakfrost of the *Quarkstorm*."

"I'd heard that the *Quarkstorm* was on her way but nothing about the *Tektite*. She must just have docked," Tallica Apnis said. "Crizz will want shore leave in that case, I expect," she added to Ahxenta. "Our chief engineer," she explained to the two from the *Nyx Warrior*. "Her son's one of the *Tektite's* senior engineers."

At the reception after the service, the *Arianrhod's* officers parted to mingle with associates that they met only rarely. It was a good way of catching up on the minutiae that was not passed on via the usual PSS channels. Both were waylaid separately by Captain Fleetskup and had the opportunity to meet his latest crew member.

"I think I'm deaf," Apnis told her captain when the two caught up later. "Commander Dyne-Bek has a loud voice."

"It could crack glass," was Ahxenta's view. "I'd like to hear what Tommy Buntle makes of her. He's had his captain's ears for more years than I can remember but *she* seems to have Fleetskup in hand."

"Roger that, Cap. I've told Flish to take a few more days out. We can do without her for Vreskota as we're up to strength in medbay and we've no serious cases. Pa's not fit to command yet and they still have crew with serious injuries aboard the *Firedrake* and in Merkat's medbay, Flick Poppet told me. By the way, Flish will be given a part of Patt: Pa is having his remains compressed into diamonds and will give one to Flish to add to the one she has of her mother. I have to say I find the idea of hanging your dear departed around your neck on a chain peculiar, but I guess it's their way."

"I guess. But back aboard for us; we need to get ready for loading those agro supplies. I've heard no more on the attack on Azular and Hills is still being cagey about those cams that security missed. Maybe you could check with Kit Biernop to see what he's heard?"

"Will do, Cap. I'll link from the shuttle in case he wants a meet, but I doubt it. I expect Crizz has heard the *Tektite's* in, but we'll want her for the trip, so she'll have to be quick if she wants to see Sim."

In the event, Biernop had heard no more than that the cams were part of a larger network along green twelve and green four that had been traced back and dismantled. He promised to keep in touch and the shuttle made the trip back to the *Arianrhod* without incident.

Azular had been busy and had called around to try to find out more about the ship that had been seen by the *Nyx Warrior*. The *Warrior's* senior science officer, Bix Holt, was young and sharp and had figured that the power use was great because the ship was cloaked and her hull highly shielded. He had also deduced that she was topping up air. He had picked up an ion trail in the local area but could not pin it to the ship, nor could he figure her drive technology or weapons. The design was new to him and a trawl through ISP records was no help.

The Berzic thanked him without offering his own points of view, made a few links to ISP sources and collated the data he had to hand on sightings of strange vessels to check if the design had been seen before. The results he was keen to pass to Kerrix at their next date, after she had finished her stint in the *Half Moon*.

The two met as arranged in her quarters on green level twelve. She was late, but had given him a key and granted him voice access.

"Merry was delayed," she said as she stripped off her work attire.

"Merry? That's unlike her," Azular said, turning from the comm where he had been busy. "She's very efficient and always has been."

"She had a date," was the arch reply, with an enigmatic smile.

"With whom?"

"None of your business, Azular Azular."

She was trying to assume an air of relaxed content and was failing, he realised. He sat meditating until she had showered and changed and then caught her in his arms as she made for the catering area.

"What's wrong, Xanna? You're as tightly strung as a harp. It's that business with Captain Holdspan and the Norvallan ship isn't it? And other things. Has Ally been pushing for answers?"

"He thinks he's bitten off more than he can chew," she chuckled. "I was a little forceful. Your captain was certainly unimpressed."

"You were rude."

"She scares the hell out of me and it's the way I cope. Is she really as awesome as half the galaxy thinks she is?"

"Stop prevaricating," he ordered, steering her to the sofa. "What's biting you and how can I help?"

"You can help by keeping hold of me," she said tensely. "I feel as if I'm coming apart. Things seem to be going very fast, Azular. There were a lot of ears in the *Half Moon* at alert and Jez said he thought he saw a guy with a recorder, but he hid it when he saw Jez watching. He wasn't a regular, though a few of *them* were gawking. I think my reactions were a tad impulsive, but seeing that ship shook me."

"Impulsive? Rash, you mean. But for all that, we didn't get the whole story did we?" Azular taxed her.

"Of course you didn't, I'm not a total fool. Captain Holdspan was taken aback, though."

"Xanna, I haven't pushed for answers and I won't, but I'd like to understand more about who and what you are and how you got to be in this situation. And no, whatever you tell me will not end up in my captain's ears – unless I deem it necessary or she orders me to tell."

She laughed. "So you're an honourable man, sir; there aren't many like you about. But in return, I want to know what you've been up to half the afternoon. You haven't been sat round here doing nothing."

"Deal," he grinned. "And then we go out to dinner, hopefully in a place that we won't be followed, shot at or otherwise unsettled. And then back to my place?"

"You live dangerously, mister."

"I somehow suspect you do the same, Xanna Kerrix."

Ahxenta and her first mate spent the next morning in inner belt two, in talks with security and marketing. After a lunch in the *Half Moon*, where Kerrix was conspicuous by her absence and Merry singing like a songbird, the two set out for their shuttle berth in green twelve, where they were to meet Azular. All three would be heading back up to *Arianrhod* to prep her for departure later in the evening. The cargo for Vreskota was aboard and was being checked and locked down, after which the ship needed only final clearances to head out.

"He'd better be on time," the captain said firmly to the first mate as the two walked along the dim passage that would take them to the entry to their shuttle bay. "It's been another eventful stop-off. I'm beginning to think that the Web isn't as safe as it used to be."

"It never *was* safe, Cap, it's just that we seem to be on more hit lists than usual these days. Some people out there have started their own little war and we're the opposition. And look who come hither," Apnis added as two forms appeared around a corner in the opposite direction. "Just come from *her* shuttle, by the look of it."

Azular was in uniform and carrying his kitbag. Kerrix was in work fatigues. A playful finger pointed at the man suggested argument but whatever it was, she stopped when she saw the two. The woman was civil when the four met. They had been installing new nav-charts into her craft, it transpired, and Azular had copied hers for the *Arianrhod*. The PSS would thus have charts that extended the mapped galactic zones into Norvallan space, at least at a basic level, he explained. He seemed inordinately pleased at the prospect.

There were few others in the vicinity and apart from one or two curious stares, none of the local foot traffic gave them more than a cursory once-over. Kerrix had just taken her leave and was trying to dissuade Azular from seeing her home when heavy footfalls coming towards them stopped and a shirring that sounded like the slither of a weapon from its housing made all four pause and half turn.

"Ahxenta!"

The voice was the hiss of a snake and was enough to alert them to trouble. Both the captain and the first mate were fast, their phase rifles in their hands in seconds. A hard thrust sent Ahxenta to the floor as she felt rather than saw the flash of a phase bolt that missed her by a fraction. The deck hit her face with a smack. She lay stunned as her world spun in weird slow motion and two more bolts rent the air. Apnis' screaming expletive echoed in her ears as she struggled to haul herself up. Her first mate cannoned into her as a savage shove by an external force bowled them both over. They fought themselves upright, trying to make sense of what had happened. There was one unmoving stranger on the deck and the rear view of another could be seen making off along green twelve.

"Azular! Azular!"

That was Kerrix and the dread and passion in her voice brought Ahxenta back to full awareness. The utter fury in the eyes that bored into the captain's was palpable.

"You look after him!" she spat. "That bastard's mine!"

She threw off Apnis' restraining hand and shot off down the passage like a streak of light.

"Let her go," Ahxenta snapped as she hauled up her communit to request immediate medical aid and a security detachment. "Make sure that other bastard can't get up," she ordered her first mate, beginning a thorough scan of her unconscious senior science officer.

The phase bolt had caught Azular in the back as he and Kerrix in one split second had thrown their weights against the captain to push her out of the way of the aimed rifle. The gunman now on the deck had also aimed at the captain but his shot had hit the bulkhead as the first mate's stun bolt caught him and brought him down.

Ahxenta was on her knees cursing volubly and calling her science officer's name. There was no response.

"Cinnabar…" Apnis began in an agonised voice.

"I'm getting a pulse," she croaked. "Any of our own medics still down here apart from Flish?"

"I'll check."

Even as the first mate was notifying duty officer Whisper Earbleat of the attack and asking for information, a team of medics hauling a gurney and emergency gear raced up, scattering the few onlookers in the way. Azular was hardly stabilised and locked into the trolley when two security guards bolted in. The captain was short. She and her first mate were for medbay: the guards could deal with the gunman on the ground *and* send more after the escaped fugitive.

The race to the medical facilities seemed to take an inordinate time, though flashing lights on the way warned of the emergency and transport tube stops were overridden to provide a fast link. A second team was waiting at an admissions station to assess him and Azular was soon out of sight. The medical officer taking the verbal report from the captain was skilled and wasted no time.

"Hell, I'm still shaking," Ahxenta admitted as soon as the man had left them in the waiting room next to the emergency admissions suite. "What the hell's happened to Kerrix and that other son of a bitch?"

"I'll see if I can get more from security, Cap," the first mate said softly. "And then we get you fixed: you've got blood on your face."

Apnis strode to a wall comm station, leaving the captain to dig up hot coffee and to contact *Arianrhod* to apprise her crew of the latest. The few on leave, apart from Ma'Lappis, were to be recalled at once, she ordered Earbleat. She had just done when Flintlock sprinted through the entry. The doctor had received word from the ship after Apnis' call and had wrapped up her business double quick.

"Any news on Azular?" the chief medic demanded. "What in hell happened to your face, Cinnabar? Sit down here," she directed. "I'll go grab an emergency aid pack."

"Nothing from security apart from a second squad's been sent to green twelve, but the officer in charge refused to give me details," the first mate reported when she came over. "Where's the doc shot off to?" she went on as she gratefully accepted the proffered cup.

As the captain explained, Flintlock appeared with the kit and came over to begin her task. Apnis brought her up to date on the doings of the previous half hour but the doctor had other news.

"Saw another emergency team prepping for action next door," she said as she swabbed the captain's face. "Someone's on their way up with a casualty; a shooting, somebody said. It sounds like they've just arrived," she noted as a cacophony of noises erupted outside.

Ahxenta turned, puzzled, to look at her two officers. "I know that voice," she said roughly as she pushed the doctor's hand away.

"So do I," Apnis agreed, and both women rose and made quickly to the door, followed seconds later by the *Arianrhod's* chief medic.

Outside, a bloody and dishevelled Captain Nathan Holdspan had just relinquished his burden to the emergency response team that had met him and was giving them a rapid run down of events, as a duo of efficient medics quickly prepped their patient for transport within.

The captain of the *Nyx Warrior* stood back to let the gurney pass, his face a mask of concern, though his tones were calm as he instructed the armed lieutenant that had escorted him to return to green twelve to assist Commander Treskitt. He would stay in medbay until he had news. As he turned to a medical officer who stood by to lead him next door to take details, he spied the three from the *Arianrhod*. He saluted them with a quick nod but his mouth was grim as he followed the man over to a side table. The others noted that he was limping and winded but his answers to the questions put to him were short, precise and audible. Apart from her physical injuries, the victim had taken a phase bolt – whether it was a crease or a ricochet, Holdspan did not know but the weapon that had dealt it was set to kill and the shock of the hit had been enough to render her unconscious.

The three officers of the *Arianrhod* had been eyeing each other in silence: they had recognised Kerrix as she was being strapped in and prepped. At length, his interview done, the captain was told by the medical officer that a medic would be sent in to deal with his injuries. Flintlock stepped up to give her credentials and state that she would attend to him. Holdspan nodded in acquiescence.

"I'll get more coffee," Apnis said shortly. "You look like you need it, Nat. Go and sit down in a comfortable chair. You too, Cap."

Flintlock had insisted that she would deal with her patient before he was allowed to pass on any details of what had happened down on green twelve and her med scanner was soon busy.

"Nothing broken; it's a strained tendon and I can strap it for now. You've used your fists. I'll take samples of what's not yours in case you need them for ID later," she added. "Now let me look at your face. Someone's hit *you* with a hard fist."

"He got the same in return," was the dry retort as he winced at the application of pressure.

Ahxenta let her chief medic finish before she faced him. "I take it you met the bastard that had Kerrix on his tail."

"Yes," he confirmed. "How is your officer, Dr Azular wasn't it?"

He could see the pain in her eyes and the creased face that told of her grief as she admitted that she had no idea: he was in surgery and they were waiting for news.

"You know what happened, then?" she asked him.

"The bare bones," he said, taking the cup Apnis offered. "Sol and I had finished in marketing and were heading for our shuttle on green twelve. We'd just got out of the transport tube when the guy ran right at us: almost bowled us over. He had a rifle and looked capable of using it. People were scattering left and right so we tried to stop him. We thought he'd committed a crime and was making a run for it. He lunged at us like a lunatic and he *was* aiming to use that gun. He had some strength and it was all Sol and I could do to hold him. Then Ms Kerrix rode in at high speed, spitting quarks. She jumped on his back, tearing at his hair, trying to pull him over. Once he was down she was like a hell-cat, kicking lumps out of him, but he was fighting back and she took a few hits before we could haul them apart."

Holdspan shook his head. "Sol hit him with a heavy stun but it didn't stop him. Hell knows *what* he is, it took another two stun shots to down him. I was trying to hang onto Ms Kerrix: she was distressed and cursing." He paused. "She threatened him with extreme violence. I think her exact words were, "If he doesn't make it, I'll dig your heart out with a blunt knife and feed it to the damn rats!" I realised at that point that it was something really serious. And then she told us that he and another had tried to kill you, Captain, but had missed and hit Dr Azular. I called security. But I'd made the mistake of assuming the maniac was out cold – he wasn't, he was far from it."

Treskitt had begun to search the man and Holdspan was trying to escort Kerrix to medbay when the first mate of the *Nyx Warrior* was driven bodily backwards by a punch. The very much awake gunman was on his knees, rifle ready and murder in his eyes. At that instant the shocked captain of the *Warrior* realised that *he* was the target. The man was looking straight at him, his finger on the trigger. A second later Holdspan felt a painful thump as Kerrix' weight sent him to the deck. He heard the bolt hit the wall as another seared through the air to hit his assailant. It was followed by a second as the first had only slowed the man. He looked up, stunned: two of his junior officers, alerted by the noise, had raced up, realised their own were in trouble and had no hesitation in shooting first and asking questions later.

"You've got them well trained," Apnis noted in an undertone.

It was as he was picking himself off the floor that the captain had noticed that Kerrix was on the deck and inert. A small dent on the bulkhead where the bolt had struck but not pierced gave him the clue and he had taken a closer look. A rip in the woman's clothing and blood across her back and shoulder told him that the shot had either struck in passing or she had caught a ricochet. Realising that Merkat's medbay was almost straight up from where they were, he decided to carry her. He told Treskitt to alert the emergency room and ordered one of his two officers to escort him to clear the way and prevent any boarders on the transport tube to green three.

"And you know the rest," he concluded. "I left Sol to clear up the mess. But who was that guy? And why did he aim for me?"

"The uniform and the rank," Apnis hazarded, "Though he called *you* by name, Cinnabar. I used heavy stun on the one I put down and it was enough to keep him there but the other one chucked me aside as if I was a rag doll. I'd guess he was a lot more cyber than human."

A trill on his wrist communit alerted Captain Holdspan to a call and he excused himself to take it; it was Treskitt, he told them.

"He's seriously shook up, despite the brave face he's putting on," Apnis said to her colleagues. "He's maybe finally realised that life in space isn't the perpetual adventure he thought it was."

"He's young; he'll learn," the captain replied, stretching. "But he's quick and he's not an easy target, I'll give him that. And he looks out for his own. He'll make a first-rate commander one of these days."

"I bet they said the same of you when you first started out," the first mate told her. "Here he is. Wonder what the news is?"

The news was that Treskitt was in security and both gunmen were under guard in medbay. The one Apnis had decked was Treskk and part of a criminal group wanted on charges including extortion and robbery with violence. The ID of the other bore the name Mek Brisk but the man had undergone recent surgery to alter his exterior and upgrade already extensive cyber implants. He had worn a chameleon vest to blanket his biosigns, but a full scan and medical tests had been sufficient to pull up a definitive ID. Security had him listed as a fugitive called Berg Brack, although they also had him under the alias Hoxiz. He was considered high risk. The reactions of his hearers told the captain of the *Nyx Warrior* that they had heard the name before and were aware of the man and his capabilities.

Ahxenta gave a quick rundown of part of their dealings with him and his associates, recalling Holdspan's theories on the nature of the crew of the ship that attacked the *Tallulah* near Silverglass. If they *had* been Hoxiz-like clones, then the medical skills the hostiles and their heirs had perfected to produce them had to be highly advanced and in use in more than one centre. Azular had suggested Minch Fettin as a site of one such facility and Hoxiz had been exposed previously as possibly hailing from zone Mu, where that planet was located. The rapidity of the alteration that he had undergone would be consistent with such advanced surgery, was Dr Flintlock's opinion.

"Worth passing the news to Thal that security here has Hoxiz?" Apnis murmured to Ahxenta. "*He* wants him and I'd bet he'd be able to keep him safer than all the security nets they have here."

"You have a point," the captain agreed wearily. "I'll call Earbleat and have her send the link. And I have another call to make."

She rose and made for the privacy of the comm booth to use her own communit. Her second link was to Vettarista to apprise her of what had befallen, although she suspected that the ISP agent already knew. Duty done, she returned to the other three and sat back down. As she did so a noise at the entry heralded the arrival of the medical officer. A strange prickle told her it was news of Azular and she rose again, motioning the others to remain seated.

"Captain Ahxenta?" the man said, coming forward.

She led him off to one side as the other three watched in anxiety. The officer left minutes later and the captain walked slowly back to her companions. Her face was calm but her own officers could tell that she was far from tranquil as she sat down again.

"Cinnabar?" the first mate asked gently.

"He's made it through surgery and he's stable. He's very weak and the final outcome can't be predicted with certainty, but he'll make it."

Apnis leaned against the captain's shoulder with a deep sigh of relief. "Thank hell."

"Axellina, I need you to find out what you can from your contacts here. And I want you to stay in the Web while we're on our trip to Vreskota. He can't be moved, obviously. I'll assign you two guards as well. Flish Ma'Lappis is still here, so she'll be your back-up."

"We're still going to Vreskota, then?" Apnis queried.

"Yes. I put my hand to a contract and they need that gear. Azular would understand. They won't let me into his bay to see him as he's still post-operative but I can have a look through the obs window — the medic told me which unit. You're with me, Doctor. Tallica, you wait here with Nat for news of Kerrix and check in with security to see if there's anything new that end."

"Aye, Cap. I'll link to the ship as well and make sure we're set to go as soon as you give the word. Want me to give the crew the news of Azular or would you prefer to do that yourself?"

"Tell them now; I won't keep them in suspense. Come on, Doc."

The chief medic was familiar with the ins and outs of medbay and led Ahxenta through a maze to the surgical wing and an area adjacent to the theatre suite. Their IDs were checked at every step but they were expected. A nurse-tech at the reception pod took them to the iso-bay and left them. Whilst Flintlock evaluated his life sign readings on the external monitor, the captain gazed through the view portal at the form wired into the intensive care cradle.

"He looks like hell," she said softly, not taking her eyes from him.

"He'll do all right," the doctor assured her. "He's a tough old bird, Cinnabar. And our uniforms have built-in shielding, so thanks be he was wearing his. The shot didn't penetrate his lungs or he *would* have been in trouble. But until the nerve damage and the spinal trauma can be fully assessed we won't know for sure how much movement he'll get back. And it'll take time, it's not something that can be fixed in a few days or weeks. But what's eating at you, Cinnabar?"

"That shot was meant for me."

"Any of us would have done the same, you know that. As you said of Nat Holdspan less than an hour ago, it's the instinct to protect your own. And like it or not, Kerrix has that same instinct."

"I suspect Azular concerned her more," was the harsh rejoinder.

"You think? Well I don't. She respects you a lot. She doesn't show it, in fact often the reverse, but it's there. And as Azular's captain, she knows how he'd feel if anything happened to you."

Ahxenta sighed. "Let's get back and see if there's news. If Kerrix doesn't make it, Azular will tear heads off. But there are a few things I want you to organise while you're here."

With a last troubled look at the cradle and its immobile occupant, she turned for the way out, outlining what she wanted put in place for the care and security of her senior science officer.

Apnis had not been idle. *Arianrhod* was being readied for her trip and two guards were on their way to provide escort for Dr Flintlock. Quarters had been arranged for them and Apnis and Holdspan had been joined by Ma'Lappis. Merkat security had scoured both areas of attack and collected samples for analysis but had not reported. The weapons toted by the gunmen were being examined but apart from their relation to high-spec hostile technology, nothing more had been found; at least, that was what Apnis had been told, but she had called Kit Biernop to update him and ask him to find out all he could.

There had been no word of Kerrix and the restless Holdspan was at a comms console making his own links. Sol Treskitt had stopped in but had been sent to make waves at marketing: the *Nyx Warrior* was awaiting a cargo and she would be off before long.

"We had a medbay rep in about fees the second you were out the door," the irate first mate notified Ahxenta. "Naturally we'll take care of our own, but Kerrix is an unknown and they want credit up front or she'll be shunted to the charity wing. Nat's furious, as she's a crime victim and the fees should come out of the Victim Support Unit's pocket. He's authorised the rep to charge her care to him meanwhile as he figures he owes her that. Cottontail's still portside as she was visiting Sim so I've got her checking our shuttle. She'll come up with us. The rest of our crew are aboard. I've got Azular's gear here for the doc to take, so we're set to go. How did he look?"

The captain gave her opinion in a quiet voice as Flintlock updated Dr Ma'Lappis on the technical details. She had almost done when the medical officer in charge of the two cases came in. Holdspan stood up quickly and he and Ahxenta crossed the floor to arrive at the door at the same time. The other three waited, reading their expressions. The relief was clear on the face of the captain of the *Nyx Warrior* but it gave way to a baffled look as the med officer began to question the captain of the *Arianrhod*. The murmuring rose to an angry buzz as the irritation in her voice grew. Holdspan looked shocked.

"The culprits were arrested, charged and prosecuted," Ahxenta said clearly. "They are now serving sentences in a penal facility. The reason Ms Kerrix was *not* brought to this medbay at the time was that she had earlier been the target of an assault here with the connivance, we suspect, of Herta, your former senior surgical officer. *She*, as I'm sure you know, was recently arrested, though she's evaded justice. That's all you're getting; and I expect to be kept informed of Ms Kerrix' condition as well as that of my officer."

"They've noticed the cuts on her back, then," the first mate said in a low voice to the two medics.

"They could hardly miss them," Flintlock replied shortly. "They were damn apparent last I saw and she point-blank refused aesthetics. But Holdspan looks thankful enough, so I guess she'll make it."

That was confirmed when the two came back. Kerrix had taken a ricochet which had resulted in extensive injuries to her back, shoulder and right arm. They were not life-threatening and she would recover more rapidly than Azular. Her biosigns were causing curiosity, as was the implant in her left shoulder that had been noted last time she was in medbay, but apart from that, all was as expected.

"Keep a close watch on her, Axellina," Ahxenta directed. "Given what happened last time she *was* in here, there may be trouble."

"I'd like a word with you, Captain, if you don't mind," Holdspan interrupted. "In private, if you please."

The captain guessed the topic, but deeming that he had a right to know part of the mystery that bit at him, she nodded. "Over there."

He surprised her with his opening resolve, but after a pause she agreed it was practical. He then came to his main point: he wanted to know more of Kerrix and her arrival in the Web. Ahxenta edified him on some points, including her implants, for if there were people out there with malice in mind, it was better he knew. But as before she insisted that he must ask Kerrix for more. He nodded, frustrated, but was wise enough to be content. There was another thing that he had to ask and did so hesitantly, gauging her reaction. At her reluctant accord, he set off to organise his people and check in with his ship.

"I take it Nat wanted more details on Kerrix than he had?" Apnis greeted the captain.

"He did and he got very few," she told her. "But the boy's savvier than I gave him credit for. He's going to post two of his own security officers down here while he's off on his next cruise, to keep watch on Kerrix and the doings in the Web and report back to him."

"Interesting," Flintlock stated, glancing over to where Holdspan stood at the far wall, clearly making links. "Has he got a crush on her or is he just covering all his bases?"

"Payback for saving his skin and he's mighty curious, given what went down in the *Half Moon* when she took over his info-pad and used it like an expert to tell him things he'd never heard. He likes to be in the know about things going on out there as he thinks it gives him an edge in trade and in keeping his ship and crew safe, and his rep intact as the hotshot of the PSS fleet. And he has a point," the captain conceded. "And no, I don't think he has a crush on her: she's old enough to be his mother."

Flintlock laughed. "So are you and he's got a crush on you."

"You'd better be joking, Doctor."

"No comment. You and Tallica ready for shipping up?"

"Yes. There's nothing more to do here and I don't intend to be grilled by security for hours. They've got the perps so they can damn well charge them with attempted murder and get them locked up for a very long time. You're with me, Tallica. If you want more time with your family, Flish, take it."

"Yes ma'am," the young medic responded.

"He'll be all right, Cap, I'll see to it," Flintlock promised, noting the concern that still shaded her eyes. "I'll send you regular updates, on him and anything else relevant. You'll only be gone a few days."

Ahxenta nodded and she and Apnis stepped over to bid farewell to Holdspan before making their way out and towards the nearest transport tube for their shuttle, where Cottontail awaited them.

It was a sober duty crew that greeted the three when they made the bridge. Earbleat quickly vacated the command chair, an enquiry after Azular on her lips. The captain was positive, aware that every ear was pricked. The second mate confirmed that Port Control was aware of their intentions and final clearances were in place; the ship could depart at her convenience.

"This'll be a fast about-turn. I want everyone sharp," Ahxenta told her bridge crew. "Box, plot a direct course to Vreskota Two, avoiding the worm-pocket off the Helix Cluster. And keep us well away from the Orriga Two asteroid field. Dox, take us out slowly. Shields up as soon as we make the bypass and long-range sensors on line. Yours too, Greffy, I'll need all the data your arrays can bring in. We need to see or hear anything before it gets within spitting distance. Tallica, liaise with Lindell and his team to make sure we're ready to drop our cargo as soon as we make port – after they've paid for it of course."

"The Vreskotans are reliable as far as payment and cargo pick-up go," Apnis soothed. "We've never had trouble in that quarter."

"There's always a first time," was the dark reply. "But one of their reps checked it this end, so it should pass muster. Chief, give us as much speed as you can without overcooking our engines."

"You got it, Cap," Cottontail returned.

"All weapons systems primed," Earbleat confirmed. "*Loki VII* standing by in her bay," she added brightly.

"Hell, nothing stops her and that damned pet cargo pod of hers, does it?" Apnis grumbled quietly to the captain.

The huge ship was loosed from her net of docking struts, their red lights shading to green as Dox slowly manoeuvred her out. Her space-pink hide glowed against the star-spangled blackness of space as with a slow turn, she banked and picked up speed to head for the nearest bypass and her route across zone Alpha.

The captain sighed. It was good to feel space around you, she said to herself, but the science station looked incomplete. As the bridge stations called in current status and the holo-grid dropped to show the starfield and their path through it, she sighed again.

"Time to bypass, Lieutenant Dox?"

"Forty minutes, Captain," Dox replied at once.

"Steady as she goes."

"Aye, ma'am. Get me the fastest route to where we're going," the helmswoman instructed her sidekick at navigation.

"On it," Box replied softly. "It won't take long once we're on the bypass," he added to fill the silence. "I expect it'll be quiet as far as Beta Zegonia, as we'll still be in ISP space."

"Don't count your cookies, we've had trouble in ISP space before. Remember last time we were heading to Silverglass? Across Epsilon, and that's almost completely ISP. We were running to the rescue of the *Tallulah* and if the *Nyx Warrior* hadn't stepped in, we'd have had been in even more trouble. And get that coffee can off my console – this is the bridge of a starship, not a frigging café."

"Route plotted and laid in," Box announced to deflect any more criticism. "Thought any more about what we were talking about last night, Romanna?" he added in a hushed tone as he leaned in closer.

"No," she said shortly. "And this is not the place to bring it up."

"I saw a really nice ring when I was down in the Web, in the green nine market on inner two. You'd like it."

"Button it and mind your boards," she instructed.

Box sighed dolefully and Apnis exchanged an amused glance with the captain. "Lindell confirms that the Vreskotans know we'll need a quick stop-off. They'll have moving gear in place and they have a rep from Agrotech Stellar out there to deal with technical details. Did you get anything else out of Nat while you were talking to him, Cap?"

"One or two things," Ahxenta replied evasively and with a lift to her lip that denoted something not to be discussed. "The *Warrior's* for Sevolb to drop a cargo and then up to Selliden to collect a load, though he wouldn't tell me what he's carrying."

The captain then gave her first mate a rundown of what she had told Holdspan of Kerrix. She was interrupted by Lindell, who wanted a private word about a contract that had just come to his attention.

"I'll head on down to his office," Ahxenta said. "I need the walk and I want to check with medbay. You have the helm, but one cheep of anything unusual and I want to know, even if it's trivial."

"Aye, ma'am. We'll hit the bypass shortly so look out for bumps."

Lindell and his team, ears always open for a good deal, had heard of a small batch of comms-grade crystals for sale at Brown Amber at a sound rate but they would have to be bid for and collected sooner rather than later. Amber was in the opposite direction to their next two arranged ports of Stinward and Tressic Major but it meant good profits if the goods could be processed at better than the going rates by the captain's contact on Freskat Six. If they could reshuffle cargo scheduling they could make Amber, but one or both of their existing contracts would have to slide a little and it would result in *Arianrhod* being away from the Web for longer, Lindell clarified tactfully.

Ahxenta sat back and reflected, stroking her chin. "I hope to get Azular back before we ship out for Stinward. Dr Flintlock is sorting things. That reminds me: once we're back in the Web she'll have a list of stores. Make sure she gets all she needs. And I can maybe call in a favour or two. Stand by on the Brown Amber deal, but see if you can get a quality guarantee on the products. I'll get back to you."

The captain's next stop was medbay for a chat with her staff there; they were two experienced medics short and she wanted to make sure they were not overstretched. All being in order, she set off for her office to make some long distance links. She had had an idea.

"What gives, Cap?" Apnis asked when Ahxenta finally reappeared.

"A smart deal on a batch of crystals from Brown Amber. Lindell's checking the quality of the goods. If it's as high as they claim it'll be worth bidding for. They've to be shifted quickly and as we're tight time-wise, I put a couple of calls out. *Obsidian's* on her way into the Web. She'll dock in a couple of hours for a quick stop for a load for Burr Two, so Grey's agreed to do a pick-up at Amber if we get the deal and will bring it into the Web if he can. *Obsidian* should make it back before we head out for Stinward. If we miss each other, he can hold onto the consignment and pass it on whenever. I've told Lindell to go ahead if the stuff's as advertised and we can sort the details of collection later."

"Grey knows what went down?" the first mate murmured.

"I told him. I didn't put it out on the UV and neither did Nat Holdspan, so I gave Grey the green light to mention it, but only in private comms. Any of the fleet shipping into Merkat will hear of it."

"Anything from Axellina?"

"No. Nor have I had anything more from Vettarista. She'd heard of the incident on green twelve but not that we were involved."

"Kit Biernop hasn't called either, but I doubt he'd link to me here as there are too many eyes and ears and itching fingers on comms his end," Apnis said. "And it's early yet, we've only been out a few hours. And so far, so good: traffic's low, none of it is close and there've been no alerts on any channels that we can pick up."

"Long may it continue. But here's Lindell. I hope it's good news."

It was. The supercargo had received the requested guarantees and had put the bid in immediately. It had been accepted.

"I'd better get back to Grey," Ahxenta said as she rose. "Even if we can't get the crystals set right off, it's profit in our back pockets."

The next day and a half passed with no alarms and little comms buzz. The flight between the Helix Cluster and the edge of the Orriga Two asteroid field was made smoothly. Flintlock had linked in, four hourly at first, with news of Azular. The details the captain kept to herself and her first mate, but she issued regular reports to let the crew know that his progress was fair. The doctor was in fact anxious: it was slow and she could not gauge the level of nerve damage. He was conscious and could talk, but was weak. He had been told about Kerrix. It had upset him but they had not met as she was in no state to be moved and Flintlock would not sanction a comms link.

Flintlock had also taken it upon herself to send on word of Kerrix to Nat Holdspan via the guards he had posted. *She* was holding her own but her previous injuries were giving rise to curiosity among the medbay staff tasked with her care, as were her novel implants. And she had had visitors, as Vetta and Merry had both called in. The news was a hot topic in the *Half Moon*, Flintlock noted in her most recent report. The doctor had gone in to notify Ally and had found that not only did he know, but his regulars were taking bets on how long it would take Ahxenta to return and shake security up over its lapses.

The two gunmen were still in medbay and under secure guard, the new chief surgical officer had assured the doctor. The Treskk would be released to custody soon as his injuries had been slight but Hoxiz had apparently taken serious hurt. Flintlock could find out very little about his forward path and had set Ensign Marks to dig up more.

That news convinced the captain that she had been right to pass word of Hoxiz' capture to Thal, but she had heard nothing from him other than confirmation that he had received the message. None of her regular contacts had heard anything of the *Kel'Moth*, although the *Kel'Beth* had called into Delta Iridium and had caused quite a stir.

Arianrhod was four hours away from Vreskota Two when a link came in for the captain. Bellfish was incredulous as he turned to inform Ahxenta that a personal and private interview was requested. The link had come in via at least four relay stations and was hemmed about with high-level security coding.

"Who the hell is it?" the first mate asked the comms officer.

"Bick Micklemouse," was the short reply.

After several minutes and a number of comments well-laced with expletives, the captain ordered the link put through to her office.

"You're with me, Tallica. Earbleat, you have the conn; keep us on course and our eyes on everything in range. And monitor each iota of this chat. Mr Bellfish, analyse that message and its source and liaise with tactical and science. I want to know how he made that link."

"Aye, ma'am," echoed around the bridge as the two stood up.

"What in blazes does the little pipsqueak want?" Apnis queried as she and Ahxenta made for the office. "Last time we saw him he was narked to be dumped at Selliden because you'd let the Port Authority in on his dealings as Froyd Melson and his links to the slimy Spendle Doosbak, who's now been deprived of his position in the Coalition Council and presumably some of his platinum level credit slips – as far as we know. He may have oozed his way back in by this time."

"No doubt we'll be given some version of a story, but I expect it'll be one word of truth in ten and he'll want a favour. Or he's been put up to it by his very devious controllers, some of whom are probably still around and operating his mouth."

"Not Hoxiz, as he's still on Merkat – the last we heard that is," the first mate added acerbically. "Maybe Thal's sprung him by now."

"You wish. If this is a game, I'm not up for playing it," the captain growled as she sat at her console and began to set up the recording and security gear. "And I want to know how he got through."

The crackling image of the trader sharpened as Bellfish brought in more relays. He looked much as usual and as far as they could make out of the view around him, he was in a tight space, possibly his ship.

"Well, what is it?" Ahxenta demanded. "I have very little time."

Micklemouse was in his ship on Lonagan, he told them glibly. The Selliden authorities had enquired, found little and sent him away with the order to stay gone. Doosbak had pulled strings to get him off the planet, but *he* had now vanished and his buddy was urgently seeking him, hence the link to *Arianrhod*. The great scope of that ship and her captain gave Micklemouse hope that she might enquire at the ports of call on her route for the missing man. He had last been seen by his friend on Lonagan Four a day before a meeting Doosbak had set up with trade contacts from Sevolb. He had now missed two meetings and his contacts wanted him found. Sceptical, the captain insisted on details of the contacts, their location and their dealings with the two. From his dithering and his glances about, the man was clearly too scared to say and was being watched. Ahxenta cited the influence and long arms of the Coalition Council as a source of help and his eyes widened. He had not gone to that body for aid.

"Pack of lies," Apnis stated roundly. "What do you *really* want and how did you manage to link to us?"

The man licked his lips and restated his concerns, but upon sharp probing let out that Doosbak had told him that the talks were about transporting small cases of high-tech nano-scale weapons parts from Lonagan to Minch Fettin, using Micklemouse's ship.

Ahxenta shook her head. "Which would mean a heap of credit for you. You always were a lousy liar and your talent in that line has not changed. You've got ten seconds to tell me how and why you made this link or I shut it down and inform every central security agency in every sector of every zone of you, your shady dealings and your very corrupt friends. Do you understand me, Mr Micklemouse?"

He looked at her, horrified. "You wouldn't!"

"The hell I wouldn't and you damn well know it. Eight seconds."

They had been here before and he did know it. "The contacts we were to meet say they don't know where he is. They told me to find him; they thought he'd gone to ground because the Coalition Council has dredged up some stuff on him and it wants to talk to him about it," he confessed sullenly. "They told me to try you and gave me the codes and the data to make the link."

"They did what?" the captain flared, aware that the man's eyes were roaming the den he was in when they were not gazing at her and her first mate as if trying to work out where they were and what they were thinking. "You're going to tell me right now who and what they are or I'll personally send someone to wipe you and your beat-up little ship off the face of the galaxy! You got me?"

Not for the first time Ahxenta wished she had Azular with her. At that point a note flashed up on her monitor. Greffy had probed the relay sequence used to bounce the link and had traced it via Orange 2334, Mizreel Point, Lonagan Four and thus to Keeant. Ahxenta's eyes blazed. Mizreel Point was an ISP relay station in zone Alpha, in Coalition space, but Keeant she knew was a remote colony world of the Friskianx League and close to the border of ISP-controlled zone Epsilon.

As the man's eyes bulged she spoke again. "Not that you're on Lonagan Four. You're on Keeant. The truth, or you *are* space dust."

"Spendle *has* disappeared," he blurted out. "They say I'll be next if I don't do what they say to get him back, because they say he took a couple of cases of the miniaturised high-tech weapons bits with him when he ran off. I *am* in my ship and I've scrambled my data output but I don't know how much they can pick up. And I don't know who they are. One of them I'm sure I saw on Mellifly, at that underground medical facility where I was treated. I think *he* was like that Hoxiz, as he felt like the same kind. The others I hadn't met before but Spendle said they were from Sevolb. I made for Keeant as it's near ISP space and I hoped I could make it into zone Epsilon, but they found me."

"And where does *Arianrhod* fit in?" Ahxenta demanded. "And how did they get the link to me?"

"I think they figured if I got you on board they could get to you. They knew you'd left the Web a short time ago and knew you'd made for the bypass on a heading for Beta Zegonia. *And* they said they'd be able to track me no matter where I went, like they did before. They know the spec of my ship and I can't ditch her, she's all I've got. But I don't know how they got the link to your ship. They've got spies all over the place, maybe even in the Trades Alliance. I don't know."

"You don't know much, do you, Micklemouse? Where's Hoxiz now?" the captain demanded.

"I don't know."

"End of conversation, Micklemouse," Ahxenta snarled, smacking her hand down to break the link. "Cut comms, bridge," she called as she rose. "I didn't like what I heard and I had the odd feeling he was stalling for time. Let's go: if they know we've taken the bypass on this heading and what our cargo manifest is, they'll have a damned good idea where we're making. Silent running!" she called out the second she entered the bridge. "Get our cloak up, helm and get those long-range scanners working overtime."

She sat down, pulled her boards across and scanned her bridge stations' output. "Good work, Greffy," she told him. "Helm, bring us about and set course for the Marridan beacon. Crank up the engines, Chief, and divert every spare iota of power from our other systems to give us speed. Box, plot a convoluted course to Vreskota and bring us in from the Velish side."

"Whoa Cinnabar! That'll take us near the Outer Reaches, between those rocks and the edge of the Orriga Two," the first mate whistled. "And it'll take us time – which we don't have."

"I know that but I also know if we stay on *this* route we're liable to meet a surprise or two. Hold the conn: I'm going to put a link out on the Ultraviolet III in case any of ours are out there. If they – whoever they are – can't get us, they'll take out anyone else just for spite."

Ahxenta was back in her chair in a very few minutes, but not for long. Bellfish, one hand to his ear, called that he had Commander Thal on the comm and asking for the captain.

"Put him through to my office," she instructed. "There's no need for him to see what my bridge stations are doing."

By the time the captain returned, the creaking of *Arianrhod's* seams indicated that she had increased speed to the maximum safe limit and all spare duty stations were filled. The first mate had called an amber alert, but they were picking up no undue disturbance in the local area.

"Thal's heard about the attack on us, from one of his spies I bet. He wanted to know more. He hadn't heard that the perp was Hoxiz, though he *had* wondered why I'd sent word that security had the creep. I told him that as he and his have the means to get him, he's welcome," Ahxenta said to her mate. "And I told him that we'd had word there were others after us out there, near Beta Zegonia 68. Not our location or our heading but if he'd heard about what went down, he'll have an idea – he'd know we shipped out. I'm also tending to give credence to his claim that he was once an undercover op sent in to infiltrate a raider set-up and got taken by the hostiles. But what his personal beef against them is I don't know."

"Personal?"

"It has to be," the captain insisted. "He always goes out of his way to take them down. Got anything on long-range scanners, Gliss?"

"No ma'am, not a cheep. But if anything out there is well-shielded we may not spot it, good as our gear is," the tactical officer answered.

"And I guess Greffy can't operate that damned Norvallan scanner that Azular's so possessive about," remarked the first mate.

"If it's linked into our ops, I don't see why not," Ahxenta replied. "But I know nothing about the nuts and bolts of the damn thing."

She unloosed her webbing and made for the science station. She was back in minutes. "He can't make it work. He reckons it's touch-activated but short of abstracting one of Azular's blood samples from medbay and smearing it on, he doesn't have another suggestion."

"One more than I would have come up with," Apnis admitted. "But so far we're showing clear. Any news on PSS channels?"

"Nary a thing. Jikelleli sent in an alert about a couple of hits she'd heard about by Keystone Kell, but no specifics. *Green Comet's* on her way across Zeta, so I sent her a reminder to steer clear of Zeta Dixt."

The next hours were a waiting game for the crew as the great ship sped through hyperspace. Her navi-helm crew had elected to stay on duty as the course changes to foil possible pursuers needed complex calculation and manoeuvring and they were the most experienced. Apnis ordered them off for a couple of hours as the bypass node that led to the remote ISP Fivepoint outpost was set. *That* station marked the convergence point of five galactic zones on the border of the

Outer Reaches and the first mate wanted her best team fresh for the passage through the Archipelago to Velish and back to Vreskota.

The captain had called Flintlock to inform her of the situation and warn her that they might be late. The doctor's news was favourable. Azular was mending but his spinal damage meant that he would lose a degree of mobility. It would be repairable in time, but until he had otherwise healed, it would have to be left. Ahxenta had a task for her: she wanted a supra-light private link to Azular set up using their own communits, any other essential gear and strict security. She told her to contact Vettarista for help and she wanted it done before Azular could talk to Kerrix. Puzzled, Flintlock agreed.

Arianrhod was on the final beacon to Vreskota when the link was finally achieved. Noses twitching, the bridge crew watched narrowly as the captain strode to her office with the order not to disturb her except in emergency. It was evident to them that she had a duty on hand that was giving her an edge of disquiet.

Ahxenta was shaken at the change in Azular but smiled and asked after his health. That he was surprised at the comm was clear, as the ship was due to return so soon. He had kept abreast of developments and had had words with Vettarista remotely but nothing else. His lack of contact with Kerrix had disturbed him, as he feared that he was being kept in the dark over the extent of her injuries.

"No, she's doing fairly well," Ahxenta assured him. "She wants to see you, but I asked Axellina to delay any get-together until I had a chance to speak to you. I gave my word to Nat Holdspan that I'd pass something on. I think you should hear it before you see her. I'd have preferred to be with you, but other things intervened."

Ahxenta shrugged ruefully and began. Azular had been given the gist of the events around the attack on Holdspan and the part played by Kerrix. He knew that the captain had swept her up in his typically heroic style and carried her to medbay to save time; his actions had in fact probably saved her a little. She had been stunned by the bolt that hit her, not having a defensive element to her clothing that a uniform would have given. She had come to in the transport tube heading up, realised what had happened and had whispered a few words, making Holdspan promise to carry out her wishes. He had naturally agreed, although he realised that she was in shock and not fully aware. He had been unable to perform the task but had asked Ahxenta to do it as a point of honour.

"Captain?" Azular queried.

Even at the distance separating them the captain could sense that he was curious but anxious. She quickly eased his mind. "Tell Azular I love him," she said slowly and distinctly. "It was the last thing she said before being taken into surgery. But I imagine you've worked it out anyway," she went on as Azular's face creased and he bit his lip.

"She also threatened Hoxiz that if you didn't pull through she'd dig his heart out with a blunt knife and feed it to some rats. Not that she knew it was Hoxiz at the time."

He laughed a little at that. "That's so like her," he said. "How she ever got to the command…" Suddenly recalling where he was and to whom he was speaking, he sighed deeply. "Thank you for telling me, Captain. I expect you know it's reciprocated?"

"That I *had* figured," she returned, with a smile and a shake of the head. "Where you go from here I can't tell but just get well. We're almost at Vreskota for one of the quickest U-turns ever and we'll be heading Web-side soon. I'd like you aboard before we ship out for our next trip. I've spoken to Axellina and she knows the score on that. You know Nat Holdspan is footing Ms Kerrix' medical bills?"

"I know, ma'am."

"On a matter of business, by the way, Dr Azular: that Norvallan scanner you plug into the bridge science station when it suits you — we could make use of it on a permanent basis."

He smiled at her. "I'll see what I can do, Captain."

"You do that. Take care. I'll go before this link packs up. And I expect you'll have one or two things on your agenda."

Ahxenta cut the link with a sigh and sat back to reflect, stretching to relieve the tension. At least that was that job done, she thought. She had not relished it and it brought its own problems, at least in her mind, but it was done. Instinctively, she tabbed her console to call up the list of the latest inward calls directed to the *Arianrhod*. Satisfied, she eased her way out of her chair and made for the bridge.

"Azular okay?" the first mate greeted her.

"Doing well," she acknowledged. "What's our status?"

"All long- and close-range scanners show clear. We'll be in orbit in less than two hours and our clients will have grapple drones ready to grab the payload as soon as the admin's done. There's only one other ship in, a small trader, and she's heading out. We've had no word of trouble, at least in this zone, but Bellfish is listening out. Question is, do we take a straight route back or do we assume that there *is* a nasty surprise out there in wait? Micklemouse is a slippery rodent, so how much credibility do we put on his tale?"

"Very little," was the acerbic response. "But why would he make the link if there was nothing in it, even if his masters were breathing down his neck? I *will* take the direct route back though and we'll be cloaked and at red alert all the way. Our armoury is up to full strength and I want all our duty crews on standby."

"I'll see to it, Cap. Any word of the *Obsidian* and our cargo from Brown Amber?"

"Grey's on his way; he's dropped his cargo pod at Burr Two and should make Amber any time now. There's been no glitch at that end of Beta as far as I know, but I only did a skim-through of comms."

The captain spent the intervening time to orbital insertion in close examination of her ship's systems and had Bellfish monitor all local channels for relevant news. The stop-off at their endpoint was as rapid and as efficient as estimated and only three hours were needed to complete the necessary exchanges. The *Arianrhod* was only minutes from departure when the tactical officer noted a massive ship on approach at the outer edges of the Vreskota system. She had been running cloaked and had only just dropped her protective shielding. She was on a direct heading for the second planet.

"Do you have an ID on her?" Ahxenta demanded.

"Bringing it up now, Captain. It's the *Kel'Moth*."

22: A STRANGE ALLIANCE

Gliss brought the image of the *Kel'Moth* into a single frame as he fine-tuned the bridge holo to pan across local orbital space. Tactical and science stations were both scanning her, as a query to Vreskotan Port Control had confirmed that she was not due in. Seconds later, Greffy called out that the planetary defence net was gearing up and Bellfish reported that a general alert had been issued. Contact must have been made with the *Kel'Moth*, for within five minutes the outer ring of the defence grid powered down to standby. The *Kel'Moth* had changed course, her trajectory indicating that her target was Vreskota Two. A unit of Vreskot fighters had been despatched as a deterrent but held off at distance as the ship drew closer.

Arianrhod's captain had ordered her own weapons arrays warmed up and the shields raised, and although Ahxenta trusted Thal up to a point, Greffy was directed to maintain scrutiny with all he had until the ship came within visual range. The science officer could tell that the *Kel'Moth's* weapons were not on line and her surface jammers had not been activated but her shields were up. Her interior shields were effectively blocking probes.

"Incoming for you, Captain: Commander Thal," Bellfish called.

"Put it on grid, Lieutenant. Let's see what this is all about."

"Bet he knew we were here," Tallica Apnis said in a low voice as the face of the commander appeared opposite.

Thal looked as sour as ever but greeted them calmly. He claimed to have come in via Kanelian Juxta and had heard that *Arianrhod* was at Vreskota. He had planned to act on her word of Hoxiz and was on his way to the Web. He had also made enquiries after her news of the possible menace lying in wait near or on the bypass close to Beta Zegonia 68. Her suspicions were warranted, he warned. He refused to disclose his sources but he had heard that two ships of a new but undeniably alien design had been spotted off Pilt 24, an uninhabited system close to the bypass entry node. He had a spec.

Ahxenta ruminated before asking for details. Thal had plainly been expecting the request for he nodded across to one of his stations and in moments Greffy had confirmed receipt of the data and set up the holo of a sleek and unmistakably hostile ship on an auxiliary grid.

"I read no zukivianite in its make-up, Captain," the science officer reported. "But the outline matches an alien design we hold – one of the newer specs in our database but *not* the same as those interceptor-types we met near the asteroid field off Kolly when we answered that fake distress from the *Watersprite*," he added cautiously.

Ahxenta took that to mean it was a fit to a hostile spec that Azular had added from Norvallan data. The ship packed a deal of power for its size, Greffy noted, a fact echoed by Thal, who seemed surprised that the design was not as new to Ahxenta as he had expected. She refused to satisfy his interest but thanked him for the data, though she was curious as to why he had given it. His reasons were clear: as both ships were heading for Merkat, it would be sensible to travel together. Should they meet with any hostile vessels, their combined firepower would be a match for them.

"Stand by, Commander. I'll get back to you," was the short reply.

"He wants them taken out," Apnis stated sharply. "And he thinks he may as well use our armaments to do it."

"Fair comment," Ahxenta agreed. "This is where we miss Azular. But he knows we're headed to the Web and if we meet trouble, he's shown his hand in our favour before; and two ships *are* better than one. But I'm sending an advisory to the fleet before we head out."

"You're going to tell him that?" the first mate asked.

"I am. He'll have to know where I stand. Open a link to the *Kel'Moth*," she ordered comms.

Thal's jaw tensed in frustration at Ahxenta's plan to notify the PSS fleet but he consented and requested her schedule. She gave him the facts, cut the link and sent the advisory. She also ordered cloaking of the decoy's bay by the response plate gear that Azular had integrated into the hull in that area as she did not want to give Thal any reason to scan her ship. All else being in order, parallel courses were set and the two ships made to leave Vreskotan space.

Greffy had meanwhile carried out an in-depth search of their files on ships and tech classified as unknown or hostile to the Norvallans, had pulled up the spec that came closest to the one Thal had sent and had run it against related files. The result was a schematic that gave an indication of the speed and weapons capability of the alien and pinpointed weak spots where firepower might be effective. If those areas had not been upgraded in the vessels that lay off the bypass, it might give the two traders an advantage. The spec under Greffy's hand also suggested that such a ship was likely to be crewed.

Ahxenta pondered as she stood by the science station studying the image of the craft revolving above the console. "There *are* differences to the ships under the control of the *Watersprite*," she admitted. "And Thal may not have given us the full story. But I don't think he'd have held back on what his people or his informants had picked up – that wouldn't be to his advantage if we *do* meet them. Greffy, get the bare bones of what you have into a tight file that we can send over to the *Kel'Moth*. Lieutenant Bellfish, get me Commander Thal on the link," she ordered as she made for her usual seat.

Both officers complied speedily and Ahxenta found herself facing Thal. Without stating the source of her data, she gave him its bearing on the current situation and advised he accept it. He did, calling it up immediately. His eyes ablaze in a mixture of curiosity and wariness, he thanked her abruptly and linked off.

"You've really put the wind up him, Cap," Apnis grunted. "He's thinking he's bitten off more than he can chew with the *Arianrhod*."

"Not he; any other commander would have asked questions and shown much more interest," the captain replied. "But it's given him something else to mull over until we get within range of Pilt 24 – if his information was correct and if these hostiles are still there."

"You mean they could be halfway along this bypass route and a lot closer than we think."

"Exactly. You'd best rotate the duty crews now. I want us all fresh when we do get close to the node at Beta Zegonia."

The next hours were uneventful. The only ships detected were distant and very little comms came in. Ahxenta was on the bridge well before they hit the bypass node at Beta Zegonia as she had little faith that a ship whose eyes were set on *Arianrhod* would stay in the same place for any length of time. She was right, for the node was achieved and passed and no alarm was raised. It was almost as the two ships were ready to quit the bypass that tactical warned that a pair of blips had been detected close to Static Cross, an automated ISP monitoring post in the Outer Zone beyond the edge of the tripoint crossing of zones Beta, Delta and Alpha.

"Show me!"

As soon as the two fast moving marks were visible in the holo, Ahxenta called Thal to tell him. He was still in the command chair of the *Kel'Moth* and was quick to call up his tactical output. He agreed and immediately ordered a red alert. Both ships set for silent running, with every defensive facility on line. The ever-cautious captain of the

Arianrhod warned her bridge crew that she would not deploy *Loki VII* and would only loose the decoy if the situation warranted it.

"Thal damn well knows about the decoy. He saw it in the firefight we were in with the *Watersprite*. But if *Arianrhod* is new to these ships, any crews aboard might not," Ahxenta said to Apnis as she tightened her webbing. "Though if Thal's not seen it in action, I don't want to give him an opportunity unless I have to. And cloak our auxiliary torpedo tube emplacements: that'll be another surprise, I hope."

The blips might not be the aggressive strike they were anticipating but both commanders had agreed that attack was the best form of defence and had set to engage whatever was off the bypass.

It soon became apparent to Ahxenta that the strangers had been tracking them and knew that two ships were on the way through, for the two blips split to take up position either side of the node exit. She cursed and made a quick link to Thal to let him know the course that the *Arianrhod* intended to take to ensure that the *Kel'Moth* would not obstruct her path. He was as grim as she, having come to the same conclusion. With a mighty burst of power the two vessels sheared off the bypass, *Arianrhod* spiralling upwards in a twisting arc that had her crew pinned. Greffy had programmed the enemy weak spots into the weapons stations and their linked arrays, and Earbleat and her teams were set to go as soon as they had acquired targets.

The fire of phase cannon bolts seared the hide of the great pink-hulled trading ship as she spun down again in a whirlpool offensive strike against the ship nearest her. As Ahxenta thundered out her commands for the launch of deflecting drones to draw any lock-on enemy bolts, the ship shook to the thwack of a high energy torpedo against her hull plates. Her own pulse cannon energy bolts hit their marks, however, Earbleat's people making every one count. But the hostile had chosen her targets well and even as the weapons officer was crowing over several sustained hits, Chief Cottontail yelled that an external relay to one energy cell emplacement in main engineering had been hit and main bridge systems integrity was compromised. As *Arianrhod* spun up and out of range of her opponent under Dox's skilful hands and the bridge officers fought to stabilise their stations and keep themselves secure where webbing had failed, it seemed that her weapons teams had indeed hit their marks: their target careened off course to split apart in a ball of fire. They could see thus much in the overhead grid but little else as emergency systems kicked in.

The *Kel'Moth* looked to be in a better state, for *Arianrhod's* tactical and science stations reported that she was intact, had disabled her own target and was sweeping up debris samples. Greffy had scanned the *Kel'Moth's* mark and was able to confirm that she was manned, although her crew quota was small. Thal, however, had his own tactics for he did not, as Ahxenta half-suspected, send in a boarding party. He had opened a comm link to the hostile ship, as Bellfish had detected an exchange, the result of which was that the vessel limped off to a safe distance to maintain station-keeping near Static Cross.

"Commander Thal's on the link for you, ma'am," the comms officer reported moments later.

One raised eyebrow was all that the *Kel'Moth's* commander gave as he took in the medics attending to injured crew who had been flung from their seats and the emergency lighting that had cut in to bathe *Arianrhod's* bridge in a red wash. He offered support but was politely rebuffed, Ahxenta's steely tones quick to inform him that they could cope. She was more interested in his next steps. The first smile she had ever seen fleetingly crossed his lips as he told her that he would head back with *Arianrhod* to the Web. The hostile ship he intended to leave at Static Cross, as he had called in one of his fleet to escort her elsewhere. Where elsewhere was he would not say. Ahxenta had her own ideas and intended to inform the ISP of the shattered hostile warship hanging off its listening post. What it did about it was its own concern, although she suspected that Thal's ship would make it in first. He concurred and also consented to pass on the data from the debris that his team had picked up from the battle zone.

"Bet we don't get all of it," the first mate commented.

"Greffy's got as much as he could and we have the Norvallan data on those ships' spec in any case. But let's see the status of our people. We're near enough to Merkat that we can call on medical aid there if we need it, but our casualty list is short," Ahxenta noted as she scanned her boards. "We'll be late leaving for Stinward but it can't be helped and I want our armoury up to scratch before we do."

"Yes ma'am," agreed Apnis. "But the blips weren't expecting what they got. I wonder what they thought when they saw us coming off the bypass. They must have known one ship was Thal's, as I imagine they have the spec of most of his fleet locked into their databanks, given they're based on their own hostile tech and they'd be well-informed on what his people are up to – Thal *did* say they had spies."

"Maybe not; those ships hailed from beyond the charted zones and as we'd not met them before, it may be that they're from as far as that Telzilt place that has meaning for Thal, or even further."

"Maybe; but that's two less and we've upped the ante and scared the socks off any other bad guys that thought we were easy pickings."

"No doubt, but I'd best send that comm to the ISP. I'll pass it to the fleet and the TA. And I may as well copy Zillah in – it's well away from her sphere of influence but ISP Central can be slow at letting its smaller hubs know what goes on. Keep on top of things and make a list of what we'll need when we ship into the Web. You may as well send it on ahead and let our suppliers there get a hands up."

"They'll be rubbing their hands in glee at the thoughts of profits," the first mate grinned as she acknowledged.

Profits aside, the news that the *Arianrhod* and the *Kel'Moth* had seen action so close to Merkat as Static Cross had given rise to a great deal of concern amongst the planetary authorities and many Web-based concerns. The result had been the despatch of an ISP heavy cruiser to Static Cross from Alto Finglas and the notching up of the usual alert level. Ahxenta and Thal had been bidden to a meeting in the Web upon arrival. Both had refused. They had other priorities.

One of Ahxenta's first tasks was a trip to medbay to see Azular. She had left her first mate to deal with Port Authority reps that were upset by her refusal to cough up the extra levies they were still intent on charging, and the Dockers' Guild, whose members would cost and carry out the repairs to *Arianrhod's* hull. She had also to dodge the Merkat Central Advisory Council and Trades Alliance agents seeking more details than she was ready to give on the foes she had faced and her means of outfacing them. She referred them to Thal, reckoning that he would be more than able to cope.

Azular's appearance alarmed his captain. He had always been lean but now he was thin and haggard, though his eyes lit up when he saw her. She knew from Flintlock that he had regained some mobility but he found walking difficult, a result of spinal nerve trauma. Aware of her reaction, he made an effort to downplay his frailty as they talked of *Arianrhod's* latest mission and its results and the interactions with Thal. Azular was keen to get out of the Web's medbay and back to the ship, but there was a hesitancy in his manner that the captain sensed. She could imagine the reason and dared to mention Kerrix.

She was doing well, better than he was, Azular admitted. They had debated the scanner she had given him and its limitations for use aboard *Arianrhod* if he was the only operator. She had promised to deal with it. Vettarista had called on her and passed on the news that charges against Hoxiz under the name Berg Brack and not Mek Brisk were being pressed. The Treskk had been charged with assault and other crimes. Both were now in maximum security cells, with Brack under medical supervision. The charges posed difficulties, for unless the two pled guilty, Kerrix would be called as a witness.

The captain's next call was on Flintlock, who was positive that the science officer could be moved to *Arianrhod's* medbay as long as extra medical provisions were in place. Ahxenta had no problem with that, though she was troubled to hear that in the doctor's opinion, Azular was not his normal cheery self mentally: he was fearful that he would not regain full physical capability. She had reassured him and had words with associates in Merkat and elsewhere. With a shrewd look to see how the captain would take it, she also mentioned that she had talked to Kerrix about it and in fact it was the Norvallan woman who had introduced the subject. She and Azular had talked over his condition, evidently, the doctor disclosed with a quirky smile.

Ahxenta's jaws tightened. "And?" she demanded dangerously.

Highly skilled technical nano-surgery had been necessary to insert the language decoder cum translator that Kerrix carried, Flintlock told her calmly. The links into her nervous system were both intricate and specific and the expertise to carry out such work *was* available. In fact the hostiles were on track to carry out similar, given the device found in Micklemouse. If they could get to a place in which such skill existed and have it exercised, they could profit from it.

Ahxenta let her go no further for she exploded in icy fury. "She's trying to persuade me to find her a way back to her own people and in my ship! And now we have the nav-charts to do it!"

"Cool it, Cinnabar," Flintlock said firmly. "She is not. She's aware of your attitude to her and that you'd not sanction bringing her on board again. Even though she tried to save your neck, though Azular bore the brunt of that," she added for good measure. "She wants to go over the data that Nat Holdspan gave to Azular – she has a copy – and find a way to get to Starfall Exit. She reckons that Holdspan might be a good bet there. *He* now owes her, though he's paid it back by paying her way in this place. But as he gets about a lot and now knows she's a bit more than he first thought, he might be curious enough to give her passage."

"In exchange for?" the captain asked sharply.

"How would I know? Expertise, probably. She's smart and she'd no doubt have that shuttle of hers."

"Yes, with *my* call-sign integrated into one of patches I gave her that's holding her hull plating together!" Ahxenta snapped wrathfully.

"You what?" the doctor exclaimed.

"Never mind. I want a word with Ms Kerrix."

"I bet you do. And she *is* well enough to be called on. But go easy, Cinnabar: if it was you, what would you do? She wants to get back to something like she had and was, but not at her own home base by what I've seen and heard; but she also doesn't want to lose sight of Azular. A cleft stick, wouldn't you say?"

"Damn her!" the captain retorted.

The details of her talk with Kerrix Ahxenta would not disclose. Azular knew that the captain had spoken to her but neither seemed keen to say more. The science officer had little time to organise his thoughts, for the *Obsidian* was on her way in and Ahxenta intended to head back up to *Arianrhod* and deal with the delivery that Captain Bluejohn had picked up for her. She also figured it would be best to be aboard when the repairs to her ship's hull began. And she wanted Azular with her, for more than one reason. A short talk that Apnis had had with Kit Biernop had brought to light suspicions that the Treskk contingent of local ruffians was highly put out by the arrest of one of their own and some were planning more mischief. Biernop had sent the news to one of his contacts with links to ISP Intelligence and was in hopes of action from that side.

Dr Flintlock had been granted another day to organise what she needed before Azular was relocated to *Arianrhod's* medbay. The chief medic had an agenda, for Kerrix had been discharged on the proviso that she returned for regular check-ups and was involved in plans of her own. The request that Greffy be sent down to help Azular was met with scepticism on the captain's side, but she had agreed.

"The four of them are up to something," Ahxenta observed to her first mate, as, fist on chin, she examined the schedules of repair and business that she had called up on her boards. "See if you can chivvy on the repair teams, Tallica, but don't promise them a bonus because I can't afford it. Grey's hauling our goods over on a shuttle and he'll want a lowdown on what's been going on before he ships out. And I need a chat with the ISP reps over the Stinward contract. I don't think they'll take it away from us but they'll want assurances that we'll be able to make the trip. And guess who's just dropped into the Web and wants a quick chat over the problems out at Static?"

"Fleetskup," the first mate said dryly. "*Tallulah's* just docked. I've organised limited shore leave as we have time and the crew needs a break, so we can hit the *Half Moon*. Flish is heading up, by the by, as the *Firedrake's* shipping out – she's up to a fair spec and has new crew to pick up at Selliden. And the Port Authority still wants a face to face over Static Cross *and* I hear that the ISP heavy cruiser sent out to pick up the bits might call in here first to get the nitty gritty."

"Let's hope it's not the *Repulse*, if she's still under Myrtleberry," Ahxenta grunted. "If it is, I *will* want Azular here, fit or otherwise."

"We'll see. What do you think to loading the Stinward payload as soon as it's ready? I know it'll mean extra security with repair teams hopping all over our hull, but it might save us a bit of time, as our cargo bays are fit. And as Lindell's sourced the gear that Crizz needs for main engineering, we'll have that installation going anyhow."

"Seems practical," the captain nodded. "We're going to be busy."

It was two days before the captain and first mate could drop into the *Half Moon*. With better things to do with her time Ahxenta had not agreed to a formal meeting with Captain Fleetskup: having fended off Colonel Ellin Myrtleberry, SSO Hills of Merkat security and the Port Authority, she was in no mood for his lack of charm. Azular was now back on board but unfit for duty and the discussion with Myrtleberry had exhausted him. Greffy had also come back and was playing with gear that the two had been gifted by Kerrix. The captain had picked up that Greffy was as partial to Kerrix as Azular but for different reasons, and was now an ally. It was her chief medic who edified her. Kerrix was a close friend of Merry Jetty and that young woman and Greffy were in a relationship that had begun when Merry, in need of subjects for her psychology degree research, had recruited him.

The captain was also mulling over other news imparted by Flish Ma'Lappis. The doctor and Commander Flick Poppet of the *Firedrake* had formalised things and were now engaged. Not that Ma'Lappis intended to quit the *Arianrhod*, but she thought it fair that her captain should be made aware. All in all, the stopover at the Web had already thrown up a lot and Ahxenta felt her overfilled plate already heavy. The last thing she needed was a dose of Fleetskup, she thought, as he and his first mate waved over from the far end of the bar, the forceful Dyne-Bek hallooing out that she would buy them a drink.

"What's the payback?" Apnis murmured as Ahxenta nodded in accord. "And where's Tallulah Tommy? In hiding?"

Fleetskup was his usual long-winded self but was friendly, asking for details of the attack off Static Cross and giving his own opinion as to how he would have dealt with it. Dyne-Bek was more interested in Thal and had a few stringent questions about him and his ship, which Ahxenta dodged effectively. *Tallulah* was headed out to Beta Zegonia 68c for her next mission and did not want to run afoul of anything out there was the excuse for the cross-examination. The captain of the *Arianrhod* was not buying that and was brusque. Dyne-Bek then came to the point that Ahxenta guessed had been her intention all along: the actions of *Arianrhod* in taking out the hostile limpet drones that had latched onto *Tallulah's* hull at their fateful encounter just off Idledott. She had read the reports, she said, as part of her briefing after signing aboard the *Tallulah*, had deemed the response needless and as the damage caused had needed extensive repair, the captain of the *Tallulah* was entitled to recompense.

That Fleetskup had admitted at the time that Ahxenta's action was justified, as the drones would certainly have pierced the *Tallulah's* hull and caused serious damage, cut no ice with Dyne-Bek. The captain was furious but continued calm. It was clear that the woman was out to prove that she was a force to be reckoned with. Ahxenta was terse. She refused to reiterate her case, produced the link to her legal rep, demanded the link to the *Tallulah's* legal rep and told Dyne-Bek that she would refer the matter to the Trades Alliance. She then paid for her own and her first mate's drinks, wished the two a good day and turned her back on the spluttering Fleetskup.

"That round to you, Captain," applauded Ally as the captain of the *Tallulah* recollected other business and he and his first mate set off.

"Damned nerve," was Tallica Apnis' opinion. "She wasn't even at Idledott. I bet she's been reading Fleetskup's watered down logs that beef up his own actions and put down everybody else's."

"And I bet her next tactics will be let's all be friends and we'll forget the whole thing," Ally put in sagaciously.

"*I* won't," Ahxenta told him curtly. "And I *will* inform my legal rep: a note from there might spoke her wheel. Where's Ms Kerrix?"

"Still on sick leave and Merry says she won't be fit for a while. It's a relief in a way," he confided. "You're not the only one asking about her – I've had a few curious enquiries."

"From whom?" Apnis queried with a quick glance at her captain as she accepted the pot of ale that Ally had placed on the counter.

"That's the point, I'm not sure. I've told them to keep their noses out, but the tale's gone round of that episode with Captain Holdspan and people are asking who and what she is. Merry's warned her. But what exactly happened down on green twelve?" the barman asked quietly. "I've not had the full story and rumours are all over."

"And what do these rumours say?" Ahxenta probed.

"That you were targeted by a pair of thugs with big guns and a grudge; that your science officer Azular took a bad hit; that *she* raced after the guy that shot Dr Azular and that he and she ran slap into Captain Holdspan and his first mate; and that *she* took a hit that was meant for Captain Holdspan. And now the two perps are in custody but they're part of a bigger conspiracy that's set to take out the PSS fleet, especially you, Captain. That's all I have."

"All?" Apnis asked. "Seems like plenty."

Ally shrugged. "I pick it up in bits and pieces. Why the PSS fleet I don't know, as there are plenty others. But you lot take on contracts that usual shipping lines don't and fight back rather than run *and* give more than you get. That seems to have annoyed a few. And some say that this war we thought was over has started again, but this time the baddies are harder to catch because they're better at hiding. At least, that's what one of the crew of one of those new transports said."

"What new transports?" Ahxenta asked harshly.

"Ones like that," Ally indicated his active info-cams that displayed the traffic in and out of the massive docking bays of the outer belts. "That's the biggest one we've had in and she's been here before, but there've been a couple of others that are similar but smaller and that nobody seems to recognise. *They* use the middle belts. Guild security can't get clear scans of them either, according to my partner."

Both officers gazed at the holo showing the *Kel'Moth*. Their keen glances were not lost on the owner of the *Half Moon*, for he smoothly continued, "She escorted you in, didn't she, Captain?"

"We both ran into the same trouble at Static Cross," was the short reply. "What have you seen of her crew and other crews from these similar ships and who is it that told you that these new baddies are harder to catch because they're better at hiding?"

"I've not seen much of *her* crew as only one or two have been in. I saw her captain once; at least I think it was him as she was the only one of her type in at the time. It was ages ago, about the time of that bang that nearly got your shuttle. He doesn't drink, or at least not ale; his crew do, the ones that came in. I asked where they were from but they wouldn't say. But crew from one of the smaller ships were in, when you were out. They're a sour lot and don't say much but Evrett heard that they're part of a trade outfit at the edge of Mu. They're independents I guess, but those armoured uniforms scare people. What do you know about them, Captain?" he added casually.

"About as much as you seem to," was the acid retort.

"I see you've got repair teams out on your hull," he said, gesturing to the holo, which was now on *Arianrhod*. "My regulars like to keep an eye out," he explained at the dangerous glint in Ahxenta's eye.

"You didn't tell me who told you about the new bad guys on the block," the captain reminded him. "One of the crew of these new transports, you said."

"Yes, ma'am. The guy's mate had gone to the hygiene so I started to chat, keeping friendly with the paying customers as I like to do. I spoke of the trouble in the war, said I was glad it was over. And *he* said it was no way over. He'd had one or two, so he let slip that there were aliens out there in hidey holes with small fast ships that could nip in and out and strike before they could be got. He'd started to say that they had spies all over the place as well, but his mate came back and she shut him up before he could spill any more. I think she was annoyed. But other people are saying there's trouble and it's those aliens again. That Ms Dyne-Bek for one," Ally hinted darkly.

"So what's she been putting about?" Apnis asked.

"Just before you and the captain came in, Commander," he said. "The *Tallulah* had been hit by two warships on the way to Silverglass but they'd got the upper hand and had them on the run. That's when you and the *Nyx Warrior* showed up, she said. Was that the scuffle off Idledott she was trying to dun you for?" he asked.

"Yes it was," Ahxenta told him, giving a few of the minor details that the ill-informed first mate of the *Tallulah* had omitted.

"I get the impression that Commander Dyne-Bek's out to impress Captain Fleetskup," was Ally's summation. "She lays it on thick and he laps it up. Maybe she likes the cut of his jib?"

"Maybe she likes the size of his wallet," Apnis said scathingly. "She's welcome. I wouldn't have him gift-wrapped."

"That I figured long ago," Ally laughed. "Do you want to order lunch, Captain, Commander? My mid-day crew's just come in."

The two turned to see a pair of the *Half Moon's* young staff sail in through the holo-veils of the door. Merry and Jez nodded to them as they passed behind the bar on the way to the staff room to change.

"We'll sit over at the back and order at the menu pad," the captain told him. "And I'd like a word with Merry, if she can spare the time."

"She can," Ally said firmly. "I'll tell her to bring your orders across once they're ready."

"About Kerrix," Apnis guessed when the two were seated. "Has Azular spoken to her since he came back aboard?" she asked slyly.

"I didn't ask him and I don't suggest you do," Ahxenta responded with a wry grin as she punched up her choice of rations. "But we'll find out how she is and what she's up to."

Kerrix was still in some pain when she had called on her earlier,

Merry told them when she brought their order, but she was about to move quarters, for last night she had been waylaid by two strangers outside her door who claimed to be journalists. They requested an interview with the promise of payment for talking to them, but would say only that it related to the events on green twelve a few days back. One of the two had tried to activate a scanner. Kerrix had snatched it, thrown it down and tried to call security. The man had grabbed her to prevent the call and was stunned by a shot from behind: Vetta had heard the ruckus on her way in from work and had taken her own steps. Vetta called security to report the incident as an assault. The female half of the duo turned to flee and was also brought down. The upshot Merry had not heard but she guessed that the two had been arrested and locked up.

Once the assistant had gone, the first mate turned to the captain. "Locked up? I wonder where?"

"So do I, and I bet Kerrix scanned *them*," Ahxenta replied. "I've not heard from Vettarista and I'm loath to call her as I don't want to risk making any links here with all these eyes on us."

She gazed intently around as she spoke and the owners of the eyes swiftly looked elsewhere.

"So things are still going on, Cap," Apnis surmised as she began to eat. "Kerrix did herself no favours when she jumped in and gave Nat Holdspan a turn. Every ear in here was pricked and you know how Ally's regulars spread gossip. And some of it ends up in the wrong ears. But on another note: what did you make of Dyne-Bek? She seemed quite keen to know more about Thal and his lot."

"So I saw. She's nosy or wants to prove that she's smart, maybe. Azular didn't report any concerns when Fleetskup introduced her to him a while back, but he had other priorities. I'll ask Jesse Inks; he's over there and I suspect he'll be no friend of hers," the captain noted nodding at the young lieutenant as she caught his eye, with a flick of her head to indicate the empty seats of their booth.

"He's sharp. He's figured you want to chat and he's heading over. I'll get him a beer and more for us. It's time he had his lieutenant commander's pips, he damn well deserves them."

After civil openings, Ahxenta cut to the chase with her customary bluntness and asked what he knew of *Tallulah's* new first mate, giving her reasons. He asked several discreet questions before telling them that he *had* enquired into the intrusive Dyne-Bek's past. She had been second officer of the *ISPPS Steel Guardian* out of Sekward Central and a lieutenant commander. Previous to that she had been security chief aboard an orbital custodial facility of the remote Skene Starn outpost. By her own admission, her posts had been too quiet and too far from civilisation. Inks did not have the authority to access her personnel files, and he would not give his personal opinion of her. As far as he knew, word that the *Tallulah* was seeking a first mate had reached her ears and she had applied. Fleetskup had been impressed by a link-up interview and had paid her transport to Copper Starn, where the *Tallulah* had trade, and met her there. He offered her the first mate's position, which she accepted. She joined them shortly afterwards.

It was plain to the two that Inks was not thrilled about his career aboard the *Tallulah* but he would not disparage his captain. After an exchange of views on the present situation, the three finished their drinks and he took his leave.

"He'd make a good bet for the *Warrior*, if Nat Holdspan didn't already have a first mate," said Apnis. "He's honest to a fault. Most of Fleetskup's merry band wouldn't think twice about criticising their captain behind his back. But what do we do now? Vettarista?"

"Yes – once we're out of here."

Ahxenta had no need to call the ISP agent as a link marked urgent had appeared on her communit. As she tabbed off the holo, she told her first mate that they had a meet in marketing in half an hour. They finished their meals in a leisurely way, bid goodbye to Ally and then set off for their rendezvous.

"At times I wonder if she has us bugged," the first mate remarked as the two walked into the marketing suite to see Vettarista in a smart business suit at one of the stands near the centre of the space.

Incisive as always, the agent set up a bug-jammer and came to the point. The two pseudo-journalists that had accosted Kerrix the night before had been hired by Kasinnick, the tech outfit known to have fingers in radical and expensive micro-medical devices. The firm had been let be and a watch set to track down its operators and backers but it was clear that the move on Kerrix had been missed. *She* was now in a billet on green eleven. One of the hirelings was Treskk, the other was from Sevolb and both had criminal records. They had been set loose under surveillance and so scared witless by threats against their persons that they were unlikely to tell their employers anything other than that their mission had failed.

Vettarista was canny and in exchange for her information wanted more on the *Kel'Moth*, her commander and her reasons for being in the Web. As far as the agent was aware, the huge transport ship had not logged a cargo manifest and none of her people were involved in ongoing trade deals. She was still hanging fire in the outer belts, did not need repair and had not requested permission to depart, although several of her crew had been seen in the inner belts.

"Shore leave?" Ahxenta posited. "I haven't seen any of her crew around, but they're adept at hiding when they want to."

At the flash of Vettarista's eyes the captain judged it wise to let her know that Thal was possibly aiming to transfer Hoxiz from security's hands into his own and she was inclined to let him do it. She gave the basics of her dealings with him and then enquired of the similar but smaller ships that Ally had described as docking in the middle belts.

"Traders," was the succinct reply.

"Since when?" the captain said sharply.

"Since not long after that mishap to your shuttle, the *Gadfly*."

"In other words, since around the time that Kerrix turned up in the Web," Ahxenta snorted. "Interesting coincidence."

"No," Vetta disagreed. "That base called Starfall has been under surveillance for a while. ISP's long-range monitoring posts are on constant scan and they show rising numbers of unknown ships in and near local systems, the inference being that there's a hidden bypass, inaccessible except to those that know the route and access codes. It may be that Thal's lot have been on the watch for hostiles coming off, which would explain why Xanna's shuttle was targeted. We think there's a major bypass node in uncharted space, in a system close to Thal's Starfall base. One arm goes from the node straight through the end of zone Mu via Canna and beyond Kirtish…"

"To at least K457:003," Ahxenta cut in. "A red-orange lithium star that Kerrix claims was the location of the node that caught her and threw her off at the Starfall Exit node. So where else does it go?"

Vettarista pursed her lips irritably. "Yes, I know that she and your science officer resolved part of her route. *We* reckon that the bypass continues from the Starfall Exit node in the opposite direction, partly through unmapped space, to an exit close to another ex-raider base off the Starglass Nebula, near Kelfennig Four."

"One of the bases the hostiles used during the war!" Apnis hissed. "We'd heard of it and alerted the ISP via Admiral Zillah of Freskat. We'd found out it was one of five key hubs of hostile activity and figured it for an ex-raider post that the hostiles took over, but maybe it wasn't. So it's now likely in the hands of Thal and his band."

"Yes, *how* you heard exercised a lot of minds in ISP Central," the agent said acidly. "But your warning about Lartzeg gave us enough heads up to face what we did at Skyrtek. In fact, your activity on that front probably helped end the war a lot sooner than otherwise *and* in our favour. Another of the reasons that the hostiles left behind are upset and want you and yours out of the picture. Care to tell…"

"No," Ahxenta retorted curtly. "My schedule's tight as the trouble on our last mission cost me more than time. I need to check on the repairs to my ship and on my loading. But I think that Thal not only knows of that extended bypass route but is active in its operation."

With that she thanked the woman and she and her first mate made off, to head down to their shuttle bay.

"Reckon she'll assist Thal to get his paws on Hoxiz, Cap?"

"Not directly: she'll not want to go near him. He's smart and if he *was* once an undercover agent, he'll know what to look for in another. But we need to get home. We've plenty to do until we ship out."

Everyone aboard had much to do before the ship was ready to leave. This would be a long haul as the captain had insisted that all her new contracts would be carried out before she returned to the Web. That meant that *Arianrhod* would be heavy, her huge outer bays full as well as her smaller inner holds. The weighty gear for Stinward would be the first drop, followed by a lengthy trip in open space with few settled systems. That would take her through zone Kappa to Tressic Major, to offload a cargo of engineering parts. The risk of raiders on that leg would be low but a lone vessel might be open to attack if her route were known. Tressic to Freskat meant crossing five galactic zones to Lambda, but much of that would be in more travelled and thus more heavily-patrolled space, where a number of eyes and ears in monitoring posts were keeping watch.

Several days had gone before *Arianrhod* was back to her standard spec, by which time the *Kel'Moth* had departed Merkat. A warrant for the extradition of Berg Brack had led to his transferral by security to an authorised prisoner transport service. Less than a day later came news that the transport had failed to reach its destination and its whereabouts were unknown. Apnis made it her business to tell Kit Biernop that her crew were not overly worried, letting him draw his own conclusions. The Treskk accomplice in the attack on *Arianrhod's* people had pled guilty and was due to be sentenced.

Ahxenta was looking forward to time away from the Web and her usual haunts. Her major concern was the health of her senior science officer. Flintlock had insisted on top-range mobility aids for him and had advised implanted cybernetics once he was fully healed, but he was loath to undergo such invasive surgery. Unlimited comms time had been sanctioned but on the doctor's advice the captain refused to allow him off ship. Flintlock's alternate proposal that he be allowed visitors was met with a negative. Kerrix, she knew, was back to part-time in the *Half Moon*. Ahxenta suspected that she was also trying to find a way out of the Web, or at least of contacting her own people.

Greffy had spent his time upgrading the bridge science stations with the gear that Kerrix had given them, with the result that Azular's Norvallan scanner, when tied in, could be used by anyone operating the stations. Earbleat had come up with the notion of replacing one of *Arianrhod's* forr'ad phase cannon arrays with a circular gun-port turret that produced focussed phase-bursts, a modification which was firmly vetoed by the captain.

With the recall of the last of her crew from leave and all her cargo safely aboard, the ship was as ready as possible and Ahxenta gave the order to prepare for departure. It felt good to be heading out, she told her first mate as she hauled her boards over for last minute checks and ordered the helmswoman to begin strut disengagement.

Several pairs of eyes were set on that part of the outer Web where the massive trading ships berthed. The pertinent holo-grid that was suspended just over the bar for the benefit of the *Half Moon's* regular clientèle was as active as ever and the two topers that held up the bar as they nursed small mugs of bargain ale were agog in anticipation.

"There she is, Malty, shiny as a new shovel," Jurry noted with a watery sniff as he pointed "*You'll* be sorry to see the stern of her," he added to Kerrix, who was ostensibly clearing glassware but answering a quick link on the comm behind the counter.

"Why don't you mind your own business and get your elbows off the bar," was the cool retort as she mopped up around the comm pad whilst sneaking a peek at the grid.

"Who's that coming in fast off the starboard side of the *Tallulah?*" Malty piped up in a rasping squeak. "Don't recognise the shape."

The tone alerted Kerrix, who looked up. "What the... Azular, there's a small ship coming in on your starboard side and using the *Tallulah* as a shield! She's fast! Get your shields up!"

23: FINDING TROUBLE

The advent of an unknown ship that had refused to respond to hails and had begun to accelerate as she moved closer into its territory and near to the outer meshes of its massive space dock had also alarmed Merkat Three's Port Authority. That body had sent out a warning to the intruder and a general alert to all ships in the area and was already scrambling the small fighter squadron based in the Web. The guard systems of the outer limits of the Web were also gearing up for action but the warning had come late and the single intruder had already breached its outer defences.

There had been disciplined activity on the bridge of the *Arianrhod* on receipt of the alert: her tactical and science teams had stepped up scanning of local space and weapons systems were ordered online. Azular's terse voice cutting through the ether calling for shields up was sufficient for the captain to repeat the order and call for red alert and the input of additional external monitors on her holo-grid. The voice of the senior science officer continued over the wail of the alert that attack was imminent on their starboard from beyond the bulk of the *Tallulah*, berthed alongside.

"Cut those struts and get the hell out!" another voice bawled over the medbay link. "She's broken off! She's coming up under you!"

Gliss had now pulled in every external visual he had and Ahxenta could see the source of the attack. "Helm, emergency strut release! Get us out of here! Earbleat, target that blip and prepare to fire."

"You touch that and you die!" the voice yelled. "*Arianrhod*, deploy high energy torpedoes, your pulse cannon won't cut it! Now!"

"Do it!" the captain ordered, her voice ice cold in fury as the ship speared upwards and banked sharply.

As everyone clung to their seats, Dox swung *Arianrhod's* great bulk round in an arc to provide the optimum firing position as a searing gout of pure white energy shot from the small craft in their direction.

"She's set to ram!" the first mate hollered as Earbleat sent three deadly torpedoes one after the other towards the hurtling craft.

The hostile ship exploded in an intense ball of light so bright that those watching the action closed their eyes to cut the sting. The flak burst outwards to rattle the hull plates of the great trading vessel.

"Damage reports!" Ahxenta bellowed over the noise, as, too late to be effective, the Web's fighter squadron sped in for an assault.

As details came in of slight damage to the shields and other ship's systems, and a growing list of minor casualties amongst those caught off-guard throughout the ship, Lieutenant Bellfish intimated that an officer of the Port Authority wanted a word.

"That'll have to wait," the captain growled. "Get that link up here that Azular has in medbay, I want a word or three with Ms Kerrix. And keep Azular on line."

"How in hell did she figure it?" the first mate wanted to know as the connections were made.

"We're about to find out," Ahxenta responded grimly as the stern face of Xanna Kerrix appeared in the overhead holo.

"Care to explain?" the captain of the *Arianrhod* asked evenly.

"I will, but I'll use Ally's office: there are far too many inquisitive eyes and ears round here," the woman replied, looking about her and for the agreement of the owner of the *Half Moon*, who with almost every other person in the place had stopped to watch the action.

"This way," he replied dazedly, his look of shock apparent.

"You put one finger on that and I cut it off; you get me?" Kerrix snarled in the passing to someone out of view.

"Yes ma'am!" was the terrified response.

"Hell, I wouldn't want to be one of *her* crew," said Apnis quietly.

"Maybe I should take it in the office," Ahxenta replied in response as she glanced around her own bridge.

"Negative on that Cap – we *all* want to know how she did it."

"Are your people okay, Captain?" were the woman's first words when the link was remade.

Despite her calm outward manner, Ahxenta could see that she was rattled and nodded as she reiterated her request for the details. Kerrix was short and to the point: the sharp exclamation from one of the spectators at the bar had alerted her to the external viewer while she was linked to *Arianrhod*. She had recognised the dense shape. It was a self-directed missile intended to be taken for a small ship. It could be pre-set for autonomous long-distance deployment and for specific targets. As far as Kerrix knew, such devices had arisen recently. She had been warned of them by an alert to her own fleet not long before the events that had led her to the Web. She remembered the odd shape – and that heavy fire would be required to take it down.

"It's their damn version of *Loki*!" the aggrieved voice of Whisper

Earbleat cut across the bridge.

As it had skirted the *Tallulah* to reach *Arianrhod*, Ahxenta's ship must have been a target held in its memory matrix, Kerrix said.

"Or the *Tallulah's* not worth the trouble," suggested Apnis.

"Or it had a priority list," the woman continued. "You won't find out now, judging by what we saw on the holo here. But I suggest you go over the specs of the craft and technology registered as hostile to Norvallan shipping that I understand you have in your databanks. If I recall aright, the basics of that beast or something similar is there."

The captain regarded her keenly "I'll bet. You've done yourself no favour in alerting us, you realise, *Ms* Kerrix? The Port Authority will be on your back for a start."

"Only if you tell it."

"Someone in the *Half Moon* will pass it on, believe me," Ahxenta warned as a note flashed up on her board; it was from Azular, who had found the relevant limited spec and linked it through.

The captain grimaced but made no other overt sign. "I suggest you watch your back, Ms Kerrix. And I guess I owe you thanks."

"Hardly, Captain; but *I* guess the customer here who spied it and gave the yell that made me look expects a drink. I'll see he gets one."

"Roger that. I'll have you put through to Dr Azular. I imagine that he'll want a word. Ahxenta out."

At a nod from the captain, Bellfish cut the link to the bridge.

"She didn't want your thanks then, Cap," the first mate observed.

"Does she ever; interesting that her people have had experience of that bloody guided missile, though, and recently by her reckoning. But let's find out what the Port Authority has to say about permitting a hostile past Web defences. I see its fighters have been called off."

"It'll want a full report and then some," predicted Apnis. "And it'll want to know why we used torpedoes in such a confined space. *And* why we tore those docking struts apart. The Dockers' Guild will be bawling over that. All that'll put the scuppers on our scheduling."

"Like hell. The Authority can pick up its own bits. It let the damn thing get so close it nearly blew a hole through our hull, though I'd like to know why it skipped past the *Tallulah* without wasting a shot. You sort out the bits and pieces here and send me through the details on our hurts and what the Guild says we've done to its dock. I'll take the PA's call in my office."

"Aye, aye, ma'am."

The captain pulled no punches. Her ship had been put in needless danger by the negligence of the PA in allowing an unknown ship that would not respond to hails so far into its space that it could penetrate its docks. Action should have been taken well before that and not when Web defences had been breached and the craft was racing in through the meshes with an obvious target in view. Ahxenta had been forced to take extreme measures for the protection of her ship and her crew. *That* had meant blowing the struts of her berth and taking out an intruder that was then likely to have turned its sights on other ships nearby, or elsewhere in the Web. That the consequences would have been more than devastating had the *Arianrhod* not taken the action she did was clear, given the very heavy firepower it took to destroy the thing and the amount of explosive it was carrying – the resulting blast when the craft was taken out made *that* very obvious.

The result was thus that the *Arianrhod* was now even more behind schedule thanks to the PA's ineptitude; and the clearly irate Ahxenta had no intention of delaying any longer than it took to clear the debris field, register the details with her insurers and send word of the incident out to the PSS fleet, her clients and relevant authorities – including the Interstellar Systems Protectorate, since Merkat sat in an ISP-controlled area that took in small sectors of zones Alpha, Beta and Delta. She also wanted the data that the Port Authority had collected on the device, including its projected route into the Merkat system, and she wanted it immediately.

By the time the captain returned to the bridge, leaving a dazed pair of PA reps wondering what had hit them and what they were going to do next, she had yet another irritation. Flak from the debris of the exploding hostile device had scored the hull of the *Tallulah* and her captain was keen for a word with the commanding officer of the vessel he held responsible. With an oath, Ahxenta ordered the link on line. She then delivered a blistering lecture similar to the one she had dealt the Port Authority, allowing Fleetskup no time to interrupt and leaving his ears ringing. His first mate sat open-mouthed at his side. Before she could say a thing, the captain of the *Arianrhod* ordered the link cut and her own people to prepare for departure with all speed.

Tallica Apnis was the only one who dared utter a word. "Sit down, Cinnabar, and cool it."

Ahxenta took her seat, still seething. "I swear I'll wring his neck for him the next time I see him," she threatened.

"I suspect you'll have to get in line," was the calm reply. "And you took the wind out of Dyne-Bek's sails. She'll think twice before she tangles with you again."

"She'd better. What's our status?"

"We'll be good to go shortly, once a few things are tidied up. The hits on our hull weren't too bad so I've had some of our repair bots sent out to patch the worst. We can get the damage repaired properly when we get to Stinward. I take it you'll be letting them in on this?"

"Roger that, once we're underway; *and* I'll be telling a few others. I'll send out the spec of the thing as well, lest any of ours meet one. The PA reps said they'd send me all they had, from the time they first logged it and I want it before we leave. What about our casualties?"

"A few minor, two serious but not life-threatening, Axellina says, so medbay can cope," Apnis reported. "It's just as well she brought a heap of stuff up from Merkat with Azular."

"Is he off the comm yet?" the captain asked, cocking an eyebrow.

"Yup; he's hauling out all he can on that beast and others similar, and on how to deal with them. He'll send it through when it's done."

"He's supposed to be resting. Flintlock will have his ears."

"She knows the score. Greffy had the stuff in his databanks but he didn't get the chance to pull it up as it was all so fast. He's scanning the debris field and he's sent out two grabbers to collect bits. There are zukivianite traces in its make-up so the PA's probes should have picked that up, given that they know zukivianite equates to hostile. But hell, Cinnabar, it was close. Where did it come from and how did it know we were here?"

"We might get a clue from what the PA sends but I won't hold my breath. Whoever started this damn personal war against us must have our spec set into every one of its ships and have agents in every port in the frigging mapped galaxy that watch our every move."

Ahxenta was interrupted by comms: a screed of data from the PA had come in. She had it transferred to Greffy and bid him examine it for extent and quality before she would send an acknowledgement. It seemed inclusive was the science officer's opinion as he connected to tactical to see if he could get a bead on the ship's route into the Web.

In the event, the best that could be deduced was that Earbleat had been close to the truth and the alien device was a huge missile created to simulate a small ship and coded for destruction of its target. It was a larger version of her *Loki*, a much-enhanced shell that was basically a guided projectile. The major difference in the alien version, apart from its size, was that it appeared to have been on a solo mission without a guiding ship, unless its mothership was nearby, an alarming possibility. Greffy and Gliss had taken the data from the PA and their limited spec and had worked out that it was capable of long-distance travel, but their joint opinion, backed by Azular, was that it would have to receive frequently updated orders. It had entered the system on a bearing that implied it had come off the local bypass, but any regular ship of that size would be unlikely to withstand hyperspace currents – though that would not hinder an unmanned vessel as resilient as the alien device.

The debris collected had been briefly screened but it showed little other than it was based on hostile tech allied to high grade explosive. Nothing could be equated to a guidance system but a thick piece of meta-jurillium in the waste still bore a traceable molecular signature. Greffy matched it to records he held for the hull plate of a hostile ship destroyed at Freskat and he knew that the material was deemed suitable for use on Norvallan ships' hulls. The implication was that the device had come from beyond the limits of mapped space. How it had been able to find *Arianrhod* was unknown but as alien-crewed ships posing as legitimate traders were about, that was one possibility.

Ahxenta had plenty to send out to the PSS fleet and others on what her teams had found and deduced, but wisely kept a few aspects under wraps lest the report ended up in the wrong ears. Several hours later than intended, *Arianrhod* finally bid farewell to Port Control and slid out of the shattered skeleton of her berth, her captain having received assurances that she would not be billed for the damage. She had decided on the fastest route to Stinward and *Arianrhod* would run with shields up and at alert. The ISP station had been primed to expedite cargo turnover and to repair the ship's residual hull damage.

The first days out passed at an even tenor, with nothing to interrupt *Arianrhod's* steady progress, but comms channels were busy. News of the attack in the Web had spread to every galactic sector, resulting in a rise in patrols by the Allied powers. The Trades Alliance had begun issuing regular bulletins to all shipping lines under its flag and there had been sporadic sightings of ships listed as alien in remote areas of zones Mu and Zeta. The Flemm system, where a node of the new zone Mu hyperspace bypass route was being built, had seen minor problems that had been handled by local units but little more had disrupted the by now well-advanced construction.

The fourth day brought a link from the *Obsidian Sky*. Aware of the attack in the Web and having dropped cargo at Cygilla Prime, Captain Bluejohn had time in hand and offered to delay there until *Arianrhod* caught up. He would join her in the trip to Stinward, as his next load was also for the new ISP dock. Ahxenta agreed: two ships were more likely to deter threats, especially when both were as well-armed and well-known as the *Arianrhod* and the *Obsidian Sky*. In the first mate's opinion, Bluejohn wanted a full account of the trouble at Merkat and a face-to-face was more secure than any comm.

Apnis was correct and the two ships had scarcely joined forces at Cygilla when Bluejohn and his first mate made the shuttle crossing for a briefing. Ahxenta held little back: Bluejohn had been more than a trusted friend for years. She also had the suspicion that he had news to pass on that he did not want to put out publicly. She was right.

The *Obsidian* had had a curious encounter near the remote Rosen, in zone Theta, where she had picked up her cargo for Cygilla. There was an unlisted transport in orbit when they made port and as usual the captain ordered a scan. The spec matched one that *Arianrhod* had sent out some time before of the cargo ship *Kel'Beth*, and much to his surprise, Bluejohn had been hailed by Commander Kismulin Ver. She knew of him and his ship and the courtesy call was to warn him of hostile activity close to Daff Six, a large uninhabited ice world on the border of zones Eta and Theta. He was not headed near the place but Ver had been shot at by what seemed to be a surface station on the planet. She had called the attack in to her own people and had no plans to inform any other authorities, but Bluejohn was welcome to pass it on to his contacts. He had asked for her data on the attack and the station and had been given visuals of a surface structure and the launch of ground to orbital missiles that the *Kel'Beth* had shot down, but that was all. Bluejohn had thanked her for the information and cut the link. His problem now was the validity of the data and the veracity of the informant. As Ahxenta had had dealings with Ver, he wanted her advice. He had brought the shard across with him.

Ahxenta and Apnis studied the images closely. It was the captain's conclusion that from what they could see, the artillery used by the *Kel'Beth* was what she would have expected from that vessel, and the woman in the link *was* Ver. Her advice was to pass the information on to the ISP, the Trades Alliance and the PSS fleet.

"So what do you make of it?" Apnis asked after their two visitors had departed. "Is Ver trying to further the notion that she and the rest of Thal's group are our friends and want to help rid us of these alien unknowns that have been popping up all over?"

"And they realise they can't do it alone," Ahxenta replied as the two made their way back to the bridge. "It could very well be. I'll get Greffy to scrutinise this and get his take on it."

"I bet it'll be that Azular should see it," said Apnis wryly. "I must pay him another visit now we're well on course. He must be cracking up with little to keep him busy. But how is he, really? The doc's cagey every time I ask and I get the impression that all's not quite right."

"His condition's no one's affair but his medical team and mine," was the evasive answer.

"I'm your first mate and a close friend of his *and* yours and you're worried, Cinnabar, I can tell."

The captain halted the transport tube to face the commander. "He may never get his full mobility back unless he has cyber implants at a specialist centre and he's refusing point blank to consider it," she said frankly. "I *can* understand why, at some level, but Axellina's worried that permanent mobility problems will dent his confidence long term. And he has other worries that he's keeping mighty quiet about but they're obvious to Flintlock – and he's refused to see Parri Millit."

"He doesn't want the ship's counsellor involved? I guess his other worries concern Kerrix, then. From one or two things I heard in the mess, he was due for some leg-pulling over his Ms Kerrix, but other things intervened and now nobody would dare."

"They'd better not," the captain said flatly. "And we have work to do. But no word of this to anyone."

"Roger that," the first mate agreed as Ahxenta released the hold.

The two ships continued across zones Zeta and Eta and into Iota. The captains had chosen to head to Stinward by New Zegonia to give Daff Six a wide berth. The details of Ver's warning had been sent to the agreed parties but only confirmations had been heard by return. They made the ISP station without incident, where berths were ready with grapples on standby to relieve both ships of their cargoes.

A few days later saw *Arianrhod's* hull back to its usual trim and she made ready to ship out. The *Obsidian* had set out for Keystone Kell as soon as she had unloaded and was long gone, but had had a trouble-free ride. Ahxenta ordered her own ship on course for Tressic Major and her forward mission.

As time slid by and duty crews changed, Lindell and his team, on constant lookout for new contracts, had found one for the transfer of agro-engineering gear from the industrial-agrarian Larrikon Seven to Vellis Prime, a route that would take them on a heading for their next scheduled stop of Freskat. Ahxenta was quick to agree terms and sat musing as she scanned route charts on the approach to Tressic space.

"We'll cut directly through Coalition space and make dead straight for Larrikon; we can use the local bypass to Rettik and then cross the zone boundary at Stook. There have been no reports of anything in that area, but it's pretty empty of Allied systems. Crizz still has some kin on Larrikon, doesn't she, in the engineering trade?"

"I'll check. Let's hope the next few days are as tedious as the last: space that looks void doesn't mean it is," Apnis yawned, stretching to ease muscles at the end of her watch. "By the way, Whisper's got a rough version of that ring-shaped gun port based on the Norvallan design on the go. She's attached a trial-sized edition to *Loki's* hull and drilled through. She's trying to link *Loki's* weapons systems into it but I've barred her from arming it, given what happened to Gem Ferry's toy boat last time. But she's run sims and reckons that its six phase-beam nubs *can* be used as one focussed burst *or* as disparate divergent bursts of fire to confuse an enemy."

"Or shoot a hole in *Loki's* own hull," Ahxenta snorted.

"Funny, that's what she said Azular said when she visited him in medbay to ask about its feasibility," the first mate grinned. *"He's* been running the data that Greffy pulled in on the alien version of *Loki* to see if he can match it definitively to the example in the Norvallan database he got from Kerrix."

"He should help Lieutenant Ferry to produce a scale model of it," Box piped up from the well of the bridge, where he and his mate were running nav-sims to pass the time. "Gem's good at that sort of thing. Then let Lieutenant Commander Earbleat loose on it with her model gun emplacement thingy. I'm sure she'd be able to work out how to blow the next one we meet to bits with the real *Loki.*"

"Will you shut your mouth?" Dox interrupted testily.

"Big ears," Apnis commented. "But it might keep Azular out of trouble and Ferry occupied. Though I doubt Gem would let Whisper anywhere near it. But that's it for now, Cap: here comes the next watch and we'll have to be back on for the final leg into Tressic. I can maybe catch up with Crizz in the mess and find out about her folks on Larrikon. She may want to pop in and see them or see if they have anything that might be of use to us."

"I'm heading to medbay. I'll find you in the mess later."

"Tell him I said hello," was the soft reply.

Azular was much as she had last seen him, Ahxenta noted as she looked in through the viewing portal of his bay. He was busy with the console he had set up across his mobility chair but his usually placid face now bore the traces of past trauma and present anxiety. Some intuition made him look up and he smiled at her.

"Punctual as always, Captain," he greeted her as she walked in.

"What are you up to?"

He turned the console to let her see. As the first mate had said, he had been comparing the actual data on the alien projectile ship to the specs of similar from Norvallan data. He had been successful and had found a close match. He had thus updated the Norvallan files with technical details and integrated the results into *Arianrhod's* science and tactical ops for rapid recognition if ever they came across similar.

The conversation turned to Earbleat's latest project and the quirky suggestions by Box for testing her circular gun-port layout at bench-level, and then moved on to various contract and other ship matters. One topic Azular blocked at every turn was his own health. Having read updates from her chief medic, the captain was aware that his progress had been less than hoped for. It was time, she decided, to take a stand. Invoking the privacy option to obscure the view panel and deter intrusion, she pulled her chair closer to his.

"Put that damn board to the side. You and I are going to talk."

As he adamantly refused to discuss anything personal on the basis that it *was* personal, Ahxenta led him to the private chat that she had had with Kerrix in Merkat's medbay a short time before Azular had been brought back aboard. As he had suspected at the time, he had been the chief subject. And despite her almost instinctive dislike of the woman, the captain let him know that she had come to respect and trust her, and to believe that her feelings for Azular were not only sincere but much stronger than she had initially realised.

"She's almost as tight-lipped about you as you are about her and we had a few sharp words over it," the captain informed him. "She came to see my point of view eventually."

"Your point of view, Captain?" Azular asked warily.

"Just let's say our conversation became more frank. I have to say I don't totally get what you see in her and what she sees in you puzzles me a tad, but whatever it is, well, it's your concern and hers, not mine. And I've obviously no idea what you discussed when you saw each other in medbay and when you talked to her from here before we were targeted by that alien missile you seem to have got the measure of." The captain paused before continuing. "Do you know that she and Dr Flintlock had a few words about you?"

His expression was still guarded but he acknowledged that Kerrix had mentioned one or two things.

Ahxenta nodded. "The doctor naturally would tell her nothing but she's capable of reading *and* interpreting medical scanner output. She recognises nerve damage when she sees it and knows what it can mean physically and mentally. After all, she went through complex technical surgery to have that language analyser fitted, so she's aware of what can happen if things go wrong. But one thing she made plain to me," Ahxenta recalled with a gentle look. "Whatever the outcome for you, it wouldn't change how she felt about you. She didn't hold back. I *did* point out that it was possible that it might be a long time, perhaps a very long time, before she saw you again. She knew you were headed back aboard and that we had a long haul in front of us."

The captain's eyes bored into his as she waited his reaction. In the face of his stubborn silence, she continued, "Did you know that she wants to get as far as Starfall Exit to see if she can find a way back to Norvallan space from there? And she figures the *Nyx Warrior* might be an option, now that Nat Holdspan seems to think he owes her?"

He nodded dumbly, looking away, but as he still looked mutinous Ahxenta decided to carry on. "So you've talked about it."

There was no response.

"Azular, whatever I think of that woman, she loves you: what you are *and* what you'll be or not be as far as she can see ahead; and she accepts that unreservedly. Haven't you grasped that? And I think very highly of you, as you're aware. I can't imagine how I'd run this ship without you. Hell, you're the longest-serving officer I have. When we get back to the Web, if Xanna Kerrix is there and needs a ride, she'll be welcome aboard *Arianrhod*. And I'll do what I can to assist her."

Azular turned in amazement. "You'd do that for me, Captain?"

"I'd do that for both of you. On condition you snap out of it and get the hell back on duty."

"Captain… Cinnabar… I don't know what to say."

"That's a first," Ahxenta replied laconically. "At least she realises your worth. But no word of this to anyone, though I suspect you'll have to put up with a bit of ear-bashing over your Ms Kerrix when you do get back in gear. And as I'm off duty and need my rations, I'll leave you to yours. Tallica says hello, by the way."

"Thank you, Captain."

Ahxenta winked as she rose, releasing the privacy screen on her way out. As she sauntered, smiling, past the chief medic's office, she was collared by Dr Flintlock.

"That was one hell of a long one-to-one. How did you find him and how is he now?"

"It was, he was miserable and now he's much better. Leave him for a while before you let anyone in. He's got thinking to do. Time you were off duty in any case. I'm for the mess; I'll see you there."

"Is that an order, Cap?"

"That's an order, Doctor."

Ahxenta found Apnis with Crizz Cottontail and most of the way through her meal when she claimed a chair in the mess.

"How's Azular?" the first mate greeted her.

"He'll do," she said briefly. "He can't keep his hands off his work, but I suppose it keeps his mind active."

"And off other things?"

"I wouldn't go that far," the captain grinned. "You okay Crizz?"

"Aye, Cap. Tallica's brought me up to date on the Larrikon pick-up after we leave Tressic. Haven't spoken to the cousins in years but if they still have their shuttle repair yard in Greencourt I'll look them up and see what's what. If you need any small technical bits, give me a list and I'll see what I can do. I have mates in various trades there still and I can give them a call as well."

"Will do. Pass what you get by Lindell; he'll be sourcing the stuff we need. You'll have a day to get your visiting in. There'll be no time for shore leave for the crew, nor will there be at Vellis Prime but we'll hang on at Freskat for the crystals to be set and to see if we can find a market for them on the way back to the Web. Those at the top of the leave rota can have some time out there."

"As the shipbuilding trade is still increasing big time, there'll be no shortage of potential customers for set comms arrays," the first mate remarked. "We might see a few on Freskat as their military is always on the lookout, Freskat being such an out of the way place."

"I'll make sure things are go for work to begin on the crystals as soon as we get them off ship," Ahxenta told her. "I'll get Azular to check them before we send them down, as his eyes and gear are the best in the business. They're still in the hold as they were handed over from the *Obsidian*. As other things got in the way, they haven't been touched. I know Lindell got a guarantee that they were high quality, but I want to make sure before we do anything to them."

"And if they're not the best?" the chief engineer asked.

"Then we head back via Brown Amber and take the place apart."

"Seems reasonable to me, Cap," Crizz Cottontail shrugged as she spooned up the last of her rations.

Tressic Major, a typical world on the edge of Coalition-run space, was close to no other centre apart from its colony Tressic Minor, but it ran three orbital repair stations for the ships that crossed zone Kappa on the way to remoter sectors. As *Arianrhod* had made good time and was back on schedule, a quick about-turn at Tressic had her on the road to her next port in less than two days standard. The trip through Kappa and into Zeta was quiet, the most positive event by the time they made Larrikon Seven being Azular's return to the bridge.

Walking was still difficult for him but he had taken more fully to his mobility chair and with facility made for locking it into his usual stations he could carry out most of his normal duties in his lab and on the bridge. The chief medic had stipulated short duty shifts for him, but his off-duty was invariably spent in the scientific ploys that absorbed him. As Flintlock noted, she had no idea what the captain had said to Azular during their lengthy dialogue, but whatever it was, he seemed to have regained his usual genial outlook and even took the veiled teasing from his shipmates on the interest he had at Merkat with no more than a resigned look and the odd sharp remark.

Word of a scale model of the alien missile and the use to which he should put it had hit Gem Ferry's ears via Box and he was interested to the extent that he had begun to produce it, although he refused to let Earbleat anywhere near his workbench. The data that Azular had built up on the device Ahxenta thought prudent to circulate over the Ultraviolet III and to Thal. There had been no word over the usual nets that such a weapon had been used against PSS or other ships but a non-direct piece of news from Thal implied that one of his vessels had faced a similar threat at the edge of Beta near Kelfar Keeth. That his people were still active in that area suggested to the captain that their destroyed base had been hugely important to them and they still held out hope that something could be salvaged.

Larrikon's major settlement was Steelspire and the captain set her team's shuttle down in the mercantile quarter, close by the offices of Spire Holdings, where she was to finalise accounts for handover of a cargo pod of heavy gear, now in an orbital freight holding point, to *Arianrhod*. Leaving their two guards with the craft, Ahxenta, Apnis and Lindell headed for the main building. None of them knew the clients although the supercargo had spoken to them by link, but they ran into one familiar figure in the reception area. A startled Spendle Doosbak stopped dead as he caught sight of the uniforms.

"The missing Mr Doosbak," Ahxenta greeted him coldly. "You're a long way from Lonagan Four and you're dressed rather smartly for a fugitive. Have you floated up out of the swamp where you were hidden or are you still on the run from your devious ex-clients?"

"I don't know what you mean," Doosbak croaked harshly.

"I think you do. Are you still toting the cases of advanced nano-weapons components that you ran off with from Lonagan or have you sold them off to the highest bidder?"

"Here are our contacts, Captain," Lindell murmured at her elbow.

Doosbak's mouth dropped in audible relief but it was short-lived.

Ahxenta eyed him frostily. "Good. It won't take long. You and I will deal with it, Lindell. Commander Apnis will keep our friend here amused until we're done, won't you, Commander? I want a word or ten with him. As I'm sure many others do."

"Aye, ma'am," the first mate replied, eyeing the man with a grin that boded ill for him. "We'll sit over there until you're done, Cap."

"I have an urgent appointment," Doosbak cringed. "I have to go."

"Tell me all about it," Tallica Apnis invited, grasping his elbow in a vice-like grip and leading him off.

The captain turned to the oncoming reps, and with a nod she and Lindell followed them out whilst Apnis propelled her quarry over to a window seat, pushed him down and unsheathed her small phase pistol. She primed it for very heavy stun.

"I know your little foibles and your implants still pack a punch, I'll bet. Now you sit quiet while I let my guards know we've met you."

Apnis left her comm open as she made the link and passed the message. She then ordered Lieutenant Goldwash to inform *Arianrhod* of the missing trader and to have tactical maintain a close watch on the lifesigns of the landing party via their locating pins. Goldwash got the message: none of the five were wearing locating pins.

"And now we'll have a nice little chat, won't we?" Apnis smiled across at the squirming man as she dug out and set up a recorder cum jammer to prevent listening in or intrusion from others and to foil the embedded data-recorder she suspected he still possessed.

The first mate had extracted little from Doosbak in the hour it took the captain to settle her business other than that he had a local berth and a local contact, but by the time Ahxenta and Lindell appeared he was hot under the collar and feared the worst. He would not discuss his doings over the weeks he had been missing or how he had ended up on Larrikon but he realised that Ahxenta would want answers.

The captain sent a link to the ship to apprise them of the results of negotiations, gave the go-ahead for loading, and sent Lindell back to the shuttle to expedite cargo-related matters. She then made for a seat opposite Doosbak. As she was certain he would try every trick he had to mislead her and to record every nuance of their interaction, she set her scanner to continuous probe, its output transferring to the ship. She knew that Greffy and Azular were both on the bridge and would examine every photon of the data as it was received.

"I'm waiting," she told the man. "And as I don't have much time, this will be short, unless you want to talk to me in my brig. You *have* after all seen it before. And as there are so many on your tail, I'm sure I'll meet someone to hand you over to on the way to my next stop."

His eyes bulged at that. "I don't know what you mean."

"Then let me clarify. Your business friends, the ones you lifted the high-tech nano-weapons bits from, are keen to get their hands on you. So keen that they made your chum Micklemouse contact me to try to hoodwink me into finding you and the missing gear, *and* so that they could get their slimy hands on me and mine."

"Bick?" he asked. "They asked him to call *you* to try to find me?"

"I don't think they actually asked him," Ahxenta said with a quirky grin. "I suspect he had little option. They had got him after all, even though he tried to run and had made it as far as Keeant. But you they still want, very badly, so Micklemouse says. So you're going to tell me who they are and why they want you – and me, for that matter."

"They got Bick?" Doosbak's eyes widened as he gaped in seeming shock, but his reaction did not convince the captain.

"As if you didn't know," Ahxenta snapped. "So you last saw him on Lonagan Four a day before some meeting you *said* you had set up with trade contacts from Sevolb about using his handy little ship to carry alleged super spec nano-weapons components from Lonagan to Minch Fettin. Did you *have* the meeting or had you already managed to get you paws on the contraband and just light out with it, figuring you could sell it on if it was so special? Answers now, Doosbak or you're for my brig and believe me, you won't enjoy the experience."

"You can't do that to me! You've no right! I'm a free citizen…"

"Are you? As far as I'm aware, you're missing. Nobody knows where you are. Or do they?" The captain scanned his pale, greasy face and the hands he was twisting together as if in high anxiety.

A vibration of her wrist communit alerted Ahxenta to a message. She read the holo, slipped her earpiece into her ear and listened. Her jaw tightened and her icy eyes bored into those of the trader.

"Commander Apnis, Mr Doosbak has set off a tracker signal from a wrist unit. Find the unit and destroy it. Break his wrist if you have to," she ordered without taking her gaze from Doosbak's face.

Apnis quickly complied, found and removed the device and fried it with her hand weapon. "End of message," she said grimly.

"Now we're going for a walk, Doosbak. There are too many eyes, ears and other things around here," the captain told him as she stood.

"Are you coming or do I have to tie you up and carry you?"

"You wouldn't dare!" he said defiantly. "There are witnesses."

"There are," she agreed, looking round. "I don't see any objecting. But as you *are* reluctant to come, I can have security here take you in charge. I'll call local law enforcement and we'll explain to them. And though we're not in Coalition space, I'm sure its Central Council will have local officials it can call in and we can talk to them."

He hesitated a fraction too long.

"As you wish," Ahxenta declared and turned to make for the main reception desk, ignoring his call behind her.

She was soon back. "Security's on its way. We'll wait here."

"Captain!" he exclaimed in anguish. "Look, I'll tell you what you want to know but you'll have to give me some time."

"You don't have time and neither do I. I suggest you sit quietly or I *will* restrain you. And as your face has been recorded by local secure cams, a lot of people know you've been in here, and still are in fact. What were you doing *in* here in any case?"

He licked his lips. "I have contacts here," he asserted shiftily.

"Agro-equipment? That's not your usual line," Apnis remarked.

"They do other things," he said, looking at her warily.

"Like what?"

"Lots of things."

"Like what?" the first mate repeated. "Not saying, huh? Oh, here comes security, Cap," she noted, her eyes skipping to the entry doors through which two tall uniformed officers were making their way.

It was then that the trader realised he had been duped: the guards were *Arianrhod* crewmen. Hanx unhooked a pair of restraints from his belt, primed them and looked enquiringly at the captain.

"Do you walk out nicely or do we truss you up like the mean little felon you are?" Ahxenta asked the man. "Cams are still on you, so if you *do* have meetings with contacts here, I'm sure someone will tell them. Or you can link from my brig. I'll set you up with the needful."

He knew he was beaten. He stood up warily, glancing round to see who was watching. The few clients visible were enough to cause him to attempt a smile, as though agreeing with his escort.

"You really don't cut as suave a figure as you think you do, Mr Doosbak," Apnis informed him as the five made their way out of the door, the captain nodding decisively over to the main desk.

"Keep walking," Ahxenta ordered. "My shuttle's over there and my guards will keep you right. Both have their phase rifles handy," she said as she unloosed her own, signalling Apnis to do likewise.

The party was not accosted as it made its way across open space to the shuttle, to be greeted by Lindell, who had been busy aboard.

"Our cargo's loaded, the manifest is in order and all our clearances have been granted, ma'am," he informed the captain. "We can leave orbit as soon as we're aboard. Lieutenant Commander Earbleat and Chief Cottontail are both aware of the situation and have altered their schedules accordingly."

"Good. Tie our guest in tightly, Mr Goldwash, and take care you don't fall foul of his implanted hardware and software, as he's able to pack quite a punch with fists *and* feet. And you'd better dispossess him of most of the fancy bits and pieces he carries about his person. The rest you can remove once we're on board."

"Aye, Captain."

Doosbak was hustled into the craft and searched diligently by his captors. He made little protest other than to say that he had gear in his billet that he needed. Ahxenta let him complain; she was intent on heading back to the ship and putting distance between *Arianrhod* and Larrikon. However he had got there, his being there concerned her. Her advent *had* seemed to shake him but otherwise he appeared to be his usual sneaky self and not what she expected in a man on the run.

Once back on the bridge and with their unwelcome lodger in the brig, the captain gave the order to depart directly for Vellis Prime.

"Too much coincidence, Cap," the first mate said in an aside once the ship was fairly on her way.

"Precisely. Once we're out of Larrikon space, we take care of it."

"What did you have in mind?"

"We get rid of Doosbak for a start. After we figure what he's been sent here to do," the captain told her.

"We were meant to pick him up?" Apnis asked.

"That's what I reckon. The questions being by whom and why."

"We'd better make sure he's not wired to go bang when he's being questioned," Lieutenant Box chipped in from the navi-helm console.

"Keep your eyes on your boards, Mr Box. And get ready to plot us a course to Rydderwild on my say so," Ahxenta ordered.

"Aye, ma'am."

"Rydderwild, Cap?" asked the first mate, puzzled.

"Rydderwild; it's Coalition and so's he. Its Central Council wants him, so it can have him. I'm sick of all these shenanigans with him and Micklemouse used as pawns in some big game to get us."

"And you think that's what this is?"

"I do. Whoever these bandits are that knew we were on Larrikon, they'll also know our next port of call. So we don't head there."

"But what about these cases of weapons bits that he's supposed to have run off with? Was that a set-up or did he really think he'd have a chance of outfoxing his slimy clients, given that he knows what they are and what they could do to him if he crossed them?"

"I wonder," Ahxenta mused. "He may have got his paws on what he thought were advanced nano-weapons parts that he could make profit of. He *was* after all arrogant enough to think he could run his own shady trade outfit and keep his place on the Coalition Council. But he set off that tracker while he was sat with us, so either it was planned or he thought he *was* in trouble and set it off in hope of rescue. I wasn't convinced that Micklemouse's capture was a surprise and our arrival may not have been the shock he made it seem. No, all in all, I reckon he was in on some of it. What I don't get is why they made it look like he had run off with the gear or had gone missing. It can't just have been to get us. There's something else going on. And where's the stuff he's supposed to have filched?"

"Maybe we'd better ask him?" was the jocular reply. "But do you think they're still tracking him?"

"We'll find out shortly – Azular's down in security with all his kit. But *I'll* be dropping Doosbak at security in Rydderwild Township. I'll advise them *and* the Coalition Central Council. If the Council wants him, it can send reps to pick him up there."

"You'll be telling him this?" the first mate enquired.

"You're damn straight I will. Enough is enough."

It was obvious to the eavesdropping members of the bridge crew that the captain was seriously put out over what had happened. They all maintained a judicious silence as the great ship sped outward.

Once well away from the Larrikon system the order was given to change route, deploy the cloak and make for Rydderwild, all speed. Ahxenta then headed to her office to take her own measures before the talk with Doosbak. Azular and Flintlock had both been busy: the man still bore implanted hardware, none of which read explosive, and an embedded data-copying port. His internal data recording facility *had* been upgraded since last they had scanned him and he had an internal tracker that could be read long distance, but Azular had blocked it by reinforcing the security field around his cell. Doosbak had been given a meal into which the chief medic had slipped a self-destructive systems inhibitor to scramble his short-term data uptake. She and Azular were in on the interview, two guards were posted outside the door and the whole procedure was being monitored.

The trader looked less anxious than the captain had expected, a sign she ascribed to his belief that he could escape his present plight. She began by going over previously-covered ground and found that he had met his Sevolb contacts at their request hours before the planned meeting. He was handed the two cases then, for delivery to Minch Fettin by his hand rather than that of his friend. The contacts had told him that the Coalition group probing his business interests had dug up more damning evidence and was about to press charges. They insinuated that they could help him out of his fix if he would help them. He was given a liberal fee as an incentive on the proviso that he vanished but held himself ready to be called on. Believing he had no option, he had carried the goods to Minch Fettin in one of his own super-spec small transports. He had then made for Larrikon at his clients' behest, where he was told to await orders. That had led him to Spire Holdings and his unexpected meeting with the captain.

The captain snorted sceptically, exchanging a glance with Azular, who shook his head fractionally.

"You're a liar, Doosbak. But what *did* you do with these cases, *if* they ever existed?" Ahxenta demanded. "Lonagan to Minch Fettin is a long way in a small ship to have made it there and back to Larrikon. Assuming you *did* make Minch Fettin, to whom did you hand the cases? Where's your transport now? And you still haven't told me who and what your clients are and what their line of business is."

The man writhed uncomfortably. "I *did* have the cases when I left. I used my ship to get to Keystone Kell. I waited there for a transport that was to pick me up for Minch Fettin. But then I was told to make for Larrikon instead, so I used my own ship to go there."

"What did you do when you checked out those cases and found that they didn't contain weapons parts?" Azular asked suddenly.

"They did!" the man exclaimed. "At least my clients *said* they did."

"They did not," the science officer countered. "You *are* smart and you were able to break the coding and get into them, weren't you?"

Ahxenta kept her peace, realising that Azular was chasing his own trail. The trader was wary, scenting a hidden agenda and not sure how to respond as the Berzic bid him reveal the identity, nature and trade of his mysterious contacts and their stated origin of Sevolb.

"Did you recognise or work out what you actually had when you broke into the cases of kit that you'd been given, Mr Doosbak?"

"I don't know what you're talking about."

"I'm talking about the cases you broke into that your contacts from Sevolb gave you," Azular said tranquilly. "You *will* tell us what they contained, what you were going to do with them, and why you thought you could outplay your Sevolb clients by setting them against your unpleasant cyber-enhanced alien associates from Mellifly. Did you think you'd get a better offer and better protection from them, but then found that they were part of the equation anyway? Or did you try to contact Hoxiz and found you couldn't? And then realised you had better confess and toe the line or else?"

"How the…"

"You'll answer every one of Dr Azular's questions now," Ahxenta snapped harshly. "I have no time for you and your time wasting."

"Look, if you let me off at Vellis Prime and no questions asked, I'll tell you all I know," the trader offered.

"You're on the edge, Doosbak, and about to fall off!" the captain hissed. "*How* did you know my ship was for Vellis Prime unless you knew the details of our contract with Spire? It's not been mentioned. Who told you to head for the reception area there at that time?"

"Or what?" the man asked, evidently scared as his eyes roamed his small cell, but still sure that the outcome would be in his favour.

"Some news for you, Doosbak: whatever you were counting on will not happen. My ship is *not* headed for Vellis. And one reason you will never see your contact Hoxiz again is that he's been taken from Merkat, where he was being held for *my* attempted murder and that of two others, to a very safe and permanent holding area where he's unlikely to see anyone he knows ever again. You savvy?"

As the man's eyes rounded in real or feigned shock, the wail of the red alert hit their ears, the call to battlestations boomed and a strident voice demanding the captain's presence on the bridge rang out.

"Too late, Doosbak!" Ahxenta hissed as the pulsating light of the alert grew around them, turning their faces to blood red.

24: THE EMERALD

The captain gave Azular her arm as support as they made a rapid exit. As soon as the panel zipped over, she ordered her guards to keep a secure watch on the prisoner and tabbed the local comm to demand the cause of the alert. Apnis was terse: they had picked up a distress from a PSS in the area and had set to intercept. Ahxenta could tell by the rising hum that *Arianrhod's* engines were straining to cope as she moved into high gear. She and Azular made for the nearest transport tube, calling on override for a straight run to the bridge and leaving the doctor to make her own way to medbay.

The first mate, her face a grim mask, rose to vacate the command chair as the two sped through the entry. Azular limped to his station. The bridge holo-grid was set to full extent and data from the tactical and science relays integrated into the ship's hull was flowing in as the grid continuously updated. Every post was manned.

"What gives?" the captain demanded as she sat, webbing herself in securely and hauling her boards across her knees.

"Alert on the PSS channel: it's the *Emerald*. Two interceptor-types burst out on top of her at Mitten, all guns blazing; positive for hostile tech so they're not raiders. She's holding her own so far but *Emerald's* a helluva lot smaller that we are and those beasts are relentless. We'll be up on them in fifteen minutes. I've dropped the cloak to give us more speed and to let the blips see we're on their horizon."

"She could have been spied and tailed or somebody put one and one together when she picked up her last cargo ahead of schedule at Fyvie Minor and lit out in this direction. She'd hit the bypass for a straight run to Mitten, so it would be a sound guess that she'd be for rendezvous with us at Vellis, because it's sure as hell known we were headed there. But Goodsocks is no panicking fool and a damn good commander – she'll make a fight of it."

"Captain! *Emerald* reports another incoming!" Bellfish hollered.

"Put her on speaker!"

"On speaker!"

The rough tones of Captain Melly Goodsocks could be heard as she called out commands to her bridge crew demanding confirmation of the identity of the newcomer off her ship's bows.

"It's a PSS!" a loud but relieved voice in the background yelled. "It's the *Nyx Warrior*, Captain!"

"Thank hell for that!" Apnis exclaimed feelingly. "It'll be all over bar the shouting by the time we get there. Nat Holdspan's no slouch when it comes to using his guns and he'll have the measure of them."

As the thunder of phase fire echoed in their ears, it was clear that the *Warrior* had leapt in directly. Ahxenta ordered comms channels kept open and alerted Holdspan to her impending arrival. The sound of spattering fire as both ships took hits was overridden by staccato commands from their captains and the responses of their crews. The two rogues quickly realised they were outclassed and outgunned and began a retreat towards the Mitten bypass node. Holdspan did not, as Ahxenta suspected he might, order pursuit, but directed his crew to stand down red alert and query the status of the *PSS Emerald*.

By the time *Arianrhod* made local space there was little to see but a heavily-damaged *Emerald* and a sound *Nyx Warrior*. Ahxenta sighed in relief as Goodsocks reported that she had several serious injuries but no fatalities. The ship was still spaceworthy thanks to the *Warrior's* aid but would need extensive repairs. There had been minor casualties aboard Holdspan's ship.

"So your plan to transfer our cargo to the *Emerald* at Rydderwild is shot, Cinnabar," Apnis grated as Goodsocks cut the link.

"Damn!" was the vexed exclamation. "And we owe Nat Holdspan again. But what's he doing in this neck of the galaxy?"

"His outer cargo bays have the meshes down so he's carrying a big payload. We're about to find out," the first mate added as Lieutenant Bellfish announced that Captain Holdspan was on the comm.

The *Nyx Warrior* had been in transit from Vrackin to Heligon's repair base with heavy engineering gear when she caught the distress. She had just passed the node at Mitten but as she had been running cloaked, she may not have been picked up by the hostiles.

"Or they were in wait for the *Emerald*," Ahxenta posited, cocking an eyebrow at the news that the *Warrior* now had a cloaking facility.

Captain Holdspan was working to a tight schedule but was willing to help escort the *Emerald* into whatever repair base she or Captain Goodsocks judged suitable. Ahxenta thanked him but refused to hold him up further and with a mutual exchange of goodwill, cut the link.

"We could have asked him to ship our stuff for Vellis," murmured the first mate. "It's not too far out of his way."

"It crossed my mind but we already owe him. The *Emerald's* not fit to ship anything, so I'll have to come up with a new plan. But we're for Rydderwild. Their orbital repair yard's expensive, not the best *and* Coalition but as we're passing Doosbak to a party that's keen to have him, I can maybe twist arms. And I want the *Emerald's* casualty list as some of ours have friends aboard, or family in the case of Bottle."

Orders were given and the crippled *Emerald* made ready to move out. Ahxenta left Apnis in command and made for her office to link to her contacts and to send a note to relevant bodies. She was spared the latter, as Holdspan had beaten her to it and sent his own.

Less than an hour later and with one and a half more to go before the two ships made Rydderwild, the captain returned to the bridge.

"Got a pick up," she told Apnis. "Our Vellis clients are happy so long as they get their goods. The *Comet* was on her way from Delta Iridium to Vellis and she's off the beacon at Peascod Colony, so Sarie will divert and take on our cargo. She's got the hold space and needs the fee as she's had engine trouble, hence her stop at Delta. The yard at Rydderwild can carry out basic repairs to the *Emerald* so we'll hang fire there and then escort her to Delta for major overhaul. It means we'll be late to Freskat but it can't be helped. We'll take on *Emerald's* cargo for Hespera and drop it off on the way in. Melly's arranging it. Her clients ought to be grateful that it wasn't blown to bits and that there *is* a ship that can take it over."

"Roger that, Cap. *Emerald's* under our flag, so she *is* our concern. I take it there's been nothing big on the PSS channels apart from us?"

"No, or little else; but I'd better give Doosbak the news that he'll be leaving our tender care and heading for the Coalition's. I didn't get the chance during our interview as those hostiles interrupted us."

"They were maybe his buddies."

"Possibly," the captain groaned, flexing aching shoulders. "Once we're in orbit get the duty crews off shift, yourself included. I'll have to head down and deal with the squad that'll be taking custody of Doosbak. I'd like to take Azular but I don't think Flintlock will allow it as he's had a long stint."

"You'll be taking an armed escort and a pilot regardless *and* you'll all have locating pins," the first mate informed her. "And I'm staying on duty until you're back aboard."

"And then I'll have to see Melly Goodsocks and her people. Best post the *Emerald's* casualty list for our people to look at. Kym Bottle's sister was hit but she's listed as a minor injury. Melly has four serious casualties that should be cared for off-ship but she's not keen to have them treated at Rydderwild and neither's her chief medic."

"I don't blame her, but didn't Axellina bring a lot of extra medical supplies up from Merkat with Azular? She and Greenwing between them should be able to fix it. He's one of the best medics in the fleet and she's another. I can organise that while you go break the news to the rat in the brig that he'll have a new cage soon."

"Good call. You do that. But first I need a word with Azular: our little chat to Doosbak ended too soon and I want to know what he worked out and how. His grilling of the rat was rather pointed."

The captain ordered Azular into her office for the talk about their captive. The first clue was the endpoint of Minch Fettin for the so-called weapons components, he explained.

"I think it also occurred to you, Captain. I deduced that they were nano-components for medical rather than military use, though it'll probably come to the same thing in the end. Doosbak was surprised that I'd picked up on it and lying when he denied it. He was smart enough to realise what he had and that his employers would not only be upset but would be liable to retaliate nastily once they'd found out he'd broken into the cases. Once he figured that the pieces *were* for complex and likely illegal medical devices and having himself been altered in the Mellifly facility, I guessed that he tried to get himself out of his dilemma by contacting his associates in that business there and selling out his Sevolb clients. That he linked to Hoxiz was a shot in the dark and I can't be sure he did, but he'd not realised at that point that his Sevolb contacts were part of the Mellifly set-up."

"But how did you work out that the Sevolb band were part of the ring of cyber-enhanced types that were into humanoid alteration for their own ends at Mellifly?" Ahxenta asked. "Ah… Micklemouse."

"Exactly. He said when he called you from Keeant at the behest of his masters that he was sure he'd met one of the Sevolb contacts at the Mellifly facility where he went through the surgical, physical *and* genetic alterations that made him an info-sent, and where his later upgrades were done. He also said the man was similar to Hoxiz – and as we know, Micklemouse is highly sensitive to his masters. It's one of the reasons he's been let loose so often to serve them."

"So once Doosbak realised he was in deep, he'd no option but to confess and do anything to get out of it. He did seem shocked to hear that Hoxiz was out of the picture, though. But it still doesn't tell us how they knew we were set for Larrikon and the meet with Spire Holdings *and* when it was – though he said he'd been there a while."

"Many people would know of the contract," Azular pointed out. "And even if *our* comms can't be breached, I expect that many of our contractors are less strict about security. And any huge loads that need shipping require equally large carriers."

"Like us. Yes, you're right. And many companies will have snoops that can be bought at the right price; most I expect. And so will larger bodies like the TA and the ISP. And hyperspace trade routes are not secret and we have to use them."

Ahxenta paused as updates on her screens advised of imminent docking. "We're coming into orbit now. You get off duty. I want a word with Doosbak before we ready him to ship down."

"Will you need me portside, Captain?" he asked.

"Dr Flintlock will have my ears if I take you. You're off duty now, mister. Move it."

"Aye, ma'am."

In his small cell, Doosbak was contemplating his fate. He had no idea what had caused the red alert or the results but had no illusions that this would be an easy ride. He looked up anxiously as the captain and two security guards entered.

"Get ready to ship out," Ahxenta stated shortly. "You're going to Rydderwild. You know the place, you've been there. You'll be held in their lock-up until the Coalition Central Council reps that are on their way to pick you up get in. Try anything on me or mine on the way down and you are toast. I take it you understand me, Doosbak?"

"You can't hand me over to the Council!" he exclaimed.

"Why not? It's better than what you and yours have been trying to do to me. Count yourself lucky I'm not bringing charges. Your pals are up for murder and attempted murder. You want to join them in the dock on those charges and I *will* arrange it. You got me?"

"Yes, Captain," he swallowed.

"Truss him up and escort him to my shuttle in alpha four," she ordered her guards. "He so much as sneezes, take him down."

Ahxenta marched out of the cell, repeated the orders to the guards outside and headed for a transport tube and the bridge. By the time she arrived the first mate had spoken to Captain Goodsocks and Dr Flintlock. The latter was even then coordinating with Dr Greenwing over the transfer of gear and expertise. There had been a call from Captain Sarie Jikelleli: the *Green Comet* had just come off the bypass and would be up on Rydderwild in a couple of hours.

"Good. Lindell's team can arrange the details for cargo transfer to the *Comet* with our clients at both ends if you'll organise the move of the goods once it's all in place. I'm going to check how far the bunch of Coalitions reps has got and then I'll head down to the Township and dispose of our living cargo to their security."

"Aye, Cap. I'll be glad to see the back of the little twerp. Hoxiz is off the board, Doosbak soon will be. So that's two down."

"And several hundred more to go," Ahxenta said ironically. "At this rate we can clear up the lot; it'll only take a year or three."

The Coalition reps were expected shortly and a local security unit was ready for Doosbak. Azular was waiting in the shuttle bay. He had been given leave by the CMO on condition that he returned to the ship immediately after. Ahxenta considered.

"Okay, done," she agreed. "I'd planned to head straight up to the *Emerald* but we can bring the shuttle back here and drop the pilot and guards off. And if there's any more we can ship over to the *Emerald* to help her out, I can pick that up and take it across."

The trip to the Township's main facilities, where the captain knew that two security guards and their senior officer awaited them, took a short time. Ahxenta's inflexible face when Doosbak made a final plea for mercy as he was hauled off the shuttle made him realise that his chances were nil. As the captain was talking to the reception party in the bay, Azular made it his business to watch the trader and saw the fear on his face give way to a resurge of hope and quiet assurance as he took in the senior SO. Azular caught Hanx' eye and he gave a warning glance that flicked to the SSO and his party as he quietly slid his hand into the pocket in which he kept his handgun.

The SSO was as swift as the two from the *Arianrhod*, realising that he had been caught out. Azular had read the man and, aware that he would not hesitate to act, drew his weapon and fired. Hanx as quickly stunned one of the others as Ahxenta's left hook caught the third.

"You going to tell me what the hell that was about?" the captain asked Azular brusquely, nursing her sore fist.

"I suspect that these are not the real escort party, Captain. The SSO's certainly not what he appears and I assume, possibly wrongly, that the other two are also imposters. Perhaps we should find out?"

"You and Hanx do that. Goldwash, check the perimeter. Marks and Ji, keep an eye on *him* and don't let him run away. If he tries, shoot him. Keep your weapons primed, all. I'll contact *Arianrhod*."

The captain had no sooner stepped down from her shuttle after a private word with her first mate than a commotion at the entry to the shuttle bay alerted her to more company.

"Take cover!" she ordered as four armed individuals burst in.

They scattered, Ji hauling Doosbak. The four were in Rydderwild Security uniforms. The lead man looked round, calling for Ahxenta.

She rose warily, phase rifle in hand and Marks at her back. She gave her ID and waited. Recognising the PSS uniform, the leader lowered his gun; his other hand he raised palm outward in token of peace. He took in the three on the deck and turned back to the captain.

"Your work?" he asked.

"You weren't quick enough," she responded acidly. "Do you mind telling me what the hell is going on and who the hell *they* are?"

"I'm SSO Sharp. We were to meet you to take custody of the guy wanted by the Council when our cams logged these three in a secure area. We didn't know them so we tailed them, but they had back-up and we were intercepted by a couple of hardnoses before we could act. We dealt with the other two but how did you pick up on *them*?"

"We're not witless," was the abrupt retort as the captain looked Sharp up and down. "And you still haven't told me who they are."

"I've no idea, Captain, but we'll find out. You two, get those three in restraints and back to the lock-up."

"I take it you have authorisation to collect Doosbak," Ahxenta stated levelly, noting that Azular was scanning the newcomers.

"Yes, ma'am," replied Sharp, calling up the pertinent holo on his wrist unit. "There are two Coalition reps on their way in to talk to him now. I take it you want to be in on his interrogation?"

"No I do not. I have much better things to do. Just make sure the reps *are* the genuine article before you let them near him. And keep a close eye on him and get him thoroughly checked over: he's got cyber implants that pack a punch and an internal data recording facility that'll record everything you say and do. Good luck."

With that she ordered the release of Doosbak to the security team and turned on her heel to catch her limping and clearly exhausted science officer by the arm to help him back into the shuttle.

"This time you're definitely off duty," she informed him on the way up the ramp. "I take it *those* three read as the real thing?"

"Yes ma'am. Doosbak recognised the leader of the others, and in fact seemed pleased to see him, so I looked at him closely. He was *not* wearing an SSO's insignia and from his expression I figured that he'd shoot first and ask questions later. Luckily Ensign Hanx read me and was ready. The leader is Friskianx; the others originate from near the Outer Zone, perhaps Treskk. But that's all my scans showed. I found no more than standard prosthetic repair implants in any of them."

"Drafted in to do the dirty work then. But by whom?"

"We could probably make a list," Azular replied dryly as he settled awkwardly into his seat and closed his eyes with a sigh.

The captain slid in beside him, giving her pilot the order to head out. It was a short trip up and by the time they had docked Flintlock and Lindell had arranged several crates of supplies for shipping to the *Emerald*. Dr Zaiklyn Oak and nurse-tech Jym Kelp were also there as the chief medic had reckoned that two extra pairs of trained hands would aid the crippled ship. Her repairs were already underway and it was hoped that two days would see her clear of Rydderwild and on track for Delta Iridium and its vast repair centre. The *Green Comet* was about to dock and measures were in place for cargo transfer.

It had been a while since Ahxenta had been aboard the *Emerald*. The adaptation of the former luxury cruiser into an efficient and well-armed medium-sized carrier was complete and the service facilities and muted colours in the shuttle bay met with the captain's approval. Goodsocks was there to meet them, with people on hand to help unload and to escort the medical staff to medbay. The extent of the damage, particularly to the ship's hull, was great and her arsenal was empty, but her captain was sure that she could be rendered fit for service in less than thirty standard days. One engine needed replaced, but her others and her auxiliaries were sound.

By the time Ahxenta had briefed the *Emerald's* senior officers, had had a tour and had visited the injured crew, the transfer of *Arianrhod's* cargo to the *Green Comet* was complete. She returned to her own ship knowing that she had left her other investment in very capable hands. She was met by a grim-faced Flintlock: Azular had severely overtaxed himself and she had ordered him back to medbay.

The news met Ahxenta on the bridge that two Coalition reps had arrived and were with Doosbak. The bogus guards were unknowns with no previous convictions and had been charged with imposture and intent to commit felony. They had refused to divulge their orders or their controllers. Apnis on behalf of the captain had declined to have any of their crew head down to give evidence.

Two days later found the *Arianrhod* and the *Emerald* on the way to the bypass for Delta Iridium; the *Green Comet* had left the day before. The reason for the attack on *Arianrhod's* crew was unclear. Interrogation of the suspects had elicited that they had been paid in advance to take down her shuttle crew and hijack their prisoner. Doosbak's fate was known only to the leader of the group, who had refused to talk. His ID had been circulated to every law enforcement agency within the Allied systems but nothing had been returned.

"Blank wall yet again," the first mate stated. "So what's new?"

"Doosbak was evidently promised by his masters that everything would be all right. Azular says the little maggot was a bit too cocky to be scared about his trip with us. So his vicious chums have messed up and he's in Council hands. And *that* means that he and they now know they're not invincible when it comes to dealing with us."

"Which means they'll be even more pissed with us. Do they never learn?" Apnis asked wryly. "You'd think they'd give up eventually."

"They may on us, but not on our concerns or our associates. Who ordered the hit on the *Emerald?*" the captain demanded.

"We know some of the outfits that once traded out of Mellifly are sources of trouble, wherever they're holed up now, and we figure that several small groups of hostiles still run ops all over the known galaxy and outside it. But Thal and his lot seem to have a handle on most of them – Zeta Dixt and Peden Post are two bases he spoke of."

"Thal and his lot," repeated Ahxenta. "How much of a lot does he have and how much control does he have over it? There were about fifteen ships at Skyrtek but he lost a few and he wasn't in command then. Kerrix said there were hulks at Starfall that looked shot to hell, so he'd need to get them back up to spec *and* find crew for them; and the same might be said for any ships in other captured bases. But what about hostile hotspots beyond Mu, past Kirtish *and* that hidden bypass they use to get out there? And Vettarista spoke of a route in the opposite direction that leads to a node by that ex-raider base by Kelfennig Four, just off the Starglass. *That's* likely in Thal's hands."

"But there are still hostiles all over the place, fewer than in the war but smarter, meaner, more difficult to identify, with a lot of average thugs to do their bidding; *and* they have it in for us," snorted Apnis.

"That's about it. But there has to be a control centre or they'd fall over each other. Minch Fettin and the Web seem to figure a lot."

"The Web's worrying. Many of the PSS fleet use it as well as ships from all over, as it's the biggest centre of trade, shipping, mercantile and everything else you can think of in the entire mapped galaxy."

"Which would make it a logical centre of operations; I wonder if that's occurred to the ISP and the other giant alliances that think they run the galaxy?" the captain posited.

"You could ask," the first mate yawned. "This'll be a long haul to Delta with *Emerald* off our bows. I'll get the crew onto drills to keep active. As Azular's itching to be doing he could link his Norvallan scanner to the hull science arrays and run long-range scans. He could do it from medbay if the doc won't let him loose."

"Good luck with arranging that," she was told.

The run did seem like a survival test but the ships met no trouble and word had been received that their Vellis cargo had been delivered safely. At Delta, with *Emerald* berthed and her worst-injured under specialist care, *Arianrhod* stopped only to take on supplies. The next leg of her trip would take her into a Non-Treaty area of Lambda for her drop at Hespera, but it was a familiar and well-patrolled route. There had been nothing bar two minor clashes with raiders, both off the beaten track, and as *Arianrhod* would come nowhere near Peden Post, the captain hoped for a peaceful passage.

The great pink-hulled ship navigated the vast spaces of zone Delta and crossed into Lambda without difficulty. The small load was safely transferred at the warm world of Hespera Two and *Arianrhod* made headway for her next port of Freskat Six.

"It's almost like coming home," Apnis remarked a little while later as the outer edges of the spectacular Ginseng Nebula brightened the dark of space and the approach to the Freskat system came upon them. "We've been out this way so many times."

"And had so many good spells of shore leave on Freskat," hinted Lieutenant Box from the navigation station.

"Don't push it," Dox warned. "We're not top of the leave rota."

"And you're slipping down my list by the minute, Mr Box," the first mate put in as she smiled across at the captain. "All fixed for the work-up of the goods?" she added quietly to Ahxenta as Lieutenant Dox announced that they were on final approach to Freskat Six.

"On standby," was the reply. "But I've a meet set up with Admiral Zillah, at her request. She knew we were due in, how I don't know, so you'll be there and so will Azular, whether or not the doc agrees."

Less than two hours later the shuttle with Ahxenta, Apnis, Azular and their two security guards aboard made planetfall on the outskirts of a small suburb of the main settlement, where the captain set off to deposit the batch of crystals with her contact. On her return, the shuttle headed out for the Freskat home fleet's main offices and their priority assignation with the admiral.

Shortly after, Ahxenta, Apnis and Azular were seated in Zillah's office with the admiral and her aide, Tealdun. Their two guards they left outside. The reason Zillah gave for the hasty meeting was the number of reports that had come across her desk from the *Arianrhod*. She wanted to know more about the actions the ship had seen, and more about the activity of the rebels that seemed to be setting up as friends rather than foes of the established order. Freskat was a distant world and vulnerable to outside influences, and with only a single member on the Interstellar Systems Protectorate Council, it was often last in line when aid was required. Ahxenta for her part wanted to know how the admiral had known she would be in the local area.

The latter was dealt with first. The news had come through as an urgent despatch a few days before via an ISP agent at an undisclosed location who had come by it and wanted Ahxenta warned that her itinerary had partly at least been known to hostile parties since she left the Web and that she was liable to be a target either on Freskat or soon after. The attack on the *Emerald* and the *Arianrhod's* subsequent actions had alerted those who had lost sight of her after Larrikon to her heading. The admiral had had her own environs scoured but was chary of alerting local spies that their actions were under surveillance. One snoop not linked to the issue had been dug out but the existence of more was suspected. Zillah had informed Freskat's ruling council's security chief, whom she could trust, but that was all.

"Since we left the Web?" the captain echoed. "So there are eyes on our cargo manifests, our clients and our usual trade routes as well as other things. That smacks of infiltration in core bodies in the Web and out of it *and* listening posts in the wider galaxy that are acting on specific instructions. How many listening posts do the ISP and their allies have and how many have been subverted for other uses?"

The admiral's eyes blazed in fury as she pondered the implications. "I don't like where you're going but I won't discount it," she said at last. "You have a damn good point and that's one big can of worms. Leave it with me. But now I want to know more on these odd friends of yours that keep popping up, not to mention what other assets you have that get you out of the trouble you seem to attract."

The captain gave a concise account of her impression of Thal and his people and her guesses of their intentions, but was obliged to admit that much of the his rationale escaped her. Of her ship and her contacts, she was direct: they were private and no-one's business. As she talked, Ahxenta was aware that Azular was brooding on some matter, and at the end of her discourse she asked him openly.

"Listening posts," he said. "Peden Post was once a raider post that now seems to be hostile. There may be many more; there *must* have been during the war, to direct the actions on several fronts. I recall the hidden post on Elf One that launched the attack on the *Tallulah* some time ago, at which we intervened. Elf One is near Delta Iridium and yet the post went undetected. I believe the captain sent the news on to you, Admiral, before your last meeting? And Captain Flintlock mentioned several attacks on small traders on routes between Delta and its colonies. They were later and blamed on raiders, but they must have known about the transports and their cargoes."

"Your point?" Zillah said abruptly.

"My point, ma'am, is that there may be more hidden listening or other posts on your doorstep or beyond that are biding their time."

Zillah agreed the possibility but argued that such places would require manpower.

"Unless they're automated?" Azular postulated. "However, if any were left over after the major conflict that *had* initially been set up by the original hostiles, *their* traces might be discernible."

"What sort of traces?"

"Zukivianite," the senior science officer stated bluntly.

"And how do you suggest we check that out over the vast areas of space that would have to be covered?" was the waspish retort.

"Unmanned probes set to scan for specifics," he replied calmly.

"I'm beginning to see why your ship has such an edge," Zillah told Ahxenta, "If all your officers are as sharp as he is."

The captain grinned. It seemed that Azular was more or less back on form despite his physical limitations. She requested closure of the meeting shortly afterwards, having had as much talking as she found palatable. The three collected their guards and made for their shuttle, where Apnis brought up a subject upon which she had been musing.

"Who was the nameless ISP agent at the secret spot who told the admiral that our schedule had been known to villains since we left the Web and that we'd be targeted wherever we went?"

"Vettarista," Ahxenta said shortly. "She must still be there and has probably picked up more on what's going on. She's got to be a damn good agent not to have been pulled out sooner."

"Or she has other interests," Azular added mildly, with a smile.

"Yes, Kerrix," the captain agreed. "I'd imagine she'd want to keep tabs on her. It's her brief after all: alien matters. The admiral's aide said little, but as we've met him before I guess he passed muster?"

"Commander Tealdun? Yes, ma'am, I sensed no ulterior motive in the close attention he was giving us. I think he's rather wary of us."

"I'll bet. But let's get back to the ship. Lindell's found a potential ISP contract I see, but on the basis of what Zillah's told us, we may have to think twice about accepting it if we win the bid."

Ahxenta piloted the shuttle and once home made for Lindell's office, Azular in tow lest his quick mind caught a detail that needed enquiry. The supercargo had the contract up on his grid.

"It's a payload of modular habitation units from Limekiln Central to Alto Finglas and they're for a new Allied Central Office that's a joint project between the ISP, the Coalition, the NTA and a number of small groups that have formed themselves into a union called the United Independents, apparently," he told the two.

"The what? That's a new one on me," the captain stated.

"United Independents – mostly the zone Mu independent leagues that have decided they'd better offer a united front, now their double bypass system is near complete," Lindell said. "It'll mean more trade routes on line as the initial node at Cassary will bring in ships from the outer reaches of zones Kappa and Iota that'll be able to go direct to Kollaskin Ambit. And it might mean it'll bring in more trouble, as *that* line takes in most of Mu and links to the small internal routes that cross zone Mu. And then from Kollaskin, the second part of the route makes across lower Mu and back into Kappa at Wild, so not far from Kellybar One. That'll cause its own problems, because it'll provide a route almost into ISP territory."

Azular wrinkled his brow as he called up a condensed holo of the relevant area. "Kollaskin Ambit is close to Kirtish and the bypass we believe extends from Starfall into uncharted space, with an exit node at K457:003. So trouble, and maybe not from where it's expected."

"Our concern's the contract," the captain reminded him. "Official ISP markers on the data?" she asked Lindell.

"Aye ma'am, it's genuine and trackable; and I know the exec in the issuing office, I've dealt with her before. And as we're on Freskat and Limekiln's on a direct line, collection will be simple. Alto Finglas is en route if we're headed back to the Web and so far we've nothing that will take us out of our way unless we get more interest in the comms wafers that we're having processed. I've sent out feelers to our usual clients and the ISP but nothing's back so far. Once I have the data on wafer quality, I'll send it out – the ISP dockyard at Alto Finglas might be keen as they've probably got a shortfall for their new ships. I'll try the Freskat Navy as well. The habitation units at Limekiln are being prepped and will be ready for shipping in eight days."

"Then we put the bid in. Azular will check over the contract with you, Lindell, just in case there's something out of line. Link the final to me for authorisation."

"Aye, Captain," both responded.

The next days passed with no external alarms for *Arianrhod* and her crew. Ahxenta's contact made steady progress with array-setting the batch of crystals and had given her some ready-set wafers, knowing that she could reach markets not open to him. Lindell had won the contract to transport the habitation units and the speed with which *Arianrhod* could carry it out meant a bonus. Ahxenta had heard from Melly Goodsocks at Delta Iridium: the *Emerald's* injured crew were all well on the way to recovery and the ship herself was in good order.

Nothing had been heard from Merkat bar general chatter and the captain was reluctant to contact anyone there unless she had a valid reason. No word had come in of Thal or his fleet and PSS channels were quiet. Aboard ship, matters were on a different footing, with a squabble in an engineering side lab between Gem Ferry and second mate Whisper Earbleat reaching such epic proportions that the first mate had been called in to arbitrate. Ferry had created a scale model of the alien projectile that had almost taken *Arianrhod* down and had gifted it with virtual firepower. As soon as Earbleat was made aware, she was desperate to try out her bench-scale phase-beam cluster gun on it and the promise that she would not use actual fire was cutting no ice with the young engineer. That Earbleat had been able to link *Loki VII's* weapons systems to the scaled-up version she had bolted on to her favourite projectile's hull and could now say that the system would work using virtual fire had likewise no effect on Gem Ferry.

"The quicker we're back in space the better," was Ahxenta's take on it as she and Apnis, in the bridge office, sifted through the work to be done before *Arianrhod* left Freskat. "Earbleat's off ship. The day of shore leave she put in for was to visit a chum that works in the orbital naval dockyard, so she said. I bet she's on the hunt for bits of free tech. She's already sounded me out on turning one of our less-used cargo pods into a mini *Loki* as back up for the original."

"You told her no way on that, I take it," Apnis stated.

"Damn straight I did. But I couldn't deny her the day as she was due the leave. So are you for that matter, Tallica."

"We both are but neither of us has time, Cap. Maybe once we're back at Merkat? I could do with a pot of Ally's ale," admitted the first mate as she stretched. "But at least we've got rid of half the comms arrays to Zillah's people and the dockyard at Alto Finglas will take the rest. That saves us time and effort *and* credit. I take it your buddy down there gets a bonus for the hard work he's put in?"

"A bonus and then some," was the dry retort. "He'll need it: he's getting hitched and needs a bigger place."

"Whoa Cinnabar! Will he let his intended in on the fact that you're his foster ma and aunt or will you still remain a secret?"

"Up to him, it's his life. I haven't met her, but she's a nurse-tech in the settlement's local hospital. I won't make the ceremony anyhow, as it's in two months Freskat time. But let's see this schedule again: if we win that contract for shipping the two new-spec military shuttles from Alto Finglas to Linza Base, we can make for the Web from Linza. One of the things I don't like about the deal is the fact that the ISP wants us to shift their pilots as well and they'll give me no gen on them at all – confidentiality and all that."

"Azular?"

"Who else," groaned the captain. "Flintlock will flay me, but what in hell I'd do without him I wouldn't like to think."

"Recruit Ms Vettarista," the first mate advised. "He thinks she's as gifted as he is and as she's ISP, she'll be military to her boot heels."

"I hope that's a joke, Commander."

"She could always entertain the crew on her off duty time; she's some sort of hostess at Azure Belle's after all," Apnis chuckled.

"Can it," Ahxenta told her. "I don't have the spec of these fancy new boats and they'll be shielded, so we'll be able to access damn all. And if we're offered the deal and take it, we'll need to free up a bay as they'll be flown in. And we'll need billets for the pilots."

"Get Whisper onto berths for the shuttles. She can fix firepower and secure cams in inner aft bay three – it's pressurised, so they can sit there. Azular can organise that holo projection camouflage tech to hide what we don't want seen and we can post the bay off limits *and* post guards. The pilots can berth alongside our own but we set a security watch on them, if ISP won't tell us who they are."

"Good call. You get Whisper organised and I'll have words with Azular. I bet he'll have his own ideas."

"Roger that, Cap. And now can we go and take a break?"

"Once we've checked over the port clearances for getting out of Freskat space; they've changed the rules again."

"Hell's teeth!"

"You said it," the captain grated as she tabbed up the data.

The *Arianrhod* shone pinkly metallic in the glow of her bay as slowly, docking struts retracting, she slipped her traces and turned in a slow waltz to pull away from Freskat Six. The captain checked her boards.

"Limekiln Central via Lamella Four helm, steady as she goes."

"Course plotted and laid in, ma'am," Dox called from her station. "Estimated time to bypass forty minutes."

"Roger that," acknowledged Ahxenta. "Feels better when things are back on an even keel," she said to her first mate.

"Let's hope they stay that way, Cap."

Her schedule for the next eight days set, the mighty trading ship slid onto the bypass. *Arianrhod* was uncloaked but her shields were up and the captain had decreed standby alert for the duration. There had been no local unrest but it was two and a half days to Limekiln and the crew was always ready to expect the unexpected.

As it was the ship met naught of concern and she made her target on time. The payload of habitation unit modules was huge and heavy grapples were needed to winch each piece into position for insertion into *Arianrhod's* vast outer bays. As soon as accounts were cleared and the cargo safely aboard and locked in, continual scans were activated and the fine-meshed safety shields released and locked down tight.

"Good job," Ahxenta commended her teams ship-wide. "All done without a hitch. Prepare for departure to Alto Finglas."

"Time for the slow road," said the first mate. "We're heavy in the beam. It must be a huge central office ISP's put up credit for. What does it get out of it apart from the company of the Co-Scutters, the NTA and all the Independents that have joined their little band?"

"Kudos and grateful friends in case the galaxy goes belly-up," the captain replied sardonically. "And the ISP will get help in kind: extra ships to bolster its defence fleet or similar. Azular's checking the scan outputs for things that shouldn't be there and he'll send hover probes in on a random basis, in case there's something shielded that can take out or jam our security gear or send out a bug once we're underway. And Goldwash is setting up special quarters for these pilots when we pick *them* up at Alto Finglas. I still haven't been told anything about them even though we've got the contract. I don't know much about the new boats either, apart from their size and weight. Nor what their armaments are; if they're armed, I'm damn well concerned."

"I *can* see ISP's point," Apnis granted. "Look at it from the pilots' and fleet's standpoints: would *you* want your ID spread if you're able to fly the latest new-spec military shuttle that's just off the production line? And *new* implies novel tech. And we'll be the ones hauling that latest high-spec novel gear and its pilots. There's got to be a heap of credit tied up in it and I bet a lot would want a piece of that action. And it's headed from one ISP base to another? I know Linza Base is small, but it's close to the Web. And look at the flak that's been flying there, much of it thrown at us, it has to be said."

"Several good points. So why were *we* awarded the contract?"

"Because the ISP knows we can handle it and we're on the run to

Alto Finglas anyway, and so well-placed for a fast delivery; though their reps wouldn't know we're for the Web after that. What I don't get is why the ISP can't use one of its own ships to transport these shuttles. There must be a few in and out of Alto Finglas on a regular basis. Doesn't the almighty Myrtleberry use it as a home base for her gunboat? If there's hot new tech, she'd be first in line for it."

"Keeping it from their own in case they fight over it," the captain grinned. "We'll find out more at Alto Finglas."

"Or maybe not, as the case may be," Apnis smiled in return.

Heavy or not, *Arianrhod* made rapid progress to her endpoint, with no obstructions. The crew was beginning to wonder if their enemies *had* decided to give up on her as a bad job, as thus far they had been unable to put a stop to her. Conflict had not ended as news had come in of more attacks on shipping lines by raiders and others, some of which had been deadly. No PSS had been hit since the *Emerald*, but the latest was enough for the Trades Alliance to up their levies, as did a number of insurance concerns, including the one Ahxenta used.

The *Arianrhod* was welcomed into Alto Finglas and directed to the largest dock of the orbital transfer station, where heavy grapples were in place to catch each part of the cargo as it was unloaded and then transfer to it massive drones that would relocate the pieces to their holding point. The procedure took some time as every unit had to be checked and passed as fit at each stage.

"What in blazes do they think we would do to the stuff?" Tallica Apnis complained to the captain, who had just returned from taking a private comm in her bridge office. "None of it would be of any blind use to us and the whole caboodle's been sat in our cargo bays untouched since it was put there at Limekiln. Have we had any more word on these fancy shuttles that we're due to move next?"

"That was the gist of the link. I'm due a meet with a rep from fleet logistics and a couple of high rankers in an hour to talk about it, and I'll get to meet these two pilots that are to fly the shuttles. It's in their orbital office, so I'll fly over there. You'll stay here to keep an eye on things. I'll take Azular and two guards: Lieutenants Goldwash and Ji, I think, as rank counts with these people. And one of our own pilots for the trip to sit in the shuttle and keep an eye on her; Elka Reef or Haze Kelsitt, whoever's next on the rota, as they're the most senior."

"If I didn't know better, I'd think you didn't trust the ISP, Cap."

"Most of them I don't. And as one of the high rankers is Colonel Myrtleberry, I'm shipping over in company," the captain snorted.

"Myrtleberry! I didn't notice the *Repulse* in orbit as we came in."

"She may be on the far side or in the dockyard for an overhaul. I wasn't about to enquire as a very little of Myrtleberry goes a very long way. And if she *is* the ISP's equivalent of a Bick Micklemouse, as we suspect she might be, I don't trust her as far as I could throw her."

"Hardly that," the first mate argued. "But Azular can read her and I bet she knows, so she may not try her needling tactics to provoke a reaction. Have you told him that she's part of the ISP delegation?"

"I have; he's not impressed."

Captain Ahxenta also thought it wise to brief her escort and pilot lest any of them were waylaid and interviewed. Her shuttle made the bay shortly before the meeting, to find a pair of ISP security on hand.

"Lieutenant Kelsitt will remain aboard my shuttle," the captain told the welcoming party crisply as introductions were made. "I'll see you later, Mr Kelsitt. Please lead on," she added to the two guides.

It took only minutes to reach the office set for the meeting. Ji and Goldwash were left outside as Ahxenta and Azular stepped in to be greeted formally by Colonel Myrtleberry, who frowned as she took in the science officer on crutches and with a case slung across his back. She introduced her aide Captain Border with her usual lack of charm and then a Commander Tarn, a fleet rep from the logistics arm of the service. The pilots would be called to the meeting later, the two from *Arianrhod* were told as they were invited to sit.

That Ahxenta set a data recorder on the table was the first bone of contention but the captain was adamant that every syllable of the talk would be logged. Azular detached and set out his info-pad, activating it to capture any relevant holos, he told the colonel as he invited her to check it. She declined, but in response she brought out a recorder and a jammer, informing the *Arianrhod's* officers that the subject was sensitive and not to be spread beyond the room. Azular immediately probed the jammer and both the captain and himself.

"I'm testing to see if our locating pins are being blocked," he said to Ahxenta. "I suspect they are. Commander Apnis will have to be informed, for she *will* take action at the loss of our signals."

Myrtleberry was furious and said so, but even as she moved to switch off the jammer to allow linkage to *Arianrhod*, there was an uproar that heralded the entry of Lieutenant Goldwash, Ji at his back, fending off two ISP security officers. Apnis had alerted them to the loss of the locating signals and wanted answers. Seething, the colonel agreed to suspend jamming and ordered the security crews out.

"Let's get on with it," she directed. "Border, set up the holo."

As Ahxenta had suspected, the new shuttles were trial craft and testing of their inbuilt novel tech was to be completed at Linza Base. As a small ISP post it was simpler to control two-way traffic there and it was less liable to be a hostile target. In answer to a direct query, the captain was told that neither shuttle contained active weaponry. Their pilots would fly them to their assigned holds on *Arianrhod* and they would remain there undisturbed until Linza was reached.

"Why my ship?" the captain wanted to know. "*You* have a fleet."

"A trading ship would not be expected to be carrying ISP military hardware out of Alto Finglas," was the firm reply. "And you're here on other business. The shuttles will fly up covertly and local sensors will be offline at the time. Commander Tarn will see to it."

Despite further questioning by Ahxenta, Myrtleberry would not be drawn on the tech carried by the shuttles. Azular was more intent on another matter and when asked for his input, was succinct.

"Are they actively shielded and impervious to regular scanning? If they are, how do we know that they're not armed and ready to blow our ship apart once we leave orbit?"

The colonel hissed in fury. "How dare you! They're ISP and we'd hardly be likely to destroy our own just to take you down. Their tech is not your concern but ours and that's the way it will stay. And do you really think we'd risk two of our best test pilots, even if such a preposterous idea was in the offing, Doctor?"

"Your pilots aren't here. They wouldn't be aware," he pointed out.

"All they're required to do is fly," Myrtleberry retorted. "And do you think ISP HQ could really be subject to such subversion?"

"Your ex-HQ at Skyrtek was and we were the target then," the science officer reminded her coldly. "It was ISP recovery teams who retrieved the salvage from the wreck of your dock off Skyrtek Prime and ISP personnel who loaded the pods, one of which contained a projectile that had been primed to self-activate and breach the pod once *Arianrhod* was well away from Skyrtek and on the route to Alto Finglas. We scanned the pods before they were brought aboard and after we had locked them down and detected nothing."

"So how did you work out there *was* an alien projectile in the pod before it burned its way out if you hadn't sensed it initially? How *did* you take out such shielded kit?" Tarn asked, his eyes raking Azular.

The Berzic officer raised an eyebrow and gazed at him as intently. "We maintain surveillance on our bays as standard," he said, "As part of our service to ensure that our cargoes remain safe and secure."

"That incident is closed," Myrtleberry interrupted icily. "And that projectile, however you were able to find *and* deal with it, was classed as an unknown device picked up inadvertently by our salvage teams."

"Interesting," Azular stated. "I believe you told the captain that your salvage pods were of a very high spec to foil scanning, Colonel; it seems a lot of trouble to go to for garbage containers. I assume that your newer military shuttles are constructed to an enhanced standard compared to waste pods, in the hope that they're totally impervious to *all forms* of scanning. Would that include your own scans?"

Myrtleberry was utterly furious. "You tread a fine line, Doctor!"

"I expect you realise that I trust no-one outside my own, and given what we've had to contend with from the ISP amongst others, I think I'm justified," Ahxenta interrupted. "And my senior science officer's questions, which you have *not* answered to my satisfaction, are also justified. And I stand by my initial assertion that the highly dangerous projectile that put my ship and my crew at risk was planted purposely. And as we did not detect it on initial scans, it was damn well hid. So what new types of gear do these shuttles carry, are they so shielded that they can't be scanned by any known probes and can your own people even read their specs?"

"And are you aware that Commander Tarn is a highly cybernetic individual that has at least one implanted data recording device?" added Azular with a quiet smile. "And a very high-tech chameleon suit to prevent your routine scans picking up his biosigns?"

Within the room an abrupt silence greeted the senior science officer's questions. It lasted only moments, for as the colonel's head slewed round to the logistics officer, her sharp eyes and hissing expletive revealing her wrath, several things happened at once. Tarn, a furious leering look on his face giving lie to the direct denials that had sprung from his lips, had reached into a pocket for a weapon. Myrtleberry, equally fast, had jumped to her feet and drawn her own, letting loose a bolt in his direction. Azular's quick reaction in striking Tarn's arm to disturb his aim blocked a shot that would have hit Ahxenta as *Arianrhod's* two guards burst through the door, the ISP duo at their backs. Realising that she was the target, the captain had dived out of her chair, her phase rifle already primed. She did not hesitate as she knew that Tarn's chameleon suit would be armoured. The multiple shots as the colonel let loose another salvo brought the man down and Ji and Goldwash had him secured in seconds.

"Commander Apnis ordered us in," Lieutenant Goldwash told the captain in answer to her question. "Dr Azular activated the alarm."

"What alarm?" Myrtleberry spat out.

"The one on my info-pad," was the science officer's cool reply.

"You people!" she flared in vexation. "You two get him to the most secure lock-up in grey seven," she ordered her guards. "Border, go with them. And he's cyber, so make sure he's under tight restraint. So what made you suspect he was trouble?" she asked Azular.

"Several things. I had scanned him and realised he was wearing a chameleon suit with inclusions that read close to hostile tech. And his quizzing of me about the cargo pod from Skyrtek: he referred to the projectile as alien, he said it had burned its way out and he said it was shielded. To the best of my knowledge none of these matters was mentioned in any briefing, so how did he know?"

"Smart," the colonel acknowledged but her sour glance suggested to him that she was not convinced she had heard the whole tale.

"But I get the impression that you were not completely surprised to find out that Tarn was an imposter, ma'am," Azular went on. "Did you already have suspicions of him?"

Myrtleberry regarded at him in annoyance. "Not your business."

"What is our business is the cargo," Ahxenta interrupted. "There's no way those shuttles go anywhere near my ship until my people have checked them and their pilots out fully. And if that means disarming their shielding then that's what will happen. *And* they'll stay that way on the trip or I won't be transporting them anywhere."

"You've agreed the contract," the colonel contended.

"I agreed a contract *provisionally*. I did not agree to be part of some underhand shenanigans that puts my people at extreme risk. And if this logistics officer of yours *is* a subversive, he'll have contacts who'll know about these shuttles, their covert transport and the pilots who'll fly them – you *did* say he'd arrange to offline local sensors. The name of the carrier will also be part of it and that means my ship. The whole deal smells like a set-up if ever there was one. And Tarn was aiming to shoot me, not you, Colonel. Have you any idea why?"

"He probably had a dozen good reasons," was the sharp retort. "But he's been smoked out now, and we'll take every precaution..."

"Smoked out?" Azular asked tersely. "Were *we* the bait that was set to smoke him out?"

"If that's the case we're going now. And I intend to lodge a formal protest with the ISP. I will also be making a full report to relevant bodies, including the Trades Alliance," Ahxenta stated icily, sheathing her firearm. "Please answer Dr Azular's question, Colonel."

Myrtleberry looked from one to the other. "You were the logical choice of carrier," she admitted. "You were heading into Alto Finglas with a cargo and the shuttles were set to move out in the near future. It was sheer chance that my people intercepted a couple of things at about the same time that led to my suspicions of Tarn and your name was part of it. So yes, I brought the shuttle schedule forward and got him in to arrange it. The plan was that we'd be ready for shipping out and at that point my trusted people would move in and take him and his associates. But thanks to your science officer's antics, Tarn's been got early but his contacts are still loose and probably close at hand."

"In other words, we *were* the bait in the trap!" the captain snapped. "And you're not pinning any of your failure to stop Tarn's associates on Dr Azular. If you weren't smart enough to work out that we'd have our own ways of checking things out, that's your problem."

"I suggest we sit and discuss this calmly," Myrtleberry said sharply. "I still want those shuttles shipped and you've just proved that you're one of the best and most secure carriers there are. Yes, you *are* more of a target than most but you're also more than capable of taking care of yourselves. So shall we discuss it? I *will* authorise upping your fees and my people will go over both vessels micron by micron – and everything else Tarn had set up."

The captain looked at her shrewdly and then at her science officer, who remained carefully neutral. "We'll discuss a *provisional* contract, Colonel. My ship will be listening in and my security will be posted outside this door. And then we'll see."

An hour and a half later and an altered contract had been agreed on the proviso that Ahxenta's people were given full authority to go over the shuttles in depth prior to transfer in, and that neither their weapons nor their shielding would be active. Azular had stipulated that all energy cells be detached during transport and only reattached when the craft left *Arianrhod*. The captain reserved the right to cancel the agreement at any point up to departure: she wanted to go through the whole with her senior officers, without Myrtleberry or any of her people listening. The last task for the session was the interview with the pilots. They had been briefed by Captain Border before entering the meeting room and were clearly peeved at having been left out of the equation, but seemed competent and loyal to the ISP.

Matters were shelved as far as Ahxenta was concerned until she and her people were back aboard their ship and to that end, she was escorted back to her shuttle. She had called for a briefing immediately after docking as it was obvious to her that Myrtleberry wanted the matter closed speedily and with any outside interest minimised.

Apnis, Cottontail, Earbleat and Flintlock were waiting in a main briefing room when Ahxenta and Azular arrived. Goldwash and Gliss were also there; Lindell was ordered to go over the new contract.

"I want this wrapped up now," Ahxenta began as she sat. "Azular, you were quick to pick up on Tarn, and it wasn't just what he said."

"No, Captain. I had set my info-pad to scan everyone because the colonel, as we found out some time back, had been genetically and physically altered to suit ISP needs. As far as I could tell she's had no further adjustments. But Tarn was different. I sensed hostility in him, and an arrogance that was difficult to pin down. And of course the tech which he was wearing and that he had implanted."

"How can an info-pad do that?" Earbleat asked. "And how come Myrtleberry didn't catch on? She's sharper than most and I bet she had a pocketful of super-tech. You'd all have been monitored from the second you landed."

"I'd upgraded my info-pad with Norvallan scanning gear."

"I bet you did," the second mate snorted.

"And shielded it to the extent that had she checked it, she would have detected nothing amiss – I hope," he added with a grin.

"Fine. How about Captain Border?" Ahxenta asked.

"I detected nothing unusual in him but a dislike of the colonel."

"He's not the only one. So how do we deal with the shuttles? The contract's now more lucrative but it's as shady a deal as ever I've met. Myrtleberry's still sure that some of her own are up to no good and even with *her* talents she hasn't been able to oust them."

Various ideas were bandied about until Cottontail came up with a solution by recalling a similar dilemma with Micklemouse's ship that they once faced. "We move their berths to the outmost docking bay, we seal it off from the rest of the ship and we set charges to blow the lock-down struts and bolts in the whole section. We didn't need to do it then, but if there *are* surprises that we can't detect, then we have insurance. And anything related to their weapons systems or scanning gear can be shipped separately in pods and kept in the same bay but well away from the two boats."

The captain was less than reassured but with little time left, she ordered her people off duty for a couple of hours and then back to the tedious tasks of dealing with the colonel's crew and making sure that their less than welcome cargo was as safe as possible.

"That's our cargo fully secured," the first mate told the captain as the final force field was set off and logged as fully stable. "Outer bay four is now sealed to space with all interior fields active, so we'll be safe if there's a breach. Charge relays are green and will be ready to blow if we need them *and* we can release the lot from the engineering station here or on the emergency bridge."

"Roger that, Tallica. Our guests are safe in their new homes?"

"Yes. I had Ji and Kelsitt escort them. They'll have a covert watch on them at all times and our pilots have been briefed to show them nothing but the bare essentials. They're used to obeying orders and this should be a quick trip once we're on the move."

"Good. Azular's satisfied with the security of the boats but we still haven't been given the details of that novel shielding they're meant to have, and he's sure they have hostile tech integrated into their hides but he can't pinpoint it. He got Greffy to plug their exterior sensor arrays and set local force fields around their weapons ports lest they *have* been armed and we can't detect it."

"I bet he keeps a continuous watch all the way and he'll use all that gear he squirrels away to see what he can find."

"He's used an external projection camouflage unit to hide our info banks and dock stations in the bay, so if there *is* something in those beasts keeping a watch, it'll be baffled," the captain stated.

"Aren't you glad he's on our side? But how could anything hidden in them get a look-see out when they're sealed as tight as drums and with no active systems apart from their engines?" Apnis asked.

"Remember the tale Kerrix told us of external sensors that Thal's super tech didn't pick up that got her visuals of the place they'd taken her? Yes, she'd a cloak that deceived them but she could bore a hole through her lower deck for air and pressure equalisation, or so she said. And *her* tech was so good that she picked up enough Inter-Lan to understand them. The ISP has had missions into uncharted space for years so who knows what they've picked up and not passed on?"

"You've a helluva suspicious mind, Cinnabar."

"That's why I've lived so long," Ahxenta replied. "But we're now well behind schedule with all this nonsense. And Myrtleberry's been bending my ear over the protest I put into ISP Central and wanting to know what I'll be sending out to the TA and our own fleet."

"What did you tell her?"

"None of her business. Most of what *she* does is none of ours so as far as I'm concerned, we're equal. But let's get this circus on the road and away from the eyes and ears of ISP."

As final checks were made and the orders given for departure, the captain was well aware that very many eyes and ears would be on the *Arianrhod* until she had cleared local space, and probably after that also. She had had some private talk with her senior science officer however, and based on that she made her own plans.

As soon as Dox had called that they were on the bypass and set for Linza Base, the captain ordered a course change for Minti, a small mining settlement off their route, silent running and full cloaking. She also ordered sporadic discharge of reflector flak in varied directions, to the perplexity of her bridge crew. Several hours into the flight, she instigated a further course change for Silshoon and then headed for her office to make long-distance highly encoded comms links. The bridge crew, scenting a mystery, observed closely and noted that their captain had returned with a smile on her face.

"What gives, Cinnabar?" the first mate demanded quietly.

"There's been a request sent out by the ISP local office at Selliden Central via Mizreel Point for us to divert with our load to Silverglass with all haste. I've responded in the affirmative."

"But we're not going to, are we?" Apnis rejoined softly.

"No Tallica, we are not. But there *will* be word out in a day or so that we've been seen beyond Silshoon and heading for Sevolb, at the edge of the Crimson Drapes."

"So come on Cinnabar, how did you swing it? And why?"

"Why, because even with all our tactics and gear, I won't discount that someone or something can pick up our signal or track us – there *have* to be secret listening posts littering mapped space. And I bet one or two ISP or Alliance stations have been breached and their comms cracked. As to how: I had words with an influential acquaintance."

"Admiral Zillah?" Apnis guessed. "But how could she orchestrate that in such a short time?"

"Not the admiral, no. I called Vettarista."

The first mate's eyes widened as she sucked in her breath. "Wasn't that risky, Cap?" she enquired in a low voice.

"It was, but given our load, our mission and the hitches we've had already, I judged it worth the risk. I want rid of this cargo, Tallica. I don't like it and I don't like what it heralds – fancy new fleet tech the ISP has developed that the hostiles already know about?"

"Can of worms there, Cap, and no mistake."

"Exactly. Maintain course for Silshoon, helm, but increase speed to full and do *not* drop our cloak. Box, plot a course for Silverglass via Silshoon. Ms Dox, we'll come off the bypass at the Silshoon node and then get straight back on. Do you copy?"

"Aye ma'am. Off the bypass at Silshoon beacon and then back on; I estimate twelve hours tops."

"Good. We'd best get some sack time before the course change as I want everyone sharp. And I expect I should go and be sociable with these two pilots for half an hour or so, if they're about."

"They'll be heading to the mess shortly," Apnis told her. "Kelsitt's keeping a tight rein and Goldwash has set an around-the-dial watch. Our pilots reckon they're both smart, Myrtleberry's hotshots they call them, but they figure they're okay. And according to Elka Reef, one's been hinting that service aboard *Arianrhod* might be an option, but Reef's quashed that. She's suggested he try the *Nyx Warrior*."

Ahxenta laughed. "If he can convince Nat Holdspan he's so keen he'll give up an ISP fleet pension for an equivalent in the PSS fleet."

The twelve hours to Silshoon were made safely and the route changes executed as intended. Back on the bypass *Arianrhod* had been ordered to set for Kelpin, a small planet in zone Beta and close by the beacon at Merkat. Ahxenta had planned to detour beyond Linza lest there were still some subversives that had realised she was not making for Silverglass. Although the diversion added two hours to their already lengthy journey, the gain in safety was worth the loss in time as far as the captain was concerned as *Arianrhod* closed in on her endpoint.

The advent of the ship was hailed with surprise as Linza had also been told that their new shuttles had been re-routed to Silverglass. In response to a wary enquiry as to her intentions, Ahxenta called for a direct link to the commanding officer and sent over a validation code. It took time and several cross-linkages to authority bodies before CO Greave would approve receipt of the shuttles and their related tackle, including the pilots. The latter flew the craft into the secure hangars set aside for them, but Ahxenta insisted that the weapons systems and scanning array modules that had been stored separately be sent out in their pods and retrieved by grapples once the shuttles had docked. The whole proceeded smoothly and Greave, happy with his new gear, was more open and grateful as *Arianrhod* set her course at last for Merkat.

As the huge outer meshes of the Web began to glow on their holo horizon, the first mate turned to the captain. "Glad to back?"

"It'll be a change," was the reply. "I'll get Lindell and his team on to scouting for deals for us. He's had to hold back as I'd no mind to give any snoops the lowdown on where we might be headed. But half the frigging galaxy will now know we're not at Silverglass and I would image a few will be vexed that they've been outfoxed yet again."

"Especially if they'd traps set from here to there in the hopes of catching us," Apnis laughed. "This has been some haul. But despite the fun ours had on Freskat, they'll be ready for another break. And you and I will be on the list, Captain."

"Roger that, Commander. Bring her in nice and slow, Ms Dox and send out our call-sign. Put me on speaker, comms. *PSS Arianrhod* to Merkat Three Port Control requesting permission to dock."

"We have you on our screens, *Arianrhod*: welcome back to Merkat Three Free Port. Stand by docking instructions."

"Docking instructions coming in, Captain," Lieutenant Dox called out. "Awaiting clearance."

"I recognise *that* hull and her peculiar shade of lilac," Apnis noted as they waited. "It's the *Tallulah*. I wonder what Fleetskup's business is, other than showing his first mate off in bars and trying to make us cough up for his scratched paint yet again."

"Maybe trade is thin on the ground out there?" Ahxenta hazarded.

"That's not all that's thin on the ground as far as *he's* concerned. I guess we'll find out in the *Half Moon*. If there's little to do here other than argue with the harbour office reps and then the Authority about the fees again, we can make it there sooner rather than later."

"That's our clearance through," Ahxenta noted. "Bring her in Dox, and lock her down. Let's see who else is in. That's the *Firedrake* and the *Urania*. I haven't seen Mikbeam for an age but his home port *is* Delta Iridium. Who's that over yonder?"

"It's the *Aqua Aura*, the oldest ship in the fleet. It's a wonder she's not been retired: most of her crew must be veterans," Apnis declared.

"Old spacers never die, they just fall into lower orbits," the voice of Lieutenant Box chimed in.

"Keep your eyes on your boards until we're secure, Mr Box," the captain reproved mildly as the lattice of docking struts began to move outward to fix *Arianrhod's* hull into place, the confining cross-pieces locking one by one, each red lit strip signifying another secure hold. The helmswoman gradually slackened off the power as she brought the ship to station-keeping.

"Boards all green, Captain, docking complete."

"Roger, helm. As soon as we're straight I'll make for the harbour office, see what's what and pay our fees."

The sojourn in the harbour office was short, for the reps there knew better than to extract more than their dues from the captain of the *Arianrhod*, especially as they had nothing new to report on the danger that the PSS had faced when last in the Web. They had found out little from the shards recovered from the hostile weapon-ship other than that it had been highly explosive. Ahxenta thus wasted no time and made for the Port Authority's HQ on green four of inner two, as their senior reps had asked for a rundown on some aspects of her last trip, and deeming it fair exchange for no increase in docking fees, she agreed. She followed that by a trip to security HQ for an update.

A short time later and Ahxenta was aback aboard. Her first mate had been busy arranging shore leave and the first shuttle was ready to set off. With no major scares since *Arianrhod* had last been in port, the shuttle was given leave to go. The captain then called a briefing to discuss potential deals. That done and the supercargo given free rein to set up contracts, all those seniors present bar the first mate left to return to duty. As the door closed, Apnis turned to the captain.

"Azular's refused shore leave. I asked, as I figured he'd request an early slot. Greffy's keen to head down so that's maybe why he said no; but the stint with Myrtleberry took it out of him, more than he'll admit. And he looks to have aged a year in the last few weeks."

"I'll speak to Flintlock. But we're for the *Half Moon* for a quick jar once all the nitty gritty here is done so we'll see what gives there. And then we have that other meet in marketing."

Dr Flintlock also voiced concern when the captain called by a little later. She had spoken to the senior science officer, who had denied any problem. The chief medic's advice was simple.

"Get Kerrix to contact *him* but make sure he's not on the bridge."

"*If* she's still here in Merkat," was the dry reply. "That may be half his concern and it's one of the reasons I want to head down sooner rather than later. If she's not, he won't know where she is and he'll have to put up with a lot of ribbing from some of our people."

"He'll have done his own checking, though I doubt that kind of data will be stored anywhere," Flintlock frowned.

"So when are *you* heading for furlough?"

"I'll miss this spell," the doctor told her. "*Karillion's* due in and a dose of my brother I can do without. Let me know what gives over Kerrix in case I have to be on standby with cookies and sympathy."

"You got it. I'll see you later."

"Enjoy your shore leave," Flintlock called after her.

The captain and first mate took the *Gadfly* down. They left her in a shuttle bay off marketing and were soon heading for the *Half Moon*.

"Welcome back, Captain, Commander," the dulcet tones of Ally greeted the two as they strode through the entry. "We saw *Arianrhod* was in and looking good. No trouble this time out?"

"Nothing we couldn't handle," Ahxenta replied, looking around. "Where's Ms Kerrix and Merry? I don't see either of them."

"In the back organising a bunch of stores," he replied as he pulled up a couple of pots of ale. "We're not busy yet."

"So what else is new?" the captain asked.

"Apart from that missile disguised as a non-reg ship that nearly blew you out of the water, except that one of my regulars spotted it and Xanna Kerrix warned you about it? And Captain Fleetskup and his first mate reckoning that they could have taken it out far more efficiently and with less flak and the *Tallulah's* hull would have got off with nary a scratch," Ally grinned.

"What?" Ahxenta demanded irately.

"That was their story after you left and it was the song they were singing last night when they and Mr Buntle hove in here. They'd just shipped in but they'd had one or two. Ms Dyne-Bek was paying."

"What else has been going on?" the captain enquired dangerously.

"The guy that shot Dr Azular was moved to a super-secure prison ship and hasn't been seen since. It's said by some that he had friends in high places that got him out. My partner saw the ship and said it wasn't like one she'd seen before, though it had ISP clearances. But there *have* been one or two of the oddballs in that nobody knows that use the middle belts and that security can't get clear scans of. The Guild thinks they're some new trading line that's started up but their crews say very little. They cause no trouble and pay their dues and as this is a free port, they're entitled. They give zone Mu as their base."

Ahxenta looked at Apnis, raised an eyebrow and shrugged. "Any more?" she asked.

"Oh, the usual mischief; and there are a few new faces in security and the Guild as they had to get rid of a bunch of bent crew. There was quite a barney over it, but my partner reckons it was about time as it was known among the duty crews that there were guys out there with sticky fingers, though nobody could prove it and anybody that tried ended up with bruises they couldn't account for. One or two crime rings have been broken too, a buddy of Merry's says. Though he apparently wouldn't say more," Ally added.

"Wonder who *he* was?" the first mate put in ironically.

Ahxenta laughed quietly and requested a private word with Kerrix, in Ally's office. Surprised, he agreed and led her around the back of the bar and into the room behind, routing out Merry and another of his staff. The captain reappeared ten minutes later, asking that Kerrix be left alone until she had ended a link. Ally was quick to agree.

"You eating here, Captain, Commander?" he continued.

"Not now," Ahxenta informed him. "We'll be back later; we've a small job to do first."

The job was a tryst with Vettarista in the marketing reception area. The agent had asked for the meeting just after *Arianrhod* had docked. As Ahxenta and Apnis had reserved rooms in green four's dorm quarter, they called there first to drop off their kit and were seated at one of the small tables when the Berzic woman joined them.

Vettarista was quick to get to the point: she was headed out of the Web soon. The matters that had held her there for so long were all but sewn up, but she wanted to warn the captain that not all the loose ends were tied and a few infiltrators remained at large, though ISP agents were digging them out. Security had been shaken up and new systems put in place to prevent future misuse of the secure cam nets. The Dockers' Guild was not yet shipshape but it was more open than it had been in years and was less likely to be a source of trouble, though it still contained a few rogues.

In her turn Ahxenta asked after the ships that Ally had mentioned that sounded like part of Thal's fleet. Vettarista agreed: she had come to the same conclusion but had not met any of the crews. There had been cargo exchanges but everything had been logged and was above board. The ships rarely stayed long in port but three different craft had been recorded, none of which matched Thal's huge vessel. The woman pulled up the spec of one which she had on her info-pad.

"It's the *Kel'Beth* or one very like," the first mate noted.

"That's what she was listed as," Vettarista concurred.

"Kismulin Ver in command and she calls herself a trader," Apnis said. "And they're being very nice to our ships. Didn't she warn Grey Bluejohn of hostile activity on Daff Six? She said she'd been targeted by missiles launched from a surface station and she'd downed them. She passed on the data and Grey sent it out to the TA and ISP."

"I'd heard," Vettarista said shortly. "The ISP is aware of them but thus far they've done nothing to merit increased attention."

"But you're still keeping an eye on them?" Ahxenta guessed.

"Both eyes," was the somewhat dry retort.

"What about Ms Kerrix? Have you eyes on her?"

"Not your concern, Captain. But she may not be in the Web for much longer, which is probably a good thing. She drew far too much attention in the *Half Moon* not too long ago, as you're aware. And there are other eyes on her that are not friendly."

"She won't be here for much longer? How do you know that?"

The Berzic woman's look was shrewd. "You know she's looking for a way off. She'll find one. She's piqued the curiosity of the captain of the *Nyx Warrior* for a start, so that's a possible ride."

"What about the ISP? Hasn't its curiosity also been piqued?"

"Don't push it," the agent advised. "We're not here to discuss her. I asked to see you to warn you that you may still have problems and to find out if you have anything useful to pass on to me. Have you?"

Ahxenta reached into a pocket and pulled out a data shard. "One or two things, including more on that projectile ship that almost got us when we were last in: spec and tech information for rapid ID and hints on how to take any similar out. And data on possible hostile bases at Zeta Dixt and Peden Post, in case you weren't posted."

With little else to discuss the meeting was ended and the two PSS officers made their way back to the *Half Moon*, where they expected a good meal and a quiet two hours. The first familiar face they saw at the bar was Captain Murmur Fleetskup. His first mate was at his side. Ahxenta nodded equably at his greeting and would have passed by but Dyne-Bek accosted her by name and asked for a word.

Sceptical of the woman's affected affability, the captain was curt. It was a quick matter, Dyne-Bek assured her. Having run several sims of the attack on *Arianrhod* by the alien weapon-ship, she had deduced that the firepower used by *Arianrhod* had been excessive and had thus caused more damage than necessary to the *Tallulah*. Her crew would have dealt with it far more efficiently.

"So why didn't you?" Ahxenta asked shortly.

"You were the target, not my ship," was the tart response.

"So you'd have held back and watched it blow us to hell," Apnis cut in acidly. "Interesting new tactics, Murmur," she added pointedly to Fleetskup. "As long as *my* ship's okay, the rest of the PSS fleet can burn? We'll remember that next time you send out a distress. And I'll make sure the rest of the PSS fleet is aware of it too."

"Don't be absurd, Commander Apnis; that is not what my first mate meant at all."

"So please explain what she *did* mean, Captain Fleetskup."

After a blustering few minutes of the captain of the *Tallulah* saying that he would never ignore a sister ship in distress, a view seconded loudly by Dyne-Bek, Ahxenta had had enough. She abruptly told the pair to save their breaths and she and her first mate turned on their heels to make for a table by the far wall. Two spectators of the scene let out their own breaths. They had hoped for fisticuffs.

"Well mate, we won't be able to dine out on that one," Jurry said glumly to his chum.

"No," Malty agreed. "But there's Kerrix looking chipper. She's off to serve them. Wonder what she and Captain Ahxenta were yapping about round the back earlier?"

"Don't ask: chipper or not, she'll bite off your head and spit down your neck. And keep your eyes away from their table or your ears will be singing when the captain boxes them for you," advised Jurry.

"What does Fleetskup see in that new first mate of his?" asked his friend. "It can't be her voice – that would shatter glass."

"Maybe he's at last realised he's not got a snowball's chance in hell with Commander Apnis and he's after comfort elsewhere. Or he likes the cut of her jib, more fool him. Tommy Buntle's not charmed by her. I heard tell he's been cut out to the extent he's stuck in the exec's office and isn't welcome on the bridge of the *Tallulah*," Jurry nodded sagely. "He'll win in the end. Tallulah Tommy's far craftier than

Commander Dyne-Bek any day. *She's* just lip and britches."

Meanwhile, Kerrix had taken the orders at the far table and had returned with two pots of ale and the news that their food was on the way. The captain sat back to view the other customers in the *Half Moon*, a sprinkling of whom were her own and other PSS crews.

"See any scallywags, Cap?" the first mate asked lazily. "There are a few of Ally's regulars in but none that are usually up for a scrap."

"A bunch of strangers by the bar, but that's it," Ahxenta noted. "I've had enough anyway, with Fleetskup and his mouthpiece. But I see Greffy's got a smile on his face; he's chatting up young Merry."

"Making a date for later," Apnis grinned. "I've heard a tale or two. What's going on at the grid that's linked to Web external channels? Pointing fingers, so there must be another big ship coming in. Ally tends to keep his main holo set to the outer belts so he can see when his favourite customers heave to."

"That would be us, would it?" the captain asked.

"Too true. But here's the man with our orders, so we can ask. Chef must have been quick off the mark."

The *Nyx Warrior* had just docked, Ally told them. The last he had heard was that she had been heading for Keystone Kell, but that was over ten days ago and it was one of the crew of the *Tallulah* that had spoken of it the day before, as they had met the *Warrior* at Salt Three. Still, to make it into the Web from Keystone meant she must have made a rapid about-turn and hit the bypass at high speed. No doubt they would find out when any of her crew called in.

The call was rather earlier than Ally had anticipated, as one of his staff, a puzzled look on her face, came over to say that he was wanted at the comm as Captain Holdspan was on the link.

"Party?" he queried as he turned to see what was going on.

He returned to the table a short time later even more perplexed to have a word with Kerrix, who was clearing glassware.

"Captain Holdspan's on his way over here," he said. "He wants to talk to you in private as soon as he gets in. He says it's important."

"What? But the *Warrior's* just in. He must have more urgent things to do than hightail it over here to see me; check in with the harbour office for a start. Isn't he supposed to haul in there and argue over the docking fees?"

The woman looked openly surprised despite the attempt at levity, Ahxenta noted. She hefted her tray and made off to the bar, the three remaining watching her.

"He seemed anxious," Ally muttered in an undertone, to foil the curious ears that had picked up part of the exchange, his eyes flicking over to his assistant. "What's she at now?"

"Checking what else is hanging off the outer belts, by the look of it," Apnis apprised him. "If you will insist on having your holo set to keep your eyes on things out there, what do you expect?"

"Finish your dinner," the captain advised. "Nat Holdspan will no doubt enlighten us as to what's going on when he gets here."

The *Half Moon* had quietened down by the time the two had eaten. Ahxenta had contacted the *Arianrhod* to have her duty officers check if there was any unusual activity in local space and after some enquiry was advised that two ships were holding station off the outer beacon, probably awaiting clearance. She had just linked back for more details when the captain of the *Nyx Warrior* and his first mate arrived.

Azular was obviously now on the bridge, for he called out that the two ships must have been cleared for they were moving in tandem towards berths not far from the *Arianrhod* but that both were highly shielded. His loud expletive as he raised a visual was sufficient to alert Ahxenta and Apnis that there was a cause for concern.

Holdspan and Treskitt had just reached the bar where Ally had set two jars of ale when Kerrix appeared from the back. She nodded to the two and was about to reply to the captain's urgent request for a chat when the first mate of the *Nyx Warrior* drew attention to the overhead holo-grid, which showed the vast lacunae of the outer belts that were home to the huge cargo vessels that used the Web.

"Damn! They made it in!" Holdspan exclaimed.

The oath uttered by the Norvallan woman when she spied the two ships was new to the locals. She had clearly recognised one or both. Customers began to converge on the bar to have a look, Ahxenta and Apnis amongst them. Ally was quick to call in one of his security to give priority elbow room to the four senior PSS officers.

"We have it on visual here, Azular," Ahxenta was saying into her communit. "That huge cargo is the *Kel'Moth*, and *that* I assume Ms Kerrix, is the *Twin Star*?" she asked the woman.

She nodded. "Yes, that is definitely the *Twin Star*. Is that what you wanted to talk to me about, Captain?" she asked, eyeing Holdspan.

"Yes. They passed us at Barfit with barely a hail and I figured they might be headed here. I asked but was told it wasn't my concern by the captain of that cargo. I recognised the double-hulled ship from our data. And our talk last time we were in here suggested it might mean trouble. We were making for here so we put on a spurt to get in ahead of those two. *Does* that ship mean trouble for you?"

She looked uneasy. "I don't know," she admitted. "And why is she being escorted by *that* ship? They're no friends of mine."

"Is that the ship you hitched a ride on when you came to Merkat months ago?" Ahxenta asked curiously.

Kerrix looked closely at the holo which showed that the two ships were now at station-keeping. "I can't be sure if that's the one but it's one out of the same yard. You know that ship?"

"That is the *Kel'Moth*. She flies out of Starfall and she's captained by Commander Vexin Thal, an ex-victim of those hostiles that caused the war not so long ago and who are active yet. He was in command of one of the ragtag ships that fought with the Alliance at Skyrtek," she stated for Holdspan's benefit. "To take revenge on the hostiles and then take over their ops, I suspect. But he and his now claim to be traders and they seem to have several bases and a fleet of ships."

"Not all as big and well-armed as that one," Apnis added. "But if he's so friendly, what's he doing flanking a Norvallan ship? And why have they hauled in here, if not for you?" she asked Kerrix.

"*I'd* like the answer to that. How did they even know I'd made it?"

"You said Thal, or at least his people, had got your spec; and your implanted ID sends out a signal," Ahxenta reminded her. "And he'd have had your shuttle's data as it was his people that intercepted you. He's smart and probably recognised *that* as the same tech. And now that he's a good guy, he'd talk first rather than shoot if he meets a ship he doesn't recognise," she continued in an ironic tone.

"We may find out," Sol Treskitt remarked. "That's a shuttle gone out from the cargo to the two-hulled ship. Picking up some friends?"

"They'd better not start anything in here," Ally hinted darkly.

Kerrix had been reflecting and eventually gave a sigh as she turned to Holdspan. "Can't do anything about it," she shrugged. "But thank you for making the effort to warn me, Captain. I owe you for that."

"You owe me nothing," he responded. "If there *is* trouble, you can count on me as back-up."

"Thank you. But until there is, I'd better get back to work."

"Cool," Treskitt remarked as she picked up a tray and moved off.

Ahxenta watched narrowly. "We may as well sit it out," she said to Apnis. "Most of the folk here won't shift until the showdown."

"You reckon there'll be a showdown, Cap?"

"I do. I also reckon Azular's watching what's going on out there with everything he's got," she went on in a low voice.

As they reclaimed their table the first mate grimaced. "If there's trouble, you can count on me as back-up? You think Nat Hotshot's flexing his muscles? And I saw Fleetskup and his mate watching from the wings and Dyne-Bek's eyes were as wide as a full moon."

An hour passed before a hum from those eyeing the holo heralded action. The *Kel'Moth's* shuttle had left the *Twin Star* with another at its back and the two were coming in. Word had gone round, for the *Half Moon* was busy and Ally had recalled his security. A woman in casual wear slipped in the door and made for a table just inside.

"Vettarista!" muttered Ahxenta. "And I see ours are all still here and they're not full of ale."

It was a further forty minutes before five strangers made their way in. Thal and one of his officers were in the lead. The other three wore uniforms not seen in the *Half Moon* before but both Ahxenta and her first mate recognised the insignia.

"One bigshot and a security detail by the look of it," the captain noted. "Big guns."

"Given the spangle on the uniform, that might be this admiral in charge of the ship," Apnis responded. "Where's Kerrix?"

"Over by Vettarista at the door and she looks narked."

Thal made straight for Ally. "We are looking for this woman," he said coldly, displaying some holo from a wrist unit.

"You've found her," a voice said at his back as Kerrix slapped her tray onto the counter. "So what do you want?"

All five turned. If the older man was Admiral Posettix then he was the canny veteran that Kerrix had claimed, for he barely twitched as he looked her over, taking in every detail. The two guards stiffened to attention, stared at her and loosed their weapons. Kerrix caught the noise and the implied threat and stepped back, her eyes still on Thal.

"What do you want?" she repeated.

Ahxenta and Apnis rose from their table and began to make their way forward, the captain tapping Greffy lightly on the shoulder as she passed with the command to stay put. Merry she had no control over and the young woman followed in their wake. Nat Holdspan and Sol Treskitt had also decided to step up.

"This is the one?" Thal asked of the older man.

"Of course this is the one," Kerrix said tartly. "What's going on and what's *your* ship doing leading the *Twin Star* on a string?"

"Belay that," the senior officer said calmly, in a voice that sounded strangely offbeat. "Your manner hasn't improved."

"Admiral Posettix," she responded clearly for the benefit of the ears listening. "Your presence here surprises me."

"Why?"

"I'd assumed I was listed as missing presumed dead and as I've no-one to give a damn, why are you here? And how did you get here? Through that bypass node called Starfall Exit that *his* people guard like the gates of hell, I expect. Sir," she added.

"Commander Thal escorted my ship here in search of you, once I'd been made aware of your survival," he replied levelly. "Norvalla has opened trade relations with the Starfall Trade Fleet and others in the zone named Mu. Travel is possible by the bypass node that your mission discovered and others on the same route. The minutiae you don't need to know. But you *are* coming back with me."

"Trade?" she questioned. "They're shady dealers getting tech from the new areas they've opened up beyond the mapped sectors of Mu, including Norvallan space it seems. Are you dealing with the hostiles out there as well?" she demanded of Thal.

"No we are not!" he hissed. "We are assisting a trade partner in pursuit of a fugitive from Norvallan fleet justice."

"You're *what*? What in hell's going on, Admiral?" she spat as the two security guards cocked their rifles.

Admiral Posettix sighed. "You're coming with me," he told her.

"I'm going nowhere until I get some answers."

"You're not making this easy, Xanna," he said quietly. "You *will* obey or my guards will have to detain you."

Her eyes sparked fire. "If you've got a charge to make, Admiral, you make it."

Into a stunned silence, he did. "Elistya Xanna Sethina Vetoyn Bet Kerrix, Lady of the Family Paramount of the Colony of Valla Key, Daughter of Clan Starwain of Telzilt and Captain of the survey vessel *NFS Sunburst*, I arrest you on a charge of insubordination, explicitly, disregard of the direct orders of your superiors in Norvallan Fleet Command, and of sundry other charges listed in the warrant under my hand."

26: FAREWELLS

The conversational hum in the *Half Moon in a Puddle* grew to a buzz as word and guesswork passed from mouth to mouth and those not in the immediate vicinity strove to get a view of the main event. It was evident to those around the bar that the charges had stunned Kerrix. She gaped at the high-ranking officer, her mouth forming a question, as one of his security officers laid a hand on her arm. She shook it off with an oath and found the business end of a rifle in her face.

"You're not resisting arrest are you, Kerrix?" the admiral asked.

"That's *Captain* Kerrix, until I'm stripped of that rank," she replied as she put a hand up to move the gun away from her eye. "Or do you hold me guilty in advance of whatever nonsense is in that warrant?"

"The outcome will be decided at your court-martial," he returned crisply. "But for now you're under arrest so you either accompany me quietly or I have you restrained and forcibly removed."

"I don't advise that," another voice broke in.

"Who are you?" the admiral demanded, turning to the speaker.

"I'm Captain Nathan Holdspan of the *PSS Nyx Warrior*. And I suggest you lower that rifle," he said to the guard.

As the admiral signalled his escort to comply, Kerrix gave a short laugh. "It's all right Captain Holdspan, he wouldn't dare shoot me. Now what exactly are these charges against me, Admiral?"

"It is not a matter open for discussion in this place. Shall we go?"

"Admiral, may I respectfully request that I'm allowed to collect my effects from my quarters if I'm to be removed to beyond the end of the mapped galaxy. And what the hell are you staring at?" she added to Thal, who had been taking in everything in a gloomy silence.

"You belong to the Clan Starwain of Telzilt?" he rasped.

"What's it to you?" she came back at him.

"That's enough," Posettix interposed. "It *is* a reasonable request," he told Kerrix. "But I and my aides will accompany you every step of the way. The party's over," he announced to the onlookers.

"Not quite." Ahxenta's icy voice cut the air as she came up. "You won't be taking Ms Kerrix anywhere she doesn't want to go."

"And who might you be?"

"I'm Captain Cinnabar Ahxenta of the *PSS Arianrhod*. And you know you have a berth aboard my ship," she added to Kerrix. "I take it you won't argue with that, Commander Thal?" she asked of the dour renegade officer, who remained silent.

"Thank you, Captain. I *am* grateful, but running away won't help. I *will* be back in to say goodbye," Kerrix soothed a clearly upset Merry. "We need to talk privately, Admiral. We can do that in my quarters."

"Hell, I need an ale," Tallica Apnis remarked to her captain as she watched the four Norvallans step out of the *Half Moon*. "Think he *will* bring her back and not spirit her away when we're not looking?"

"He will," Ahxenta murmured in reply. "Vettarista's tailing them and she'll have caught every word."

Ally's security had dispersed the crowd around them by the time the two turned to the bar to claim two jars. Thal and his officer stood there still, the commander looking acutely morose. He eyed Ahxenta and she had the impression that he wanted a word but the advent of Captain Fleetskup and his first mate put paid to it. Nat Holdspan and his first mate also remained close by but forbore to intrude.

"Two ales on my tab," Fleetskup ordered heavily before facing the commander of the *Arianrhod*. "What was that about, Captain? She's a fugitive from outside, an alien hiding out in the *Half Moon*?"

"Don't be absurd," she spat, echoing his earlier rebuke to Apnis.

"But you know about her, don't you, Captain?" Dyne-Bek put in, her eyes gleaming in curiosity. "So who and what is she?"

Ahxenta shook her head with an expressive grimace of distaste, leaving the question hanging in the air.

"I met a few like her in my former post in the Prison Service," the *Tallulah's* first mate continued blithely. "They think they can get away with bending the rules and are too smart to get caught. So why did you give her a job here?" the woman asked Ally. "Surely she must have struck you as a bit shifty?"

"*She* didn't; not like some I could mention," was his barbed retort.

"We'll sit," Ahxenta said to Apnis. "I've a private link to take."

Several pairs of eyes followed the two as they made their way to their table. The captain set privacy and tabbed her wrist communit.

"Azular," the first mate predicted. "He's figured something's up."

An hour passed, the *Half Moon* settled into to its typical evening tenor and the Norvallans had not yet returned. Holdspan and Treskitt had joined the two from *Arianrhod*. Thal and his second were sat nearby, as were various PSS officers and sundry others keen to see the finale.

"Would you have believed it?" Jurry asked of his mate for the fifth time. "I always said she was something else, that Kerrix."

"And you're still saying it," Malty pointed out. "I'd better go and get us another couple of jars or Ally will charge us rent on these seats. This is turning into an expensive night. I hope it's worth it."

"Oh it will be," predicted Jurry. "In fact, hurry up, there they are now and would you look at her get-up!"

The sudden stir was well-founded for Kerrix had changed into an outfit that Ahxenta and Apnis recognised. She was wearing her flight jacket, its ranking pips sparkling like gems; one badge matched those worn by the others. She carried a kitbag but seemed to be unarmed. She set her bag on a stool by the bar and turned to speak to Ally. That caused Fleetskup and Dyne-Bek to draw near but after an angry earful from the Norvallan woman they pulled back.

She made next to a table where a few of *Arianrhod's* junior officers and Merry sat. The admiral and his guards were at her back taking note, to her obvious irritation. She exchanged a few words with her friend even so, and then handed over a token.

"It's the key to my quarters," she said crossly to the admiral as she waved him and his escort away. "Perhaps you and Vetta will go over the place and take or dispose of anything left? And then hand the key to the agents?" she asked the clearly distressed younger woman.

"They can't take you away like this!" Merry cried. "It's not right."

"They can you know. But you haven't seen the last of me, Merry. I haven't done anything to merit being locked up. It *will* be all right. And thanks for everything. You've been a true friend."

Ahxenta and her colleagues rose as Kerrix made her way to them, her minders a few steps behind. She bid them all farewell by name.

"I meant what I said. You have a berth aboard my ship for as long as you want," Ahxenta said, with a steely look at the three at her tail.

"Thank you, Captain, but it's not an option."

"What *is* the story? How did they get here and what did you do that they want you so badly?"

Kerrix inclined her head, glancing over her shoulder. "You *have* a right to know. I ignored an order from Fleet Command to call off my mission and return directly to base: a court-martial offence. We were responding to what we thought was a distress and had located that anomaly I once told you of. I didn't inform my first officer of the order, continued on mission and took my personal sci-shuttle out to investigate. My first officer took command after my shuttle was lost, found the order and followed it. He left a warning beacon."

"What was in the order that he left you behind without attempting a rescue?" Nat Holdspan asked indignantly.

"All ships of the fleet registered at Valla Key and not engaged in vital duties were ordered home directly for a fly-by to celebrate the inauguration of the colony's new Protector," she said dryly. "In other words, they were wanted to make a big show at a party."

"Belay that!" Posettix interrupted in a testy voice.

"By the time they *did* send a rescue party they found the anomaly was as we'd suspected, the node of an ancient hyperspace route, only it was now operational. As far as I know, it *had* been in use covertly by hostiles to access various systems and bring down any ships that came upon it but *his* people at Starfall had upgraded it from their side to use for their own ends," she said, casting a bitter glance at Thal, who eyed her sharply but said nothing.

"Trade with worlds beyond the node for novel tech and similar made it useful to *them*, and they found the Norvallan beacon. When a rescue ship arrived, contact was made. The Norvallans are ever-open to new trade deals, so the admiral's ship was sent in on a fact-finding diplomatic mission. And met *him*," she added. "And as he'd come across me when I'd made it through and had my ID signal, *and* I'd used one of his ships to hitch a ride here, the link was made."

"Why hitch a ride here?" Holdspan asked curiously.

"I didn't know I was headed here, Captain. I was only anxious to escape *his* people, who had been trying to do me harm at the time."

"You've said your goodbyes," Posettix broke in, reaching over to tap her on the shoulder. "We leave now."

Kerrix nodded. "Of course, Admiral, but I'd like a private word with Captain Ahxenta – if you don't mind."

"This is as private as it gets," he answered sharply, stepping back a little and gesturing his bodyguards to give her space.

Apnis and the two from the *Nyx Warrior*, with quick looks at one another, withdrew to their table whilst those in the immediate vicinity shuffled and backed off a little, most looking away when the captain of the *Arianrhod* fixed them with an icy glare.

Kerrix bit her lip and half-smiled at Ahxenta. She pulled her hands out of her pockets and lifted them to her neck to undo the fine chain with the tiny locket that the captain remembered she said had been her mother's. She removed and re-fastened the chain, holding it up to let the jewelled locket catch the light as it spun.

"Captain, I… do you mind?" she flared at one of the guards, who had closed in. "This is private… Captain, would you be so kind as to give this to Dr Azular and tell him to keep it and all it represents as a reminder of me? Please tell him I…" she glanced over her shoulder again as she dropped the token into her other hand to pass it over. "Tell him I… I'll… see him on the flipside one of these days," she said in a voice that cracked as Ahxenta put her hand out to catch the gift and deposit it swiftly into her own pocket.

The captain nodded. "I'll tell him," she promised, her eyebrows flicking up as she looked directly at Kerrix. "Good luck," she said with a wry smile. "I suspect you might need it."

"I have it," she smiled back. "The admiral will represent me at my court-martial – he's an expert in fleet law and very high in rank. My people set more store by status than anything else, sense included."

"He says he'll fight your case?" Ahxenta asked.

"He will. He's fought impossible cases before, including one for my father, who was his best friend. Ask Azular: he knows the story."

Again the captain's eyebrows rose expressively. "I'll do that. Your people are getting restive," she noted.

Kerrix nodded once, smiled around at her friends and raised a farewell hand. Her escort fell in at her heels as she collected her bag from the bar stool and bid another goodbye to a sincerely affected Ally. The four made their way out of the *Half Moon*, shadowed by Thal and his officer and watched by every eye in the place.

"That's a tale and no mistake," Jurry whispered to his sidekick.

Captain Ahxenta had no sooner settled back down at her table with a thoughtful look on her face when her first mate leaned over.

"So what did Kerrix slip you with that necklet?" she whispered.

"Mind you own business," she was told.

It was two hours later that the captain and first mate made it back to *Arianrhod*. A grim-faced senior science officer awaited them on the far side of the shuttle bay. He had noted the return of the Norvallan shuttle to the *Twin Star* and Thal's craft to the *Kel'Moth* earlier but both ships still held position in the outer belts.

"Tallica, you head up to the bridge. We're making for your office, Azular. We'll talk there."

If the first mate was disappointed not to be in on the chat she did not show it: the captain had alerted her to its content. The bridge was humming when she strode in, the duty crew speculating as to what had gone down portside. Apnis gave no hint and took her place.

The captain faced Azular across his office table, noting his creased brow. She had kept him abreast of part of what had gone on in the

Half Moon and he was aware that Kerrix had left with the admiral. The news that she had been arrested pending court-martial shocked him and as Ahxenta related the details, he grew more downcast.

"And she left you this," she ended, holding out the shiny trinket. "She once told me it was her mother's."

He cupped the chain in his hand, a grieved look on his face, and looked across at her. "Did she say anything?"

"Not much; there were too many eyes and ears. But she slipped me this and asked me to tell you to keep it and *all it represents* as a reminder of her," she said as she slid a small metallic piece across the table. "Congratulations, Azular. If it's what I think it is, you now own a Norvallan science shuttle. I take it you know her berth?"

He nodded, stunned, his hands clasped around the two objects, as the captain repeated Kerrix' last words to him and her belief that the outcome of her trial would be favourable, given the support and legal expertise of Admiral Posettix.

"Tell me about this admiral," she invited. "She said you knew a tale about him and a legal case he fought for her father."

Azular repeated much of what he had garnered from Kerrix as he turned the shuttle key in his hand, examining it closely.

"That's an odd-looking key," Ahxenta said conversationally. "It's coded for authorised personnel only, I guess?"

"Yes. It unfolds like this," he explained. "There are two insertion points in the shuttle's flank. It needs an authorised user, which I am," he smiled sadly. "It's docked in bay six one eight on green eleven; she moved it to a secured bay as a deterrent."

"We're here for at least another day or two as Lindell's setting up local meetings and half our crew are still on shore leave. Let me know how you want to proceed and take time out as you need it."

"Yes ma'am," he responded dully. "Thank you, ma'am."

The captain left him alone and made for medbay for a word with Flintlock before heading to the bridge to check in. She was tired and groaned as she sat, automatically pulling her status boards across.

"Hard day, Cap," Apnis consoled. "How is he?" she asked softly.

"Shaken," was the equally soft reply. "And no doubt it'll be all over the Web in twelve hours and embellished to boot. You know what the bigmouths in Ally's are like."

"Only too well. Azular's heading down tomorrow?"

"I expect so. Make sure he's not on for a bridge shift and give him any time out he wants," Ahxenta said as she called up her external tactical relays and homed in.

"Aye ma'am. Time we were off duty as well. We *were* supposed to be on shore leave and we had billets reserved. *Karillion's* just docked and I see those two ships are still there," Apnis noted, leaning over.

"They are," the captain replied. "What Thal is up to I don't know, but something Azular said about Kerrix begins to make sense. She's only part-Norvallan; her mother was apparently out of Telzilt."

"Ah, that daughter of some clan or other that was part of that list of titles she seems to have," the first mate recalled.

"That's it; the Norvallans are stuck on rank, apparently. But Thal was mightily reticent about the Telzilt system and was taken aback to hear that she had a link to it. And I got the feeling he wanted a chat about her and it when Fleetskup and his best buddy butted in. And now he seems to be sticking to the *Twin Star*."

"Maybe he's hoping for a heads up on her tech, although if it *is* obsolete by Norvallan standards, he's maybe got better aboard the *Kel'Moth*," Apnis postulated. "Mess-time," she hinted heavily.

"Let's go."

The mess was well-populated when the two officers reached it. The hum of conversation fell at their entry, causing the first mate to tilt her head and huff. "Curiosity's killing them."

"They'll find out soon enough. But any ribbing of Azular and I'll have their heads."

"I'll make sure they know, Cap. But as he's able to give as good as he gets any day, I don't think you need worry."

Word had come in that the *Twin Star* and the *Kel'Moth* had departed overnight. The captain had deferred leave to attend early trade talks Lindell had set up with ISP reps. She took Apnis and two guards, as with Kerrix gone she figured that *her* erstwhile pursuers might aim elsewhere. Azular joined them for the trip but set off on his own.

"I'm not going to ask," the first mate murmured as she watched the science officer limp slowly down the passage. "Will he be safe?"

"He's still sharp despite his injuries and Flintlock's advised that he be let loose to do what he wants. He's got a locating pin and a meditag and he's well-armed. I figure he's got people to see as he says he's staying over. We will too as we have those quarters booked *and* we've more business tomorrow: so much for shore leave."

"People? What people?" asked Apnis, her mind elsewhere.

"Vettarista and Merry, I suspect. And Ally. But we have this meet, so let's get to it. Lindell will catch up with us in the lobby."

The talks took two hours and the follow-up with the supercargo another one, by which time the captain and first mate were in sore need of refreshment. They dismissed their escort and made the short ride to the *Half Moon* to hear the upshot of the previous evening. The place was quiet bar Ally's usual hangers-on and a handful of off-duty crew from ships in port and workers from nearby offices. Ally had lately returned from a foray outside and stopped to chat.

"Looking for more bar staff," he replied to Ahxenta's question. "Merry wants to cut her hours to focus on her studies, Evrett's doing full-time as it is, Jez and Lotty are too young for more responsibility and Xanna's gone. And the rest on call only do evenings and off-days. The team in the kitchen's fine as is, but I can't call on any of them – chef would freak out."

"Not many applicants, then?" Apnis commiserated.

"Oh there are a few but most of them are not suitable – they just think the *Half Moon's* the place for a piece of the action. My best bet's getting buddies of the ones I have already."

"Good idea," the first mate agreed. "Merry's friend Vetta might have an idea or three. But what's this about a piece of the action?"

"The story about Xanna, or Captain Kerrix I should call her, has got round. I had a pair of security officers in here earlier asking what I knew! I told them to get lost. And one or two of my regulars have been digging. They reckon I knew about it. I mean, I'd worked out that she was a lot more than a drifter down on her luck but who would have figured her for a fleet officer and a captain at that?"

"One or two," Ahxenta told him with a wry smile. "Who else?"

"Give it time. But that nosy Commander Dyne-Bek got in early and was stroppy: asked where Xanna lived and who her friends were. I told her it was private and if she tried her tactics on my staff I'd report her. She got all uppity, but a couple of my regulars waylaid her and dunned her for drinks. Here's Captain Holdspan and his first mate. They've been in marketing, I expect. I had a couple of ISP reps in here for breakfast that said they were up for a busy day."

The two from the *Nyx Warrior* had indeed come from marketing and the *Warrior's* next trip would end at her home port of Nyx. She was due out soon to Beta Zegonia 68c for a cargo of hull plating, part of which was bound for the Alto Finglas shipyard and the remainder for Freskat Six, from where it was a short hop to Nyx with her other payload of medical supplies. Ahxenta exchanged a glance with Apnis: her supercargo had bid for the plating cargo but had lost as *Arianrhod* had already agreed to hold fire at Merkat for a load for the ISP base at Stinward, which would be replaced there by another for the ISP's

Kellybar One outpost. As the latter halt would take the ship close to the zone Mu border and the scene of past trouble, higher fees had been agreed for that portion of the trip.

The four officers shared a table for lunch, after which Holdspan and Treskitt took leave. The two from *Arianrhod* did not have long to wait for more company, for a short hiss from her first mate let the captain know that the latest comers were not welcome.

"Hasn't the *Tallulah* got commissions to fulfil?" Ahxenta groaned.

"We could ask Tallulah Tommy. I see he's part of the party."

"May we join you?" Captain Fleetskup asked, sitting down quickly.

"Looks like you have," Ahxenta noted mordantly. "How are you, Mr Buntle? We haven't seen you about much lately."

He had been busy aboard was his excuse as he eyed her askew: she had never been his friend. Dyne-Bek interposed volubly to clarify. As exec, Buntle had tasks to tie him to his desk, including those that she was far too busy to handle. Her priorities lay in aiding the captain and keeping the crew in line, duties that the former first mate had plainly neglected, as Buntle had been so often on the bridge. The slur cast on Goodsocks Fleetskup could not ignore; it led him to interject that she had been a very capable first mate and he had been sorry to lose her.

"She certainly got *your* feet out of the mire and saved the necks of your crew more than once," Apnis scathingly reminded him. "At the battle for Freskat for one, but you missed that didn't you, Murmur?"

"You know very well I was incapacitated at the time, Commander Apnis," he said in annoyance.

"Where's Lieutenant Inks? Holding the bridge in your absence?"

"As acting second mate that *is* his post when the captain and first mate are elsewhere," was the ponderous response.

"Naturally," Dyne-Bek agreed and held on that tack for a moment or two, before coming to what her real objective seemed to be: the two ships that had come in the night before and what the officers of the *Arianrhod* knew about them. The reason for her interest she glibly decreed to be the necessity for information lest her ship met them.

"So what *do* you know, Captain?" the woman finished.

"Very much more than you do, Commander," was the cool retort. "And until you explain precisely what your unwarranted interest is in those ships and matters related to them, I'm telling you nothing."

She was piqued, but whether she was too in awe of Ahxenta to speak or was planning another strategy was unclear.

"The huge cargo hails from around zone Mu and there are two or three similar around," Tommy Buntle said casually. "The other one's an unknown but it's reckoned she's from beyond mapped space."

"Mr Buntle seems to have all the data you need at his fingertips," Ahxenta told Dyne-Bek with some irony. "But I see I have an urgent link to take, so please excuse me."

The captain sat back waiting until the three from the *Tallulah* rose and walked off to take up their station at a nearby table.

"Point to Tommy Buntle," Apnis remarked quietly as she set the privacy shield. "Who's on the comm?"

"Business associate that wants a meet in the *Sunlight* ASAP."

"Got you," the first mate acknowledged. "We'd best get to it."

As Apnis had inferred, the contact was Vettarista, but their goal was not the *Sunlight Subspace Diner*. That line was to mislead the *Half Moon's* lip readers. They made for the *Pink Kettle* on green six.

The Berzic woman was there, her table set for privacy. She wore a flight suit, she was armed and she bore a new facial scar. Her aim was to let them know that she was leaving, but before she did she wanted to tidy up loose ends, including learning the fate of Norvallan shuttle. She and Merry had cleared Kerrix' billet but had not found any non-standard piece of personal property or the shuttle key.

Ahxenta reflected for an instant and then let her know the key's fate. Vettarista accepted it calmly and handed on a shard of details on local corrupt traders to avoid and on possible infiltration in legitimate businesses. The data was also with Merkat security, but that body was unlikely to pass it on to any PSS officer. The captain in her turn asked if the Berzic woman knew anything of Commander Dyne-Bek, given her undue interest in Kerrix and the renegade ships that Admiral Posettix had referred to as the Starfall Trade Fleet.

"*She's* an aggressive fortune-seeker with a big mouth," Vettarista said irately. "She was a senior security officer aboard the *ISPS Resolve* but was reduced in rank and shunted into the prison service after a ruckus including suspected bribery. It resulted in charges against her and a posting to Skene Starn orbital detention facility, which is as far from civilisation as you can get. She got out by toeing the line until she was promoted to second officer of a prison ship out of Sekward Central. *That* was even further out and she wanted a place to flex her muscles and call the shots. She fancies a command role but she's not as smart or smooth as she thinks she is. Now she's aboard a PSS, she'll be looking for any links that give her an advantage."

"She's already referring to the *Tallulah* as *her* ship," Apnis noted. "Why Fleetskup didn't make Jesse Inks first mate escapes me, he's an outstanding officer. But how come you know so much about her?"

The woman raised a mocking lip. "I checked. I was named by one of the barflies in the *Half Moon* as a friend of Xanna Kerrix and she dug me out at Azure Belle's this morning to ask about her. She hadn't spotted me last night so I played stunned and asked what she knew, which is no more than rumour. But Xanna's gone so there's little more she'll find out, despite her big ears and sticky fingers."

Vettarista left after a few more exchanges, promising to keep in touch. Apnis signalled the nearby assistant to order more coffees and mentioned in passing that if she was looking for another job, the *Half Moon in a Puddle* on green two was in need of staff. Wekki Munnet gave her a wry look, thanked her and agreed to keep it in mind.

"She'll probably dig up more there than in the *Green Diamond* or here and it *is* closer to what passes as culture in the Web."

"Roger that. But I've a note from Azular requesting approval to bring his shuttle up tomorrow. *Arianrhod's* call-sign *is* integral to her hull so there shouldn't be noses twitching," Ahxenta stated dryly. "I'll alert Earbleat that there'll be a new craft and we'll need a bay, but I'll give her no more than that. *Her* nose will twitch and Cottontail will have to be in on it so I'd best be back on board when she comes in. She can be berthed in an outer bay."

"You realise he'll never be away from the damn thing?" warned Apnis. "And you'll have to let the senior officers in on exactly what she is, which means that Earbleat will never be off his back."

"I know but it should keep the pair of them out of trouble for a bit. The news *will* filter down to the rest of the crew once he starts on it. But I want to see what's on this data shard; if there are people out there to avoid or to watch, I want to know."

The remainder of the afternoon was spent by the captain and her first mate in catching up with sundry acquaintances and in dodging others. They met again for dinner in the *Half Moon*, where they were accosted by Ally, whose ears were still being been buzzed by curious parties. The latest tale was that the *Half Moon* had been aiding an alien who had escaped pursuit by hostiles and had washed up in the Web. Ally had been at pains to tone down the more lurid stories and to paint a tale of ill luck and ingenuity that had ended with unfounded charges against her and Kerrix being removed by her own, who were hardly alien as they hailed from just off zone Mu, but he had had an uphill struggle. It had at least brought an influx of clients eager for details.

"You're part of the story, Captain," he warned Ahxenta as he left. "Don't be surprised if there are a few busybodies that want a chat."

"Here's one," Apnis grated. "Is he so dense he doesn't get the hint that he's not wanted? And where's his pet minder?"

"She's chatting up a few of ours," Ahxenta told her as she nodded over to a group of *Arianrhod's* crew that included Greffy, Box, Dox, Ji and Ferry. "Dox is savvy enough to keep the rest in line and Greffy won't stand for it if she starts to get nosy about Azular," she added as Fleetskup hauled up with a request for a few words.

"Sit," his fellow captain said shortly. "You won't mind us carrying on with our meal?"

"Of course not, Captain," he sighed.

"Your first mate's busy," noted Apnis. "I'm surprised she's not on board, with all her vital duties to keep the *Tallulah* on track."

"She's still learning the ropes," he answered heavily. "A PSS isn't like the military ships she's used to. She'll be an asset as she's efficient and can get things done. Where are you headed next?"

"Is that what you wanted to talk about?" Ahxenta enquired acidly. "Because if it is, I can't tell you. You *are* aware that clients prefer that their business is not spread around, especially in places like the *Half Moon*, where every ear is open and every tongue is ready to wag?"

As Fleetskup bleated on about talking in general and the two from *Arianrhod* ate their way through their rations, a stir at the entry caused all three to look up. Azular had arrived with Merry, the latter making straight for the staff ready room to change for her shift.

"Your science officer is still limping," Captain Fleetskup observed.

"We know," Apnis replied caustically as Ahxenta waved him over.

He nodded and made for the bar, to be intercepted by Box, who with his sidekick was collecting drinks. They exchanged a few words. Box looked baffled but smiled and carried on. Dox looked skyward, seeming to apologise to Azular for her mate. The science officer gave a quiet smile and soon joined the captain's table, a hot drink in hand.

His response to Captain Fleetskup's gruff greeting was equable as he sat down stiffly. He had not ordered a meal, he replied in answer to Ahxenta, not being hungry. She and the first mate did not intrude on his silence but talked quietly to the *Tallulah's* captain. Their peace was soon shattered by Dyne-Bek's jarring voice. Her eyes as well as those of others had noted the new arrival.

"Damn!" Apnis hissed quietly as Fleetskup invited his first mate to sit, which she did with alacrity.

The woman was not subtle and after a few compliments aimed at her captain began on the events of the previous day. Ahxenta let her talk, figuring she may as well find out what Dyne-Bek knew and what she had been pestering *Arianrhod's* crewmen about. It seemed that several conflicting reports were going round and the *Tallulah's* first mate had picked up on most. She queried the allusions to Azular, as a number of ears had recorded the request that Kerrix had made of Ahxenta and a few mouths had exaggerated the content.

By this point the captain and first mate of *Arianrhod* were trading troubled glances. The Berzic officer's face had set hard and it was evident to them that he was holding onto his temper. Ahxenta finally had as much as she could stomach.

"That's enough," she rapped. "Whatever affects me and mine is *not* your concern Commander, and repeating ill-founded gossip is not what I would expect of a senior officer of any fleet. I suggest you and Captain Fleetskup leave us to our table and our own company."

"With respect, Captain, that's hardly the tone for a senior officer to use," Dyne-Bek replied, jerking up in irritation. "And I'm sure my captain *and* Commander Apnis and Dr Azular agree with me."

Apnis hissed in fury. "You are way out of line, Dyne-Bek!"

Azular stared at the woman, his eyes angry and his voice ice-cold. "I suggest you go to hell, or you'll find yourself on your way there with my boot up your backside."

As she bridled in wrath, Ahxenta stepped in. "Captain Fleetskup, I advise that you and your first mate find other seats. I also advise that you ask her about those charges she faced as a senior security officer aboard the *ISPS Resolve* that resulted in demotion and transfer to the prison service. And if I find that *any* of yours have spread rumours about me or mine, I *will* file charges. Good evening."

"How did...?" Dyne-Bek began.

Fleetskup gathered his wits and stood. "I find your reaction totally unreasonable, Captain Ahxenta."

"And I find your behaviour inexcusable. Leave, now."

The three pairs of hostile eyes that surveyed the pair were enough to make them retreat and with a stiff nod, Fleetskup signalled his first mate to make tracks. As they headed to the exit, most of the heads in the *Half Moon* turned to follow them.

"Now that's a chat I'd have given my eye-teeth to hear," Malty said to Jurry from the safety of their dark corner as the privacy shield intensified around the distant table. "Fleetskup was green about the gills and that first mate of his was livid over something."

"No-one takes on the captain of the *Arianrhod* and wins," his mate sniffed. "Commander Dyne-Bek had better learn that lesson before she gets into real trouble."

At their table, Ahxenta viewed her science officer in disquiet. "Tell me about your day, Azular," she said softly.

He disclosed that he had spent much of it in the shuttle bay but he had talked to both Vetta and Merry. The agent he knew was headed back to her unit, but from what she did *not* say he was sure that her remit would still involve alien matters, including the Norvallans and their contacts in mapped space. As for the shuttle, she was ready to leave as soon as a bay aboard the *Arianrhod* was available.

"Why don't you take her back up tonight, Azular? I'll clear it with the duty crew. There's a berth ready for her," the captain told him.

He considered and nodded. "Yes ma'am, and thank you."

Ahxenta was quick to contact her second mate, who seemed more than keen for a look at the new craft earlier than anticipated.

"You will ensure that measures are in place for Dr Azular to dock his shuttle in the allotted bay. He and only he will have access. There will be no incursion into the bay by anyone unless authorised by Dr Azular or by me. Anyone breaching that will answer to me personally. Are you absolutely crystal clear on that, Ms Earbleat?"

"Yes ma'am, absolutely."

"He'll let you know when he's heading up. Ahxenta out."

"You've put the wind up Whisper," Apnis remarked.

"Good. Let's finish up and get the hell out of here. We still have a resupply backlog and we have cargo manifests to check."

The next day saw more early meetings for Ahxenta that led to a deal for a cargo for Selliden Central that could be dropped off en route to Stinward. For many reasons the captain wanted business over quickly and the ship out in space and she pushed for early loading of the ISP payload. *Arianrhod* was busy traffic-wise as most of the crew on leave were shuttled up over the next twenty hours, but by the time the last batch of freight had been secured, everyone was back in post.

It was noted that Azular spent much of his time in the shuttle bay that held his new acquisition. Only the captain, the chief engineer and Greffy had been inside the craft since she had been brought up and none of them would be drawn on the subject but rumour was rife. By the time *Arianrhod* was ready to depart, all of her crew had heard of the drama in the Web and most were curious as to the outcome.

"Doc Azular's got it bad," Box remarked to his mate at the navi-helm console as he set their onward course. "He refused that mug of ale from me in the *Half Moon*. It's unheard of."

"You shouldn't have asked him to tell you all about it and then bawl out that a problem shared is a problem solved," was the short reply. "I'm surprised he didn't paste you. He knows as well as the rest of us that a problem or anything private shared with you becomes common knowledge in every bar in the sector before the day's out. I suggest you shut up and keep your eyes on your boards."

"He should've made it official and handed over a ring. So should we, Romanna; why don't we make it very official and get hitched?"

"Rewind to the last time you asked me that, and play back the answer I gave you then," Dox advised him.

"Will you two keep your personal lives for your off-duty and keep your minds on your work," Commander Apnis ordered tartly. "And keep Dr Azular's personal life out of your conversation, Box, or he *will* have your head for a hockey ball."

As the captain appeared on the bridge and took her chair, the duty officers jerked visibly upright but kept their eyes on their consoles.

"I take it there's nothing coming at us from empty space," she asked of the first mate.

"We've had no warning of anything untoward and I bet every eye in the Port Authority's on it."

"Good. Our heading's Selliden Central, Mr Box, the quickest way. It'll take us a few days so let's get ready for the bypass. Best speed, Lieutenant Dox, once we're out of the Web."

"We're cleared for departure," Apnis reported.

As her docking struts retracted, *Arianrhod* slipped from her bay and made for the bypass that would take her across zone Alpha and on course for Selliden, to the standard farewell of Port Control.

"Course laid in; I estimate we'll make the bypass in thirty minutes, ma'am," Dox announced.

"Roger that," Ahxenta said as she scanned her boards. "No other traffic in the local area, so let's hope this is a quiet trip."

"You said it, Cap," the first mate sighed, and settled back to watch the stars go by.

Box was still musing on the rebuff he had received from Dox as he collected his rations in the mess later. He ambled over to the table occupied by Greffy, sat down heavily and began to impart his woes.

"I don't know why she doesn't want to share my personal space," he continued to grumble. "We share everything else."

"I saw your personal space at your last birthday party," the science officer told him. "Maybe if you tidied it up she'd be more willing."

"I like a bit of comfort," the navigation officer responded cheerily.

"On another note, how's Doc Azular? Still missing Captain Kerrix?"

"Don't go there," Greffy said shortly. "Why does everyone on this ship think that Dr Azular is carrying a torch for Captain Kerrix?"

"Isn't he?"

"It's none of my business. I suggest you make it none of yours."

The huge port of Selliden Central was made without incident. The captain had asked for a meeting with reps from the local ISP office to check up on any recent incidents in the area that had not been sent out over regular channels. That she received a direct assent gave her a moment's unrest but she left her first mate to handle cargo delivery and set off with Azular in tow, knowing that he would be useful to sift out truth from idle talk. Apnis had insisted on an armed escort despite the high security of the port and the four made their way to the designated office. They were greeted by an envoy who introduced himself as Lieutenant Greenbow as he invited them in.

Ahxenta left her guards outside and she and Azular stepped in. A newly-arrived senior officer was on her way, Greenbow told them. She had asked to be in on the talks but was due out soon, hence the hasty organisation. The captain had no time for more than a prickle of tension before the door opened to admit the officer. The uniform was ISP, the ranking pips denoted commander and the insignia was novel but both *Arianrhod* officers recognised the face as Greenbow introduced Levettiza of the Intelligence Division.

"Well met, Captain, Doctor," she greeted them. "I'll take it from here, Lieutenant," she said to the junior officer, waving dismissal.

"You must have made *very* good time from Merkat, *Commander*," Ahxenta stated calmly once the entry panel had closed over.

"Our ships are fast and I left before you did."

"You knew we were headed here?" the captain asked sharply.

"I did. I made it my business to find out after I received an alert related to an adversary of yours that may affect you and your ship."

"Hoxiz," Azular guessed.

"Very good, Doctor," Levettiza replied. "*He's* out of the picture, but we've since found that he's not one of a kind. He's a clone with many genetically parallel but non-identical counterparts. They've been altered to fit into various ops and have a number of mandates, one of which is to engineer the take-down of any vessel or fleet that's likely to do the same to them. The *Arianrhod* is explicitly on that list as part of the PSS fleet, though the list covers most large fleets. The ISP via the Alliance is drafting an alert to be sent out over the usual channels, but it'll be in general terms as anything specific will sound alarms. But your actions raised hackles in many parts, Captain, after you blew that hostile yard at Mellifly to flak. It put paid to more than shipbuilding in the area – so my people think at any rate."

"Including various illicit operations that depended on the support of the hostiles, or at least on the trouble that they caused," Azular put in with a quiet nod. "Hence our trouble with the Treskk."

"That's so," Vetta agreed. "Vexin Thal's fleet is also on the list, as he's shown he'll side with the ISP and its allies in certain matters."

"When it doesn't put him out," Ahxenta stated dryly. "He pursues his own agenda otherwise. But who exactly is he? We've had what he says he was but that's not the whole truth, not by a long way. And your people are investigating him. You told us so."

"We've probed his claims that he was once an agent from a group infiltrating raider packs, though with no definite bio or other data we can't be sure. As agencies we have links to *have* lost agents over time, it's possible; and as your scans say he's part-Friskianx, he may have been Coalition. But not only does he command a fleet of ex-hostile and other ships that he and his people are restoring, he's been active in reinforcing ancient bypass systems that were likely used by hostiles *and* maybe by raiders. His main problem now is that his set-up is so big that he's reliant on others to control parts of it and that's how subversives are still undermining him from within and without."

"What are Thal's links to the Norvallans?" Azular enquired.

"They've begun trade relations but we don't know what exchanges have been made, if any," Levettiza said. "We'd be unlikely to, as both sides are close-lipped. The Starfall Trade Fleet is using a bypass node near their main base to reach K457; *that* links via a few hyperspace routes to a local exit at Norvalla. As Posettix referred to other nodes beyond Starfall, we checked: the bypass cuts across mostly unknown space to a node near that ex-hostile base by the Starglass. The base is tagged Sunrise, so the node will no doubt be Sunrise Exit. There may be more. And there's a cross-way into Mu as a node's been built near Canna to allow a jump into the Brittle to Minch Fettin bypass."

"I don't get it," the captain interrupted. "How in blazes can Thal have taken over so many hostile bases and the hyperspace bypasses that we guessed existed for hostile use?"

"We'll never know the nitty gritty but the rebels have been around for years, recruiting more of their kind, piling up and improving on hostile tech in several refuges. It was only when the war began to get out of hand and their ex-masters looked like winning that they burst out of sector sixteen of Beta. Thal was likely high in the command chain at Skyrtek. There *is* a chain of command with local leaders, and to hijack a hyperspace route that's already there doesn't need a lot of tech, just damn smart recalibration and new defences. You take the base and you inherit the local bypass, if you can reconfigure it."

"Has there been more than one Norvallan ship spotted in charted space?" Azular persisted.

Vetta smiled, seeing where the question was going. "No, only the *Twin Star* and she's on a route out. We have a signal and our outposts are tracking her. The last I have is that she'd passed Needle Beacon on a track across Epsilon via Skyrtek, but that was two standard days ago. The *Kel'Moth* was still escorting her."

"What else should we know?" the captain asked. "I asked for this meet to see if there had been local trouble recently that hadn't been sent out on the usual channels and you haven't mentioned any."

"No more than the usual hit and run by raider packs and not close to here. And reports of small hostile-spec ships at Orange 2334 again, but no contact. A moonbase of Lesser Kirrin did report being buzzed by a small craft so fast and so shielded that they couldn't get a fix but that was it. On another note, I expect you recall Dr Mazy Herta?"

"I do," Ahxenta agreed as Azular raised his brows.

"You know she's wanted on a few charges. Intelligence is involved because of her dealings in rogue med-tech. Her trail's been picked up. She's had help to cover it but we're pretty certain where it leads."

As Vetta paused, Azular eyed her acutely. "Minch Fettin."

"You *are* sharp and that's what our agents reckon, which opens a can of worms. Your theory that there's a facility there churning out info-sents and other altered sentients has been looked into and we've reason to believe you're right. If Herta *is* a recruit, one of the options they're exploring may be implanted micro- and nano-tech that gives them even more of an edge."

The science officer's brow creased in worried concentration as he looked at the other two. "Thal needs to know," he said sharply.

"How do you figure that?" Ahxenta asked.

"The *Twin Star* and the *Kel'Moth* are headed to Starfall. That much is clear. *Your* people won't be the only ones tracking them," he said to Vetta. "They'll pass Minch Fettin and I'd guess that Xanna's not the only one aboard the *Twin Star* with implanted language analysis and translation devices. The admiral at least must have one. *And* his ship will be bristling with novel tech."

"The *Twin Star* and the *Kel'Moth* are massive ships and from what we've seen they're both well-armed and very capable of taking care of themselves," the captain interposed.

"That depends on what they come up against," he said stubbornly.

Ahxenta leaned back. "Your opinion?" she asked the ISP agent.

"It's a good point but an ISP link to Thal isn't an option. He's not likely to trust it and as he doesn't know Herta or what she's involved in, it might be hard to convince him."

"I wouldn't be too sure," Azular argued. "He seized Flatt and he knew who and what he was. Flatt knew him and *that* affair involved Minch Fettin. We have a link to Thal and he trusts us as much as he trusts anyone," he added to the captain.

"I can see this getting messy," she said wearily. "We don't know what Thal's real interest is in the *Twin Star*: perhaps more than trade."

"Possibly, but all we would have to do is warn him that he may have a problem. Thal knew Flatt; he's aware of a facility for genetic and cyber alteration on Minch Fettin that's under alien influence and how significant the tech carried by the *Twin Star* might be to hostile factions. In fact it may be one reason he's acting as escort. But there's no point in second-guessing him."

Reluctantly, Ahxenta agreed, deciding that the call would be made once the ship was on her way to reduce the risk of interception. With a promise that she would keep them updated as far as it lay within her power, Levettiza cut the meeting as she had to leave. Ahxenta and Azular collected their guards and made their way out.

Less than an hour later and with all her pieces in place, Ahxenta called a briefing with her senior officers to apprise them of the latest from ISP. The identity of her contact planetside she kept from all but her first mate at the request of the ISP agent but the news that there were clones of the hostile Hoxiz out there and that *Arianrhod* was on their hit list to be taken down was an unpleasant surprise.

"*Now* can we replace one of our forr'ad phase cannon arrays with a ring-array of gun-ports, Cap?" Earbleat enquired. "I can get the last bits before we leave here and all it'll need is a bit of hard graft from a couple of Crizz's engineers and my team. We could have it ready by the time we make Stinward and use their yards for the placement."

"No we could not," Ahxenta said firmly.

Apnis shook her head. "Haven't you given up on that, Whisper?"

"No Commander," she replied cheerfully. "But you're a weapons expert so why not have a look at my test runs on the simulator?"

"You can continue with the prototype you attached to *Loki*," the captain told her. "But that's it. You will *not* bring the subject up again in any briefing unless specifically asked. Is that clear?"

"Yes ma'am."

Ahxenta closed the meeting and ordered her officers back to their posts to ready *Arianrhod* for departure. It had been a long day already, it was scarcely done yet and she had the feeling that there would be more to come before she saw the back of it.

Selliden was a star on the edge of sight when Lynxi Bellfish called out an incoming. It was ISP and was tagged urgent and confidential. With a word to her first mate to keep them on course, the captain made for her bridge office. The crew mused on the content of the link as half an hour slid past before she returned. She looked severe.

"Change of course," Ahxenta directed as she settled into her chair. "Plot a direct route to Silverglass Station, Mr Box, and get us there as fast as you can, helm. We're picking up an extra cargo for Stinward."

"You don't look happy about it, Cinnabar," Apnis noted.

"I'm not. It's a state-of-the-art military combat shuttle straight off the design board. It's not a gnat's whisker off those two shuttles we shipped from Alto Finglas to Linza but it can withstand a whole lot more, including hyperspace currents. It's to finish it's outfitting at the new yard at Stinward and be tested there. It won't be armed but it will have a test pilot and the officer overseeing the whole shebang."

"And who would that be?" the first mate asked, suspecting from the captain's face that she might know the answer.

"Colonel Ellin Myrtleberry."

"She gets about," Apnis said cynically. "ISP's shifted the schedule to fit it in and threatened no more business if we don't comply?"

"That about covers it," the captain agreed. "Where her ship is I don't know, but I don't need her on mine. I'd better warn Azular as he'll want to make sure his new shuttle is well out of scanning range. And I still have that link to Thal. Dammit! Bellfish, have Azular meet me in my office right now, and prepare a highly secure channel for linking to Commander Vexin Thal aboard the *Kel'Moth*."

"If he's awake," the commander grinned.

"He'd better be," Ahxenta grunted as she rose.

It was a good hour before the captain returned to the bridge, by which time the *Arianrhod* was well on her way to Silverglass.

"You spoke to Thal, then," the first mate greeted her.

"I did. He'd heard about the shake-up in Merkat medbay but not about Herta. He's aware of the hostile-guided med facility on Minch Fettin, though not the specifics, but he's also heard there's another close by on Ellas. His people suspect the hostiles use it for upgrading their own. As Ellas is supposed to be empty, no-one goes there. He's known for a while that his fleet was being hunted, but not the extent, nor of the Hoxiz clones. He *was* evasive about his interest in the *Twin Star* and Azular rode him a bit over it, but Thal reckons the *Kel'Moth* will see her safe beyond Mu. I told him he and the *Twin Star* had been tracked past Needle Beacon and he might be in for a nasty surprise at Starfall. Azular told him he should change course and make for the node by his base at Sunrise," the captain laughed quietly.

"Bet he was put out you'd heard of Sunrise."

"He was, especially after Azular advised him to set up an ambush at the Starfall bypass before anyone tried to do it to him. His people there need to be alerted but we've no proof they'll be targeted as it *is* just conjecture. He cut the link quickly, so he has a bit to think about but we've done all we can. What he tells Posettix is up to him."

"What's Azular got to say about Colonel Myrtleberry?"

"He's pissed," Ahxenta snorted. "He'll shield his shuttle and move her to a secure cargo bay but he doesn't want a guard as that will only raise Myrtleberry's curiosity if she finds out. But as soon as that ISP shuttle's aboard we'll head top speed for Stinward, cloaked and at alert all the way. And colonel or no, she'll be marked at every step."

It was a short hop to Silverglass and by the time *Arianrhod* had made it, the bay was ready for the shuttle, which was prepped to load. The captain had insisted that her crew go over the craft before she would let her aboard, despite the colonel's obvious haste to be off. Ahxenta remained adamant, demanding details and safety assurances. As she reminded her, the last time they met, the colonel had used *Arianrhod's* team as bait to trap Tarn, exposing them to considerable danger.

The ISP officer had little option but to comply. The reason for the craft's presence at Silverglass was that she had been built there from units shipped in over time to foil discovery and being near complete, she was ready for final fitting and trials. The new high-spec shipyard at Stinward was the ideal testing ground and had the means to finish the prep. As for the *ISPS Repulse*, the colonel would catch up with her ship at Stinward, as she was also undergoing refit.

They had been given half a story was the first mate's opinion, and Azular agreed that the colonel was holding back after a meeting they had had with her, her pilot and local cargo transfer experts. Ahxenta had stipulated that the shuttle's ops systems be locked down after transfer and that her energy cells be taken out. She was to be held in the bay recently occupied by Azular's shuttle, as he had augmented it with every security device he had available.

Scans within and outside the craft and the narrow spec they had been given raised no issues and the shuttle was flown up by her pilot, the colonel riding beside him. The ship was tracked from *Arianrhod's* bridge and the landing observed from outside the bay by the captain, Azular, and the three engineers tasked with rendering the craft safe. Guards had been posted at the entries to the docking area but it was a model landing. As soon as the space pressurised, Ahxenta and her team made their way in to meet Myrtleberry and the pilot, Horn.

The senior science officer greeted the two and then headed to the shuttle ramp with two of the engineers to ensure that the ops systems were locked down and to carry out the agreed energy cell removal. The third remained at an external station to monitor the procedures. At a sharp command from the colonel, Horn followed the trio to the shuttle, Myrtleberry's eyes on them until they disappeared inside.

Several minutes passed as the monitoring officer reported a steady drop in shuttle power output. As one engineer emerged hefting two energy cells, the captain leant over to check the readings, a prickle of unease down her spine. She watched as the output continued to drop. The other engineer appeared with a third cell but he had no sooner made the end of the access ramp when a noise at his back disturbed him. Ahxenta wasted no time and sprinted over to the shuttle and up the ramp, Myrtleberry at her back. She could hear the sounds of the security team, alerted by Apnis, making their way into the bay.

Seconds later and the colonel found herself in a heap on the bay's deck, her pilot alongside. Ahxenta's fist had connected with Horn's jaw so solidly that he had been bowled over, taking his superior officer with him as he rolled out of the shuttle and down the slope.

Colonel Myrtleberry shook herself and sat up to find the sharp end of a phase rifle in her face. She turned sideways to see Horn lying flat on his back; he was also staring into a rifle barrel. Two more guards had stepped in and flashing lights indicated that an alert had been called. The colonel's furious threats raised no response from the guards and she was in no doubt that they would take action if necessary. She rose to her feet slowly, her eyes on the entry of her combat shuttle, and waited. The bay entry parted again to admit Crizz Cottontail, who made straight for the monitoring station.

"Status?" the chief engineer barked at her officer.

"She's still reading a power output above station-keeping. With no energy cells, it's more than it should be. There's an energy source in the aft cargo bay but as I don't have its spec and it's well-shielded, I can't tell if it's a standard unit. From what I *can* get, it's a complex set-up. It looks like a network of integrated databanks linked by singly-shielded nodes, and each one has a trip to prevent disablement."

"Let's see," Cottontail said, flicking the console controls. "I need Azular: I think I know what this is, but he's the expert."

As she spoke, the captain appeared at the top of the shuttle ramp, supporting her senior science officer. She helped him down and called on one of her guards to assist.

"There's a medic on the way," she said to her chief engineer, who had turned in concern. "Lieutenant Corvus, Ensign Marks, disarm Mr Horn, escort him to the brig and lock him up. Post a full detail."

The colonel began to object vociferously but was silenced by the blazing voice of the captain of the *Arianrhod*.

"Enough! Any more and you'll be with him, colonel or not. *No-one* assaults my officer or tries to prevent him probing a highly-shielded compartment not listed in the details and not part of the shuttle spec I got. *And* which did not show up on scans, as it had been cleverly masked by the output of the spare energy cell and internal shielding. Did you think we wouldn't find your cyber suite, Colonel?"

"Kindly clarify what you're talking about," Myrtleberry said coldly.

"You know precisely what I'm talking about," was the equally icy retort. "The section integrated into one side of the aft cargo bay that looks like the spare energy cell housing unit. Take out the cell and the housing's still active, *and* it's better shielded than the galactic credit union's mint. What kind of info-sent are you that you can utilise such a miniaturised cyber suite? And what made you think we'd miss it?"

The ISP officer cast her eyes around the bay at the listening crew. She pursed her mouth, shaking her head. "I'm saying nothing here."

"Then you'll be escorted to my brig and I'll be speaking to ISP HQ at Alto Finglas. Guards!"

"Just a minute, Captain! You have no authority…"

"Aboard my ship I have all the authority there is. I will not be the pawn in whatever game you're playing, Colonel. Ji, make sure she has no weapons, take her to the brig and post a watch."

Ahxenta turned on her heel to attend Azular, who was seated on the deck with his back against the monitoring station. Ma'Lappis had appeared with a full medical kit and was kneeling alongside.

The colonel shook off the guard that had taken her arm, stating that she would comply. She extracted her weaponry, handing the lot to Lieutenant Ji, who with Ensign Hanx had their guns on her.

"I won't talk here with all these eyes and ears *and* those security cams looking on. But I object to being taken to the brig."

"Escort the colonel to the brig," the captain told the guards. "I'll be there once I've ascertained the status of Dr Azular and gone over every micron of that shuttle. Your every step will be monitored from the bridge," she added to Myrtleberry.

Once the three had moved out, Cottontail turned to the group on the floor. "Are you okay, Azular? What in hell went down?"

"Lieutenant Horn isn't what he seems," he grimaced painfully. "He's not as advanced as the colonel but I guess he's not far off an ISP version of an info-sent. I'd scanned him *and* every internal shuttle system and realised there was a potential problem."

"You logged the cyber transfer unit and so did the monitor," she said. "It ran comparisons and pulled up that suite on Micklemouse's ship as the closest to what it registered, but how did it produce that holo-spec? You've upgraded this station with Norvallan tech haven't you? And you were using that precious scanner of yours."

"Later, Chief," Ahxenta ordered. "Doctor?"

"You'll do," Ma'Lappis told Azular. "But you're for medbay with me. There's a hairline fracture to your jaw that needs repair and you have a fair amount of bruising elsewhere. What happened?"

"I was trying to shut down the cyber unit. I'm not sure what it's capable of and I didn't want to run the risk of leaving it active. Horn realised that I knew what it was; he moved faster than I anticipated and landed the punch on my jaw. I retaliated, but he's strong. He was incensed and I suspect his judgement was clouded. He *did* pull back when he realised he'd overstepped a mark, by which time the captain had come aboard and took a hand. But that unit must be shut off."

"Greffy can do it," the captain said firmly. "Clear up here, Crizz, get him in and totally shut down that shuttle without injuring yourself or *Arianrhod*. I'm for medbay with Azular. And then we'll see."

It was her senior science officer's view that the colonel had been genetically altered again since last they had met her. The captain was not surprised, figuring that the ISP was upping the ante. The unit in the new shuttle was clearly the latest in download and data retrieval gear and it had been shielded with the newest secure tech. Had it not been for *his* novel scanner, Azular guessed, he would not have found it. Why the unit had been integrated into the shuttle was another question but as the pilot Horn was also an info-sent, albeit inferior to Myrtleberry, it was possibly meant to be the standard vessel for such individuals. Ahxenta expected an interesting talk with the colonel.

"How is your officer?" Myrtleberry asked in seeming concern when the captain, with surveillance gear set, had sat down opposite her.

"He's in medbay with a fractured jaw and extensive bruising. I will not be conveying Horn anywhere other than off my ship and you'll tell me everything, or I won't be transporting you or your shuttle either. And believe me, I *will* be making waves about this."

As they talked, the captain realised that Box's off-the-cuff remark that the ISP had not curtailed the medical facility at Mellifly in order to produce its own variant of info-sents was close to the truth. It was hoped that they could sniff out spies inside and outside ISP *and* trace enemy info-sents, but the colonel admitted that Horn's alteration had been poor and had left him with side-effects that included a short fuse. It was also clear that the ISP officer was curious about the gear that had detected the cyber unit. Ahxenta declined to enlighten her.

By the time the chat was over Greffy had decreed the shuttle as shut down as possible, though the cyber unit was still using minimal power. On that basis and on Myrtleberry's word that she would cause no trouble, she was set loose to settle matters with the Silverglass authorities, who had been querying irately why *Arianrhod* was still in orbit. She relieved Horn of duty and had him shipped to the station pending review. As Ahxenta had refused to take on another pilot, the colonel decided to fly the shuttle out herself at Stinward.

"We should be in line for a bonus after what we've had to put up with from the ISP," the first mate grouched as the captain settled into her chair and *Arianrhod* made to leave orbit. "We've had no report of trouble ahead, but that's no guarantee. *Obsidian* linked about a hit on a carrier off the node of the new Mu bypass at Batsok II. She lost her cargo pods but she got out. A huge ship with a fleet of small craft, so maybe they're back to the mothership-fighter pack tactics. I sent a confirmatory. Our guest settled into her new berth?"

"She has and I've posted a watch – and she knows. She offered to have the *Repulse* come out to meet us at Polstarn and escort us in."

"You said no," Apnis postulated wryly.

"Damn straight I did," Ahxenta growled. "She's still pushing to know how we found her secret cyber unit as it's resistant to every ISP scan system there is. She reckons we've got our hands on alien tech."

"She's right. On which note, how's Azular? He looked pretty ropy from what we saw on the bridge."

"Doing okay but he won't be fit for duty for a bit. I made a formal complaint to Fleet Command at Alto Finglas and the head of the ISP unit at Silverglass but I've had no more than a strap line that it'll be looked into and Horn will be charged. Myrtleberry's furious but that's her problem. At least we've been paid our deposit for this trip and they'll remit the balance before they get their shuttle; the colonel they can have back at no charge."

"How do we stop her reading our people if she's an info-sent, as we don't know her full capabilities?" Apnis asked. "We can't doctor her rations as she'd pick it up, nor can we set Azular on her."

"We keep her under surveillance; she knows we know what she is. We trust her up to a point but she'll have to use the mess as I'm not having one of ours wait on her. The rest of the time she can keep to quarters. We should make Stinward in four days at top speed."

The titanic facility had expanded again when *Arianrhod* finally made berth, the ISP shipyard stretching into infinity. Ahxenta lost no time in settling the contract and having the shuttle prepped for exit. The colonel upheld an icy civility as she made her farewells but voiced the hope that she and Ahxenta would meet again when the galactic state improved. The captain gave her a curt nod: she had cargo to load.

The supplies for Kellybar One were ready in ISP-sealed pods. As the goods were being inspected by Lindell's team prior to stowage, Azular was carrying out his own checks in the secure bay before he re-berthed his prized Norvallan shuttle. He had decided not to move her until they were out of range of Stinward lest high-spec sensory gear was trained on them. Gem Ferry was assisting and as they were slotting the data got from the combat shuttle into the main console, they were interrupted by the second mate. She wanted Azular's input in fine-tuning *Loki VII's* Norvallan-based phase-beam cluster gun prior to a test run in space once *Arianrhod* was in flight. Ferry had refused to let her try out and tune her model of the device in the lab using his model of the hostile missile ship as the target.

Earbleat had gone over the data a dozen times, she cheerfully told the two, and was convinced that with tweaking, an actual test could be carried out using virtual fire. The new circular gun port assembly was now tightly linked into *Loki's* weapons system and with the data they had on the hostile missile ship, she was sure that if they met another they could deal with it effectively. Azular regarded her warily, suspicious that she had chosen to bring the matter up at that point so as to get a view of what he had put in place to protect his shuttle.

"Later, Lieutenant Commander," he informed her briefly. "You can link me the data and I'll have a look once I get back to my lab."

"I've got it here," was the instant response as she set a shard into a reading port on the console and swiftly called up the holo.

Azular was curious despite his other pressing concerns and with a sigh he began to run her pre-set simulations. He soon realised that his hours of dissecting data on alien ships, weapons and ops had given him an instinctive grasp of what would work and what was less useful in terms of neutralising threats from outside and as he manipulated firing patterns and phase-beam angles, the other two could see the efficiency rating of the cluster gun array rise.

They were interrupted by the request that Earbleat report to the bridge, as *Arianrhod* was prepping to depart. She made off, with Azular's promise to complete the fine tuning and send her the results. He was headed to his lab, despite his official sick-leave status.

The bridge was buzzing as duty crew reported in. With the cargo locked down and credit transfers in order, final clearances had been issued. The only drawback was that the *Repulse* was under orders to ship out and as their route lay together as far as Hervesta Tertius, Myrtleberry again offered her ship as escort. Ahxenta firmly refused and gave orders to get under way as rapidly as possible.

"Where's the *Repulse* headed after Hervesta?" Apnis asked. "Off to investigate the first section of the new zone Mu bypass at Cassary or the trouble at Batsok?"

"Or maybe off checking out something beyond mapped space," the captain replied. "We'll cut through to Skitter via Tressic Minor. After that we're in ISP territory to Kellybar."

"That's a lot of empty space, Cinnabar."

"And the quicker we're through it the better. I'll leave you to set tactical drills to keep the crew on its toes, lest we run into trouble."

"Will do, Cap, given trouble's what we always seem to run into."

Although subtle shifts in hyperspace currents marked the passage of other craft on the bypass, the next hours *were* calm. Such being the case, the captain authorised a test run of *Loki VII* using virtual fire at the next node shift, Azular having completed his fine-tuning of her weapons system. The science officer made his way to the bridge to observe as *Arianrhod* made the crossover node at Hellatrix, but it was obvious to his fellow crewmates that he was not yet back to fitness.

Loki was launched from her bay to a static locus off *Arianrhod's* hull where the basics of the ringed array could be observed. Earbleat was elated as she exhibited sequential, random or simultaneous bursts of the six phase beams, straight or angled inward or outward. A fail-safe mechanism had been incorporated to ensure that a stray beam would not interact with another and cause a strike on *Loki's* own hull. The final test was a focussed burst, where the beams were brought together to a single point. The second mate sent the small cargo pod-based craft into a dizzy upward spiral and then back down towards the *Arianrhod*, raining virtual fire on her mothership.

"Belay that, Lieutenant Commander!" Ahxenta yelled. "That's the end of testing. Bring *Loki* back aboard. And you try that again against my ship and you'll be in the brig!"

"But Cap, she's using virtual fire, she won't hurt *Arianrhod!*"

"That is *not* the point, Ms Earbleat," the second mate was crisply informed. "You call the test a success, Azular?"

"I do, Captain; the array will make an impressive weapon when armed, though only at close range and for a short time. I advise extra guidance and recognition coding to ensure that loss of contact with *Arianrhod* won't halt her progress should that occur."

"And self-destruct if anyone tries to pick her up," Earbleat added. "But even as she is, that new emplacement's a beauty and well worth the time and effort spent on it."

"And the cost," Apnis added dryly from the sidelines.

The ship passed Hervesta and was halfway to Tressic Minor when an ISP report came in of raider clashes by Ripple Seven in zone Gamma and by Fivepoint, on the edge of the Outer Reaches Archipelago in Epsilon. The captain thought it expedient on the basis of Fivepoint to alert Thal, as there was an ex-hostile base close by that his people had probably taken over. He replied a little later with thanks and the advice to steer clear of the Astrella Nine asteroid field, as one of his ships had been lost in the area while chasing up a report of hostile activity, and he had lost contact with another sent in to investigate. The *Kel'Moth* and the *Twin Star* had crossed Epsilon and were in the ISP-controlled sector of Zeta, but that was all he would say. The captain gave Azular the news privately. He took it quietly, only stating that it was likely that Thal had taken the advice to head for his Sunrise base in view of likely problems at Starfall.

Arianrhod had come off the bypass at Tressic Minor to renew her air supply. The world was on the edge of Coalition space but was friendly and air recharge was rapid, the only cost being an exchange of news. Ahxenta left that to her first mate as she had links to make, including enquiries of her contacts about hostile activity by Astrella Nine. By the time the ship was ready to leave there had been a note from Captain Coxen of the *Hexameter* about an attack close to the Dice Gold system, on a fast cargo ship out of the remote Kell Lyne, on the Iota-Kappa border. The cargo was a radical armoured carrier that had been making for Cassary. She had shaken off pursuit but had captured readings of the enemy which pointed to a hostile rather than a typical raider spec and the attacker had been low on both power and weaponry. Coxen sent on the spec.

"Let's hope the next stage is as quiet," Apnis said as the order was given to prepare *Arianrhod* for bypass entry and set direct for Skitter.

"Roger that," Ahxenta replied with a sigh. "I'm stiff as a board. Once we're well on the road I'll do the rounds and stretch my legs."

"Entry to bypass successful, Captain," Dox announced from her station. "Time to Skitter sixteen point five hours at present speed."

The words were no sooner spoken than Lynxi Bellfish let out a yell. "Distress call, Captain! It's faint and it's repeated: just a signal, no message. I don't recognise the code."

Gliss at tactical and Greffy at science began immediate sweeps of the area as the captain called for the signal to be put on audio. The minutes trickled by as the cyclic tone sounded across the bridge.

"Got it!" Greffy crowed as Azular appeared to see what was going on. "It's very close. It must be a tiny ship or escape craft, but how it's survived the hyperspace currents I can't imagine. No other ships detectable, unless they're very well shielded."

"I get no other vessels nearby," Gliss verified as the tactical holo spun and enlarged to show what looked like a streamlined shuttle.

"It's highly protected and has surface jammers but it's seen a bit of action and we can get through the shielding, partly at least," Greffy noted. "The hull structure's complex…"

"And we've seen it before," Azular continued as he slid into his accustomed chair and called up his own readings.

"You what?" the captain asked.

"The structure," he amended. "It's similar in construction to the *Kel'Moth* and *Kel'Beth* but very small. It's a shuttle, immensely strong and possibly designed as an escape craft. I get no lifeform readings but that may be down to the high-density shielding."

"There's maybe no life," the navigator intoned. "It might just be a big bang waiting to go off."

"Button it, Mr Box," Ahxenta instructed. "Slow us to match speed but don't get too close," she ordered the helmswoman. "Try to raise her, comms. Tell her who we are and ask what help they need."

"How long has she been on the bypass?" Apnis questioned as Bellfish reported that no response had been received to their hails.

"I need a positive ID on that craft," the captain called. "Keep our targeting eyes on her but do *not* power weapons. She's bound to be reading us, if there *is* anyone aboard that is. And repeat our hail."

"Long-range scanners show no other ships nearby on bypass," Gliss reported. "Nor any ion trails that indicate recent passage."

"So where's the ship, if that *is* an escape shuttle?" Apnis asked.

"We have a response to our hail, Captain!" Bellfish interjected. "Visual's patchy but audio's clear enough."

"Let's hear and see it," Ahxenta ordered.

The thin, hawk-like features were wary as the man acknowledged the hail. He and four others were aboard an escape shuttle from a vessel that had been attacked close to Axle Lexo. They were short of rations and almost out of air. In response to the captain's questions he told her they were one of three shuttles to escape their ship and they had been in flight for close to nine days standard. He was Lieutenant Lek; his ship was the *Kel'Tarn*. As he was speaking, Gliss called up a holo of the relevant area. Axle Lexo was in a remote system between Tressic Minor and Dice Gold and was claimed by no authority, but was within range of the Astrella asteroid field. Azular had also been busy and had captured a clearer visual of the man and two others. The dark, rigid uniforms were those of Thal's people.

"What was your mission?" the captain demanded suddenly.

"Search and rescue," Lek responded jadedly. "One of our ships had been reported missing in the area. We were sent in to look for her, picked up a distress, went in and were ambushed."

A few more searching questions and answers later and the captain gave the command to bring the craft aboard. Lek had confirmed Thal as his commander and had allowed a full scan of his shuttle. Ahxenta ordered an outer bay cleared and security and medical teams standing by. The crew were to be taken directly to medbay.

The five were utterly weary and in very poor condition when they alighted. Flintlock had made a cursory scan of each and insisted that questioning be left until later. Lek asked that the shuttle remain sealed but agreed to a sortie by Greffy and two engineers to ascertain safety. He gave the names of his crew at Ahxenta's request. She planned to contact Thal to confirm their identity and have them picked up. She also wanted the *Kel'Tarn's* data, taking it as read that it had been sent to the home fleet and that the escape shuttle had a copy.

Ahxenta minced no words when her request to speak directly to Thal was denied. She had not linked supra-light to talk to a deputy, the matter was highly urgent and the comms officer was liable to have his head in his hands if his commander was not summoned at once, she told him. She also insisted that the link be private.

Thal knew the captain sufficiently well to take her comm in his quarters. The name *Kel'Tarn* caused a sharp hiss as he confirmed that the ship was one of his, a medium-range cruiser. They had suspected she had gone down. He called up the crew roll to verify the names on Ahxenta's list and asked to speak to Lek but accepted her veto on that. She passed on the coordinates of the pick up and the news that two other escape craft were possibly out there but that her ship had not detected them. She also told him that she expected his crew to be removed from her ship quickly and that she wanted the data that the *Kel'Tarn* had sent in to her fleet. He agreed, indicating that he would link back with relevant arrangements, but refused to give her anything on his own movements.

"*Arianrhod* is heading to Skitter. We'll be there in sixteen hours if we make good speed and meet no obstacles," Ahxenta stated. "That would be the obvious place to hand over your people. I'll be sending out the details of the action around Axle Lexo, as there was also an incident close to Dice Gold that one of my fleet reported – I'll link you that data. I will not mention the *Kel'Tarn* or your escape craft but I'd like to know more about that shuttle: that it survived the currents in hyperspace is pretty impressive for such a small craft."

"I expect you would," he replied evenly. "I'll be in touch when I've arranged matters. Thank you for looking after my people."

"Welcome. Ahxenta out."

"So how was grumpy Commander Thal?" Tallica Apnis queried as the captain resumed the bridge.

"Same as usual, though he did seem grateful that we rescued his crewmen. He'll link again when he's arranged their pick-up. I asked about that shuttle but I doubt we'll get much more."

"That shuttle of Kerrix' made it through rough currents, so it's got a few tricks we could use on ours," the first mate noted.

"Azular's on it. I take it he's back in his lab? But that shuttle's strength is down to hull structure, as it's similar to their damn smart ships and based on hostile tech. But it looks like there's a hostile base near Axle Lexo, because how else could they take out two ships?"

"Bet Thal will send in a squadron of his best battlecruisers to find out," prophesied Apnis. "But he won't haul in to pick up his own if he's escorting the *Twin Star*. They must be close to leaving charted space, if they haven't already done so. He didn't mention where he was or what he was up to, I take it?"

"Nary a word. But they got him out of his bunk, I'm pretty sure – he wasn't in uniform."

"He doesn't sleep in his uniform? I *am* surprised," Apnis grinned.

"Stow it. Any word from Flintlock on our passengers?"

"No major injuries but all pretty shook up and anxious about their other shuttles. Tactical's on long-distance scan but not a thing."

"I passed the news onto ours. If any of them are in the area, they'll keep a lookout. I sent a report to the ISP as well and they can send it on as they see fit. But that's now three new hostile bases that may be out there. How many more?" Ahxenta asked.

"Worrying, but if we have Thal on board it might even the odds a bit. If he and his *have* taken over the four working ex-hostile bases, he must need a hell of a lot of organisation to run them. We know about Starfall and Sunrise, but what's he called the others and do they all have secret bypass nodes linked to who knows where?"

"Looks like the mapped galaxy's getting bigger all the time," Box whispered to his mate at the navi-helm console.

"Just keep your eyes on our course and make sure we avoid any sources of trouble," Dox responded irritably.

Thal must have had several pieces in place, for he was back on line in forty minutes to advise Ahxenta that the *Kel'Beth* would meet *Arianrhod* at Skitter to take on the shuttle and her crew. He also told her that a distress from a second escape craft had been detected and one of his own was chasing it up. He sent on the data they had from the *Kel'Tarn* before she was hit but made no mention of data on the shuttle. The captain brought *that* up and with one or two other topics she introduced, it was over an hour before she resumed the bridge.

"So what took so long?" the first mate asked curiously.

"Mind your own business," was the cryptic response.

She gave the news of pick-up by the *Kel'Beth*, however, and then made for medbay to inform Thal's crew. Her next stop was Azular's lab, where he had set up their scans of the super-strong shuttle.

"I've had a talk with Commander Thal," Ahxenta said frankly.

She took a seat, summarised the gist of their dialogue and handed over the data the commander had sent across, which did not include the spec of the escape shuttle. "He's been aboard the *Twin Star*. He's seen Ms Kerrix," she finished.

There was a pause before he reacted. "How is she?"

"Not in the brig: confined to quarters mostly and always escorted, but treated with respect. He's talked to her but not alone." Ahxenta gave a quirky smile. "Thal says she questioned *him* about his ships and set-up. She's confident the charges against her won't stick."

"May I ask how Ms Kerrix came up in the conversation, ma'am?"

"Thal brought it up. The *Kel'Moth* escorted the *Twin Star* to Merkat and he led the admiral and his lackeys to the *Half Moon*; *and* he was listening to every word. He's no fool; he's linked her to me and you and reckons we know more than we're saying. In fact he tried to get more on her background out of me. I told him nothing he didn't know but he alluded to the Telzilt system. He has some link to it and I get the feeling it haunts him, but he'll not tell. Though I recall he once said that hostiles had set up a base by force on the third planet. Did Kerrix tell you anything? She must have known about it."

The science officer looked serious as he nodded. "You know that Xanna's half-Telziltic on her mother's side? An alien force attacked Telzilt Three after her parents' marriage. Her mother was an officer aboard one of three Norvallan ships sent out in answer to the call for aid; all three ships were lost. She was very young at the time. She won't talk much about Telzilt either, or any links she has there."

The captain looked at him sympathetically. "Tough," she agreed. "But *Captain* Kerrix can take care of herself. And she *has* promised to see you on the flipside one of these days. If Thal and his like can come and go in and out of the charted zones with ease, she'll find a way. And *he* seems to be sticking like glue to the *Twin Star*."

"Are you trying to cheer me up, Captain?"

"Yes," Ahxenta smiled. "Is it working?"

"Barely," he admitted. "But thank you for the effort."

"Anytime. I'm off to do the rounds. You take it easy."

Arianrhod made Skitter fourteen hours later. The *Kel'Beth* was in orbit around the only habitable planet. Ver had been briefed and proposed that Lek fly the shuttle and his crew over to her ship. Ahxenta agreed: in her view, the faster the shuttle was off her ship the better. The five were far healthier than they had been at their rescue and grateful for their treatment, but eager to be amongst their own. The transfer was carried out with little exchange. Ver verified that another shuttle from the *Kel'Tarn* had been found with the crew alive, but that was all. She thanked Ahxenta, agreed to send on updates and took her leave.

"Do none of the crews of those ships smile?" Apnis asked.

"Maybe they think their faces will crack," the ever-eavesdropping Box put in brightly. "If they *are* partially cyber, it's a possibility."

"If that's a joke, it's not funny," Dox told him. "And if you're serious, you need to see the ship's psychologist."

"Just cut the chat and plot us a course for Kellybar, Mr Box," the captain said. "Straight across; there should be nothing between here and there to divert for, if the latest comms are accurate."

"Course plotted and laid in, Captain, on a line for the beacon just off Kellybar," was the rapid response.

"Hit it, helm. Everyone else stay sharp; we won't cloak but shields up and scanners at max. And all weapons at standby, Ms Earbleat."

"Aye, Captain. *Loki VII* primed for release on your mark."

"Let's hope we don't have to deploy her," the first mate stated.

"Roger that, Commander Apnis — we're heading for a busy part of the galaxy as far as trouble is concerned."

In the event the hours passed peaceably, with little traffic on the bypass. The cargo for Kellybar was delivered without a hitch and the crew was beginning to relax in the knowledge that two more lucrative contracts had been agreed that would take the ship to friendly parts.

Arianrhod's next port of call was Arrissia Five in the ISP region of Zeta for pick-up of two cargoes of weapons parts, one for Heligon repair base and the other for Delta Iridium. The second stage would be a long haul but Lindell was finalising details of a contract with Coronis Comms at Delta to pick up a load of comms equipment for the ISP dockyard at Alto Finglas in zone Beta.

After several hours into the trip and almost at Arrissia, the captain was called to the bridge by an alert from the duty officer.

"Picking up a distress, ma'am," Lieutenant Redmoss informed her as he vacated the command chair. "On a PSS channel and near to Flint Wolf but we can't pinpoint it accurately."

Flint Wolf was a giant red star with no habitable planets and close to their endpoint. Redmoss had called an amber alert and ordered the cloak. He had not responded to the distress but the system was up in the view grid with the probable locus of the signal highlighted.

"Thought it was too good to last," Apnis panted as she raced up. "At least we can yell for help from Arrissia if things get out of hand."

Ahxenta ordered red alert and the bridge began to buzz as duty crews sprinted in to man their emergency stations.

"Any word on what we've got, comms?"

"It's clearing, Cap... it's the *PSS Hexameter*! Reporting incoming from two hostiles!"

"Battlestations! Prepare for jump into free space! Gunnery crews, hot them up! Comms, let *Hexameter* know we're on our way. On my mark, jump. Mark!"

As the holo-grid stretched they could see their damaged sister ship swerving off to avoid a huge vessel intent on coming up under her.

"Readings match the ships we met off Kolly Beacon!" Azular's strident voice rang out. "Heavy weaponry and they know we're here!"

As *Arianrhod* jumped in, Ahxenta could see that one of them had veered off towards her. "Azular, ready the decoy but do not launch! Weapons, target oncoming blip and fire when ready! Dox, keep us out of the way of those phase beams!"

"They're deploying limpet drones from hull pockets!" Gliss yelled as he expanded an area of the tactical holo.

"Confirmed!" Azular bawled.

"Earbleat, get one team focussed on those drones! And ready *Loki* we may need her! Tallica, man auxiliaries and target any that get by."

The holo revolved as Dox sent the ship veering crosswise to avoid lock-on by a closing phalanx of drones and status updates confirmed that the shields had taken damage from glancing phase-beam fire and shards from torpedoes that the busy gunnery crews had destroyed.

"Fire intensifying, Cap!" roared Earbleat.

"She's launched a massive escape craft!" Gliss called. "It looks like that projectile ship that nearly got us in the Web!"

The captain could see that as Azular had sent his readings to tactical. "Earbleat..."

"*Loki* away!" the weapons officer sang. "On it... on it..."

Even as *Loki* spun and dove, the nubs of her gun-port focussing lancing beams into a potent burst of deadly fire, a massive torpedo glanced off one of *Arianrhod's* outer holds. The impact sent a shock wave through her hull but Dox held steady to allow Earbleat to guide *Loki's* targeting. The intense gush of fire as the projectile exploded rocked the ship, flinging the crew about in their seats. As she steadied in the currents, another fire-burst lit the space around them.

"What the hell was that?" the captain roared.

"That self-directed missile blew apart too close to its mothership and destabilised her," Gliss replied loudly. "She's out of control..."

Dox needed no bidding to pull *Arianrhod* out of the path of the huge hostile as Earbleat reeled *Loki* back in and ordered one of her crews to send a spread of torpedoes after the stricken vessel.

"That's her down!" a voice called out.

"Status of *Hexameter?*" Ahxenta bellowed above the hubbub.

"Lost a lot of power, but still fighting," Azular responded. "She was not targeted by drones. I've no trace of them on the hull of the second hostile, nor did it launch a projectile."

"Bring us about to assist, helm! Take that ship down!"

The *Hexameter* had held her own against her opponent and though battered and almost out of firepower, she had shield integrity enough to take a final barrage that made it through before *Arianrhod* sent the lethal volley into the hostile amidships that put an end to the fight.

"Get me the *Hexameter*, comms," the captain ordered as the dust settled and both great ships moved out of the expanding debris field.

"Captain Coxen for you, ma'am; on grid," Bellfish called.

"What help do you need, Bee?" Ahxenta asked practically as Coxen's face appeared and they could see the damage to her bridge.

"Escort to Arrissia, if you're headed there, Cinnabar. I'm near out of power, though I can still manoeuvre," Coxen replied, checking her boards. "Thanks for the assist: we'd have had hard work without it."

"You're welcome. What happened?"

"We'd just come off the beacon when they jumped out on top of us. They were so well-shielded we didn't pick them up until too late, but we're well-armed and we're fast. I'd have run for Arrissia if you hadn't showed, though we may not have made it without *Arianrhod*. I'll send you what my tactical and science stations got. At least my cargo's intact; it's for Arrissia, so I can drop it and use the fees to get part of the work done that *Hexameter* needs. The planetary authority will have to know – this is too close to their border for comfort."

"Get your helm to link to mine and we'll set for towing," Ahxenta told her. "Bellfish, warn Arrissia we're coming in. What else can we do?" she added to her counterpart. "How's your medbay coping?"

"We'll do," was the short reply as various comms passed between both ships and the *Hexameter's* first mate Rosee Charellis, several cuts to her face, slid into the seat next to her captain.

The next twenty minutes were spent readying for departure and collecting data on the two wrecks that drifted across the spaceways. The order had just been given to make way when Bellfish broke in.

"We have another ship coming off the bypass, Captain: a PSS. It's the *Tallulah*. Captain Fleetskup's hailing us."

"Hell, who invited him to the party?" Apnis enquired acidly. "And he's late as usual."

"The *Tallulah's* sent out scavenger pods to collect debris!" an irate Greffy announced as the large face of Murmur Fleetskup appeared in the grid, his sycophantic first mate at his side.

"What do you want, Captain Fleetskup?" Ahxenta asked curtly.

"Do you require assistance, Captain?"

"No. Though the *Hexameter* does, or hadn't you noticed?"

"You're towing her," Dyne-Bek observed coldly. "We can add our weight to yours to bring her safe in."

"We have it under control and we're on the move. *You'll* have to hold to recall your scavengers, so you'll have your hands full," was the tart reply. "I'll notify *Hexameter* of your concern. Ahxenta out."

"What in hell was that about?" Apnis barked as a call was ordered to Coxen to inform her of the exchange.

"Grabbing a piece of the action and as many bits as she can scoop up," Ahxenta snorted as an irritated Coxen called in with queries.

The captain of the *Hexameter* was unimpressed by the offer from the *Tallulah* in view of her actions. "And if she's headed to Arrissia, it'll be a barrel of laughs," she predicted.

"Captain?" Azular called over.

"Stand by, Bee; what is it, Azular?"

"As far as we can work out, neither of those ships was manned."

"What? Are you sure?"

"Not entirely, ma'am, but the debris we pulled in and the scans we got point to it. *Hexameter's* data verifies ours, unless the crew were so well-shielded that we can't find their traces. Though that's unlikely."

"Or the crew was completely cyber," the navigator piped up.

"Similar to those ships we met at Kolly but we reckoned they were controlled by the *Watersprite*," Azular continued, ignoring Box. "Our long distance scans don't indicate another ship close by that may be a control vessel – unless it's also very heavily shielded."

"Or it's the *Tallulah*," Box suggested.

"Shut up," Dox advised. "It's more likely to be a land station or some boat that's hightailed it to Arrissia or some nearby base. There may be a hidden base in the Flint Wolf system."

"Or they've upgraded a bit since last we met them," Box persisted.

"Button it, both of you," instructed Ahxenta. "Keep on it, Azular. And get me Captain Coxen back, Lieutenant Bellfish."

Once updated, Coxen was as puzzled as the *Arianrhod's* officers. If the ships were under auto-control then the coding behind them was highly complex or they were being distance-controlled – which would also imply high-level equipment.

"Have you pulled out any more, Azular?" Ahxenta called over.

"The ship that attacked us was slightly different in contour to the other and the ships at Kolly but these hull insertions match what we had last time. From that I'd guess that they originate outside charted space by Kirtish, towards K457 and Telzilt," he noted quietly. "I've cross-matched with Norvallan data but I don't have a direct parallel – although the limpet drones *are* similar to those we've met before and which penetrated the hull of the *Obsidian Sky*."

"So bad bits of work," Ahxenta grunted. "We'll have a more in-depth when we make Arrissia and you've seen to your people and your ship," she assured her fellow captain. "We'll be there in less than an hour. I see *Tallulah's* packed her traps and is heading after us."

"Trying to beat us in," Box conjectured.

He was almost correct as all three ships arrived at the main orbital docking station of Arrissia together. The *Hexameter* was given priority and having seen her safely enmeshed in holding struts in the largest repair bay of the facility, *Arianrhod* made her way to her pick-up point to collect her next cargoes, her captain declining an invitation from Captain Fleetskup for a cosy chat in one of the local meeting places.

"We'll no doubt see Fleetskup around," Apnis guessed as she and the captain made for the *Cosmic Blue*, a diner in one of Arrissia's orbital trade stations. "There aren't many other places to meet."

"Too bad; we're here to see Bee and her senior science officer and we're not about to discuss our doings with Fleetskup and his excuse for a first mate listening in," Ahxenta said firmly.

"*Hexameter's* in for a long haul but this is a good repair centre and she'll get decent rates. Lucky her cargo was in one piece – and lucky we're in the right place at the right time to take on her next contract for that load from Coronis, as we're headed to Delta Iridium anyway. It means a trip to Freskat, but as the stuff for ISP's shipyard at Alto Finglas isn't ready yet, we can spare the time. And it'll give you a chance to call in at your buddy's place. He got hitched yet?"

"Haven't heard," the captain smiled wryly. "Long distance comms can be tricky and I don't like calling him in case it leads to trouble."

"Roger that. There's Bee and I guess that's her senior SO. We've not met him before. They've set privacy. They've seen us."

The two headed over to join them. The talk revolved around Flint Wolf, the data got and a report to the Arrissians. Ahxenta passed on a data shard from Azular, who had not flown over on Flintlock's advice, as she was still anxious over his current fitness.

"Never fails," Apnis groaned as a motion at the entry caught her eye and she spied the captain and first mate of the *Tallulah*. "It's as well we're done: he's never slow to ignore privacy when it suits him."

"I'd like to know what his scavengers picked up," admitted Coxen. "If he'll tell us, that is."

"We tell him what we got as a trade, which is *only* what we'll be sending to the Trades Alliance and the ISP," Ahxenta said dryly.

Fleetskup quickly asked to join them, a tad surprised at the cordial response, given the last stormy encounter he had had with the two from *Arianrhod*. Dyne-Bek was plainly ignoring the incident, for she greeted them heartily. The strike at Flint Wolf was her chief topic and she introduced it after trivial prattle about trade. Mentions of limpet drones and the projectile similar to the rogue that had attacked at Merkat gave Coxen the chance to bring up the *Tallulah's* scavengers and the results of their activity. The unhelpful Dyne-Bek stated coolly that the analyses were the business of her ship and no-one else.

"I see," Coxen replied. "You want all we have but you refuse to give us anything. In that case, this talk's over. I *will* report your refusal to assist your fellow PSS officers by passing on highly relevant data when I send in my report of the attack to the TA and the ISP. Come on Zib, we've work to do. Cinnabar, Tallica, if I don't see you later, have a good trip. And I'll copy you in on my reports, naturally."

With a wink at Ahxenta she and her science officer set off without a backward glance. Dyne-Bek's disapproving eyes followed her.

"How rude!" she exclaimed.

"Have you realised, Murmur, that your recent behaviour is pissing off the entire PSS fleet?" Apnis asked Fleetskup genially.

"What do you mean, Commander Apnis?"

"Your unreasonable demands for compensation, your ingratitude when you're assisted out of trouble and now a refusal to share what is very useful information. *Tallulah's* a top-range ship after all, with the best tech available and a well-trained crew that knows how to use it. But you're becoming a byword for perversity."

"There's no basis for that statement, Commander," Dyne-Bek rumbled at her opposite number.

"I was talking to Captain Fleetskup," was the calm but pointed reply as Apnis smiled at the uncomfortable commanding officer.

"You've made your point, Tallica, but *we* have duty aboard. Have a profitable trip to wherever you're headed, Murmur," Ahxenta said as she rose. "I won't ask, as I'm sure that's also classified."

"We're for Milkit Major," Fleetskup replied to their back view as the two officers made off towards the counter to settle their bill.

"Interesting," Apnis murmured. "Seems he's heading home; you think he's planning to introduce Dyne-Bek to his mother?"

The captain chortled. "If he is, I bet Tommy Buntle put him up to it. From what I've heard of Tallulah Fleetskup, she has a tongue that could scorch a dragon. She'll wipe the floor with Dyne-Bek and hang her out to dry. She'd probably make a far better captain than her precious son, though she'd be just as short on willing crew. And you've really irritated Dyne-Bek by sweet-talking Fleetskup."

"That was the idea," Apnis replied as Ahxenta's communit trilled.

"Our cargoes are aboard and approvals are in order. So we hit the trail for a fast drop at Heligon and a high-speed crossing to Delta Iridium. There may even be a bonus for early delivery at Delta."

"Don't tell Box or he'll pull out every stop to cut corners and get us into real trouble," the first mate advised.

"I'll have his ears if he tries," the captain grunted.

In the event, three hours later *Arianrhod* was again in space and on course for the nearest bypass node for a quick hop to Heligon Station and the release of their first load. Copies of the reports of the attack to the TA and the ISP were received from the *Hexameter* as promised, but Ahxenta was amused to find a short note of what the *Tallulah's* scavengers had brought in, with tags denoting that it had also been sent to the TA and the ISP.

Cargo handover at Heligon was smooth and the ship was quickly out of port, with her heading set for the crossover into zone Epsilon at Vellis Prime. The captain had decided to take the most rapid route from Vellis to Delta Iridium via Peascod Secundo, despite the latter's closeness to the edge of a Coalition-run sector, as with the Alliance of major governing bodies still strong, she reckoned on little trouble.

Duty crews had changed over several times and *Arianrhod* had passed Vellis and was well into Epsilon when an urgent message came in for Ahxenta from Ver of the *Kel'Beth*. The captain was on the bridge and ordered the link sent to her office. She was gone some time but just as Apnis was wondering what had happened, she reappeared.

"What gives, Cinnabar?" the commander asked.

The captain glanced quickly across the deck at the science station where Azular sat and shook her head. He was diligently conning over something that seemed to have grabbed his attention.

"Ver's people have sighted a convoy of five ships that read hostile off Kelfennig. She estimates on their current course and speed they'll hit zone Zeta somewhere near Alpha 412 in about ten hours. You got the data, Azular? What's your reading of it?" she called over.

"The data's not totally clear but it matches what we have on newer hostile interceptor designs. The blips were in tight formation when this data was captured, as if they had an end in view. I concur with Commander Ver's assessment," he stated, turning to look at her.

"Good. Ver asked that I send it to the ISP as it's the major power in that area and she reckons it won't give her credence. I've done that via Admiral Zillah and I notified the Trades. I put it out on the UV-III as well, lest any of ours are in that area. Ver's mobilising as many ships from her local bases as she can but says there won't be many."

Apnis voiced the interest of the listening crew. "Ver's taking a lot on herself. I thought she commanded one cargo ship in Thal's huge fleet but now she's mustering that fleet because of a potential threat from what seem to be a bunch of regrouping hostiles and warning the local governing powers? What's up, Cap? What's Thal got to say about it, or has he delegated command?"

With a serious look at Azular, who was still watching her intently, the captain turned back to the first mate. "The Starfall fleet has lost contact with the *Kel'Moth* and the *Twin Star*. They were last heard of off the beacon at K457:003. They'd dropped out of hyperspace at the end node there and were set on a heading for Norvalla. That was three days ago standard."

Almost every eye on the bridge turned to Azular to see how he would take the news. His face was impassive, apart from his tightening jaw. Apnis, a grave look on her face, asked if there was any more. Ahxenta nodded. Ver had sent in two of her best-equipped heavy cruisers but had had no news back other than that comms relays were active. The inevitable conclusion was that the *Kel'Moth* and the *Twin Star* had met trouble, but until she had proof, Ver refused to assume that they had been attacked. The *Kel'Moth* was one of the largest and best-armed of any of their vessels and she was certain that Thal could hold his own in most situations.

"We can only hope they *did* hold their own if they were hit," the first mate said. "But if they were on track for Norvalla, the *Twin Star* could have called for aid, surely? She's an admiral's flagship."

"Their last known position had them quite a way from Norvalla, but what other places they could call on for help I don't know – and neither does Ver," the captain told her.

"What do *we* do?" Apnis asked softly.

"Continue on mission; we're too far away to help and the ISP is aware of possible hostile incursion into zone Zeta. Zillah will update me even if ISP HQ sits on it and we'll see her at Freskat. But as it's a potential alien threat, the ISP Intelligence Division will be involved. Levettiza said that its outposts were tracking the *Twin Star* as they had her signal, but I've no more on that."

"Hostiles off Kelfennig," Apnis mused. "The hostiles in the war were offshoots of colonists sent out from there eons ago, as far as we've been told. And the energy forms that were all that was left of the original Kelfennig population had a part in lending the rest of us a hand in dealing with their sinister descendants by giving us vital info. You don't think this latest batch is up for revenge do you?"

"That would waste time and energy if they've an endpoint in view. Ver's concern is what it might be. They were heading into mapped space, so it wasn't her Sunrise Base. Heligon's the nearest big settled centre, it's non-military but it *has* a heap of hardware in its yards. Mr Bellfish, keep an ear on all ISP and Alliance comms and let me know immediately if there's anything pertaining to the situation."

"Aye, ma'am."

Three hours had passed when Apnis indicated a bright yellow star in the holo-grid. "We're coming up on Merlin. No habitable planets but there was a Coalition comms post on the major satellite of the third once upon a time, which is why the bypass route crosses here. Maybe we should check if it's still there?"

The captain reflected, hand on chin. "We won't leave the bypass but we can slow and take readings. Helm, reduce to dropout speed. Tactical, scan the Merlin system; you too, Azular. It may be too well-shielded, but it's worth the risk of our scan beams being spotted."

"As long as nothing's based down there and ready to pounce if it figures we're up here," Box murmured dourly from the nav-station.

"Ever the optimist," Apnis commented. "Just keep our course, Mr Box, and make sure our route ahead is clear."

The tactical and science officers were quick and both reported an energy spike that denoted activity but *Arianrhod* was too far off to decode specifics. The inference was that the post was in situ and in use. They could not detect comms, but as the order to cease scan was given, Gliss let out a shout.

"Something's scanning us! And not from the direction of Merlin!"

"Confirm!" Ahxenta spat out.

"Source is ahead and just off the bypass, Captain!" Azular called.

"Return the favour and scan them!"

"She reads as a small cargo, Cap," Gliss affirmed. "She's damaged so her comms may be down, but I don't get why she hasn't sent out a distress. She's maybe afraid of what will answer. Her energy output reads low, so she'd not make the bypass. But who hit her? I don't read any other ships in the area."

"Azular, your take on it?" demanded Ahxenta.

"Too many maybes," he replied grimly. "If she was hit, why didn't the attackers finish her? And her hull reads oddly… Surface readings imply she's a standard cargo but they're shifting… just a moment… it's a chameleon cloak! Linking in all scanners! I suspect she's not a cargo and she's not crippled, Captain," he said shortly. "If I can cut through it I may be able to clarify… aha! I'm sensing structural units with trace zukivianite. That suggests hostile origin, but she *is* small. I estimate similar in the size to the *Firewave* and the *Watersprite*."

"So it's a trap!" Apnis blazed.

"But are *we* the target?" the captain questioned.

"Give you one guess," the first mate answered. "Do we jump off the bypass and pretend we've fallen for it?"

"Not without back-up we don't. She may have buddies lurking in the shadow of one of Merlin's planetary bodies that we can't detect."

"I'm getting a distress now, Captain!" Bellfish called across. "She claims to be the cargo vessel *SS Seafoam* out of Kell Lyne."

"Don't say who we are but ask her status. Are any of the PSS fleet close enough to assist?"

"I'll send a general hail on PSS channels with an alert tag," stated Apnis, making for auxiliary comms. "Tactical, long-range scans for other traffic: there may be one of ours close enough to pick it up."

"Long-distance scans operative," Ishbel Larai replied. "Nothing detected close in, but if it's shielded we may not be able to read it."

Minutes passed with no response from the *Seafoam* bar a repeated distress. Azular and Gliss were tracking the source as it coasted closer to their position. Greffy called in from the lab that no shipping line of Kell Lyne listed an *SS Seafoam* and a search on independents had drawn a blank. The only *Seafoam* on record was a luxury cruiser out of Cygilla and her trade was unlikely to bring her into the area.

"Warm up our weapons, Earbleat, and have your auxiliaries stand by. And prep *Loki* for launch. Azular, ready the decoy but keep it in reserve. I'd rather not use it as many of our opponents have seen it and I'm betting word's got round," Ahxenta growled.

"So you expect the worst?" Apnis asked, tying herself back in.

"I always expect the worst," was the abrupt retort.

"It's why we're all still here," Box muttered to the bridge at large.

"Dammit!" Gliss spat. "She's changed her heading and is speeding up! And there's another blip coming in from beyond Merlin!"

"So there *was* something hiding out there!" the first mate snarled. "Do we jump out and risk a fight or do we run?"

"We run. Battlestations! Helm, evasive! Power up the shields, keep those weapons hot and make sure our aft torpedo tubes are on line!"

Dox altered course at speed to confuse the advancing vessels. Both were homing in and were ready to jump onto the bypass.

"Ready deflecting drones!" the captain called.

"Not a good place to fight from!" declared Apnis sharply. "But look at the size of that second ship! And they're both headed after us! They surely can't match our speed on the bypass?"

"Don't count on it," was the grim response. "We're hauling a big load. I bet they know about it and that second blip's close to our size. Any response to our hails on the PSS channels, comms?"

"None, ma'am."

"Those damn things are gaining!" the first mate hissed in a fury. "They can't be manned, they're all speed and weaponry."

"You've hit it," the captain agreed. "That means their mandate is to take us out any way they can. Azular, deploy our decoy to our rear on my mark and with every trick in place to keep them guessing. If there are no sentients in control, it'll maybe fox them."

"On it," he responded briefly as Ahxenta ordered Dox to liaise and assist in decoy release.

"They're closing," Apnis warned, pointing to the main holo-grid. "They want us badly, but they're both on straight trajectories."

"Change our heading to mark ten by three and make for Pelt Tipp as soon as the decoy drops, helm! Ready decoy for release, Azular! Steady as she goes… Decoy on my mark… Mark!"

"Decoy away!"

"Mark ten by three!" the helmswoman called out a split second later as she sent the great ship on a tight curve at increased speed.

"Decoy's camouflage and part-cloak operational," Azular's voice echoed. "Her call-sign identifies her as us. I've programmed her to project a detached cargo pod if she's fired upon."

As the minutes ticked by and tactical tracked their pursuers, they could see that both had followed the decoy and were gaining. Shots were loosed at the virtual ship but as Azular confirmed the success of external image projection, the larger of the two pursuing craft broke off in a tight arc on a heading directly on their tail.

"Hell's teeth!" the captain cursed. "They're not buying it! Reel in the decoy, Azular, they know it's a trick."

"Too late, Captain, that ship's too close: she's trying to capture it!" he spat in fury, wrestling with his controls. "Initiating self-destruct," he called as *Arianrhod* shook in the shock wave of a long-range enemy torpedo that burst just off her flanks.

"Hell that was close!" Apnis yelled. "Get us more speed, helm!"

"They've launched a missile spread!" warned Gliss.

"One less on our tail!" Azular bellowed above the din as Dox sent the ship into a tight spiral to get her out of the path of the phalanx of deadly warheads that was attempting a lock-on. "Decoy's destruct has immobilised the smaller ship."

"Captain, another ship on the bypass!" Larai yelled from second tactical. "Edge of range but she's heading in!"

"Identify!" Ahxenta ordered as she took in the starfield in the grid.

Earbleat was meanwhile letting loose a string of invective as her gunnery crews could not get weapons lock on the shifting hide of the approaching enemy. She exhorted them to anticipate hostile tactics and fire blind as a stream of pulsed photon fire lanced towards them.

"Weapons station two, launch deflecting drones, wide spread!" the captain ordered. "Helm, come about! Time we faced her out," she ruled as her eyes swept the colossal shape in the bridge holo that was the result of the data that her tactical stations had pulled in from the hostile. "Earbleat, target our forr'ad torpedoes on her nose!"

A call from Cottontail warned her that they had lost port shielding but *Arianrhod* rode the wave of a spread of incoming fire and burst through to come steeply down on top of the attacking vessel.

"Nice move, helm!" Apnis called as she loosed her webbing and made for auxiliary weapons. "Any word on what's coming in?"

"Can't get a fix; she's shielded and we've lost scanning capacity," Larai responded. "And there goes *another* scanning node!"

"Station two, target those incoming missiles!" Earbleat bawled.

"Keep a distance!" Azular roared. "She's packing explosive!"

"Maintain fire! They've upped missile intensity!" Earbleat's voice cracked in fury. "*Loki* ready to go on your mark, Captain!"

"Belay! I want her in reserve…"

"Target her underside aft! There's a weak point in her shields!" the senior science officer interjected. "Sending data to tactical grid!"

Dox brought *Arianrhod* into optimum firing range and in a rain of fire that rattled her shields, a massive salvo was released at the hostile.

The voice of Bellfish cut through the uproar with a yell. "I have a link! It's the *Comet*! Repeat, *PSS Green Comet* coming in!"

"Roger that," Ensign Larai confirmed. "I now read her as a PSS."

"Got her!" Earbleat screamed as her torpedoes hit their mark and a gout of fire spewed from a gaping hole in the hostile's underbelly.

"Get us out of here, Dox! She's set to blow!" Ahxenta roared.

The great pink-hulled ship streaked off, her engines groaning as she strove to outfly the expanding bloom that was the death throes of the hostile vessel. She caught the wash of the edge of the energy field and rocked dangerously.

"We're clear!" Gliss called.

"Haul back on the helm, Dox and let's get the damage reports," the captain breathed heavily, loosening her restraints. "Where's the *Comet*?" she demanded of her tactical lead.

"She'll be up with us in fifteen minutes, Captain."

"I have Captain Jikelleli for you, ma'am," interrupted Bellfish.

"Put her on grid."

Sarie Jikelleli looked serious as she took in the dishevelled bridge crew of the *Arianrhod*. "You've been to hell and back, Cinnabar," she greeted her fellow captain. "What in blazes was that ship? We can't get her ID. More importantly, what can we do to help you? Sorry we couldn't make it in sooner, we're heavy-loaded."

"Likewise," Ahxenta said. "But thanks for the response. They may have held back because they knew you were headed in and wanted to have enough firepower to deal with you as well. I'll link you what we got once we've made sense of it. There's another wreck out there that may not be totally dead in the water. But we sorely need energy cells and weapons. My casualty list's low and my cargo's in one piece, but almost every system has taken a beating, I've lost hull shielding and some of my hull plates are buckled. Our stop at Delta Iridium will be longer than anticipated, but at least we can still fly."

"I'm headed to Delta Iridium, so I'll escort you," Jikelleli assured her. "If you give us the details of that other ship you spoke of, we'll scan on the way to you. What went on?"

As Ahxenta updated Jikelleli, Apnis, back in her own seat, collated damage reports and shrewdly eyed the bridge crew as they reset their consoles. Once she had sent the final report tally to the captain's board she rose and made her way over to the primary science station.

"So it's a new one based on an old one," she remarked to Azular, who had a holo of the large ship suspended above his console.

"Yes, Commander. It may even have been a retrofitted original. A number of the large destroyers we faced at Skyrtek had an aft gap on their undersides but *this* one had no crew as far as I've been able to tell. And it was autonomous, unless there's a hidden control ship out there. The hull was cloaked in a shifting camouflage to deflect scans, and I suspect the ops were geared to detection and destruction."

"You mean if it finds what's perceived as an enemy, it's pre-set to take it out and if that means blowing itself up, that's the price?"

"Speculation of course; but the original hostiles we faced did seem that way inclined, even in manned ships."

"But who's sending them out? The *Seafoam* was the lure, I guess. And as we're on hostile hit lists and we pass by, it thinks jackpot. But if we take *it* out, does the news get back to some HQ? And how did that thing know it was us?"

"I can't answer that, Commander. It must have been able to read us, but we weren't cloaked. I'd like to see what's left of the *Seafoam*, to confirm if she was parallel to the *Firewave* and the *Watersprite*, despite her chameleon appearance."

"We'll have to make sure she's dead anyway," Apnis frowned. "So how come the decoy took her out? What was with the self-destruct?"

"That was Ms Earbleat's idea," he admitted. "It has a certain logic and she *did* integrate it into *Loki*. I sent the captain an updated spec."

"She must have missed it," was the dry reply. "But once we're on the road, you're taking time out – you've been on a long shift."

He shook his head. "Not necessary, Commander, I have plenty to keep me busy here."

The first mate rested a hand on his shoulder. "The *Twin Star* will have made it through," she told him softly. "It *will* be all right. And you're taking a break once we're on line for Delta Iridium."

In the hours that followed, the two trading ships coordinated their ops and made their way to the scene of the demise of the *Seafoam*. There was nothing left of the decoy but dust and the hulk that was once the disguised cargo was quiescent. As Azular had suspected, it was similar in size to the *Firewave* and the *Watersprite* but there were subtle differences. The zukivianite levels were alike but the surviving hull plating incorporated minute novel units that he inferred were the source of the chameleon cloak and possibly also served to emit fake signals. There were no remains that indicated organic crew but the payload of explosive had been large.

"We're not bringing samples of it aboard," the captain told the science officer when he suggested it. "I've sent an alert to our fleet, the ISP and the TA. We're for Delta Iridium and refit. They know the score. We're still ahead of schedule so we'll take stock once we get there and find out how long it'll take to get us up to scratch. If we can't take on the comms load for Freskat, the *Comet* may be able to."

"Perhaps Commander Ver should also be informed of this latest threat?" Azular proposed quietly.

"I'll see to it," Ahxenta agreed with a sigh. "Now we hit the trail."

The two vessels made direct for their endpoint via Peascod Secundo. No local incursions had been reported and both captains wanted to make good time. Apart from a request from the Peascod authorities for a report on Merlin, nothing disturbed them. *Arianrhod's* crew were kept busy on the minor repairs possible on a ship in hyperspace. Despite having been ordered on medical leave, Azular consulted Cottontail with plans for a new decoy and spent the balance of his time locked in his shuttle, to Flintlock's concern and the irritation of Earbleat: *she* wanted his input on a new version of *Loki*, once she had coaxed the captain to release a cargo pod for alteration.

News had filtered in that the hostile convoy on course for Zeta had made mapped space. It had been sighted several times and was being tracked by the ISP and others, but had not been engaged. The group had kept its line and passed Heligon. The main detail was that all five ships had sustained damage detectable to local probes. An advisory from Ver had confirmed that her people were also tracking them and had come to much the same conclusion.

It was four days later and well into zone Delta that a link came in from Ver for the captain. Ahxenta was on the bridge and about to go off duty but had it instantly patched through to her office. She was gone only a short time but every eye was on her when she returned.

"What is it, Cap?" Apnis anxiously enquired in a low voice.

The captain remained standing, her gaze flicking over to Azular, now back on duty. "Ver's heard from the ships she sent after the *Kel'Moth*," she said evenly. "They've heard from Thal. The *Kel'Moth* and the *Twin Star* met trouble and then got caught in a web of local jammers, hence the signal loss. Jamming's still causing headaches, conflict is ongoing near Telzilt and Thal's ordered the two cruisers in as support. Ver's got no more than that both the *Kel'Moth* and the *Twin Star* are operational. She'll keep me updated."

The first mate let out a gusty sigh. "So no news is good news?"

"Looks like. And we're off duty. You have conn, Mr Snow," she added to one of her senior tactical officers.

"Aye, ma'am," the efficient lieutenant responded.

As the various bridge stations handed over to replacement crew, Ahxenta collared Azular. "My office," she ordered. "I'll see you in the mess shortly, Tallica."

Shortly was half an hour later and Apnis was pondering on Ver's message when the captain hove to with her rations and sat alongside.

"Crew's wondering what you had to say to Azular, Cinnabar."

"They can wonder," was the curt reply.

"What did Ver tell you that you didn't tell us?"

"Very little," the captain stated. "Thal's in one piece but his ship's been hard hit. So why he ordered his other two ships in I don't know. Ver said it might be related to the hostile stronghold on Telzilt but she was giving nothing away."

"And the *Twin Star*?" Apnis persisted.

"Also badly hit but operational; and whatever fight they're in, they're seeing it out. Ver says they've called for back-up from allies."

"Cinnabar…"

"I've nothing on any of her crew except the admiral: he sustained an injury that put him out of action. Who's in command Ver doesn't know and she's had no word on Kerrix."

"I take it Azular knows?"

"He knows. He's more hopeful than he was," Ahxenta continued at her first mate's questioning look. "And as for that hostile convoy, Ver thinks they might be making for Zeta Dixt. They're on a straight line and they're not keen to interact with anyone on the way. And it's been confirmed that all five ships have taken a beating."

"I'd be suspicious that they're using the kind of cloaking that the *Seafoam* had and they're just huge travelling bombs," Apnis grunted. "If they're reading as on their last retros and not trying it on, it smells fishy to me. Waiting for some fool to make the first move on them?"

"That's a good point. Once I'm done I'll send the technical specs of the *Seafoam* and her buddy boat to the ISP and Ver and warn them not to get too close. They can always deploy artillery from a distance. Hell, I'll be glad to see Delta Iridium."

"You and me both; the crew will too, so I'll organise shore leave rotas once we've moved our cargo, as we'll be there for a while."

"Do it, but leave Earbleat off your list or she'll start foraging for bits for her new design of *Loki* and handing me the bills."

"Roger that, Cap. A *Loki* fleet we can do without."

The starships were expected at Delta Iridium and berths were already assigned. The *Green Comet* dropped her cargo quickly and loaded her next for delivery to Delta's Flag Delta outpost. Ahxenta and Lindell had gone over their schedules and concluded that they would have to give up the comms cargo for Freskat. *Arianrhod's* refit would take ten days and the contract for the ISP dockyard was the priority. Jikelleli was sounded out and agreed to take it on. With accord between the parties involved, the transfer was made.

Most of the ensuing days were spent in bringing *Arianrhod* back up to her usual polish. Ahxenta was adamant that the best gear and skills were utilised and cost-cutting was not an option. It was towards the end of her stay that a long-distance call came in. A very surprised Lynxi Bellfish turned to the command chair.

"It's a private link for you, Captain, high security and encoded. It's supra-light and it's come a very long way on a very directional beam."

"Who's it from?" Ahxenta enquired, alerted by the officer's tone.

"It's requested that you take it privately, ma'am," Bellfish told her guardedly, aware that all his colleagues were listening in.

"My office."

"Yes, ma'am."

The captain was some time and the comms officer had been called more than once to restore the link, which was obviously breaking up. Curious eyes were on Ahxenta as she resumed her chair but she gave nothing away as she drew her status boards over to scan for updates. Apnis knew that she would be told eventually but was aware that her commander was overly pensive.

A briefing of senior officers was called to discuss the news two hours later. The captain began by commending her first mate on her reading of the advancing hostile convoy.

"Good call, Tallica: two ISP ships went in, sent in a pawn to close-probe and it was destroyed. But it did its job – the ships *were* crewed but all were packing enough explosive to take out a small moon. And they were under the remote control of a covert small ship up ahead."

"So what happened?" Apnis demanded.

"The ISP ships sent in a wave of torpedoes and took the five out."

"What! Even though they were manned?"

"By a few highly-cyber hostiles. But they got the control ship. It was headed for Zeta Dixt, which has now been confirmed as a hostile base, along with Peden Post and Axle Lexo. The Elf One outpost is gone, but there's one in a system listed as Cox 455, off the edge of Beta near Coalition space. I've a note of other suspected hideouts – a few were once listening posts belonging to Alliance worlds."

The captain called up the data and summarised the evidence. She then displayed the records of the captured control ship and the being in command, who clearly resembled their old adversary, Hoxiz.

"May I ask why this was linked to you, Captain, and by whom?" Azular asked as he reviewed the material.

"And from where," the first mate added. "It was long-distance."

"Commander Levettiza of ISP's Intelligence Division: she's now aboard the *ISPS Advance*, a survey ship on patrol beyond zone Mu. In the vicinity of system K457:003," she added with a look at Azular.

"How in blazes did she get that far out in so short a time? And why?" Apnis asked suspiciously.

"She's a senior ISP Intelligence officer and her mandate includes alien incursion," Ahxenta reminded her. "She told us of the clutch of Hoxiz-clones out there with orders to take apart any ship that's liable to put a stop to their activities and the list included us. That control ship they got had one aboard, as well as details of *our* current route."

Earbleat whistled. "That's worrying," she noted.

"Which does not entirely explain why Ms Levettiza linked to *you* from beyond zone edge, Captain," the science officer pointed out.

"You remember she *did* promise to keep us up to date on relevant issues, Azular? The *Advance* was alerted to the conflict at Telzilt as she was in the area, and was sent in to observe. I don't have the full story, but the *Advance* appears to live up to her name: she's the best the ISP has, with a lot of high tech that I bet includes the ISP version of a chameleon hull. Levettiza isn't in command but she persuaded the captain to jump in and with Thal's ships, the *Twin Star*, a resistance group on Telzilt, *and* back-up ships sent in by their allies, the hostile influence on Telzilt has been totally wiped out. The planet will take ages to recover as the aliens had been there for years but it looks like there's a hostile exodus from bases beyond Mu and they're heading our way. The science officers aboard the *Advance* figured from one convoy that passed by that four ships matched the *Seafoam's* spec: a zukivianite-rich hull seeded with units they suspect can be coded for various ops such as specific signals emission. The blips *are* being tracked and will be dealt with but there may be more out there with Hoxiz-types aboard and our name on a hit list."

"Who's tracking the blips, Captain?" Azular asked tensely.

"At the moment, a federated body that includes the Norvallans and others. The ISP and its allies will take over once they're in range – if the convoy isn't blasted out of existence first. But now the ISP has the specifics of what to look for and how to deal with it, the mop-up should be simpler. That's how the story goes, at least."

"So Levettiza's in a super-fast, super-spec ship that has contacted civilisations beyond mapped space and having taken part in an action is now a buddy? Quick work!" snorted Apnis. "So when does the ISP join hands with this federated group and bring it into the family?"

"Search me, though the *Advance* is a survey vessel and first contact will be part of her mandate," Ahxenta replied. "But why the hostiles are heading our way is another question; it can't be *our* rep. We now know they have bases in local space but do they have a control centre as well, even though most of their original dens were outside charted zones? And are some of them making for that centre?"

"You figured Minch Fettin or the Web as logical places for an ops centre, Cap, as I recall," the first mate said. "And if it's the Web, it's a doozie of a problem. I hope you mentioned it to Levettiza."

"In the passing and ISP has reached much the same conclusion," she smiled. "But that's it for now. We carry on as normal but remain aware that we're a target and a lot of bad guys out there know about our business. Everyone back to work, we're about to start loading our cargo for Alto Finglas. Not you, Azular, I want a word."

The science officer's face was a study in anxiety, the captain noted, as the others cleared the room.

"Your Ms Kerrix is all right," Ahxenta said succinctly. "She took a tumble when a bolt penetrated the hull of the *Twin Star* and blew her bridge station but she was lucky: they've lost a number of crew."

"Bridge? What was she doing on the bridge?"

"The admiral had posted her to the science station before he was hit as he needed every able-bodied officer. She took command when the two most senior bridge officers went down, Levettiza said," the captain grinned crookedly. "But the conflict at Telzilt is over. They're picking up the pieces and Thal for some reason is holding fast there. Ver's taken charge of the Starfall fleet this side of the line..."

"What's the status of Admiral Posettix and the *Twin Star*, do you know, Captain?" Azular interrupted.

"The admiral will make it; they have top notch medical staff on board. But the *Twin Star's* a wreck and the *Advance* and a Telziltic ship are towing her to Norvalla. Levettiza will keep in touch as far as she can but no guarantees. You look puzzled, Azular."

"I'd like to know what Commander Levettiza's role *is* aboard the *Advance* if she's not in command," he stated.

"Good question and she wouldn't say. She's Intelligence; that may be a discrete role aboard an ISP survey ship or be part of tactical ops. She's ranked commander so she must be near the top, but why she's now aboard a ship rather than station-based I don't know. Her link to Kerrix, perhaps," the captain posited. "In any case, if and when I hear more, I'll let you know. It may be a while," she warned.

He nodded. "Thank you for your... understanding, Captain."

"Welcome. Let's get to the bridge and see how far loading's got."

Three huge cargo pods were on the way to one of the ship's outer bays by the time the two made the bridge. *Arianrhod's* skilled loading teams were on standby to receive and lock the goods down securely and Greffy was already in post carrying out the necessary scans.

"No surprises and we're on schedule," Apnis reported. "Coronis are old clients, so we'll be loaded in no time. The crew will be glad to be back out there and so will I. We've been here long enough."

"Roger that. It's a short haul to Alto Finglas but we'll make there via Istrel Statice and keep clear of Quartic Cross. I've had no more reports of raider attacks but we keep all our long-range gear on line."

It took a couple of hours for the release orders to be ratified but once done, *Arianrhod* made her way out of her berth and into the wider spaces beyond. The bypass was reached easily and it was with relief that tactical could confirm that their forward path read clear.

"They're never grateful, are they?" Apnis observed with asperity as, business concluded, *Arianrhod* was given approval to leave local space around the ISP docks. "Now this Allied Central Office is setting up, with ISP, Coalition, NTA and Independents sharing the space, you'd think they'd be polite at least, as they'll need a helluva lot more gear hauled in. And I noted a heap of activity around those half-finished hulls that we could see from our berth. Setting up a bloody new fleet by the look of it. Where the credit's coming from, I wonder?"

"Our pockets," the captain said sourly. "Trades Alliance is upping the levies again and Lindell's carping about reduced profit margins. *Emerald's* in the same fix; Goodsocks has seen a drop-off in passenger numbers, but at least as a smaller vessel she can take on the shorter routes that local mercantile lines are too scared to run. UV-III's been quiet but I had a short link from Ver that her people are tracking two hostiles that slipped into mapped space by the Curtain Nebula. *They* match the specs that Thal sent out and the ISP circulated. Seems her lot has a station close by the Curtain but she was evasive about how long it's been there. She hasn't a ship she can send out, but I've passed the details to Zillah as it's mighty close to her backyard. Ver figured they may be making for Peden Post, as there's a whole lot of empty space to cross at the far end of Lambda, but how they got as far as the Curtain if they came in from outer Mu I can't imagine."

"Unless Ver's station *is* an ex-hostile base we didn't know about and there's a bypass sheer across space from their Sunrise place?"

"Hell's teeth! I don't even want to think about it," Ahxenta told her mate. "But there *are* likely to be one or two hostile enclaves we know nothing about that are still active and they're being called up."

"Another showdown we don't need," Apnis groaned. "And here's Lindell with a meet he's set up in the Web for two days after we haul in," she noted, tapping her ops board. "So no peace for us."

The great ship sped onwards, her cloak at full capacity and extra watches set on long-range scanners. Her holds were near-empty, an unusual position for the *Arianrhod*. A small pick-up of pharmaceutical supplies was scheduled at Silshoon that was destined for the home planet of Merkat Three, to be delivered to a holding point in the Web. A few comms from fellow PSS captains had confirmed that trade was slack, a reaction to the buzz on open channels that random attacks on shipping were on the increase. ISP and other Allied vessels that usually patrolled the space lanes were concentrating on the larger issues of incursions by small but deadly bands of hostiles, leaving the lesser-equipped but still dangerous rat-packs to flourish.

Cargo pick-up at Silshoon was smooth and rapid, and sooner than expected, *Arianrhod* made berth in the Web. Her payload was swiftly released to the orbital offices of the Merkat-based medical company and with accounts settled, the captain and first mate paid a visit to the harbour office to complete the usual formalities for a stay in the port facilities, surprised that there had been no dispute over fees.

As Apnis had had a link from Kit Biernop immediately the ship had docked requesting an urgent meeting with her and the captain, the two carried on to inner two. Biernop had refused to disclose the topic but had proposed the general meeting area of main marketing as a venue as it was a well-populated and patrolled space. The officers found a booth in a corner and as their contact had not arrived they spent the time watching for known and unknown faces.

Biernop hailed them as if the encounter had been chance. Pleasant smiles were traded but he soon invoked privacy to talk. A reshuffle of Guild and Merkat security had laid bare substantial felony but details had been suppressed by order of Merkat Central Advisory Council, the body that directed routine running of the Web. Several covert ops had been mopped up and contraband seized that included advanced tech and data. The whole was now in the hands of ISP Intelligence but Kit had heard from a contact that part of the booty comprised a note of public and private groups to be infiltrated, harassed or taken out. His Guild and Merkat security were listed, as were the ISP, its allies and the Trades Alliance. And *Arianrhod* was at the top of a list of vessels that were to be stopped by any means necessary.

Security had lost many of its no-goods but was now short-handed, despite the extension of its higher-grade secure facilities and an influx of new blood. That had led the Advisory Council to demand the early release of low-life serving short sentences and more use of automated security measures. The upshot was a rise in minor crime and in more petty crooks on the loose and ripe for exploitation by bigger villains. And Biernop could not pass on the data directly as practically every public space had auto-eyes on the watch and it would be noted and logged. He took his leave, with a promise to keep in touch.

"Wonder if *Tallulah's* on that list he spoke of," commented Apnis. "But we'd better warn our friends that they're liable to be hit if they stop by. Here's Nat Holdspan in: we can wave him over and pretend we've been waiting for him, if all these spy-cams are up there."

The captain had come directly from his home port of Nyx with a small but valuable cargo for Merkat and was waiting the release of his next payload, he told them as he sat. He had other contracts in train and had just left a meeting. The three swapped stories and it seemed that the incursion of two strange ships into local space at the edge of Lambda by the Curtain Nebula had been noted and reported to the authorities on both Nyx and Aoria. The last Holdspan had heard, the two vessels were on a track into an empty region known as the Star Desert – which would put them on course for Peden Post, Ahxenta noted in passing. Bar that, attacks against merchant lines were causing concern, as the specs of the attackers were sparse. Rumour blamed hostile influences but with no proof, blame could not be cast.

By common consent the three left marketing to make their way to the *Half Moon*, where comfortable seats and more news could be got. As the two ships had been out for some time, Ally was pleased to see them. He had new staff in place, he was quick to point out, and both Ahxenta and Apnis were amused to spot Wekki Munnet at a distant table. Merry was still there but off shift, they were told.

The recent shake-up of main Web ops was causing unease, Ally disclosed, but Merkat medbay had also had its share of trouble, with more cases resulting from violence related to the closure of a number of trading premises. And external aid had been called in, the owner of the *Half Moon* said in a whisper. He had had people in his place that he'd never seen before asking questions of him and his staff and they looked both capable *and* dangerous, was his opinion. And there was still interest in Xanna Kerrix, but that was tailing off now that she was gone. As the three sipped their ales, Ally described one or two of the strangers that were still around, none of whom seemed familiar to the PSS officers. Their enquiries had largely related to local matters such as attempted bribery, coercion by unsavoury types and transfer of small goods – and the *Half Moon* had been witness to one result of the investigations, for two Treskk nationals had been seized in the place and had put up a fight. The rumours around them were to the effect that they had run a small trading outfit as a sideline but were shipping illegal goods in and out using willing and unwilling pawns and with the connivance of certain official parties Web-side. Ally had taken it all with a pinch of salt, but was inclined to give most of the outsiders who dropped in a wide berth.

Two pairs of eyes were watching the talk at the bar and had noted other clients who also had covert eyes on the trio of uniforms. From the safety of their small booth, Jurry turned to his buddy.

"Does it look to you as if that bozo over there in the brown suit is setting up something that might be a nasty surprise, Malty? He's been giving Ahxenta shifty looks since she came in."

"Could be. Do you think we should warn her?" Malty asked.

"Might be an ale in it but if we're wrong, it'll be her left hook."

"I'll take the chance," Malty rumbled. "Hand over your mug."

He ambled over to the bar and close to his quarry to set down the mugs. In the face of Ally's rebuke and a curt aside that he would be dealt with shortly, Malty broached the subject in a low voice.

"I thought you should know, ma'am," he ended with a hiccup.

Ally eyed him in distaste but filled fresh mugs, his gaze flicking to the far table, as Apnis turned to inspect the loner. An odd familiarity about him caused her lips to tighten and she loosed her phase rifle. Malty heard the noise, grabbed his drinks and scuttled for safety.

"You've done it now," Jurry greeted him. "Ahxenta's looking over now and the bozo figures he's been spotted. You'd best sit down."

"As long as I don't get blamed," Malty puffed as he slid in.

"You won't," was the quick retort. "He's not too sharp. He looks scared and he's started to pack his traps for a getaway."

Others had noted the stranger, for Wekki Munnet had disposed of the contents of her tray and was heading for his table. She came to a halt as the captain and first mate of the *Arianrhod* reached it. They had left Holdspan at the bar to watch lest there were others nearby.

Ahxenta's hand came down on the thin arm. "You've a new face but you're still not subtle, Micklemouse. How did you get here and why? You were a long way off last time we spoke and you were trying to do me harm then. *And* you were firmly in hostile clutches."

"I don't know what you mean…" his voice trailed off as the sharp end of a phase rifle made contact with his temple.

"Talk," Tallica Apnis ordered coldly.

Even as she spoke the sharp hiss of a phase bolt cutting the air and a crash at the entry caused several heads to slew round. A split second later and the sound of metal hitting flesh and bone resounded as Wekki Munnet's tray met the face of a squarely-built man at the adjacent table who had risen up, a primed weapon in his hands.

The captain of the *Arianrhod* had taken in the situation instantly. She told Apnis to keep Micklemouse pinned as a glance at Wekki Munnet indicated that the woman had calmly stunned the other man with his own gun and then disarmed it. Ahxenta nodded and with phase rifle poised, she strode to the entry. Nathan Holdspan had already reached the spot: two insensible but heavily armed bodies were on the deck.

"Good shot, Nat," his fellow captain commended as she took in the pair. "Armoured outfits; your rifle packs a punch."

She looked around. Almost everyone in the place had taken refuge under a table or behind a friend. Ally had called in back-up in the form of his security guard Jox, who was hovering at the bar.

"They'll be out for a couple of hours," Holdspan said levelly. "I've seen suits like that on Nyx – on a pair of heavies who tried to waylay a couple of my crew at our last stopover. They didn't succeed."

"Who were they?" she asked, raising an eyebrow: he had not mentioned *that* during their chat in marketing.

"Hell knows," was the sanguine reply. "Our readings then implied natives of Salt Three, but that was of little use. We left them with the Nyx planetary authorities and I've heard no more."

Ahxenta stirred the nearest carcass with her toe. "Looks average: a pawn, I guess, sent to do someone's bidding. The question is whose."

Holdspan was scanning the two. "They've been surgically altered. Prosthetics for strength, so set up for trouble, but that's it. Here are the cavalry," he added as three Merkat security officers raced up.

After a quick chat the captains left security to deal with the pair and made for Apnis and Micklemouse. The latter was visibly quaking. Ahxenta turned to the man Munnet had whacked. He was still on the deck and she suspected that the agent had slipped him a knock-out drug to keep him that way. Holdspan's scanner was again in use.

"He has far more implants than an average thug and I'm getting a lot of hostile cyber-tech. He could do serious damage, and that gun's not one I've ever seen before."

"Right on," Ahxenta replied sharply. "He's a cloned hostile agent. The original was called Hoxiz."

"Hell, another one?" *Arianrhod's* first mate cut in. "He's a friend of yours?" she enquired of Micklemouse, prodding his ear with her rifle.

"I've never seen him before," the trader quavered.

"Liar," Apnis said evenly. "I called the ship," she told her captain. "They don't know the full score but they know about this trickster."

Ahxenta glanced at Munnet, who stood waiting. "These two will need extra-special berths," she stated calmly as Ally approached.

"I'll call in more security," was the woman's pointed reply. "This guy will need to be tied down, but as your pal hasn't done much bar try to deploy what he's got there, they may not want him. I'll see."

Munnet walked off with a wink to Ahxenta. The captain turned to Ally to give him the gist of the matter, suggesting that he get his bar settled and quell the inquisitives who were already furtively collecting visuals for use later – and get her a copy of his own secure-cam data.

"You'll have it, Captain, but *their* records will be wiped: this isn't a damn circus," he promised as he left.

One of the newly-arrived guards came over, scratching his head, to talk about the inert felon and the shaky Micklemouse. He seemed relieved that matters were in hand and notified the officers that the other two were unknowns and were headed to new high-security cells on level green one. The possession of high-spec weaponry set to kill was enough to have them charged, until such times as the *Half Moon's* cam record could be analysed to determine their intentions.

"They targeted Captain Ahxenta and Commander Apnis as soon as they came in," the steely voice of Nat Holdspan apprised him.

The guard nodded sagely and repeated that vis-evidence would be used. For now, as Captain Holdspan had dealt them very heavy stun blows, he would be expected to provide a statement.

"I just have," was the terse reply. "I have business. You know my ship, you can contact me there. But I want to be kept up to date on those two, when you find out who and what they are."

Once the guard was out of earshot, Holdspan asked for details on the trader. Apnis had examined the device he had been trying to set up, suspecting it to be a target-specific bio-reader and tracker with various covert uses. Micklemouse had not assisted her enquiries but a search of his person had turned up other goods, now set out on the table. They included a small but powerful handgun and a case of data shards. A trill from Ahxenta's wrist unit interrupted. It was Azular.

"Stand by," she told him, for Wekki Munnet had just returned.

"On the way," the waitress stated. "They'll sort the cyber guy out and they can take your friend off your hands if you want him stored safely. He'll be held in the new security wing and you'll be able to interview him. SSO Hills is aware of the situation."

The captain nodded. "Thank you. I'll take Azular's call over the earpiece, Tallica. Can you hold on 'til the security team arrives, Nat?"

Holdspan agreed, watching Munnet closely as she made to clear a nearby table. He was plainly a little doubtful of her.

Azular had been quick and immediately Apnis' link came through, he began to check the smaller berths around the Web as far as he was able, calling Kit Biernop for information on the latest arrivals. One Comet Six had come in three days before and was docked in the middle belts. Its spec fitted the old boat that was Bick Micklemouse's usual ride. The news troubled Ahxenta: three days implied that it was known that the *Arianrhod* was headed for the Web, if indeed she had been the prime target of the attack. She ordered Azular, Flintlock and two guards down and deferred shore leave for the rest of the crew.

The security duo that appeared to arrest the gunman made for the three officers at the back, stated their duty, showed their passes and unloaded a gurney. They swiftly scanned the man and relieved him of a number of articles before loading him up, telling Ahxenta that they would keep her informed. They also offered to offload Micklemouse at the new facilities on green one on a charge of possession of illegal materials; the gear on his table looked to fit that bill.

Ahxenta shook her head, but the trader's relief was short-lived. "I want to chat to him first. But tell me where I can drop him off, and then you can have him – and that stuff."

"As you wish, Captain. I'll make sure you get the details as soon as I confirm with my HQ," the leading guard agreed.

As they watched the party move off, Apnis glanced at her captain. "Those two are far too efficient to be usual Merkat security types. I bet they'll make mincemeat out of the cyber-thug."

"What is he?" Holdspan asked. "You seem to recognise the type."

"Over here," Ahxenta inclined her head to a private spot, out of earshot. "You recall that scuffle that the *Tallulah* had with hostiles by Idledott and our talk in the ISP office on Silverglass a while back? You suggested that the hostiles had honed their skills in altering their own to produce human-like versions just as scary, for crews for these new ships we've seen and for other uses? You were right. And they've been around long enough to cause a lot of trouble, they and more advanced types. That cyber-clone's one. That's all I can give you, and don't spread it around. You've got his readings. You meet another, you shoot first and don't ask questions. And now I want to speak to that pipsqueak. I'll keep you up to speed. Watch your back."

"I will," he replied soberly as she turned to make for her target.

Apnis gave her a quirky grin. "So where are we going for our cosy chat with this one, before we hand him over to the authorities?"

"Ally's office. We can wait for Azular there."

"Who'll tell Ally?"

"I will. I want a word with that waitress as well," was the response as she took Micklemouse by the arm and hauled him to his feet.

Two pairs of eyes watched as the three made across the floor to the bar. "Huh! She might have stood us a jar!" Jurry sniffed.

"She's got other things on her mind," Malty told him. "We'll drop the hints later. And I wasn't charged for these," he added, waving his empty mug. "I'll go and see what I can do."

"Hang back a bit," Jurry advised. "There's Nat Hotshot looking like a lost pup. We could chat him up."

"You're kidding! Though he's young, he's savvy and he'll have your guts for garters. But look! Fleetskup and his minder have come in. They'll be as welcome as toothache, so we may as well wander over in a bit and give them the time of day."

Ahxenta had talked to Ally, taken a last look round and then made off behind the bar, towing the reluctant trader. Moments later, Ally walked over to the booth at which the two topers sat.

"These are on Captain Ahxenta. Don't expect more," he growled tetchily as he set down two large jugs of ale.

"I take it all back, Malty! Here's to the captain of the *Arianrhod*! Long may she drink in the *Half Moon*!"

The staff room was empty bar Munnet when the officers walked in, the silent Micklemouse between them. The captain halted to talk to the waitress whilst Apnis steered the man into Ally's office. She pushed him into a chair and sat on the edge of the desk, phase rifle ready, watching him quizzically until Ahxenta came in. The captain let fall the man's goods on the table, sorted them and began a scan.

"I know what these are," she told him as she sat opposite. "You'll now tell me how you came to be here and why; when, where and why you were altered; and, who your crony at the next table was. And that's just the start," she warned. "Get on with it."

"Why should I tell you anything if you're going to hand me over to security?" he parried.

"That's *one* option. You're facing a charge of attempted murder — and accomplice to murder if you're linked to your friend at the next table. Your ship's been impounded and your quarters on green nine are locked down. You've nowhere to run. And your chum Doosbak's awaiting sentence in a high-security cell in Skene Starn's detention facility," she continued harshly as he gaped. "He's been found guilty of offences that also concern you, so it's likely you won't see him for a very long time – unless you end up in the same place."

Thirty minutes later Azular, Flintlock and their escort arrived, by which time the trader had confessed that he had been picked up at Keeant after his abortive talk to the captain. He had then been taken to Minch Fettin for surgery to which he had not consented and had been there until recently. He was told that part of his cyber-ware had been removed, as it posed a danger both to him and to his masters. His new face and identity were to protect him but let him operate with less risk to himself. His ship had been refitted, though he could not judge the extent. The man at the adjacent table had met him on arrival; he had seen *him* before on Sevolb. As for his ride – he and his ship had been dropped off the local bypass by a large transport.

Ahxenta posted her guards at the door. Azular and Flintlock were then directed to check the man out. The doctor had just confirmed that he had lost part of his internal hardware and software when a tap at the door disclosed Hanx with the news that someone needed to speak to the captain urgently. Ahxenta looked out to see Munnet.

The dialogue outside was short and Ahxenta was back in minutes. She did no more than shake her head at her crew and continue to press for answers from the man in the chair as to his mission and his means of accomplishing it, and to have Azular scan him again from head to foot for anything that could pose a direct threat.

"New and intricate implants and much of the original *has* been removed, Captain. I estimate that this is experimental and part of it is set to keep tabs on him from a distance. Dr Herta's work, perhaps?" he added, looking Micklemouse squarely in the eye.

The trader's shocked expression gave him away: he knew.

"Her interest *was* complex embedded micro-medical tools such as language analyser-translators – helpful in opening up new areas for good or ill for those who trade in chaos. Being able to monitor and track your spy and his contacts at distance would be a useful feature of such implants and would render redundant much of an info-sent's capacity, particularly when he's conversant with your quarry."

"You mean he's being monitored now, which means so are we?" Flintlock interjected.

"Unknown, but his implanted devices may be under test. I detect short-range emissions and he's gathering data from this location."

"Your mission was?" Ahxenta demanded of the man. "Now!" she barked. "I don't have all day, and believe me mister, neither do you."

Micklemouse had been told that *Arianrhod* was headed to Merkat Three. His brief had been to get close enough to her or her crew to inject internal bugs that would read the individual and transmit data that could be tracked at distance by a bio-reader. As he was familiar with the senior officers of the ship, he was a logical choice.

"Inject!" the captain hissed.

"Using this," Azular held up a gun. "It would need an accurate shot and the volatile delivery system would deliver a sharp but brief sting. These shards are to store data from the bio-reader tracker and he could download it into his implanted data port. The credit slips are advance payment and these are the keys to his ship and his billet.

"I had no choice!" the trader cried, but even as the words left his lips, he gave an involuntary scream and cringed in pain.

"What the...!" exclaimed Apnis as he writhed in his chair.

Ahxenta held up her hand. "Bang," she said. "So you *are* linked to your ship in some way."

"Captain?" Azular asked as Ahxenta checked her wrist communit.

"Go over him again and confirm he's not rigged to self-destruct," she ordered. "And his gear, as we'll be handing it over. Your ship is dust, Micklemouse. It was fitted with enough explosive to take out a warship. Your contact is locked up tightly with no outside access, as are those gunmen that were set to get us if you failed or your cover was broken. And they were quick, so they had to be ready to move the second I figured *you*. So you're going to tell me more, aren't you? Or I hand you over to people who are less tolerant that I am."

He knew little more than that his handlers seemed antsy that their strategies were failing, with their ships being taken down, their moles traced and their operations undermined. Their current tactics aimed to remove the agents they held liable: the forces of order and those seen as aiding them. The aim of the invaders he did not know, but he guessed it was control, as they were part-cyber and very powerful.

"And that makes them think they're better than us and more suited to be in charge," Apnis sneered. "And what do they do with the power once they've got it? Sit back and rake in the profits?"

The captain pressed for more on where their centres of operation were, but Micklemouse either did not know or was too scared to tell.

"You'll get no more, Cap," the first mate said eventually.

"I agree. In that case, we're going for a walk," she told the trader. "Azular, take his stuff: you're with me. Tallica, you and the doc head to our shuttle; take Corvus and get back to the ship. I'll take Hanx and we'll come back in the other shuttle once we've dealt with *him*."

The captain's later briefing was short. "Micklemouse will cause us no more trouble. He's headed for a secret ISP facility where he, his toys and his implants will be studied by experts and his brains picked for what he knows. I'm sure there's a strong ISP Intelligence presence here still, though my contact was evasive. But the Web's a key control centre for hostile activity, so I've been *advised* to get out now as our being here is seen as provocative, as has Nat Holdspan. With us and a few others out of the way, I gather that an impending face-off can go ahead that will shut down hostile ops here for good."

"You mean we're being used to take the heat off?" the first mate indignantly demanded. "We head out and some of them follow?"

"Yes, and I've agreed," was the direct reply. "Lindell, sort us what you can of non-local contracts, even if the fees are below our usual terms. We need to be out of the Web for sixty days standard at least – but we have other ports we can call home for the duration."

The captain held up her hand as the voices rose around her. "The situation is risky: ISP has to act fast as this place is riddled with spies. No going port-side, we'll deal with everything from here. Order what you need from our usual suppliers but take nothing as read and check every micron before it's brought aboard. Crizz and Azular, if you can source the needful to start on a new decoy do it, but the ship comes first. Keep comms minimal, especially personal. I'll keep you all informed. Dismissed. Stay, Tallica, we have things to sort out."

"That was to the point, Cap," Apnis said dryly as the door slid to. "You missed out a lot, such as who told you this, why, and why you believe it. Warweft? And she doesn't want us blowing her cover?"

"Exactly. As Munnet, she sees and hears a lot. We met her after we dropped Micklemouse. Her people found out about his ship, used drones to move it out and blew it. As for a hostile base here: a certain party snitched about a place in the guts of the Web where he met people, carried goods and got orders and the link was made."

"What certain party?"

"She didn't say but I'd guess Doosbak. What other villain would have such insider gen and be spineless enough to squeak when his neck was in a noose? But Minch Fettin's now verified as a facility for hostile clone production, so it'll be shut down. Not that we've seen the last of this alien infiltration, I bet. There may be plenty Alliance ships out there to deal with the hostile fleets that seem to be heading into charted space, but organising them into a coherent defensive force will be a headache for someone."

"Myrtleberry maybe; it would keep her out of our hair," the first mate said scathingly. "I know Warweft's ISP, but you're getting us out of here on the strength of her story?"

"Azular was with me," was the wry retort.

"Talking of whom – I see he's still down in the mouth. Any news of what's going on outside known galactic borders?"

The captain shook her head. "Not a word. But hyperspace comms links can be transient and relays can be subverted or bugged. I've not heard from Ver so I expect Thal is still out there. But we have a ship to get on the move, so we'd best get a few good deals in place."

"Some of the crew will be sore at missing shore leave. Greffy for a start – you know he's seeing young Merry from the *Half Moon*."

"That place has got a lot to answer for."

Arianrhod was cleared for departure three days later. The ship's first duty was a run through heavily-populated parts to Brown Amber to drop off mining gear and pick up two batches of crystals. Amber had never been friendly but trade was trade and *Arianrhod's* was handled quickly. The ship had three more stops in Beta. Zandee, on the edge of a Coalition sector, was the first, for a load of heavy gear for the ISP dockyard at Alto Finglas, their third port. They ran cloaked and silent: the sector ran to the edge of unmapped space and was uneasily close to Cox 455 and its alleged hostile base. Lindell had been careful in setting up contracts but Ahxenta was suspicious that an inkling of their current schedule was known to undesirables.

Eight days standard after their departure from the Web and with cargo uplift at Zandee in progress, a call came in for the captain. The link was quick and the content sufficiently vital that she called a staff briefing before *Arianrhod* left orbit. A major control base of hostile ops had been crushed at Merkat and operatives and gear seized. Once word spread to other alien hotspots there would be an impact, most likely in the form of reprisal, and it would come soon. The safety of her ship and crew being critical, Ahxenta had decided that a straight run to their next port of Minti was too risky. They would head out of Zandee on a direct line but at Violet they would cut across Coalition space to sector sixteen and the Riptide system, and head for Minti from there. At top speed, they would only be a day behind schedule.

"Sector sixteen of Beta!" more than one voice objected.

"Those are our tactics from here on in, until we've discharged the contracts set up in the Web. I've warned the fleet. I'll see what the score is when we make Alto Finglas, but as I'm damn sure the ISP and its hangers-on still have a few suspects in their ranks, we don't discount trouble in that area either. Back to work people."

Despite the disquiet created by crossing Coalition space, most of the bridge crew were relieved to leave the busier route. Signs of other craft on the bypass had increased by the time *Arianrhod* made Violet, some not friendly, but hyperspace noise had dwindled to almost zero as Riptide was passed. Ahxenta had not given the customary notice of approach to Minti and was mildly amused that the port authority of the settlement seemed surprised at their advent.

Cargo transfer and related transactions were made from the ship. As there had been no news of local upset the captain decided that a straight run to Alto Finglas at top speed was their best approach, with cloaking and silent running ordered. It would take two days and with luck, those tracking her progress would expect *Arianrhod* to use tactics similar to the ones employed out of Zandee.

That her departure from Minti *had* been marked was confirmed when *Arianrhod's* arrival was logged by Alto Finglas Port Authority, for her docking triggered a signal that the captain should stand by for a link-up. Ordering her first mate to proceed with cargo discharge, Ahxenta made for her office to accept the call. She had a vague idea of the identity of the party, as her tactical officer had reported a fair number of ISP and other Alliance ships in nearby berths.

"Myrtleberry," was the sour reply to Apnis' query on the captain's return. "She's up to date on the situation in the Web and told me that an ISP cruiser had logged two hostiles sitting off-beacon at Pocket eight days ago. The cruiser called for back-up and took them down."

"Pocket! If we'd carried on from Violet, *that* would have been the next main node!"

"Exactly. But how *she* came to know of our itinerary she wouldn't say. Her own spies, I guess. She wanted to know how we'd avoided them. I wouldn't tell her and she was put out but she did mention that the ISP, its buddies and the Trades Alliance are having a meet at their new cosy centre to discuss tactics. I advised her to get them to check out every listening post each of them has, in use and defunct. I bet a few have been subverted for alien purposes, given the speed that our business and theirs gets passed around the damn galaxy."

"Bellfish reported a new Allied Central Office channel among the comms he picked up, so maybe they're boasting overmuch," the first mate grinned. "And the reason ISP wants comms-grade crystals is that it's set up its own hub for churning out arrays for its dockyard. Couldn't find out how many warships are in prep, nobody would say, but by what we *could* scan, there must be a small fleet. Anything else?"

"She hinted about a contract with an urgent tag on it to bring in a load of hull plating from Beta Zegonia to here if I could fit it in, but I didn't bite: if it's on the cards, Lindell will hear about it."

"She's a tricksy customer at best. She's maybe trying to find out where we're next headed," Apnis conjectured.

"Could be. But if *she* doesn't know, it might mean we're off the hostiles' antenna, though I won't count on it. How's drop-off going?"

"On target; the loads are not huge so they're easy to shift. Lindell is hunting up more trade and Perla Jute's handling the paperwork. If this Beta Zegonia deal is above board, do we go for it?"

Ahxenta mused. "I'm not keen. Given the goings-on in the Web, there'll be a lot of eyes on local space. And I want away from the eyes here. The ISP's grand alliance has a few members that don't like us."

"Coalition members like the Friskianx, for example," said Apnis.

"Right on. But here's a memo from Lindell so I'll hop down to his office to see what's what. Let me know when the drop's complete."

"Aye, Captain."

The supercargo had checked out several sources and had two potential contracts that he wanted the captain's go-ahead to bid for. After a full check, Ahxenta agreed. The second batch of crystals in one of *Arianrhod's* inner holds was earmarked for Freskat Six, and the deals would take them in that direction, albeit not directly.

"If we get them, our next stop would be Bistra for food supplies for Delta Iridium," she told her first mate as she reclaimed her chair. "At Delta we'd have a wait for a load of construct units for Lamella Four and that would put us on a course for Freskat for crystal drop."

"Any word on your buddy's move to bigger premises?"

"No; a freeze on personal comms applies to me as well," was the smiling response. "But the workshop will be in the same place."

"So once we're out of here?" asked Apnis.

"We aim for the beacon for Silshoon to foil the eyes here and then switch for the Crimson Drapes and Bistra. Ceres Corp on Delta is an old client, so I'm sure we'll get the deal," the captain said.

A short time later and the supercargo confirmed that both trades were in place and it was with a feeling akin to relief that Ahxenta gave the command to head out as soon as clearances were granted.

The trip to Bistra for cargo collection took days and was trouble-free, leading the crew to hope that whoever had wished them ill had either given up or was now incapable of causing mischief. The habitually wary captain had insisted on cloaking and silent running at departure. Her measures were justified, for three days out, long-range scans picked up a distress by a star cluster known as the Triple Pinks.

"Fake or real?" Apnis asked disparagingly.

"Likely genuine," Azular said. "Her call-sign identifies her as the Vreskot supply ship *Marjenna* and I know her Berzic supercargo. I've not seen him or his ship in a while but we owe them: they redirected part of a food cargo *Arianrhod's* way after our fight at Kifferbuck."

"Then we go in," Ahxenta decided. "But we don't discount it's a trap and we don't drop the cloak. Warm up our weapons, Lieutenant Commander Earbleat. Set for battle-readiness but hold the red alert for the moment. We're without our decoy so we go cautiously."

As *Arianrhod* came into range of the signal she read three distinct outlines, two of which were hostile. At that point, the captain called battlestations and under the skilled hands of Dox, the ship speared off the bypass, shields up, cloak down and weapons primed. That the two attacking ships were aware of her approach was obvious, for one instantly veered off target to make for the PSS.

The captain's curse rang out over the wailing alert and the hum of powering systems. "That was damn quick! Earbleat, target that near blip, I want it gone! Evasive, helm, she's got our mark!"

As searing bolts of fire missed the great pink hull by a fraction and *Arianrhod's* own weapons blazed, the first mate scanned her boards. "Small but dangerous: her hull's shielded but she's got phase cannon, torpedoes, slicer beams and fighters *and* she matches the interceptors we met at Orange! They must have kept some in reserve! Those are not battered old has-beens, they're spanking new!"

"So we take the shine off them!" the captain snarled as Gliss called out that the second ship had turned to try and outflank them.

"Then let's get this one! We've been here before. Dox, get us close enough to target main engines. Tactical, assist targeting of her comms and Tallica, take auxiliary weapons and cover our rear."

As *Arianrhod* slewed upwards to confuse enemy targeting, the first ship matched course and speed.

"It's sticking like glue!" the helmswoman hissed.

"Earbleat…"

"On it, Cap! *Loki* away and she's set to spit down its throat!"

The weapons officer had readied her prized craft and in a blink a streak of fire shot out of *Arianrhod's* hull in a twisting line, a stream of deflecting drones spreading out either side. Her final upward spiral and drop down gave Earbleat the time to fine-tune her firing pattern to focus a sustained burst at the hostile craft's main engine housing.

"Second blip closing!" Gliss sang out as the first ship veered away, on fire amidships and clearly down. "Wide-spread missile salvo!"

A reverberating boom signalled a direct hit to the hull as the chief engineer called out the loss of aft shielding and Dox sent the ship into a downward curve to protect her stern.

"Another ship coming off the bypass!" called Larai. "She's ISP!"

"It's the *Repulse*," Azular's measured tones resonated.

Earbleat's quick brain had taken in the implications and she pulled *Loki* quickly back to her bay as Dox fought to put distance between *Arianrhod* and her attacker. The ISP vessel's priority was clearly the active alien: she spared no firepower to overwhelm the ship but was careful to target weapons, auxiliary engines, comms and fighter bays.

"Disable, not destroy!" Ahxenta whistled as she slackened her seat restraints, the better to view the holo of the ISP cruiser and her prey. "Stand down battlestations but keep weapons on line. Bring us round and towards the *Marjenna*, helm. Bellfish, raise them and get their status. They seem to be pretty banged up."

"Where in hell did Myrtleberry's boat come from?" Tallica Apnis demanded as she came over. "Was she tracking us or them?"

"Guesstimate as to our position. But I bet ISP relays were tailing *them*. Levettiza said that the ISP and its allies would take over tracking those ships heading our way from outer Mu, and they're now well up on the specs of alien ships and how to deal with them."

"Captain Jedinlok from the *Marjenna*, Captain!" the comms officer alerted her. "Visual on holo."

The Vreskot captain was grateful for the aid; his vessel would not likely have survived the attack, she was seriously damaged and he had many casualties. A check of her boards told Ahxenta that her ship's aft shielding was out and her hull plating was buckled but her engines were intact and she still had weapons power. Jedinlok accepted the offer to tow his crippled ship to Delta Iridium and as *Arianrhod* set up for the task, Bellfish called that Colonel Myrtleberry was on the link.

"She's got that hostile tied up and in her tractors," the first mate noted. "The other's stardust. Bet this is short and sour."

It was: the purport of the message was to learn the status of the *Arianrhod* and the *Marjenna*, ask that the tactical and science data both ships had picked up be handed over and announce that the *Repulse* was headed to an ISP base to take the hostile apart bolt by bolt.

"Does that include the crew?" was Ahxenta's waspish retort.

The question was ignored as the colonel repeated her request. She was told curtly that the ISP would be given copies of the reports that both captains would make as and when they were complete, as would their respective fleets and other bodies that should be made aware. Meanwhile, with the *Marjenna* in such a poor state, *Arianrhod's* priority was to see her safe. Delta Iridium was the closest large repair facility and that would be their target. Ahxenta ordered the link cut before the irate Myrtleberry could respond, and sat back to ruminate.

"Does she *ever* take a hint?" Apnis asked wearily. "All linkages in place now, Cap, we're good to go and Jedinlok's given the green light. I wonder if she figured we were bound for Delta Iridium anyhow?"

"With her net of spies, I bet she had a clue. Hit it, helm: best speed to Delta Iridium Colony, and remember we're heavy."

The Colony was quiet as the two ships hove in barely a day and a half later. Berths were ready and as *Arianrhod's* cargo was undamaged, she unloaded before she prepared to engage with the repair equipment and teams that were charged with bringing her back up to spec.

The captain ordered shore leave for those of the crew that could be released. Repairs would take at least five days and until those were complete, Ahxenta was loath to bring up the cargo for Lamella. Her supercargo was hunting up trade, and as a spin-off of their rescue of the Vreskot ship, he was asked if *Arianrhod* could take on what would have been the *Marjenna's* next but one load, agricultural gear from Hespera Two for Nyx. As it would fit with *Arianrhod's* schedule, the trade was agreed. Diversion to Hespera meant a minor route change on the way to Lamella and Nyx was close to Aoria, where Ahxenta planned to stop after Freskat for weapons emplacement upgrades.

Two days into their forced stopover at Delta, a long-distance link came in for the captain. She had been off-duty and at dinner but had made directly for her office. The voice of the duty comms officer as he reported that it was ISP, security-coded and on a tight beam gave her a notion of the identity of the sender.

Forty minutes later Ahxenta headed back to the mess to continue her interrupted meal. Her first mate was still there, curious as to the content of the message. She had been joined by Dr Flintlock and the two had been sitting quietly talking over various crew matters.

"Levettiza?" Apnis enquired softly.

The reply was a short nod and the news that several small packs of hostile ships had been sighted in various parts of the galactic sector in which Norvalla and its colonies were located, and which the *Advance* was scouting. Local systems had sent ships in to deal with them but a few had broken off and crossed into mapped sectors. The ISP and its allies were aware and several posts and ships were trying to track the intruders. It was suspected that the hostiles had made use not only of hyperspace routes known to them but of local nodes in zone Mu, including those on the new bypass route. The consensus was that the ships sighted were making for their own bases.

"So why don't the ISP and its allies take out the suspected bases and leave them nowhere to run?" Apnis asked. "They have a list."

"Suspected doesn't mean they are," the captain pointed out. "And as some were Alliance listening posts, the owners want them back."

"And why is Levettiza telling you?" the first mate queried archly.

"One, she said she would keep me updated, and two, Thal asked her to pass it on."

"Thal! What's going on out there, Cinnabar?"

"The *Kel'Moth's* made it to Norvalla, for reasons Levettiza won't give, and as *her* ship is out on patrol for much of the time, Thal hears things she and her people don't," was the silky reply.

"Cinnabar! What else did she say? About Kerrix, for a start?"

"Keep your voice down, Commander, our crew has big ears."

"Cut it, Cap. What gives? She didn't link all this way just to tell you what the ISP will no doubt put out in a few days."

"The *Advance's* remit is exploration and first contact and she and her people have set up the necessary for the ISP to continue, but she obviously can't discuss the specifics. And alien matters of course. As for Kerrix: she's okay and that's all you need to know."

"Azular…"

"Is my affair," Ahxenta told her. "Finish your rations and scoot."

"Is that a dismissal?"

"Make it one, Tallica," Flintlock interrupted. "I want to talk to the Cap about a private matter and this is as good a time as any."

"Azular," Apnis said resignedly as she stood to go.

Once the coast was clear, the doctor began. "I've called a friend of mine here, a highly-skilled neuro-surgeon and an expert in his field. I didn't mention the finer details but he's agreed to give his opinion, so I want approval to pass him Azular's case notes *and* get his help, if I can persuade our stiff-necked senior SO to cooperate. Delta Colony's medical school is outstanding and my friend's a director and a senior consultant surgeon in the teaching hospital."

Ahxenta ruminated for a moment. "You trust him?"

Flintlock nodded. "He's the best there is, Cinnabar. He and I both trained here and I've seen *him* in action since. He might even be able to repair the damage without using cyber implants."

"Okay, you can sound him out; but you go down to talk and hand over notes, I want nothing of this on any channel. But not a word to him until I give the go-ahead: I need to tell Azular something first."

"I hope it's good news," the doctor said dryly.

"Mind your own business," the captain directed.

A little later, Ahxenta sought Azular out in his lair, where he spent much of his off-duty. Her trained eyes took in what he was doing.

"You're refining our nav-charts. I thought you'd already updated them with the data you put together for Kerrix when you updated her shuttle's on-board charts with the route home using the outline star charts that Admiral Zillah handed over."

"Indeed, Captain; my priority then was the route to Norvalla but now I have that and the shuttle's more complex nav-system charts, I can extend ours to take in sectors mapped by the Norvallans – and enrich our databanks with other data held in the shuttle's ops system. It may serve us if we meet something we haven't seen before."

Ahxenta looked at him steadily. "You're filling your time to stop you thinking, aren't you?" she asked. "No, don't answer that. I've just had a link from Commander Levettiza," she told him, and proceeded to give a condensed version of her news.

"She didn't say much about Kerrix except she's over her hurts and her court-martial; the outcome I don't know but she had the Admiral, a Telzilt officer *and* crew from the *Twin Star* as support. You may find out more from this," Ahxenta said, holding up a data shard.

"Captain?"

"A private coded message to you from Kerrix. Even Levettiza has no idea what's in it. She transmitted the datastream over the link and I loaded it on this. You'll have to decode it. If you need to talk, you know where I am. It's been a while since you last heard news of her."

"Forty point five days," he smiled crookedly as he took the shard. "And the last I spoke to her was the day she was taken."

"Make for your own quarters. You won't be disturbed there."

"Aye, ma'am. Thank you, ma'am."

Two hours later and it was obvious to his crewmates that Azular was chipper about something. The captain inferred from that that he had decoded his message and was cheered by its content. She notified her first mate and Flintlock privately of the link and gave the latter approval to see her friend, pass on the details and take his advice, but to delay a talk to Azular. The doctor took the next shuttle down.

Dr Jink Burr was as skilful and thorough as Flintlock had claimed. The captain had her own sources and had checked with them before she allowed her chief medic to raise the issue with Azular. *He* realised that he had been the subject of debate but his annoyance lasted no longer than it took him to appreciate that the captain and Flintlock had his welfare at heart and he agreed: the surgery advised by Burr was viable and the probability of total success high. Burr's advice that Azular remain on Delta for ten days afterwards he refused to agree to, however. He was determined to leave with *Arianrhod*, for reasons he refused to disclose. Ahxenta suspected that they related to Kerrix, but did not press the point and instead authorised a further forty eight hours on Delta, though it would curtail their time on Freskat.

The ensuing days brought the ship up to high spec, although many of the crew queried the worth of it, as she would likely meet more hard luck on the next leg of her cruise. Cargo lift for Lamella was however smooth, orbital exit from the Colony swift and the halt at Hespera Two for pick-up of the *Marjenna's* load short; eight days after leaving Delta the sight of the glowing Ginseng Nebula filled the holo-grid.

The brief stopover planned for Freskat Six had to give way, as an urgent comm from Admiral Zillah came in that resulted in Ahxenta and her first mate taking an early trip down to Fleet HQ. The captain had delivered the small batch of crystals to her contact's workshop, stopping only to hear the latest news and pass on good wishes and a gift of credit. It had been welcome, she told Apnis on her return; the small home close by his studio that had served him when single was being extended, a less costly option than finding a new place.

"The fun of housekeeping on Freskat," the first mate replied. "So what does Zillah want to say that she won't put on an open link?"

"About to find out," the captain responded as she brought their small shuttle into a landing pad handy for Fleet HQ.

The intelligence was relevant and personal, Ahxenta was told as she and Apnis took seats in the admiral's office. Twenty days before, a Freski Navy ship had taken custody of the remnants of a small alien craft that had been on a line for what they now knew was a hidden base off the Curtain Nebula. That the base was a target was likely: the alien had been carrying a great deal of high explosive in external pods that had been blown off by one of Thal's ships. The latter had hailed the Freski in passing and left the shattered shell. Zillah had ordered the Fleet ship to tow the hulk into Freskat space, and Intelligence had been sifting through it ever since. Evidence indicated that it had been crewed by a handful of advanced humanoids and scoring on the hull showed that it had passed through the Star Desert but had not spent long in space. Data gleaned from its ops systems had been decrypted and sent to the ISP Council but that body had not issued a bulletin, deeming it unconfirmed. But amongst lists of the type that had been found in various places, there were plans of main institutions, specs of ships including *Arianrhod* and orders to target specific individuals.

"You'll be on that list, Captain," Apnis said shortly.

"You both are, as are firms and people who are held to be trading contacts or linked to you, including me. Your contacts here include Greskitty Comms, who supply us. *They've* been told but your other local contacts listed have not," she said, passing over her info-pad.

"Damn!" Ahxenta spat.

"Hell!" the first mate breathed as she scanned the names. "This is not good. How many copies of this are out there?"

"We don't know – not many is the consensus, as the ship we have, or what's left of it, is a design neither my people nor the ISP have on any database," the admiral replied. "We therefore reckon it's recent in construction and this data may be the latest. Certainly, much of the info Fleet Intelligence decrypted is not on any other lists we know of, and what *is* here is interestingly specific, much of it related to the outer sectors of zones Lambda and Delta but not beyond."

"So somebody's been watching us *and* you from close to here and passing on the news," Ahxenta said. "Who and for how long? I take it your own people have been cleared, Admiral?"

"As I once said of you, you don't pull punches, Captain. And yes they have. If there are spies on Freskat, they're well-hidden but they must be in posts that can access confidential data, including trades data. My people and local and ISP Intelligence units are on the case. You're not the only PSS that has been linked to concerns here either. All you might need to know is on this shard. Be wary in sharing it."

"Of course, Admiral. And thank you."

The two officers of the *Arianrhod* made their farewell and headed straight to their shuttle.

"Zillah took a risk in giving us that," Apnis noted once they had settled into their seats. "You heading across to see your buddy?"

"No, I can't risk it. But he needs to know he'll have to watch his back. I'll find a way to drop some protective gear off that will help."

"Give Earbleat a free day to cadge a bunch of high-grade tech to upgrade *Loki* into an even more lethal weapon and send her down in one of our old shuttles. She can park it in a berth on the outskirts by his place and you can sneak out at dusk to do the needful."

"Very funny. But I have an idea that's not a whisker off that. Let's get back aboard. I need to see Flintlock."

The doctor found Ahxenta's idea reckless and at first rejected it. The captain knew her people, however, and Azular was very willing to comply. He was still weak and under medical care, but was gaining strength daily and his mind was as sharp as it had always been. Apnis insisted on one guard and had agreed with Azular on Ji Lerro. As she had been inside his Norvallan shuttle, she was the only choice as far as he was concerned. It was thus much later and after dusk in the settlement that the cloaked craft left *Arianrhod* to make landfall close to the outskirts of the small suburb where scattered workshops and homes made up the space. Azular activated the shuttle's chameleon facility once within the atmosphere and skilfully piloted her to a berth close to the captain's target. Her call-sign had been altered to identify her as a small runabout from a local shuttle-hire company and Azular had named her *Xanna* in honour of her previous owner.

The captain and Lieutenant Ji were both in protective clothing and well-armed. Azular was to be left aboard the shuttle, both to protect it and to maintain scans on his colleagues and on the local area. His initial probe had shown that the small house was occupied by two individuals, which complicated things in Ahxenta's eyes but could not be helped. She used the *Xanna's* comms to make a quick connection, using her own voice to alert her nephew to her identity.

"Interrupting dinner," was all she said as she and Ji collected their gear. "Lock down and set her signals to read empty after we've gone but keep the links to us open. Anything goes down, I want to know. And on no account leave this shuttle. You copy, Azular?"

"Yes ma'am."

The captain evidently had much talking to do for an hour passed without a word, but as Azular stretched to ease his cramped limbs a chirp from his ops board alerted him to traffic. He brought up the visual to see a robust land craft heading in. It was scanning as it went, the beams sliding over his shuttle. That rang alarm bells: no typical runaround had gear of that kind aboard. As it passed, he sent out his own probe beams and tabbed the emergency voice link.

"Captain, we have a problem."

Captain Ahxenta's reply to the alarm was prompt and her responses rapid. She called Ji inside and ordered her science officer to sit tight, monitor the area and inform *Arianrhod*. Apnis was equally as reactive: she scrambled the *Gadfly*. Azular had alerted her and the captain that the heavy vehicle advancing on the lonely steading, outwardly typical, was solidly-plated and armed with weaponry that could reduce the structures to rubble. As his covert probing had logged three lifeforms emitting cyber signals, it made for a very risky situation.

The dark transport was moving slowly, scanning as it went, but its aft scanners had cut on passing the Norvallan shuttle, evidently rating her non-threatening. The vehicle stopped, a light emanating from its underside marking the exit. The occupants stepped out, one moving towards the front of the dimly-lit house whilst the other two slid off either side. Azular saw one of the latter halt at the unlit workshop to focus a hand-held probe on the building. The shadowy shape moved on seconds later, probably sensing nothing off-beam. The three met in the doorway, scanners directed at the interior. Brief words were exchanged and the trio moved backwards.

"They're going to storm the entry!" Azular's voice hissed through the link. "All are armed with heavy weaponry!"

"Copy," Ahxenta intoned in response.

The front door broke apart in a shower of splinters as the three leapt into the brightly-lit long lobby. The leader had no hesitation in making for the furthest door that led off it, kicking it open. The gang burst in with rifles set, to find that the occupiers had made ready to defend themselves and had taken cover behind the upended dining table. A bolt aimed aloft carved a hole in the ceiling, causing a drift of fine flakes as the leader's guttural voice ordered the pair to come out with hands raised. Three seconds ticked by before the answer came.

"Now!"

Two shapes hurtled from either side of the solid table, bunching up and rolling over before releasing a firestorm from high-powered rifles. The attackers stood their ground, secure in the awareness of their own resistant nature but mortal enough to pause as they took in what was happening. That was sufficient for the first barrage to bring one down. A retreat was called, and dragging their injured mate, the two on their feet made for the door. The captain stood to take better aim but was too savvy to lower her guard, making use of the scanty cover that the simply-fitted room offered as she followed them.

Their vehicle was sufficiently close that they could reach it quickly and to deter pursuit the unhurt pair loosed streams of deadly fire to cover their backs. Ahxenta cursed, shielding herself behind the door jamb, aware that Ji had sustained an injury and that she had civilians close by. If they reached their craft they could deploy its weaponry and that thought propelled her forward. A searing stab of pain to her arm sent her reeling back into the room but even as she gathered her strength for another effort, her ears caught a dull boom from beyond. A sudden pause in firing and harsh angry cries let her know that her assailants had new targets on the outside. The scream of weapons fire cut the air and she knew that she had no more to do. She crawled over to her injured officer, who was trying to sit up.

"I'll live, Captain," Lieutenant Ji assured her, wincing. "Got my leg and my foot. Are *you* okay, ma'am?"

"Just a scratch. Ahxenta to Azular: what in blazes is going on out there? It sounds like a circus."

"Admiral Zillah sent in a team," was the calm reply. "Commander Apnis called her for back-up as she knew the *Gadfly* wouldn't make it down in time. They're wrapping up now; they have the three."

Ahxenta had other priorities and linked to *Arianrhod* to alert Apnis to Ji's injuries and ascertain ship's status. Leaving her officer as easy as possible she made for the basement to release the two there; as a nurse-tech in the local hospital, her nephew's partner would be of more use than she would. That done, Ahxenta made for the smashed door and the relative quiet that had replaced the earlier racket, being curious as to the source of the rumble she had heard. She noted in surprise that the Norvallan shuttle was not where she had last seen it, but closer to the house. And what had been the intruders' craft was a listing heap of part-fused metal. In the low lighting she made out an armed man making for her. She turned to greet him, recognising the uniform of the Freskat Home Fleet.

It was hours before Ahxenta saw the inside of her ship. The criminals were under arrest in a secure fleet facility, their craft now in the hands of Zillah's team, and the captain had given as much of an account as she was inclined. Apnis had sent Ma'Lappis down with the *Gadfly* and

Ji was now in medbay, for Earbleat, in command of the rescue party, had rounded up all she could, called in a local friend to carry out emergency repairs to the homestead and flown all the crew bar the captain and Azular back aboard.

As the captain had concluded, the wreck of the armoured car was Azular's doing. He had moved his shuttle into an optimum position to disable it with directed bursts without activating its weapons. The senior officer at the scene had not been amused. Neither was Zillah when she arrived but as she had the suspects and their goods, she did not push the issue. The admiral also agreed to the captain's request that her contact would not be subject to further intrusion: Zillah was conscious that she would never hear the full story and also acutely aware that the two PSS officers were not as fit as they should be. The wound Ahxenta had sustained had been patched by Ma'Lappis but required further treatment and Azular's exertions had weakened him. Both had been ordered directly to medbay once back aboard.

A concerned Apnis awaited them in *Arianrhod's* medical facilities to hear the parts of the story she had missed and the captain gave a brief rundown as Dr Flintlock worked on her injured arm. In a short exchange with the couple, they had been warned that their place was likely to be targeted, hence the kit that Ahxenta had brought. Azular's alert resulted in the two being ordered to the cellar, a shielded space used as storage for the costly crystal elements of the young man's work. The captain and Ji then set the table on its side as a barrier and were ready when the trio burst in. As Azular had been ordered not to leave his shuttle, he had moved her in stealth mode to a spot where on-board scanners could very precisely target the hostile vehicle. His probe beams had also found that it had been strengthened by meta-jurillium plating that bore inclusions indicative of alien extraction.

"You're both here for the rest of the night – no arguments," the first mate told the two. "No doubt we'll hear more from Zillah in the morning. And this will mean a delay to our schedule yet again."

"It won't," the captain said decidedly. "We're for Nyx to drop the agro-gear that's still in our hold. It's close enough to here that any details from the admiral can be sent out on a tight beam. She knows."

"I hope you said thanks: I interrupted her at dinner."

"I did. But she's got the perps and a ball of tech to play with so she's not lost out. And it's three off our tail. Hell, I need a shower."

"When I say so," interrupted Flintlock. "And has it crossed your mind that three more out of action might mean fewer to worry about but the ones still around will be even more miffed once they hear?"

"Yes it has. And let me off this couch. Once you're done with Dr Azular, Dr Oak, I want to speak to him."

"Ma'am?" the science officer queried.

"Malicious obedience," growled the captain. "You're ordered not to leave the shuttle so you just move her and blow up the evidence."

"They may have made it to their craft and used its weapons…"

"The CMO's office, mister," Ahxenta directed. "And if you could rustle us up some rations, doc, I'd be grateful. I want my dinner."

The captain faced her senior science officer squarely in the privacy of Flintlock's office. "What did you not want Zillah to find?"

"Captain, I was motivated by the knowledge that they could use their weapons to destroy…"

"That I know and don't think I'm not grateful. But you *could* have used your precious shuttle to take *them* out or stop them boarding that battle-car. Those shots were pretty specific. What did they have in there that you thought Zillah had better not see?"

"I have no suspicion of Admiral Zillah but in view of events, it's clear that there's a mole or perhaps more than one close to her. That land-car was carrying a miniaturised cyber suite much like the one we found in Colonel Myrtleberry's high-spec shuttle a while ago *and* an array of what registered as highly complex micro-medical devices that were possibly for implantation. Both loads were encased in hard-alloy shells as if for shipping and that may have been their next mission, after dealing with your contact on Freskat. There may be a ship due here soon for pick-up or perhaps a shuttle ready to leave to meet up with such a vessel. The admiral should be informed, but covertly."

"One helluva lot of speculation, mister, that gave you no right to blow up that cargo! If you're right, that stuff is not only evidence but would be very useful to the Alliance."

"Or very detrimental in the wrong hands, and with a mole in the admiral's inner circle, that's where it's likely to end up. Besides, I have fairly clear schematics of the devices and the Alliance has similar in its own hands – Colonel Myrtleberry's cyber suite for one."

"That damn Norvallan shuttle!"

"It has an imaging scanner able to penetrate heavy plating. I first saw it in action as a hand-held months ago and it's standard as part of the ops of the shuttle. The details are not perfect, obviously."

Ahxenta shook her head. "Damn you, Azular! That those bozos might have made it to their transport and turned its weapons on us is the reason I'll have to give to the admiral for your actions. I expect you took out its firing ops as well?"

"Yes, ma'am."

"Let's get our rations; Flintlock won't let either of us loose until the morning, so we'll see what's what then."

The action of the previous night meant that *Arianrhod* was still in port and without clearance to leave. Ahxenta had been bidden to an early closed session with Zillah. She had taken Azular in spite of her chief medic's protests, she was armed and had security in tow. The admiral was alone in her office and tolerant when the captain set up a jammer after Azular scanned the room: her own suspicious mind had figured that she had a leak close by that her people had not found. The three culprits had been questioned. All were cyber-enhanced but not equal to the highly-cyber hostile agents that had surfaced here and there, Zillah told them. Their base and their contacts were being traced but they were recent arrivals on Freskat via a commercial liner out of Delta Iridium and had not been tracked further. The biosigns of the two males implied an origin in the Drosophila Systems in zone Eta, whilst the female was from Botrix in Gamma. The origin of their ride was less easy to work out, now that it had been partially destroyed.

The captain's account caused the admiral's jaw to tighten and it was clear that she was still irked. Her irritation was enhanced by the data that Azular had obtained and his assertion that had the goods been passed on, more trouble was likely to result. She was sanguine enough to know that nothing could be done now but to assume that the cargo had been for transfer off planet and investigate that. Azular then pointed out that endpoints for such a payload included Mellifly and Minch Fettin and if the latter, a likely recipient could be Dr Mazy Herta, late of the Web's medbay. The *origin* of the devices was also a mystery; was it possible that the ISP had lost novel medical gear?

A short time later the two officers collected their guards and made for their shuttle. Nothing was said on the way up to the ship but once aboard, the captain ordered Azular into her office.

"How did you pick up on the missing ISP tech?"

"The admiral: her anger at me had more to it than the loss of alien tech and when Colonel Myrtleberry's cyber suite was raised, albeit indirectly, she displayed an involuntary awareness. It was a calculated guess on my part but her reaction to it confirmed my hunch."

"She was livid but at least she's admitted there's been a theft. So the ISP has a secret centre that's creating med-tech and such gear and the enemy's either found it or is able to hit the transports that carry it. I suppose *that* led you to figure that her local mole could be in her own or ISP's Fleet Intelligence? Well, it's given her something to mull over *and* it's pushed her to release the block she put on our departure. Anything else you dig up from the readings you got, I want to know at once. But you're still on sick-leave, so don't overdo it. Dismissed."

Back on the bridge, the captain found action already underway for breaking orbit. She had made her personal farewells and was grateful to be heading for the liberty of open space. The run to their next port would be short and as soon as possible, she gave the order to free *Arianrhod* from her docking struts and make for the bypass.

It was a three day run to Nyx and with nothing to hinder progress, the ship made good time. It was the crew's collective opinion that the bust-up on Freskat had scared off their ill-wishers and any out there would think carefully before trying to waylay them. The tale had done the rounds it seemed, for as cargo delivery began, a call came in for the captain from the recently-arrived *Nyx Warrior*.

"So what did Nat Hotshot want?" Tallica Apnis enquired of the captain on her return from her office.

"To ask after us and to confirm what the ISP reported of a rise in actions against Privates. And to see if what a Freski contact told him about our trouble could be believed. He's got contracts in hand that'll take him right across to the edge of Zeta, so he wanted facts."

"Smart boy."

"He's learning," agreed Ahxenta. "But he's next for Aoria to drop a cargo and as that's our next stop he'll hang fire and wait. Any raider out there will think twice about taking on two Privates."

"Especially *Arianrhod;* and the *Warrior's* making a name for herself – or maybe it's her captain's personality," Apnis added wryly. "So where's he for after Aoria, or didn't he say?"

"Across to Delta via Hespera with gear he's loading at Aoria; he didn't elaborate and I didn't ask but as Lindell's been grouchy, I think it's that arms cargo *he* bid for and lost due to scheduling constraints. We're for Freskat to collect the crystal arrays for Coronis Comms – they should be done by the time we get there, despite the glitches."

"Your buddy's partner's now aware of who and what you are, I take it?" the first mate asked in a barely audible whisper.

"She is, but she's clever and in her job she knows how to keep her mouth shut. But I see Lindell's won the contract to carry the grain supplies from Delta to Vellisa Colony and as we have the deal for the parts for Heligon sealed, we'll be going in the right direction."

Ahxenta updated her senior staff at a briefing she held after the ship had left Nyx and was on the way to Aoria Six, a familiar place, as the materials for *Arianrhod's* hull emplacements and many of her arms were sourced there. *Arianrhod* would hold for three days for upgrades and extra armaments, as the captain had a niggling suspicion that the current quiet would give way to chaos sooner or later.

The fitters of Aoria's orbital repair bays were efficient and the ship's overhaul proceeded smoothly. It was almost complete when the first hint of upset came in via Captain Bluejohn of the *Obsidian Sky*. The ISP and its allies had sent out convoys in simultaneous hits on the small groups of hostiles that had been tracked into charted space and on their known and alleged bases. The mission had limited success. A few worlds, baulking at attacks on their own ex-posts, had held back and some attacks had been expected, implying that advance warnings had been leaked. The *Obsidian* had intervened to assist two frigates from ISP's Kellybar One in a clash with three hostiles who had tried to take out the end node of zone Mu's new bypass route at Wild. How far the wave of invaders had advanced was unknown, but the Allied powers were no doubt hoping that it had been slowed.

Arianrhod's captain had noted the silence of the usual channels on aggressive activity over the past few days but such action by the ISP and its allies had not crossed her mind. Zillah must have been aware and ISP Intelligence would have been a party, she figured, but as some of the hostiles had been alerted, there were still holes to plug. And with ragtag hostile bands trying to regroup, random strikes would be likely at civilian, merchant and military targets. Bluejohn had no data on how many had escaped or been missed, but given the nature of the enemy, its disregard for its own safety and its relentless crusade against certain groups and people, the PSS fleet would still be under fire. If those giving orders were silenced, those left would no doubt pursue their previous agendas.

After the link to the *Obsidian Sky* had been cut, Ahxenta spent the last few hours of their time at Nyx in exchanges with other contacts she could reach over secure channels. She had little more to go on by the time *Arianrhod* slipped her moorings and made for open space.

Armed with the news from Bluejohn, all security measures were in place for the return to Freskat. The bypass was quiet and three days later the ship reached the outer limits of the system, the glow of the Ginseng Nebula lighting their way. The orbital space around the sixth planet was far from quiet, however.

"What gives?" demanded Apnis, scanning the bridge holo as

Arianrhod came in. "How many ships do we have in port?"

"Too many," was the grim retort. "And a few are reading as ISP."

"As long as Myrtleberry's ride isn't one of them," the first mate returned. "Have they seen action do you think, and no-one told us?"

"Port Authority's granted us clearance so it's not lockdown," the captain noted from her boards. "And nobody's targeting us, but we sure as hell had better not try to scan or target any of them."

"Maybe they're all on furlough," the bright voice of Box piped up. "If they *have* been in action, they'd need a break."

"If that's a hint, Mr Box, I didn't hear it," Apnis told him. "This is a quick stopover. And you're taking two guards down with you, Cap. Anything from Zillah? She must have been informed we've come in."

"Not yet; she's probably busy."

"Or doesn't want to talk, given what happened last time."

"I've local comms to make before I head down, so we'll see," said Ahxenta as Dox called out that docking was complete and the ship was at station-keeping. "I'd better call the Port Authority in case they have any issues for us, so I'll do that first. You check in with Lindell and make sure we have everything in place to hand over the fees. I'll send him a final total once I know the score."

"Roger that, Cap."

It was almost three hours before the captain's shuttle left her bay and late afternoon in the main settlement, as a talk with Zillah over a closed link had taken up a deal of time. She made a rapid sortie to her contact's place to find that the goods were ready despite the damage and the well-meant visits of nosy neighbours. By the time the *Gadfly* had resumed her berth and the small but costly cargo was safely stored in a secure hold, Ahxenta was more than ready for off-duty.

Arianrhod left Freskat space the ensuing planetary day, the short delay allowing for a flying visit by the *Emerald* with a cargo of reflector flak from Limekiln. The transfer was made quickly, for the *Emerald* had another matter on Freskat that Goodsocks assured Ahxenta would be handled discreetly and only by her own. Noses twitching, *Arianrhod's* bridge crew were no wiser as the order was given to break orbit.

Apnis found out later in a quiet moment in the mess. *Emerald* was carrying prefabricated sections of a small habitation unit for drop-off at Ahxenta's nephew's home. It was recompense for the upset he and his partner had gone through. And as Zillah had informed her that two moles had been dug out of her fleet's Intelligence section, it was hoped that there would be no repeat in that quarter.

"Doesn't explain the number of ships we saw in orbit," the first mate commented sourly.

"Zillah wouldn't say, but I suspect it was to do with an attack near Peden Post – a couple of my other contacts spoke of a base that had folded close to there and a few of the ships hauling into Freskat had been hit by more than space dust. But we're for Delta and as it's all set up, we should be out in just over two days Delta time."

"We've been a long time away from the Web this bout," Apnis noted. "That sixty days standard have come and gone."

"We'll be out longer still. Lindell's been savvy about finding trade and *Emerald's* catering for our regular clients closer in. Vellisa's after Delta, then Heligon. That'll place us as far away as dammit from the Web, and if a new deal he's looking at comes off we'll be even further out: Wester 287. It's heavy agro gear we can pick up at Vellisa. Our aft cargo bays will be empty after we drop their grain and the Wester authorities want the gear to up their own food production."

"The only person aboard that'll cheer is Azular. Closer to Mu and the boundary to uncharted space – though I bet *he's* got it as well-charted as the ISP and their explorer fleet. But it makes sense: the Westies still depend on imported food as they're a newish colony."

"Well, let's to it. The ship won't fly herself."

"I wouldn't bet on that," the first mate chuckled.

Five days later and the vast port of Delta Iridium was achieved. As well as offloading the cargo of crystal arrays and taking on the huge loads for their next deliveries, the captain ordered essential resupply. That meant that nearly every section aboard was running full-tilt and most of the crew were looking forward to down-time once *Arianrhod* was back in the space lanes. Lieutenant Box was no exception.

"It'll be good to have time off," he sighed to his usual partner at the helm. "I seem to be glued in place here."

"You've been twiddling your thumbs," he was accused. "I suggest you plot our forward routes now we know what they are, *and* build in plenty of alternatives in case we hit snags. We don't want to run afoul of local or inter-system disputes or over-zealous patrols that want to prove they're worth their pay. Lynxi Bellfish will get you the latest comms. And as Doc Azular's taken the trouble to generate new nav-charts, it'll be worth your while to get your head around them."

"But we won't be flying outside the charted zones," Box objected.

"Ha! Not *now* we won't but things'll change, mark my words," was Dox's enigmatic reply.

"What've you heard?" Box whispered, his eyes lighting at the hint of gossip. "Dr Azular heard from Captain Kerrix again, has he?"

Ahxenta and Apnis traded wry smiles. News had evidently filtered down the grapevine that kept the inquisitives of *Arianrhod's* crew up to date on private matters. The captain had had a short link from Levettiza. The *Advance* had been ordered to hold around Norvalla as the ongoing presence of Thal's ship, allegedly for repairs, was making ISP upper ranks antsy, and a diplomatic ship was on its way as backup. From the standpoint of the PSS fleet and other targets, a number of hostile ships had been foiled in attempts to cross to Alliance space, thus lessening the hazard, but it still existed despite the strike against the enemy and its strongholds. Thal's fleet had been badly hit, with ships lost or wrecked, and his people had faced incursions over the past thirty days into what they held to be their space. Ver was holding the reins but Thal planned to head out shortly, once a few things had been set in place about which he was saying nothing. Levettiza had also passed another coded message to Azular from Kerrix. Her courtmartial had left her record and her rank intact, though it was unlikely that she would be offered a command in the Norvallan fleet. Matters were, however, moving ahead positively.

The news had raised more questions than answers but what was in the private message to their senior science officer had not caused him grief and he continued his latest allotted task of building a new decoy with a quiet humming that Cottontail grumbled was driving her crazy.

The first mate's opinion was that Thal was fostering relations with contacts in the areas opening up in order to gain first dibs on radical tech and an advantage over other trading fleets. The captain was less sure, but it was of small concern. Her priorities lay in maintaining her own trade foothold whilst keeping her crew and her ship safe.

"Get on with your work," was all that Box was told by his mate, but the sly wink as the words were uttered caused him to grin.

"Can't keep a good crew down," Apnis smiled at the captain. "But I'd best see how far resupply has got. Air recharge was the last job."

As final tasks were nearing completion, orders were given to ready the ship to leave. In less than two hours *Arianrhod* had shaken loose her traces and was in a line to the bypass and Vellisa Colony on the edge of zone Delta, the most remote outpost of Vellis Prime. With her ship up to full spec the captain had ordered silent running and cloaking; despite the lull in hostilities she wanted no undue interest in her doings and was aware that her destination and likely route were known to many besides her own people and her clients. It would be a long haul of about ten days across a belt of empty space and would mean a cut by the Coalition-controlled sector near Peascod Secundo.

The trip had been more tedious than expected, Box was grousing to his friend Gem Ferry over early rations in the mess near the end of the time. They had passed no other ships, the only comm noises had been a hum of distant traffic and the drills that the first mate insisted on during quiet times were no fun. He had clashed with Dox over how to spend their next leave, always assuming a next leave, and she had deserted him to start her bridge shift early. The words were no sooner spoken than the distinctive shrill of the red alert pierced the air and the call to duty stations rang out.

"You and your mouth!" exclaimed Ferry as he jumped to his feet.

Box grabbed a last bite, dropped everything else and sped off in the wake of several of his mates.

The bridge was in a state of ordered efficiency but the main holo-grid was expanding as senior duty crew took their places. The captain was already in her chair, her fingers on her boards calling up data.

"Damn typical!" Apnis was grunting. "But we're only reading one ship and that's the *Tallulah*, by the call-sign."

"Cut the cloak Dox, and bring us off the bypass on an intercept to the *Tallulah*," Ahxenta ordered. "Keep the shields up. Comms try to patch me through. What in hell's going on that she's sent a distress?"

"Detecting missile fire and a restraint beam from the third planet of the Pellucid system!" Azular called.

"They've got her!" the tactical officer verified.

"What? But it's uninhabited – supposedly. Gliss, get all you can on what's there and how we can go in without getting trapped. Earbleat, triangulate the sources of the tractor and the missiles and use long-distance torpedoes to take them out as soon as we're in range."

"Just as well we got those upgrades at Aoria," the first mate said tightly. "Not even lost their shine and we're deploying them."

The *Tallulah* had evidently been given similar orders for she was bombarding the surface with those of her weapons she could use.

"As much speed as we can without compromising targeting," the captain called. "But do *not* head in close. I don't want to risk there being another tractor with our name on it."

Streaks of fire shot out from the recently-upgraded torpedo tubes and within two minutes the weapons officer declared their targets out of action. The tractor was certainly out, for the *Tallulah* had speared away from the vicinity of the third planet with all haste.

"Scan for anything unusual down there and prepare to disable it,"

Ahxenta directed her science and tactical ops. "Dox, bring us round in tight orbits to cover the whole surface but don't get too close."

"Aye, ma'am."

Another missile launching site was found and destroyed but there were no biosigns, suggesting that the systems were automatic and had been triggered by the *Tallulah's* approach. She had now slowed and was heaving to. Damage appeared to be minimal, Azular reported.

"That's your link now, ma'am! Captain Fleetskup on the comm!"

"So what happened, Captain?" Ahxenta queried acidly, noting the flushed and unsmiling face of his first mate at his side.

Tallulah had left Milkit Major for Vellisa, Fleetskup told her. They had come off the bypass at Pellucid in response to a distress from the luxury liner *SS Sea of Stars* of Cygilla Prime. A garbled comm claimed that she had lost hull integrity on impact with a rogue asteroid. They could find no trace of the ship or debris but had picked up a repeat distress from the third planet and headed in. At that point the tractor and missile attack had begun. Fleetskup admitted that he had not checked the registry for an *SS Sea of Stars* from Cygilla or elsewhere, his first mate angrily butting in that rescue was the priority. Hardly, if there was nothing to rescue, was Ahxenta's acerbic retort.

"He looks hunted," Apnis noted as the link was cut, the captain of the *Tallulah* insisting that he could make Vellisa on his own, though he did give a grudging note of thanks. "But Dyne-Beck's shifty eyes were looking at anything but us, as if she'd been caught out."

"We'll maybe find out more at Vellisa; it'll take time to unload the grain and then ship up the Wester 287 stuff, as that's still planetside. I want it checked before it gets near the ship and as I've not dealt with Crosscorp before, I'd like to meet their people. And if they're smart they'll want to know who they're dealing with. I'll take Azular to make sure the goods and the clients are as advertised. We'll meet the reps in that bar for visitors in the main trades centre."

"And that's where Fleetskup's likely to be if he was headed in for trade, but what he'd be carrying from Milkit I can't think. Or maybe he's picking up. What was he doing at home anyway, another visit to ma? Or maybe he'd been there for a while?"

"Don't give a damn," was the laconic reply.

Several hours later and the ship made orbit around Vellisa. Cargo release was rapid for the port was set up for orbital transport and the service was efficient. The *Tallulah* had a load to deliver, for two pods had been quickly shunted out of her aft bays by grapples. It seemed her transport crews were proficient at any rate, Ahxenta mused as she cast her eyes over her own accounts and authorised the indents.

"All clear, let's go," she instructed Apnis. "We'll meet Azular in the shuttle bay. It'll be a break for him from setting up the decoy."

"And a break for Crizz's ears – she says he sounds like a tuneless bee trapped in a glass jar. But nice to know we'll have a decoy again."

The *Satellite Bar* was bright and busy for all that few trading ships were in. The three from *Arianrhod* were quick to spot their contacts, for one bore an info-pad with a prominent company logo and both hastened towards the team the second they entered the door.

"Our rep precedes us," Apnis whispered. "They look nervous."

The captain declined refreshment prior to the trip to Crosscorp's despatch depot where the cargo pods awaited her review. The ride to the trade premises was short and two senior managers were on hand to meet the party. The visit advanced smoothly and in under an hour the three officers were back in the comfort of the *Satellite Bar*, having shaken off the persistent company reps.

"You'd think nobody had ever wanted to check what they were shipping up before," the first mate stated. "At least it read okay. I got the impression they were a bit overawed, even the managers."

"They were," Azular smiled. "Now we have the readings of what's to be carried, we'll know if there's been tampering. But the pods are standard hard-alloy, they have relevant tags in place and our grapples will have no problem with them. And Captain Fleetskup, his first mate and Mr Buntle have arrived with a senior officer I don't know, though he's wearing the uniform of the *Tallulah*."

"But he's not wearing a smile," Apnis noted. "Here they come."

Dr Mill Steen was *Tallulah's* new chief medic. He had joined her at Milkit and subtle probing implied that Fleetskup family strings had been pulled to recruit him and others, including a senior scientist.

"Don't you believe in promoting the crew you have, Murmur?" Tallica Apnis asked slyly.

"*If* they are capable and *if* they deserve it," Dyne-Bek put in with a caustic look at her. "At least, that should be the protocol."

"Inks rated confirmation as second mate," Fleetskup said huffily.

"But evidently not the pips that went with the job," Buntle added in an ironic tone that inferred he knew something.

The *Tallulah* was in Vellisa with cargo from Nyx but would now have to wait for costly repair, an issue that was taxing her captain. Apnis adeptly drew him into chat to find out why he and Dyne-Bek were at odds but it was Buntle's malicious interjections that told her that despite cautions from his science and tactical stations that the signal read false, Fleetskup had heeded his first mate and gone in.

Ahxenta called a halt an hour later, citing business aboard as the excuse, and once out of earshot and on the way to the shuttle bay, she let out a deep breath. "Now we know the story."

"And Tallulah Tommy's keen to spread it," snickered Apnis. "All Dyne-Bek could see was the salvage fee for rescuing a luxury liner. But Jesse Inks didn't rate lieutenant commander's pips? Dyne-Bek, I bet. *Tallulah's* paid the price if Inks left the ship at Nyx. Fleetskup must have her measure now, but he'd best rein her in or he'll have no crew left. So Fleetskup had to call in at Milkit to pick up his new people. What do you make of his new CMO, Cap?"

"He's seen shipboard action if he's been on trade routes but he'll find the *Tallulah* a trial with the command crew she's got. What was your take on him, Azular? I saw you had a few words."

"He was ill-at-ease," the science officer replied. "I sensed no liking for either of his senior officers or Mr Buntle, and he was unsure as to why he'd been taken to meet us – which *was* one of the points of the visit to the *Satellite*, at Ms Dyne-Bek's instigation."

"To find out what we're up to and see if there's profit in it – and to rile me, I suspect," Ahxenta said testily. "Levettiza checked her out and told us she was a freebooter with big ideas out to grab what she could and wasn't above taking backhanders."

"And now Fleetskup's stuck," Apnis chuckled. "I almost feel sorry for him. He'll have a mutiny on his hands if he's not careful."

The ensuing day saw *Arianrhod* preparing to leave Vellisa for Heligon Station repair base. A straight run would take her across Epsilon and into the ISP-run sector of Zeta but it would mean crossing an ill-patrolled area with no known settled systems.

"We take the direct road," the captain decided after keen scrutiny of the latest updates. "It's across ISP space and we know fleet ships are out there in response to the latest incursions. And even if there *is* a hidden bypass between Thal's Sunrise station and that base by the Curtain that Ver's so cagey about, it's far enough off the edge."

"Makes sense to me," Apnis said. "The Freski confirmed there *is* a base and as part of a hostile set-up, there would have had to be ways in and out that didn't cream their ships at hyper-speeds."

"You've convinced me. Let's hit the trail. Nice and easy out, helm; I don't want to suggest we're in a hurry. Set an initial heading of Vellis Prime, Mr Box, just in case anyone's got beady eyes on us."

The only eyes on them as they made the bypass were the scanners of the *PSS Urania*. She was on course for her home port of Delta Iridium via Vellisa Colony and exchanged greetings in passing. They had had no alarms, Captain Mikbeam told Ahxenta. After dropping his cargo at Arrissia Five he had returned via Heligon, and the bypass had been empty of trade traffic, although they had met a couple of ISP cruisers on patrol who warned of an incident involving hostiles near to Flint Wolf. It had been dealt with.

"Seems a popular place for a scrap," Tallica Apnis remarked after Mikbeam had signed off. "Last time we had that kind of trouble was when the *Hexameter* was hit. Maybe it's a hostile stop-off as it's on the edge and nobody lives there – at least nobody we know about."

"We'll keep it in mind when we're en route to Wester," the captain told her. "For now, it should be quiet as far as Heligon – I hope."

The captain's hope was fulfilled, for the four standard days that it took to cross the near-empty space was peaceful apart from the hint of distant comms and a hail from an ISP patrol ship. *Arianrhod* was uncloaked but had been running silent, the inference being that the ship had new-spec gear that could pick her up. The patrol reported no known dangers as far as Heligon but advised caution if they were travelling further through zone Zeta. Such being the case, Ahxenta ordered an extra day at Heligon to take on additional armaments and quiz the locals about any known hazards. She also decided to detour via Arrissia on the way to Wester 287 on the chance of learning more about conditions further out.

The three day crossing to the Arrissia system brought the hum of remote comms that implied other ships on the bypass, signals passing through or hazards to trap the unwary. The space around the fifth and only inhabited planet of the system was active, with a number of vessels in orbit. The *Nyx Warrior* was one and a link from Captain Holdspan alerted Ahxenta to a clash at zone edges that had merited the presence of two ISP warships as well as one that he had identified as similar to but smaller than the *Kel'Moth*. He had hailed her and had been told that she was the *Kel'Seth* under a Commander Nil Mint, but that was all he got. The *Warrior* had dropped her cargo at Wemm and had been on her way back when she came upon the trio. Their quarry was little more than dispersed wreckage but had once been a pair of hostile warships that the ISP ships *Defender* and *Trueheart* had been warned were inbound. The *Kel'Seth* was on their tail: she had tracked the blips into charted space where they had jumped off at a node of what was suspected to be part of a covert bypass that cut through the outer reaches of Zeta just beyond Wemm. The ISP ships had added their fire to the *Kel'Seth's* to take them out, the captain of the *Defender* had told Holdspan. The ISP ships were holding station in the area to salvage what they could for analysis but as they had no authority over the *Kel'Seth*, they had no reason either to question or detain her.

Ahxenta expressed her thanks and told him what she knew of the ex-hostile but most likely fully-operational bypass that cut clear from unmapped space across a swathe of Mu from Kirtish to Canna and then to exit nodes by Thal's Starfall and Sunrise bases by the Enigma and Starglass Nebulae respectively, dipping into Zeta by Wemm.

Nat Holdspan's brow wrinkled as he digested the data. "I bet it doesn't stop at the Starglass," he mused.

"Clever boy," Tallica Apnis muttered *sotto voce* as Ahxenta smiled and told him that there were suspicions that it continued, possibly on a direct bearing, to where another hidden base had been detected just off zone edge and close to the Curtain Nebula.

"So it skirts the charted zones, and possibly clips the edge of Delta if it ends at the Lambda edge of the Curtain Nebula. No wonder the hostiles got about during the war," Holdspan continued.

Captain Ahxenta agreed but refused to divulge more, other than that the base by the Curtain was under Thal's aegis and thus not likely to be a source of trouble to him if he was headed home to Nyx.

"So trouble where *we're* headed," Apnis stated after the link had been cut. "The *Warrior* trades at the edge if she's been to Wemm."

"It pays a lot," was the dry answer. "Why do you think there are more Privates out here than other commercial lines?"

"Because we're the only ones cocky enough to take the risk, or at least some of us; I can't see the *Tallulah* putting herself out. But it's probably as well we cut in here. Looks like ISP patrols are out there."

"It's not those that bother me but we'll have to stay sharp: we're heavy and it'll slow us. It's a nine day crossing to Wester, assuming no trouble en route. And I always assume trouble en route."

In view of Nat Holdspan's news, Ahxenta had Lindell scour trades concerns on Arrissia for extra gear to ensure that *Arianrhod* would run at full efficiency. Azular and Cottontail were in the final throes of completing the new decoy and were given free rein to order anything needed. The same licence was not given Earbleat, who still yearned for a new version of her own piece of quirky tech, but spare parts for *Loki VII* she was permitted to order.

"Ready as we'll ever be," the first mate announced when, all stores aboard and all boards at green, *Arianrhod* was powering up to leave.

"Roger that, Commander Apnis. Take us out, Ms Dox and plot us a straight run, Mr Box. We'll cut by Mercy Four, as there's an old ISP listening post that may be active, given the current spate of disorder around here. But as soon as we're on the bypass and away from local scanners, we cloak. Long-range sensors, tactical, and get everything you can probe with on line, Azular."

The hours passed slowly for all the rapid progress the ship made. The constantly upgrading holo-grid tracked their line across the dark and empty spaces as the watches changed and very little came in over any channel. The highly-secure Ultraviolet III that the PSS fleet used to link between vessels was empty of any noise that affected the outer region of zone Zeta, although regular updates suggested that one or two of *Arianrhod's* sister ships were out there.

The Mercy Four system was passed with no detectable signal to suggest an active post on the third planet. *Arianrhod* crossed into zone Kappa on schedule and had just dropped off the bypass for the short hop to Wester 287 when a problem arose. Her long-range tactical and science sensors picked up a drift of recent wreckage. The remains hinted at a small ship, possibly a trader, as pieces of hard-alloy rather than meta-jurillium were all that was left of her hull and of those, no identifying signs were detectable. Residual ion trails indicated two ships, implying that the attacker had been a lone hunter, but whatever it was it had gone, possibly towards zone Mu.

The captain ordered her stations to pick up what data they could and then called for best speed to Wester 287. The ship's cloak was dropped but other protective systems were kept on line. Ahxenta had advised the authorities of her imminent arrival and sent on details of the wreckage and trails. Azular's analysis had included meta-jurillium traces that matched known hostile hull materials, suggesting that the small ship had put up a fight and had stung her opponent.

In a little over four hours *Arianrhod* had made orbit, had finalised transfer of the huge cargo to waiting grapples and was in process of completing the relevant formalities when an urgent message from the Wester defence agency came in asking for a briefing. A local trading ship, the *SS Shade*, had been reported as missing. Ahxenta was terse, agreeing only to a very brief comms link-up within the hour. She had other concerns: they had received a short unidentified comm that she suspected was from one of Thal's fleet warning of aggressive activity just over the border in zone Mu and close to Minch Fettin. Bellfish had traced the link as far as he was able and with Azular's aid had worked out that it had come from the general direction of zone edge, probably by Kirtish. A trawl of ISP and other channels had brought up nothing similar. In view of the situation, the captain decided that she would not retrace their route but would head further into zone Kappa and make for the ISP's Kellybar One Station.

Once back in the command chair, Ahxenta checked her boards. The deal had gone through without a hitch, payment had been made and they waited only clearance to leave orbit. It had been one of the longest trips away from their usual haunt of the Web at Merkat, over one hundred standard days, and the captain was well aware that her crew needed a break. She sighed as the go-ahead came through.

"Hit it, helm. Let's see what the rest of Kappa has to show."

"A peaceful trip to the Web, I hope," Apnis said at her elbow.

As Wester 287 receded and their projected course lit up on the holo, the ship gained speed to make for the local bypass entry node. She rode the current and set her head on a bearing that would take her close to the large ISP sector within Kappa. The minutes trickled by, the hum of her engines and the muted reports of the bridge crew making a soothing background. It was shattered by the strident voice of Lieutenant Bellfish.

"Distress call! It's on a PSS channel!"

31: MOONSTONE

The captain sat bolt upright in her chair, cursing as she slammed her fist down. Her voice rang out calling for details as the officers around her readied for action. Bellfish was wrestling with his boards in an attempt to clear the static that crackled over the signal. A half-familiar but disjointed voice echoed around the bridge as tactical and science officers strained to pinpoint the source. As the order for red alert and battlestations rang out the bridge became a hive of activity, with duty crews jumping in to man every station amid the wails of the siren and a pulsing red glow from every bulkhead. The rising hum of engines gearing up for fast manoeuvring could be heard as the crew made ready for what was coming in. Earbleat's voice was louder than the engines as she yelled at her teams to heat up every weapon.

"Got it!" Bellfish roared. "It's the *Obsidian Sky*! Repeat, *Obsidian*!"

"Get her position, tactical! Comms, tell her we're on our way! Get that grid full down and home in! Where in hell is she?" Ahxenta's voice rang out. "Helm, prepare to come off the bypass at speed once we have her. All stations, web in!"

"Aye, ma'am!" various voices replied as the captain's boards came alive with ship's departments signalling readiness for action.

"Just over the boundary in Mu space!" called Gliss.

The captain's eyes were fixed on the grid as she spat out orders. "Box, plot an intercept direct to her position! Dox, get us there now! Earbleat, run weapons hot and get *Loki* ready to ride! Prep secondary bridge, Tallica. Any more on what *Obsidian's* facing?"

"She has three hostiles on her! Repeat, three hostiles, Cap! Signal's breaking up but getting more data now: they're warships, huge and they're getting through her defences!" Bellfish hollered.

"Confirm we're on our way! Crizz, I want every last ion of power out of those engines! Cook it, helm!"

By the time *Arianrhod* had crossed into Mu and come within range, the *Obsidian* was hard beset. The three hostiles *were* huge and Azular was quick to confirm that they were similar to craft they had met in the war, with lifesigns that read as highly cybernetic. As *Arianrhod* was ordered into the attack with no holds barred, Azular called out that the enemy was poorly manned, low on weaponry and with scarred hulls indicative of previous conflict. That did not lessen the barrage that was searing the fast-moving *Obsidian* and the black-hulled ship was returning fire even as she wove an intricate pattern to outwit her adversaries, her strength weakening as shield after shield cut out.

"Helm, take us in close to that nearest ship, under her!" bellowed Ahxenta. "Target forr'ad torpedoes on that weak spot and punch a hole! Gunnery crews, fire at will; take out anything in your sights."

"Second ship is turning to engage!" Gliss bawled. "She's targeting! Incoming missiles! *Obsidian's* pulling back, she's got nothing left!"

Arianrhod's hull plates vibrated to deadly fire but her shields held. Her wave of torpedoes cut through her target's weak defences like a blade through butter and a section of hostile hull blew off in a gout of flame, but the great hulk turned in a slow arc and came on, oblivious to the rain of fire that seared her flanks.

"Dox get us out of here!" Ahxenta roared. "She's going to ram!"

Arianrhod spun away from the burning craft but the second ship was closing and letting loose torpedoes. Suddenly a phalanx of tiny lights speared out from one of her side bays.

"Damn! They're deploying fighters!" the first mate hissed.

"Tallica, man auxiliary weapons and get that ship! Gunnery crew two, take down those fighters! Earbleat, deploy *Loki* now and send her after that beast on the *Obsidian*. Hit it with everything you have!"

"Another ship coming in but not off the bypass!" yelled Gliss. "Unknown configuration! She's big and she's fast!"

"Trajectory suggests she's come from Starfall!" Greffy called out.

Ahxenta had no time to take in the stranger as Dox had propelled the ship into an upward spiral to avoid a torpedo spread that had got lock-on and she was thrown to the side, her seat restraints straining to cope. As the chief engineer called out that they had lost a chunk of aft shielding and an auxiliary engine, their first adversary exploded in an almighty ball of fire, the energy of the explosion spreading out in a wave that caught *Arianrhod* and sent her spinning off into space.

Emergency lighting had kicked in and almost every ship's station was calling in damage. The secondary bridge stood ready for power transfer but Dox had regained helm control and was coaxing the ship back on line. The holo-grid spun as external probes captured visuals and tactical and science stations strove to bring their arrays to bear to augment data flow. Enemy fire on the hull had ceased and Ahxenta could see that *Arianrhod* had been hurled a good way out. The ship closing on them had also been caught in the backlash and was way off to their starboard but seemed still to be in one piece.

"Status of *Obsidian*!" the captain hollered, trying to find her fellow PSS in the shifting holo.

"On grid!" Gliss yelled in reply. "*Loki* impacted on target hostile but caused minimal damage. What the hell… unknown ship is taking it on! Repeat, unknown is firing on third hostile vessel!"

The latest arrived craft was massive but smaller than *Arianrhod* and of an odd, almost trilateral shape. Ahxenta had seen nothing like it. The ship could move and was under formidable helm control for she swept across in a zigzag curve to come so close to her quarry that they almost touched. The bridge crew had no time to wonder for a shout from tactical warned that their late antagonist was heading back in at speed. A quick look at her ops boards told the captain that her arsenal was seriously depleted and her defences well below par.

"Helm, evasive! Try to outrun her but bring us into a position that we can use our aft torpedo arrays: they still pack a punch."

As *Arianrhod* strained in a tightening curve to outwit the hostile on her tail, an exclamation from Gliss caused heads to slew round.

"She's breaking up! Unknown is breaking up!"

Seconds later, Azular called out to contradict the assertion.

"Negative on break-up! She's split in two! Unknown ship has split and both units are fully operational!"

"Track them!" the captain thundered.

"One unit heading this way! The other is maintaining an assault on *Obsidian's* opponent!" That was Azular, who had his arrays set on the incoming stranger and was trying to scan for everything he could.

The wedge-shaped part-ship had been marked by the hostile and deemed unfriendly, for the attack on *Arianrhod* abruptly ceased as the vast alien turned to face the newcomer, spears of phase-fire spewing from her forr'ad weapons emplacements.

"Hostile reads low in energy and she's slowing, Captain!" Greffy called over. "That half-ship's dancing all over her!"

"Then let's give her a hand," Ahxenta barked. "Dox, get us close enough to loose aft torpedoes! Earbleat, target her main engines and send all we have left down her throat!"

The weapons officer lost no time and as soon as she had the range she sent the final salvo herself. "That's for *Loki*, you great bastard!"

The hostile slewed and moments later her main hull imploded into a mass of metal and flame. Dox had quickly pulled out to avoid the eruptive flak. The main holo-grid stabilised as the ship was brought back to an even keel. Ahxenta stared at the fluid starfield, trying to identify the stranger amongst the shapes drifting across. It was Azular who located her and highlighted her in a ring of light. He had every scanner under his control aimed at her position.

"Tallica, take the damage reports," the captain instructed the first mate, who had reclaimed her usual position. "Comms, get me a link to the *Obsidian* and to whoever's in command of *that*, if you can."

Even as she spoke, Bellfish broke in. "Captain! Captain Bluejohn for you, ma'am!"

"Put him on speaker and try to get a visual. Tactical, check for any other hostiles close by, including those fighters that were loosed. And Azular, get a fix on whatever *that* is holding position out there."

Bellfish sent the link through to the main holo-grid and Bluejohn's tired face materialised. His bridge was in chaos.

"Grey! Are you okay?"

"Barely," he grimaced. "I've hardly a shield to my name and not enough firepower to warm my hands. We had a hull breach close to main engineering but we managed to seal it. Casualty list's stretching as well," he added bleakly as he scanned his boards. "You?"

"Shielding and hull plates hit bad and I've lost an auxiliary engine but we're in better shape than you. But what in blazes is that ship that hauled in out of some other bypass at that speed? My science team reckoned it came from beyond zone edge."

"We're about to find out," Apnis warned. "The unit that flew to our assist is closing – trying to get clear of the debris field, I think."

"Captain!" Azular's voice cracked in emotion. "Her shape's novel and she has structural elements I can't identify, but her hull comp's reading Norvallan." He looked dazed.

"Are you sure?"

"Yes, ma'am. And the second unit is heading this way. She must have taken out the hostile facing the *Obsidian*, as I read nothing left of that but flak."

"Tactical, confirm!"

"Reading no more hostiles, ma'am; but the second blip *is* on a line to the first. She's a tad larger but essentially similar in shape."

"I read a lot of damage to her hull, Captain," Azular put in. "She's intact but she's taken a beating."

Ahxenta traded a look with Bluejohn but before either could say a word, Bellfish cut in. "Captain! I have a link from the closer unit!"

"Put it on speaker!"

"*Arianrhod*, request a visual link," a voice crackled.

"Put it up and make sure the *Obsidian* stays on channel."

As the holo sharpened, the features of the uniformed individual in the command chair of the Norvallan half-ship could be made out. It was a known face but not one that anyone on the *Arianrhod* expected to see. Even Ahxenta's jaw dropped.

"Lieutenant Inks! What in blazes are you doing there?"

"Commander Inks," he corrected her with a quirky smile. "And I'm about to attempt to reconnect to the main hull of my ship. She's losing stability and we need to move quickly but her comms are out."

"Your ship? You're in command of a Norvallan ship?"

"First mate of a free trader," he clarified as a call from one of his officers alerted him that the primary hull was closing for alignment.

"Stand by, Captain," he said abruptly as his eyes took in his holo-grid and his boards and he leaned over to his right to check a nearby station. "Get her on fine grid! Comms, do we have them yet?"

"What the… she's deployed external comms and data units!" was the strident reply. "We've got them! Signal clear – patching through."

"All stations, ready for conjunction! Helm, link guidance systems and bring us to optimum position; steady as she goes!" Inks called.

"Optimum aye: confirm all intersects show stable, Commander!" a voice responded. "Both hulls read go for conjunction!"

"Deploy tractors to keep her steady and link at your discretion, helm! Engineering, ready us for post link-up!" Inks commanded.

On *Arianrhod's* bridge Ahxenta had ordered the main holo-grid to show the slow dance as the two great wedges came together. Contact with the Norvallan ship had been held on a separate channel and the crew could hear staccato commentary as the units were brought ever closer, to merge with a final lock-on of external clamps. It took time for numerous couplings to be made and conditions to be equalised in both hulls. As they watched, the lustre of an outer defence cloak grew and one by one a net of tiny lights spread over the entire shape.

"Linkage fully established! Main systems read operational!" a voice heavy with released tension called out. "Hull auto-repairs initiated!"

The auxiliary monitor that had maintained the visual to the bridge of the Norvallan half-ship showed Inks' look of immense relief as his fingers scampered over his ops boards. "Comms, get me the main bridge! *Arianrhod* and *Obsidian Sky*, stand by."

Inks was back on line in minutes. "Our systems are stabilising," he told the two captains. "We have hook-ups to make but we're on it. What direct help do you need, Captain Bluejohn, Captain Ahxenta? I suggest we get out of here as soon as possible as it's not safe."

"The *Obsidian's* the priority, Commander," Ahxenta declared as she took a closer look at Inks.

Her scrutiny took in his uniform and she realised that he was not in Norvallan garb. In fact it looked more like the armoured suiting that Thal's people favoured. "Who do you fly for, and what's your ship called, Mr Inks? You haven't told us."

Jesse Inks smiled tranquilly. "We fly for the Starfall fleet and my ship is the *SS Moonstone*, Captain. This is the *Stone*; our main hull's the *Moon*. Captain Bluejohn, what are your immediate requirements?"

Bluejohn swiftly listed his most urgent wants. Only minutes later the efficient Inks notified him that an auto shuttle was loading and once his ship was stable she would head in closer to *Obsidian* to send it across. A medic Inks could not spare, however, as he had several injured personnel and the *Moonstone* was under-crewed, being on her shakedown cruise.

"That must have been a damn short shakedown cruise," Ahxenta commented as Inks requested *Arianrhod's* pressing needs.

"Just done final testing and training the crew up on her handling," he stated as a note on his boards caught his eye. "If you'd send your list across to my comms, Captain Ahxenta, I'll link back from the main bridge. I'm heading there now and I'm sure my captain would like a word with you and Captain Bluejohn. Inks out."

"He was always smart, but how did he end up in Thal's fleet in a Norvallan ship that looks like a glitzy slice of cake?" Apnis asked.

"I've no doubt we'll find out. Prepare to manoeuvre us closer to the *Obsidian*, helm, once the *Moonstone* is on the move. Did you catch all that, Grey?" Ahxenta asked her opposite number.

"Did I ever. That's one story I want to hear over a long beer, once I've got my crew patched up and my ship back on an even keel. But where do we head? Wester 287 and Minch Fettin are the nearest but I don't reckon on either of them. And I'll need towed: I won't make it under my own power."

"There *is* one place that's probably closer," Azular stated aloud.

"You've got to be kidding, Doc!" Greffy turned, round-eyed – he had noted the star charts the senior science officer was examining.

"I'm not going to like this, am I?" the captain questioned.

"Starfall," was the calm reply.

As a joint outrush of breath swept the bridge and the first mate's eyes shot wide, Ahxenta raised a sardonic eyebrow. "I thought so: I don't like it. I want a word or three with Commander Inks and this captain of his. Any thoughts on who it might be, Dr Azular?"

The reply was a long-suffering look as Azular turned back to his station and the captain and first mate exchanged looks. Ten minutes later, Bellfish announced that he had the *Moonstone* on the comm for the captains of both PSS vessels.

The bridge of the primary hull of the *Moonstone* was larger than her secondary bridge but not equal to those of the *Vanguard* class ships. A smaller space, it was more colourful than the utilitarian PSS vessels and linked consoles stretched from deck to overheads, with an upper gallery behind the control position. All the details were assimilated in an instant, for the eyes of the bridge crews of the *Arianrhod* and the *Obsidian Sky* were caught by the two in the dual command chair. Jesse Inks had made it back and was seated on the left of his captain.

The *Moonstone's* commander gave a token nod. "Captain Ahxenta: good to see you again. Captain Bluejohn, a pleasure to meet you."

"Captain Kerrix," Ahxenta declared. "I'm not greatly surprised to see you aboard a Norvallan ship but I *am* surprised to see you in that uniform. I didn't think you and Commander Thal saw eye to eye."

"No comment," she replied dryly. "But we need to get away from here as there's trouble by Canna and we don't want to run into it if it spreads. We're preparing to move to your position, Captain Bluejohn. The shuttle with your supplies is ready to go. I have hull auto-repair drones that can be sent over to reinforce your hull breach externally and I have enough patches to shore up some of your hull plates also, Captain Ahxenta, at least until we can get to our repair base."

"And your repair base would be?" Ahxenta questioned.

"Starfall, as I'm sure you're aware. I believe it's changed since last I was there. Hit it, helm," she ordered. "If you follow us, Captain Ahxenta, we can send a cargo pod over with your requisites."

"Agreed."

"I'll be in touch," Kerrix told the two captains.

As her hand moved to cut the link her eyes slid over the holo that was before her to *Arianrhod's* science station, where Azular was avidly watching. Her face softened into a smile as her image faded.

"Aw!" came the dulcet tones of Box from the navi-helm console.

"You hush your mouth!" his mate warned in a furious hiss as she prepared *Arianrhod* to follow the *Moonstone* to the *Obsidian's* position.

The crew of the three ships had much to do and the exchange of comms over the next two hours related to supply runs and makeshift repairs to the PSS craft. The *Moonstone* was well-equipped, as she was a novel design direct from the Norvallan fleet dockyard. She was also stocked with gear for her new home of Starfall base and had been on the way there when her tactical ops picked up the hostiles on a long-range scan and realised they had a target.

Captains Ahxenta and Bluejohn had exchanged rapid private links on the issue of accepting hospitality from the Starfall fleet. Bluejohn knew less than did his fellow captain but despite having had a brief history of Kerrix, he was wary. Their dilemma was that there was no other base closer that did not pose danger and neither the *Obsidian* nor the *Arianrhod* was in a fit state to argue if they met opposition. Ahxenta was clear: they call Kerrix and ask awkward questions.

Kerrix took the comm in her office and was open about her ship and her links to Thal. The minor details she would not articulate but the *Moonstone* had been ready for trials and with the aid of Admiral Posettix, the Telziltic captain and Thal she had claimed her. Her own fleet had refused her a command on the direct order of the Protector of her home colony of Valla Key but he had approved the transfer of the *Moonstone* to her at a price. She had taken on many of the crew of the defunct *Twin Star*, as well as a few disaffected others.

Ahxenta shook her head, disbelieving, seeing Bluejohn looking incredulous. "You were just handed a ship? I don't believe it."

"I mentioned a price. The Protector of Valla Key is my younger half-brother. Admiral Posettix, backed by Captain Heltakt of Telzilt, broadcast publicly that my maternal line is more high-ranking than inferred. And as I had long been legitimised as my father's daughter, it was pointed out to the Protector that not only did I rank him, I had more right to sit in his seat than he did. It gave him enough of a jolt to trade. I'm no longer a Norvallan citizen and I've resigned all rights to my hereditary property and to any position on Norvalla or any of her colonies. But I have a damn good ship and she's unique: she was designed as the new Protector's flagship but she was so expensive to build that his advisers won't give him free rein to build another."

"You're stateless, so you've signed on with Thal and his fleet of beweaponed renegades for a cheap berth at Starfall and the use of the smart tech they've been able to lift over the years? What does he get out of this cosy partnership?" Ahxenta asked cynically.

"I'm half-Telziltic, Captain. And Commander Thal needs all the ships he can get. He's taken heavy losses recently, some of them in aiding the ISP Alliance and a few of *your* people, so I've heard. I get a base for my ship and my people; he gets an extra ship and contacts. I have links beyond the mapped zones and I know my way around."

"How convenient," Ahxenta retorted. "And what's *his* link to this Telzilt place? He's got some issue there that eats at him."

"He has, it does and I won't tell you. It's his concern and highly private. If you want to know you'll have to ask him, but I do *not* advise it. He's at Starfall and I've spoken to him about this attack."

Ahxenta was sceptical but continued icily, "So you're saying we'll be welcome at Starfall?"

"I wouldn't go that far. But Thal *has* sanctioned it. And you'll have the wherewithal to repair your ships."

"And how much will *that* cost us?" Bluejohn snapped harshly.

"It won't." Kerrix was short as she tapped a key on her board in response to a message that had flashed up.

"What about Inks? Where and when did you recruit him? And how?" the captain of the *Arianrhod* demanded.

"We do *not* have time for this, Captain. We can discuss it in more depth at Starfall but we have to leave. I've had word that there's been a skirmish this side of Minch Fettin and that's too close for comfort. I realise that you find it difficult to trust me, though you don't have much option," she said ruefully, eyeing them. "But there *is* someone that might convince *you* at least, Captain Ahxenta. Come in," she said into her communit, to someone who had clearly been awaiting the signal, for the door opened almost at once.

"Meet my second mate, who's also tactical and security chief, *and* the one who persuaded Mr Inks to sign on with us. Sit," she invited.

"Captain Ahxenta," the officer acknowledged. "I don't think I've met you before, Captain Bluejohn."

"Commander Levettiza of ISP's Intelligence Division! Did you leave of your own accord or were you booted out of the service?" the captain of the *Arianrhod* enquired waspishly.

"Azular's itching for a word with Kerrix," Apnis murmured to the captain as the three ships, in support formation, manoeuvred slowly away from the assault scene on a course that would take them into unfamiliar territory and Starfall base.

"He can itch," was the equally low response. "Have you got those new nav-charts incorporated, Mr Box?" she added more loudly.

"Aye, ma'am; there's a small hyperspace track through and it's all but straight if we don't meet trouble."

"Trouble's already riding alongside," Ahxenta noted trenchantly.

"What induced Levettiza to join the *Moonstone*?" the first mate continued quietly. "I doubt it's the pay."

"I imagine she's still working for the ISP. She was aboard an ISP ship last time we spoke and she said things were moving positively, so the *Moonstone* must have been a deal at that point. Alien incursion is her speciality and now she's got all the aliens she wants. But if she *is* still ISP, Kerrix is in on it: whatever I think of *her*, she's savvy."

"If Levettiza was out there, how did she recruit Inks? And what's this Starfall base like and how come we don't have to cough up for refit? There must be a price; there's always a price," Apnis frowned.

"I've no doubt Thal will tell us when we see him."

The first thing they saw a few clicks off the bypass crossover point named Starfall Exit was the massive Starfall repair base. It circled an all but dead planet and bore little similarity to the sketchy holo of the huge scrapyard that Kerrix had given the captain months ago. There were ships under repair and under construction and the designs were as varied as the proportions. One or two were uniquely Norvallan in outline, Azular reported, as a strict voice directed them to an assigned berth. The three ships had been allocated adjoining moorings in an inner ring that was close to what looked like movable rigs.

"Call for you, ma'am, Captain Kerrix," Bellfish called over as soon as the docking struts had locked and *Arianrhod* was at station-keeping.

The *Moonstone's* captain was aware that Ahxenta would let no one near her ship unless she had triple checked them and was able to log their every move. Thal had thus grudgingly given permission for the use of *Arianrhod's* scanners for local surveillance and for a link-up to the rig that would be used for her repairs. Captain Bluejohn would be accorded the same freedom. And as Ahxenta wanted more answers, Kerrix was open to a meeting at an agreed time with both captains.

"I suggest my ship. Commander Thal will be there as I expect you have several questions for him. I'll send Commander Inks over in a shuttle to collect you. Please feel free to bring your own aides but no more than three additional officers, if you please."

"Two security and who else?" asked Apnis archly as the holo cut.

Captain Ahxenta's only reply was a warning look.

As the first mate and most of the bridge crew had expected, the senior science officer accompanied the captain to the *Moonstone* at the agreed time, four hours later. Inks had stopped off at the *Obsidian Sky* to pick up her captain and his first mate. Bluejohn had elected not to bring his own security, deeming the *Arianrhod's* sufficient.

The shuttle was the first surprise: she was sleek on the outside and smart on the inside and the flight deck could be screened, although Inks had not implemented that. Azular requested a seat alongside him and paid close attention to the flight ops. Kerrix and Levettiza were in the bay to meet them and escort them to a nearby briefing room along decks that were far from the plain and serviceable spaces with which the PSS officers were familiar.

"They came with the ship," Kerrix replied ironically to a remark by Azular that snack points and art niches were not ordinarily found along bulkheads. "They'll be replaced by storage as soon as possible."

Ahxenta noted that Kerrix had posted guards outside the allotted briefing room and so left her own there. They found Thal alone in the sizeable space, where refreshment facilities were indicated and the officers invited to help themselves and choose seats.

"You're welcome to set up your own jammers and recorders," the captains were told after the taciturn commander of Starfall had been introduced to Bluejohn and his first mate, Stone. Both did: Thal had his own devices clearly in view.

Captain Bluejohn's initial concern was the return required for the first rate repairs to the *Obsidian Sky* that were now in progress. Such quality gear and services were expensive and he did not for a moment imagine that his thanks would be sufficient. Thal's only response was a gesture towards Kerrix, as if inviting her comment.

"I did Commander Thal a favour and it's payback," she said.

"It must have been one helluva favour," Ginger Stone remarked.

"Not your concern," she replied.

Ahxenta, her nose twitching, had her own ideas. "It wouldn't be related to your overriding interest in that Telzilt place would it?"

His indrawn breath of fury was palpable, but it was Kerrix' intense stare, her warning shake of the head and quick cutthroat gesture that alerted the captain that this was a taboo topic. "Leave it be, Captain, it's no business of yours," she cautioned with a look of deep concern at the evidently enraged Thal.

"Your pity I don't need!" he snarled, having read her face.

"I advise that you keep that anger of yours ice cold, Commander. Cold preserves; it means you can serve your revenge at the right time *and* to deadly effect," she advised frostily, her eyes narrowing in ire.

Azular, sitting to the left of the captain of the *Moonstone*, had been taking in the scene and had turned his sharp eyes and his pet scanner on Thal. "You no longer have external cyber-attachments but you *do* have new shielded implants. Would that be part of the price?"

The commander's furious hiss was interrupted by a soft laugh as Kerrix turned to the Berzic man. "You don't miss a trick, do you?"

The pressure of her hand on his thigh tightened as her keen glance and slight shake of the head warned him not to pursue the topic. His captain was not so constrained.

"Well? Answer the questions. We're not here for the good of our health and you know as well as I do that information is the key to any battle, personal or otherwise. You don't do all this for us for nothing and as it's more than clear that you want to rid the known galaxy and elsewhere of these damn hostiles, you must have a damn good reason that you'd risk so many ships and lives to do it."

Thal was terse to the point of rudeness. The favour had involved the removal of the last vestiges of the technology that tied him and the crew of the *Kel'Moth* to their hostile ex-masters – and in his case, implantation of a Norvallan language analyser-translator and a visual insert enabling him to scan others for metallic adjuncts. The latter would boost his innate sensitivity to those altered like himself and give him an edge in finding the last of the spies that he was certain were still undermining his operation. It was one of those spies that had betrayed the position of a base that he and his people had set up outside the Gamma-Beta border near sector sixteen to cater for the vulnerable of their kind and the base and everyone and everything on it and around it had been utterly destroyed.

Ahxenta glanced at Levettiza; the captain had heard of the base from Thal months before and the ISP had known of action in the area but had assumed it was an old raider stronghold, she told him. She was sorry for the losses suffered by his people. But that still did not explain the Telzilt connection, she continued remorselessly.

"My partner was Telziltic. She and our child were on that base, as were almost all the children of my people." Thal smiled dourly at the shock on Ahxenta's face. "Yes, children: we *are* still human, most of us. And we've been fighting for our lives and our rights for longer than you or most are aware. I was taken twelve standard galactic years ago. Some of my people were taken twenty or more years ago, as children, as adults, as elders. We've had a long fight. We want it done. And now that the hole in space you call the mapped galaxy and the wider spaces outside its borders are involved, it's their fight too. And once it *is* over – we want real lives and our own place."

"You were right, way back," Ahxenta nodded at Levettiza. "A need for a stable future, security, a living where you won't be hunted. Yes, you deserve that," she agreed. "Your organisation must be vast and very well controlled. You once said you had spies in a number of salient places, Commander Thal. Does that include the ISP?"

"Not me, if that's what you're hinting, Captain," Levettiza cut in.

"That is not your concern, Captain Ahxenta. What else do you deem it imperative to know?"

"You, Mr Inks," was the reply as she turned to the first mate of the *Moonstone.* "What's your story?"

"Now that *does* concern me," Levettiza conceded. "The captain had asked for my help in finding crew for the *Moonstone.* She's a big ship, only so many signed on from Norvalla and her colonies and she had need of people familiar with our sectors, since that's where much of her trade will inevitably be based. I'd heard through my sources of the *Tallulah's* problems so I called an Intelligence friend on Nyx and asked him to contact Jesse and sound him out; and attest that it *was* a genuine offer. Naturally, he insisted on a whole lot more," she smiled at Inks. "So I linked to him and persuaded him that the *Moonstone* was a good bet. He would be first mate and ranked commander. I'd heard enough about him to know that he was an exceptional officer. The *Kel'Beth* out of Twilight station off the Curtain Nebula picked him up at Nyx and he came through to Norvalla on her."

"I know the *Kel'Beth.* But why did you leave the *Tallulah* at Nyx, apart from the obvious reason of Dyne-Bek?" Ahxenta asked.

"I have contacts there."

"And?"

"With respect, it's none of your business, Captain."

"Precisely," Kerrix interrupted. "Anything else, Captain Ahxenta, Captain Bluejohn?"

"A heck of a lot," Bluejohn said tersely. "Why are our ships being targeted? We're traders, we don't go out of our way to interfere with these damn hostiles."

"They're greedy. They want total control and every advantage that keeps them on top. *That* means as much advanced technology as they can steal and the upper hand of anyone that might be more or have more than them," Thal said bluntly. "That's why one of their moles on my ship *and* others devised the tracking of and attacks on Captain Kerrix months ago. And they bear grudges: it's inherent in some of them. That's why you've been a repeated target, Captain Ahxenta. It's become their objective to take you down and as so far they've failed, you motivate others to resist; *and* you scare them."

"She scares a lot of people," Kerrix commented quietly.

"The PSS fleet tends to fight rather than run from opposition, unlike most," Thal said stiffly. "And you inflicted heavy losses on them, Captain, particularly at Mellifly. Many of them, their allies and their hangers-on fled and found bolt-holes elsewhere including in the Web at Merkat and other important centres of various kinds."

"A hostile med facility on Minch Fettin," Ahxenta remarked.

"Minch Fettin was already on line, but as a result of the influx it expanded to Ellas. And there are hostile bases that still build ships, worlds they've subverted or overrun over the years. But we, you and others are grinding them down. What else do you wish to know?"

"I don't see how this language analyser you spoke of and surgery to your crew can be worth the price of refitting two starships, given the damage we sustained," Ginger Stone said suspiciously.

"Believe me Commander, that device and its implantation alone cost much more than the refit of the *Arianrhod* and the *Obsidian Sky*," Azular told him. "So how *did* you contrive it?" he asked of Kerrix.

"I called in favours and resorted to bribery," she stated equably. "But I got an expert surgeon as a chief medical officer out of it."

"So Thal gets even more radical tech, your very fancy ship as part of his fleet, your contacts from beyond the edge; and apart from a berth here and a heap of hassle, what do you get?" asked Ahxenta.

"I got out of where I was, Captain, and the trip home. It was Thal who led the *Twin Star* to Merkat and guided her through to Norvalla. Not that that quite worked as planned," she shrugged. "I owed him for that and for his testimony at my court-martial. As I owed you for the help you've given me, despite the fact that I stole your shuttle."

"We're even on that score," the captain shot back, not amused.

She conceded that with a slight inclination of her head but refused to be drawn on her present business, the role of Levettiza aboard her ship and her place within a vast operation that encompassed so many ships and bases. Thal was equally as uncooperative and with a look at Bluejohn, Ahxenta realised she would get no more, called a halt and began to wrap up her gear.

Once back at the shuttle bay and away from the prying ears of the few crewmen about the *Moonstone*, Ahxenta turned to Kerrix.

"You trust Thal?" she asked forthrightly. "He's never been open, he's ill-tempered, he's sour and he has a streak of inflexibility in him that blinds him to the needs or the worth of others."

"He always was sour, possibly a reaction to what happened to him after he was abducted. And I suspect obstinacy is part of his nature and what helped him free himself. But when that base was destroyed a bit of him died inside; it's been dead ever since and it's now his main reason for this single-minded vendetta against the hostiles."

"How does he control such a huge outfit and not come unstuck?"

"I suggest you ask him," was the cool reply. "I'm not party to his mind or his methods. Mr Inks will pilot you back to the *Arianrhod*."

"Clan Starwain," Ahxenta persisted. "His ears pricked up at that back in the *Half Moon*. What's his connection to that – and you?"

"He told you. His partner was Telziltic, an intelligence agent, I think, and involved in the set-up of his group and his fleet. She was taken when the hostiles first jumped in to set up a base on Telzilt. She belonged to that Clan, as do I. It shook him when he found out. It still does. Perhaps one of the reasons he was keen to help me."

"And why are you so keen to help me?"

"You're damn well aware of part of the reason," Kerrix fired back hotly. "Your shuttle, Captain. I'll no doubt talk to you again."

"Count on it," was the mordant return.

"What in hell was that about, Cinnabar?" Bluejohn asked her in a low voice once the party was safely strapped in for the first leg of the short trip to the *Obsidian*.

"Long story. For now, what do you make of all this?"

"Can we trust them – and her?"

Ahxenta nodded. "Oddly enough, yes I think we can. Her at least; I know enough of her to know that she's straight as a die, mostly. As for Thal – he's still a loose cannon and I'd keep my guard up. And as soon as our repairs are done, we head back to safer places. I'll hang on until *Obsidian's* fit to move out and see what else I can find out. I noticed Levettiza made off the second the meeting was done – to track us from the bridge, I expect."

Ahxenta had to field more searching questions before Bluejohn and Stone were set down and *Arianrhod* was reached. As soon as she and her crew were aboard she dismissed her escort and told Azular to accompany her to the briefing room where her senior officers had been bidden to hear the results of the meeting.

The captain gave a quick summary before Azular was directed to give his views of what had not been said. He was confident that the three from the *Moonstone* had been largely open, although some issues had been veiled. One thing had struck him as they were led through the ship: his scans on the way had included two crewmen with cyber-implants that bore the scars of recent surgery. His inference was that they were originally part of the Starfall fleet. The ship *was* still acutely short-handed; he had learned thus much from Kerrix. As for Thal, he was unreadable for the most part and there was a deep anger in him that still burned, but not for them. Deeply protective of his people and controlling by nature, the science officer believed he would stop at little to deal with anyone or anything that got in his way.

"Including us," Crizz Cottontail grunted shortly.

"Indeed, Chief. But as I believe Commander Levettiza once told you, Captain, the ISP had been watching Thal and his fleet for some while – and I wonder if that was part of the reason that Levettiza was released to join the *Moonstone*."

"Didn't your Ms Kerrix tell you?" asked Earbleat sarcastically.

"No, *Captain* Kerrix did not. I sense that we can trust Thal up to a point but I recommend that we don't outstay our welcome."

"I still think this deal that we and the *Obsidian* get refitted as Thal owes a favour to Kerrix is fishy," sniffed Earbleat.

"I'm sure Thal's getting more out of the Norvallan connection than he's saying," the captain agreed. "But he won't tell. Back to post, all of you. Not you, Tallica, I want a word."

"Judging by the smile on his face and the gleam in his eye, he was not let down by his reception," Apnis smirked as the door closed. "Was he holding her hand under the table?"

"They both behaved like the officers they are," was the dry retort. "But I need you to keep a tight grip on all ship's sections and make sure that our people keep their beady eyes and sharp noses on what's going on around the ship. A fly sneezes and I want to know about it. Any crew from Starfall come aboard and they have security on them. I've spoken to Grey and he's doing the same. The faster we're done the better. And now I have to see Lindell about what trade we can pick up and I'll try to get the *Emerald* online and see how she's fixed."

"Aye, Cap. And Azular?"

"I'll be having words there as well; now he's got a girlfriend in the Starfall fleet, we may as well profit by it."

"Good luck with that, Cap, you'll need it."

Ahxenta found out little else about the misfit fleet and its aloof leader but Kerrix called her two days later to notify her of the results of the clash near Minch Fettin that had expedited their run to Starfall. It had involved a Treskk heavy carrier, a shot-up hostile interceptor and two ISP warships. The carrier was being tracked by the ISP on suspicion of hauling contraband when her master decided that the chance-met interceptor would make an easy target. He was wrong and the hostile had all but taken his vessel apart when the ISP ships stepped in, ended the action and netted the interceptor. *She* had tried to run and a boarding party found out why: as well as a load of complex micro-medical gear, she was carrying human cargo, some of whom had boarded willingly and some who had not. One of the former was Dr Mazy Herta. The craft also had a small crew of human-like beings, all of whom were now with ISP Intelligence. The ship had been set for Canna and a node on the covert bypass that crossed Mu to K457:003.

Her destination beyond that was unknown.

The source of the information had been Levettiza and Kerrix was frank over her second mate's links to the ISP: the advantages to her of a highly skilled Berzic officer, contacts within mapped sectors and ways into ISP nets far offset any negatives. Ahxenta held her peace and consulted Azular, who had had a few recent exchanges with the captain of the *Moonstone*. He agreed with Kerrix and as far as he was aware, Levettiza's first loyalty was to her captain and her ship and not the ISP. Azular was also aware of a subtle nuance, difficult to define, that led him to suspect that there were plans afoot that involved the future of the Starfall fleet, but what these were escaped him and Xanna would tell him nothing. His request for a trip to the *Moonstone*, if Captain Kerrix could be persuaded to grant a tour, was quashed by his captain. As long as they were in Thal's stronghold, she would not sanction unnecessary excursions.

Another three days brought the *Obsidian Sky* up to a spec where she could fly. Ahxenta had been in frequent contact with Bluejohn and both captains were impressed by the speed and quality of the repairs to their ships. Neither had heard from Thal over that time but his ship was still in dock. The reason became clear when, repair rigs retracted and extraneous kit removed, they were hailed with the news that the *Kel'Moth* would escort them out. Thal's suggested route was via his base by Sunrise Exit to Arrissia, where the two ships should have safe onward passage. He had business elsewhere.

Ahxenta and Bluejohn agreed. Both were eager to be on their way and their weary crews were looking forward to normality. The former had put out feelers for current news in her regular trading ports and had been assured that things were quieter. A late link to Levettiza had confirmed that the ISP and its Allies were gaining ground and the number of run-ins was markedly down.

"So maybe our war's over," Tallica Apnis commented as she set her boards in preparation for departure.

"I'm not counting on it," Ahxenta replied gruffly. "There's always a bully out there with stones to throw. But let's hit the flightpath. The quicker we're back in free space the better. Course laid in, Mr Box?"

"Yes ma'am."

"Then let's wave goodbye and get us the hell out of here. Shake us loose, Ms Dox and prepare to follow our sheepdog to the bypass."

"Aye, ma'am."

Their sheepdog turned into a pair for the *Kel'Moth* had no sooner swung out ahead of the two PSS vessels than the *Moonstone* hove in behind. That ship would join them as far as Sunrise, they were told, and then continue on the line that led to the new Starfall fleet base of Twilight Station off the edge of zone Lambda.

Ahxenta used the hours that it took to traverse the bypass to scout for trade along her intended route back to *Arianrhod's* usual haven of the Web. She was given unexpected help from Levettiza, for a link with news of an ISP contract to transport four huge cargo pods from Arrissia to the ISP holding station of Silverglass was on the table. The captain was suspicious and called for details. The pods held the goods from the Treskk ship that had been downed near Minch Fettin, she was told. The ISP wanted them closer to an inspection point where they could be sifted out thoroughly and had no spare ships to convey them. And the ISP was not about to trust the Starfall fleet with such a cargo. Ahxenta was welcome to carry out whatever checks she chose on the payload. And the fee was substantial. She agreed.

The captain was wary enough to check in with other contacts and those with whom she was able to connect verified that trade was on the rise. There had been fewer raids over the past month, although sporadic skirmishes had been marked by their ferocity and the direct involvement of ISP and Allied vessels. Almost every zone had seen conflict but Lambda and Delta had been the most recently affected and on that basis, the captain called Admiral Zillah at Freskat Six for an update. The response gave her food for thought.

Freskat had seen little trouble close to home since last they talked, but the admiral disclosed that there *had* been action near Hespera and a failed raid on Blue Delta further out. She would say no more and on impulse, Ahxenta contacted her nephew. He was worried: the Freskat home fleet was on alert and local hospitals had been advised to expect casualties, according to his partner. A few odd ships had come into port and by their descriptions Ahxenta deduced that they were part of the Starfall fleet. As she scrutinised the holo of the two systems mentioned by the admiral her eyes were drawn to the hostile listening post of Peden that Thal had once told her of – it sat almost equidistantly between Hespera Two and Blue Delta. She called the *Moonstone* to have a word with Captain Kerrix about her destination and was curtly told that it was not her concern.

32: ENDGAMES

The commander of the *Kel'Moth* made an abrupt farewell at the node of Sunrise Exit. His course implied that he was en route to his nearby base, but that may have been a blind in Ahxenta's view. The parting with the *Moonstone* had been civil as she was to remain on the bypass, but a vague disquiet implied that Kerrix did not relish her next task and Azular had been unable to prise the details from her. The captain of the *Arianrhod* sighed deeply as she ordered their onward course set for Arrissia. The *Obsidian Sky* would hold there for a cargo, Bluejohn had told her, and he also wanted to inspect the new armaments with which his ship had been fitted at Starfall base. He was still doubtful of Thal's motives for the aid he had given them.

Azular was aware that his captain had learned something that was giving her unease and at the first opportunity he asked for a private talk. Ahxenta had already ordered comms to track every ISP and other network available for news on any hostile or related activity and had sent out a query on the Ultraviolet III. That had raised a reply from Goodsocks of the *Emerald*. She had been shifting small loads between Stella Triplet and Stella Marina and had noted the increased presence of military vessels just off the node at the latter. Goodsocks' hunch was that the Alliance was building up to some intense action. Azular had his own concerns. He had been brooding on the elusive atmosphere of plans in the wind that he had detected on their short visit to the *Moonstone* and in his later talks to Kerrix. It involved Thal's fleet, he was certain. The captain had also been turning ideas around and recalling the less than effective first attempt to take out a number of hostile bases and ships in one fell swoop, was suspicious that this was a repeat. One of the targets had to be Peden Post, but as Freskat was on alert and local medical facilities had been mobilised, there had to be more to it. It was possibly that if leaks in the chain of command *had* led to the glitches in the previous ISP mission, the present action was likely to come unstuck unless the leaks had been corked.

"Has Thal thrown in his lot with the ISP and its allies?" Azular asked, more of himself than Ahxenta. "He claims to be a trader but many of his ships are battlecruisers and better equipped than Alliance dreadnoughts. He says he lost a large number but he still seems to have some in reserve – including the *Moonstone*."

"We've seen her in a fight and she'll hold her own," the captain said incisively. "But what's scaring the socks off people about what's expected to go down? And what does Thal get at the end of the day if he pitches in for the Alliance? But there's nothing we can do. We're for Arrissia and we look after our own. Our friends in the war zone, *if* that's what it is, will have to look out for themselves."

There was an ISP corvette awaiting *Arianrhod* at their endpoint to oversee the loading of the Silverglass cargo. The task was finished as quickly as an in-depth series of tactical and science scans allowed. Captain Bluejohn in the interim had called every local contact he had for any news in relation to military or other action. He drew a blank.

It was with deep relief that Ahxenta gave the order to move out. She had decided on a direct route to Silverglass as every source she tried bore out the general report that the way was clear. It would be a long trip but it would bring *Arianrhod* into familiar territory. The *Obsidian* was hanging fire, as her promised cargo for Fyvie Major was not ready to load. She would be on *Arianrhod's* tail in a day or so.

As hours stretched into days, comms channels were ominously free of all but routine. There had been no whisper of hostile action and one link to her nephew let the captain know that nothing had shaken Freskat's peace. *Arianrhod* had been on a fast run through the bypass for fifteen days when alarm bells rang. From garbled messages and bulletins spearing across space, it seemed that the hostiles had called in outside forces and were attempting to do to the Alliance what it had planned to do to them. Freskat was under attack from ships out of an unnamed world near Peden Post and from a hiding place in the Star Desert. An attack force had made into the minor Coalition-held sector of zone Beta and there were rumours of actions elsewhere.

Arianrhod by that time had passed Vrackin Twelve and the misty glow of the Silverglass Nebula was off starboard. As far as Ahxenta knew, the only known nearby hostile outpost of Zeta Dixt had been destroyed, it was behind them and it was too far off the bypass to cause them harm. She ordered weapons on standby and intensified shielding and cloaking even so, and held the ship at amber alert. They were closing on Silverglass and would make the station in a matter of hours. As a safeguard, she did not call in their approach.

"What the... Cap! Two ships have jumped *onto* the bypass! There must be an unlisted node! Armed and making for us!" Gliss hollered.

Ahxenta had called battlestations and ordered all weapons on line before the tactical officer had set the holo-grid to full stretch.

"Nearest locus is Ochre Valley; no data to suggest any life there," Azular called over as the two blips appeared in the grid. "They're fast, they're closing and they're hostile!"

"Turn and engage! Give them no time to think!" barked Ahxenta. "Azular, deploy the decoy astern and show it arming. Comms, warn Starglass they may have a hostile base on their doorstep. Triangulate! I want to know where they're from!"

A full-on attack had not been anticipated and the two interceptors broke formation to come in on *Arianrhod's* flanks. Earbleat let loose with a battery of the high-grade torpedoes that had been loaded at Starfall and followed them up with a barrage of phase-cannon.

"Whatever they were expecting, it wasn't this!" bawled the first mate above the scream of the engines as Dox outflew their foes to give the gunners every advantage.

Huge shards of flak blew off into space as both hostiles were cut to pieces and the captain ordered the return of the decoy. The initial angle of attack had been analysed and the probable origin was Ochre Valley, a system on the edge of nebular space with no liveable planets and no known resources. Azular had been conning over the data and the wreckage expanding abaft of them and he turned, perplexed.

"The ships were very sparsely manned, poorly armed and from what I have of their hull structure, they were recently constructed."

"Say again?" demanded Ahxenta.

"They were of recent construction. They hadn't lost their shine."

"Comms, get me whoever's in charge at Silverglass…"

"Already on comm, Cap: they want to know what's going on."

The long-distance relays of the ISP station had detected signs of the conflict and were keen to know what had transpired. The captain was sharp and advised they notify ISP HQ and send a well-armed scout to check out Ochre Valley without delay. The data collected by her teams she sent on. She also despatched an urgent message to the PSS fleet, ensuring that Bluejohn was aware, as the *Obsidian* was but a couple of days behind them.

The news alarmed the command staff of Silverglass to the extent that they called in back-up: as a fleet holding station, they had vast stores of supplies and were a prize worth picking. *Arianrhod* had no sooner docked than the captain was bidden to a classified meeting.

Three hours later Ahxenta and Apnis returned to the ship to find that the cargo had been offloaded, the fee paid and the holds made ready to take on more. Lindell had been busy and had secured a payload for Linza base that only waited the captain's approval. Consent was given and half a day later the freight was aboard. It was as final clearances were in process that another PSS made orbit. It was the *Tallulah*. She had come in via Bream on her way to Cygilla Prime to sniff out what she could, having noted the recent alert sent out by Ahxenta.

A dose of Murmur Fleetskup the captain of the *Arianrhod* did not need but she reiterated their recent encounter for his benefit when he linked in. His first mate's interjections she parried with as much grace as she could muster and called a halt as soon as she could, leaving the two to their ploys. They intended to call in at the ISP office.

"Let's get out of here before he thinks up another thing to annoy me with," Ahxenta said to the first mate. "The ISP here will keep us abreast of what goes down once they send the troops into Ochre."

"What he thinks he'll get at the office I don't know. He seems on better terms with Dyne-Bek, but he's not happy. And *she's* still far too nosy, asking where we're for next and with what. Damn cheek!"

"I noticed Tommy Buntle in the background, so he's a step closer to where he used to be," the captain commented.

"I'm not surprised Jesse Inks told them where to stick it. And I'd like to be there when they find out where and what he is now."

"You and me both," Ahxenta agreed with a wry smile as she scrutinised her boards and gave the order to move out.

Constant comms-checks on events in the charted zones had been ordered but it was a while before news began to filter in. The attack on Freskat had been repulsed thanks to aid from non-Alliance ships. A call to Zillah verified that they were part of Thal's fleet. *Arianrhod's* quick actions to defeat the hostiles off Silverglass had repercussions and the scouts sent in had found a small but well set-up shipbuilding operation. The ISP swiftly put an end to it, having deduced that it had been back-up for the now-defunct hostile base of Zeta Dixt.

"Thal's been a busy bee," the captain remarked to the first mate as ISP's relay station at Mizreel Point was passed and she resumed her chair after taking two private links. "Looks like a few of his were in salient positions including off the edge of Beta near Mellifly when the balloon went up and lent their guns to the Alliance. I've just had Myrtleberry asking about the latest I have on him. She's had reports and they're bugging her. She reckons he's up to something."

"He's always up to something," Apnis replied. "Why doesn't she ask Levettiza? She's ISP or was and is aboard one of his fleet ships."

"I did *not* mention her or anything about her ship. And the colonel told me little else other than to watch my back. One of her people intercepted a poorly-coded message to what they think was a moving transmit-receive station in Lesser Kirrin space, source unknown. The names Silverglass, *Arianrhod* and Linza were part of it."

"Damn! A *moving* relay station? That means a ship. And that data's recent. So who knows we're carrying an ISP load to an ISP base?"

"That was worrying Myrtleberry, as it might mean an ISP leak."

"What did Grey have to say that he wanted a private word?"

"*Tallulah* was still in Silverglass when the *Obsidian* made it in and they hailed him. All very civil but quizzing about his route, his cargo and about what he'd been doing for the past while. He was pissed as they refused point blank to say what they were up to. He'd no trouble on the way in but thought he'd best check his out-route to Selliden. It *was* clear, but a contact there has now sent him word of a sighting of a hostile by Matty. As he knew we were bound for Linza Base with an ISP cargo from Silverglass he thought he'd better pass it on."

"Hold a sec, Cap: Matty to Lesser Kirrin isn't more than a day's ride. And how did Grey know we were for Linza with an ISP cargo?"

"That struck me. Fleetskup told him. Naturally, Grey asked him how *he'd* got to know. He said he'd found out in the ISP office. A big mouth there had mentioned it in passing, evidently."

"Meaning Fleetskup or Dyne-Bek had asked," said Apnis.

"Looks like. Grey registered a complaint with the ISP office over it, but I doubt anything will get done. But if there are messages about us getting out there, the leak could be ISP."

"So who do you tell? Our old buddy Zillah?"

"Zillah will have her hands full."

"Levettiza?" Apnis said quietly. "She must still have ISP links."

Ahxenta cast a quick look at Azular. "I couldn't raise a link. But from here on in we're at amber alert and we run cloaked and silent."

"Aye, Cap. Recommend we detour via Silshoon, just in case."

"Good call; it'll make us a day late, but tough."

The captain gave the course change orders and sat back to think.

A little later and with long-distance scans clear, Ahxenta called a briefing over the worrying news that details about them were crossing space to shipboard relays. An ISP leak as the only source made no sense, as *Arianrhod* had been targeted too often by outfits that knew where she was likely to be. Trade reps and other client staff would know what payloads were going where, the identity of the carrier and scheduling, but routes would be unknown and those details would be insufficient to plan and execute the attacks *Arianrhod* had faced.

Hyperspace comms breaches in ISP or other large concerns could provide a store of accurate data, in Cottontail's view. Listening posts and relays were prevalent, and most were secret. Subversion of cam systems in the Web at an unheard-of scale had caused untold harm there and it was feasible that similar could be done on a wider scale if the various pieces could be pooled to form a coherent picture.

Azular disagreed. Such an operation would require a degree of cooperation that simply did not exist. It was more likely that there were several agents out there with watching briefs on the activities of individuals or concerns, who reported to a central unit. Infiltration of data relays could not be discounted, nor could the use of legitimate sources for illicit intent. The question was what sources carried news of *Arianrhod* and her doings and who had access to them.

Various possible sources and informants were debated and it was soon clear that there must be several, which made tracing them tough. The senior science officer had listened but said little else.

"So what's biting you, Azular?" the captain asked outright.

"One potential source has not been mentioned: the Ultraviolet III channel," he stated austerely.

"No way!" declared Cottontail emphatically. "Who could crack that? And it's not dependent on external relays."

"I agree it would be difficult to subvert. But there *has* been a spate of complex, high-tech tools coming in: the cargo Flatt tried to ship to Minch Fettin; Herta's illicit medical devices; Doosbak's cases of tech; maybe the Treskk contraband we delivered to Silverglass. There's also the remote possibility that the news carried on the UV-III could reach the wrong ears. Not all PSS personnel are tight-lipped."

The captain broke the silence that met Azular's statement. "I hope you're wrong. The problem with you is that you're so often right."

"Damn you," Cottontail added for good measure.

Little arose over the next days to disturb routine as *Arianrhod* sped on to her goal. There had been no news of action close to Linza or its environs but the captain refused to notify the base of their imminent arrival. She found out that there was concern that a mishap to the ship had occurred when, uncloaked and off the bypass, Ahxenta at last made the link. That *Arianrhod* had made her destination would no doubt be broadcast, as the area that they were now in was one of the busiest in the charted zones. With that in mind, cargo transfer was rapid and the ship readied for the short hop to the Web at Merkat.

She had been a long time away, months by Merkat time, and the crew expected to see changes. What they did not expect to see when they made the outer belts and their berth was the *Tallulah*.

"How in hell did *she* make it in so fast?" Apnis demanded.

"At least she's not the only PSS," the captain grunted. "The *Comet* and the *Warrior* are this side and the *Ice Spar's* further out. Once we're logged in I'll head to the harbour office and see who's there. Check in with Kit Biernop if he's about for news on Guild and security issues and if it's quiet, start the shore leave rotas. Our people need a break."

Ahxenta found Nat Holdspan in the harbour office when she paid her requisite visit. The *Nyx Warrior* had just come in from Kanelian Juxta, he told her, where he had had a run-in with a large but scarred warship intent on excising his cargo pods. The fight had been short: an unfamiliar vessel had intervened and destroyed his attacker. The stranger claimed to be the *Kel'Lath* of the Starfall fleet, from a nearby base that her commander, Olith Dun, referred to as Nexus Station.

"She was as open as that Commander Thal," Holdspan said. "But the *Kel'Lath* had seen action – she had bent hull plates and was low on arms. She wouldn't accept help and left as quickly as she'd come."

On their way to the local shuttle bay and their respective rides, the captain of the *Nyx Warrior* made discreet enquiries about Thal's ship, the *Twin Star* and Kerrix. Ahxenta bluntly told him that the *Twin Star* was gone but all else was well the last time she *had* heard, saying little more but warning him to be prudent in asking similar questions.

Back aboard, the captain found that the Web was back to as near normal as ever, apart from a heightened security status, the result of the recent all-out assault on hostile elements that had penetrated the near and far reaches of the settled zones. The first mate had begun to organise leave rotas, resupply and minor refit. Earbleat, in hope, had put in various requests for the means to produce *Loki VIII*. The market was picking up and Lindell had refused furlough on the basis that if he didn't jump in quickly, other trade ships certainly would.

"So meetings for us," Ahxenta sighed as she ran over the logs that Apnis had brought to her notice in a session in the bridge office.

"Looks like, Cap, and it *is* what we're here for. But we can stop in at the *Half Moon* and hear how things are," she added expressively. "Azular's refused shore leave. He reckons Greffy needs it more. He'll be spending his off-duty scouring info-channels and trying to make personal links. Anything new come up in the harbour office?"

Apart from the short talk with Holdspan, the only topics were the effects that the existing situation and its clean-up would have on Web business and a suspicion that the surface calm hid undercurrents that might erupt into tidal waves of trouble, Ahxenta told her.

"So same old, same old. Azular will be keen to hear about Nexus Station, so I'll pass it on. But we had a courtesy call from Fleetskup."

"Since when has he ever been courteous?"

"Since never. He asked after our health and our trip in and hoped to see us in the *Half Moon* at some point. I didn't encourage him but as Dyne-Bek was listening in, I didn't tell him more than he knew. He made the run straight from Silverglass to here but wouldn't say with what or why. Looking for business, I reckon. Or more crew."

It was two days before Ahxenta and her first mate made it to the *Half Moon* and that was after a long morning debating contracts and fees with reps in marketing. The captain was adamant that her crew would have plenty of time for furlough as they had had such a long stint, and was unwilling to take on urgent cargoes. Ally was delighted to welcome his pet customers back in and had two pots of ale on the counter as they reached it. Lunch, should they want it, was on the house, provided they gave him an account on what they had been up to since last he saw them. Rumours had abounded that both the *Arianrhod* and the *Obsidian Sky* had vanished without trace for weeks and then popped up again with nary a scratch. There had been word of attacks where *Arianrhod* had played a part – by Triple Pinks and off Wester 287 for example – brought in by crews from some of the ships that had been in and out, but most of those he had taken with a pinch of salt. But still there were strangers asking about *Arianrhod* and her people. He pulled up images of two netted by his secure cams but neither was known to Ahxenta or her first mate. The captain copied them to her wrist communit and let it go for the present to give Ally as much as she deemed should be known.

Shortly afterwards, at a private table and with food before them, the two talked of contracts in hand, ship's business and the news they had picked up from Ally. Their jammers were clearly set out and their wary eyes missed little. The place was busy with lunchtime patrons, regulars and crews from ships that were in, including their own.

"I see Greffy's making a date with Merry," Apnis grinned, tilting her head towards the duo. "And there's Gem Ferry and Hanx with… dammit! Thought it was too good to last. It's Fleetskup, with Buntle *and* his first mate. So Tallulah Tommy's worming his way back into his captain's back pocket."

"No supercargo; maybe he's in marketing trying to drum up more business," Ahxenta replied with a snort. "And here they come."

"I'd better polish the smile. It annoys the hell out of Dyne-Bek and for some curious reason, that tickles me," was the sardonic reply.

The ponderous captain of the *Tallulah* made his way over but as the two from *Arianrhod* had chosen to dine at a small table, he and his entourage had to sit nearby. Fleetskup began with a few nothings but was interrupted all too soon by soothing flattery from his first mate and hints from Buntle that things aboard ship were less smooth than they might be. Subtle questioning elicited the fact that Fleetskup had had no news of his ex-second mate and had assigned his chief tactical officer to the post, new ranking pips included. Blatant enquiries from Dyne-Bek on *Arianrhod's* latest trade deals brought Ahxenta's eyes on her in some wrath, suspecting that the woman was trying to outflank her by undercutting. It was Buntle who interposed to remind Dyne-Bek of the privacy due to commerce but the captain had had enough and brought the chat to an end on the basis of imminent meetings.

The afternoon session with trade reps from various local concerns had the captain wishing she was back aboard. There was an odd buzz about the place that she could not fathom and as a result she decided to bring Azular down with her for talks over the next few days and leave Apnis aboard to deal with the logistics of resupply.

The following day brought an encounter with Captain Fleetskup, Tommy Buntle and the *Tallulah's* supercargo in the marketing area on green four. There were lines of worry around Fleetskup's face but his exec was mightily amused about something. His supercargo had been given a tongue-lashing and was darkly muttering about finding a new post. *Tallulah* was expecting a very important visitor, Buntle disclosed quietly. The main investor in the vessel had been so put out by the slackness of recent trade that she was taking the trouble to cross the whole of zone Delta to deal with it herself. Fleetskup was terrified.

Ahxenta spotted one possible cause of the tension in the air when she spied a uniform she had never before seen in marketing. The lone individual was talking to a trade rep in a quiet corner and he wore the dark armoured outfit favoured by the Starfall fleet.

"Interesting," the science officer observed. "Their ships have been visiting the Web for some time and they come to trade, allegedly."

"Competition," was Lindell's quick response. "Wonder if they give discounts as they're new to the business?"

"*We* don't," the captain told him. "And there's our trade rep."

After a lengthy sitting and an eventual contract for a cargo to be loaded some twelve days down the line, Ahxenta ordered lunch at the *Half Moon* before two afternoon stints for long-term commissions. As these were with regular clients, she was in hopes that talks would be brief and she could factor in some personal time. The diner was busy as usual and she and her team joined Nat Holdspan and his first mate at their table. He also had later meetings, he said, but his ship would be out the next day on a short trip to Beta Zegonia. Ally had been at pains to have a word with the PSS officers and brought their orders across himself. There had been casual queries about their ships earlier from a stranger: Merry had been asked when their captains had last been in the *Half Moon* and if she knew if the ships were staying in port or were due out. She pled ignorance, as the man had scared her in a way she could not define. She had caught an image of him before he left. She had planned to pass the details on to Greffy, Ally winked, but as the captains were here, they had best see it immediately.

"Damn!" Ahxenta swore softly. "That looks like a hard face to me and it reminds me of someone."

"There *is* a vague likeness to Hoxiz," Azular noted. "But we can't be certain as Ally's secure cams don't have inbuilt scanning capacity. It would however explain Merry's aversion to him."

"Watch your back, Nat. And we watch ours. I'll call it in but I'm not blocking shore leave. We need it," Ahxenta said decisively.

The first mate of the *Arianrhod* thought it wise to alert Kit Biernop to a potential threat. He was in a position to notify Merkat security to be on the lookout and post a watch in known hotspots such as bars. And before they left the *Half Moon*, Ahxenta had a word with Wekki Munnet, who was still one of the diner's serving staff.

The hours dripped by, filled with further meetings over the next two days. By the end of the final session the senior officers were feeling the strain and the captain had decreed dinner in the *Half Moon* by way of a celebratory. They were almost through their extended meal when a holo-note came through to Azular from the bridge. Ahxenta felt the jolt of electricity that shook him as he scanned the brief memo on his communit. A private link had come in that he would like to respond to from the ship as soon as possible, he explained self-consciously.

"In that case, we'd better all head up," she said, a smile playing around her lips. "It's been a long day."

"Looks like it's going to be longer," Apnis noted wickedly.

Their shuttle was docked in green four and was quick to reach. In a little over half an hour they were back aboard, where Azular rapidly excused himself and made off. The captain did not see him again for an hour, at which point he asked for a private chat. The gist of the talk was relayed to Apnis over a nightcap in the mess some time later.

The call had been from Captain Kerrix, as they had figured. The *Moonstone* was under refit in a small orbital shipyard at Berzic, having left Alto Finglas, where she had been delayed by unspecified business for over a week local time. Overhaul would be complete in two days, at which time the *Moonstone* would head to Merkat.

"So how wide was his grin?" Apnis demanded.

The captain held up her hand for silence. "There was a message to me. Her first mate's organising a reception in the events suite in main marketing. Senior PSS officers mostly, but any of our crew are free to attend. Other invites are going out. The *Nyx Warrior* will be back so her people will be there, and Fleetskup and his. The reason for the social is to meet the *Moonstone's* crew but Levettiza wants a chat with me about an issue that she won't pass on over any channel. So there's something going on. But what Kerrix and her ship have been up to over the past several weeks is beyond me and Azular's no wiser. She *was* sent in to the defence of Freskat and came out in one piece and with credit, but that's all he's got. As the ship's at Berzic for refit just now I suspect Levettiza's had a hand in what's afoot."

"The events suite in marketing's a big space; seems a lot of trouble and expense just to introduce yourself around," Apnis shrugged. "So when's the party and do we have to wear dress uniform?"

"Three days from now, nineteen hundred hours, and I don't get dressed up for anybody. But I'd like to know what in hell's going on and what Levettiza's so keen to pass on."

"And *I* want to see the look on Fleetskup's face when he meets Commander Jesse Inks," Apnis snickered. "Azular's happy, then?"

"And then some. He's suggested we take the *Xanna* down for the talks tomorrow to give her an airing and I'll bet he'll have his shore leave request in first thing."

"You said no to the *Xanna*."

"Damn straight I did. But make sure he gets his time off; he's had one of the roughest rides of us all."

"Aye, Captain."

Three days later, the captain of the *Arianrhod* gaped as she gazed at her bridge holo-grid. "What in the name of hell…"

At her side, Commander Apnis began to laugh softly. "Azular, did you know about this?" she called over to the science officer, who had been at his post for hours awaiting the arrival of the *Moonstone*.

"No ma'am, though I *did* suspect something in the wind."

"We're being hailed, Captain," Bellfish alerted her from comms. "Captain Kerrix on the link."

As the face of Xanna Kerrix materialised in the grid, Ahxenta eyed her keenly, aware that most of her bridge crew were doing the same. "Captain Kerrix: I'm surprised to find you in command of a PSS."

"I'm sure you are, Captain Ahxenta. You'd best be set for more surprises. The *Moonstone* isn't the only new ship in the PSS register. The *PSS Kel'Moth*, Captain Vexin Thal in command, is on her way in as we speak. And the *PSS Kel'Beth* is also out there. We're the first of several of the Starfall fleet that will fly the Trades Alliance flag."

Apnis exhaled sharply. "Competition looks to be hotting up then, Cap. We'd best be on our toes."

"So it does," Ahxenta retorted thickly. "But as the charted galaxy seems to be expanding, there's space for us all. Thank you for your invitation for this evening, Captain, by the way. I'll see you there."

"I hope you *and* your officers will be able to attend. I only linked in to confirm. Several of my crew would like to meet you and yours."

With an exchange of courtesies Kerrix cut comms. The captain sat back and traded a glance with her first mate.

"*Captain* Vexin Thal? Myrtleberry's going to be furious."

"Why? She's been proved right. He *was* up to something, only not what she expected it was. The *PSS Kel'Moth*? Life is going to be even more of a ball from here on in," Apnis laughed.

"That's what she was doing at Alto Finglas, then – the HQ of the Trades Alliance. And with the help that Thal and his ragtag fleet have given the ISP and its allies, the TA couldn't say no."

"The TA couldn't say no to the credit it'll make out of them, you mean, Cap. And the refit at Berzic was mostly the paint jobs on her hull and call-sign integration."

"She *is* reading as the *PSS Moonstone*, Captain," Azular confirmed.

"*Captain* Kerrix will have a lot to do here," Ahxenta stated flatly. "Check in with the local TA office for a start. But Jesse Inks will have a handle on most things as he's flown with the PSS fleet for years. And with Levettiza as second mate, she'll be well-informed. Starfall as her ship's home base! It's right off the edge. I wonder what other crew she's picked up since last we saw her."

The captain and her senior officers were fated to find out that and more when they made the events suite at nineteen hundred. Captain

Kerrix and her senior officers were there to greet them. Her chief medic was Norvallan, her chief engineer a Marridani veteran of the Starfall fleet and her Friskianx senior science officer one of Thal's ex-crew. Levettiza was on hand and Commander Jesse Inks stood by his captain. The officers of *Arianrhod* were invited to enjoy the hospitality and to introduce themselves to others of the *Moonstone's* crew, several of whom were around, as more guests arrived. Ahxenta noted from the newcomers that every PSS in port was represented. The open invitation to her own crew had been heeded for a number had turned up to view their new associates. Amongst a smattering of non-PSS guests she spotted Ally and Merry and waved them across.

Merry's face was alight as she came up, looking around in delight, but her boss was grumpy. She breathlessly explained. Her Master's degree in psychology was almost complete and she had been offered the prospect of earning a living as a psych-counsellor whilst training and carrying out the research to gain her PhD. She would very soon be ship's counsellor aboard the *PSS Moonstone*.

"Captain Kerrix thinks of everything," Azular remarked, the grin creasing his face suggesting to his captain that he knew more. "But there's Captain Fleetskup with his senior officers and Mr Buntle."

That both Fleetskup and Dyne-Bek were stunned was obvious to everyone nearby but Ahxenta had little time to enjoy their reactions, for she found Levettiza at her elbow with the request for a word in one of the private offices off-suite. She nodded to Apnis and made her way out with the second mate of the *Moonstone*.

Ten minutes had barely elapsed when the two returned. Ahxenta's set jaw indicated to her officers that she had heard news that had incensed her but she renewed her smile to join in the chat. Levettiza moved off to continue her social duties and to relieve her captain and first mate, both of whom had matters in hand of their own: Captain Vexin Thal and his officers had appeared.

"I take it you'll be staying over tonight?" his captain asked Azular in a quiet moment, to his embarrassment. "Captain Kerrix will update you and I'll link over in the morning. Stay sharp." She turned away as the captain of the *Moonstone* finally made her way over to them, having spoken to most of her guests.

"How did Captain Fleetskup take Commander Inks' promotion?" Ahxenta asked matter-of-factly.

"Speechless," was the laconic reply. "A first for him, I guess. Ms Dyne-Bek had one or two snide remarks, but she's not sure how to take me. And she's as nosy as ever about my plans, but no wiser."

After a little small talk the group split, having shrewdly noted that Azular and Kerrix craved personal space. The two moved off to the peripheries, ostensibly to examine some of the artwork that clad the walls of the huge room, carefully avoiding physical contact until they reached a vacant sofa with none occupied nearby. They sat.

"I've missed you," Kerrix said softly, her hand reaching discreetly across to touch his leg.

Azular deposited his glass on the low table and leant back, smiling teasingly at her. "I've booked a suite over the way," he murmured. "If you're free, I hope you'll be my guest tonight?"

She laughed huskily as she slapped his jacket. "I've heard that line before, a lifetime ago. And I still can't resist those big dark eyes."

He reached across to kiss her on the lips, his arm sliding around her in a tight embrace. Several jaws dropped as the two linked.

"Looks like her crew's now latching on to what was plain to most of ours months ago," Apnis remarked to Ahxenta with a chuckle.

"Looks like," was the ironic response.

"Aw! That's cute!" Lieutenant Box enthused to his mate from the sidelines. "Think they'll get hitched?"

"Don't be a fool. She's got that great ship to command and he's *Arianrhod's* senior science officer," Lieutenant Dox reminded him.

"She could take him on as *her* senior science officer," argued the nav-officer artlessly.

"At times I swear you're dumber than a bag of dead quarks," Dox told him harshly. "Point one, the Cap would never let him go even if he wanted to, which is unlikely in any case; point two, Captain Kerrix wouldn't ask him to leave *Arianrhod* on her account; and, point three, the *Moonstone* already has a senior science officer. We met him. He's one of Captain Thal's ex-officers."

"That doesn't prevent them tying the knot," Box contradicted stubbornly. "Dr Ma'Lappis got engaged to Commander Poppet of the *Firedrake*. They serve on different ships. Nice thing, a wedding," he added in a suggestive tone. "Time we had one aboard, don't you think? We could do the honours on that front, Romanna."

"How many times do I have to say no?"

"I'll keep pestering you until you say yes, you realise that?"

"Only too well," the helmswoman groaned, raising her eyes to the roof. "If I did say yes, would it shut you up?"

He nodded, a beatific smile splitting his face as his eyes lit up. He waited, watching her reaction, his eyebrows rising questioningly. She let him wait. And wait.

"Oh, okay," she at last sighed, shrugging.

"Yahoo!" his voice cut the air like a siren. "She said yes!" he called out jubilantly to the room at large. "We're engaged!"

"I thought you said you would shut up!" Dox accused indignantly.

"But I didn't say for how long," Box tranquilly told her.

"You realise you'll be footing the bill for that party, Cap?" her first mate warned Captain Ahxenta as they joined in the applause.

"Like hell I will. They can pay for their own celebration."

"What's Mr Box's name other than Box?" Ally wanted to know. "That's all I've ever heard him called."

"Trust me, don't call him anything else," said Apnis. "It's Blue."

"Blue Box? You're kidding, Commander."

"Nope. But I think his parents might have been."

"Where's Merry?" he continued, looking around.

"Chatting to Greffy," she said dryly. "There must be something in the drink. And here's Nat Holdspan looking for company; it's going to be a long night."

The captain of the *Arianrhod* did not intend it to be a long night. She had other matters in hand, one of which was to schedule a very early and urgent briefing for the following morning. Taking it to be connected with Levettiza's news, most of her senior officers headed back aboard at a reasonable hour.

Captain Ahxenta had arranged to meet Captain Fleetskup in the *Half Moon in a Puddle* at noon. She had brought her first mate and two security guards and the group arrived in good time to meet Azular, Kerrix, Inks and Levettiza. The latter had been busy, for three ISP security officers sat discreetly by the far wall.

"Who in hell's that?" Apnis asked as the *Half Moon* fell silent at the entrance of a stout, shrewish woman, past middle years, the awkward Murmur Fleetskup behind and his own people trailing him.

"The forbidding Tallulah Fleetskup," Levettiza edified her with a chuckle. "She got in three hours ago. She's here to sort out her son and his business and to hand out Dyne-Bek's marching orders."

"She knows?" Ahxenta asked.

"She knows Dyne-Bek's been involved in shady dealings that have feathered her own nest at the *Tallulah's* expense – backhanders from suppliers and the like. The sly Mr Buntle handed on relevant details and I'm sure he's had a hand in this little farce: he wants the galaxy as witness so that Dyne-Bek will have no fall-back."

"Well, he knows all about shady dealings," Apnis remarked tartly.

"He's been doing the same for years, only not quite so inanely and not enough that he got caught. So we bide our time?"

"So we bide our time," Levettiza agreed.

Fleetskup spied Ahxenta, muttered a few words to his parent and headed to the bar. "You wanted a word, Captain," he said agitatedly.

"You appear to have business of your own, Captain Fleetskup. I suggest you deal with that first," she said equably as she returned Ms Fleetskup's hawk-like gaze with one equally as searching.

"If you don't Murmur, *I* will," a sharp voice that matched the face of his mother cut the air. "Though why you picked *this* place to deal with this matter I can't imagine."

Dyne-Bek must have had an inkling of what was to come, for she looked ill-at-ease but mutinous. She drew herself up and eyeballed her captain. "You have something to say to me, Captain?"

"I have plenty to say to you, Modis," he said uncomfortably as he drew out a tiny info-pad and scrolled through its contents.

Over the next two minutes he read out a detailed list of offences as Buntle smirked triumphantly behind him and Dyne-Bek's mouth tightened, her eyes blazing in fury. At the end of the recital, he told his first mate that she was off his ship forthwith and he would not provide a reference.

"It's a pack of lies! You can prove none of it and you can't dismiss me on the word of a shifty-eyed weasel like Thomas Buntle! What's more, I won't go and there's zip you can do about it!" she hissed.

"Oh but we can," Buntle put in. "The captain has the proof..."

"I doubt it and I *will* seek legal redress. You are an interfering old busybody," she shot at Ms Fleetskup. "And you, Buntle, are a slimy, arrogant and criminally underhand ass!"

She straightened up, her brash gaze raking the room. Most of the patrons sat gawping, giggling and nudging one another, speculating on what was about to happen next.

"Tommy Buntle's got her over a barrel," Malty mumbled to his mate in their safe haven in a dark corner. "She's standing on shaky legs and she knows it."

"Bet she doesn't," Jurry replied. "She's as dense as a dead ferret."

Azular had meanwhile been talking quietly to Kerrix when a wary Merry slid up for a whispered conversation. The result was a stealthy scan by the science officer of Dyne-Bek and others in the *Half Moon* and a quick order from the captain of the *Moonstone* to her first mate, who made off towards the back.

Levettiza, monitoring the action at the bar, nodded to the three

ISP officers, who rose to make their way forward. A shot followed by a crash at their side caused the three to spin and most of the heads in the place to whip round. Jesse Inks was calmly locking his phase rifle. The crash had been caused by a lone diner hitting the deck.

"You can deal with *him* after you've dealt with her," he said to the three. "He's going nowhere."

The senior ISP officer strode up to Dyne-Bek. "I'd like a word."

"I've got nothing to say to you."

"I have plenty to say to you," he replied in an echo of Fleetskup.

He stated his name and rank and called up a holo-list of charges, the major one being that she had supplied information for financial gain on the activities of a number of ships and personnel to persons unknown, from the *Tallulah* and elsewhere, by means of a complex comms encoding unit linked to roving transmit-receive stations.

"You can't prove it!" she stated harshly, her eyes flicking rapidly.

"You shouldn't have used your prison officer ID number as your call-sign," he said deprecatingly. "Bad move. And we have your name and that number – and other names and numbers – on lists that have been found aboard vessels hostile to the ISP and the Alliance."

"That proves nothing, only that people out there have my details! I am a commander in the PSS fleet and this is a set-up! I bet you had a hand in it," she rounded on Tommy Buntle.

"We'll require access to your vessel, Captain Fleetskup, in order to search Ms Dyne-Bek's quarters," one of the other ISP officers told the open-mouthed captain.

"I'd search her person, if I were you," the cold voice of Azular advised at his back. "Try her wrist communit; you'll find it does more than most. That's her comms encoding unit. She has a data download port implanted in her left arm as well. When did they get to you?" he asked the woman civilly. "Before or after you joined the *Tallulah*?"

Dyne-Bek's lip curled in contempt. "You think you're smart with your clever gadgets and your high-spec boat and your alien girlfriend. I bet *she's* more than she says on her packet, for sure. You've not heard the last of this. *Arianrhod* and her high-handed captain…"

"Good call," Ahxenta commended her senior science officer over the spluttering of the ex-first mate of the *Tallulah*. "Who's the one that Commander Inks got?"

"The stranger who was asking questions in here not so long ago – Merry recognised him. As he was cyber-enhanced and packing a kick that could dent a bulkhead, Mr Inks took him down rather heavily."

"We owe you thanks," the captain said to Levettiza, who had done scanning the seething and still belligerent Dyne-Bek. "And your team; you deciphered the coordinates pretty quickly to get to those ship-based stations and work out who they'd been sending to."

"It *was* my job. And now my job's protecting my own," she smiled at Kerrix, who with most of the rest of those within earshot, was listening. "You can take your prisoners, though I think you'll need a gurney for the thug at the back," she said to the ISP officers.

"Don't think you've heard the last of me," Dyne-Bek threatened a shocked Captain Fleetskup. "Nor you," she snarled at Ahxenta. "And there's nothing you can do about it."

"Oh no?" was the cool reply as the *Arianrhod's* captain drew back her left arm and let loose. "You'll need two gurneys," she told the security team as she surveyed the prone form on the deck and poked it with her foot. "Beats listening to her at any rate."

"Captain Ahxenta's got a persuasive way with her, Malty," Jurry noted astutely from his viewpoint by the wall.

"Aye, Jurry my lad: with a left hook like that, she'll win any argument," Malty agreed.

"It's a well-known fact," his friend replied with a hiccup, "You'll get more by sweet words and a good sock on the jaw than you ever will with just the sweet words."

The captain of the *Arianrhod* was rubbing her left hand with her right, her retractable hand shield plainly not having had the protective power to field the effects of a hard jaw. "Commander Apnis, I need a drink," she announced.

"Roger that, Cap. You paying?"

"No, you are."

"Aye ma'am. Ally, set me up a tab!" *Arianrhod's* first mate called over. "I think we all need a drink."

"Nice to see things are getting back to normal around here," Jurry observed placidly. "Plenty of action, plenty of folks to stand us a jar if we tell them all about it and Captain Ahxenta's left hook by way of a bonus."

FINIS

ABOUT THE AUTHOR

SANDI CAYLESS is the author of *Arianrhod*, the first in *The Pirates'
Web* series, and of the Mars-based *Sub Martis* series of novels: *Dome
Lowell*, *Dome Beagle* and *Starship*. Her other literary works include both
fiction and non-fiction. For more on the worlds of *The Pirates' Web*
and *Sub Martis* see the website, www.submartis.com, where you can
find stuff to download, maps to help you find your way around the
charted galaxy and Mars domes Lowell and Beagle, and information
on other strange places such as the *Half Moon in a Puddle*.
www.submartis.com